Kate Elliott lives in Pennsylvania with her husband and three children. In addition to the Crown of Stars series, she has collaborated with Melanie Rawn and Jennifer Roberson on *The Golden Key*.

Find out more about Kate Elliott and other Orbit authors by registering for the free monthly newsletter at www.orbitbooks.co.uk

Also by Kate Elliott

CROWN OF STARS
Volume One: King's Dragon
Volume Two: Prince of Dogs
Volume Three: The Burning Stone
Volume Four: Child of Flame

THE GATHERING STORM

Volume Five of
CROWN OF STARS

Kate Elliott

www.orbitbooks.co.uk

An *Orbit* Book

First published in Great Britain by Orbit 2003
This edition published 2003

Copyright © 2003 by Katrina Elliott

The moral right of the author has been asserted.

Map by Michael Gilbert

A CIP catalogue record for this book is available
from the British Library.

ISBN 1 84149 200 0

Typeset in Ehrhardt by
Palimpsest Book Production Limited, Polmont, Stirlingshire
Printed and bound in Great Britain by
Mackays of Chatham plc, Chatham, Kent

Orbit
An imprint of
Time Warner Books UK
Brettenham House
Lancaster Place
London WC2E 7EN

AUTHOR'S NOTE

To my readers – thank you for waiting. I'm sorry it took so long but it proved to be a lot more complicated to write than even I thought it would be. The sixth and final volume will be titled 'Crown of Stars.'

ACKNOWLEDGMENTS

I offer a particular thank you to Sherwood Smith whose cogent commentary on the penultimate draft caused me to add an all important fifteen minutes of additional screen time to one of the final scenes and revise a crucial scene in the middle of the book. My editor Sheila Gilbert remained patient and insightful throughout the long and arduous writing period; Debra Euler and the rest of the staff at DAW Books who did not hesitate to make fun of me when necessary. The usual suspects gave me support and advice – you know who you are.

ACKNOWLEDGMENTS

To Jeanne

MAP LEGEND

RECENT RULERS OF WENDAR AND VARRE

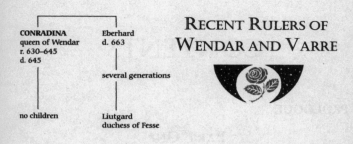

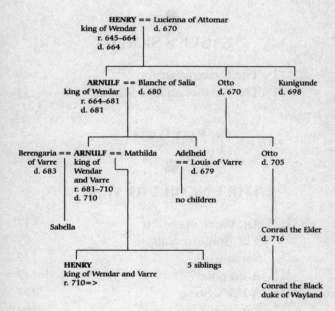

CONRADINA
queen of Wendar
r. 630–645
d. 645

Eberhard
d. 663

several generations

no children

Liutgard
duchess of Fesse

HENRY == Lucienna of Attomar
king of Wendar
r. 645–664
d. 664

d. 670

ARNULF == Blanche of Salia
king of Wendar
r. 664–681
d. 681

d. 680

Otto
d. 670

Kunigunde
d. 698

Berengaria == **ARNULF** == Mathilda
of Varre   king of
d. 683   Wendar
              and Varre
              r. 681–710
              d. 710

Adelheid
== Louis of Varre
d. 679

Otto
d. 705

Sabella

no children

Conrad the Elder
d. 716

HENRY
king of Wendar and Varre
r. 710=>

5 siblings

Conrad the Black
duke of Wayland

== married
r. reigned
d. died

CONTENTS

PART THREE

CAUDA DRACONIS

PROLOGUE

She dreamed.

In the vault of heaven spin wheels of gold, winking and dazzling. The thrum of their turning births a wind that spills throughout creation, so hot and wet that it becomes a haze. This mist clears to reveal the tomb of the Emperor Taillefer, his carved effigy atop a marble coffin. His stern face is caught eternally in repose. Stone fingers clutch the precious crown, symbol of his rule, each of the seven points set with a gem: gleaming pearl, lapis lazuli, pale sapphire, carnelian, ruby, emerald, and a banded orange-brown sardonyx.

Movement shudders inside each gem, a whisper, a shadow, a glimpse.

Villam's son Berthold rests peacefully on a bed of gold and gems, surrounded by six sleeping companions. He sighs, turning in his sleep, and smiles.

A hand scratches at the door of a hovel woven out of sticks, the one in which Brother Fidelis sheltered. As the door opens, the shadow of a man appears, framed by dying sunlight, his face obscured. He is tall and fair-haired, not Brother Fidelis at all. Crying out in fear, he runs away as a lion stalks into view.

Candlelight illuminates Hugh of Austra as he turns the page of a book, his expression calm, his gaze intent. He follows the stream of words, his lips forming each one although he does not speak aloud. A wind through the open window makes the flame waver and shudder until she sees in that flame the horrible lie whispered to her by Hugh.

Heresy.

She knelt in the place of St. Thecla as the holy saint witnessed the cruel punishment meted out by the empress of the Dariyan Empire to those who rebelled against her authority.

The blessed Daisan ascended to the sacrificial platform. He was bound onto a bronze wheel. Never did his smile falter although the priests flayed the skin from his body. Joy overwhelmed her, for was she not among the elect privileged to witness his death and redemption?

The floodwaters of joy wash back over her to burn her.

Is this not the heretical poison introduced into her soul by Hugh's lies?

Yet what if Hugh isn't lying? Has he really discovered a suppressed account of the redemption? It surpasses understanding.

In her confusion, the dream twists on a flare of light.

In a high hall burn lamps molded into the shapes of phoenixes. Their flames rise from wicks cunningly fixed into their brass tail feathers. Here the skopos presides over a synod called to pass judgment over the heretics. The accused do not beg for mercy; they demand that the truth be spoken at last. Her young brother Ivar stands boldly at the forefront. Who will interrogate them? Who will interrogate the church itself? If the Redemption is true, if the blessed Daisan redeemed the sins of humankind by dying rather than being lifted bodily into heaven in the Ekstasis while he prayed, then have the church mothers hidden the truth? Or only lost it?

Who is the liar?

'Sister, I pray you. Wake up.'

Dark and damp swept out from the dream to enclose her, and the cold prison of stone walls dragged her back to Earth. Light stung her eyes. She shut them. A warm hand touched her shoulder, and she heard Brother Fortunatus speak again, although his voice had a catch in it.

'Sister Rosvita! God have mercy. Can you speak?'

With an effort she sat up, opening her eyes. Every joint ached. The chill of the dungeon had poisoned her to the bone. 'I pray you,' she said hoarsely, 'move the light. It is too bright.'

Only after the light moved to one side could she see Fortunatus' face. He was crying.

Her wits returned as in a flood. 'How long have I been

here? Without the sun, I cannot mark the passing of days. I do not hear the changing of any guard through that door.'

He choked back tears. 'Three months, Sister.'

Three months!

A spasm of fear and horror overcame her, and she almost retched, but her stomach was empty and she dared not give in to weakness now. Strength of mind was all that had kept her sane in the interminable days that had passed since that awful night when she had heard the voice of a daimone speak through Henry's mouth.

'What of King Henry? What of Queen Adelheid? Has she not even asked after me? Have none spoken for me, or asked what became of me? God above, Brother, what I saw—'

'Sister Rosvita,' he said sharply, 'I fear you are made light-headed by your confinement. I have brought you spelt porridge flavored with egg yolks, to strengthen your blood, and roasted quince, for your lungs.'

They were not alone. The man holding the lamp was Petrus, a presbyter in the skopos' court, Hugh's admirer and ally. What she needed to say could not be said in front of him, because she dared not implicate Brother Fortunatus, the girls – Heriburg, Ruoda, Gerwita – and the rest of her faithful clerics. If she could not protect herself, then certainly she had no hope of protecting them. Her father's rank and her own notoriety gave her some shelter, which was probably the only reason she was not dead; she doubted Fortunatus and the others could hope for even such small mercies as being thrown into a cell beneath the skopos' palace.

Fortunatus went on. 'Sister Ruoda and Sister Heriburg bring soup and bread every day, Sister Rosvita, just after Sext, although I do not know if you receive it then.'

He watched her with an expression of alarmed concern as she worked her way down to the bottom of the bowl. She was so hungry, and she supposed she must smell very bad since she was never given water to wash. But no disgust showed on Fortunatus' lean face. He looked ready to begin weeping again.

'You have not been eating well either, Brother. Have you been ill?'

'Only worried, Sister. You wandered off in a sleeping dream that night, as you are wont to do, and never returned. It did not take us long to discover where you had wandered to in your delirium, alas.'

He smiled and nodded as if she were a simpleton whom he was soothing, but she read a different message in the tightening of his eyes and the twitch of his lips.

'Three months,' she echoed, scarcely able to believe it. In that time she had meditated and prayed, and slept, knowing that whatever she suffered at the hands of men would only test the certainty of her faith in God. Yet who had lied to her? Hugh? Or the church mothers? She could not shake that last desperate dream from her thoughts.

'Truly, the weeks have passed,' Fortunatus continued blandly. 'King Henry has ridden south with his army to fight the rebel lords, the Arethousan interlopers, and the Jinna bandits in southern Aosta. Queen Adelheid and her advisers rode with him. Since I could not go to the king, I asked for an audience with the skopos. After eight weeks of patient waiting, for you know that the cares of the world and of the heavens weigh upon her, I was admitted to her holy presence two days ago, on the feast day of St. Callista. She refused to release you, but she agreed that you ought to be allowed exercise in the corridor each day between the hours of Sext and Nones. Her generosity is without measure!'

Amazing, really, how he kept his voice steady, how he managed to keep sarcasm from his tone. The horrors of her confinement, the intense focus of mind she had brought to her prayer to keep herself from utter despair, were lightened by hearing him and by clasping his hand.

'The Holy Mother also gave me permission to pray with you every Hefensday. So do you find me here, Sister, with such provisions as I was allowed to carry as well as a blanket. As long as I am allowed, I will come every Hefensday to pray.'

'Then it is almost the first day of Decial. The dark of the sun.' Facts were a rope to cling to in a storm at sea. Knowing that she lay confined in this dungeon while, above, the good folk of Darre celebrated the feast day of St. Peter the Disciple, on the longest night of the year, amused her with its irony. 'Does the Holy Mother wish me kept in this cell indefinitely?'

'If it is the Enemy's doing that causes you to walk in your sleep, Sister, then you must be kept apart to avoid contaminating others. There will be a special guard to walk with you at your exercise, one who is both mute and deaf.'

She bowed her head. 'So be it.'

They would never be left alone, and even if they thought they were alone, Anne could still spy on them by means of magic. She could no longer speak frankly to him, nor he to her. Hugh knew that she had seen the king ensorcelled by a daimone and Helmut Villam killed by subtle magic at Hugh's hands, and yet Hugh still had not had her killed.

She was ill, she was hungry, and she was imprisoned in darkness in the dungeon beneath the holy palace, but by God she was not dead yet.

'Let us pray, then, Brother, as we will pray every Hefensday, if God so will it.'

She knelt. The straw cushioned her knees, and she had grown accustomed to the aggravation of fleas and the scrabbling of rats. If her limbs were unsteady and her voice ragged, and if she shifted the wrong way because the glare of the lamp hurt her eyes, at least she had not lost her wits.

God willing, she would never lose her wits.

As Fortunatus began the service of Vespers, she knew at last what time of day it was: evening song. To this scrap she clung with joy. In an appropriate place she chose a psalm, as one added prayers of thanksgiving or pleading in honor of the saint whose feast day it was.

'It is good to give thanks to God
for Their love endures forever.
Those who lost their way in the wilderness
found no city to shelter in.
Hungry and thirsty, they lost heart,
and they cried out to God,
and God rescued them from their trouble.
God turn rivers into desert

and the desert into an oasis,
fruitful land becomes wasteland
and the wilderness a place of shelter.
The wise one takes note of these things
as she considers God's love.'

When they had finished, Fortunatus answered her with a second psalm.

'Blessed be the Lord and Lady,
who snatched us out of the haunts of the scorpions.
Like a bird, we have escaped from the fowler's snare.
The snare is broken, and we have flown.
Blessed be God,
who together have made heaven and Earth.'

Too soon, he had to leave. He kissed her hands as servant to master, wept again, and promised to return in one week. It was hard to see him, and the light, go. It was agony to hear the door scrape shut, the bar thud into place, and the sound of their footsteps fade. Fortunatus might return in a week, as he had promised, or he might never return. She might languish here for a month, or for ten years. She might die here, of hunger, of lung fever, or of despair, eaten by rats. It was hard to remain hopeful in the blackness where Hugh had cast her.

But she had heard the promise implicit in Fortunatus' choice of prayer:

Like a bird, we have escaped from the fowler's snare.

The King's Eagle, Hathui, had escaped and flown north to seek justice.

PART ONE

EAGLE'S SIGHT

I
THE STRIKE
OF AN AX

1

The air smelled of rain, heavy and unseasonably warm, and the wind blowing in from the east brought with it the smells of the village: woodsmoke, ripe privies, and the stink of offal from the afternoon's slaughter of five pigs. Just yesterday Hanna and the cohort of Lions and sundry milites who were her escort had journeyed through snow flurries. Now it was temperate enough to tuck away gloves and set aside cloaks as they ate a supper of freshly roasted pig as well as cold porridge and a bitter ale commandeered from the village larder. Yet neither the food nor the familiar smells of the Wendish countryside brought her comfort. East lay the object of her hatred, still living, still eating. Her choked fury was like a scab ripped open every single day.

'Come now, Hanna,' said Ingo. 'You're not eating enough. If this cut of roast won't tempt you, I can surely dig up some worms.'

She ate obediently, knowing how her mother would have scolded her for the unthinkable sin of refusing to eat meat when it was available, but her heart was numb. Hate had congealed in her gut, and she could not shake it loose.

'Ai, Lady,' said Folquin. 'You've got that look on your face again. I told you I would kill him for you. I'd have snuck right into his tent when he was asleep and stabbed him through the heart.'

For months, as a prisoner of the Quman, she had shed no tears. Now every little thing, a stubbed toe, a child's giggle, a friend's helpless grimace, made her cry. 'I can't believe Prince Sanglant let him live,' she said hoarsely. 'He should have hanged him!'

'So said Princess Sapientia,' commented Leo, 'and so she's no doubt continuing to say, I suppose, for all the good it will do her.'

'Anything could have happened since we left the army,' suggested Stephen quietly. 'Prince Sanglant could have changed his mind about killing him. Once the army reaches Handelburg, then the holy biscop might agree with Princess Sapientia and demand his execution. Princess Sapientia is the rightful heir, after all, isn't she? Prince Sanglant is only a bastard, so even though he's the elder, doesn't he have to do what she says?'

Ingo glanced around to make sure none but the five of them were close enough to hear. Other campfires sparked and smoked in the meadow, each with its complement of soldiers eating and chatting in the gray autumn twilight, but certainly far fewer Lions were marching west back into Wendar than had marched east over a year ago.

'You don't understand the way of the world yet, lad. Princess Sapientia can't rule if there's none who will follow her.'

'What about God's law?' asked Stephen.

Ingo had a world-weary smirk that he dragged out when dealing with the youngest and most naive members of the Lions. 'The one who rules the army rules.'

'Hush,' said Leo.

Captain Thiadbold walked toward them through the overgrazed meadow, withered grass snapping under his feet. Trees rose behind the clearing, the vanguard of the Thurin Forest.

Ingo rose when Thiadbold halted by the fire's light. 'Captain. Is all quiet?'

'As quiet as it can be. I thought those villagers would never stop squealing. You'd think they were the pigs being led to the slaughter. They've forgotten that if they want the protection of the king, then they have to feed his army.' Thiadbold brushed back his red hair as he looked at Hanna. 'I've had a talk with the elders, now that they've calmed down. It seems an Eagle rode through just yesterday. Princess Theophanu's not at Quedlinhame any longer. She's ridden north with her retinue to Gent.'

Sometimes it was difficult to remember that the world kept on although she'd been frozen in place.

When she did not speak, Ingo answered. 'Will we be turning north to Gent?'

'Quedlinhame is closer,' objected Hanna wearily. 'We'll be another ten days or more on the road if we turn north to Gent.'

Thiadbold frowned, still watching her. 'Prince Sanglant charged us to deliver his message, and the king's Lions, to his sister and none other. We must follow Princess Theophanu.'

The others murmured agreement, but Hanna, remembering duty, touched the emerald ring on her finger that King Henry himself had given her as a reward for her loyalty. Duty and loyalty were the only things that had kept her alive for so long. 'So Prince Sanglant said, but what will serve King Henry best? The king needs to know what has transpired in his kingdom. His sister rules over Quedlinhame convent. We might deliver ourselves to Mother Scholastica with no shame. She will know what to do.'

'If Prince Sanglant had wanted us to deliver his message to Mother Scholastica, he could have sent us to her. It seems to me he meant his message, and these Lions, for Theophanu.'

'Not for Henry?' Rising, she winced at the painful ache in her hips, still not healed after the bad fall she had taken fourteen days ago during the battle at the Veser River. Pain had worn her right through, but she had to keep going. 'Is your loyalty to the king, or to his bastard son?'

'Hanna!' Folquin's whisper came too late.

Thiadbold studied her, a considering frown still curving
his lips. She liked Thiadbold better than most; he was a good
captain, even-tempered and clever, and unflappable in battle.
The Lions under his command trusted him, and Prince
Sanglant had brought him into his councils. 'I beg pardon for
saying so,' he said finally, 'but it's the chains you stubbornly
carry of your own will that weigh you down the most. No use
carrying stones in your sack if you've no need to.'

'I'll thank you, Captain, to leave me to walk my own road
in peace. You didn't see the things I saw.'

'Nay, so I did not, nor would I wish any person to see
what you saw, nor any to suffer it, but—'

She limped away, unwilling to hear more. He swore and
hurried after her.

'Truce, then,' he said as he came up beside her. 'I'll speak
no more on this subject, only I must warn you—'

'I pray you, do not.'

He raised his hands in surrender, and his lips twisted in
something resembling a smile but concealing unspoken words
and a wealth of emotion. A spark of feeling flared in her heart,
unbidden and unexpected. She had to concede he was well
enough looking, with broad shoulders and that shock of red
hair. Was it possible the interest he had taken in her over the
last two weeks, after the battle and then once Prince Sanglant
had sent them away from the main army to track down
Theophanu, was more than comradely? Was he, however
mildly, courting her? Did she find him attractive?

But to think of a man at all in that way made her think of
Bulkezu, and anger and hatred scoured her clean in a tide of
loathing.

Maybe Bulkezu had died of the wound to his face that he
had received at the Veser. Maybe it had festered and poisoned
him. But her Eagle's Sight told her otherwise.

She halted beside a pile of wood under the spreading
branches of an oak tree that stood at the edge of the forest.
Acorns slipped under her feet. Most of the wood had been

split by the Lions and taken away to feed campfires, but a few unsplit logs remained. Thiadbold crossed his arms, not watching her directly, and said nothing. There was still enough light to distinguish his mutilated ear, the lobe cut cleanly away and long since healed in a dimple of white scar tissue. He had a new scar on his chin, taken at the Veser.

Ai, God, so many people had died at the hands of Bulkezu.

Rolling a log into place between several rocks, she grabbed the ax and started chopping. Yet not even the gleeful strike of the ax into wood could cut the rage and sorrow out of her.

The wind gusted as a hard rain swept over them. Soldiers scrambled for the shelter of their canvas tents. She retreated under the sheltering canopy of the oak. Out in the open, campfires wavered under the storm's force. One went right out, drowned by the heavy rain, and the dozen others flickered and began to die. Distant lightning flashed, and a few heartbeats later, thunder cracked and rumbled.

'That came on fast,' remarked Thiadbold. 'Usually you can hear them coming.'

'I felt it. They should have taken shelter sooner.'

'So must we all. Prince Sanglant is a man who hears the tide of battle before the rest of us quite know what is about to hit us. He's like a hound that way, hearing and smelling danger before an ordinary man knows there's a beast ready to pounce. If he fears for the kingdom, if he fears that his father will not listen while black sorcery threatens Wendar, then I, for one, trust his instinct.'

'Or his ambition?'

'Do you think so? That all this talk of a sorcerous cabal is only a cloak for vanity and greed? That he is simply a rebel intent on his own gain and glory?'

'What did the great nobles care when the common folk were murdered and enslaved by the Quman? How many came to the aid of the farmers and cottagers? They only thought to defend themselves and their treasure, to nurse along their own petty quarrels. They left their people behind to suffer at the hands of monsters.'

'So that may be. I will hardly be the one to defend the likes of Lord Wichman, though it was God's will that he be born the son of a duchess and set above you and me. Some say that the Quman were a punishment sent from God against the wicked.'

'Innocent children!'

'Martyrs now, each one. Yet who can say whom God favor? It was Prince Sanglant who defeated the Quman in the end.'

She could think of no answer to this and so fumed as rain pelted down, drumming merrily on the earth. Drenched and shivering, she wrapped her arms around herself. A gust of wind raked the trees while thunder cracked. Branches splintered, torn free by the wind, and crashed to the ground a stone's toss away. Out in the meadow, a tent tore free of the stakes pinning it to the ground, exposing the poor soldiers huddled within. She recognized three wounded men who couldn't yet move well; one had lost a hand, another had a broken leg in a splint, and the third had both his arms up in slings to protect his injured shoulders. The canvas flapped like a great wing in the gale, trying to pull free of the remaining stakes.

Thiadbold swore, laughing, and ran out into the full force of the storm. For a moment she simply stood there in the wind and rain, staring, slack. Then a branch snapped above her, like a warning, and leaves showered down. She bolted after Thiadbold and together, with the belated help of other Lions, they got the tent staked down again while their injured comrades made jokes, humor being their only shield against their helpless condition.

At last Thiadbold insisted she walk over to the village and ask for Eagle's shelter at a hearth fire. There she dried out her clothing and dozed away the night in relative comfort on a sheepskin laid over a sleeping platform near the hearth. She woke periodically to cough or because the ache in her hip felt like the intermittent stabbing of a knife, thrust deep into the joint.

Would she never be rid of the pain?

The next day they chose a lanky youth from the village

to take a message to Mother Scholastica at Quedlinhame. No person among them, none of the Lions and certainly not any of the villagers, could write, so the lad had to be drilled until Hanna was sure he had the words right and could repeat them back at need. He proved quick and eager, learning the message thoroughly although eventually they had to chase away a chorus of onlookers who kept interrupting him to be helpful.

'I'd be an Eagle, if I could,' he confided, glancing back to make sure his father could not hear. The old man was complaining to Thiadbold about losing the boy's labor for the week it would take him to walk to Quedlinhame and back at this time of year when the fields were being turned under and mast shaken down for the pigs and wood split. 'It must be a good life, being an Eagle and serving the king.'

'If you don't mind death and misery.' He looked startled, then hurt, and a twinge of guilt made her shrug her shoulders. She hated the way his expression lit hopefully as he waited for her to go on. 'It's a hard life. I've seen worse things than I can bear to speak of—' She could not go on so stood instead, fighting the agony in her hip as tears came to her eyes.

But he was young and stupid, as she had been once.

'I wouldn't mind it,' he said as he followed her to the door of his father's small but neat cottage. 'I'm not afraid of cold or bandits. I've got a good memory. I know all the psalms by heart. Everyone says I'm quick. The deacon who comes Ladysday to lead mass sometimes asks me to lead the singing. B-but, I don't know how to ride a horse. I've been on the back of a donkey many a time, so surely that means I can easily learn how to sit a horse.'

She wiped tears from her cheeks and swung back to look at him, with his work-scarred hands and an undistinguished but good-natured face that made her think of poor Manfred, killed at Gent. She'd salvaged Manfred's Eagle's brooch after Bulkezu had torn it from her cloak, that day the Quman had captured her. She'd clung to that brass brooch and to the emerald ring Henry had given her. Together with her

Eagle's oath, these things had allowed her to survive.

The lad seemed so young, yet surely he wasn't any younger than she had been the day Wolfhere had asked her mother if it was her wish that her daughter be invested into the king's service. In times of trouble, Wolfhere had said, there was always a need for suitable young persons to ride messages for the royal family.

'Is it your wish to be invested as an Eagle?' she asked finally.

The boy's strangled gasp and the spasmodic twitch of his shoulders was answer enough. Even the father fell silent as the enormity of her question hit him. His younger sister, left behind when the loitering villagers were chased out, burst into tears.

'Yes,' he whispered, and could not choke out more words because his sister flung herself on him and began to wail.

'Ernst! My son! A king's Eagle!' The father's tone was querulous, and Hanna thought he was on the verge of breaking into a rage. But hate had clouded her sight. Overcome by emotion, his complaints forgotten, the old man knelt on the dirt floor of his poor house because his legs would not support him. Tears streaked his face. 'It's a great honor for a child of this village to be called to serve the king.'

So was it done, although she hadn't really realized she had the authority to deputize a young person so easily. Yet hadn't Bulkezu taught her the terrible power borne by the one who can choose who lives and who dies, who will suffer and who survive?

'If you mean to earn the right to speak the Eagle's oath, then you must deliver this message to Mother Scholastica and bring her answer to me where I will bide with Princess Theophanu. If you can do that, you'll have proved yourself worthy of an Eagle's training.' She unfastened her brooch and swung her much-mended cloak off her shoulders. 'You haven't earned the Eagle's badge yet, my friend, nor will you happily do so. But wear this cloak as the badge of your apprenticeship. It will bring you safe passage.' She turned to regard Thiadbold, who had kept silent as he watched the unfolding scene. 'Give the lad the dun pony.

He can nurse it along the whole journey, or perhaps Mother Scholastica will grant him a better mount when he leaves Quedlinhame.'

The lad's family wept, but he seemed sorry only to leave the sister. The company of Lions marched out in the late morning with the sky clearing and yesterday's rain glistening on the trees and on wayside nettles grown up where foliage had been cut back from the path. Hanna and the Lions took the turning north and rode for Gent. The lad was soon lost around the bend as he continued west toward Quedlinhame along the northern skirt of the Thurin Forest, but for what seemed a long time afterward she could still hear the poor, artless fool singing cheerfully as he rode into his new life.

2

'Hanna? Hanna!'

Blearily she recognized Folquin's voice and his strong hand on her elbow, propping her up. She had fallen asleep on the horse again, slumped over. In a panic she began whispering the message from the prince which she had committed to memory, afraid that it had vanished, stolen by her nightmares. But as he pushed her up, an agony of pain lancing through her hip tore her thoughts apart. Tears blurred her vision. She blinked them away to focus, at last, on the sight that had caught the attention of her companions.

After many days of miserable rainy weather, their path had brought them to an escarpment at the border of hilly country, and from this height they had a good view north along the river valley. A broad stream wound north through pastureland and autumn fields, and she recognized where they were with a clarity so ruthless that it pinched. Here among fields of rye the Eika and their dogs had attacked them, when she,

Manfred, Wolfhere, Liath, and Hathui had ridden toward Gent in pursuit of Prince Sanglant and his Dragons. Here, when King Henry had come with his army to fight Bloodheart, she had seen the chaos of battle close at hand as Princess Sapientia had urged her troops forward to descend on the Eika ships beached on the river's shore.

'Hanna?' Folquin's tone was sharp with concern. 'Are you well? You didn't finish your porridge last night nor eat the cold this midday.'

'Nay, it's nothing.' She sneezed. Each breath made a whistle as she drew it into her aching lungs. Yet what difference did it make if she hurt? If she shivered? If she went hungry or thirsty? Nothing mattered, except that Bulkezu still lived.

Harvested fields lay at peace. Cattle grazed on strips of pasture. The rotund shapes of sheep dotted the northwestern slopes, up away from the river bottom lands where grain flourished. A few tendrils of smoke drifted lazily into the heavens from the walled city of Gent. The cathedral tower and the mayor's palace were easily seen from this distance, their backdrop the broad river and the white-blue sky, empty of clouds today. Was that the regent's silk fluttering from the gates, marking Theophanu's presence? The chill wind nipped her face, and she shuddered.

'Best we move on quickly,' murmured Leo in a voice so low she thought he did not mean for her to hear him.

At the western bridge, a welcoming party greeted them: thirty milites braced in a shield wall in case the approaching soldiers were marauders or enemies. One of Princess Theophanu's stewards stepped out from behind the shields to greet them as Hanna rode forward beside Thiadbold.

'I bring a message from Prince Sanglant, from the east,' Hanna said. 'The prince sends as well these Lions, to strengthen Her Highness' retinue.'

'God be praised,' muttered the steward. She gave a command, and the shield wall dispersed.

As the Gent milites clattered back through the gates, they swept through a little market of beggars and poor folk gathered in the broad forecourt beyond the ramparts, almost trampling a ragged woman with a basket of herbs for sale. The milites did not even notice their victim, tumbled in the dirt while the folk around her muttered uneasily, but Hanna hurried over to help the beggar woman to her feet, only to be spat at for her pains.

'Here, now,' said Thiadbold as he came up beside Hanna, 'never a good deed but goes unpunished by the frightened.' His smile melted the old woman's anger, and she allowed him to gather up marjoram, cinquefoil, and dried nettle. 'No harm done, mother, once it's all set to rights.'

Hanna felt as if she'd been kicked in the stomach. Her heart thumped annoyingly, and her breath came in short gasps.

'Come, now, friend,' Thiadbold said as he took hold of the reins of her horse so she could mount again, 'she was scared, and acted out of fear.'

'Next time those soldiers will cripple some poor soul, and never bother to look back to see what they've wrought. Ai, God.' She got her leg over the saddle, but the effort left her shaking. 'I still have nightmares about the ones who cursed me.'

'There was nothing you could have done to help them. You were as much a prisoner as they were. You did your duty as an Eagle. You stayed alive.'

Words choked in her throat.

'What are you speaking of?' demanded the steward, who had waited behind to escort them. 'We've heard rumors of Quman, of plague, of drought, and of foul sorcery, but seen nothing. Rumor is the speech of the Enemy. Lord Hrodik rode off with Prince Sanglant. There's been no news of him. We've been praying every day for news from the east.'

'In good time,' replied Thiadbold, glancing at Hanna.

The steward sighed heavily, then laughed. She was a short, stout woman, with a clever, impatient face and, apparently, a sense of humor. 'So do God teach us patience! Come now. Her Highness, Princess Theophanu, will be eager to hear news of her brother.'

They made their way through the streets of Gent, their

path cleared by Theophanu's milites. Once their party entered the palace compound, the steward directed Thiadbold and the Lions to the barracks above the stables but took Hanna immediately to the opulent chamber where Theophanu held court. The vivid colors made her dizzy: a purple carpet, gold silk hangings on either side of the royal chair where Theophanu sat studying a chessboard, a dozen noble companions garbed in reds and blues and greens. Four braziers heated the chamber, but the atmosphere of the chattering women gave it life and energy. As Hanna entered, the women looked at her expectantly, murmuring one to the other.

'From the east!'

'From Sapientia, do you think? I recognize her. She is the Eagle who served Sapientia before.'

'Make haste to speak, Eagle!'

'I pray you, let us have a moment's calm.' Theophanu rose. At her gesture, a serving woman hurried out of the shadows cast by the silk hangings and carried the chessboard away to a side table. 'You look pale, Eagle. Let ale be brought and some bread, so that she may refresh herself. And water, so that she may wash her hands and face.'

Her companions were not so patient. 'How can you stand it? After all these months!'

'After everything we've suffered, waiting and wondering! After Conrad's insolence at Barenberg!'

'Yes!' cried others. 'Let her speak first, and eat after.'

Theophanu did not need to raise her voice. 'Let her eat. We will not die of waiting, not today. I pray you, Eagle, sit down.'

Two servants carried forward a bench padded with an embroidered pillow onto which Hanna sank gratefully. Ale was brought as well as a fine white bread so soft that it might have been a cloud, melting in Hanna's mouth. A servingwoman brought a pitcher of warmed water, a basin, and a cloth, and washed Hanna's hands and face herself, as though Hanna were a noblewoman. The women around Theophanu muttered to each other under their breath, pacing, fiddling with chess pieces, quite beside themselves to hear the message she had brought. One dark-haired woman dressed in a handsome green gown turned the corner of the carpet up and down with her foot, up and down, while servants gathered at the open doors, spilling back into the corridor, eager to hear news from the east. Theophanu alone showed no sign of impatience as she sat in her chair, as easy as if she already knew what Hanna was going to say.

It was hard to really enjoy one's food and drink under such circumstances, and better, perhaps, simply to have done with the message she had carried in her memory for so many long and weary days. When she rose at last to stand before the princess, she heard the crowd exhale in anticipation, and then, like an angry toddler making ready to scream, fall silent as they each one drew in breath.

Hanna shut her eyes to call the message to her tongue.

'This message I bring from Prince Sanglant, to his most glorious, wise, and beloved sister, Princess Theophanu. With these words I relate to you the events which have transpired by Osterburg and in the east.'

She had repeated the words to herself so many times that they flowed more easily the less she thought of which word must come next. Not even the wheeze in her chest or her frequent coughs could tangle the message now as she recounted the events of the last two years.

King Henry had sent her and two cohorts of Lions east to aid his daughter. Their party had met up with Princess Sapientia and Prince Bayan and soon after faced a Quman army under the command of Bulkezu. Only Bayan's wits had saved the army from a catastrophic defeat. That terrible retreat toward Handelburg with a battered army had been the best of a bad year. It had started going worse once they had reached Handelburg, where Biscop Alberada had condemned Prince Ekkehard as a heretic. Sapientia's jealousy had made Hanna a target, too, and so she had ridden out with Ekkehard and the other excommunicated heretics into winter's heartless grip.

Better not to think of what had happened next, if she could speak the words without listening to what she was

saying. Better not to think of the Quman invasion of the
marchlands and eastern Wendar that had caught her in its
net. Better not to think of the destruction Bulkezu had
inflicted on the poor souls unfortunate enough to stand in
the path of his army. Plague and misery had stalked them,
and only after much suffering had she caught a glimpse
through fire, with her Eagle's Sight, of the war council held
by Bayan and Sanglant. Was it she who had persuaded
Bulkezu to ride to the city of Osterburg? Or was it God who
had inspired her voice? Outside Osterburg, on the Veser River
plain, Sanglant had defeated the Quman, but Bayan had been
killed in the battle together with so many others, including
Lord Hrodik. The Lions had been particularly hard hit, losing
fully a third of those left to them, two proud cohorts shrunk
to one.

She had to stop; the effort of speaking was too great. The
crowd stood shocked into silence at her litany of war, famine,
drought, plague, disease, heresy, and countless villages and
towns destroyed.

Theophanu lifted a hand, a gesture as casual as a lazy swipe
at a fly. 'All of which,' she said, with a hint of sarcasm in her
tone although no trace of emotion blotted her smoothly handsome face, 'are not unknown to me. We saw each other last
at Barenberg, Eagle, where I was helpless to combat the
invaders and had no recourse left me except to pay them off
temporarily. I am glad you survived your captivity.'

Hanna really looked at her then, seeing in her dark eyes,
steady gaze, and firm mouth the mark of a personality not
tumbled every which way by the prevailing wind. 'That is not
all, Your Highness. Indeed, according to your brother Prince
Sanglant, that is the least of it.'

Theophanu had the intelligence of a churchwoman, hidden
at times by the inscrutable eastern temperament she had inherited from her mother. She rose to her feet before Hanna could
continue. 'My brother speaks, I believe, of a sorcerous cabal
whose plotting will destroy Wendar and bring a cataclysm
upon the land.'

'That is so.' Surprised, Hanna lost track of her laboriously memorized words. 'If I may have a moment, Your Highness, to collect my thoughts . . .'

A fit of coughing seized her.

Theophanu waited her out before going on. 'Do not forget that I was at Angenheim when Sanglant came with his child and his mother. I heard him speak. Yet I heard nothing to make me fear sorcery more than I already do. It seemed to me that he spoke rebellion against our father, the king. Perhaps he does not know his own mind. Perhaps his mother's blood taints him—'

'Or it is a madness set on him by the witch he married?' said one of her courtiers.

'Perhaps,' replied Theophanu so skeptically that it took Hanna a moment to realize that the 'witch' they spoke of was Liath. 'But if a cataclysm does threaten us, then surely our enemy are the Lost Ones, not those who would protect us against them. I cannot believe that my brother acts wisely in this case. But I am grateful to him for sending me what remains of the Lions who marched east last summer. Why did he not come himself?'

'When I left him, he meant to escort the body of Prince Bayan to Ungria, Your Highness. From Ungria he intends to journey farther east into the lands where sorcerers and griffins may be found.'

'Can such stories of the east be true?' demanded the woman in the green dress. She had pressed forward to listen, and now sat on a pillow beside Theophanu's chair. 'Marvels and wonders. Snakes that drink blood. One-legged men who hop everywhere. Did you see such things in the marchlands, Eagle?'

'Nay, I did not, my lady, but we did not ride even so far as the kingdom of Ungria. Most of the time I was in the march of the Villams, or in Avaria and even here into Saony. I do not know what lies beyond Ungria—'

Except that in her dreams she did know, for she had seen the Kerayit princess Sorgatani wandering in desert lands or through forests of grass growing higher than a man's head. She had felt the claws of a living griffin grip her shoulders.

She had touched the silver-and-gold scales of dragons heaped into dunes on the edge of habitable lands. She had seen the tents of the fabled Bwr people, whose bodies combined those of humankind and horse.

'Any expedition to the east must prove dangerous, and might take years to complete, if he even returns at all.' Theophanu beckoned. A servingwoman brought forward a silver cup on a wooden platter with sides carved in the likeness of twining ivy. 'Here, Leoba.' She offered the cup to the noblewoman sitting at her feet.

'Is Aosta closed to us?' Leoba took the cup but did not drink. 'How can it be that a messenger comes to us from Prince Sanglant, but not from King Henry? Why have we heard no news from Aosta when so many troubles assail us here? Where is the king?'

'And where is your venerable husband?' Theophanu smiled fondly at her companion. 'I am no less troubled than you. It seems strange to me that I have sent three Eagles separately to Aosta and yet no word has come to us from my father.'

'With winter setting in, there'll be none who can cross the Alfar Mountains.' Like Theophanu, Leoba was young and robust, but she had a hound's eagerness in her face, ready to fling herself forward into the hunt, in contrast to Theophanu's calm.

'We must wait.' Theophanu took the cup and sipped while her attendants whispered. A tapestry hung in the room between shuttered windows, so darkly woven that lamplight barely illuminated the images depicted there: a saintly figure impaled by knives. Hanna's hip twinged as if in sympathy as she shifted on the bench. A servant padded forward to refill the wine cup, and the princess sipped, eyes shuttered, as though she were mulling over a difficult question. She spoke in an altered voice, so smooth it seemed doubly dangerous.

'There is one thing that puzzles me, Eagle. You bring me a message from my brother, Sanglant. You speak of the death of Prince Bayan of Ungria, and of other worthy folk, in the battle against the Quman invaders. But you have spoken no

word of Princess Sapientia. You served her once, I believe.
What has become of her?'

The question startled Hanna, although she ought to have
expected it. 'She lives, Your Highness.'

'Where is she? Where is her army? Why have these Lions
been sent at Sanglant's order, and not hers? Is she injured?
Lost? Separated from the army?'

'Nay, Your Highness. She rides with Prince Sanglant.'

'How can it be that my brother sends me greetings, but
my sister does not? Wasn't she named by Henry as heir to
the throne of Wendar and Varre?'

Spiteful words came easily to her tongue. 'Prince Sanglant
commands the army, Your Highness. Princess Sapientia does
not.'

The courtiers murmured, a warm buzz of surprise and
speculation.

Only Theophanu seemed unmoved by Hanna's statement.
'Are you saying he has taken from her what is rightfully hers
to command?'

'I cannot know what is in the mind of princes, Your
Highness. I can only witness, and report.'

'Where goes Sapientia now?'

'East to Ungria with Prince Bayan's body.'

'Did she consent to this journey, or was it forced on her?'

All the anger boiled back. Hadn't Sanglant betrayed her
and all those who had suffered at the hands of Bulkezu by
leaving Bulkezu alive? Perhaps it was true that Sanglant was
fit to rule, and Sapientia was not. But he was a bastard and
meant for another position in life; he had usurped his sister's
place. He had let Bulkezu live. She could no longer trust a
man who would let a monster go on living after so many had
died under its trampling rampage. Sapientia would have
ordered Bulkezu hanged. Sapientia would not have saved him
in the vain hope that he would somehow serve Wendar better
alive than dead. Sapientia's choices would have been different, had she been allowed to make the decision, as was her
right as Henry's eldest legitimate child.

But she hadn't had the choice. '*This is* my *army now,*'

Sanglant had said after the battle at the Veser. He might as well have torn the crown from her head. Yet no one in that host had refused him.

'The command was taken from her against her will,' Hanna said.

Everyone in the chamber began talking at once, and Hanna's words were repeated back into the mob of lesser courtiers and servants crowded into the corridor.

'Silence,' said Theophanu without raising her voice. After a moment of hissed demands for quiet and a few last hasty comments, the gathered folk fell quiet. Like Sanglant, Theophanu had the habit of command, but she hadn't his warmth and charisma; she hadn't fought and suffered beside an army, as he had; she didn't shine with the regnant's luck, as he did.

'If that is not rebellion against Henry's rule, then I do not know what is. So be it. Nothing can be done today. Eagle, I pray you, eat and drink well and rest this night. Tomorrow I will interview you at more length.'

Hanna slipped forward off the bench to kneel, shaking, too tired even to walk. 'I pray you, Your Highness, may I keep company with the Lions? I have traveled a long road with them. I trust them.'

'Let it be so.' Theophanu dismissed her. Calling for her chess set, she returned to her amusements. Hanna admired her for her composure. No great heights of emotion for her, however unnatural that might seem in a family whose passions, hatreds, joys, and rages were played out in public for all to see. She was like a still, smooth pond, untroubled by the tides of feeling that racked Hanna. Theophanu, surely, would not succumb to jealousy or greed, lust or pride. Not like the others.

A servingwoman came forward to help Hanna up. Even standing hurt her, and she could not help but gasp out loud, but the gasp only turned into a painful cough.

'I beg pardon, Eagle. Let me help you out to the barracks. I can see you need some coltsfoot tea. Are you also injured?'

'I took a fall some days ago and landed on my hip.'

'I have an ointment that might help, if you'll let me serve you. It came to me from my grandmother, may she rest at peace in the Chamber of Light.'

They moved out through the door, and the servants in the corridor had enough courtesy to stand back to let the two of them pass through, although it was obvious by their whispering and anxious looks that they wished to hear more extensive news of the troubles plaguing the borderlands and the southerly parts of the kingdom. Gent might lie peacefully now, but they had not forgotten what Gent had suffered under the Eika invasion just two years before.

'I'll take any help you'll give me, and thank you for it,' said Hanna. Weight pressed into her chest with each hacking cough. 'Has the plague reached here?'

'Nay, it has not, thank God. But we've heard many stories from the south. They say that in the duchy of Avaria the plague killed as many as the Quman did. I don't know if it's true.'

Outside the palace they paused on a broad porch while Hanna rested, sucking in each breath with an effort. Such a short walk shouldn't have tired her so much, but it had, and her hip hurt so badly that her vision blurred. A drizzle wet the dirt courtyard. The barracks lay across that impossibly wide expanse.

'You're white,' said her companion. 'Sit down. I'll bring some lads to carry you over. You shouldn't be walking.'

'Nay, no need. I can walk.'

The servingwoman shook her head as she helped Hanna to sit on the wooden planks. 'You haven't caught the plague, have you?'

'I pray not.' She leaned against the railing, shivering, aching, and with a dismal pain throbbing through her head and hip and chest. 'It starts in the gut, not the lungs.' She glanced up, sensing the other woman's movement, and got a good look at her for the first time: a handsome woman, not much older than she was, with a scar whitening her lip and a bright, intelligent, compassionate gaze. 'What's your name? It's kind of you to be so . . . kind.'

The servingwoman laughed curtly, but Hanna could tell that the anger wasn't directed at *her*. 'It takes so little to be kind. I'm called Frederun.' She hesitated, cheeks flushed. Her unexpected reserve and the color suffusing her face made her beautiful, the kind of woman who might be plagued by men lusting after her face and body. The kind of woman Bulkezu would have taken to his bed and later discarded. 'Is it true you traveled with Prince Sanglant? Has he really rebelled against his father, the king?'

'What does it matter to you?' Hanna blurted out, and was sorry at once, throwing sharp words where she had only received consideration. Was sorry, twice over, because the answer was obvious as soon as the words were spoken.

'No matter to me,' said Frederun too quickly, turning her face away to hide her expression. 'I only wondered. He and his retinue spent the winter here last year, on their way east.'

'You don't grieve that Lord Hrodik is dead?'

Frederun shrugged. 'I'm sorry any man must die. He was no worse than most of them are. He was very young. But I'm glad Princess Theophanu came, seeing that we have no lord or lady here in Gent. That will keep the vultures away.'

'But not forever.'

'Nay. Not forever.' As if she had overstepped an unmarked boundary, she rose. 'Here, now, sit quietly and wait for me.'

As soon as she left, shame consumed Hanna. What right had she to torment a kindly woman like Frederun? She pulled herself to her feet and, jaw set against the pain, hobbled across the courtyard as rain misted down around her. She could walk, even if each step sent a sword's thrust of pain up her hip, through her torso, and into her temple. She could walk even if she could not catch her breath. She could walk, by the Lady, and she *would* walk, just as Bulkezu's prisoners had walked without aid for all those months, sick and dying. She was no better than they were. She deserved no more than they had received.

She was staggering by the time she reached the barracks, and for some reason Folquin was there, scolding her, and then Leo was carrying her back to a stall filled with hay. The smell of horse and hay made her cough. A spasm took her in the ribs.

'Ai, God,' said Ingo. 'She's hot. Feel her face.'

'I'll get the captain,' said Folquin.

'Maybe they have a healer here in the palace,' said Stephen.

'Hanna!' said Leo. 'Can you hear me?'

She choked on hatred and despair. Dizziness swept her as on a tide, and she was borne away on the currents of a swollen river. She dreamed.

In her nightmare, Bulkezu savors his food and guzzles his mead and enjoys his women, and even the gruesome wound is healing so well that folk who should know better turn their heads to watch him ride by. How dare he still be handsome? How can God allow monsters to be beautiful? To live even in defeat?

Or is she the monster, because despite everything she still sees beauty in him? Wise, simple Agnetha, forced to become his concubine, called him ugly. Surely it is Hanna's sin that she stubbornly allows her eyes to remain clouded by the Enemy's wiles.

A veil of mist obscures her dreaming, a fog rolling out of marshy ground beside which she glimpses the pitched tents of the centaur folk. Sorgatani walks through the reeds at the shore of the marsh. The fog conceals the world, and she knows that something massive is creeping up on her, or on the Kerayit princess, but Hanna cannot see it, nor does she sense from what direction it means to attack.

A woman appears, shifting out of the fog as though a mist has created her: she is as much mare as woman. Green-and-gold paint stripes her face and woman's torso.

Sorgatani cries out in anger. 'I have fulfilled all the tasks you set me! I have been patient! How much longer must I wait?'

'You have been patient.' When the shaman glances up at the heavens, her coarse mane of pale hair sweeps down her back to the place where woman-hips meet mare-shoulders. 'That lesson you learned well. The elders have met. Your wish is granted.'

'We will ride west to seek my luck?'

The centaur shifts sideways, listening, and after a moment replies. 'Nay, little one. She must suffer the fate she chose. But we are weak and diminished. We cannot fight alone—'

She rears back, startled by a sharp noise, the crack of a staff on rock. 'Who is there?'

The hot breath of some huge creature blows on Hanna's neck, lifting her hair. She feels its maw opening to bite. Whirling, she strikes out frantically with a fist, but when her hand parts the mist, she stumbles forward into the salty brine of a shallow estuary, water splashing her lips and stinging her eyes as reeds scrape along her thighs.

She is alone, yet she hears a confusing medley of voices and feels the press of hands as from a distance, jostling her.

'It's the lung fever. She's very bad.'

'Hush. We'll see her through this. She's survived worse.'

A woman's voice: 'I've boiled up coltsfoot and licorice for the congestion.'

'I thank you, Frederun.'

Each time she strikes ax into wood and splits a log, she swears, as though she's trying to chop fury and grief out of herself, but she will never be rid of it all.

Better if she lets the tide sweep her onward through the spreading delta channels of the lazy river and out onto a wide and restless sea. Yet even here, the horror is not done with her. Fire boils up under the sea, washing a wave of destruction over a vast whorled city hidden in its depths. Corpses bob on the swells and sharks feed. Survivors flee in terror, leaving everything behind, until the earth heaves again as the sea floor rises.

A phoenix flies, as bright as fire. Or is it a phoenix at all but rather a woman with wings of flame? Delirium makes the woman-figure appear with a familiar face. Is that Liath, come back to haunt her? Is she an angel now, flying in the vault of heaven, all ablaze? As the creature rises, she lifts the slender figure of a man and two great hounds with her. But their weight is too great and with a cry of anguish and frustration the Liath-angel loses her grip on them and they fall away, lost

as the fog of dreams rolls across the sky to conceal them.
    Hanna falls with them.
    'How is she?'
    'She's delirious most of the time, Your Highness.'
    'Will she live?'
    'So we must pray, Your Highness.'

II
THE ACHE OF AN OLD WOUND

1

'Hanna?'

Someone held a light close to her face. Squeezing her eyes shut, she turned away from the harsh glare.

'Hanna.' More insistently.

She smelled horse on his tunic. A breeze tickled her ear, and she cracked open one eye and realized that it was not lamplight but sunlight that lit the chamber. She lay in a neatly appointed chamber with a second rope-frame bed opposite hers, a table and bench, a chest for clothing, and several basins set here and there about the room, five on the floor and two small copper ones on the table. Through open shutters she glimpsed an apple tree in bloom.

Ingo knelt beside her bed. 'Hanna?'

She grunted, reaching out to grasp his shoulder, not sure if he were real or another vivid dream like the ones that plagued her. Even moving her arm took an effort. She was terribly weak, but she could breathe without pain. 'You're really here,' she said, mildly surprised that her voice worked.

'Aye, indeed, lass,' he replied with a crooked grin. He wiped a tear from his cheek. 'I've been here many a day over the winter, but you didn't know it. We've all watched over you. I thank God that you look likely to live.'

'Ah.' All she remembered was the dreaming, although she knew that long stretches had passed in which she was intermittently aware of the struggle it took to draw a single breath, of fever and chills washing through her as though she were racked by a tidal flow.

'Listen, Hanna.' He took hold of her hand. 'We're leaving Gent. Princess Theophanu is marching with her retinue to Osterburg. Duchess Rotrudis has died at last. The princess must go there swiftly to make sure the old duchess' heirs don't tear Saony into pieces.'

'Yes.' She had a vague recollection that Prince Sanglant had given her a message to take to his sister, and an even mistier memory that she had, perhaps, delivered it.

'We leave after Sext. Today.'

Her head throbbed with the effort of thinking. 'How long?'

'A week or more—'

'She's asking how long she's been sick,' said a second voice from the door.

'Folquin?'

He hurried in to kneel beside her, and suddenly Leo and Stephen pressed into the room as well.

'Captain said that until she's stronger—' began Stephen hesitantly.

'She might as well know from us.' Folquin's shoulders were so broad that they blocked her view out the open window. He bent close to her, setting a huge hand on her shoulder as gently as if she were a newborn baby. She didn't remember them all being so large and so very robust. 'You've been sick with the lung fever all winter. You almost died. It's spring. Mariansmass has come and gone. It will be Avril soon.'

Her mouth was so dry that her tongue felt swollen. Still, she managed to smile despite cracked lips. The passing of seasons meant little to her. It was just nice to see their familiar faces, but exhaustion already had its grip on her again. She wanted to sleep. Yet would she be abandoned once they left? Ingo and the others had rescued her from Bulkezu, after all.

'Who will look after me?'

'There's a good woman here, by name of Frederun. She's been nursing you all winter. She's head of the servant's hall here at the palace. Princess Theophanu thinks well enough of you to leave her good companion, Lady Leoba, as lady over Gent. You'll travel to Osterburg once you're strong enough to ride. We'll see you soon, friend.'

They fussed over her for a little longer before being called away, but in truth she was relieved to be able to rest. She'd forgotten how exhausting they were, yet she had an idea that they hadn't always seemed so, back before her illness, before Bulkezu.

Days passed, quiet and unspeakably dreary. Her hip had healed, but even to stand tired her and walking from her bed to the door and back again seemed so impossible a task that she despaired of ever regaining her strength. Her ribs stuck out, and her abdomen was a hollow, skin stretched tight over hipbones. Some days she hadn't the will to eat, yet Frederun coaxed her with bowls of porridge and lukewarm broths.

The passing days became weeks. Avril flowered, and with it the feast day of St. Eusebë, when apprentices sealed themselves into service to a new master. She had recovered enough that she could walk to a chair set outside in the sun, in the broad courtyard, and watch as a dozen youths were accepted into the palace, seven years' service in exchange for a place to sleep and two meals every day. Lady Leoba herself came by to speak with her, and Hanna even managed to rise, to show the new lady of Gent proper respect.

'I see you are healing, Eagle.' The lady looked her over as carefully as she might a prized mare whom she had feared lost to colic. 'My lady Princess Theophanu hoped we could join her by the Feast of the Queen, but I've sent a messenger to let her know we'll be delayed until the month of Sormas. It was a lad who said you had deputized him as an Eagle. He went by the name of Ernst. Do you remember him?'

At first she did not, but when Lady Leoba gave her leave

to sit down again, a hazy memory brushed her: the village, the thunderstorm, the eager youth Ernst. For some reason, tears filled her eyes. She didn't cry as much now but that was only because the world seemed so stretched and thin that it was difficult to get up enough energy to cry.

'Hanna?' Frederun appeared at her side. She had sent the new apprentices to their duties in stable, hall, kitchens, or carpentry. Dressed in a fine calf-length tunic worn over a linen underdress, she looked quite striking with her bountiful dark hair caught back in a scarf and her cheeks rosy with sun. 'You look tired again.'

'I'd like to go back to bed.'

'Nay, you must take three turns around the courtyard first. Otherwise you'll not get stronger.'

Hanna did not have the stamina to resist Frederun's commands. She did as she was told, because it was easier to obey than to fight. Yet, in fact, she did get stronger. The invalid's spelt porridge soon had a hank of freshly baked bread to supplement it, and infusions of galingale and feverfew gave way to cups of mead and mulled wine. Light broths became soups, and soon after that she could eat chicken stewed in wine, fish soup, and periwinkles cooked up with peas. By the beginning of the month of Sormas she took her meals in the servants' hall rather than alone in her room. Gent remained peaceful, a haven, but its quiet did not soothe her. She did not care to explore the city and kept to herself within the confines of the palace compound. Those like Frederun, who tried to befriend her, she kept at arm's length; the others she ignored. When young Ernst returned late in the month of Sormas with an urgent summons for Lady Leoba, Hanna greeted his arrival with relief. It was time to move on.

Leoba and her retinue rode out the day after Luciasmass, the first day of summer. Fields of winter wheat and rye had grown high over the spring, turning gold as summer crept in. Gardens neatly fenced off from the depredations of wild creatures and wandering sheep stood around hamlets sprung up along the road. Children ran out to watch them ride by. Some enterprising farmers had planted apple orchards to replace those chopped down during the Eika occupation, but these were young trees not yet bearing fruit. As they rode south along the river, fields gave way to pasturelands and a series of enclosed fields of flax and hemp near palisaded villages built up in the last two years to replace those burned by Bloodheart and his marauding army. The cathedral tower remained a beacon for a long while as they rode, but eventually it was lost behind trees. Settlements grew sparser and children more shy of standing at the roadside to stare.

Ernst insisted on riding beside her. 'I've never seen such fine ladies as those in the princess' court! Do you see the clothes they wear for riding? All those colors! I've never seen so much gold and silver. God must truly love those to whom They grant so much wealth. I have so much food to eat that every night I have a full stomach! Sometimes I'm allowed to eat the leftovers off the platters the noble folk eat from. I had swan, but some spice in it made my tongue burn!'

He sat a horse well. It hadn't taken him long to learn, but his simple belief in the glamour of an Eagle's life would prove a more stubborn obstacle to overcome. She kept silent, and eventually he shut up.

The warm days and cloudless sky of Quadrii did not cheer her. Each league they traveled seemed much like the last, although there was always something new to look at and plenty of folk willing to offer them a meal of porridge and bread in exchange for news. The local farmers and manor-born field hands had heard rumors of bandits, cursed shades, and plague, but hadn't seen any for themselves, nor had any of them heard until now of the great battle at Osterburg. Again and again she felt obliged to repeat the story. It was her duty, after all.

Would it have been better to have stayed in Gent, safe behind bland walls? Yet she had grown tired of the friendliness of Gent's servants and of her caretaker, Frederun. Everyone knew Frederun had been Prince Sanglant's concubine when he'd wintered over in Gent the year before, on the road east; they spoke of it still, although never in Frederun's hearing. He had given her certain small tokens, but she had stayed behind, bound to the palace, when he had ridden on. The prince had had a child with him, but no one knew what had happened to his wife, only that she had, evidently, vanished when the daughter was still a newborn infant.

What had happened to Liath?

When she closed her eyes, she saw the fever dream that had chased her through her illness, the hazy vision of a woman winged with flame whose face looked exactly like Liath's. At night, she sought Liath through fire, but she never found her. King Henry, Hathui, even Prince Sanglant no longer appeared to her Eagle's Sight, and Sorgatani came to her only in stuttering glimpses, clouded by smoke and sparks. It had been so long since she had seen Wolfhere that she had trouble recalling his features. Only Bulkezu's beautiful, monstrous face coalesced without fail when she stared into the flames. Even Ivar was lost to her, invisible to her Eagle's Sight although she sought him with increasing desperation. Had her sight failed her? Or were they all, at last, dead?

She felt dead, withered like a leaf wilting under the sun's glare.

Rain delayed them. 'It will ruin the harvest,' Ernst muttered more than once, surveying sodden fields, but Hanna had no answer to give. She had seen so much ruin already.

After twenty days, they rode into Osterburg under cover of a weary summer drizzle that just would not let up. A gray mist hung over the fields, half of them abandoned or left fallow after the trampling they had received from two armies but the rest planted with spring-sown oats and barley and a scattering of fenced gardens confining turnips, peas, beans, and onions. Stonemasons worked on scaffolds along the worst gaps in Osterburg's walls, but although there were still a number of gaps and tumbled sections, the worst stretch had been repaired. Inside, the streets seemed narrow and choked with refuse after so many days out on the open road.

Stable hands took their horses in the courtyard of the ducal palace. She and Ernst walked at the rear of Lady Leoba's escort as they crowded into the great hall, glad to get out of the rain. A steward, the same stout, intelligent woman who

had met the Lions outside Gent, escorted them up stairs to
the grand chamber where Princess Theophanu held court.

Despite the rain, it was warm enough that the shutters
had been taken down to let in the breeze. Theophanu reclined
at her ease on a fabulously padded couch, playing chess with
one of her ladies while her companions looked on in restful
silence. Two women Hanna did not know but who bore a
passing resemblance to the notorious Lord Wichman fidgeted on chairs on either side of Theophanu; it was hard at
first glance to tell which one was more bored, irritable, and
sour.

'Ah.' Theophanu looked up with a flash of genuine pleas-
ure. 'Leoba!' They embraced. Theophanu turned to address
the women sitting to either side of her. 'Cousin Sophie. Cousin
Imma. Here is my best companion, Leoba. She is out of the
Hesbaye clan, and was married last summer to Margrave
Villam.'

'But isn't she dead yet?' asked the one called Sophie, with
a leer. 'How many wives has Villam outlasted?'

'Nay, it will be a test of the Hesbaye and Villam clans to
see which one can outlast the other on fourth and fifth mar-
riages,' retorted her sister.

Leoba colored, but Theophanu drew her attention away,
making room on the couch for Leoba to sit beside her. 'How
fares Gent?'

'Well enough. A spring sowing of oats and barley was put
in on the fallow fields. The winter wheat and rye crop has
flourished. There are four excellent weaving houses. Each one
produced enough cloth over the winter and spring that there
is surplus for trade. The market brings in folk from three
days' walk away. Merchants have sailed in from as far as
Medemelacha. They pay the regnant's tax willingly enough.
The year the city lay under Eika rule hurt their custom and
their routes to the east. There's to be a harvest fair that will
likely bring folk from a week's walk. Gent is a prosperous
place. I have brought five chests of coin and treasure to give
into your coffers.'

'That is Saony's tax!' cried Imma. 'It belongs to our family.'

'Nay, Imma,' said Theophanu mildly, 'it belongs to the regnant, and to Saony. You have not been named as duchess, I think?'

'Because I am the elder!' said Sophie triumphantly.

'You are not!'

'I pray you, Cousins, let us not hear this argument again. I have been left as regent while King Henry remains in Aosta. I must judge. As I have already told you, I mean to let my father decide who will succeed my aunt, may she rest in peace, as duchess of Saony. I have only been waiting for an experienced Eagle, one who has traveled before across the Alfar Mountains.'

Every person in the chamber turned to look at Hanna.

'Dare you send another?' asked Leoba. 'You have sent all three of the Eagles left in your care south to Aosta and not heard one word from any of them, whether they lived or died or even reached the king.'

'Do I dare *not* send one more? You did not hear the news, Leoba? My cousin Conrad the Black celebrated Penitire in Mainni as though he were king! He allowed the biscop to receive him outside the city and escort him into the palace as she would if it were my father who had come. The feasting lasted a full three days in the royal manner. He has taken Tallia of Arconia as wife and got her pregnant. She rides with Conrad rather than remaining in the custody of my aunt Constance, in Autun, as my father decreed. If this is not rebellion, then I don't know what is.'

'Conrad would support my claim to Saony,' said Sophie, her expression shifting with animal cunning, 'if I offered to support him and Tallia. You forget that, Theophanu. You are not my only recourse.'

'But Conrad is not here, you stupid cow,' said her sister, 'nor is he king of Wendar, although it seems he would like to lay claim to the kingship of Varre by right of the body and blood of his new wife.'

'Where is the king of Wendar?' demanded Sophie. 'Can he be king if he has abandoned his people?'

'Henry is king over Wendar and Varre,' said Theophanu,

'and God have given their blessing to him. I trust you will remember that, Cousins.'

'I remember seeing your troops ride in after your brother stripped us of half our mounted soldiers for his mad journey east! Yet you haven't half the army Sanglant has, nor could you drive out the Quman invaders. And you can't do anything to stop Conrad!' Sophie's peevish expression vanished abruptly as she glanced at her sister who, like a cat, seemed ready to wash her paws with disdainful triumph, seeing that her enemy was about to fall into a trap of her own making.

'Do not think I am unsympathetic to your plight, Theophanu,' Sophie went on quickly. 'If Sapientia cannot rule after your father, then you are the rightful heir. You have not received what you deserve.'

'But you'll have honey poured on you now.' Imma sneered as she reached for her wine cup. 'Whom do you mean to flatter and cozen, Sophie? Conrad, or Theophanu?'

'It's true enough, nor can any of you admit otherwise!' said Sophie. 'Theophanu was left to be regent for King Henry but given no support. Henry has an army in Aosta, and Sanglant rides east with the army that defeated the Quman. What are you left with, Cousin?'

'My wits.' With an enigmatic smile, Theophanu gestured toward the windows. 'It seems the rain has passed. I intend to ride today. My head is quite stuffy from all this chattering. Eagle, you will attend me.'

In this way, Hanna found herself back on a horse and riding beside the princess along the verge of muddy fields where, last autumn, battle lines had been drawn and armies had clashed. Beyond the western shore of the Veser lay the hills where the Quman army had made its camp and where Bulkezu's prisoners had huddled in those last desperate hours. To the east she recognized the ragged band of forest that concealed the Veserling, where Ingo and the others had rescued her.

'Where are the Lions, Your Highness? They came to you early in the spring, did they not?'

Theophanu nodded. 'I keep them in the city to remind my cousins of my authority. These days, they work on the wall.

It was let fall into shameful disrepair by my aunt, may she be at peace. I think she must not have been at all well these past few years.'

Together with two stewards, three servants, and a half dozen of the princess' noble companions, they skirted several ditches half full of rainwater, an attempt to drain off the excess water collecting on the fields, and approached a low hill that rose out of the plain like a bubble. Theophanu waved her companions back but beckoned Hanna forward with her, and with some difficulty the two women urged their mounts up the slippery rise to the top. Alder and oak had been cut back here only recently, and they had to be careful of burned out stumps laying traps for their mounts' hooves. Wood rush and bramble bush proliferated. Dill had taken root, flowering in yellow clusters alongside cream-colored bells of comfrey. Yet at the height of the hill, in one man-sized spot, the lush greenery turned to blackened ground, as bare as if salt had been sown on the earth.

'It's said that this is where Bayan died.' Theophanu pulled her mare up beside the barren patch of ground, surveying it dispassionately. 'I never met him. What was he like?'

Hanna dismounted, kneeling to touch the earth. A wasp sting came alive in her chest as her fingers brushed the scorched ground. She knew in her bones that Bayan had been killed here, but the eerie sensation that coursed up her hand lasted only an instant. It was only dirt, after all. Catching her breath, she rose. 'He was a good man, Your Highness, may he rest at peace in the Chamber of Light. He was no fool.'

'A good match for Sapientia.' Was that sarcasm in Theophanu's tone? Hanna could not tell.

'She trusted him, Your Highness. With his guidance she gained in wisdom.'

'Then my father chose wisely.'

'In truth, I believe he did. Bayan's death grieved Princess Sapientia mightily. Things might have turned out differently for all of us, and for the kingdom, if Prince Bayan had not died at Bulkezu's hand.'

'The Quman prince himself killed Bayan, in combat?'

'Nay, Quman magic killed Prince Bayan. And his mother.'

Such a complicated expression swept over Theophanu's face that Hanna looked away, embarrassed. But when Theophanu spoke again, no trace of emotion sullied her voice.

'Have you command of the Eagle's Sight?'

No one stood near enough to hear them. The rest of their party waited obediently at the base of the little hill. 'I do, Your Highness.'

'Surely you have sought sight of my father.'

Ashamed, she lowered her gaze. 'My Eagle's Sight is clouded, Your Highness. I have looked for him, but I cannot see him.'

'Is it possible that another hand has clouded your sight?'

What a fool she had been! Cherbu had concealed Bulkezu's army for many months with magic. Surely a knowledgeable sorcerer could shield herself against the Eagle's Sight. Yet Wolfhere had never spoken of such things to her. Perhaps he had not wanted her to know, so that he could always keep an eye on her.

'It could be possible,' she admitted. 'I know little about magic, and less about the Eagle's Sight save that I can seek for visions of those I know through fire and sometimes hear them speak.'

'You have done nothing wrong, Hanna. The king himself rewarded you with that ring you wear, and therefore I know that he considered you a faithful and trustworthy subject. That is why I am glad you are with me now. My father must understand that I am in an impossible position. The duchy of Saony cannot go to one of Rotrudis' children. Their greed and mismanagement will only weaken the duchy. But I haven't troops or authority to install another in their place, and either one of my cousins will ride straight to Conrad if she thinks he will take her part. I have no army, or little enough of one—' She gestured impatiently toward distant Osterburg. '—and Sanglant has taken the rest.'

'It seems a large army for even a commander with Sanglant's reputation to march so far into the wilderness, Your Highness. They must all be fed and housed.'

'It's true enough. We've heard reports from various places that all of the infantry was dispersed after the battle, sent home to tend to planting. Villam's daughter is said to be supporting Sanglant. It's rumored that she's holding a portion of his army in reserve, in the marchlands, for when he returns from Ungria and the east. It could be true. She wanted to marry him once, but it wasn't allowed because he was only a bastard.'

Wind tugged at the princess' hair, bound up with silver pins, but no trace of feeling troubled her expression. Was it possible that the calmer Theophanu looked on the outside the more she raged in her inner heart? No wonder many in the king's court dared not trust her, if she concealed the truth of her heart behind a veil of composure. Yet after watching Bulkezu do as he willed, giving his whims and frenzies full rein, Hanna could admire a person who had the fortitude and discipline to hold herself in check.

'I might have been allowed more, born a bastard,' Theophanu murmured. As if she had just heard herself, she looked directly, almost defiantly, at Hanna, who gazed back steadily, unafraid.

'I beg your pardon, Your Highness, for speaking so boldly. I am also a third child, and what was granted to my elder siblings was not possible for me. That is why I joined the Eagles, rather than accept a marriage I would have found distasteful. I am proud to serve King Henry.'

Theophanu's smile was thin. 'Then you and I are perhaps the last folk here in Wendar who remain faithful of our own will to the rightful king. Do you fear magic, Eagle?'

'I fear it, Your Highness, but I have seen too much now to let the threat of magic halt my steps.'

'I am glad to hear you say so, because I must rest all my hopes on you. I have sent three Eagles to Aosta, but none have returned to me although I sent the first more than a year ago. You must travel to Aosta and find my father. I will give you a message to bring to him, but in truth it will be up to you to make him understand that his position here in Wendar is weakening, even here in Saony, our clan's ancient home.

Conrad troubles the west while Sanglant troubles the east. My cousin Tallia is a dangerous pawn in Conrad's hands, and I have heard no message from my aunt Constance in Autun for many months. I cannot hold here in the center for long, when even my cousins plot to seek help from those who would undermine Henry's authority. Not when famine and plague afflict Avaria. Not when we hear rumors of civil war from Salia. If the king hears your tale of the Quman invasion and the terrible destruction brought down onto Wendish lands, if he knows the extent of the plots whispered against his rule, surely he will return.'

2

'Hanna? Did you hear that? Hanna?'

Hanna had been lost in thought, repeating Theophanu's message to herself for the hundredth time, but the pitch of anxiety in Ernst's voice started her into alertness. 'I didn't hear anything.'

'You weren't listening. Hush. It will come again.'

Fog swathed the beech forest in the central uplands of Avaria through which she and Ernst rode, thirty or more days out of Osterburg; she had lost count because the weather had not favored their journey. They had suffered many delays because of day-long downpours, swamped roads, and pockets of plague they'd had to take detours to avoid. This clinging fog was the least of the hindrances they had faced.

Above, the sky appeared gray-white, almost glaring, while around them slender trees faded into the fog, their shapes blurred by the mist. Deer darted away, vanishing quickly into the fog, but otherwise there was no sign of life except for the chuckling calls of thrushes, the exuberant song of a blackcap, and the occasional rustle of some small animal thrashing away through the dense field layer of wood rush, or into a stand of honeysuckle. Although the world was obscured, these sounds carried easily enough.

She listened.

Nothing, except for the steady clop of hooves, two mounts and two spares. Nothing, except for the sough of an east wind through the summer leaves. East lay memories, and no matter how hard she tried to squeeze them out of herself, they still swelled inside her with the ache of an old wound. On a chill summer's day like today, her hip hurt. Where fog wrapped its tendrils around trees, she kept catching glimpses of strange figures from her dreams: centaur women stalking warriors with the bodies of humans and the faces of wolves and lynx; Sorgatani kneeling among reeds at the margin of a vast swamp; a pair of griffins hunting in the tall grass; a longship ghosting through a tide of mist like a beast swimming upriver toward unsuspecting prey; men with humanlike faces and the tails of fish swimming through the fogbound trees as through a pillared underwater city.

'Nothing,' said Ernst with disgust. 'But I know I heard something. It sounded like fighting.'

His indignation made her smile. To her surprise, the youth had proved to be a decent traveling companion. He no longer talked too much, he did his share of the work, and he never faltered or complained.

'If I never see any fighting again, I will be content,' she said.

All at once the wind shifted, and she heard the distinctive clap of weapons striking.

'It's ahead of us. Come on.'

She slipped her staff free from its harness across her back and, laying it ready over her thighs, pressed her horse forward along the path. With a gasp of excitement, or fear, Ernst drew the short sword the princess had given him and rode after.

Because of the swallowing fog they came upon the skirmish unexpectedly where the forest opened into a clearing marked by a tumble of stones and a crossroads. A tall woman in a battered Eagle's cloak had taken shelter with her back to the remains of a stone wall, fending off three ragged bandits armed with staves and a knife.

'Hai! For King Henry!' cried Hanna.

'For King Henry!' bellowed Ernst behind her, voice cracking.

Hanna got in a good whack at one of the bandits before they ran like panicked hogs into the trees, dropping their weapons in their haste to flee.

'Do we go after them?' shouted Ernst, barely remembering to rein his horse back from the fence of beech trees.

'Hold!' Hanna peered into the forest, but the fog shielded the bandits' flight, although she heard branches cracking and shouts fading into the distance. Her heart raced from the exertion, but her hands were perfectly steady. Was she glad they had got away? Or would she have gladly killed them?

Maybe it was better not to know.

She turned to see the Eagle doubled over.

'Comrade! Are you hurt?' Dismounting, she ran over, grabbed the woman's arm, and saw who it was. 'Hathui!' The shock caused her to step back, and she slammed hard into stone.

'Nay. A cut on the arm, that's all.' Hathui straightened with a grimace. 'Hanna! How is it you come here? Where are the bandits?'

'Fled,' called Ernst cheerfully from the forest's edge. 'We routed them!'

He dismounted to collect the two staves. The horses bent their heads to graze. The fog seemed to be making an effort to lift, and they could see pretty far into the forest by now. Far back into the misty haze among the trees, nothing moved.

'God above,' swore Hathui. Blood trickled through her fingers where she held them clamped tight just below her left shoulder. 'Have you something I can bind this with? He slashed me. Lad, look for my horse. She can't have strayed far.'

Hanna's shoulders throbbed where she'd hit the stone wall. Lichen slipped under her fingers as she pushed forward, finally sweeping away the grip of shock. 'Ernst! Go on! Keep your eyes open. We don't want those men creeping back with their friends to attack us.'

She had nothing to say to Hathui. Surprise had mangled her tongue. She hurried to the horse tied on behind the saddled gelding and fished out the roll of linen in their stores packed by Theophanu's stewards for just such an eventuality.

Hathui limped over to a ramp of stone half overgrown by a bramble bush heavy with berries. With a grunt, she eased down to sit on the stone and carefully released her fingers. Blood leaked through a gash in her sleeve. The cloth had been mended once, just above the fresh rip, tidy white stitches set into the dirty gray wool that matched a dozen mended tears in her Eagle's cloak. Her dark hair was caught back in an untidy pony's tail, and a smudge of dirt darkened her hawk's nose. Fresh blood smeared one corner of her mouth.

'Best move quickly,' she said without raising her head as she delicately pulled aside torn cloth to examine the cut. She was breathing hard but did not look likely to faint.

Hanna had seen worse wounds. The blade had caught the surface of the skin and torn it back raggedly, but not deeply. She unfastened Hathui's Eagle's brooch and helped her pull off the tunic, then painted a paste of crushed marigold flowers over the cut before binding it up with a strip of linen. Hathui got her tunic on, wincing, just as Ernst returned triumphantly, leading the sorriest-looking mare Hanna had ever seen.

'My thanks, lad.' Hathui limped forward to take the reins from him. 'I'm called Hathui. Are you one of us?'

'I'm called Ernst,' said the youth, staring at her with admiration. Hathui was not, Hanna supposed, a handsome woman, but she was impressive: tough, proud, and looking like she'd ridden through a storm of demons and survived. 'I mean to be an Eagle. That's why I'm riding with Hanna.'

'Well met.' After greeting him, Hathui rubbed the mare's nose affectionately and checked her saddlebag, which seemed to hold nothing more than half a loaf of dry bread and an empty wineskin. Finally, she looked up. 'Ai, God, Hanna, it's good to see you. Where are you bound?'

'Aosta. What news, Hathui? Have you come from the king?

I've been sent with an urgent message from Princess Theophanu—'

Hathui's face drained to white, bled dry, and she sank down onto the fallen stone with a grimace of pain. 'You must ride straight back to Princess Theophanu!'

'The king's *dead*?'

'Not dead when I left him.' Hathui spoke so quietly it was difficult to hear her voice. 'I pray he is not dead now.' Tears trickled down her cheeks, and her breathing became harsh. 'That I should take so long to get even this far! And I do not know how far I have left to go.'

Her expression made Hanna tremble as the older Eagle grabbed her sword hilt and pushed herself up, looking grim and determined. 'We must make haste, you to Princess Theophanu and I— Can you tell me, Hanna? Where is Prince Sanglant? I have followed rumors that lead me east, but I may be following a cold trail, God help me, for he is veiled to my Eagle's Sight. I must reach Prince Sanglant.'

Ernst had wandered close to listen, but Hanna chased him off. 'You're sentry, Ernst! You must keep watch. Those brigands could come sneaking back and kill us while we're not looking!'

She picked up one of the bandits' captured staves, which was not much more than a stout walking stick carved to a nasty point at one end, and beat down the bramble bush around the stone bench so she and Hathui could sit without fear of thorns. It felt good to batter down the bramble bush, to hear the snap of vines and watch bits of leaf spill like chaff onto the ground, revealing more of the old stone ruin. By the pattern of the tumbled stones and their neatly dressed edges, she guessed this had once been an old Dariyan way station. Dariyan messengers, folk like herself, had sheltered here long ago.

'Sit down,' she said. Hathui sat, shaking and still pale. 'You must tell the whole.'

Haltingly she did, although Hanna had never before heard Hathui sound so unlike the confident, sharp-tongued Eagle she had met in Heart's Rest five years ago. While she talked,

Ernst paced out the edge of the clearing, riding a short way down each of the three paths that branched out from the clearing: one led north back toward Theophanu, one east, and one southwest. Each time he returned he glanced over at them and their hushed conversation before resuming his circuit of the forest's edge.

Hathui spoke more with rasp than voice. 'I bring no message from King Henry, only news of his betrayal. Hugh of Austra has connived with Queen Adelheid and the skopos herself, the Holy Mother Anne, to make Henry their creature in all ways. I know not with what black spells Hugh has sullied his hands, but he trapped an unearthly daimone and forced it into the king, who was all unsuspecting. Now the king speaks with the daimone's voice, for the daimone controls his speech and his movements.'

'How came Hugh of Austra into the councils of Queen Adelheid and the skopos?'

'He is a presbyter now, forgiven for all his sins,' said Hathui bitterly. 'I know little of the new skopos save that she claims to be the granddaughter of the Emperor Taillefer. She also claims to be Liath's mother.'

Could it be true? Hanna had seen Liath's child, with Sanglant, in the few days she had remained at the prince's side beyond the Veser, when the prince himself had interviewed her at length about the time she had spent as a prisoner of Bulkezu and the Quman army. Before he had sent her away to carry word of his victory and his plans to his sister. She had heard this tale herself, but it seemed as unlikely then as it did now.

Or perhaps it was the only explanation that made sense.

Wind made the leaves dance and murmur. A brown wren came to light among the brambles, eyeing Hanna and Hathui with its alert gaze before fluttering off.

'There is more,' said Hathui at last, sounding exhausted, her shoulders slumped. 'The infant Mathilda is to be named as heir. Adelheid wanted Henry to stay in Aosta to fight in the south, although it was his intent to return to Wendar. That is why they bound him with the daimone. Now he only does what they wish.'

'Why go to Sanglant, then?'

'He must be told what has happened.'

'He is himself a rebel against the king. You must take this news to Theophanu at once!'

'Nay, to Sanglant. So Rosvita counseled me. She said . . .' Hathui grasped her injured arm again, shutting her eyes, remembering. Her words were almost inaudible. 'She said, "a bastard will show his true mettle when temptation is thrown in his path and the worst tales he can imagine are brought to his attention." Ai, Lady. She allowed herself to be taken prisoner so that I might escape. I do not know if she lives, after all this time. I have searched with my Eagle's Sight, but I see only darkness.' To Hanna's horror, indomitable Hathui began to weep. 'I fear she is dead.'

Rosvita meant little to Hanna beyond being Ivar's elder and half sister. 'When did this happen? How long have you been traveling?'

She wiped her cheeks with the back of a hand. 'Months. Since last year. I had to ride west, toward Salia. Even then I came too late to the mountains. Snow had already closed the pass. So I laid low and lived as I could, all winter. They hunted me. A dozen times or more I saw soldiers wearing Queen Adelheid's livery along the roads. It was only three months ago that I was able to fight my way through the snow and into Salia, and then I had to travel in the wilderness, or at night, until I came at last to Wayland. There I found that Duke Conrad's soldiers would as soon throw me in prison as aid me. I have not come easily to this place.' She patted the cold stone, almost with affection. 'Those bandits were the least of the troubles I've faced. I fear I have a long and difficult journey still ahead of me.'

'So you do, if you will not turn north to bring your tidings to Theophanu. Prince Sanglant rides to Ungria. He left last autumn from Osterburg, after the battle there, although I do not know how he fared this past winter. He is hidden to my Eagle's Sight as well. You would be a fool to ride east after him. You must take this news to Princess Theophanu—'

'Nay!' She rose, striding toward her horse. 'I must ride to

Sanglant! I will do as Sister Rosvita commanded me, for she is the last one I know who is loyal to the king now that Hugh has murdered Margrave Villam.'

'Villam!' The words came at her like barbs, pricking and venomous. 'May God save us if it's true.' *And yet* . . . 'We've heard no news from Aosta. Nothing. Princess Theophanu sent three Eagles to her father with desperate tidings—'

'One at least delivered that message, but she has been detained in Darre. Perhaps the others have as well, if they reached the court after I fled. They will not let Theophanu's Eagles leave Aosta now. King Henry knew that he was needed in Wendar! He meant to return!' She halted beside the tallest segment of wall, which came to her shoulder; a pair of fallen wooden roof beams lay covered in nettles and moss at her feet. Her expression was set and stubborn. Unshakable. 'I go to Sanglant, Hanna. Sanglant will avenge his father's betrayal. He will save Henry. No one else can.'

'Sanglant is not the man you think he is, Hathui. Do not ride to him, I beg you. Princess Theophanu—'

'No.' Hathui tied a stave to her saddle and made ready to mount. 'I will not be bent from my task.'

This was the stubbornness that King Henry had admired so much that he had made Hathui his favored Eagle and, indeed, an intimate counselor whose opinion he consulted and trusted. Hathui loved the king.

But she was wrong about Sanglant.

'Very well,' said Hanna at last. 'Ernst will return to Theophanu.'

The answer gave Hathui pause as she swung onto her mare and, turning, gazed with an expression of dismay at Hanna. 'What do you mean to do?'

'I mean to do as Princess Theophanu commanded me. I will ride to Aosta to the king.'

'Hanna!'

'I can be as stubborn as you, Hathui.' But as she spoke the words, she felt the wasp sting burn in her heart. Was she turning away from Sorgatani because the Kerayit princess had not rescued her from the Quman? Was she punishing

Sanglant, who had betrayed his own people by letting Bulkezu live? Or was she only doing what was right?

'You can't have understood what I've told you—'

'I understand it well enough. I will deliver Theophanu's message, as is my duty. I will deliver my report about the Quman invasion to King Henry, as I swore I would. I shall see for myself how he responds.'

'You cannot trust them! What they might do to you—'

'They can do nothing worse to me than what I've already suffered.'

Imperceptibly, as they spoke, the sun had burned off the fog, and now light broke across the clearing. Dew sparkled on nettles and glistened on ripe berries, quickly wicked away by the heat of the sun. The morning breeze faded and a drowsy summer glamour settled over the green wood, broken only by the song of birds and the caw of an irritated crow.

The light of camaraderie had fled from Hathui's face, replaced by the expression of a woman who has seen the thing she loves best poisoned and trampled. 'So be it. You have chosen your path. I have chosen mine.'

Enough, thought Hanna. *I have made my choice.* The core of rage that these days never left her had hardened into iron. As long as Bulkezu lived, she would never give loyalty, aid, or trust to the man who had refused to punish him as he deserved.

'So be it,' she echoed.

There were three paths leading out of the clearing. She would ride hers alone.

PART TWO

THE UNCOILING
YEAR

III

AN ADDER IN THE PIT

1

In the east, so it was said, the priests of the Jinna god Astareos read omens in fire. They interpreted the leap and crackle of flames, the shifting of ash along charred sticks, and the gleam of coals sinking into patterns among the cinders, finding in each trifling movement a message from the god revealing his will and the fate of those who worshiped him. But no matter how hard Zacharias stared at the twisting glare of the campfire, he could not tease any meaning from the blaze. It looked like a common fire to him, cheerfully devouring sticks and logs. Like fire, the passage of time devoured all things, even a man's life, until it was utterly consumed. Afterward, there was only the cold beauty of an infinite universe indifferent to the fate of one insignificant human soul.

He shuddered, although on this balmy summer's night he ought not to be cold.

'What do you think, Brother Zacharias? Do you believe the stories about the phoenix and the redemption?'

Startled, he glanced up from the fire at Chustaffus. The

stocky soldier regarded him with an affable smile on his homely face. 'What phoenix?' he asked.

'He wasn't listening,' said Surly. 'He never does.'

'He's seeing dragons in the fire,' retorted Lewenhardt, the archer.

'Or our future,' said quiet Den.

'Or that damned phoenix you won't shut up about, Chuf,' added Surly, punching Chustaffus on the shoulder.

They all laughed, but in a friendly way, and resumed their gossip as they ate their supper of meat, porridge, and ale around their campfire, one of about fifty such fires scattered throughout pasturelands outside the Ungrian settlement of Nabanya. Why Prince Sanglant's loyal soldiers tolerated a ragged, cowardly, apostate frater in their midst Zacharias could never understand, but he was grateful for their comradeship all the same. It allowed him to escape, from time to time, the prince's court, where he served as interpreter, and the grim presence of his worst enemy who was, unfortunately, not dead yet.

'Prince Ekkehard was a traitor,' said Den. 'I don't think we should believe anything he said.'

'But he wasn't the only one who spoke of such stories,' insisted Chustaffus. 'Men died because they believed in the redemption. They were willing to die. Takes a powerful belief to embrace martyrdom like that.'

'Or a powerful stupidity.' Surly drained his cup and searched around for more ale, but they had drunk their ration. 'I don't believe it.'

'It wasn't heresy that saved Prince Ekkehard,' said black-haired Everwin, who spoke rarely but always at length. 'I hear he was treated like a lord by the Quman. If that Eagle's testimony was true, and I don't see any reason why I shouldn't believe it, then there's many honest, God-fearing folk who died while Prince Ekkehard ate his fill of their plundered food and drank stolen wine and dandled women, none of them willing to have been thrown into his bed. They might have been any of our sisters forced to please him or die.'

'Prince Ekkehard wasn't the only one who survived,'

objected Chustaffus. 'Don't forget Sergeant Gotfrid of the Lions, and his men. They escaped the Quman, and shades in the forest, *and* bandits who sold them into slavery before the prince redeemed him. Gotfrid is a good man. He believed in the phoenix. Even that Lord Wichman admits he saw the phoenix.'

'Give it a rest, Chuf,' said Lewenhardt. 'If I have to hear about that damned phoenix one more time, I swear I'm going to put an arrow through the next one I see.'

Den, Johannes, and Everwin laughed longest at this sally, but Chustaffus took offense, and it fell to Zacharias to coax the glower off the young soldier's face. As a slave to the Quman, he'd learned how to use his facility for words to quiet his former master's dangerously sudden vexations.

'Many a tale is truer than people can believe, and yet others are as false as a wolf's heart. I wonder sometimes if I really saw that dragon up in the Alfar Mountains. It might have been a dream. Yet, if I close my eyes, I can still see it gleaming in the heavens, with its tail lashing the snow on the high mountain peaks. What am I to make of that?'

The soldiers never got tired of his story of the dragon.

'Were its scales really the size and color of iron shields?' asked Lewenhardt, who had a master archer's knack for remembering small details.

'Nothing that big can fly,' said Surly.

'Not like a bird, maybe,' said Lewenhardt. 'It might be that dragons have a kind of magic that keeps them aloft. If they're made of fire, maybe the earth repels them.'

'Kind of like you and women, eh?' asked the Karronishman, Johannes, who only spoke to tease.

'Did I show you where that Ungrian whore bit me?' Lewenhardt pulled up his tunic.

'Nay, mercy!' cried Johannes with a laugh. 'I can dig up worms enough to get the idea.'

'Someone's been eating worms,' said Surly suddenly, 'and not liking the taste. There's been talk that King Geza is going to divorce his wife and marry Princess Sapientia. That's the best way for the prince to get rid of her.'

'Prince Sanglant would never allow that!' objected Lewenhardt. 'That would give King Geza a claim to the Wendish throne through his children by the princess.'

'Hush,' said Den.

Captain Fulk approached through flowering feather grass and luxuriant fescue whose stalks shushed along his knees and thighs. Beyond him, poplars swayed in the evening's breeze where they grew along the banks of a river whose name Zacharias did not yet know. Where the river curved around a hill, an old, refurbished ring fort rose, seat of the local Ungrian noble family. Beyond its confines a settlement sprawled haphazardly, protected by a palisade and ditch but distinctively Ungrian because of the many stinking corrals. Every Ungrian soldier kept ten horses, it seemed, and folk who walked instead of riding were scorned as slaves and dogs. Yet who tilled the fields and kept the gardens? The farmers Zacharias had seen working in hamlets and fortified villages as Prince Sanglant and his army followed King Geza's progress through the Ungrian kingdom were smaller and darker than the Ungrian nobles who ruled over them. Such folk were forbidden to own the very horses they were scorned for not riding.

All the men rose when Fulk halted by the fire's light.

Lewenhardt spoke. 'Captain. Is all quiet?'

'As quiet as it can be, with the army marching out in the morning.' Fulk surveyed the encampment before looking back over the six soldiers seated around the fire. 'I posted you out here to keep alert, not to gossip.' He nodded at Zacharias. 'Brother, I come from the prince. You're to attend him.'

'I thought he had Brother Breschius to interpret for him tonight. Isn't it only Ungrians and Wendishmen at the feast?'

'I don't answer for His Highness. You're to come at once.'

Surly began whistling a dirge, breaking off only after Chustaffus punched his arm.

'You take your watch at midnight,' said Fulk to his soldiers. 'I'll be back to check up on you.'

That sobered them. Zacharias rose with a sigh and followed Fulk. They walked along the river, listening to the wind

sighing in the poplars. Although the sun had set, the clouds
to the west were still stained an intense rose-orange, the color
lightening toward the zenith before fading along the eastern
hills to a dusky gray.

'I miss the beech woods of home,' Fulk said. 'They say
we'll ride through grasslands and river bottom all the way to
the Heretic's Sea. There are even salt marshes, the same as
you'd see on the Wendish coast, but lying far from the
seashore. When I left home to join the king's service, I never
thought to journey so far east. But I suppose you've seen these
lands before.'

'I have not. I traveled east the first time through Polenie
lands.'

'Did you see any one-legged men? Women with dogs'
heads? Two-headed babies?'

'Only slaves and tyrants, the same as anywhere.'

Fulk grunted, something like a laugh. Like all of Sanglant's
personal guard, he wore a pale gold tabard marked with the
sigil of a black dragon. 'The Ungrians are a queer folk,' he
continued, humoring Zacharias' curtness. 'As friendly as you
please, and good fighters, yet I know their mothers didn't
worship God in Unity. I'd wager that half of them still sacrifice to their old gods. One of the lads said he saw a white
stallion being led out at midwinter from the king's palace, and
he never saw it come in again for all that King Geza spent
the Feast of St. Peter on his knees in church. God know
they're half heretics themselves, for it was Arethousan
churchmen who first brought the word of the blessed Daisan
to these lands.'

'It is Brother Breschius who presides over mass, not an
Arethousan priest.'

'True enough. It's said the last of the Arethousans fled
Ungria when we arrived with Prince Bayan's body last
autumn. They're worse than rats, skulking about and spreading their lies and their heresy.'

'It seems to me that there's heresy enough in the ranks of
Prince Sanglant's army. I hear whispers of it, the phoenix and
the redemption.'

Fulk had a deceptively mild expression for a man who had survived any number of hard-fought battles and had abandoned King Henry to join the war band of that king's rebel son. His lips twitched up, as though he meant to smile, but his gaze was sharp. 'If you toss an adder into a pit without water and leave it alone, it will shrivel up and die soon enough. But if you worry at it, then it will bite you and live.'

In silence they left the river and followed the track across an overgrazed pasture to the palisade gate. The ring fort had been built along the bend in the river, but in recent times houses, craftsmen's yards, and shepherds' hovels had crept out below the circular ramparts and been ringed in their turn by a ditch and log palisade.

The two men crossed the plank bridge thrown over the palisade ditch and greeted the guards lounging at the open gates. With the king in residence, the Quman defeated, and a good-sized army camped in the fields beyond, the watch kept the gates open all night because of the steady traffic between town and camp.

In Ungria, peace reigned.

Half a dozen soldiers were waiting for Fulk just beyond the gate, leaning at their ease on the rails of an empty corral. As soon as they saw their captain, they fell in smartly behind him.

'A captain cannot appear before the prince without a retinue, lest he be thought unworthy of his captain's rank,' said Fulk wryly.

'You came alone to get me.'

'So I did. I wanted to get a good look at camp without being noticed. Smell the mood of the men.'

The settlement had a lively air. A summer's evening market thrived near the tanners' yard, although the stench of offal, urine, and dung at times threatened to overpower the folk out bargaining over rugs, bronze buckets, drinking horns, pots of dye, woolen cloth, and an impressive variety of shields. Small children with feet caked in dried mud ran about naked. A woman sat beside a crate of scrawny hens, calling out in an incomprehensible tongue that seemed only half Ungrian to

Zacharias' ears, shot through with a coarser language closer to that spoken out on the grasslands.

Horses pounded up behind them. Zacharias glanced back just as Fulk swore irritably. A sweep of pale wings brushed the dark sky; in an instant the riders would be upon him. The frater shrieked out loud and dropped hard to the ground, clapping his hands over his head. Death came swiftly from the Quman. They would strike him down and cut off his head. Terror made him lose control; a hot gush of urine spilled down his legs.

But the horsemen swept past, ignoring him, although in their passage they overturned the crate. Freed chickens ran squawking out into the market. One of the birds ran right over Zacharias, claws digging into his neck.

'Here, now,' said Fulk, grasping his arm to pull him up. 'Did you get hit?'

They hadn't been Quman after all, come to behead him. It was only a group of Ungrian cavalrymen wearing white cloaks, the mark of King Geza's honor guard.

Fulk's soldiers ran down the chickens and returned them to the woman, who was cursing and yelling. At least the commotion hid Zacharias as he staggered to his feet. The darkness hid the stain on his robe, but nothing could hide the stink of a coward. As long as he feared the Quman, and Bulkezu, he was still a slave. Blinking back tears of shame and fear, he tottered over to the dirty watering trough and plunged in as Fulk and his soldiers shouted in surprise. Chickens, goats, and children made an ear-splitting noise as they scattered from his splashing. He was sopping wet from the chest down when he climbed out. Someone in the crowd threw a rotten apple at him. He ducked, but not quickly enough, and it splattered against his chest.

'For God's sake,' swore Fulk, dragging him along. 'What madness has gotten into you now, Brother?' The ground sloped steeply up and the ramparts loomed dark and solid above them.

'I fell into a stinking pile of horse shit. Whew! I couldn't attend the prince smelling like the stables.' As they walked into the deeper shadow of the rampart gates, lit by a single sentry's torch, he found himself shaking still. 'Next time those Ungrian soldiers will cripple some poor soul and never bother to look back to see what they've wrought.'

'Here, now,' said Fulk, taken aback by his ferocity but obviously thrown well off the scent, 'it's a miracle you weren't trampled, falling like you did.'

The passage through the ramparts took a sharp turn to the left, and to the right again, lit by torches. Sentries chatted above them, up on the walls from which they watched the passage below. One of the soldiers was singing a mournful tune, his song overwhelmed by the hubbub as they came into the central courtyard of the inner fort.

The nobles were feasting in the hall, late into the summer night, in honor of St. Edward Lloyd, a cunning and pious Alban merchant who had brought the faith of the Unities as well as tin into the east. Zacharias heard singing and laughter and saw the rich glow of a score of lamps through the open doors. Servants rushed from the kitchens into the hall, bearing full platters and pitchers, and retreated with the scraps to feed the serving folk, the beggars, and the dogs.

Fulk gave the bright hall scarcely a glance and headed straight for the stables, currently inhabited by the rest of Sanglant's personal guard and a sizable contingent of Ungrian cavalrymen. Wolfhere met them at the door.

'It isn't raining,' the old Eagle said, looking Zacharias up and down in that annoyingly supercilious way he had, as though he had guessed the means and nature of the injury and found the frater wanting yet again.

'An accident.' The words grated, harsh and defensive.

Wolfhere shrugged. 'This way, Captain. We got her por-ridge and ale, as the prince requested. She said she'd rest and bathe *after* she'd delivered her report.'

Instead of heading up a ladder to the loft where the soldiers quartered, the old Eagle led them past stalls, about half of them stabling a horse and the rest storing arms, armor, or barrels of grain and ale, down to an empty stall where Heribert and Sergeant Cobbo hovered beside a tall, dark-haired, big-boned woman who had a stained Eagle's cloak thrown around her shoulders and a mug of ale at her lips.

Was the floor heaving and buckling? His knees folded under him so fast that he had to brace himself against the wall to stay upright.

'Well met, Eagle.' Fulk stepped into the halo of lamplight. 'You've ridden far.' Straw slipped under his boots as he moved forward and the Eagle, lowering her mug, stood up to greet him.

Hathui.

Only a strangled gasp escaped Zacharias' throat. He tugged at his hood, pulling it up to conceal his face, but she had already seen him. For the length of time it might take a skilled butcher to cut a calf's throat she stared at him, puzzled, her hawk's gaze as sharp as a spear's point. He was so changed that she did not know him. If he was careful, he could make sure that she would never know who he was, never be ashamed by what he had become. He turned to hide his face in the shadows.

Her eyes widened as recognition flared. She dropped the mug. Ale spilled down her leggings; the mug hit and shattered on the plank floor. Her lips formed his name, but no sound came out. Staggering, she folded forward and fell as though she'd been slugged and, reflexively, as he'd always done when she was only his little sister and had got into trouble yet again, he leaped forward to catch her.

She clutched him hard. 'Ai, God.' She was as tall as he was, with a strong grip and a rank smell. 'I thought you were dead.'

I am dead. I am not the brother you knew. But he could not speak.

'God's mercy,' said Wolfhere softly, much surprised. 'I knew you had a brother, Hathui, who walked into the east as a frater and was lost. Can this man be the same one?'

She wept, although she'd never been one to weep as a child, scorning those who cried; her beloved older brother had been the only soul ever allowed to see her rare bouts of tears.

'Hush,' he said, remembering those days bitterly. Memories swept over him with such strength that he felt nauseated. Now she would know. Now she would despise him.

'I thought you were dead,' she repeated, voice hollow. Tears still coursed down her face, but her expression had changed, taut and determined, the hawk's glare focused again on its distant prey. 'All things are possible, if you are truly alive after all this time. My God, Zacharias, there is so much for us to speak of, but first I must deliver my news to the prince.'

She nodded to the others and strode out of the stables. He was left behind to follow in her wake, fearing the worst: that she brought ill news, and that he had been called because Prince Sanglant intended to bring in the captive Quman and needed Zacharias to interpret. Yet why not? Let the worst be known at once, so that her repudiation of him would come now, the pain of her rejection suffered immediately. That was better than to be left lingering, malignant with hope.

They pushed into the hall past servants and hangers-on, brushing aside a pack of hopeful dogs waiting for bones. Hathui walked with a pronounced limp, as if she had aggravated the old childhood injury that had left her with a slight hitch in her stride. Was it really almost two years ago when he had glimpsed her that day in Helmut Villam's presence? Zacharias had kept back in the shadows, and Hathui had not recognized him. Since that day, she'd grown thin and weary and worn, and her sunken cheeks made her hawk's nose more prominent, bold and sharp. But when they pushed through the crowd and came before the high table where King Geza presided over the feast, she stood proudly in her patched Eagle's cloak and tattered clothing and spoke in the voice he remembered so well, confident and proud.

'My lord king of Ungria, may all be well in your kingdom. I pray you, forgive my abruptness.'

The hall grew quiet as the feasting nobles settled down to listen. Sapientia sat in the seat of honor to Geza's right while Sanglant sat between the robust but gray-haired King Geza and Lady Ilona, a ripely handsome and fabulously rich

Ungrian widow. Brother Breschius leaned down to whisper into Geza's ear as Hathui turned her attention to the royal siblings.

'Your Highness, Princess Sapientia, I come from Aosta bearing news. My lord prince, my lady, I have traveled a long and difficult road to reach you. It has taken me almost two years to come so far, and I have escaped death more than once.'

Sanglant rose to his feet, holding a cup of wine. He wore a rich gold tunic embroidered with the sigil of the black dragon and finished with red braid, and his black hair had been trimmed back from his beardless face. No person could look at him and forget that his mother was not born of human-kind.

Yet neither could they forget that he was a prince, com-mander of the army that had defeated the Quman. Even, and especially, Sapientia, dressed in all the finery appropriate to a noblewoman, looked as insignificant as a goldfinch perched next to a mighty dragon.

'You bring ill news,' said Sanglant.

Hathui almost choked on the words. 'I bring ill news, Your Highness, may God help us all. King Henry has been bewitched, ensorcelled with the connivance of his own queen and his trusted counselor. He lives as a prisoner in his own body. You are the only one who can save him.'

2

Blessing had a disconcerting habit of leaning so far out tower windows that it seemed in the next instant she would fall, or fly.

'Look!' She had crawled up into the embrasure of an archer's loophole and was still – barely – small enough to push into the narrow opening so that she could look down into the forecourt. 'My father has left the feasting hall. I don't like it when he makes me stay here, like I'm in prison. Doesn't he have enough prisoners to lord it over? Why does he pick on me?'

'Your lord father does not like it when you behave as you did this morning,' said Anna for the tenth time that evening. 'When you act like a barbarian, then you must be treated as one.'

Matto sat by the cold hearth, a lit lamp dangling above him. He had made use of the long and dreary afternoon to oil the young princess' harness until it gleamed. Looking up, he winked slyly, and Anna blushed, gratified and irritated at the same time.

Blessing forced her shoulders through the loophole. Anna hastily grabbed her trailing feet just as the girl called out, words muffled by the stone. 'Who's that with him? It looks like an Eagle! He's coming back here!'

Anna tugged, grunting, but Blessing was either stuck or was holding on. 'Matto!'

He was more than happy to set down the harness and help her, because it gave him an excuse to put his arms around her as he grasped hold of Blessing's ankles as well. 'Your Highness!' he said. 'I pray you, do not get stuck in there or we will be the ones who will face your father's anger.'

There was a pause.

Blessing wriggled backward, half slid down the stair-step embrasure, and hopped to the carpeted floor. Despite everything, the girl had a profound sense of fairness and did not like to see her attendants blamed for her misadventures.

'Well, there *is* an Eagle with him,' she said defiantly. 'I don't know where she came from, or how she could have found us out here in Ungria. I hate Ungria.'

'We all know you hate Ungria, Your Highness,' said Anna wearily, allowing herself to lean against Matto's broad chest. His hand tightened on her shoulder.

'Thiemo won't like that.' Blessing had a sweet face still, although she stood as tall as many a nine- or ten-year-old child, but her expression was sharpened by a spark of malicious glee as she bared her teeth in something resembling a grin. 'I hear him coming up the stairs now.'

Anna stepped out from under Matto's arm.

'I'm not afraid of him!' Matto muttered as the latch flipped up.

The door had a hitch to it, and the floor was warped, so it took Thiemo a moment to shove it open. To be safe, Anna took two more steps away from Matto.

'My lord prince is returning,' said Thiemo, addressing Blessing. 'Your Highness.' His gaze quickly assessed Anna, and Matto, and the distance between them, and then he grinned winsomely at Anna, the smile that always made her dizzy. How could it be that a lord like Thiemo even noticed a common-born girl with skin stained nut-brown from the tanning pits?

Blessing's tunic was twisted around from climbing. As Anna helped the girl to straighten herself and found a comb to brush her untidy hair, Thiemo and Matto gathered up the harness, neatened up the chamber, and did not speak one word to each other. The two young men had never been friends, since the gulf in their stations did not truly permit such intimacy, but had once been friendly companions in Blessing's service. Not anymore.

The clamor of footsteps and voices echoed up from below. Lamplight glimmered and, all at once, fully a dozen people crowded into the tower chamber. Blessing scrambled up to hide in the stair-step embrasure, crouching there like a sweetly featured gargoyle with Thiemo and Matto standing as guards to either side of the opening. Anna retreated to the hearth while Prince Sanglant and his noble companions and loyal followers took up places around the chamber. His sister seated herself at the table with her faithful companion Lady Brigida at her side and the others ranged about the room, standing respectfully or sitting comfortably on the bed or the other bench, according to their station. It was the usual retinue: Lady Bertha of Austra, Brother Heribert, Wolfhere, that nasty Brother Zacharias, whose robes were damp, Captain Fulk, kind Brother Breschius, even-tempered Lord Druthmar, who commanded a contingent of Villam cavalry, and the one they all called the Rutting Beast, the notorious Lord Wichman. The only Ungrian present was Istvan, a noble if rather grim captain who, like Brother Breschius, had thrown his loyalty to Sanglant after Prince Bayan's death at the Veser. Anna had expected to see the prince's mistress, Lady Ilona, whose favorite gown Blessing had so thoroughly ruined this morning, but evidently she did not hold an intimate enough rank within the prince's personal circle to be invited into this private assembly.

Sanglant paced, wearing a path from the door to the window and back again, but his attention remained fixed on the battered Eagle who had been given Anna's stool for a seat, the only common-born person in the room not on her feet. This was no arrogant privilege granted her by reason of her Eagle's status; she looked too exhausted to stand on her own. But although her shoulders drooped, her keen gaze did not waver from the prince's restless figure.

'So it's true,' Sanglant said at last. 'Wolfhere glimpsed the truth with his Eagle's Sight, but we had no way to confirm what he had seen.' He glanced at Wolfhere, who regarded the other Eagle with a thoughtful frown, as though the news she had brought were nothing more troubling than the screech of a jay.

'We must march on Aosta at once!' cried Sapientia.

Sanglant barely glanced at her, nor did she try to interrupt him when he spoke. 'With what magic will we combat those who have imprisoned the king? Nay. This changes nothing, and in truth only makes our course more clear. We must continue east. That is the only way to defeat our enemies.'

'But, Your Highness,' objected the Eagle, 'I have been already two *years* seeking you. How can we know what has befallen King Henry in that time? He is hidden to my Eagle's Sight. He may be dead. They may do any foul deed to him that they wish!'

'And so may they continue to do,' said Heribert quietly. 'I have seen the power of the sorcery they wield. We cannot fight it with spears or swords.'

'But, Your Highness,' pleaded the Eagle, 'if you ride east, into unknown country and the lands where the Quman breed, it may be years until you return to Wendar. What will happen to your father meanwhile?' She knelt at the prince's feet, her presence forcing him to stand still.

'They need Henry alive in order to rule through him,' said Sanglant. 'His Wendish armies will desert Adelheid and her advisers if Henry dies. The nobles and their retinues will return to Wendar without the king to lead them.'

'There is the child, Your Highness.' The Eagle's voice was soft, but Sapientia all at once burst into noisy exclamations.

'Abandoned! Set aside! And for a toddling brat!'

Wichman snorted, but fell silent at a glance from the prince.

'It is true that the child can become queen in Henry's place, but she cannot yet be three years of age.' Sanglant looked toward the embrasure where his unnatural daughter had concealed herself in the shadows of the window's stone archway. Blessing was not more than three years old, but she appeared so much older that King Geza had suggested to Sanglant that he betroth her to Geza's favorite child, a brash fifteen-year-old boy whom many whispered had been all but anointed as heir despite having a dozen older brothers.

'Regents have ruled through three-year-old children before, Your Highness,' said Wolfhere. 'This girl, Mathilda, would no doubt be easier to control than a mature man of Henry's stature and experience.'

'Are you suggesting we give up our quest?'

'Nay, I do not, my lord prince, but I implore you to listen carefully to what Hathui has seen and heard. I trained her myself, and King Henry saw her worth and raised her up to stand at his right hand as a trusted adviser.'

Sanglant's lips twitched, as though he wasn't sure whether to smile or frown. 'Just as you stood beside my grandfather, King Arnulf?'

Wolfhere shrugged, unwilling to be drawn into an argument so old that Anna could only guess at its contours. Intimately involved as she was in the care of Blessing, she often witnessed the interactions between Sanglant and his closest counselors. Despite Wolfhere's status as a respected elder, she had seen tempers flare and accusations thrown like knives.

Sanglant returned his gaze to the younger Eagle. 'I do not question your loyalty to my father, Hathui. You have proved it by riding so far to seek my help.'

'What of the king?' she demanded.

'To fight the rebellious lords of Aosta, to fight the Jinna bandits and the Arethousan usurpers, it seems to me they must have Henry to lead the army. Why kill him if they can control him with sorcery? Why control him with sorcery if they felt powerful enough to kill him and still keep the crown of Wendar on the child's head? Nay, let us pray that my father lives, and that his queen and her counselors will keep him alive until the child is old enough to stand up at the war council herself.' He glanced again toward the embrasure, but the shadows hid his daughter from view. Only her eyes winked there, two sparks of fire. 'We cannot fight the sorcerers unless we have a hope of winning, and we have no hope of winning unless we can protect ourselves against their magic.'

'Griffin feathers,' murmured Zacharias. His face was flushed, and he was perspiring.

'I fear the Kerayit will not care about Wendish troubles, Your Highness,' said Breschius softly. 'They may not choose to aid you.'

'So you have said before. I do not neglect your counsel, Brother. But Anne's plotting threatens the Kerayit as much as any people. No place on earth will be safe.'

'And we could all die tomorrow,' added Lady Bertha cheerfully.

Wichman guffawed, caught sight of Anna, and gave her a wink. She shifted nervously. He had tried to grope her once, although Sanglant had put a stop to it, but the duchess' unruly son still made her uneasy.

'Set aside for a babe in arms!' muttered Sapientia. Yet it had been months since anyone had paid much attention to her, and although she still had the luster of the royal blood, she had faded in an intangible way, like silver left unpolished. 'Did the Wendish nobles not hear my father confirm me as heir? How can they bow before an infant in Aosta?'

'What of Wendar itself, my lord prince?' Hathui asked.

He paced to the door, pausing there with his back to the assembly.

'I should return to Wendar!' cried Sapientia.

'I wonder if my sisters still quarrel over Saony,' remarked Wichman, 'and if Ekkehard has managed to stick his key into his wife's treasure chest yet.'

Sanglant ignored these comments as he replied to the Eagle. 'I commanded a cohort of Lions to attend Theophanu. I sent many levies of fighters back to their farms. As you can see, I rode east with less than a thousand soldiers. Two thirds of the army we had at the Veser no longer rides with me. They must defend Wendar until I return.'

'Can they?' Grimacing with pain and favoring a leg, Hathui rose to stand defiantly in the middle of the room. 'Do you know what I have seen in the two years I have traveled, struggling to reach you, my lord prince?'

From no other common-born person might a noble lord hear such a tone, but it had long been understood that Eagles had to have a certain amount of freedom to speak their mind if their information was to be of any use to their regnant. She went on without asking his leave.

'Salia lies torn apart by civil war, plague, and drought. Bandits lurk along every road. I heard little news of Varre as I rode through Wayland, and received nothing but scorn from the retainers of Conrad the Black. It is said that he celebrated Penitire in Mainni as if he were king, with Sabella's daughter Tallia beside him as his new wife. Avaria has been swept by plague. I rode through more than one empty hamlet, and as many where the path was blocked by fallen trees and villagers standing there with scythes and shovels to guard themselves from any who might bring the contagion into their homes.

'Princess Theophanu refuses to name any of Duchess Rotrudis' children as heir to the duchy of Saony, but both the daughters have threatened to seek Conrad's aid to gain the ducal seat.'

'Two sows rooting in the mud while the boar looks on!'

'I pray you, Wichman,' said Sanglant, 'let the Eagle finish her report without interruption.'

Hathui continued. 'Cousins fight among themselves to gain lands and titles come free because there have been so many deaths in the recent wars. Riding through the marchlands, I saw fields withered by drought. I saw children laid low by famine, with their stomachs swollen and their eyes sunk in like those of corpses. In Eastfall, it rained every day for two months straight and black rot destroyed half their stores of rye. Heretics preach a story of a phoenix offering redemption. It is no wonder that people listen. The common folk fear that the end of the world is coming.'

Wichman laughed. 'What evil does *not* plague Wendar?'

Hathui was not so easily cowed. 'I have heard no report of locusts, my lord, nor has there been any news of Eika raids along the northern shores these past two years.'

'A spitfire! Do your claws come out in the bed, too?'

Impatiently, she turned back to Prince Sanglant. 'Princess Theophanu has sent three Eagles to Aosta and heard no answer from her father in reply to her pleas for help. I crossed paths with a fourth—' Anger creased her lips, quickly fled. '—last summer, who rode south to seek the king. I saw with my Eagle's Sight that she crossed the Alfar Mountains safely this spring, but as soon as she came near to Darre she was lost in the sorcerer's veil.

'Conrad of Wayland acts as if he is king, not duke. Yolanda of Varingia is embroiled in the Salian wars. Biscop Constance remains silent in Arconia. Liutgard of Fesse and Burchard of Avaria ride at Henry's side in Aosta. Saony has no duke. Theophanu cannot act with the meager forces she has at her disposal. Who will save Wendar, my lord prince? Who will save the king?'

Sanglant said nothing. Within the embrasure, Blessing shifted, feet rubbing on stone. Sapientia wept quietly while Brigida comforted her. The others waited. Anna glanced over toward the window to see both Thiemo and Matto looking at her. Heat scalded her cheeks, and she looked down. What would happen if they came to blows? Would Prince Sanglant banish them for creating trouble? She didn't want to lose either of them, but matters could not remain in this tense stalemate. She was going to have to choose. And she didn't want to.

'You have the army and the leadership, my lord prince,' continued Hathui. 'Turn your army home.'

'I cannot.'

'You can! Henry left Wendar in a time of trial. If he had stayed in Wendar, he would not have become bewitched. He ought to have stayed in Wendar and not ridden off to Aosta in search of a crown. And neither should you!'

'I am not riding to Aosta in search of a crown.' Anna heard the edge creep into the prince's voice that meant the Eagle's words had angered him, but perhaps the Eagle did not care, or did not know him well enough, to heed the warning.

'But you are riding east, in search of other tokens of power. Some have named you as a rebel against your father. I see for myself that you have usurped your sister's command of this army.'

Silence, cold and deadly.

Yet wasn't it true? Even though nobody said so?

A sharp *snap* caused everyone to jump, but it was only Wolfhere treading on a twig carried up to the room in the crowd. Lord Wichman chuckled, looking at Sapientia to see what she would do, thus challenged. Lady Bertha folded her arms across her chest, her smile thin and wicked.

Sapientia stared up at her elder brother, waiting. In a strange way, thought Anna, Prince Bayan had trained her to listen to him and wait for his approval before acting or reacting. Now she looked to Sanglant in the same way. Over the last three years she had been broken of the habit of leading.

'I have done what I must.' The hoarse scrape of his voice lent a note of urgency and passion to his words; but then, he always sounded like that. 'I have never rebelled against my father. Nor will I. But the war is not won yet. Adelheid and her supporters have traded in the king for a pawn who speaks with the king's voice but without Henry's will. Who will act as regnant now? I say, the one who can save him by acting against Anne and her sorcerers.'

Heribert cleared his throat and spoke diffidently. 'Do not forget that Anne sits on the skopos' throne. She is no mere "Sister." She is Holy Mother over us all. To go against her, my lord prince, you must war against the church itself.'

'Even those who call themselves holy may be agents of the Enemy,' murmured Wolfhere.

'As you well know,' replied Sanglant with a mordant laugh, moving restlessly toward the table. 'Is there wine?'

'Return to Wendar, my lord prince,' said Hathui stubbornly. 'Raise an army, and ride to Aosta to save the king. I beg you.'

He allowed Heribert to pour him a full cup of wine, which he drained. 'No.' He set down the cup so hard that the base rang hollowly on the wooden table. 'I ride east, to hunt griffins.'

3

After the conference with the king's Eagle, Sanglant made his way to the privacy of Lady Ilona's bedchamber. Her four attendants slept soundly on pallets lined up along the far wall, and Ilona lay naked on her stomach among the tangled bedclothes. Smiling slightly, she watched him as he stripped, then raised an eyebrow when he went to the unshuttered window instead of coming immediately to her bed.

'What are you thinking?' she asked.

Sanglant lingered by the window, staring east, yet all he saw was stars and campfires and, beyond them, unknown country lost in darkness. The moon had not yet risen. The night was mild, the breeze a caress against his skin. 'That my daughter is impossible.'

'She is only jealous. She wants you to herself. She does not like this attention you pay to a woman. It was only one gown. I have others.'

'You are very forgiving.'

'No. I am patient. She grows quickly, your daughter. Soon enough she will become a woman, and she will desire men herself.'

'Oh, God,' he groaned.

'Then you will be jealous,' she said with a chuckle, 'because you will no longer be first in her heart. She will be torn between father and lover. If she is wise and fortunate, she will choose to follow her own destiny in the end, not that of a man.'

'I am chastened,' he replied, clapping a hand over his heart. 'Now I realize that you have not given that gown a second thought, although its fate has been nagging at me all day. What are you thinking of, then?'

She smiled, stretching. The single lamp gave off enough light for him to admire the mole on her left hip, the curve of her buttocks, and a glimpse of rosy nipple as she shifted. With an exaggerated sigh, drawn out and almost musical, she rolled up onto her side. He felt the familiar stirring, heat suffusing his skin.

He had met the persuasive widow last autumn, when they had finally arrived at King Geza's court in Erztegom. She had propositioned him within a week of their first encounter, but it wasn't until the winter, when they were confined by a succession of blizzards within the town walls, that he had finally allowed her to seduce him. The arrangement had lasted through the spring.

He crossed the room to sit on the bed.

'I am thinking of the sorrow in my heart,' she said warmly, 'now that we journey close to the borderlands.'

'Are you sorry I'm leaving?'

'But of course! Now that you are leaving they are at me again, all those grasping relatives! Marry this lord! Marry that lord! Don't be selfish with your wealth and independence! How good it was when they could not insult me with their offers because they feared to anger you!'

He grinned, twining a strand of her copper hair between his fingers. 'You could enter a convent.'

'I think not! All this praying would be very bad for my knees. I am very careful of my knees. Among my people it is said that after too much kneeling, you can no longer ride a horse.'

'Then will you let your uncle choose a husband for you?'

'That old fool! It is very lucky he cannot touch my inheritance, or he would have married me himself even if the church would call him a whore for it. Is that the right word?'

He withdrew his hand from her hair. 'That would be incest.'

'So it would. I am thinking of marrying the one they call the White Stallion, Prince Arhad's eldest son by the Arethousan woman.'

'Ah. The lady with the white-blonde hair.'

'Yes, that one. Why is it that men find her so fascinating? Already she is an old woman, at least forty. I cannot see it.'

'Women can be beautiful in many different ways.' He traced the shape of her body from the shoulder, along the dip of her waist, and up along the ample curve of her hip. Her copper-colored hair and lush figure did not make him think of Liath each time he set eyes on her. Ilona had her own exceedingly pleasant charms.

She stretched to savor the touch of his hand. 'Men who find so many women beautiful in so many different ways are the ones who break their hearts and steal their treasure!'

'Ilona, has any man ever broken your heart?'

'Of course not!'

'Or stolen your treasure?'

'Do not laugh at me, you heartless man. My mother chose my first husband very carefully!' She burst into the laughter he found so attractive. 'When she found us in bed together! It was a good thing he was the son of a princely family. Alas that he died so young. My second husband smelled bad. I am determined not to make this mistake two times.'

'Thus the White Stallion? He's handsome enough, a good fighter, young, and he looks clean and maybe he even smells good.' That was another thing he liked about Ilona: she smelled good. She burned perfumed oils in the lamps that lit her chamber, oil of violets, if she had them, or vervain or sage. Tonight a garland of sweet woodruff hung on a nail above the window, stirred by the soft breeze. Even from this distance he could smell its dusky scent.

'He is not so powerful in Geza's court that he will think he can rule me. I do not like to be ruled.' She shifted onto her back and eased herself up onto the bolster that lay along the head of the bed, resting her head on a bent arm. 'You would make a bad husband for me, Sanglant.'

'You're not the first to have said so.'

She laughed again and let her free hand caress his shoulder. 'Ah, yes. What was I going to say?' She seemed distracted by the feel of his skin, and certainly the way she stroked him made it difficult for him to pay attention to her words. 'Of course. The White Stallion. My mother as a girl spent three years among the veiled priestesses. They serve the Blind Mother, who is one of the gods worshiped by those who follow the old ways. My mother would be amused to think that even though I abandoned her ways to embrace the God in Unity, I will have brought a man called by the name of the Blind Mother's companion to serve in my bed.'

By this time he had relaxed onto one elbow, beside her, but the comment made him sit bolt upright. 'Do you mean that when a white stallion is sacrificed at midwinter, he is going to be husband to the Blind Mother? That is not how I heard the ritual explained.'

'You heard what the men say. This is what the women know. Our grandmothers brought the old ways from the grasslands when we came to Ungria four generations ago. Out in the wild lands, the Kerayit shaman women still take a handsome young man as a companion, to keep their bed warm.'

'As a slave, Brother Breschius told me. A *pura*, which means "horse" in the Kerayit speech.' For an instant,

Sanglant had the uneasy feeling that Ilona had been playing with him all along, these past months, as though she were pretending that *he* were her pura. Maybe she wasn't as fond of him as he had become of her. But it was impossible to guess anything when she laughed like that, and maybe it didn't really matter.

'The White Stallion, the *pura*, is also a sacrifice, for the well being of the tribe. Be careful that the Kerayit women do not demand you for a *pura*, Sanglant, in exchange for their help to defeat your western sorcerers. Because there will be a price. The Kerayit and their masters make no bargain without exacting a steep price in return.'

4

'I'm afraid to go to sleep.' Hathui clutched Zacharias' hand as they sat together on the lip of the stone water trough set in the broad courtyard in front of the stables. 'When I wake up, you might not be here any more.'

'I'll be here.' He wanted to weep. How could he be so happy, reunited with his beloved sister, and yet so terrified? 'I won't be going anywhere.'

'I'm sorry I thought you were dead,' she replied, lips curving in an ironic smile. The moon had finally risen, chasing scattered clouds, and because he knew her expressions so well he could interpret them although there wasn't really enough light to see her clearly. 'Not very faithful of me.'

'Nay, do not say so. You couldn't have known.'

Her hand tightened on his as she stared across the silent courtyard. A spear's throw away, two guards walked the ramparts. Their figures paused beside a torch set in a tripod above the gate; the flickering firelight glimmered on their helmets. 'Zacharias, can I trust him? Is he worth giving my loyalty to, until the king is restored?'

'What other choice do you have, except to return to Aosta?'

'I can go to Princess Theophanu. That's what Hanna said I should do. Had I done it last summer, when I met Hanna, we might be in Aosta with an army by now.'

He shuffled his feet in the dirt, blotting the lines where a servant had raked away manure and litter earlier that evening. The smell of horse lay heavily over them. Nearby a dog barked, then fell silent when a man scolded it. He saw the dog suddenly, a dark shape scrambling along the rampart in the company of a guard, its leash pulled taut. Choking him.

He rubbed his throat as the nasty whispers surfaced in his mind. She would hate him when she found out the truth. She would despise him, which would be worse. It was bad enough being a coward, but he could not bear it if she turned away from him with contempt.

'Yet who else?' she asked, unaware of his silence, his struggle, his agony. 'Who else can save Henry? Who can fight Hugh of Austra, and Holy Mother Anne? Princess Sapientia is like a lapdog, suffered to eat and bark but kept on a chain. She cannot lead this army. Yet what can Princess Theophanu do against Hugh of Austra's sorcery? She fell under his spell once before. She might do so again.'

He did not need to answer, simply to listen as she worked her way through her own argument. She wasn't really asking for his advice; she was trying to convince herself because she was desperate.

'Sister Rosvita told me to come here. She must have known the prince's worth. She must have had a reason. She has served the king loyally, and wisely. What else do I have to go on?'

'You'd better sleep. The path will show more clearly in the morning.' Up on the ramparts, the guard dog growled. A person emerged from the stable carrying a candle; its light splashed shadows around them. Without turning, he knew who had come to look for her.

'Hathui? You'd best sleep.' Wolfhere sounded concerned, even affectionate. All those humiliating years while Zacharias

had lived as a slave among the Quman, Wolfhere had trained
and ridden with Hathui, her mentor among the Eagles. She
respected Wolfhere; she'd said so herself, as they'd eaten in
the soldiers' barracks after being dismissed from the prince's
chamber.

She would never respect her own dear brother, not once
she knew the truth.

She let go of Zacharias' hand. 'True enough, old man. So
many times in the past months I despaired of finding Prince
Sanglant. Yet now that I'm here, my path seems just as
troubled. Where will it end? Have you an answer?'

'You say it was Sister Rosvita who sent you to find my
lord prince,' the old Eagle answered. 'She is a wise woman,
and a faithful counselor to King Henry. Stay with us, Hathui.
That is the only way to save Henry.'

She grunted, half a chuckle, rising to her feet with a
grimace. 'Spoken by the man whom King Henry put under
ban. You've never liked him.'

'Nay. I've never disliked him. It is Henry who did not trust
me.'

'Wisely,' muttered Zacharias, but neither heard him.
Hathui had already begun moving away, pausing when she
realized he wasn't following her.

'Where do you sleep, Zachri?' she asked, using the pet
name she'd called him when she was too young to fit his entire
name to her tongue.

'Elsewhere,' he said softly, hoping Wolfhere would not
hear. It hurt to hear her use that fond old name. He was no
longer her cherished older brother, the one she followed everywhere. He was no better than the dogs, sleeping wherever he
found a corner to curl up in. No one tolerated him enough
that he had a regular pallet – or perhaps it was more fair to
say that Anna could not stand him, he could not himself bear
to sleep near Wolfhere, and the camaraderie of the soldiers
grew painful after a few nights. He could only exist on the
edge, never in the heart.

She came back to hug him. 'There's room enough in the
stall where I've been given straw—'

'Nay, nay,' he said hastily. Tears stung his eyes. 'Go to sleep, Hathui. I'll see you in the morning.'

She remained there a few breaths longer, staring at him in the hazy halo of light wavering off Wolfhere's candle. She was trying to understand his hesitation, knowing him well enough to see that there was something wrong. But she could not yet see what he had become. She still saw the older brother who had walked proudly into the east to bring the light of the Unities to the barbarians. How could she know that he had become lost in the umbra? That he had compromised his honor, submitted to the worst indignities, and licked the feet of those who owned him, in order to stay alive? It was only when they had threatened to cut out his tongue that he had fled. Shouldn't he have offered up his tongue, his very life, before he had sacrificed his faith and his honor?

'You look tired, Zacharias,' she said at last, leaning down to kiss him on the cheek. 'You should sleep, too. I'll be looking for you at first light, to make sure you aren't a dream.'

She went inside the stables with Wolfhere. The light fled. So small a thing had the candle's flame been, to cast so harsh a light onto his soul.

When she found out the truth, she would hate him. And she would find out the truth in the end, because the one person who knew everything still traveled with Sanglant's army and had no better way to amuse himself. *He* would know. *He* would see Zacharias' weakness, his fears, and his hopes. *He* would destroy Zacharias' last chance for redemption, as long as he still lived.

Zacharias got to his feet and staggered like an old man to the door of the stable. It was dark inside, Wolfhere's candle vanished entirely, although he heard a murmur of voices that faded. Half of the stalls were empty; at this time of year, and in a peaceful city, many of the horses had been put out to pasture beyond the inner walls. But soldiers stored other things here as well.

Groping, as quietly as he could, he found a stout spear leaning with its brothers in a stall. He slipped his fingers around it, eased it free, and crept out of the stable. Hands trembling, breath coming in gasps, he hugged the shadows, having to steady himself on the butt of the spear every time his knees started to give out. The haft kept wanting to spring right out of his grasp, but he clutched it tightly.

He would not lose Hathui, not after losing everything else.

Beside the great hall lay the old keep, said by the locals to have been built in the time of the ancient Dariyans, although Heribert had firmly proclaimed that it could not possibly have been built by Dariyan engineers: the technique and stonework were too crude. With a new hall and stables now built inside the ring fort's restored walls, the old keep was considered too drafty and damp for the king and his court. But stone made good prison walls.

The two Ungrian soldiers standing guard at the entrance to the keep knew him by sight and let him pass. Up the winding stairs lay the tower rooms where King Geza kept certain prisoners who traveled with him wherever he went – his first wife, an unrepentant pagan whom he had divorced on his conversion to the Daisanite faith and whom he was forced to hold hostage so that her angry kinfolk did not murder him for the insult; an Arethousan priest who had poisoned a young Ungrian princeling but whom Geza dared not execute because of the priest's connections to the Arethousan royal court; an albino boy who was either a witch or a saint, too crazy to be allowed to roam about on his own and too valuable to be given into anyone else's care.

Others, too, slept confined in chambers, but they weren't the dangerous ones, only hostages. Usually the dangerous ones were killed outright.

As *he* should have been killed, the day they captured him.

Zacharias used the butt of the spear to feel his way down the curving stairs to the lower level, where stone foundations plumbed the ground. It was cooler here, damp, smelling of mold and decay.

'Who's there?' asked the guard in Wendish, rising from the stool where he waited out the night in the dank, dark dungeon. An oil lamp hung from a ring set into the wall. The light barely illuminated the hole cut into the plank floor and the ladder lying on the planks beside it. 'Oh, it's just you, Brother. What brings you here so late?'

Would his trembling hands and sweating brow give him away? He must not falter now. His glib tongue had always saved him before.

'My lord prince has sent me to interrogate the prisoner.'

'In the middle of the night?'

He raised a finger to his lips and beckoned the soldier closer, so that they wouldn't wake the prisoner. 'Malbert, when did you come on watch? Did you hear that an Eagle rode in?'

'An Eagle? Nay, I've heard no such news. From Princess Theophanu? News of Wendar?' Malbert came from the northern coast of Wendar, near Gent, and was always eager for news of the region where he'd grown up.

'Nay, she brings news from Aosta. King Henry is ill. He's being poisoned by sorcery.'

'God save him!'

'Prince Sanglant doesn't know whether to ride east or return to Aosta. I'm to ask the prisoner again of the eastern lands. See if he'll talk, give us any information.'

Malbert snorted. 'As if he would! He'll laugh at you.'

But not for long.

'If he's groggy from sleep, he might reveal something. How many days to the eastern swamps. Where the griffins hunt.'

'Hasn't the prince come to listen and watch? Where is he?'

'Well. Well. Just where most men wish they were in the dead of night. Heh, yes. He's gone to his bed.'

Malbert grinned. 'I wish I were in as sweet a bed as he's in now. But I can't come down with you. You know the rule.'

'It's better if he thinks I'm alone. I've got this spear with me to keep him honest.'

He bit his tongue to hold back the frantic words that wanted to spill out: *to silence him.*

That was the only way. Hathui must never know.

Malbert had an open face and was himself too honest not to let his skepticism show. They all knew how disgracefully Zacharias had behaved in a skirmish before. 'So you say. I'll keep watch from above.'

They slid the ladder down through the hole until it rested on the dirt beneath. Malbert held the lamp over the opening to light Zacharias' descent. With the spear tucked under one arm, he climbed down into the pit.

Although the prince had had the pit swept clean the day they had arrived here, it still stank of garbage, urine, and feces. Dirt squeaked under his feet as Zacharias steadied himself. Malbert lowered a second, newly lit oil lamp to hang from a hook hammered into the underside of the plank floor. Drops of water beaded on the stone walls, dripping onto the soil. The stink of closed-in air almost choked him, but hatred drove him on.

The prisoner lay silent, still asleep, on a heap of straw. Chains draped his recumbent body, iron links fastened to the wall. Without chains he was too dangerous, so the prince had discovered. No matter that Zacharias had warned him. Two servants had died and three soldiers been injured in that first and only escape attempt one month after the battle at the Veser. Yet even the heavy chains did not weaken him. They barely contained him.

Do it now, while the fever burned. Do it for Hathui, so she need never know. So she need never spit in her brother's face.

Sweat dripped in his eyes and tickled the back of his neck. Flushed, heart pounding as though he were running, he stumbled forward. Triumph flooded him as his hands wrapped tight around the haft of the spear and he thrust hard at the exposed back of the man lying in the straw.

He should have done this long ago.

Lithe as a serpent, the shadowed figure twisted, and his manacled forearm batted the spear aside. The point drove into the dirt beneath the straw. Quick as a striking snake, he grabbed the haft with his right hand and with his left wrapped the chains shackling his arms around the point. Linked by the shaft of wood, the two men stared at each other. A smile quivered on Bulkezu's lips as he slithered to his feet, confined only by the limit of his chains.

The wound that had torn a flap of skin half off his cheek

had healed remarkably well, but the ragged scar marred his beauty. No one could possibly look at him now and wonder how a man so handsome could be so monstrous. It had never been true that God so wrought the world that those things They lavished loving care on by granting them beauty were, because of their beautiful nature, therefore also good. Sometimes you met evil in the guise of beauty. You had to be careful.

'So the worm comes with a long knife to poke at the lion.'

Bulkezu thrust. Propelled backward, Zacharias hit the opposite wall, first his back, then his head colliding with cold stone. His shriek was cut short as the butt of the spear, still with his own hands clutching it, jammed hard into his gut, pinning him against the wall.

'Impotent worm,' said Bulkezu in his soft voice. Now that he had hold of one end of the spear, he could reach anywhere in the cell. 'But worms aren't men, they're only worms. They can't even bark like dogs or rut like them, can they?'

How he hated that voice, and the bubbling laughter, sweet with delight and with the cunning madness that had made Bulkezu the greatest chieftain of his day, that had allowed him to unite many of the Quman tribes into an army with which to ravage Wendar. All he could do was grasp the haft more tightly.

If he let go, it was all over.

Adjusting his grip, bending slightly at his knees, Bulkezu lifted Zacharias from the floor and slammed him against the wall again. A second time the Quman pitched him against the stone as Zacharias screamed with anger and pain.

Malbert's face appeared above like some sort of angel illuminated by the lamp's glow. He shouted down unintelligible words as Bulkezu kept battering Zacharias against the wall and Zacharias kept holding on.

Was that the sound of footsteps, clattering on the floor above? Impossible to tell. Again and again, Bulkezu slammed him against the wall as spots sparked like fire before Zacharias' eyes and sound roared in his ears. A stone fell from above, then a second, but the angle was wrong, the trapdoor set too far to one side. The guards could not reach Bulkezu as he battered Zacharias against the wall again, and again. Yet was that frustration growing in the monster's laugh?

If he could only hold on a moment longer. He had escaped the Quman in the first place simply by holding on, by not giving up. He had to remember that.

A new voice rang above the fray.

'Zacharias!'

Horror gripped him, and his throat burned as bile rose.

Hathui would witness it all.

Again, Bulkezu thrust, and Zacharias smashed into the stone behind him, but this time when his head hit his vision hazed and darkened. The shaft of the spear slid out of his weakening grip. His legs no longer held him up. He toppled over, hit the ground and, as his sight faded, he braced himself for the final, killing thrust.

5

He could not sleep. Again. Not even the soft bed and the voluptuous woman breathing softly beside him, her full breasts pressed against his arm, could soothe his agitated thoughts tonight. He slipped from the bed as quietly as he could, pulled on his tunic, swept up leggings and belt and court shoes from the bench where they had been left in a heap. Ilona did not wake. She never did, when he was restless – not as Liath had, attentive to his moods – or perhaps she only pretended to sleep, having got what she wanted out of him and being unwilling to give more of herself than her body.

She was loyal to Ungria, not to him, loyal to her estates and her young children, who would inherit her portion when the time came. No reason she should offer him her heart, her confidences, any intimacy beyond that shared in the bed, two lonely people finding release.

For some reason it bothered him mightily that, as much as she enjoyed his company, she seemed to harbor no actual love nor even any particular companionable affection for him at all.

One of her serving women woke and, with barely a glance at him, no more than a respectful bob to acknowledge his princely rank, opened the door to let him out. In this same way she would let out a scratching dog.

He walked barefoot down the hall, down the stairs, feeling his way by touch to the entrance to the great hall. The feast had ended. Men snored in the hall, reeking of drink and urine. A dog growled, and he growled right back, silencing it.

The whole world seemed asleep, able to rest – as he could not.

Yet that wasn't all that was bothering him. Something wasn't right; he could smell it. The hair on the back of his neck prickled, and he stepped out into the open air, taking in a deep breath, listening. His hearing had always been as good as that of a dog.

Shouts and motion roiled the night over by the old keep, where the prisoners were kept.

He ran, reaching the door to the keep just as Wolfhere did. 'Trouble?' he asked.

From inside a guardsman shouted unintelligible words and he heard the voice of the Eagle, Hathui, raised in fear. Taking the stairs three at a time, he fetched up beside a clot of guardsmen, all crying out and exclaiming, one of them on his knees dropping stones through the open trapdoor.

'Damn fool,' cursed one as Hathui tried to push past him to get to the ladder. 'The damn fool took a spear. Now the prisoner's got hold of it.'

'Give me a sword,' said Sanglant.

Malbert handed him a sword. He grabbed it before dropping down through the trap, practically sliding down the rungs and slats with a single hand for balance. His eyes had already adjusted for the dim light, although an oil lamp swung unsteadily to his right, creaking.

Movement flashed in his vision.

Leaping from the ladder he spun, sword raised, breaking the spear in two as Bulkezu thrust at the prostrate figure slumped against the opposite wall. Left with only a splintered half, the Quman chieftain hefted it and threw it as a javelin at Sanglant's torso. With a cut of his sword, the prince struck it down in flight.

Bulkezu hit the limit of his chains and came up short, jerked back by unyielding stone. He was shaking – with laughter or with rage. It was impossible to tell. Was he mad, or merely feigning madness? How could any man stand to be chained and a prisoner for as long as Bulkezu had been without succumbing to insane delusions?

That ungodly cackle echoed within the stones. 'I'm a cleaner man than you, prince, because I rid myself of the worms that crawl into my tent.'

'This one still lives.'

'Oh, God, Zacharias.' Without being asked, Hathui scrambled down the ladder to crouch beside her brother, who moaned and struggled, trying to get up. 'Nay, don't try to stand. You're safe now.'

'Does the worm have a paramour?' Bulkezu whispered.

In the lamp's mellow glow, Sanglant saw the chieftain's lips still fixed in that mad smile.

Hathui looked up, more curious than frightened now that her brother's assailant was disarmed. 'Who is this, my lord prince?' Then her expression changed so entirely that Sanglant stepped sideways, startled, as if her gaze were an arrow that he had to avoid.

'I know who you are!' she exclaimed as Zacharias climbed groggily to his feet, a hand clapped to the back of his head.

Bulkezu's smile vanished. His eyes narrowed as he stared at the Eagle, annoyed and puzzled. He was always at his most dangerous when exasperated.

'Hathui.' Zacharias staggered forward between his sister and the chained prisoner. 'He's dangerous.'

'I know that.' She stepped past him to confront Sanglant. 'My lord prince, I demand satisfaction. His Majesty King Arnulf the Younger sent his subjects east to settle pagan lands and in exchange he promised they could rule themselves with the king alone, and no lady or lord, set over them as their ruler. The king's law sets a price for certain crimes, does it not?'

'So it does,' said Sanglant, glancing at Bulkezu. The prisoner clearly had no more idea than his captor did what she was talking about.

'This man raped me when I was a virgin of but fourteen years of age. He cut me, too, and after that the wisewoman of my village said I would not be able to bear children. So I set my sights on the King's Eagles. Otherwise, I would have stayed in my village and inherited my mother's lands, and had daughters of my own to inherit in their turn. Do I not have a claim, my lord prince?'

'*He* raped you, Hathui?' croaked Zacharias. He looked around wildly, grabbed the broken haft of the spear, and hoisted it.

'Stay.' Sanglant yanked the spear out of the frater's hand and tossed it against the ladder. 'Do nothing rash, Brother. Is this true, Prince Bulkezu?'

Bulkezu laughed again. 'One looks like another. I don't remember. It must have been years ago. But I recall clearly what I did to the worm. Does she know, your paramour, that you have no cock, Zach'rias? That we cut it off because you told us you'd rather lose your cock than your tongue? Does she know that you let men use you as a woman, just so you could stay alive? Does she know that you watched others die, because you wanted yourself to live? That it is you who taught me to speak the Wendish language, so that I could understand the speech of my enemy without them knowing?'

Zacharias screamed with rage and leaped toward Bulkezu. Sanglant swung to grab him, but Hathui had already got hold of her older brother. She stood almost as tall and had the strength of a woman who has spent years riding at the king's behest.

'Stay, Brother, do nothing rash,' she said, echoing Sanglant's words. 'What does it matter what this prisoner says to you or about you?'

Despite himself, Sanglant took a half step away from the ragged frater, a little disgusted by Bulkezu's accusations and repelled by the thought of a man so mutilated. What kind of man would watch his own kind die without doing all he could to prevent it? What kind of man would submit to any indignity, just to save his own life? For God's sake, what kind of man would rather lose his penis than his tongue?

'What answer do you make to these accusations?' he asked, struggling to keep contempt out of his tone. It was remarkably easy to believe that Zacharias had done these vile things. The frater never acted like a real man. Whatever drove him – and he wasn't without courage – he so often faltered, recoiled, and hid. Nor had he ever truly become a full member of Sanglant's court. He loitered on the fringe, not quite accepted, never able to push himself forward to join with the others.

To the prince's surprise, the frater wept frustrated tears. 'All true,' he gasped. 'And worse.' His expression was so bleak that pity swelled in Sanglant's heart. 'I'm sorry, Hathui. Scorn me if you must—'

'*Sorry* for having been a slave for seven years to this monster?' She dropped Zacharias' arm, took three steps forward, and spat into Bulkezu's face. The Quman chieftain flinched back from her anger, surprised rather than scared. 'I will lay my case before the prince and demand full recompense. *And* for the crimes you committed against my brother as well.' She did not wait for his response. 'Come, Zacharias. It was foolish of you to come down here, but I suppose you were afraid that I would turn away from you if I knew the truth.' Her anger hadn't subsided; it spilled out to wash over her hapless brother. 'I would never turn away from you. What a man suffers when he is a prisoner and a slave, under duress, cannot be held against him. Come now, let's get out of this stinking pit.'

Zacharias croaked out her name, broken and pathetic, but he followed her obediently up the ladder. Malbert's face appeared.

'My lord prince?'

'I'm coming,' said Sanglant, turning to pick up the two halves of the spear.

Bulkezu wasn't finished. 'She wore the badge of an Eagle. Are all the king's Eagles also his whores?'

'A weak thrust, Prince Bulkezu, and unworthy of you.' He set a foot on the lowest rung, stretched, and handed the broken spear to Malbert, then passed up the sword as well.

Bulkezu's lips had a way of quivering, almost a twitch, that Sanglant had learned to recognize as a prelude to his worst rages. 'What weapons do you give me?' he asked in that voice, as soft as feathers but poisoned at its heart.

'I'll give you a spear, as I promised, once you have guided me to the hunting grounds of the griffins. On that day you'll go free—'

'And until that day? You'd have done better to kill me if you're so afraid of me that you must shackle me, as a dog must a lion. At least Zach'rias is an honest worm. You call yourself a man but you act like a dog, slinking and cowering.'

Sanglant laughed. That surge of restlessness that had driven him from Ilona's bed swept back twice as strong. For two years they'd made their slow and circuitous way eastward, delayed by blizzards, snow, high water, rains, and bouts of illness in the troops and the horses. He had never seen as much rain and snow as he had in the year and a half since the battle at the Veser. Rain had drenched the land, causing floods and mildew in the grain, and snow had buried it for two winters running, as if God were punishing them for their sins.

But God's hand alone had not caused all their troubles. They had also been delayed by the necessity of making nice to King Geza, whose lands they had to cross. He didn't like Geza nearly as much as he'd liked Bayan, and Sapientia's presence was a rankling sore, a constant source of frustration.

Or perhaps it had just been too long since he'd had a good fight.

'Malbert!'

'Yes, my lord prince.'

'Throw me down the key and pull up the ladder.'

'My lord!'

'The key!'

Cursing under his breath, Malbert hauled up the ladder through the trapdoor, then threw down the key, which Sanglant caught in his left hand. Bulkezu did not move as Sanglant unlocked his wrists and tossed the key to the wall, but he struck first, still quick after months of being chained. Sanglant ducked the blow. Catching wrist and arm, he drove his foe headfirst against the stone wall. Staggered, Bulkezu dropped to his knees, only to dive for Sanglant's legs. They went down together, rolling and punching, until Bulkezu sat for an instant atop Sanglant's chest. Bulkezu's hands closed on his throat, but he twisted out of the choking grip, flipped the Quman over, and sprang back to his feet, laughing breathlessly, flushed, his heart pounding in a most gratifying manner as he allowed Bulkezu to crawl back to his feet in grim silence.

Above, the lantern rocked as men crowded around the trapdoor to stare down. He heard their whispers as they laid wagers on how many blows it would take their prince to lay the prisoner out flat.

All at once he was tired of the charade. What kind of contest was it, really, to fight a man chained up for almost two years? Bulkezu remained remarkably strong, yet what kind of man was he, to torment another as Bloodheart had once tormented him?

Bulkezu struck for his face. Sanglant blocked the blow and delivered his own to Bulkezu's gut, knocking him back, then stepped in, turning sideways as Bulkezu kicked out so the blow glanced off his thigh. As he closed, Bulkezu lunged for his throat. Sanglant seized his wrists and they froze a moment, locked, motionless.

'No creature male or female may kill me,' Sanglant muttered, 'so it was never a fair fight.'

With a curse, Bulkezu twisted his hands free, spinning to strike with his elbow. Sanglant caught the blow on his forearm and delivered a sharp punch below the ribs followed by a flurry of blows that made the men watching from above cheer. Bulkezu collapsed limply to the ground.

'On that day you'll go free,' Sanglant repeated, 'and we'll see which man wins griffin feathers.'

Malbert pushed down the ladder and climbed down, eager to help shackle the prisoner.

'Nay, I will do it.' Let him do the dirty work himself, chaining a warrior who would rather die fighting than leashed like a slave – or a dog. But perhaps Bulkezu deserved no better than the fate he had meted out to the many people he had enslaved and murdered.

What was justice? What was right?

'Here's the key,' he said, handing it to Malbert, glad to be rid of it, although he would never be rid of the responsibility for what he chose to do.

Yet his night's work wasn't done. He crawled up the ladder to discover that King Geza had been alerted by his own guard. Sanglant met him just outside the keep. The king came attended by a half dozen of his white-cloaked honor guard, young men with long mustaches and scant beards. Geza was about ten years older than Bayan, rather more burly, gone a little to fat, and keenly intelligent. He had the luck of the king, that powerful presence, but he lacked the wicked sense of humor that had made Bayan a good companion.

'A problem with the prisoner?' he asked through his interpreter. Was he suspicious, or amused?

'He insulted my father,' replied Sanglant.

'Ah.' Geza spat on the ground to show his contempt for the prisoner. 'Is he dead now?'

'Not until he's given me what I need.'

Geza nodded and took his leave, returning to his bed. He had been grateful enough to get Bayan's body back, and he had stinted in no way in making Sanglant a welcome guest in the kingdom of Ungria, yet it remained clear that he was only waiting for Sanglant and his army to leave and that he was by no means happy at the thought of that same army returning to cross Ungrian lands on their road back to Wendar. He had even suggested that Sanglant take his army north into the war-torn Polenie lands. Yet he didn't want to

fight Wendish troops either; after all, he and King Henry
were nominally allies. When Geza had offered one of his sons
as a new husband for Sapientia, Sanglant had actually flirted
with the idea – for the space of three breaths.

As Geza and his entourage crossed the courtyard to the
hall, Sanglant caught sight of Hathui and Zacharias over by
the stables, she with her arm around his waist as if she were
holding him up. Wolfhere stood by the doorway, lighting
their way with a lamp as they ducked inside. How had
Zacharias hidden his mutilation all these months? No one
had even suspected. But then, Zacharias kept to himself,
never truly part of the group, and in truth he stank because
he so rarely washed.

'My lord prince!' Heribert hurried up, hair mussed and
face puffy with sleep. 'Everyone is saying you killed Bulkezu.'

'Rumor has already flown, I see. Thank the Lord we're
moving on tomorrow. These Ungrians sing too much.'

'You haven't complained of Lady Ilona's attentions.'

'She's worst of all! I'm nothing more than a stallion to her,
brought in to breed the mare. No more women, Heribert.'

The cleric chuckled. 'Isn't that what you said in Gent?'

'I mean it this time!'

Mercifully, Heribert did not answer, merely cocked an
eyebrow, looking skeptical as he ran his fingers through his
hair, trying to comb it down. The first predawn birds cried
out, heralding the day to come.

'The Ungrian camp followers will stay behind when we
leave Geza's kingdom. Who will be left to tempt me? Pray
God the sorcerers we find will know how to get Liath back.'

'Yet what lies beyond Ungria? A trackless plain, so they
say. How will we find these griffins and sorcerers you seek?'

Sanglant smiled, but in his heart he felt no peace, knowing that some choices were ugly, made for expediency's sake
rather than being ruled by what was just. '*That* is why
Bulkezu still lives. He'll guide me to the griffins in exchange
for his freedom – and a chance to kill me.'

IV
THE SUMMER SUN

1

At the Ungrian town of Vidinyi, King Geza made his farewells and turned his court west to return to the heartland of his kingdom. A small fleet of broad-beamed merchant ships and a dozen smaller, swifter galleys had been put at the disposal of Prince Sanglant. After off-loading their cargoes of wine, oil, and silk from the Arethousan Empire, they took on grain for the return journey downriver as well as the two thousand horses, eight hundred soldiers, and two hundred or more servants with their miscellaneous carts and pack animals.

The river seemed as broad as a lake to Sanglant as he stood on deck, Heribert beside him, watching the lengthy and difficult process of coaxing horses up onto the ships. Beyond the wharves, earth-covered fires burned along the strand. Because there was no wind and the air lay heavy and humid, wraith-like streamers of smoke from these fires stretched out along the shoreline, screening willow scrub and sapling poplars.

'They can't get much more charcoal near town,' Heribert said. 'Look how far back the woodland is cut.'

'They're using charcoal for their ironworks, to forge more weapons. Ungria grows stronger every year and expands its border eastward.' Sanglant gestured toward the new palisade wall surrounding Vidinyi. 'They say it's a seven-day trip downriver to the Heretic's Sea. We won't be gone from Ungria fast enough for my taste.'

'Missing Lady Ilona already?'

'I suppose I deserve that! Missing Bayan, more like. He was the best of them.'

'If what Brother Breschius and Zacharias say is true, and considering the example of Bulkezu, you may look more kindly on the Ungrians once we are out on the plains at the mercy of the Quman and the Kerayit.'

'Maybe so. But Geza delayed us here for his own reasons. He's a stubborn man and more conniving than he seems.'

'Hoping to convince Sapientia to marry one of his sons? Or hoping to loose us into the wild lands so late in the season that the winter finishes us off?'

'Hard to say. He's not simple. No doubt the barbarians are more honest about what they want.'

'Our heads? Our horses?'

'Our selves as their slaves and puras?' He laughed curtly, wiping sweat from the back of his neck. 'Something like that.'

The woodland had indeed been cut back on all sides of the town, but when they at long last cast off and the press of the current took them round a bend out of sight of Vidinyi, forest gradually took hold on either side until it became a monotonous fence of trees broken at intervals by clusters of low houses dug into the ground. The folk about their daily chores stared as they passed; some of the children shouted greetings; then the little village would be lost behind a new screen of forest as if it had never existed.

In those stretches of wilderness between holdings, he heard nothing except the intermittent beat of oars keeping them in the main channel and the lap of water at the bows. Once he saw a hawk half hidden among the branches of a poplar. Above, the sky was a vivid blue. In the distance the rugged mountains lifted up from a horizon untouched by haze, as though the air were somehow purer there, closer to the heavenly aether.

If he looked hard enough, could he see Liath shining in the heavens? But the air was clear, only scraps of clouds and the bright sun, concealing neither angels nor daimones. He had seen no sign of her since that awful day at Gent. Two and a half years had passed since then; it was almost as though their brief life together was only a dream remembered as if it were real.

'Do you suppose she is dead, Heribert?' he asked finally.

Heribert sighed. The slender cleric had never been one to tell him only what he wanted to hear. That was why Sanglant prized his companionship. 'How can we know? I'm sorry.'

'Papa! Look at me!'

Blessing had got herself into the furled rigging of the lateen sail and shinnied halfway up the mast, clinging to a rope.

'Oh, God!' Heribert hurried toward her, unsteady enough on the rocking ship that he careened into one of the sailors.

'No matter,' called Sanglant after him, laughing. 'She'll either fall and kill herself, or she won't.'

But it quickly became clear that the captain of the ship wished no brat getting in the way, and soon enough Sanglant found himself presiding over his sullen daughter at the bow of the ship.

'On this boat, you obey the captain, who is like the regnant.'

'He's only a common man, Papa.'

'In your first battle, will you tell Captain Fulk he's wrong when he gives you advice just because he was born the son of a steward and you are a prince's daughter? A wise ruler knows how to listen to those who may know something she does not, and seeks out advisers who tell her the truth rather than those who simply flatter.'

Ai, God, she was well grown enough to pout, arms crossed and shoulders hunched as she stared at the river. Here, as forest gave way to marsh, a heron took wing, slow flaps along the shallows until it was lost in the haze that clung to the waters. Would her life pass as swiftly as the bird's flight? Would she become an old woman before he reached thirty? He could not bear to think of losing her in such an unnatural way, having to watch as age captured her and made her its prisoner. How soon would she flower and be ready to wed? She still had a child's body, all innocent grace and coltish limbs, as lively and strong as any creature let run free. Thank the Lady she was not yet showing signs of the woman she would become; the longer he could put off such considerations the better. Yet he would have to choose carefully what man she married, because she would need every advantage when it came time to restore to her what was due her: her birthright as a descendant of the Emperor Taillefer.

In such moments, watching her, he despaired. She had much the look of Liath about her, delicate features, that creamy brown complexion, and unexpectedly blue eyes, but she had the night-black hair of the Aoi and a cast of features that reminded him of his own mother. The older she grew, the more the resemblance sharpened. By appearance alone, no one would take her for Taillefer's heir; she had not the look of the west at all. Maybe there was something of Henry in her – she had his rages, after all, and his generous ability to forgive – but as hard as ever he looked he could see no resemblance to Anne, not one bit. That made him glad.

She had such a fierce expression of affronted ire on her sweet face that he almost laughed, but he knew better than to laugh *at* her. She struggled, lower lip thrust out and quivering, a tear welling from one eye to slide down a cheek. Heribert moved forward to console her, but Sanglant checked him with a gesture. Anna, Thiemo, and Matto, standing alertly nearby, knew better than to intervene when he had laid down a punishment.

'Papa,' she said finally, gaze still stubbornly fixed downriver. The prow of the ship cut the current to either side as the oars pulled them on and the current pressed them forward. Ahead, the gray-green waters purled around a snag that thrust up out of the water. 'I *would* listen to Captain Fulk. I would. When can I start training to arms?'

'You're too young—' he began, the old refrain, then broke off. Why deny what was obvious to any fool traveling with his army, of whom he was obviously the chief example? He had himself been sent at the age of seven to begin his training.

Six months ago she had been too young, but for Blessing a few months was like to a year for any normal person. If he did not start training her now, it might be too late, she might be grown and past her prime before she had a chance to prove herself. If she were doomed to a brief life, at least he must try to give to her all that he could, including her heart's wish: to be a soldier like her father.

'Look!' she shrieked as a cry rose from the warship running before them, the vanguard of their fleet.

The spar had grown to reveal itself as the topmost ruins of an ancient tower, now drowned in the shallows of the river by rising waters and a change in the river's course. Like all earthly power, the fortification had fallen in the end, its builders and queens long forgotten. But in the eddy where the river parted around that base of crumbling stone, something waited and watched. Shouts shattered the silence as other oarsmen and sailors saw what lashed in the murky water. Their cries rang out with fear and horror. Yet there it floated, a creature from nightmare, more fish than man with flat red eyes, a lipless mouth, and no nose, only slits for breathing. Each strand of its writhing hair was as thick as an eel with beady little eyes and a snapping mouth.

'Lord save us,' murmured Heribert, clinging to the rail. He had gone white.

Thiemo cursed and drew the Circle of Unity at his breast, and Matto grabbed Anna as though to shield her from the sight of that ghastly thing, but she shook him off, shaking and stuttering as she gaped.

'Look, Papa!' cried Blessing, as blissful as a child who sees the first snow of winter swirling down to the ground. 'It's a man-fish! I want to swim with it!'

He grabbed hold of her as they shot past, the current pouring them through a narrowing funnel between high bluffs. Yet it seemed for a long while after that he could hear the cries and alarmed shouts behind them as the other ships passed, one by one.

'What does it portend?' demanded the captain of the ship, his words translated by Brother Breschius. 'An evil thing, to see one of the sea brothers swimming up the river.'

'Have they a name?' asked Sanglant.

'Nay, my lord prince. My grandfather spoke of them, for he was a ship-master as well. He said they were just a legend.' He gestured, spitting on the deck and stamping his left foot, then recalled where he was and before whom he stood, and hastily drew the Circle of Unity at his chest as would any God-fearing man. 'An evil omen, my lord prince.'

'Perhaps. Did your grandfather say whether such creatures had intelligence, or whether they were only dumb beasts?'

'They have cunning, my lord prince, and hunger. It was always said they would eat any man who fell overboard.'

'Yet did your grandfather or any man who sailed with him ever see such a man-fish?'

'Nay. They had only heard tales.'

Tales aplenty ran round their camp that evening when they lay up alongside the shore for the night in a stretch of marshy wilderness teeming with birds. From the deck Sanglant could see five ships, one ahead and four behind, as well as a few fires burning on the strand upriver, but only the foolhardy or the thick-skinned ventured to shore, where gnats and sting-ing flies swarmed. It was, if anything, hotter and stickier than it had been earlier in the day.

When Captain Fulk rowed back from the foremost galley and Bertha, Wichman, Druthmar, and Istvan arrived from upriver, rather fly-bitten, he called a council. Many old tales came to light but only after he had gone round his council to hear what each member had to say did he see Zacharias standing at the back of the gathering between Hathui and Wolfhere. The frater's expression gave Sanglant pause.

'Have you something to say, Brother Zacharias?'

The frater stammered out a meaningless denial. 'N-n-no, my lord prince. N-nothing.'

'Have you ever seen such a creature yourself?'

The hesitation betrayed him.

'Tell me,' he commanded.

Hathui bent closer to her brother and said a few words into his ear, too quietly even for Sanglant to hear above the whispering of the folk around him and the lap of water against the ship's hull. The wind brought the smell of the marsh, heavy with decay.

'It was a dream, my lord prince, a vision. You know that I traveled for a time with your mother, who took me to a place she called the Palace of Coils.'

'The spiral gate!' muttered Wolfhere, but Zacharias paid him no heed as he went on.

'There I saw many visions, but it also seemed to me that for a short time I became such a creature as we saw today. I swam with my fellows, out in the salt sea, following a fleet of ships.'

Zacharias shuddered. 'That's all.'

He was lying; there was more, but Sanglant doubted he could coax it out of him. Perhaps Hathui could.

'That is all?'

'First we hear tales of a phoenix and now we see a merman,' remarked Lady Bertha with pleasure. Strife and difficulty amused her.

'It was damned ugly,' said Wichman. 'I thought mermaids had great milky breasts huge enough to smother a man. This was a nasty fiend!'

Bertha smiled. 'It's said that in the end times all the ancient creatures of legend will crawl out of their hiding places to stalk the earth once again.'

'Now we shall see the truth of it,' said Sanglant, looking at Wolfhere as he spoke. The old Eagle made no reply as he crossed to the railing to stare at the scattering of fires along the shoreline.

They returned to their places, but no man washed in the river water. No one knew how close in to shore the merfolk could swim. As he did every night, Sanglant gave orders to bring the chained Bulkezu up from the hold to take the night air, under guard. Only a few men were fit for the task, since Bulkezu might in the middle of the night taunt them in his soft voice, which was his only weapon, trying to make them angry enough to get within his reach.

After Bulkezu was chained to the mast, Blessing crept up

close to her father where he stood at the stem of the ship; she stared at the Quman chief. His chains clanked and rattled as he stretched, flexing his muscles, testing the limit and strength of the chains. Bulkezu never stopped testing those chains. He never despaired. Perhaps he was too crazy to do so. Perhaps he was too cunning, or too sane. It was the only way he had to keep up his strength.

'I would rather be dead than a prisoner like that,' Blessing whispered, leaning against her father and wrapping her arms around his waist. Her head came almost to his chest. 'Wouldn't it be more merciful to kill him? He must hate you.'

As I hated Bloodheart.

'No prisoner loves his jailer,' he said at last.

'Do you think if I'd jumped in the river that merman would have eaten me?'

'I don't know.'

The river flowed past, more sluggish now as it was glutted with waters leaking out of the marshland. A chorus of frogs chirped, then fell silent as though a passing owl had frightened them. There came a moment of deeper silence, with the flowing waters of the river and the steady lap of waves against the hull the only sound. A hard *slap* hit water out on the river, answered by a second and a third.

'They're talking,' said Blessing.

'Who is talking?'

'The merfolk.'

'How can beasts talk?'

'They *do!* They're watching us.'

He smiled, but an itchy feeling between his shoulder blades made him reluctant to laugh at her comment. 'It's too dark to see them.'

'No, it isn't. There are eleven of them. They travel in packs. Like dogs. They came to spy on us.'

Was she just making up a fanciful story to amuse herself on the long journey? Or had she inherited an uncanny sense from the blood of her parents?

'Is there more you can see that you haven't told me?'

'Well, I can see Mama sometimes.'

The casual comment came like a jolt, like a man riding a placid gelding that suddenly bucks and bolts. He broke out in a sweat, skin tingling as if he were beset by a swarm of gnats. 'What do you mean?'

'Only sometimes. She's still trapped in the burning stone. She's trying to find her way back.'

How difficult it was to keep his voice calm. 'Is there anything we can do to help her?'

She shrugged, painfully unconcerned. 'We just have to wait. The merfolk are waiting, too, you know.'

'What are they waiting for?'

He could feel her concentration by the way her small body tensed against his. At the mast, chains scraped against wood as Bulkezu shifted position again. His guards – Malbert and Den tonight – chatted quietly with each other, reminiscing about a card game they'd lost to a pair of cheating Ungrian soldiers.

'Oh!' said Blessing, sounding surprised and a little intrigued. 'They're waiting for revenge.'

2

As the river broadened and grew sluggish winding its way through marshy wilderness, Zacharias spent more time on deck watching the riot of birds that flocked everywhere: ducks, egrets, storks, terns that skimmed along the flat sheet of the water, cormorants. Once, but only once, a gray crane. Hathui never moved far from his side unless she was called away by the prince. It seemed strange and terrible to him to stand beside his beloved younger sister in this companionable silence. He kept waiting for Hathui to come to her senses and repudiate him, but she never did.

Instead, she questioned him about Sanglant's retinue, their names and character. 'And the three young folk who attend

Princess Blessing? There's trouble brewing there.'

He glanced toward the bow where Anna stood between the two young men. Matto was shorter but broader through the shoulders, strong enough to wield an ax with deadly measure. Thiemo, half a head taller, still retained a whippet's slenderness, but he had a cool head in most circumstances, a loyal heart, and a charming smile.

Anna had changed markedly since that day in Gent when Sanglant had taken her into his retinue. She had bloomed.

'True enough,' he said. 'She was a scrawny thing when she first became Princess Blessing's nurse.' Anna would never be truly pretty, but she had a quality of candor about her that made her as attractive as girls with unblemished complexions and handsomer features. She had also matured quite startlingly, with a voluptuous body that any sane man would crawl a hundred miles to worship.

'They're like dogs snarling over a bitch in heat. Doesn't anyone else see it?'

'What's to be done? They're young. They can't help it.'

'Poor girl,' she said disapprovingly, but her gaze was caught by a thicket of dense shrubs hugging the shoreline, branches brilliant with red berries. 'Look at the hawthorn!' she cried with real passion.

Briefly the land rose out of the mire, and poplars and willows took hold, leaves flashing as the wind disturbed them, before the ground leveled again into grassy banks that looked inviting but were more likely sodden, swampy traps infested by the ubiquitous stinging flies. He scratched his chin, batting away a swarm of gnats; it was bad enough out on the water.

'Hathui . . .' He wanted to speak, but he was too afraid.

'Yes?' When he did not reply, she went on. 'Did you mean to say something?'

'No, no. A strange country, this one. There aren't many people living in these reaches. I admit I never thought a river could seem more like a marsh or a lake than a river.'

'Yet there's still a current that pulls us east. Have you seen the Heretic's Sea?'

'I have.'

'What is it like?'

'Filled with water.' Slavers had captured him within sight of those waters. 'The shores are crawling with heretics and infidels. Thus the name.'

'What do the heretics and infidels call the sea?'

Surprised, he looked at her, but she was studying the shore, smiling as she watched sheep grazing on a spit of land watched over by a skinny boy and his companionable dog which ran to the edge of the water and barked enthusiastically, tail wagging. She kept her gaze on them until they were lost to sight and at last she said, 'I'm sorry. What did you say?'

Nothing, he wanted to say sourly, but he was ashamed of his ill temper. 'The infidels, who worship the Fire God whom they name Astareos, call it the Northern Sea, because it lies north of their own country. I don't know what the Arethousans call it. Maybe they call it the Heretic's Sea, too.'

'Why would they do that?'

'Because they think *we* are heretics!' he said with a laugh, but Hathui stared at him.

'How could they think we are heretics when we are the ones who worship God in Unity in the proper manner? The skopos is God's deacon on Earth.' Her expression darkened as it always did when she thought of Darre, and Aosta, and the stricken king. 'I pray we will find what we seek, and quickly.'

'The grasslands are wide. Do not think it will be so easy to find anything on those trackless wastes, and especially not griffins and sorcerer women.'

'Have you ever seen these Kerayit?'

'I saw one of their war bands but I've never seen the cart of one of their sorcery women. Nor have I seen their masters, the Bwr people, the ones who were born half of humankind and half of a mare.'

'Are there really such creatures?'

The water slipped past, a mottled brown ripe with vegetation and dirt. 'I have seen one in my dreams. I was never more frightened than at that moment.'

'Never?' she asked softly.

He flushed. 'What do you mean?'

'*Never*, Zacharias?'

He said nothing, and when it was clear to her that he would not answer, she glanced toward the prince and spoke in a different tone, as if introducing a new subject. 'What about the merfolk?'

'Let it be, Hathui! I beg you. Let well enough alone.'

But he had exasperated her, although it was the last thing he wanted. 'You can never be content, can you?' she said. 'That's why you left the village, isn't it? You can't find peace.'

'Peace was torn from me by Bulkezu! It's his fault I can't find peace!'

'Nay. You won't let yourself be at peace. You suffered. You did what you had to, to survive. I don't blame you for that. We've all done things we aren't proud of. But don't think you can run away from the Enemy. The demons can't give up their grip on you until you let them go.'

He did not answer, and at last she let him be. For a long time they simply stood at the rail together, watching the shoreline slide past. It was a measure of peace. It was as much as he could ever hope for, that much and no more.

3

By the next morning the grassy banks became overrun with reeds until all through the afternoon it seemed they sailed upon a brown ribbon cast through a green sea that stretched to the horizon on all sides. So many channels cut through the reeds that Anna marveled that the ship-master could navigate so unerringly along the main channel, if there even was one anymore. They tied up that night alongside a spit of land, but no one dared disembark because of the flies, and because they had not forgotten that glimpse of the merfolk.

At dawn they set out again, passing spits of land overgrown

with rushes. There seemed to be nothing but reeds, water, and sky; they had left the land behind them but not yet entered the sea. Yet in the end the last islands of rushes fell behind and the brown water of the river poured into the blue of the Heretic's Sea, mingling until the earthy color was utterly lost. The rushy delta lay green in the west. All else was either the blue of sky or sea.

Anna stood next to Blessing at the railing. She had never seen anything so vast in her life. Even Blessing, for once, was stricken to silence by the immensity of the waters and the answering sky, mottled with clouds. The wind whipped her braid along her shoulders and rippled her clothing across her skin like a caress.

'I've seen the sea before,' Thiemo was saying boastfully to Matto. 'The Northern Sea. I rode there with Prince Ekkehard, when we were at Gent.'

'I'm just a poor country boy, my lord,' retorted Matto in a tone that made her wince. 'I've never seen such sights.'

They both chose that moment to look at *her*, testing her reaction, and she flushed and looked away over the waters.

'They're following us,' said Blessing, head turned to gaze at the ships behind.

'Of course, my lady. We'll all sail together, just as we marched together.'

'No. I mean the men-fish. They want to know where we're going. They're following us. But I don't think they can follow us up onto land.'

Anna shuddered, but although she peered at their wake, she saw no merfolk.

For seven days they sailed north and east along the sea, always in sight of land and mostly in good weather, disturbed by one bracing squall out of the north. They often saw other ships sailing southeast, and three times the ship-master caught sight of a sail that looked like a skulking privateer, but no lone pirate wished to attack a fleet and so they continued on their way unmolested. On the eighth day they put into the port of Sordaia.

At least five hundred Arethousan soldiers stood in tidy ranks along the waterfront, alerted by the number of ships, and it quickly became obvious that any attempt to disembark would be met with force. The governor of the town, an Arethousan potentate from the imperial capital, had sent a representative to speak to the arrivals. The Most Honorable Lord High Chamberlain in Charge of the Governor's Treasure, Basil, had no beard but was not a priest. He was, Brother Breschius explained, a eunuch.

'He's had his balls cut off?' exclaimed Matto, horrified. He glanced at Anna and blushed.

'Like Brother Zacharias,' said Thiemo, 'but this one doesn't look the same. He looks softer.'

'What was done to Brother Zacharias was nothing like this,' said Breschius gently. 'That was mutilation. No doubt the operation on this man – if we can call him such – was carried out when he was a boy. It's considered a great honor.'

Thiemo laughed nervously, and Matto was too embarrassed and appalled to speak. After lengthy introductions and some kind of tedious speech on the part of the eunuch, Sanglant sent Brother Heribert, who spoke Arethousan, to the palace with an assortment of gifts – a cloak trimmed with marten fur, a gold treasure box, delicately carved ivory spoons, and an altar cloth embroidered with gold thread. The negotiations took the rest of the day, ending in the late afternoon after Prince Sanglant agreed to go with a small party to the palace the next day as a hostage for the good behavior of his troops.

'The Most Honorable Lord High Chamberlain Basil informs me that we are allowed to set up camp in an abandoned fort built by the former Jinna overlords outside the town walls,' said Heribert, still flushed and sweating from traveling back and forth between harbor and palace in the hot summer sun.

'There won't be time to disembark many before it gets dark,' said the ship-master, examining the sun. 'Maybe it's better done tomorrow.'

'Or we could send a smaller force tonight to begin setting up,' said Fulk. 'That's what I recommend.'

'Is it safe?' asked Hathui. 'The few who disembark tonight will be easy to kill, if these Arethousans intend treachery.'

'It seems a foolish way to provoke our anger,' said Sanglant. 'We can disembark fighting, if need be. How would it benefit them to anger us in such a petty way?'

'They *are* Arethousans, my lord prince,' remarked Lady Bertha, who had been rowed over from another ship. 'They imbibe treachery with their mother's milk. You can't trust them.'

'Nor do I. Nevertheless, Captain Fulk has the right of it. Captain, send one hundred men tonight. Not Wichman or any of his company. There should be time for them to reach the fort and reconnoiter before it's too dark to see.'

'I want to go! I want to go!' cried Blessing.

'No.' Sanglant beckoned to Breschius. 'I need Heribert to attend me at the palace and you to remain here with the ships until everyone is off. You are the only ones who can speak Arethousan. There must be no misunderstandings.'

'Yes, my lord prince.'

'I want to go see the palace tomorrow with you, Papa!'

'No. You'll stay with the army.'

'I don't want to stay! I want to go!' The girl grabbed the railing ready to fling herself over the side and swim for shore.

'*No.*'

The confinement of a sea voyage had not improved Sanglant's temper, nor had a day cooling his heels in the harbor made him patient. When he grabbed his daughter's arm, the girl whimpered.

'I *will.*' Her mouth quivered, but her gaze remained defiant.

'You will *not.*' The prince turned to Anna. 'You'll go, Anna, to set up camp for your mistress. And take—' his gaze flicked to Matto and Thiemo, pushed to the back during the day's negotiations. 'Lord Thiemo, you'll go as well.'

'I want to go!' Blessing tried to wriggle out of her father's unforgiving grasp.

'If you give me any trouble tonight, Blessing,' her father added softly, 'you won't even be allowed off this ship

tomorrow when the troops disembark. You'll stay here locked
in the cabin until we leave this port. Is that understood?'

Fighting back tears, she nodded but did not resist when
Sanglant thrust her into Matto's care. Yet Matto's furious
expression could have wilted flowers as he watched Anna.
She felt his gaze like the prick of an arrow on her back as
she descended the gangplank. Although she stood on solid
earth, the ground still moved and it was difficult to keep her
feet under her. With Matto and Blessing both so angry, she
dared not look back as they marched away. The unsteady
ground made her a little nauseated, and the flap of canvas
from the rolled-up tent she was carrying that got loose from
the ropes and flipped over her eyes only made the dizziness
worse. She staggered as they ascended a broad avenue
through the town. With the canvas obscuring her vision she
could only see her feet, garbage, and an occasional pile of
dog shit. The town stank in a way the ship had not; there
wasn't enough wind to chase out the smell. Voices rang all
around her – the streets were crowded – but she heard not
a single recognizable word.

How had she ever come so far from Gent? What if she
died here in this land of barbarians and foreigners? Was this
God's punishment upon her for her sins? Tears welled in her
eyes, but she bit her lip hard until the pain calmed her down.
Crying never did any good.

Yet it seemed a long and lonely walk out to the fort. Sunset
washed the land with pale gold when she finally negotiated a
narrow plank bridge over a steep-sided ditch, a yawning abyss
that made her tremble, and found herself in the fort. She
allowed the rolled-up canvas to slide down onto the ground.
Her shoulders ached, but at least the ground had stopped
swaying. It was good to be back on dirt.

As she stretched the knots out of her shoulders, she examined the empty fort. A wall built of stamped clay surrounded
the interior buildings, which resembled a bee's hive, a series
of cell-like rooms built haphazardly in sprawling units. A
number of soldiers wandered out to explore. She followed
them.

'Those infidels lived like pigs,' observed Lewenhardt as he retreated from yet another chamber filled with mounds of rubbish and dried excrement.

'Or else they kept their animals stabled here,' said Den.

'Don't look like *cow* shit to me,' said Surly.

'What do you think, Brother Zacharias?' asked Chustaffus. 'Do infidel kings stable their soldiers like beasts? Is there no hall for the men to eat together with their lord?'

Zacharias shaded a hand against the sun. 'I don't know the customs of the Jinna, but I see no hall, only these small rooms.'

'This one is empty!' shouted Lewenhardt, who had gone on to the next. The majority of the little chambers lay empty, each one just big enough to sleep four men, but no more than that, more like stone tents than proper barracks.

'Enough of that!' called Sergeant Cobbo. 'Get to work. We'll need tents set up, and you lot haul whatever you can find over to that gate to build a barrier.'

Anna was helping Den post rope lines to keep horses from straying into the tented area when the last of the advance force arrived: a dozen horsemen who had to dismount by the gate in order to lead their horses across the plank bridge over the pit. It wasn't precisely a true gate. The old gates had long since fallen down and, evidently, been carted away, and only the deep ditch protected the entrance, although a fair bit of debris – posts, planks, discarded wheels – had been dragged over to form a makeshift wall on the inner side of the pit.

Was that Thiemo among them? She shaded her eyes to get a better look.

'Hey!' said Den. 'Don't let the rope go slack!'

She went back to work, but as it began to get dark, there was no point in doing more. She wandered over to the horse lines but did not find him there. What was she thinking? Usually she shared a bed with Blessing every night. She wasn't used to so much freedom.

She could not stop thinking about finding him, yet she didn't want to appear to be seeking him out. She climbed a narrow staircase that led up to the walkway along the wall, to survey the camp. A pinkish-purple glow rimmed the western horizon, although the east lay in darkness. The town revealed itself as glimmers of distant lamplight. Below, campfires burned and Sergeant Cobbo began singing. A footstep scuffed on the wall, but it was the watchman in the corner watch-tower.

'Anna.'

When he took hold of her arm, out of the dark, she gasped, and he slipped an arm around her, pressing her close. He was a head taller than her, broad through the shoulders but with a young man's slenderness in the torso and hips.

'I have something to show you,' he whispered, breath sweet against her ear. 'Come with me.'

'I have to go back—' she began, suddenly nervous. Suddenly elated.

'We're stuck here for the night, Anna. There's no one else who needs us. Come this way.'

'I can't see.'

'Shhh. We'll go slowly.'

In the dark it wasn't easy to retrace their path along the wall, where they could have tumbled off the inner side at any moment and fallen two man-lengths to the hard-packed dirt below. It took a fair bit of groping, and tangling, and hold-ing on to each other, to negotiate the worn steps, and by the time they reached the ground they were both giggling yet trying not to, fearing that Cobbo or some other soldier would find them.

'This way.'

Thiemo still had hold of her hand, but as he started along the base of the wall, she hesitated. He turned back to her, ran a hand up her arm to her shoulder to caress the curve of her neck.

'Anna? I found a place where no one will find us. It's clean, too. I left a blanket there.'

She wanted him so badly. Even to touch him made her hot in a way the sun's heat never did.

'What will happen then?' The future opened before her like the wide waters of the sea, fathomless.

His lips brushed hers, light as a butterfly's kiss at first, suddenly insistent. When he finally pulled back, they were both breathing in gasps. Anna clung to him.

'We could be dead tomorrow,' he murmured.

What about Matto? But she could not speak Matto's name out loud. Matto would be in Thiemo's place now, had Prince Sanglant sent one and not the other. And if it were the prince himself, holding her in the darkness?

She dared not walk down that path. Thiemo was a lord, but only the eighth child of a minor count. That was why he had been sent to ride in Prince Ekkehard's retinue, to make his own way as a noble servant to a higher born man. He was disposable, the kind of boy sent into the Dragons. Maybe that was why he wasn't as haughty as the other nobles, because he was assured of so little.

'Death is sure,' she whispered, and if not now, then later. Someday. None of them knew what kind of trouble the prince was leading them into. Maybe the prince himself did not know. Anything could happen.

Anything.

'Thiemo.' The top of her head barely came to his chin, but it wasn't difficult to wrap her arms around his neck and pull him down to kiss him again.

What would she be sorry for, the day she died?

Not this.

V

SORDAIA

1

In the morning Zacharias slept late, having made a bed for himself in blessed solitude in one of the little chambers. By the time he stumbled bleary-eyed into the hammer of the late morning sun, all men, beasts, and belongings were accounted for, Captain Fulk had posted guards at the gate and lookouts on top of the wall, and the men were assembling on the open ground in front of the gates. Lord Wichman, Lord Druthmar, and the other nobles watched from beneath the shaded luxury of spacious awnings, lounging at their ease while they sipped wine and played chess and listened to one of their number playing a lute.

Fulk's speech to the soldiers was stern.

'You will not go into the town unless you have been commanded to by myself or by Prince Sanglant. No markets. No brothels. No taverns. Is that understood?'

Dismissed, they sulked in the dusty fort, having nothing more to look at than each other and nothing more than sour beer to drink.

'No wonder this place looks like prison,' said Surly. 'That's what it is.'

'I always wondered what Jinna women look like,' mused Lewenhardt. 'Is it true they dance naked through fire to worship their god?'

'You might wish,' laughed Johannes, 'until you had to do the same thing. And then the fire would burn off your—'

'Hush,' said Den. 'Here comes the captain.'

'Brother Zacharias!' Captain Fulk nodded at his soldiers and they moved away. 'The prince wishes a small party to investigate the market, to scout what's available for provisions and guides for the journey east. You've lived in the grasslands, Brother. You'll know what kinds of things we must look for.'

'Wagons.' He remembered wagons too well.

'You've said so before,' said Fulk with the skepticism any westerner might show who did not understand the grasslands. 'We don't know how long we'll be delayed here. We'll need supplies and plenty of ale or wine to drink, with this hot sun. Wolfhere will go with you, as will Lady Bertha's healer, Robert, who can speak somewhat of the Arethousan language.'

Their departure was delayed at the gate when Blessing ran up. 'Take me with you! I hate it here!'

'My lady!' Matto arrived, huffing from the exertion in the heat. 'You must come back to the tent now. You know what your father the prince told you.'

'I don't want to stay here! I want to go see the governor's palace. I want to see people with big ears like tents. Maybe they have a phoenix in the market.' Matto started, looking guilty, as the girl crossed her arms over her chest and glowered. 'I want to go with *them*.'

Wolfhere softened as that glare was directed at him. 'What harm if she comes with us?'

'Has the sun cooked your head?' demanded Zacharias. 'There's a slave market in this port!'

'I want to see the slave market!'

Anger made him clench his jaw, but he struggled to remember that she was only a child. 'It's no merry thing to be sold in a slave market, my lady, as I should know. What's to stop some Arethousan thief from seeing what a proud, fine noblewoman you are and stealing you away and selling you to the infidels?'

'I'd bite him!'

'He'd slap you so hard you'd lose your wits,' retorted Zacharias, earning himself a sharp glance from Fulk.

Blessing was hopping from one foot to the other; she hadn't heard. 'I'd bite him five times, until he let me go!'

'For God's sake, Wolfhere, dissuade her from this foolish notion!'

'A day of freedom would not harm the child,' muttered Wolfhere irritably. 'I don't like the heat and the dust any better than she does. This is an unnatural place.'

'Unnatural, indeed! How can you think it safe for her to go wandering in the market when we don't even know how we'll be greeted by the townsfolk?'

Blessing screwed up that adorable face and put her fists on her hips; she was steering hard for a big storm.

'My lady.' Captain Fulk motioned for Matto to step back. 'I will personally escort you into the market, but not today. Any disruption may harm your father's negotiations with the governor. You would not want that.'

Captain Fulk was the only person besides her father she truly respected. Everyone else she either ignored or had wrapped up tight on a leash like an adoring dog. Her frown was so terrible that Zacharias was surprised that it didn't draw in clouds to cover the heartless sun.

'I'll go anyway,' she muttered.

'I must obey as your royal father commanded me, Your Highness, and keep you in this camp. If I do not, he will strip me of my rank and cast me out of his war band, and he would be right to do so.'

She could never bear the thought of any one of those she had a fondness for being torn from her. With a wounded sigh, she stalked away, Matto hastening after her while Fulk shook his head helplessly.

'Where is Anna?' the captain asked, but no one knew.

'Let's get out of here,' Zacharias said to his companions, 'while we still can.'

'A willful child,' observed Lady Bertha's healer as they hurried toward the gate. Robert was bald, short, and fat, but he had neat hands, nimble fingers, and an easy smile – remarkable considering how much suffering he must have seen in the course of his work. 'Yet it seems to me that her body grows faster than her mind does. When shall the one catch up to the other?'

'When, indeed?' murmured Wolfhere.

The guards offered suggestions about what they wanted most from town: wine, women, or at least a sweet apple. Then they had to walk the plank bridge.

The entrance to the fort was guarded by an exceptionally deep, vertically-sided ditch, too steep to climb and dug all the way across the opening. Into this chasm Fulk had lowered Bulkezu. Zacharias saw the Quman begh pacing below. The prisoner looked up at the sound of men crossing the plank bridge that provided the only access into the fort.

'I smell the worm creeping out. Do you go to sell yourself in the slave market, worm? Do you miss it so?'

Zacharias stumbled forward, leaping for solid ground, and did not wait for the others as he hastened along the dirt track that circled around the wall and back toward town. But they caught up to him nevertheless. Mercifully, they did not mention Bulkezu.

'The builders seem to have feared the steppe more than the sea,' observed Wolfhere as he surveyed the placement of the fort, with its gates facing the water, not the land.

'They say there are men in the grasslands who can turn themselves into wolves,' said Robert.

'Do you listen to everything you hear?' asked Wolfhere with a laugh.

'I hear many strange things, and I've found it unwise *not* to listen to them.' Robert was a westerner from the borderlands between Varingia and Salia. He had never explained how he had come into the service of marchland nobles, far to the east of his birthplace, and Zacharias did not choose to ask, considering that he had once glimpsed a slave brand on Robert's right shoulder. He'd met a few Salians sold into slavery among the Quman tribes, cast out of their homes by debt or poverty. Those whom hunger or abuse hadn't killed had died of despair.

They soon came to the sprawling borderlands of the town, gardens, corrals, orchards, and the hovels and houses of those who could not afford a space to live inside the wall. Children trotted alongside, shouting in their gibberish tongues. They had all sorts of faces; they might be kin to Quman horseman or Aostan merchant, to Arethousan sailor and Jinna priest, to dark Kartiakans or to the sly and powerful Sazdakh warrior women with their broad faces and green eyes. Yet there were no blond heads among this pack. Wolfhere stood out like a proud silver wolf among mangy, mongrel dogs.

The guards at the gate did not wish to admit them into town, but Robert had a few Ungrian coppers for bribes.

They crossed through a tunnel cut into the wide turf wall and emerged into the streets. The lanes stank alarmingly, strewn with refuse baking in the heat, and yet even so they were crowded with folk busy about their errands and mindful of where they set their feet.

'Beware pickpockets,' said Zacharias. A few heads turned to look at him, hearing an unfamiliar language. Wolfhere's hair caught attention, too, but mostly they were left alone. Too many travelers came into a port like Sordaia for three scruffy visitors to create lasting wonder.

They passed windowless walled compounds, all locked away, a dozen of the distinctive octagonal Arethousan churches, and once a circular Jinna temple with its stair-stepped roof and central pillar jutting up toward the heavens, tattered streamers of red cloth flapping idly from the exposed portion of the pillar as a lazy wind out of the north teased them into motion. The barest ribbon of smoke spun up along the pillar's length, suggesting the fire within.

'Is it true they burn worshipers alive?' whispered Robert as soon as the temple was lost to view. 'That their priestesses copulate with any man brave enough to walk into the fire?'

Wolfhere snorted.

'I don't know.' Zacharias glanced around nervously. 'But

it's death for any person who has witnessed those rites to speak of them. Be careful what you say lest you hit on something true, and find a knife between your ribs.'

'Can anyone here understand us?' asked Robert. 'I haven't heard a single soul speaking Wendish.'

It was more obvious still once they reached the marketplace that sprawled in a semicircle around the harbor with its docks and warehouses. Zacharias heard a dozen languages thrown one upon the other and melding together into a babble, but he never heard one clear Wendish word out of that stew. Here, in the port of Sordaia, the north traded with the south but they had journeyed so far into the east that the west, their own land, seemed only a tale told to children. Ships unloaded cloth and spices and precious jade trinkets for the rich beghs of the grasslands, those who cared to trade rather than rob. Timber floated down the river from the northern forests lay stacked, ready for loading, beside fenced yards heaped with fox and bear furs and soft marten pelts. Open sheds sheltered amphorae of grain destined to feed the great city where the Arethousan emperors reigned supreme over their country of heretics.

The slave market was always open.

Even Robert stopped to stare at a line of fair-skinned, red-headed, and entirely naked young women who, roped together, were prodded up onto a platform so buyers could examine them. Jinna merchants with their hair covered, Hessi women with their faces veiled, Arethousan eunuchs with beardless chins, and other folk whose faces and apparel Zacharias did not recognize fondled legs for strength and breasts for firmness, tapped teeth, and studied the lines of palms.

'Must we watch?' demanded Zacharias, sweating heavily, seeing the tears on their faces as their bodies were sold away to new masters. If he stood here any longer, he would have to recall the day it had happened to him. 'They don't need onlookers staring at them in their misery!'

They moved on to the wharves where two ships were just mooring as the noon sun began its fall westward. The ships that had ferried Sanglant's army here were already taking on cargo, eager to depart. Robert and Wolfhere went to find the ship-master who had sailed with Sanglant, since the man knew Sordaia well and had promised to recommend honest merchants. Zacharias did not follow them at once, his attention caught by the interplay between a groom and the magnificent gray stallion the man was trying to coax down the gangplank of a newly arrived merchant ship. A step forward was followed by a nervous shy back, while meanwhile a traveler waited impatiently on the deck, eager to disembark but impeded by the skittish horse. The man hopped aside to avoid being kicked.

A westerner, Zacharias thought, noting the light cloak and broad-brimmed hat worn by the waiting traveler. Although not a particularly tall man, his arrogant stance marked him as a person of noble birth, and his robes and the carved ebony staff he leaned on suggested a man of clerical vocation. He had a servant with him, a stocky, stoop-shouldered fellow whose torso was slung about with rolled-up bundles and a small sealed wooden chest, almost too much for a single person to carry. The groom coaxed the stallion forward again. It took a step, snorted, and shied back.

That was enough for the westerner. He made some comment to the groom, and the man, sweating profusely, bobbed his head as though a thousand apologies would not suffice and reined the stallion aside with an effort, the horse sidestepping and tossing its head, restless and unhappy. It was a beautiful beast, not unlike Prince Sanglant in its fierce, masculine beauty, alive to the touch of the wind and the pitch of the ship on the waters as it rubbed up against the pilings. Others had come to watch; such superb creatures were not seen every day. No doubt it was for this reason that women admired Prince Sanglant so very much.

A person bumped into him; it was the heavyset servant from the ship clearing a way through the gathered crowd for his master. Dressed in clerical robes, the nobleman passed next to Zacharias, the brim of his hat tilted in such a way that the frater got a look at his face: a dark-haired man, clean-shaven like a churchman, with a pursed, judgmental mouth.

His gaze swept the crowd, skipping past Zacharias as he moved briskly after his servant.

Was there something familiar about him? Or was it only that any westerner looked familiar in a land filled with barbarians?

The press of the crowd had cut him off from Wolfhere and Robert. He was alone. Ai, God, it was in a place like this that he had been taken by slavers. The shaking hit so suddenly that he thought his feet would drop out from under him. His throat closed tightly and he couldn't draw breath. He swayed, dizzy, and his palms became clammy.

No one else was troubled by the shaking ground. It was only him. Frantically, he plunged through the crowd and, glancing beyond the turbaned heads of Arethousan market-wives and the red caps and ponytails of Jinna merchants, saw Wolfhere pushing his way through the crowd. Robert was nowhere in sight.

Zacharias raised a trembling hand, meaning to call out, but no words came.

Wolfhere's expression changed as abruptly as an avalanche alters the side of a hill. His eyes widened in surprise, eyebrows lifting. His seamed face opened with a glimpse of panic, or joy, before closing tight into a stony mask as he turned, saw Zacharias, and shoved through the crowd toward him.

Zacharias' heart was pounding so hard he was out of breath. He could not fight against the crowd as it shoved him away from Wolfhere. The stallion trumpeted in fury and fear, and he was half spun about by the force of a man knocking into him in time to see the horse break away from the hapless groom. With a graceful leap, the stallion plunged down the gangplank and landed in the midst of the crowd, trampling a hapless bystander. People screamed and scattered.

Zacharias yelped out loud, too terrified to move. The crowd surged around him as people fought to get out of the way of the frenzied horse, now bucking and kicking like a demon.

'Fool of a groom!' Wolfhere, emerging from the mob, grabbed hold of Zacharias' wrist. 'He should have waited until evening and peace—' The next word lodged in his throat.

Only a croak came out. 'God help us!'

Screaming, the stallion reared. It had cleared the space around it, although a dozen people lay on the ground, some stirring and crawling away, others lying motionless where they had fallen. Blood smeared the stones. The groom was shouting to his fellows on the ship, and they had brought rope, but they didn't leap into the fray quickly enough.

Because one bold soul strode forward to confront the gray stallion. One person was eager to test herself against the wild creature that now terrorized the docks. One small, stubborn, and recklessly foolhardy child too spoiled to understand the meaning of caution or the strength of an animal many times her size and vastly more powerful.

'Blessing!' Wolfhere was trapped behind a brace of brawny sailors loudly laying bets on whether the girl would go down under the horse's hooves.

'Brother Lupus!' cried a voice triumphantly from behind Zacharias. 'I have tracked you down at last!'

2

To Sanglant's surprise, the Arethousan governor did not greet her visitors at the marble portico to the governor's palace house but made them wait in the sun without offering them even the shade provided by the colonnade that ran along the forecourt. A smooth-cheeked eunuch declared – in Arethousan – that he had to properly learn their names and titles before they could be announced to the Most Exalted Lady Eudokia.

'We're being snubbed,' murmured Sapientia, her skin flushed either from heat or annoyance. 'Treated as if we're impoverished supplicants! Made to stand out in the sun like commoners! The governor should have met us personally and escorted us in!'

'Hush.' In truth Sanglant did not know what to make of the eunuch's supercilious attitude, looking them over as though they were a prize lot of horses brought in for the master of the house to consider buying. Sapientia quieted, still fuming. 'Heribert, I pray you, do what you can.'

While Heribert haggled with the eunuch in Arethousan, Sanglant glanced at the other companions he had chosen to accompany him: Lady Bertha, because she had insisted on coming, Captain Istvan because he had traveled to Arethousan towns before, three young lords who had the sense to remain silent, Hathui, and twenty of his most levelheaded soldiers. All sweated profusely. It was nearing midday, when the sun's hammer seemed doubly strong. Bertha winked at him. She alone seemed to be enjoying herself.

No doubt the heat accounted for Heribert's rising anger as he and the eunuch, looking cool in his linen robe and jeweled slippers, descended into a snappish disagreement. It ended when the eunuch retreated through the doors.

'What were you arguing about?' Sanglant asked when Heribert returned to him.

'The title by which you and Princess Sapientia will be introduced to the governor, my lord prince. The chamberlain insisted that the word meaning "lord" and "lady" will do, a title I refused to accept. We struck a bargain. The soldiers will remain outside, in decent shade, within shouting distance, and you and Her Highness shall be referred to as "princeps."'

'Ah.'

'Do not trust the Arethousans, my lord prince. They are devious, greedy, and will flatter you while they steal your purse. Rank means everything to them. Bargain where you must, but do not give way in any matter that will make you seem low in their eyes.'

'Why do we accept these insults?' demanded Sapientia. 'We should just leave!'

'We'll need the assistance of the governor to fully equip ourselves for a trip into the grasslands,' said Sanglant, rather tired of having to point this out to Sapientia once again. 'We'll need guides as well.'

'Don't we have Bulkezu for a guide?' she retorted. 'Is that not why you spared his life?'

'I would not put my trust in him alone, but I promise you, Sister, he *will* serve us in the end. As for the governor, we must travel as diplomatically as we can. Better we leave no trouble in our wake that we must deal with on our way back.'

The heavy doors opened silently, hauled back by unseen figures, and the eunuch reappeared, his jade-green robes swirling about his legs as he indicated that they could follow him. Once within the palace, the heat became bearable. Marble floors graced the colonnades. The palace had the appearance of great wealth considering its location in a frontier trading town. They passed several courtyards with fountains running merrily and glimpsed chambers fitted with gold-and-ivory ornamentation and jewel-studded divans. Finally, they entered a shaded arbor overgrown by thick grapevines and screened off by cunningly worked lattices. A dozen soldiers stood at guard, holding spears. A trio of eunuchs whispered in one shadowy corner beside a table laden with wine and fruit. Two slaves worked fans on either side of a couch, whose occupant reclined at leisure, eyeing them as though they were toads got in where they did not belong. She was past the prime of life, with gray showing in her elaborate coiffure and two coarse black hairs growing out of her chin, but the precious rings on her stubby fingers and the gleam of gold weighing heavily at her neck indicated her rank. A simple gold circlet crowned her head.

Sanglant could get no good idea of her height or shape because of the light blanket draped over her form. For all he knew, she could have been a lamia, hiding a serpent's body where her legs were supposed to be. Certainly she had no welcoming smile in her expression, nor did her tiny molelike eyes examine him with interest, only with contempt.

Two rickety stools had been placed before her, the kind of seat a stable boy might sit on while milking his cows.

'Are we meant to sit on *those*?' hissed Sapientia.

'Surely there is another couch,' said Sanglant to Heribert before he turned to the eunuch who had led him in. He knew how to edge his smile into a threat. He knew how to step forward in a manner that was not aggressive but made best use of his size. He knew how to loom. 'I cannot sit on such a humble seat, but I can stand over my dear cousin, the Exalted Lady Eudokia, if need be.'

Of course, it did not do for him to seem so large and threatening and the governor to seem an invalid in his presence. A pair of servants lugged in a second couch and set it down at a discreet distance from the governor.

Sapientia sat first, at the head. Sanglant waited until Bertha and Captain Istvan took the stools, on either side, and the others ranged behind him in an orderly half circle appropriate to their respective stations before seating himself at the foot of the couch. It was so low that he had to stretch out his long legs, an obstacle for the eunuchs hurrying forward to offer wine.

Despite his thirst, he could barely drink the noxious combination that tasted like pitch, resin, and plaster mixed into a nasty brew.

Abruptly, the governor spoke. She had a remarkably mellow voice, quite at odds with the unpleasant lineaments of her face, and it was impossible to tell from her tone what manner of words she uttered. Heribert flushed, hot color in his cheeks.

'So speaks the Most Exalted Lady, Eudokia,' he said, stalwartly forcing a placid expression onto his face. '"I am duty bound to give a courteous reception to those of noble blood who come to my province. I know you are the daughter of Princess Sophia, my cousin, who was exiled to the barbarian kingdoms because of her sins. Yet how can I entertain in good faith the children of a master who has most impiously invaded lands in Aosta long sworn to serve the Most Just and Holy Emperor of Arethousa, my kinsman? This hostile invader has captured the holy city of Darre which rightfully belongs to those of us who profess the true faith. He has forced my countryfolk into exile. He has burned cities who pledge their faith to the Most Just and Holy Emperor, he has massacred loyal citizens. He sends his heretic priests to roam in our westernmost province of Dalmiaka, plotting what manner of evil and mischief I cannot guess.""

Sapientia had got so red that she looked fit to swoon, but Sanglant laughed curtly, laying a steadying hand on her arm. 'If that is to be our welcome, Heribert, then I pray you let her exalted ladyship know our response.' A eunuch bowed before him, offering him more wine, but he waved him away. 'My father did not invade Aosta. The embattled citizens begged him to save them from murderers and bandits. The rightful queen was assaulted in her own palace by usurpers, so it came to my father to restore to her what had been stolen from her by rebels and traitors. Your most exalted emperor would have done the same thing to lords who had sworn fealty to him and then revolted against him. Furthermore, it is well known that all of Aosta once knelt before the Emperor Taillefer, whose greatness is known even into the east. It is only in later years that it came under the hand of the east. The folk of the south speak the same language as those of the north. They belong as one kingdom, not sundered into many.'

The Most Exalted Lady Eudokia raised her thick eyebrows. She had rouge-reddened cheeks, not enough to disguise her age, but her hands were as soft and white as a girl's, as though she had done nothing more strenuous in her life than dip them in rose-scented baths.

'With what force of ships will your master defend the south?' she asked through Heribert. 'Last year he rode south from Darre with his wife and all his army, his Wendish and his Varrens, with Aostans and Karronish, yet he could not take one small city. His soldiers are gluttons and drunks. They run from mice. What will they do when my cousin the Most Just and Holy Emperor sends troops against your master to take back what he has stolen?'

'Well, then, you shall see the worth of Wendish soldiers, will you not? I have fully eight hundreds of good, tried soldiers at my back, encamped outside the city. We will willingly take the field against your own troops if you are impatient to test our strength.'

She gestured to her servants, who hurried forward with a

platter of peeled grapes. She chose among them, popping the
most succulent into her mouth. As she chewed, her cunning
gaze flicked from Sanglant to Sapientia and back again. No
wind stirred the arbor except that created by the slaves, who
were dripping with sweat. The heat was bearable mostly
because he was not moving. Oddly enough, his irritation with
his host's arrogance made him patient, although Sapientia
shifted restlessly, gulping at the wine and then wincing at its
wicked bite.

'Let me speak bluntly.' Lady Eudokia waited for Heribert
to translate before she went on. 'Why are you here? If you
had wanted another princess for your master, you would have
traveled to Arethousa, for it is only the Most Just and Holy
Emperor who can dispose of his cousins and sisters and daughters. In any case, it is well known that your master married
the Aostan widow. I have not heard that your people follow
the idolatrous Jinna custom of marrying more than one spouse
at a time, or is it possible that you are still as barbaric as the
Ungrians?'

Captain Istvan snorted audibly, but said nothing.

'Perhaps it is you who wish a princess for your own bed,'
she went on, confronting Sanglant with her gaze but still refusing to use his name or dignify him with any kind of title.

'I am already married,' he said sweetly, 'or else surely I
would ask for your hand in marriage, Lady Eudokia.'

Was that amusement or anger that made her lips twitch?
She beckoned for the servant and ate another dozen grapes
before indicating that the man should offer the platter to her
guests. Sapientia ate eagerly, but Sanglant waved him away.

'Then what brings you here? Have you come to embrace
the true faith and cast aside the apostate heresy that the
Dariyan clerics preach?'

'Outrageous!' exclaimed Sapientia, a grape poised before
her lips.

'Do you not suppose,' Sanglant murmured, 'that there
stand among the servants one who can understand Wendish?
Do not be incautious.'

'Oh!' She studied the attendant servants as if she could

puzzle out their linguistic skills simply by the cut of their faces.

'How do I respond, my lord prince?' asked Heribert.

'Say this, Heribert.' Battling with wits he found himself nervous, palms damp. He smoothed his tunic over his thighs, the movement draining off a sliver of his tension, and continued. 'Most Exalted Lady Eudokia. What do you know of sorcery?'

Sapientia turned to him, startled, and grasped his wrist, but Eudokia, amazingly, chuckled. She clapped her plump hands. A eunuch bowed before her while she whispered into his ear. He left the arbor by a side door.

They waited in silence while the servants brought around grapes, figs, and sliced apples, still moist. Sanglant touched nothing. A sense of foreboding crept along his spine like the brush of venomous fingers. He shifted, marking Lady Bertha and seeing that she, too, sat erect, watchful, ready, as did Captain Istvan. The Eagle, Hathui, dipped her chin to show that she was alert. Sapientia nibbled anxiously on grapes, frowning between bites.

The eunuchs returned. One waited in the corner while the other knelt before Lady Eudokia, pale golden robes rustling into folds around him. He held a lidded ceramic pot. Lady Eudokia began to hum, slipping sideways into a wordless chant, as she removed the lid and slowly lowered her hand into the pot. Was that a bead of sweat on the eunuch's face, trickling alongside his nose? Probably it was only the heat.

'God Above!' whispered Sapientia, hand tightening on Sanglant's wrist as Lady Eudokia removed her hand from the pot.

A banded asp twisted upward to encircle her wrist. It reared its head back, hood flaring, and struck the hapless eunuch on the forearm.

Sapientia gasped. One of the lordlings shrieked.

The pot slipped from the servant's hands and shattered on the floor, shards scattering everywhere. He cried out, choking, as he slapped a hand over the bite, but already the flesh swelled horribly, a red mortification creeping onto the offended hand.

Lady Bertha and Captain Istvan leaped to their feet, but Sanglant raised a hand to caution them, and they paused with knives half drawn, unwilling to sit down again but respecting Sanglant's command.

One of the other eunuchs hurried over with an uncovered pot into which Lady Eudokia gently deposited the writhing snake. He clapped a lid over it and placed the pot on the floor beside the stricken man, who was gasping for breath as a drop of blood squeezed out of his right eye. The noise of his labored breathing and his whimpering moans was the only sound in the arbor except for the wheeze of the bellows worked by the slaves. The sleeve of his robe, covering the bitten arm, had gone tight because of swelling flesh.

'Basil.' The green–robed eunuch padded forward and offered Lady Eudokia a gold cup and a shallow bowl filled with fragrant herbs. She took hold of the stem in her right hand and with her left sprinkled crushed herbs into the cup while muttering all the while words whose meaning Sanglant did not understand.

'Beroush. Beroush . . . keddish gedoul.' She switched into the familiar cadences of Arethousan, and Heribert bent down to whisper a translation.

'"I invoke and beseech you, in the name of the seven blessed angels, in the name of the blessed Daisan who rebuked the poisonous serpents, let this become a cup of healing and cleansing, let the one who drinks from it be cured of poison. I adjure you, holy one, nameless one. Quickly! Quickly!"'

The stricken eunuch collapsed onto his back, clawing at his throat as beads of blood dripped out of the side of his mouth. His arm had grown to monstrous proportions, swollen all the way to the shoulder, and his face, too, had begun to swell. Sanglant had never seen poison work so fast.

Basil knelt beside his fellow eunuch and captured his head between his hands, prying his teeth open so Lady Eudokia could let droplets fall into the man's mouth. He thrashed weakly, fading, as blood leaked from his eyes like tears. Stilled, and went limp.

'He's dead,' whispered Sapientia.

'No,' said Sanglant. 'He is still breathing.'

Lady Eudokia poured the rest of the wine into her servant's slack mouth, although most of it slipped down his cheeks to stream away along the cracks in the flagstones. Already his face looked less swollen, and the wine had washed away the last of the blood, red drowning red.

'Sorcery,' said Lady Bertha. 'Look at his hand.'

'Sorcery,' said Lady Eudokia, although it wasn't clear if she were responding to Bertha's comment. Heribert kept up a running translation. 'I am familiar with sorcery, son of Henry. It runs in the blood of the women of my house, but we do not spend it unwisely, because sorcery exacts other costs, not so evident to you now but dangerous just the same. Is it sorcery you have come for?'

'You are not alone in commanding sorcery, Most Exalted Lady. Not every person who wields such powers uses them wisely, or well, or to the advantage of humankind.'

'An odd notion, Prince Sanglant. I use sorcery to the advantage of my family. Why should I use it to benefit others, who might be my enemies? Have you come to seek help from me against your barbarian magi? I will not interfere in quarrels that are beneath my notice.'

'What if this one is not beneath your notice? Sorcery can be harnessed in many ways. Its effects can cause tremors far beyond its point of origin. Do you know of the ones we call the mathematici, who weave threads of starlight into crowns formed of stone?'

Her color changed. Like the man bitten by the snake, her skin flushed and a tremor passed through her body. She dropped the cup, which landed squarely on the body of the prone eunuch before rolling off his chest to ring as it struck stone. The bitten eunuch groaned and sat up, rubbing his arm.

A door opened and closed, and a young eunuch in gold robes hurried in to whisper a message into Basil's ear. Basil, in turn, bent down to speak to the lady. Her color restored, she nodded and spoke a command.

'Go, now.' Basil's green robes flared as he stepped away

from the couch. 'A suite has been made ready. You can retire there. We will call you when it is time to dine.'

'But—' Sapientia rose.

'Nay, Sister, let us do as we are bid. The army should be safely settled in by now, with a market close at hand. We must be patient.'

'It could be a trap!' she muttered.

He bent close, to whisper in her ear. 'I think we can fight our way free of a palace protected by slippered eunuchs.'

'Bayan never insulted the worth of the Arethousan legions. He fought them once. Have you?'

Stung, Sanglant turned away from her and walked after the eunuch. The others followed obediently, murmuring together.

Basil showed them into two adjoining rooms which opened onto a porch looking over a sere garden. A fountain burbled merrily out in the sun. The spray made rainbows, quickly wicked away. A bed of rosemary was the only ornament; other plots of earth lay barren.

Within the suite a small group of attendants loitered and with gestures offered to bathe their hands and feet, to set up a chessboard, to settle them on divans piled with pillows so that they could rest. Silken tapestries graced the walls, depicting scenes of elaborate feasts and girls picking flowers.

'What do you make of it?' Heribert asked.

'My sister, or these handsome rooms?'

Heribert raised an eyebrow, wickedly, but shook his head. 'Which man was bitten by the snake?' he asked. 'Nay, I refer to the Most Exalted Lady Eudokia.'

'I expect that the walls, and the servants, have ears. If I were the master of this house, I would make sure that at least one among these attendants could speak Wendish.'

He sat down on one of the couches, stretching out amongst the pillows, yawning. All that sun, riding up to the palace, had made him tired, and he did not plot intrigue well when he was tired. It was easier to fight.

He dozed fitfully, waking frequently while around him his retinue talked quietly among themselves or napped. Breschius played chess with Lady Bertha. Sapientia snored softly. Flashes of dream brightened and faded as he twisted in and out of sleep. Liath weaving light among standing stones. Severed threads curling and writhing like beheaded snakes, like the serpent winding its way up Eudokia's wrist. Bells. An arrow flowering into flame. Bayan, dead, and Sapientia walking in chains, a prisoner. Who had done this to her?

He started awake, troubled and restless, and this time got to his feet. Walking outside, he staggered when he hit the sunlight; in the shady arbor, he had forgotten its strength. Hathui strolled up beside him.

'By the fountain we are surely safe from listening ears, my lord prince.'

The fountain's spray beckoned. He sat on the lip of the fountain and let the cooling mist float over him, beads collecting on his neck, sliding under the heavy torque, moistening his lips and hands. Hathui followed, shading her eyes with an arm. The rest of them prudently waited in the shade, watching him – or still sleeping away the heat of the day.

'Do you think she knows of the Seven Sleepers?' Hathui asked once she stood within the corona of the fountain's noisy spray. 'Or is in league with them?'

'I don't know. The church condemned the mathematici a hundred years ago. I do not know if the Arethousan patriarch did the same. Perhaps Brother Breschius knows. I suppose it will be difficult to tease out the truth.'

'Do you think the asp was really poisonous?'

He laughed. 'It seemed poisonous enough to me. Just as well I left my daughter back at the fort for safekeeping, since she would insist on handling the serpent herself. The question we must ask is whether it was magic, or herb-craft, that saved the eunuch. We cannot trust the Arethousans, nor should we try to bring them into affairs they are better left out of. If it's true that my father wars against their agents and vassals in southern Aosta, then they will either seek to hinder us in order to harm him, or they will help us hoping to weaken him.'

'You would rather trust to barbarians and pagans, my lord prince? To these Kerayit that Brother Breschius speaks of?'

'They have less to gain whether we succeed or fail, do they not?'

'Yet how do we find them?'

'How do we find them?' he echoed. 'Or am I simply a fool to think I can pit myself against Anne?'

'Someone must, my lord prince. Do not forget your father, the king.'

Here in the courtyard, open to the air, he heard noises from the town, a stallion's defiant trumpeting, the rumble of cartwheels along cobbles, a man shouting.

He smiled grimly. 'Nay, I do not forget him. Am I not his obedient son?'

'Alas, my lord prince, not always.'

He grinned as he looked up at her, delighted by her dead-pan expression and the lift of her eyebrows. 'It is no wonder that my father trusted you, Eagle.'

'Nor have I ever betrayed that trust. Nor do I mean to do so now.'

'Still, you sought me out.'

'Because I believe that you are the only one who can save King Henry—'

A shout disturbed the drowsy afternoon. Feet clattered on stone in counterpoint to cries and objections. He jumped to his feet and called out to the others just as the door into the suite was thrown open and a soldier thrust inside as if on the points of spears.

'My lord prince!' The man was too short of breath to croak out more than the title. 'Prince Sanglant!'

'Here I am.' Sanglant strode into the shadow of the white-washed porch. 'What is it, Malbert?'

'Your Grace!' The eunuch Basil shoved past Malbert with a furious expression. His Wendish was startlingly fluent. 'This man invaded the sanctuary of the palace. He injured one of my—'

'I beg you, silence!'

The eunuch faltered, mouth working, face a study in contempt and insulted dignity. But he kept quiet.

'Malbert?'

The soldier still breathed hard. 'My lord prince,' he gasped, fighting for air. 'Your daughter – is missing.'

3

Zacharias was too terrified to move as the stallion gathered itself to bolt. The groom edged down the gangplank. Wolfhere shoved at the backs of the sailors who, like the rest of the crowd, backed away fearfully to give the frightened horse room. Only Blessing stood her ground.

'Brother Lupus!' The cleric appeared out of the crowd and grasped Wolfhere by the shoulder. 'I thought I might find you tracking Prince Sanglant as well. Come. We must hasten.'

'Now is not the time!' Wolfhere pulled free of the cleric, not difficult since he stood half a head taller and had the build of a man who has spent his life in the saddle, not in court.

'My God.' The other man looked beyond him as the sailors shrank away, leaving a gap between which one could see the tableau, stallion poised, girl motionless. 'Is that the child, grown so large? I had thought her no more than three. Or is this another bastard child belonging to the prince?'

The stallion danced sideways, tossing its head. The groom reached the base of the plank.

'No time to waste,' murmured the cleric.

Something about the way he tilted up his chin and squinted his eyes skyward triggered a cascade of memories. Something about the way he lifted his left hand, as if giving a benediction or a command, spilled recognition into plain sight.

Zacharias had seen him before. He was one of those who had remained in the valley after Kansi-a-lari defeated the sorcerers. He was one of the Seven Sleepers.

As was Wolfhere.

Light flashed around the cleric's head. The sky darkened as a cloud scudded in to cover the sun, and that same wisp of light caressed Zacharias' neck before flitting on to twist across the sprawl of bodies. It tangled within the mane of the restive stallion curling around its ears. Was he hallucinating? The stallion snorted and backed so hard into the groom that the poor man tumbled off the wharf and fell with a shriek and a splash into the filthy water.

Blessing took another step forward. The stallion reared, trumpeting.

Zacharias could not shift his feet. Wolfhere thrust past the men blocking his way and sprinted to her, bearing her bodily into the safety of the crowd as Blessing shouted in protest and kicked him. The cleric turned.

'Who are you?' the man asked in his prim voice, his lips set in a terse line. 'Too late for questions, since you have already seen me.'

A breath of wind teased his ear. A flutter of breeze wrapped around his face and choked off the air. Light crackled before his eyes. Faded.

He fell.

Woke, sick to his stomach and with the ground heaving beneath him. He rolled backward, bumped up against a lumpy sack, and opened his eyes. It was dark except for a dull glow beyond his feet, too diffuse to make out. He could not tell where he was, but the splintered wood planks stank of old vomit and dried piss and the floor kept tilting gently up and down, up and down.

He heard footsteps, the scrape of an object dragged over the ground, and hurriedly shut his eyes.

'*I'll* search him, then.' That was the cleric speaking in his thickly accented Wendish. Zacharias willed his breathing to slow, his body to relax, so the cleric would think him asleep. Hands patted his body, an intimate but efficient touch. 'God have mercy. Does the man never wash?'

'He doesn't like his disfigurement to be seen, so I suppose that accounts for him not bathing. I told you it was rash to grab him, Marcus. Couldn't you have left well enough alone? Now we'll have to kill him.'

Even after the years he had survived as a slave, the years he had learned to absorb whatever humiliation was meted out to him, it was hard not to suck in his breath, not to whimper in fear.

That was Wolfhere's voice.

Hadn't he guessed all along that Wolfhere could not be trusted?

'I take no chances,' said the other man, not to be distracted from his search. 'He saw me with you and might carry tales back to the prince.' Quickly enough those hands found the little pocket sewn into Zacharias' robes; those hands extracted the folded parchment and retreated. By some miracle, Zacharias kept his breathing steady, did not open his eyes.

Do not let them know. Wait it out. Patience is its own reward.

'Do you recognize this?' asked Marcus.

'The scratchings of a mathematicus. You know I am not skilled in calculation.'

'Nor in intrigue. This bears the mark of Liathano's idle musings. How did the eunuch come to possess it?'

'I do not know. He is a secretive man, much taken by an interest in arcane matters. He believes he has seen some vision, a glimpse into the secret nature of the cosmos. I do not claim to understand it. But he will ever have at me, wanting to be taught the hidden knowledge of the universe.'

'Is that so? Hmm.'

Wolfhere's laugh was sharp. 'Do you think to recruit him? He is a coward. Not to be trusted. He says so himself. I have witnessed his cowardice with my own eyes.'

'I was thinking more of throwing him over the side once we are well out at sea. But I wonder what it is that he thought you could teach him. Why he thought you were traveling with Prince Sanglant.'

A good question, but Zacharias could scarcely concentrate; it was hard enough to hold his bladder so he wouldn't piss himself from fear. *Throwing him over the side.* No wonder the ground rocked beneath him. He was on a ship.

'One of us must watch those who present the most danger.

Hasn't that always been my task? I am the messenger who rides in the world.'

'Not you alone. I have done my part among the presbyters and clerics in Darre.'

'It is not the same.'

'No, it is not, for they are all cultured men and women. You have fulfilled the part your birth suited you for. Now you are needed to play your part elsewhere, Brother Lupus.'

'I am needed here. Prince Sanglant poses a threat. One of us must watch him.'

'I do not disagree with you, but we no longer have the luxury of letting you range at will. The wheel of the heavens turns, whether we will it or no. You know what part you are meant to play.'

'Is there not another one who can be trained? Surely there is still time.'

'Unlike Eagles, Sleepers do not retire, Brother. They die and are replaced. Sister Zoë no longer stands with us. Alas.'

'She is truly dead?'

'So she is, in the same conflagration in which we lost Liathano. I will miss her, the good woman. But we have found a strong mind to replace hers. He is called Hugh of Austra. Perhaps you know of him.'

'Hugh of Austra! Margrave Judith's bastard son?'

'The same. With his help, Anne has unlocked the secret of the crowns and how the movement of the stars acts in concert with the stones. Now we are close to understanding the weaving by which our ancestors rid themselves of the Lost Ones.'

'The seven circles—'

'We are far beyond that. Seven circles, each of seven stones. We were deceived by erroneous notions. Sister Anne believed that the crown at Verna was the key, but it is not. Meriam now believes that the crowns were laid out to surround the land of the Aoi, that in this way the ancient sorcerers bound that land within the circle of the spell. Therefore, there must be at least one crown south of the middle sea, one east of it, one west, and so on. We have discovered unexpected allies in

Alba among the tree sorcerers and their queen. With their help, we know where the westernmost circle lies. Brother Severus will journey there after he has identified the second circle, which we believe lies in southern Salia. I have myself in the course of my long search for you discovered a crown here in the east, in the wilderness between Ungria and Handelburg, at a place called Queen's Grave. Do you know of it?'

'Bayan and Sapientia fought the Quman at a spot called Queen's Grave about three years ago. There was a tumulus there erected in ancient days, so I heard—'

'The same. I ventured into the burial chamber, but it had been disturbed by grave robbers. I also saw the leavings from the battle, bones of horses and men picked clean, countless shards of arrows. There is a crown on top of the hill. The local folk were easily persuaded that it was in their interest to hoist the fallen stones upright with rope and dirt ramps, under my supervision. Yet you were not there when the battle was fought, were you, Wolfhere? How is it that we lost track of you? I see that you wear an amulet to protect yourself from aetherical sight. Are you hiding from us?'

'Nay. I was trapped by the cunning of one of my own comrades, an Eagle. My old nemesis, who hates me sorely. She retired to the service of Waltharia, the eldest child of Helmut Villam. When we passed by that way, she convinced Prince Sanglant that if he sought to act against sorcerers he must protect himself by means of such amulets. I couldn't refuse to wear one without making him distrust me.'

'You should have left him months ago. It serves no purpose.'

'Do you think Prince Sanglant poses no threat to Sister Clothilde's hopes and plans?'

'I think even if he can succeed in gaining allies, and these griffin feathers you speak of, that it will be too late, and too little, against us.'

'Perhaps. But how will we know how great a threat he poses if none of us are witness to what he is doing?'

'Any person can spy on Prince Sanglant.'

'Not any person can gain his trust.'

'That may be. I do not know how much of a dog's instinct he has for enemies. But it matters not, Brother.'

'If you think it does not matter, then you are a fool.'

'You forget yourself! You were raised as Anne's servant, not as our peer!'

The silence stank of anger and old resentment. Zacharias might have cheered to see Wolfhere spoken to in such a way, but he had himself been born to freeholders who had risked farming in the marchlands in order to be beholden to no lord, only to the regnant.

'I crave your pardon, my lord,' said Wolfhere at last in a tight voice.

'So you must. I expect you not to forget your place again. Now. As soon as my servant returns with slaves, we will cast off. There's little enough tide in these waters.'

'Where do we go?' Was Wolfhere's tone ironic? Or angry? Did the needle of rank still jab him? Was he humbled by Marcus' disdain? He had such a hold over his emotions, and the muffling effect of the dark hold muted his voice just enough, that Zacharias could not guess how he felt. 'Do we return to Darre?'

'Nay. We are to journey south to assist Sister Meriam in her search in the lands south of the middle sea. We hear stories of a crown set near the ruins of Kartiako. Meriam believes that another crown must lie south of the holy city of Saïs. It will be a pilgrimage into a new land.'

'A dangerous one. Jinna idolaters rule those lands.'

'It is difficult to know who truly rules the desert. But first I must deliver my cargo, and the child, to Darre.'

'The child.' The words, spoken so softly, barely reached Zacharias' ears although he lay not a body's length from the two men. 'I am against it. It is dangerous to act so boldly.'

'As the time approaches, we must not fear to take risks. We have hidden for too long.'

'If we kidnap the child, Prince Sanglant will not rest until he recovers her.'

'Then he cannot hunt griffin feathers and sorcerous allies

in the east, can he? He will have to choose. One, or the other.'

All at once, Zacharias realized that he lay not against a sack but against a body, limp and small. It was Blessing, unconscious and, presumably, tied up as he was. With some effort, he wiggled his arms until his hands touched her body. His searching hands brushed her fingers.

She responded. Her small hands, tied back as his were, clenched hard, tightening over his thumb. She squeezed again, a signal, and he squeezed back, then traced the pattern of the rope binding her wrists, seeking the knot. She made no sound, nor did she move except for that brief, fierce, silent communication.

The rope was wet and swollen, impossible to unknot especially at the angle he was forced to work on it. He despaired. He would be thrown to the fish, and she carried off to Darre as a hostage. Prince Sanglant had fought so hard to protect her, but it appeared that, after all, the sorcerers would win.

A ghost of a breeze tickled his nose, making him sniffle and snort.

'What's that?' asked Marcus, standing.

Footsteps sounded on the deck above them and a voice called down through the hatch in clear but understandable Aostan. 'Your man has returned, my lord cleric. He's brought a dozen likely looking slaves, half of them Quman by the looks of them and the rest foreign creatures from the east. It isn't often we get a coffle of only male slaves. Most buyers prefer women. Shall we quarter them below, or on deck?'

No breeze could penetrate belowdecks, but a breeze played around him nonetheless. As Marcus moved away to the ladder, Blessing whispered.

'Yes. Free me.'

Of course he would try, but he could not work miracles! God had forsaken him, or he had forsaken God. . . .

She was not talking to him. She was talking to the spirit of air that played around his head. A cool touch swirled around his fingers. The strands of rope that bound her hands softened and parted, unraveling like so much rhetted flax. She flexed her wrists, and the rope fell away, leaving her free.

'Yes.' Her voice had no more force than the stirring of a breeze against the skin. 'Him, too.'

His bonds loosened and he slipped swollen hands forward to his chest. A sensation as of a thousand pricking needles infested his palms and fingers as the blood and humors rushed back.

Free.

But still trapped.

Chains rattled above.

'Anna says you're a sinner and an unbeliever,' murmured Blessing under cover of the thump and scrape of chains on the ladder as slaves descended into the hold. 'Are you?'

'I don't know what I believe, Your Highness,' he whispered. 'But I think we had better consider how to escape rather than whether I'm apostate.'

'But what about your soul? Won't you be cast into the Abyss? Doesn't that scare you?'

'Nay, Your Highness. I have seen a vision of the cosmos. I am not afraid.'

'Aren't you? Everyone says you're a coward.' She said it without malice.

He twisted to see. The hold lay low and long, its far end shrouded in gloom. The cleric stood with his back to his prisoners, directing his own servant as that man prodded the slaves forward into the hold. Poor suffering souls. Zacharias wondered briefly what horrible fate awaited them at the hands of their new master.

Wolfhere stood in profile, but he turned his head and noticed Zacharias' movement. Lamp glow and shadow mixed on his face, making his expression impossible to read. He did not move.

'Be ready,' whispered Blessing.

A shout rang out from the coffled slaves. Chains clattered to the floor as iron manacles fell open. Blessing leaped to her feet.

'Follow me!' she shouted, jumping for the ladder. 'You are free!'

Zacharias found himself on his feet before he realized he

meant to obey. The slaves hesitated, dumbfounded or in a stupor. How long had they been captives, heeding the call of the whip, the binding of shackles?

Marcus spun around as Blessing reached the ladder. He leaped forward to grab the girl around the legs. Zacharias charged past the motionless Wolfhere and slammed into the small cleric. All three – cleric, frater, and child – fell sprawling on the floor. One of the slaves bolted, striking down Marcus' servant, and in his wake the others erupted into motion. Trying to untangle himself from Marcus, who lay on top of him, Zacharias saw only a blur of bodies before a figure paused beside him, legs wreathed in the tattoos marking those Quman who had chosen the shaman's path.

'The child,' said the man in a recognizable Quman dialect. 'The child with magic saves us.'

The sounds of fighting carried down from above decks. Marcus swore, kicking, as the slave tugged Blessing free. She shrieked with triumph and rushed up the ladder as effortlessly as a spider. Zacharias fought to his knees, lunged for the ladder as the last of the slaves made their escape.

'Stop him!' barked Marcus. 'Wolfhere! For God's sake, go after her!'

The servant raised his staff as Zacharias grabbed the rungs.

A blow smashed into the back of his head.

Then, nothing.

VI

A PROPOSAL

1

'My daughter is out of control! How can it be that she escaped your care and was almost kidnapped?'

Anna knelt with her back to Prince Sanglant, trembling, waiting for the switch to fall on her shoulders. He was in a rage like none she had ever seen. Matto had got twenty strokes, and Thiemo had demanded that he receive the same number even though as a noble lord he did not have to be humbled in such a way. She would have lost respect for him if he hadn't shared the punishment. Both she and Thiemo knew who was truly to blame.

Now it was her turn.

'It was my fault, my lord prince,' she said through her tears. 'I did not keep her at my side. She asked leave to go dice with the soldiers, but I didn't go with her. That was when she ran away. She must have crept out through the drainage ditch.'

She had been crying all day, first in anger because of the terrible fight that morning between Matto and Thiemo, then with fear when she had discovered Blessing missing, and later out of relief when the girl had returned late in the day with an unexpected retinue in tow. Now, at last, she wept silently, in terror. Better to crumble to dust than endure the prince's fury.

'And to add to the injury, this insult! Have you corrupted my daughter with these whispers about the phoenix?'

At least the whole troop wasn't looking on, only Captain Fulk, Sergeant Cobbo, Brother Breschius, and the Eagle, her face drawn and serious. In the distance she heard Blessing shrieking with thwarted anger. Sanglant had ordered the girl shut up in one of the little cells. Maybe he was ready to whip his daughter, too. Maybe he was going there next, once he had finished with her.

The heat made the earthen walls and the dusty ground bake. The sun's glare on her face made her squint. Sweat trickled down her spine.

'Is it true?' he roared.

The switch whistled past her back. The tip stung a shoulder blade as it whipped past, barely touching her. She burst into tears, shaking hysterically.

'I crave your pardon, my lord prince. But the words I spoke are only the truth.' Flinging herself forward onto the ground, she pressed her face into the dirt.

He cursed so furiously that she imagined him transforming from man into rabid dog, back into a beast like the ragged, stinking daimone she had once thought him when she had seen him years ago as a captive in the cathedral of Gent.

'My lord prince,' said Brother Breschius in the mildest of voices, 'she is only a girl, barely a woman. What purpose does it serve to terrorize her in this way?'

She sobbed helplessly as the prince slapped the switch into the ground, once, twice, thrice, to emphasize his words. Dirt sprayed up with each bite, spitting into her face.

'My daughter is a willful. Spoiled. Impossible. *Brat!* Now it transpires that she is soaked in heresy as well. And has the nerve to tell her own father that I am damned!'

'It cannot have helped to find her surrounded by a brace of slaves who worship her as the magician who freed them,' said Breschius. 'It must be a frightening sight, my lord prince, to see your daughter growing into her heritage.'

Sometimes silence was worse than shouting.

All she saw were his boots, six steps, a sharp turn, and six steps back, turn again. Only a very, very angry man paced like that, each step clipped and short. Anger flooded out of him until she thought she would drown. Sobs shook her entire body no matter how much she tried to hold them in.

Fully a woman now, in the old tradition. Oh, God, why had she done it?

Now Matto and Thiemo hated each other, and she had selfishly and stupidly and dishonorably neglected her duty to Blessing. What did people do who were turned out in the midst of a foreign country with no kinfolk to aid them? Didn't she deserve to be sold as a slave or murdered by beggars for her shoes?

'What of your brother, Eagle?' the prince demanded harshly, still pacing.

'I beg your pardon, my lord prince. My own sorrow clouds my mind. Did Zacharias choose to stay with the traitors rather than follow her to freedom? I pray it is not so. Yet if he wanted to follow but could not, then he may now be a prisoner. Or dead.'

'I should not have let Wolfhere and Brother Zacharias go into town, my lord prince,' said Captain Fulk. 'I should have known that Princess Blessing would try to follow them. I should not have let Wolfhere go unattended. . . .'

'Nay.' The boots stopped a hand's breadth from Anna's nose. Her tears had dampened the pale dirt, turning it dark. 'I am to blame. I should never have trusted Wolfhere. I knew what he was. My father is not a poor judge of character, but I let my anger blind me. So be it. Get up, Anna.'

No one disobeyed that tone.

She scrambled up. Dirt streaked her tunic and leggings, smeared her face. Her nose was runny, but she dared not raise a hand to wipe her face clean. She swallowed another sob.

'I have unfinished business,' he said to the others. 'Lady Eudokia will not be pleased that I left the palace so abruptly. She'll consider it an insult.'

'But you left Princess Sapientia and Brother Heribert and most of the rest of the party behind,' said Breschius.

'Yes. Now I must retrieve them and complete the negotiations. Brother Breschius, remain here with Captain Fulk.' He paused, glancing toward the cell where Blessing was confined. The girl's screams and protests had not diminished, although her actual words were muffled by the earthen walls. She was a persistent child. Wiser and less stubborn ones would have given up shrieking by now, silenced by fear of what was to come or even by an idea that it was better to placate than to annoy.

Not Blessing.

The slaves she had freed knelt beside the door, forbidden to see her although they refused to move away.

'Faithful servants,' the prince observed sardonically. 'Let them remain there until I can deal with them. Very well, Captain. You're in charge.'

He left with a few soldiers hurrying after him.

'Go on, child,' said Brother Breschius kindly. 'You've sinned, and been punished. Now go and make it right.'

'How can I make it right? Will the prince turn me out?'

'Not this time. Ask forgiveness from the one you've harmed the most, and swear to never again neglect your duty. Princess Blessing wasn't lost. Think of it as a warning to not allow yourself to be distracted again.'

Did he know? She flushed. Surely only she and Matto and Thiemo knew what had transpired last night. She ducked her head respectfully and ran off to the dark cell near to the one where Blessing was confined. The door was so low that she had to crawl inside, but within it was blessedly cool and dark. She smelled blood and sweat and saw the shape of two prone figures in the dim filtering light. Even those unmoving shapes still had the power to awaken in her the desires that had broken free last night. What a fool she was!

'Anna?' Matto groaned and shifted.

'Don't move,' she whispered, touching his ankle. 'Has anyone put a salve on your back?'

'Sergeant Cobbo did,' said Matto, 'and swore at me the

whole time. Oh, God, Anna. Why did you have to do it?'

'You're not the only one who suffered,' exclaimed Thiemo.

'You sorry excuse for a man. You only took those lashes because you were afraid that Anna would comfort *me* if I was hurt and you weren't!'

'You've no right to speak to me in that way!'

'That's right! I'm only a poor common boy, your randy lordship. Nor should I covet what you've already taken for your own, isn't that right?'

'Shut up!' Anna kicked Thiemo in the leg before he could respond. It was hard to feel affectionate toward him, smelling the whipping he and Matto had taken, remembering how close that switch had come to her own back.

'Serves you right,' hissed Matto, rearing up. 'Serves you right, you stinking goat—'

Unthinkingly, she set a hand on his back to press him down, and he howled with pain. She jerked back her hand; it came away wet with blood.

'Shut up!' She wanted to cry, but her chest was too tight. 'Haven't we done enough harm?'

2

The doors to the governor's palace were closed and Sanglant and his small retinue were, once again, forced to wait outside while the eunuch who acted as gatekeeper vanished into the interior. At this time of day, however, the shadows slanting away from the palace's bulk gave them some respite from the heat. He had only a dozen men with him; the rest he had left with his sister within the palace courtyard a few hours before.

As he waited, he fretted. He had thought himself so clever, leaving Blessing with the main body of troops in the fort while he negotiated with Lady Eudokia. That way Blessing would stay out of trouble and could not be used as a hostage if the worst happened and the governor plotted intrigue.

But Blessing was getting older every day, far too quickly. Thinking of what had happened made him so angry that he had to twist his fear and fury into a knot and thrust it out of sight. He could not let such feelings cripple him.

Ai, for the love of God, how had Blessing got so wild? What had he done wrong?

He heard the tread of many feet a moment before the heavy doors were thrust open from inside and a troop of Arethousan soldiers marched out. In their midst strode a general, or lord, recognizable by his soldier's posture and his shrewd, arrogant gaze as he looked over Sanglant and offered him a swift grin that marked Sanglant as his accomplice, or his dupe. The man had broad shoulders, powerful arms, and only one eye, the other lost, no doubt, in battle. He was a fighting man.

Sanglant nodded, recognizing a kindred spirit whether that man were ally or enemy, and they assessed each other a moment more before the general was hailed by one of his officers and turned his attention away. The troop crossed the broad plaza to the stables, where saddled horses were being led out.

Basil appeared in the entryway, recognizable by his jade-green robes although his round, dark, smooth Arethousan face looked much like that of the other eunuchs: ageless and sexless.

'My lord prince,' he said. 'You are welcome to dine.'

They entered through the long hall and Sanglant was brought to a broad forecourt where a servant washed his hands and face in warm water poured out of a silver ewer. The soldiers remained behind as the prince was shown into an arbor whose vines were all artifice, gold leaves and stems twining around a wood trellis. Cloth wings slit at intervals offered shade but allowed the breeze to waft through. No breath of wind had stirred the air outside; he heard the wheeze and groan from the fans as the slaves stood out in the sun, hidden from view behind the cloth as they worked the bellows to keep those beneath the arbor comfortable.

The Most Exalted Lady Eudokia had already seated herself

to dine at a long, narrow table with a cloth covering the area just before her while the rest of the long table lay bare. Princess Sapientia reclined in the place of honor to Eudokia's right, and a boy of some ten years of age, a dark-haired youth with little beauty and a slack expression, fidgeted on a couch placed to the lady's left, at the end of the table. Two servants attended him, spooning food into his mouth and wiping his chin and lips when he dribbled. A dozen courtiers ate in frightful silence as servants brought around platters all of which reeked of garlic, onion, leeks, oil, and fish sauce. Lady Bertha had been given a place fifteen places down from the head of the table; the rest of the party he had left behind with his sister was absent, all but Heribert, who stood behind the princess with a composed expression and one hand clenched.

Sapientia looked up and smiled as Sanglant entered. Lady Eudokia gestured to Basil, who indicated that he should take the only seat left vacant: on the couch beside the youth. The child wore princely regalia but in all other ways seemed inconsequential, and Sapientia's smirk confirmed that Lady Eudokia was, in her petty, Arethousan way, taking revenge on him for their earlier verbal sparring and his precipitous departure.

'I pray you, Prince Sanglant,' said Lady Eudokia through Basil, who remained beside her as her interpreter, 'drink to my health if you will.' He drank a liquor that tasted of fish, bravely managing not to gag, and she went on. 'Her Royal Highness my dear cousin Princess Sapientia has entertained me with a recounting of the many barbaric customs of your father's people. Is it true that a prince must prove himself a man by breeding a bastard upon a woman, any creature no matter how lowborn or unattractive, and only thereafter can he be recognized as heir to the regnant? Are you the whelp produced out of such a union?'

Sapientia's cheeks were red with satisfaction.

'I am,' he said.

'A half-breed, spawn of the Cursed Ones, is that so as well?'

'It is!' exclaimed Sapientia.

'They are all gone, eradicated millennia ago,' objected Eudokia. 'It can't be true.'

'It is true,' said Sanglant evenly. He would not give Sapientia the satisfaction of seeing that her dart had struck home.

'You might be Jinna born and bred, or your dam might have been a whore transported westward from beyond the eastern deserts to suit the pleasure of a prince.'

Sapientia giggled, then covered her lapse with a sip of wine. The servants brought around a platter of some kind of meat swimming in a foul brine that stank of rancid oil. The courtiers gobbled it down. Sanglant could not bring himself to eat more than a bite.

'A bastard, yet like a eunuch you wear no beard. Is it true you have fathered a bastard of your own who travels with you?'

'My daughter is no bastard.' He set down his knife for fear he would otherwise fling it at her – or at Sapientia, who glared at him, caught between glee and embarrassment. 'I am married, and she is legitimately born to myself and my wife.'

'Do they let bastards marry among the barbarians? We do not allow such a thing here. It would taint the blood of the noble lineages, but no doubt the Wendish themselves are a bastard race so it is no surprise they should allow their blood to become polluted. Yet, if you wish, I will foster the child with me. Bastards' get are notorious for the trouble they get wrapped up in. I can raise her as befits a noble servant and make sure she is not led astray by the Dariyan heresy.'

'I think not,' said Sanglant.

'What else do you mean to do with her?' demanded Sapientia. She drained her cup of wine, as if for courage. 'There's nothing for her in Wendar, Brother. She's got no land and no prospects, no matter what you say. And she's a brat. I say, be rid of her, and we'd all be happier. Don't think that I don't suspect that you hope to use her to usurp my position, as I've told my dear cousin Eudokia while you've been gone chasing after her. Oh. Dear. Did you find her again?'

All that saved Sanglant from a furious retort was the sight of Heribert, quite pale, brushing a finger along his closed lips as a warning. Instead, he downed a cup of the noxious-tasting liquor and let the burn sear away the edge of his anger. 'She is safe. She will remain so. So have I sworn. So, I pray, will you remember.'

'I will remember,' she muttered, flushed, her cheeks sheeny with sweat.

Lady Eudokia smiled unctuously, clearly amused by their unseemly sparring. 'It is ever the way with brothers and sisters to quarrel.' She reached over to pat the youth's flaccid cheek with a pudgy hand. 'Alas that I quarreled with my own brother in the past, but now he is dead in battle and his sweet child come to bide with me.'

The boy smiled uncertainly at her, glanced at Sanglant with fear, and spoke, in a whisper, words Sanglant could not understand. At once, servants brought him a tray of sweets and he picked daintily at them as Sapientia brooded and Sanglant fought the urge to jump up and walk anywhere as long as it got him away from that which plagued him, which at this moment was just about everything. He found refuge in a strategic retreat.

'I had hoped to discuss with you what arrangements we may make for our journey east.'

'I am sure you do. But before we do so, I pray you, tell me which synods does the holy church of Wendar recognize? Or perhaps it is too young to recognize any, for truly we have heard no word of it here where we live. As you know, Arethousa is the ancient home of the Witnesser, St. Thecla. We were first to accept the Proclamation of the blessed Daisan.'

'Do you think, Sapientia,' he said hours later as afternoon waned when at last they could break free of the long feast and return on horseback to the fort, 'that by belittling me and my daughter in front of our enemy you have made Wendish-folk look like lions or like fools?'

'Who is to say she is our enemy?'

'Can she be otherwise? Did she say anything except words meant to sneer and laugh and gloat? You were just as angry as I at her insults, when we first came into her audience chamber this morning!'

'Maybe I changed my mind while you were gone.' Sapientia's cheeks were still red. She lifted her chin, but her smile trembled as if it might collapse at any instant. 'You have stolen what is mine and you might as well be holding me prisoner just like Bulkezu for all that you listen to me, although you pretend to the others that we command jointly. Don't think I am too stupid to know what you intend by your daughter! You want her to rule in my place, and if not her, what is to stop you from supporting Queen Adelheid and her infant daughter? You were jealous of Bayan, and now you're jealous of me. I won't rest until I have back what is mine by right of birth.'

'I have taken nothing from you! I have never betrayed you.'

Her gaze had an uncanny glamour, and for once he was chastened by her anger. 'What do you take me for? A lion? Or a fool?'

3

'You sorry fool.'

Out of nowhere, cold water drenched Zacharias' head and shoulders. Sucking and gasping, he inhaled salt water, nasty and stinging. He gagged but had nothing in his stomach and finally fell back, clutching his belly and moaning.

The dead didn't suffer like this.

Footsteps padded over the planks.

'God Above, but it stinks down here,' said the cultured voice of Brother Marcus. 'So. He's still alive.'

'Were you hoping he would die?'

That voice certainly did belong to Wolfhere, but Zacharias

could not recall where he was or why Wolfhere would be talking about him while the floor rocked so nauseatingly up and down.

'It would make my life easier, would it not? We'll throw him overboard once we're far enough away from land that there's no hope he can swim to shore.'

'If he can swim.'

'I'll take no chances.'

'Will you throw him over yourself or have your servant do the deed?'

'I will do what I must. You know the cause we serve.' The words were spoken so coolly that Zacharias shuddered into full consciousness, his mind awake and his nausea dulled by fear. Bulkezu had at least killed for the joy of being cruel. This man would take no pleasure out of killing, but neither would he shrink from it, if he thought it necessary.

'Monster,' Zacharias croaked, spitting out the dregs of sea-water and bile. He struggled to sit up. His chest hurt. The back of his head throbbed so badly that he might as well have had a cap of iron tightening inexorably around his skull.

'Brother Zacharias.' A hand settled firmly on his shoulder. 'Do not move, I pray you. You've taken a bad blow to the head.'

'I can swim. I escaped Bulkezu by swimming. It'll do you no good to throw me overboard.'

'Who is Bulkezu?' asked Marcus.

'A Quman prince,' answered Wolfhere. 'Perhaps you have forgotten – or never knew – the devastation the Quman army wrought upon Wendar. King Henry never returned from Aosta to drive them out. It was left to Prince Sanglant to do so.'

'Are you the bastard's champion? I'm surprised at you, Brother Lupus. What matters it to us what transpires on Earth? A worse cataclysm will come regardless to all of humankind, unless we do our part.'

Blinking, Zacharias raised his hands to block the light of a lamp, squinting as he studied the other man. 'Are you a mathematicus?' he asked, groping at his chest for the scrap of paper he had held close all these long months.

It was gone.

Panic brought tears.

'Is it this you seek?' Marcus displayed the parchment that bore the diagrams and numbers that betrayed the hand of a mathematicus, a sorcerer who studied the workings of the heavens. 'Where did you come by it?'

'In a valley in the Alfar Mountains. After I escaped from the Quman, I traveled for a time with the Aoi woman who calls herself Prince Sanglant's mother, but she abandoned me after the conflagration.' His physical hurts bothered him far less than the sight of that precious scrap in the hands of another man. He wanted to grab it greedily to himself, but something about the other man's shadowed expression made him prudent, even hopeful. If he could only say the right thing, he might save himself. 'I found that parchment in a little cabin up on the slope of the valley. I knew then that I sought the one who had written these things. You see, when I wandered with Kansi-a-lari, she took me to a place she called the Palace of Coils. There I saw—'

He faltered because Marcus leaned forward, mouth slightly parted. 'The Palace of Coils? What manner of place was it?'

'It lay out in the sea, on the coast of Salia. We had to walk there at low tide. Yet some manner of ancient magic lay over that island. We ascended by means of a path. I thought only a single night passed as we climbed, but instead many months did. The year lay coiled around the palace, and it was the year we were ascending, not the island. I cannot explain it—'

'You do well enough. Did you see the Aoi woman work her sorcery?'

'I did. I saw her defeat Bulkezu. I saw her breathe visions into fire. I saw her save her son with enchanted arrows. Oh, God.' A coughing fit took him and he spat up bile.

'Get him wine,' said Marcus. 'I will hear what he has to say. Why did you not tell me that he traveled with Prince Sanglant's mother? He can't know what he saw, but careful examination may reveal much to an educated ear.'

'Better just to kill him and have done with it!' insisted Wolfhere.

'Nay!' Zacharias choked out the word. 'She led me through the spirit world. I saw—' His throat burned. 'I saw a vision of the cosmos!'

Spasms shook his entire body and made the bruise at the base of his neck come alive with a grinding, horrible pain. He folded forward, almost passing out.

After an unknown while, he struggled out of the haze to find himself bent double over his arms. Wolfhere had returned with a wine sack. Gratefully he guzzled it, spat up half of it all over his fetid robe before he remembered to nurse along his roiling stomach. He must go slowly. He had to use his wits.

'What is this vision of the cosmos that you saw?' asked Marcus when Zacharias set down the wineskin.

'If I tell you everything I know, then you'll have no reason to keep me alive. It's true I followed Prince Sanglant, my lord, but I only followed him because I hoped he would lead me to his wife, the one called Liathano. It's her I seek.'

Marcus had an exceedingly clever face and expressive eyebrows, lifted now with surprise. 'Why do you seek her?'

'I seek any person who can teach me. I wish to understand the mysteries of the heavens.'

'As do we all.'

'I will do anything for the person who will teach me, my lord.'

'Anything? Will you murder my dear friend Brother Lupus, if I tell you to?' He gestured toward Wolfhere, crouched within the pale aura given off by the lamp, his seamed and aged face quiet as he watched the two men negotiate.

A breath of air teased Zacharias' matted hair, curling around his ear. Was this the whisper of a daimone? Was Marcus a maleficus, who controlled forbidden magic and unholy creatures? He shuddered, his resolve curdled by a flood of misgivings. Yet he couldn't stop now. He was a prisoner. He was as good as dead. 'I am no murderer, my lord. I haven't the stomach for it. But I am clever, and I have an excellent memory.'

'Do you?'

'I do, my lord. That is why I was allowed to take the oath of a frater although I cannot read or write. I know the Holy Verses, all of them, and many other things besides—'

'That's true enough,' commented Wolfhere. 'He has a prodigious memory.'

'Is he clever?'

The old man sighed sharply. Why did he look so distressed? 'Clever enough. He survived seven years as a slave among the Quman, so he says. Escaped on his own, so he says. Sought and found Prince Sanglant with no help from any other, so he says. He talks often enough of this vision of the cosmos that he was vouchsafed in the Palace of Coils. He entertains the soldiers with the tale. He says he saw a dragon.'

'I only tell them the truth!'

'Well,' said Marcus speculatively. 'A dragon. Perhaps you're too valuable to throw overboard to drown, Zacharias. Perhaps you can serve the Holy Mother in another fashion. Perhaps I will teach you what I know after all. That will serve as well as killing you will, in the end.'

Zacharias dared not weep. 'You will find me a good student, my lord. I will not fail you.'

'We shall see.' Marcus fanned his hand before his face. 'You must clean up. I cannot bear your stench. Brother Lupus?'

Wolfhere's lips were pressed as tight as those of a man determined not to swallow the bitter brew now on his tongue. 'Do you intend to go ahead with this?'

'We are few, and our enemies are many.' Marcus had a cherub's grin that made Zacharias nervous. The cleric's riotous black curls gave his round, rather bland face an angelic appearance, almost innocent.

Almost.

'If this man can and will serve us, then why should I cast him away? We can all serve God in one manner or another. This is the lesson I learned from the one who leads us.'

'So you did,' said Wolfhere sardonically. 'Very well. Are you satisfied, Zacharias? Will you do as Brother Marcus says?'

Such a thrill of hope coursed through Zacharias that he forgot his nausea, and his pain. 'You will teach me?'

'I will teach you everything that I can,' agreed Marcus with an ironic smile, 'as long as you will serve me as a student must serve his master. Do as I say. Be obedient. Do not question.'

'I can do that!'

Did Wolfhere whisper, again, 'You sorry fool!'? It was only the creak of the ship rolling in the waves. It was only memory, mocking him.

'Let it be done,' said Marcus, who had heard nothing unto-ward. 'I will teach you the secrets of the heavens, Brother Zacharias. I admit you into our holy fellowship.'

'Then I am yours,' cried Zacharias, beginning to weep. After so long, he had found what he sought. 'I am yours.'

4

'Bring the slaves.'

Sanglant indicated the thirteen men who knelt in front of the cell where Blessing was confined. Sergeant Cobbo herded them over. These were not foolish men, although they were barbarians and infidels. They recognized him for what he was, even if they seemed to have offered their allegiance to his young daughter. They knelt before him, a ragged but defiant looking crew, half naked, sweating profusely in the heat, but unbowed by his appraisal.

Six were Quman, stripped down to loincloths. Despite the dirt streaking their bodies, they had made an effort to keep their hair neat, tying it back into loose braids with strips of cloth. They had pleasant, almost docile expressions. They looked like the kind of young soldiers who are happiest singing a song around the fire, good-natured, easy to please, and unlikely to fight among themselves. The seventh of their number bore tattoos all over his torso, twisted animals amid scenes of battle and carnage, griffins eating deer, lions rending hapless men, and a belled rider mounted on an eight-legged horse riding over corpses.

Of the other six, four might have been any manner of heathen – Salavii, Polenie, Starviki, or otherwise – with matted dark hair, wiry arms, and thick shoulders, and stolid expressions that did not conceal a rebellious spark in their gaze although their ankles and wrists bore the oozing scars of shackles.

'Are any of these men Daisanites?' asked Sanglant.

Breschius knew an amazing store of languages, and he spoke several now, getting responses from all four of the men.

'They are all heathens, my lord prince. Sold into slavery by raiders. This Salavii man says it was Wendish bandits who took him prisoner and sold him to an Arethousan merchant. He wishes to return to his home. The other three say they will gladly enter the service of your daughter if they will be allowed a servant's portion, a meal every day, and her promise as their lord never to abandon them.'

'Let the Salavii go, then. I want no slaves in my army.'

Breschius spoke in a guttural tongue. The Salavii man rose nervously, looking as though he expected a whip to descend.

'It is a long road to Salavii lands,' remarked Captain Fulk. 'If he can make it home safely, then he's both strong and clever.'

'Give him bread, ale, and a tunic,' said Sanglant. 'I'll not have it said I turned him out naked.'

Even as Breschius began to speak, the man bolted for the gate, ready for a spear thrust to take him in the back. Fulk whistled, a piercing signal, and the guards leaped back so the man could sprint out of the fort unobstructed. The remaining three heathens shifted fearfully, but Breschius calmed them with a few words.

'He had no reason to trust us,' said Sanglant, 'but I doubt me he'll get far.' He turned his attention to the last two slaves. They were much darker and wore torn robes and ragged pointy felt caps over cropped hair. Sanglant frowned as he studied them. These two kept their heads bowed, their gazes lowered, although they also looked to be young, strong men.

'These two are Jinna, are they not?' he asked Breschius. 'Are they believers?'

'Do you see the brand on their cheeks?'

'Is that their slave mark?'

'Nay, my lord prince. Or rather, I should say, yes, but not in the way you think. Every young Jinna man marks himself in this way when he becomes an adult. It is the way he enslaves himself to the god's worship. No Jinna man may marry if he has not branded himself a slave to their fire god.'

'Yet it's men who made them slaves on Earth, not their god. Tell them they may go free if they wish.'

'I do not speak their language, my lord prince.' He spoke to them anyway, giving up when they made no response. 'They must not be merchants, my lord, or they would know at least one of the languages commonly used by traders.'

'Then we must hope that gesture will suffice. What of these Quman? But you do not speak Quman as well as did Brother Zacharias, do you, Breschius?'

Anger flowed back quickly, although he had thought he had banished it. He clenched his left fist and glanced toward Blessing's cell. In the interval while he was gone she had fallen quiet. Maybe she had just screamed herself hoarse.

'Very poorly, my lord prince. I never preached among the Quman. I beg your pardon—'

Before Sanglant could respond, the old tattooed Quman man lifted both hands, palms facing the heavens. 'Great lord,' he said in passable Wendish, 'hear me, who goes by the name Gyasi. Many seasons ago, when I am young, the spirits speak into my ear at that day when the moon is dark and hungry. They tell – told – me that in the time to come, a child will save me from the iron rope. Her I must serve. So it happens, this day, that their prophecy comes to pass. I act as the spirits tell me. I do not disobey my ancestors. I will be as a slave to your daughter. These sons of my tribe will also follow her.'

'Where did you learn to speak Wendish?' asked Sanglant.

'In our tribe, we keep slaves from the western people. I can speak the language of all the slaves of my tribe. This way, they obey the *begh* and his mother. There is less trouble.'

'On their left shoulder they bear scars,' said Breschius. 'The wolf's muzzle, the mark of the Kirshat clan.'

'How did you come to be a slave?' asked Sanglant. 'You wear the markings of a shaman. How can such a powerful man become a slave?'

'I refused to heed the call of the Pechanek *begh* when he calls for war against the western lands. I tell – told – the war council that Kirshat clan should not follow that Pechanek whore, Bulkezu. But they send their sons to him because they fear him. As punishment for bad advice, they sell – sold – me and my sisters' sons into slavery. Three have died. These six, the strong ones, survive.'

'Bulkezu!' Sanglant laughed. 'Bulkezu will trouble you no more. I hold him as my prisoner, here in this camp.'

The old shaman nodded, unmoved by this revelation. 'The spirits told me of Bulkezu's fate.' He turned to his nephews, speaking in the Quman language. Two spat on the ground. A third laughed; the last two grinned. There was something uncomfortable about the merry gleam in their expressions, the crinkling of eyes, and the gleeful baring of teeth as they contemplated the downfall of their enemy.

'You are a great lord, in truth,' added Gyasi, 'to humble Bulkezu. But you wear no griffin wings. How can you defeat the man who killed two griffins? Bulkezu is still greater than you.'

'We shall see. I march east to hunt griffins.'

The shaman's eyes widened. He tapped his forehead twice on a clenched hand, touched both shoulders, and patted his chest over his breastbone, across a tattoo depicting a bare-headed man copulating with a crested griffin. 'That is a fearsome path, great lord. You may die.'

Sanglant smiled, although he had long since ceased to find his mother's curse amusing. 'No creature male nor female may kill me. I do not fear the griffins. Can you guide me across the grasslands to the nesting grounds of the griffins?'

'Nay, great lord. Mine is the power of the wolf, to stalk the ibex and the deer. I am not a griffin fighter. The secrets of the nesting grounds have been lost to our people. No warrior in three generations among the Kirshat tribe has worn griffin wings. We are a weak clan now. Our mothers die young. Our *beghs* have forgotten how to listen to the wisdom of old women. That is why the war council did not refuse when Bulkezu demanded soldiers for his army.'

A shout rose from the guard on watch, followed by the call of the horn, three blats, signifying that an enemy approached. Soldiers hurried out of the shade where they had been resting, lifting shields, hoisting bows or spears, and headed for the vulnerable gate. The slaves looked up, but did not rise. Sanglant jogged over to the guard tower that flanked the gate. Up on the walls facing northeast, men gestured and pointed. Fulk and Hathui followed him while Sergeant Cobbo herded the remaining slaves back to the cell where Blessing broke her silence and began to cry out again.

'Let me out! Let me out! Anna! I want you! *Daddy!*'

Sanglant clambered up on the wall to the crumbling guard tower with Fulk and Hathui beside him. The pair of guards on duty – Sibold and Fremen – muttered to each other as they watched. They had marked the riders because of dust, although the troop was still too far away to make out numbers and identifying marks.

Below, in the gate, a dozen men were pulling back the bridge of planks thrown over the pit. Shadow concealed the depths of that steep-sided ditch where Bulkezu was imprisoned. Was Bulkezu moving along the base of the pit, alert to the new development? Already Sanglant heard the unmistakable flutter and whir of wings, faint but distinctive. He shaded his eyes as he squinted westward at the riders approaching the fort through rolling grasslands that stretched out north and west to the horizon.

'Quman,' he said to Fulk.

Fulk shouted down into the courtyard. 'Get Lewenhardt up here!' He shaded his eyes, peering at the cloud of dust. 'Are you sure, my lord prince? I can't see well enough.'

'I hear wings.'

'Sibold,' ordered Fulk, 'sound the horn again. I want every

man along the wall and a barrier thrown up at the gate to reinforce the ditch. *Quman*.'

Sibold swore merrily before blowing three sharp blats on the horn. Half the men had assembled and the rest came running, buckling on helmets or fastening leather brigandines around their torsos. Above the clatter and shouting Sanglant heard his daughter's muffled shrieks from the cell where he had ordered her shut in.

'My lord prince!' Lewenhardt scrambled up the ladder to the watchtower platform and leaned out as far as he dared over the railing. He wore a ridiculous floppy-brimmed hat that shaded his eyes better than a hand could.

Sanglant set fists on the wall, rubbing the coarse bricks until all thought of Blessing was rubbed out of his mind and he could concentrate on the distant sound that he alone, so far, could hear. He blocked out all other distractions, the sound of planks being dragged across dirt, boots scraping on steps and ladders as men climbed into position along the walls, the sobs of Blessing, a bell ringing in the town . . . as he listened for the sough of wind through grass, the beat of the sun on earth, the rumble of distant hooves, and the whistle of wings. He listened to their pitch and intensity.

'Griffin wings.' He braced himself to get a better look.

Was that a thin shriek caught on the wind, a man crying out in fear and pain? It happened too fast, cut short. He could not be sure.

The wings sang, not in a great chorus and yet more than a few individual voices.

'Not much more than fifty,' he said. 'Certainly less than one hundred.'

'That's a fair lot of dust they're kicking up,' commented Fulk. 'Can they be so few?'

'More than one hundred,' said Lewenhardt. 'Perhaps as many as two hundred. They don't all have wings.'

'How can they not have wings?' demanded Fulk.

'Where is Brother Breschius?' asked Sanglant.

'Fremen,' said Fulk, 'fetch the good brother.'

Sanglant looked back toward town, visible from here as a

jumble of walls and roofs broken by the high tower of the governor's palace and the pale dome marking the Jinna temple. The steady slope of the ground toward the sea caused the land to melt into a shimmering dark flat, the expanse of peaceful waters. Ships were cutting loose from the quay, oars beating as they moved away from the port to escape a possible attack on the town. The ship Wolfhere had escaped on was already out of sight; according to Robert of Salia, who had found Blessing and her new retinue and escorted them back to the camp, that ship had left the harbor before Sanglant had even got the message that Blessing had vanished.

Ai, God, what was he to do with his unnatural daughter?

How had he been so stupid as to trust Wolfhere?

'I see their wings!' cried Sibold triumphantly.

'God Above!' swore Lewenhardt as other men along the wall got a better look at the riders. The restless glimmer of wings flashed in the light drawn out across grass, sun caught in white and gray feathers.

'What do you see?' He brushed his fingers along his sword hilt.

'I see griffin wings, my lord prince. One pair. And towers, fitted with gold.'

Men hammered away down, knocking beams and wagons into place on either side of the pit.

'A hard barrier to cross,' observed Sanglant as he looked down, 'but not impossible. Here comes the frater. Perhaps he knows the secret of these "towers."'

Fremen came running back with the middle-aged frater in tow. Breschius had some trouble with the ladder because he only had the one hand, but he used his elbow to hook the rungs and hold himself while he shifted his remaining hand and moved up his feet. By the time he got to the top, the approaching riders were slowing down as they neared the fort. The soldiers setting the barricade in place on the outer side of the pit ran across the last two planks, which were then drawn back into the fort. The town had sealed its gates. The great bell ceased tolling.

'We're on our own,' said Fulk, a little amused. 'We've no

friends among the townsfolk. Did the governor not like you, my lord prince?'

'The governor does not trust us, Captain. Why should she welcome an army of our size into her territory? If she fights us, she may win, but she and her troops and her town will suffer. If she loses, then she loses all. I suppose she hopes we'll take the brunt of the attack and allow her to finish off the rest.'

'But we outnumber them.'

'The governor? Or those Quman?'

Fulk laughed. 'They are wise to fear you, my lord prince.'

'Are they?' Or was he simply a fool, chasing madness? The moment he first saw the port town and the broad grasslands spreading north from the sea, he knew he had ridden into a world unlike anything he had ever experienced. With Zacharias gone and possibly dead, he was more than ever dependent on Bulkezu's knowledge. Bulkezu would have many opportunities to betray him or lead him and his army astray. Bulkezu was smart enough to kill them, if he chose to sacrifice himself with them. Yet in such a vast expanse, how could Sanglant track down griffins and sorcerers without the help of someone who knew the land?

'Women!' said Lewenhardt, laughing. 'There are Quman warriors with that troop, but there are women as well. Those towers are their crowns. They're hats, of a kind.'

'I didn't know the Quman had women,' said Sibold, hefting his spear. 'I thought they bred with wolf bitches and she-cats.'

'It's true that Quman women wear crowns like these towers,' said Breschius. 'I've seen none of them close at hand, myself.'

'Not more than two hundred riders,' said Fulk. 'Look at their standard. They bear the mark of the Pechanek tribe.'

'Ah.' Sanglant nodded. 'That makes sense. They've come for Bulkezu.'

'Do you think so, my lord prince? How would they know we were here, and that we had him?'

'Their shamans have power,' said Breschius, 'although nothing compared to the power of the Kerayit sorcerer women.'

'Quman magic killed Bayan,' said Sanglant.

'My lord!' said Fulk. 'If they are after you—!'

'Nay, do not fear for *me*, Captain. Their magic cannot harm me.' He touched the amulet that hung at his chest, but the stone made him think of Wolfhere and that made him angry all over again. He must not think about the Eagle's betrayal, and his own gullibility. He must concentrate on what lay before him.

The riders came to a stop at about the limit of the range of a ballista, close enough to get a good estimate of their numbers and appearance but not so close that the men in the fort could pick out details and faces. No more than sixty wore wings, but the griffin-winged rider shone beyond the rest, glittering and perilous. About thirty of the riders wore conical hats trimmed with gold plates. One of these hats was so tall, at least as long as Sanglant's arm, that he could not imagine how a person could ride and keep it on her head.

A youthful figure wearing neither wings nor one of the towering hats broke forward from the group, balancing a limp burden across the withers of the horse.

'Lewenhardt, what is it the rider bears before him?'

'It is a corpse, my lord prince.'

When the rider reached the halfway point between the Quman and the fort, he tipped the burden off the horse and onto the ground.

Lewenhardt winced. 'I think that corpse may be the slave who ran from us, my lord prince.'

'And into their grasp, may God have mercy on his soul. Captain, fetch the shaman, the one who calls himself Gyasi.'

'Can you trust him, my lord prince?'

'We've no one else who can interpret for us. He can prove his worth, or the lack of it.'

Fulk clambered down the ladder.

The rider approached to within arrow shot of the walls before reining in his horse.

'That boy's not more than twelve or fourteen years of age, I should think,' said Lewenhardt.

'Showing off,' asked Sanglant, 'or expendable?'

'I know little enough about the customs of the Quman, my lord prince,' said Breschius, 'but no boy among them can call himself a man and wear wings on his back until he has killed a man. Thus, the heads they carry.'

Sibold shuddered all over. 'A nasty piece of work, those shrunken heads.' He had a sly gaze, a little impertinent, but part of his particular value as a soldier was his reckless streak. 'They say that Lady Bertha didn't bury her mother's head when she took it off Bulkezu but carries it with her as a talisman. Is that true, my lord prince?'

'You can ask her yourself, Sibold.'

The soldier laughed. 'I pray you will not command me to, my lord. She frightens me. She's cold, that one. I think she may be half mad.'

'Sibold.'

He ducked his head, but the grin still flashed. 'Begging your pardon, my lord prince.'

'Here is the shaman, my lord prince.' Breschius moved aside to make room on the platform as Fulk returned with Gyasi.

'What does this mean?' Sanglant indicated the single horseman and the mass of riders beyond.

'He are a messenger, great lord.' He lifted his hands to frame his mouth and let loose a trilling yell.

The rider started noticeably but recovered quickly and urged his mount forward again, halting just beyond the shadow of the wall. He called out in the Quman tongue.

'Great lord, this young worm names himself as the messenger of the mother of Bulkezu, who have come seeking the man who keeps as a prisoner her son.'

'Go on.'

'The mother of Bulkezu wish to know what you want to trade for her son.'

'What I wish to trade?' Sanglant leaned against the wall. The heat of the sun washed his face, the swell of wind tugged at his hair. 'Which of those is the mother of Bulkezu? Do you know?'

'They are the mother of Bulkezu,' agreed Gyasi, nodding

toward the troop of women and their winged escort.

Sanglant glanced at Breschius, but the frater shrugged. It was hard to tell how well Gyasi understood Wendish. 'I cannot trade Bulkezu. I have defeated him in battle and kept him alive in exchange for a chance to win his freedom. I need him to guide my army safely through the grasslands and lead us to the lands where we may hunt griffins and meet sorcerers.'

'Is this what you truly wish, great lord? It is a troublesome road. Many troubles will kiss you.'

'This is what I truly wish. I cannot give up Bulkezu. Yet what bargain might I strike with his tribe, so that they will not hinder me?'

Gyasi hummed to himself in a singsong manner, a man pondering deep thoughts. 'People are tricky. One man may promise life to his brother and after this stab him in the back.'

'There are those who are still angry that you allowed Bulkezu to survive the battle whole and healthy, my lord prince,' said Breschius. 'I do not forget that he was the one responsible for Prince Bayan's death. Neither does Princess Sapientia.'

'Yet you ride with me, Brother Breschius.'

'As does Princess Sapientia. Yet I do not think she had much choice in the matter, although she is the heir.'

'Is she? King Henry has other children. He has a child by Queen Adelheid, do not forget, whom he may favor. Why do you remain with me, Brother Breschius? Whom do you serve?'

'I serve the truth, my lord prince, and God.'

'And me?'

Breschius' smile brought light to his face. He was a man too humble to be in love with his own cleverness but too wise to denigrate himself. 'Whatever risk you may pose, my lord prince, I believe we are in more danger from those who seek to wield sorcery without constraint than from your ambition.'

'I pray you, my lord prince,' said Hathui, who had remained silent until now. 'I would object to Bulkezu returning to his tribe. He has never paid what he owes me for the damage he did to my person.'

Sanglant turned back to the Quman shaman. 'Tell the boy

all I have said and say also that there is one among my servants who has a personal grievance against Bulkezu, who stole
her honor and harmed her body. She seeks recompense. For
these reasons, we will not release him. Yet we do not seek
war with his people. Once I have my griffins and have met
my sorcerers, Bulkezu can go free. Until then, perhaps they
will consider a truce.'

Gyasi relayed the offer, and the messenger gave a shout of
acknowledgment before returning to the troop. They watched
him pull up beside the rank of women. After some time, the
boy returned with two riders beside him, one of whom wore
a tall, conical hat sheathed in gold plates, dazzling in the sun,
and draped with bright orange-and-ivory beads strung
together like falling curtains of color. Her tunic was bright
blue, cut away at knee length and slit for riding, and beneath
it she wore striped trousers of blue and green with beads sewn
around the knee and the ankle. Beneath the weight of her
garments he could barely make out her face, dark, unsmiling,
with broad cheekbones and pale lips. The other rider was also
a woman, but she wore only a soft felt hat, drab and unorna-
mented, against the sun, and a plain leather tunic with loose
trousers underneath. Her hair had the golden brown sheen of
a westerner or a hill-woman; surely she was no Quman, most
likely a slave if the thick bronze bracelets on either wrist indicated her status.

The boy delivered his message and, once he had done
speaking, tossed a cloth bundle onto the ground. Wings of
cloth spread to reveal a dozen gold necklaces.

'What does he say?' demanded Sanglant.

'The gold, to pay for honor stolen.'

Hathui's eyes widened as she leaned over the brick rampart, staring at the bounty of gold lying below. 'I accept!' she
said breathlessly. 'God Above! I can dower my nephews and
nieces with such riches!'

'And the two women?' Sanglant asked.

Gyasi scratched the tattoo of the eight-legged horse and
its rider decorating his scrawny chest. The rider wore a conical
hat like those of the mothers, but its features showed no

markedly female cast. He hummed and mumbled to himself, bobbing his head and hopping on one foot like a nervous crow. At last, he spoke. 'The mother will see Bulkezu before she negotiate further. That way she can see if he are truly living, and not dead.'

Sanglant grinned, feeling the familiar rush of exhilaration as he considered not whether but how far to leap. He called to the men at the gate. 'I'm coming down. Throw a plank over the ditch. Keep your arrows and spears ready.'

'My lord!' Their astonished cries were answer enough, but they obeyed, as they always did. Otherwise they would not have followed him so far and on such a dangerous road.

He scrambled down the ladder, leaving most of his attendants above to keep watch, and jogged over to the barrier. Clambering over the wagons, he set foot on a broad plank just now thrust out over the ditch by one of the soldiers. From below, Bulkezu's mocking laughter rose to greet him. The prisoner's figure stood half lost in the shadow, face upturned to study him, features ghostly and indistinct.

'Is the prince come to fight me? Will the dog leap into the pit to battle the griffin? Or does it fear me still?'

Sanglant heard the approaching hooves, and his blood sang with the pitch of approaching battle as he strode over the plank. The wood rocked beneath him, but he did not lose his balance. He did not fear a fall.

'Throw down the worm, so that I might make a meal of it. Or does the dog-prince take his pleasures with the crawling things?'

He jumped lightly onto solid ground as the riders rounded the corner of the fort and stopped, as he stopped. They faced each other. The woman was too young, surely, to be Bulkezu's mother; her nose was too flat, more stub than nose, for her to be handsome, but she had brilliant black eyes, as wicked as those of a hawk, and a ferocious frown so marked that his grin faded and he paused, wondering if he had miscalculated their intentions.

The slave woman beside her looked Sanglant over quite frankly, as though appraising his worth and his possibilities

for stud, while her mistress, ignoring Sanglant, rode to the
lip of the ditch and looked down. The slave really had quite
an attractive shape under that leather tunic, full, round breasts,
red lips, an amorous gaze –

It was too quiet. No one was talking.

Looking down into the pit, he was so startled he almost
lost his balance and fell.

Bulkezu had bolted away from the shadow of his
kinswoman. Up against the far end of the pit, he cowered like
a rabbit run into a corner. The fearsome begh who had united
the Quman hordes, slaughtered untold hapless Wendish-folk,
and defeated Prince Bayan in battle was utterly terrified.

Sanglant's soldiers cried out, jeering at the man they had
all come to hate. They pressed up along the walls, against the
wall of wagons, every one of them, crowding next to each
other to see him shamed.

'Silence!' cried Sanglant.

They gave him silence.

The woman lifted her gaze to look at Sanglant. A hawk
might look so, measuring its prey. He kept his gaze steady on
hers, neither retreating nor advancing, and after a moment
she reined her mount away. By now, Gyasi had reached the
wall of wagons, standing up on the bed of one to survey the
scene with alarm.

'Great lord! Have a care!'

The gold-crowned woman reached her attendants and
spoke to the lad. When she had finished, the boy spoke.

'What does he say?' asked Sanglant when the lad stopped.

'She ask if you are the stallion to be held in kind until
Bulkezu is returned to them.'

'She wants a hostage to ensure our good faith.'

'It is common among the tribes to exchange a valued daughter or son for another, to keep the peace. She makes a powerful offer, great lord. If you give her yourself in surety, then
her tribesmen will grant you escort across the plains. This we
call the gift for the knives.'

'The gift for the knives?'

'So no man will stab you in the back.'

'Will other Quman tribes respect that, should we come across them?'

'Perhaps, great lord. They scatter to the winds after the fall of Bulkezu. Maybe there are wolves who will nip at your heels, but no army will fight you when you have so many soldiers to yourself. No tribe will be so bold to fight the man who defeated the dreaded Bulkezu. He is the man who killed two griffins. No other begh in the generations of our tribes have done so.'

'An escort and a pledge of safe conduct – in exchange for a hostage? One valuable enough to me, and to them, that they will expect me not to abandon my hostage into their hands? One of worthy rank? One too valuable to lose?'

'Until you depart this land and return Bulkezu.'

Brother Breschius appeared beside Gyasi, looking wan and troubled. 'You know what savages the Quman are, my lord prince. How can you seal a treaty with them, knowing they are Wendar's great enemy?'

'Who is not, these days? I do not trust the Arethousans, nor have I any reason to believe they have guides who can lead us where we need to go. Nay. Lady Eudokia cannot help us, nor can we trust her.'

'Do you know the customs of the steppe peoples, my lord prince?' Breschius pressed his case fervently. 'If the lady wishes you to attend her tribe as a hostage, it is not only your presence she wants. You are a great lord strong enough to defeat her son. Among these people, the old mothers breed men like horses. They'll want your seed for her bloodline and her tribe.'

'God help me,' said Sanglant. 'A stallion brought in to breed the mares.' Lady Ilona had warned him, in her own way. But he hadn't believed her. He hadn't thought he'd be making bargains so soon.

The sun bled gold across the grass as its rim touched the western hills. Soon it would be dark. The soldiers waited in a remarkably uneasy silence. Even Blessing had, at long last, stopped shrieking.

'Yet I am not the only valuable hostage in this troop,' he

said with a thrill of triumph coursing through his heart. He laughed. Sometimes it *was* possible to kill two birds with one stone.

'Gyasi, tell the mother of Bulkezu that I have a proposal. Tell her, I pray you, that I have a noble princess who would be most suitable to travel with the mothers of Bulkezu as surety for his safe return.'

VII
A BEE'S STING

1

The longships ghosted out of the fog wreathing the Temes River to beach along the strand below the walled city of Hefenfelthe. Two river gates pierced the massive wall, but they remained chained and sealed, as impregnable, so it was rumored, as the land gates and the infamous sewer canal. Behind the wall, the towering hall and citadel built by the Alban queens rose like the prow of a mighty ship. Stronghand knew its reputation. Because of the power of the queens and their tree sorcerers, Hefenfelthe had never been taken in war, although many armies had broken their strength on those walls in the hope of gaining the riches guarded within.

Tenth Son lifted the battle standard. The first wave of Eika swarmed from the lead ship, followed by their brothers up and down the strand. The shroud of fog concealed them, but Stronghand could sense each one, whether running on two feet or on four. Even the dogs ran silently. They knew what reward awaited those who survived the day.

The red glare of a torch flared by the easternmost river gate. Gate chains rumbled and, as the vanguard raced up to the wall, the gate swung open. Three men scuttled out through the gate, arms waving as they signaled the army to pour into the city.

One moment only Stronghand had to study them: three rich merchants clothed in silk and linen, weighted down by necklaces of gold and rings studded with gems. When brought before him at the emporium of Sliesby, they had proved eager to betray their queen in exchange for coin and the promise of new markets to conquer. But no man can serve two masters. Tenth Son himself, running in the lead, cut the first one down, and the others followed, hacked down by swift strokes. They didn't have a chance to cry out. His army rushed heedlessly past the bodies, although some of the dogs stopped to feed on the corpses and had to be driven forward through the open gate.

He waited on the stem of his ship as the sun rose, still obscured by a mist steaming off the waters. The chain of the western gate growled, and a second portal opened into the city. Torches sparked into life along the walls of the citadel as the Alban soldiers and their queen came awake to danger. A shrill horn, a clanging bell, and a piercing scream sounded from inside, but it was too late. Smoke twisted from buildings close by the outer wall, melding with mist. Fire rose from the houses within, lifting on those flames the cries, curses, and anguished wails of the beleaguered inhabitants, a terrible, beautiful clamor. The sun cleared the low-lying bank of river fog and poured its light across the mighty walls of Hefenfelthe, proof against weapons but not against treachery.

Those who resisted were killed; for the rest, chance ruled. Some were spared because they remained hidden, others because they fled. As many died begging for mercy as fell fighting. Hefenfelthe had shut its gates against the RockChildren and would therefore serve as an example to all the Alban towns, villages, and farms that it was better to surrender to Stronghand's authority than to struggle against it.

By the second night of the battle, the narrow streets of Hefenfelthe were deserted and the fires quenched, since he did not want to burn the whole city. With his troops ranged around the citadel walls, Stronghand watched as the Alban queen appeared high above, on her tower. Torches and lamps hung around her made her gleam. She wore bright armor; a wolf's helm masked her features. A golden banner marked with the image of a white stag streamed beside her in the wind called up by her sorcerers. She raised a horn to her lips. As the note sang in the air, flights of burning arrows streaked out from the citadel battlements to strike the roofs of buildings far out in every direction.

She intended to burn down the city around them, but she would not succeed.

'Let the men hew down buildings on all sides of the fire in a ring around the citadel,' he said to Tenth Son, who stood sooty and bloodstained beside him. 'That way the fire can only burn back in toward their refuge.'

He led the assault on the fire with his own ax, and in the end they cut a wide trail in a ring around the city and wet down the roofs on the far side of that gap. By dawn the towering wall of the citadel caught fire along its eastern front, and smoke choked its defenders, blown back against them by the very wind the tree sorcerers had called up to harry the fire against their foes. He cried out the order for the final assault himself, although he let others lead the charge, the young ones, the foolish, those who sought to prove their worth, attract his notice, or gain a larger share of treasure.

Battering rams were carried forward. Their thick wooden heads, carved to resemble the horned sheep who lived in the mountains, clove in the citadel gates. As his warriors pressed forward, the smoke gave them an unassailable advantage. The Alban soldiers drowned in it, but fire and smoke were no particular threat to RockChildren born in the long ago times when the blood of dragons had fused human flesh to wakening stone.

He followed the vanguard in through the broken gate and marched with his picked guard, his litter brothers, and the warriors of Rikin Fjord along the trail left by the assault. Bodies lay everywhere, but the dense smoke choked the smell of blood. Battle raged around the entrance to the long hall as the RockChildren tried to force an entry. Arrows drove into shields in a furious hail. Spear points thunked against wood. Shutters cracked and stove in under a press of ax blows, but in each newly-shattered opening spears bristled as Alban soldiers placed their bodies in the gap, shouting for reinforcements, crying out curses. Arrow shot and hot oil poured down the sides of the tower. The blank sides of that huge stone edifice – the largest he had ever seen – offered no purchase. The first course of stone, rising four times his height, had no windows at all, and in the three higher levels the windows were only slits. The only way into the tower was through the hall.

'Throw in torches,' he said to Tenth Son. 'Burn them out.'

Yet although the citadel walls burned as soon as fire touched them, the heavy-beamed hall had a roof of slate. Fire guttered out on these shingles. A few thrown torches slipped in through broken shutters but were quickly stamped out by the defenders. Already, dark clouds gathered, called by the tree sorcerers to put out the fires. Lightning ripped through the sky, and thunder boomed. The first patter of rain washed over his upturned face.

Warriors threw up a line of shields to protect the men with the ram from arrow shot. He took a turn himself. The pounding of ram against reinforced doors shuddered down his arms. The noise of its impact crashed above the clash of arms. Rain came down in sheets over them, turning to sleet and then to a battering hail. But what might have confounded a human foe did nothing to his kind. His standard protected them against magic, and their tough hides protected them against almost everything else. Iron might cut them. A hot enough fire would kill them, in the end, and they could drown. But the RockChildren were not weak like humankind. The strength of stone was part of their flesh, and their greatest weakness had always been their tendency to rely on strength alone instead of on the intelligence and cunning that were their inheritance from that part of themselves that derived from that human ancestors.

The door into the great hall buckled and groaned and on the next strike shattered, planks splintering as they gave way. With a shout, warriors leaped into the gap. Many fell back, wounded or dead, but more pressed onward, and the weight of numbers and the haze of smoke everywhere gave them the advantage. Once the fight swelled forward to fill the smoky great hall, it was only a matter of time.

He pushed through with his guard around him. The hall had been built to abut the tower, one end built right up against the lower course of the western face. Stairs led up to a loft, a broad balcony where Alban soldiers now made their stand, holding the single door that led into the queen's tower. The fight was long and bloody, but once his troops controlled the stairs they could hang back and, with their shields to protect them, pick off the defenders one by one.

He could be patient. He had time.

Night came, and the struggle went on with torches ablaze to light their way. Smoke wound in hazy streamers along the beams, curling like aery snakes, half formed and lazy. Sometimes all he heard was the breathing of the soldiers as they rested, waiting for a shield to drop, waiting for an opening when one man leaned too far away from another. Now and again came a whispered comment from among the Albans, a shift in their ranks as a fresh man squeezed forward to take his place from one who was injured or flagging. He admired their loyalty, their prowess, and their toughness, these ones who stayed to the bitter end. It was, in truth, a shame that such fighters would all have to die.

Midway through the night, Tenth Son reported that the rest of the citadel had fallen and the fires had been quenched. Except for the tower, the RockChildren ruled Hefenfelthe now. Once they captured and killed the queen and her tree sorcerers, the rest of Alba would capitulate.

Foolish to believe it would be so easy.

Just before dawn, thunder rumbled so low and heavy that it shuddered through his feet. As the sound faded, he sensed a strange weakening in the Alban soldiers, shields drooping, a spate of unseen movement within the tower. Pressing the advantage, his troops stormed the door and overwhelmed the score of men who had held that gap all night. Stronghand followed the vanguard as they mounted the ladder steps. The tower had fully four stories, each one a broad chamber fitted with the rich furniture and tapestries proper to a royal house. No one remained to resist them, and the rooms were empty, abandoned – until they came to the battlements, the high tower height where he had watched his enemy launch her final, desperate attack.

There the Alban queen waited for them. He had not expected her to be so young, pale-haired, with the blue eyes common to humans bred in northern climates. Her skin was creamy smooth, untouched by sun, and her expression proud and fixed. She wore robes woven of a shimmering silver cloth, chased with gold thread, and a seven-tined circlet of silver at her brow. An old man bearing a staff of living wood crowned with seven sapling-green branches knelt beside her. With his head bowed, he appeared ready for death. Could it be possible she had only one sorcerer to aid her? Or was she herself a sorcerer? Five children huddled against her skirts, silent except for the youngest, who struggled not to sob and so made a gulping sound instead, erratic and irritating.

Beyond the battlements, the city of Hefenfelthe lay in uncanny silence as the sun cleared the river mist and day came. Crows circled above the buildings and smoking ruins.

Seeing him, the queen picked up the smallest child and stood waiting, eager, face flushed and eyes bright. At that moment, he realized she had no magic to protect herself. Even the old man, tree sorcerer though he clearly was, was too weak to protect her.

She expected her enemies to kill her and her companions.

He had been tricked.

He of all people, having witnessed the victory, and loss, at Gent, should have remembered human cunning.

'Where are they?' he demanded, but she did not know the Wendish tongue. Shouts rose to him from below as Tenth Son appeared on the ladder stairs.

'There's a tunnel out of the lowest level.'

'The queen and her sorcerers escaped.' Fury clawed him. They had outwitted him! How had he not seen this coming?

'They collapsed the tunnel behind them. I have slaves

digging it out. I've ordered patrols out beyond the walls.'

But it was already too late. He knew it, as did Tenth Son. As did the girl and her aged companion and the five little ones, left behind to face his wrath.

Sacrifices.

The Alban queens ruled in the old way, offering blood to their gods in exchange for power. The circle god of Alain's people did not reign unchallenged here. Even the gods warred among humankind, seeking preeminence.

Let it be done, then. If these seven had been left behind, then they could not even be worth enough to his enemies to hold for ransom or as a bargaining chip. Lifting his sword, he stepped forward

his feet hit the ground so hard that all breath is sucked from his lungs. He staggers, gasping for air so that he can call out to her, but Adica is lost to him, torn away into the whirlwind. He grabs for her, but his hands close on dirt. Grass tickles his face. He smells rain and hears a muted roar, like that of a lion, but it is only the wind caught in trees or perhaps the rush of unseen wings, fading.

Gone.

The hounds lick his face, whining and whimpering, nosing at him, trying to get him to stand. He lifts his head.

Huge shapes surround him. He has fallen into the center of a pristine circle of raised stones. Beyond the circle, four mounds mark the perimeter, grown high with grass and a scattering of flowers. His heart quickens with hope.

But this is not the place he knew and came to love. An encircling forest cuts off any view he might have of lands beyond the clearing. The tumulus, the graves of the queens, the winding river, and the village are all gone. What peace he found will be denied him. Adica's love, given to him freely, has been ripped away.

She is dead.

He knew it from the first when he was dragged unknowing into her country, but maybe he never believed. Maybe he thought he really had died. After all, he ought to have died.

He had been so close to death after the battle with the Lions on that ancient tumulus that a part of him had chosen to believe he wasn't living anymore but rather had passed over to the other side, the field of paradise that borders the Chamber of Light, where his soul could rest at last in peace.

Ai, God. Peace mocks him, for what he has seen and experienced this night is surely more horrible than the worst of his fears.

How could the Hallowed Ones have done it? Did they know what they wrought? Was it worth such destruction to spare a few?

The hound Sorrow shoves his head under Alain's stomach and pushes. Rage tugs at his hand. Struggling, he gets to his feet, but he no longer knows where he is or what lies in store for him. The hounds herd him toward the forest's edge where a track snakes away into the trees. Face whipped by branches, he presses along the trail. Eventually, it broadens into a path padded by a carpet of pine needles. He just walks. He must not think. He must not remember. If he only walks, then maybe he can forget that he is still alive.

But maybe it is never possible just to walk, just to exist. Fate acts, and the heart and mind respond. The path breaks out of the forest onto a ridgeline. A log lies along the ground like a bench, and he pauses here to catch his breath. The hounds lick his hands as he stares at the vista opening before him.

A river valley spreads out below, a handful of villages strung along its length like clusters of grapes. Closer lie the plaster-and-timber buildings of a monastery and its estate. The bleat of a horn carries to him on the stiff wind that blows into his face, making tears start up from his eyes. An entourage emerges from woodland, following the ribbon of a road. He counts about a dozen people: four mounted and six walking alongside two wagons pulled by oxen. Bright pennants flutter in the breeze.

He has to speak, he has to warn them.

Running, he pounds down the path. He has to stop and rest at intervals, but grief and panic drive him on. Always he gets up again, heart still racing, breath labored, and hurries down the path until it levels off and emerges out of forest onto a trim estate, fields laid down in rows, orchard plots marked off by pruned hedges, the buildings sitting back behind a row of cypress. Bees buzz around his head and one lights on his ear, as if tasting for nectar. Geese honk overhead, flying south.

A trio of men in the robes of lay brothers work one of the fields, preparing the ground for winter wheat. One leads an ox while another steadies the plow, but it is the third who sees Alain stumbling out of the woodland. He runs forward with hoe in hand, held there as if he has forgotten it or, perhaps, as if he may use it as a weapon.

Lifting a hand in the sign of peace, the lay brother halts a safe distance from Alain and calls out a greeting. 'Greetings, Brother. You look to be in distress. How may we help you?' His comrades have stopped their work, and one of them has already hurried away toward the orchard, where other figures can be seen at work among the trees.

Alain feels the delicate tread of the bee along his lobe and the tickle of its antenna on his skin. Its wings flutter, purring against his ear, but it does not fly.

'Can you speak, Brother?' asks the man gently as, behind him, several robed figures emerge from the orchard and hasten toward them. 'Do not fear. No harm will come to you here.'

The bee stings. The hot poison strikes deep into him, coursing straight into the heart of memory. Weeping, he drops to his knees as images flood over him, obliterating him:

In an instant, magic ripped the world asunder.

Earthquakes rippled across the land, but what was seen on the surface was as nothing compared to the devastation left in their wake underground. Caverns collapsed into rubble. Tunnels slammed shut like bellows snapped tight. The magnificent cities of the goblinkin, hidden from human sight and therefore unknown and disregarded, vanished in cave-ins so massive that the land above was irrevocably altered. The sea's water poured away into cracks riven in the earth, down and down and down, meeting molten fire and spilling steam hissing and spitting into every crevice until the backwash disgorged steam and sizzling water back into the sea.

Rivers ran backward. The seaports of the southern tribes were swallowed beneath the rising waters, or left high and dry when the sea was sucked away, so that they abruptly lay separated from the sea by long stretches of sand that once marked the shallows. Deltas ran dry. Mountains smoked with fire, and liquid red rock slid downslope, burning everything that stood in its way.

In the north, a dragon plunged to earth and ossified in that eye blink into a stone ridge.

The land where the Cursed Ones made their home was ripped right up by the roots, like a tree wrenched out of its soil by the hand of a giant. Where that hand flung it, he could not see.

Only Adica, dead.

Wings of flame enveloped him, blinding him.

'I didn't mean to leave her, but I couldn't see.' He has been speaking all along, a spate of words as engulfing as the flood-tide. 'The light blinded me.'

'Hush, friend.'

Voices speak all around him, a chorus close by and yet utterly distant, because his grief has not moved them to stand beside him in their hearts.

'Those are big dogs,' mutters one.

'Monsters,' agrees another. 'Think you they'll bite?'

'Here comes Brother Infirmarian.'

A portly man presses forward through the throng and bravely, if cautiously, approaches. Rage and Sorrow sit.

'Come, lad,' he says, kneeling beside Alain. 'You're safe here. What is your name? Where have you come from?'

'Ai, God. So many dead. No more death, please God. No more killing.'

'What have you seen, Son?' asks the monk kindly.

So much suffering. It all spills out in a rush of words, unbidden. Once started, he has to go to the end, just as the spell wove itself to completion, unstoppable once it had been threaded into the loom.

The caves in which Horn's people have sheltered flood

with steaming water, trapping the dead and the dying in the blind dark. A storm of earth and debris buries Shu-Sha's palace. Halfway up the Screaming Rocks, Shevros falls beneath a massive avalanche. Waves obliterate a string of peaceful villages along the shores of Falling-down's island. Children scream helplessly for their parents as they flail in the surging water.

The blood and viscera of stricken dragons rains down on the humans desperately and uselessly taking shelter against seven stones, burning flesh into rock. A sandstorm buries the oasis where the desert people have camped, trees flattened under the blast of the wind. The lion women race ahead of the storm wave but, in the end, they too are buried beneath a mountain of sand. Gales scatter the tents of the Horse people, winds so strong that what is not flattened outright is flung heavenward and tossed back to earth like so much chaff. All the trees for leagues around Queen's Grave erupt into flame, and White Deer villagers fall, dying, where arrows and war had spared them. Ai, God, where are Maklos and Agalleos? Hani and Dorren?

Where is Kel?

They are all dead.

Is this the means by which the sorcerers hoped to bring peace? Did they really know what they were doing? Can it be possible they understood what would happen?

'Adica can't have known. She'd never have agreed to lend herself to so much destruction if she'd known.'

He has to believe it is true.

But he will always wonder if she knew and, knowing, acted with the others anyway, knowing the cost. Did they really hate the Cursed Ones so much?

'It was all for nothing. They're still here. I've seen them.'

Ghost shapes, more shadow than substance, walk the interstices between Earth and the Other Side, caught forever betwixt and between. Those Cursed Ones who did not stand in their homeland when it was torn out of the earth were pulled outward with it; they exist not entirely on Earth and yet not severed from it, as all that comes of earth is bound to earth.

Yet isn't it true that no full-blooded Cursed One walks the same soil as humankind now? Didn't the human sorcerers get what they wanted? Isn't Earth free of the Cursed Ones?

'We can never know peace,' he cries, turning to the men who have flocked around him. He has to make them understand. 'What is bound to earth will return to earth. The suffering isn't over. The cataclysm will happen again when that which was torn asunder returns to its original place.'

'Thank the Lady, Father,' says the infirmarian as the gathered brothers let a new figure through. 'You've come.'

The abbot is a young man, vigorous and handsome, son of a noble house. He has a sarcastic eye and a gleam of humor in his expression, but he sobers quickly as he examines Alain and the placid but menacing hounds. The portly infirmarian keeps a light touch on Alain's wrist, nothing harsh, ready to grab him if he bolts.

'It's a wanderer, Father Ortulfus,' says the infirmarian. His fingers flutter along Alain's skin. Like the bee, he seems to be probing, but he hasn't stung yet.

'Another one?' The abbot has wildly blue eyes and pale hair, northern coloring. Adica's people were darker, stockier, black-haired. 'I've never seen so many wanderers on the roads as this summer. Is he a heretic?'

'Not so we've noticed, Father,' says one of the monks nervously. 'He's babbling about the end times. He's right out of his mind.'

'Hush, Adso,' scolds the infirmarian before he addresses the abbot. The calm words slip from his mouth smoothly. 'He's not violent, just troubled.' He turns to regard Alain with compassion. 'Here, now, son. You'll not be running away, will you? Don't think you'll come to any harm among us. We've a bed you can sleep in, and porridge, and work to keep your hands busy. That will ease your mind out of these fancies. You'll find healing here.'

The hot poison strikes deep. These words hurt far worse than any bee's sting.

No one will believe him.

And Adica is dead. No one will mourn her with him,

because they cannot. They do not even know, nor can they believe, that she exists. He has come home as a stranger, having lost everything that mattered. Having, in the end, not even kept his promise to die with her.

What point is there in living?

Stronghand's foot hit, jolting him into awareness. One step he had taken, only one. The sky lightened, and the river's silver band glinted as sunlight drove the mist off the waters, dazzling his eyes. A torrent of images washed over him. All of the colors of Alain's being had overflowed in that vision to drown him.

Joy ran like a deluge. Yet joy had spoken in a terrible voice.

So many dead. No more death, please God. No more killing.

'No more killing.' Hearing his own voice, he shook himself free of the trance. The girl turned to throw the youngest child over the battlements.

He leaped forward and wrenched the child out of her grasp, knocking the kneeling sorcerer aside. The girl scrambled onto the battlements herself, making ready to jump.

'Stop her!'

Quickly all seven of the Albans were taken into custody. The child he held squirmed and began to sob outright in fear.

'Hush!'

It ceased its weeping.

'No more killing.' His voice seemed unrecognizable to him, yet it sounded no different than it ever had. Was it wisdom that made him speak? For better or worse, he was scarred by the strength of the contact between him and Alain, bound by a weaving that even the WiseMothers did not comprehend.

Where had Alain gone? He had vanished from Stronghand's dreams and apparently from Earth itself for over three years. What was the meaning of this vision of destruction on such a scale that it dwarfed even the slow deliberations of the WiseMothers?

In those years when Alain had been gone, the span of months between the battle at Kjalmarsfjord and this day's rejoining, he had thought and planned and acted the same as ever, but something had been missing. It was as if the world had gone gray and only now did he see its colors. For truly the world was a beautiful place, worn down by suffering, painted by light, never at rest.

He could never be free of that connection. He did not want to be. Before Alain had freed him from the cage at Lavas Holding, he had been, like his brothers, a slave to the single-minded lust for killing, war, and plunder that imprisoned his kind. He had been no better than the rest of them and, because of his smaller stature, at a disadvantage.

Was it Alain's dreaming influence that had altered some essential thread that wound through his being?

Around him, his troops murmured restlessly, still filled with battle lust. They had taken Hefenfelthe, but they had no clear victory.

'Why kill these hostages?' he asked, turning to look at them, one by one. These would carry the message to his army, each brother to another, spreading the word of Stronghand's wisdom. 'The queen of Alba and her sorcerers gain power by sacrificing the blood of their subjects. They left these ones behind as sacrifices, knowing we would kill them in anger once we had seen we were thwarted of our prey. So if we kill them, we do their will and strengthen their magic. Therefore we will not kill them. They will become our prisoners. The power of the queen and her sorcerers will become a slave to our power.'

The girl wept when she understood that she would not serve her queen as she had been commanded.

One of his Rikin brothers emerged from the tower, carrying his standard. Stronghand sheathed his sword and, with the child still held in his left arm, walked to the battlements and hoisted his standard high, so his army, below, could see him. A roar lifted from their ranks, echoing through the conquered city. The magic that lived in the staff hummed against his palm. The breeze made the charms that hung from the standard sing, bone flutes whistling, beads and chains chiming softly, melding with the clack and scrape of wood, leather, and bones. Once again, the magic woven by the priests of his people had protected him against the magic wielded by his enemies.

Out in the fields beyond the walls the last refugees, those who had crept out of their homes while the battle raged around the citadel, fled into the shelter of distant trees. The fields and forest of Alba stretched away in all directions, cut by the broad river and a nearby tributary. It was a rich land.

But it was not his land yet.

'We seek the queen and her sorcerers.'

'Where can we find them?' asked Tenth Son.

Stronghand glanced at the weeping girl with her silver circlet and its seven tines. Six sacrifices waited with her, seven souls in all. It could be no accident that Alain appeared to him after so long in the embrace of a stone circle so like the circle made by the WiseMothers on the fjall above Rikin Fjord.

'They will retreat to a place of power. Alert the forward parties and the scouts. All prisoners will be questioned about forts or marshes where a small force can defend itself. But we should also seek a standing circle of stones, perhaps one with seven stones. I believe that is where we will find the queen.'

VIII
RATS AND LIONS

1

Sunlight washed the plank floor of the attic room, illuminating three months' worth of dust that layered the floor and empty pallets as well as the trail of Hanna's footsteps cutting a straight line from the trapdoor to the window. It was so hot up here that she could scarcely breathe. She stumbled against one of the shutters, unhooked and laid on the floor, and kicked it aside before leaning out to gulp in fresh air.

In late spring the king had ridden south with Queen Adelheid to fight the Jinna pirates infesting the southeastern provinces. Hanna had arrived in midsummer after a grueling trip over the mountains, but the palace stewards had not allowed her to ride after Henry's army. She could not expect, they told her, that her cloak and Eagle's badge would grant her safe passage in those parts of the country not yet loyal to the king.

She had to wait.

She wiped sweat from her forehead and ducked back into shadow, but decided that the blast of the sun in the open air was preferable to the smothering heat of the attic sleeping quarters. Adjusting her brimmed hat to ward off the worst of the direct glare, she leaned out again. A stew of smells rose from the surrounding buildings: manure, piss, slops, roasting pig, and a hint of incense almost lost beneath the perfume of human living. From this angle and height, she looked out over rooftops toward the delicate spire marking the royal chapel and beyond that the outer walls and the gulf of air shimmering above the lower city with its massive stone edifices. The river cut a thread of molten iron through streets hazy with heat, dust, and cook fires.

Unbelievably vast, Darre seemed a warren of alleys and avenues, with so many houses that no person could possibly count them. Beyond the outermost walls lay fields and vineyards and, farther out, distant hills and a dark ribbon marking the route to the sea. Wisps of cloud pushed over those sere heights, promising relief against the heat later in the day. Was that smoke drifting up from the tallest peak? Had someone lit a fire at its height? She couldn't tell, and it seemed a strange thing to do in any case.

Hanna had explored as many corners, sinks, and privies, as many balconies, shady arbors, and storage pits as she was allowed into in the regnant's palace. She had even toured the prison down in the city, and the tower where other Aostan regnants had confined their enemies, although Adelheid kept no hostages now. All the tower rooms lay empty, stripped of furniture, heavy with dust.

She had asked about Margrave Villam.

Dead of a tragic fall when he was drunk.

She had asked about Duchess Liutgard of Fesse and Duke Burchard of Avaria.

Ridden south with the king.

She had asked about Sister Rosvita, the king's counselor.

Neither dead nor gone.

How could a person be neither dead nor gone? How could the stewards of the palace and the legions of servants not hoard rumors of her fate? Rosvita had been here when King Henry arrived; now she was not. Hanna had discovered no transition between arrival and departure. She found again and again that her thoughts turned to Hathui's accusations. Either Hathui was lying, or the Aostan stewards were.

She leaned out farther, dizzy from the height, but even from this angle she could only see one corner of the skopos' palace. She had hoped to find answers there, but the guards would not let her inside.

With a sigh, she ducked back into the shadow, fighting to get in a lungful of the overheated air.

A footfall sounded on the ladder. She spun, drawing her knife. A broom's handle poked through the open trap, followed by the rest of the broom, thrust up and falling sideways to clatter onto the floor. A woman emerged awkwardly, grasped the broom, and rose, then gasped, seeing Hanna.

'Oh, Lord in Heaven!' she exclaimed. 'You surprised me!' She wore a serviceable tunic covered with a dusty tabard and a plain linen scarf concealing her hair. Not as young as Hanna, she wasn't yet old. 'Begging your pardon. I didn't expect to find anyone else up here.'

'Neither did I.'

The servant gave a companionable chuckle, a little forced. 'Well, now, I suppose that means that neither of us have eyes in the backs of our heads, to see around corners and through walls.'

Hanna stayed by the window but sheathed the knife as the woman walked away from her to the other end of the long attic room. There, she stooped to allow for the pitched roof and began sweeping. Dust rose in clouds around her, and she paused to tie up her tabard over her mouth and nose.

'Always the worst when it's the first cleaning,' she said cheerfully as Hanna watched with surprise.

'It seems awfully hot to be thinking of cleaning out these sleeping rooms.' The heat all summer had been like a battering ram. She had never got used to it.

'True enough. But the weather can turn cold suddenly now that the season is turning from summer to autumn, if you call this autumn. We have to start thinking of inhabiting these rooms again. Last year you can't believe how hot it was, hotter than this, and with unseasonable rains, too, and a terrible hailstorm.'

'I hear the king was taken sorely ill, last year.'

The servant looked up at her, expression hidden except for her eyes. Her gaze had a queer, searching intensity. But as the silence stretched out uncomfortably, she returned to sweeping.

'Last summer, yes, he was taken ill with the shivering fever. He was laid in bed for two months, and the armies fought all summer and autumn without him. They had no victories, nor any defeats. So they say.' Again that searching glance scrutinized Hanna. 'That's if they say what's true, but how are we simple servants to know what's truth and what's not?'

'Eagles know.'

'Where are all the Eagles? Gone with the king, all but that poor redheaded fellow who got so sick.'

'Rufus?'

'That's right,' she continued amiably, her voice muffled by the cloth. 'He came south last year at the command of Biscop Constance in Autun, didn't he?'

'So he told me.' Carrying a message very like the ones sent by Theophanu, but the king had not heeded him.

'Yes, poor lad. He was so sick even the palace healers thought he would die from the shivering. That's why he had to be left behind this past spring when the king rode south.'

'Yet all the other Eagles rode south with the king, didn't they? Why haven't any of them brought reports back to Darre? Why is it always the queen's Aostan messengers we see?'

'How can I know the king's mind? I can only thank the Lord and Lady that his army has won victories over both the infidels and the heretics. *And* over a few Aostan nobles who would prefer no regnant placed above their heads. So we're told.'

Her account tallied with the news Rufus had given Hanna. 'I've heard talk that the king and queen will be crowned with *imperial* crowns before the end of the year.'

'That talk has been going on as long as I've been here, these two and a half years. Maybe it will finally happen.'

With the steady *scritch* of the broom against wood like an accompaniment to her thoughts, Hanna finally realized what was strangest about this industrious woman. 'You're Wendish.'

'So I am. I'm called Aurea, from the estate of Landelbach in Fesse. You're that new Eagle what rode in a few months back.'

'Yes. My name is Hanna Birta's-daughter, from the North Mark. I come from a place called Heart's Rest.' A low rumble shook through the floor and the entire building swayed.

Hanna shrieked. 'What is *that*?'

The rumbling faded, the building stilled, and Aurea kept sweeping. 'Haven't you felt one yet? An earthquake? We feel them every few months.'

'Nay, no earthquakes. Nor weather anywhere near as hot as what I've suffered through here.' She was still trembling.

'True enough. It's hot here for weeks on end, too, not just for a short spell as it would be up north where I come from. It isn't *natural*.'

Hanna exhaled, still trying to steady her nerves. 'An old friend of mine would say that Aosta lies nearer to the Sun. That's why it's hotter here.'

'Is it? That seems a strange story to me. Nearer to the sun!' Aurea hummed under her breath. 'But no stranger than many a tale I've heard here in Darre. Sister Heriburg says that in the east there's snakes who suckle milk right from the cow. In the south no plants can grow because the sun shines so hot, and the folk who live there have great, huge ears that they use like tents during the day to protect them from the sun. Even here, there's stories about godly clerics who abide in the skopos' dungeons like rats, hidden from the sight of most people, but I don't suppose those are any more true than that tale my old grandmam told me about a dragon turned into stone in the north country. It lies there still, they say, by the sea, but nothing can bring it back to life.'

She kept her gaze on the warped floorboards where dust collected in cracks. Hanna thought she would choke in air now polluted with a swirling cloud of dust, but she dared not move. She had to think. How strange to speak of clerics hidden away in dungeons.

Maybe it was only a figure of speech, an old tale spun by the palace servants to pass the time.

But maybe it wasn't.

'I've heard stories of men who can turn themselves into wolves,' she said at last, cautiously, 'but never any of clerics who can turn themselves into rats. I've heard that story about the dragon, too, though, the one turned into stone. When there's a great storm come in off the Northern Sea, you can hear the dragons keening. That's what my old grandmother always said.'

'Lots of stories of dragons,' agreed the servant woman without looking up from her sweeping, 'but I've never heard tell of a single person who'd ever seen such a beast. Rats, now. Rats I've seen aplenty.'

'There must be an army of rats in a great palace like this one.'

'And the biggest ones of all down in the dungeons. I don't doubt they're caught down there somehow, between stone walls. There's only the one staircase, guarded by the Holy Mother's faithful guards, and they're sharp-eyed, those fellows. Everyone says so. As likely to skewer a rat on the point of their knife if it comes scurrying up the stairs. A woman here I know said it happens every year, and then they roast those rats they've caught and throw their burned carcasses to the dogs.'

She looked up then, her gaze like a sharp rap on the head.

'It would take a lot of rats to fill a dog's belly,' answered Hanna, floundering.

'Not if they've grown as big as a dog themselves, or bigger even, human-sized or some say as big as a horse. A horse!' She bent back to her task with a curt chuckle. 'I'm not believing such foolish tales. No rat can grow to be the size of a horse, and where would it hide, then? But I suppose they could become mighty big, nibbling on scraps and prisoners' fingers and toes.'

That sharp look made Hanna cautious. Was there a veiled purpose to Aurea's talking, or was she just nattering to pass the time?

'I remember stories that my grandmother told me.' Hanna moved along the attic until she came to the open trapdoor.

She squinted down the length of the ladder but saw no lurking shadow, no listening accomplice. 'I do love to trade old stories, about dragons and rats and wolves. I have a few stories of my own to tell.'

'So it might well be, you being an Eagle and all,' agreed the woman, sweeping past Hanna toward the window. Tidy piles of dirt and dust marked her path like droppings. 'Eagles see all kinds of things the rest of us can't, don't you? Travel to strange and distant lands with urgent messages on behalf of the king. You're welcome to join those of us servants from Wendar when we attend Vespers in St. Asella's chapel, by the west gate of the city. There's a cleric from Wendar called Brother Fortunatus who gives the sermon in Wendish there. Only on Hefensday, mind. That's when we're allowed to go.'

Since there were a dozen chapels within the regnant's palace alone and a rumored five hundred or more within the walls of the lower city, Hanna could not guess which one the woman meant. Most of them she only recognized by the image of the saint that marked the portico. Yet she could not help herself. Clerics hidden like rats in the dungeon. Eyes that could see through walls, and traveling Eagles.

Perhaps she was making a conspiracy where none existed, but it wouldn't hurt to follow this path a bit farther.

'I don't know of St. Asella. If I go down to the west gate, is there some way to know which chapel is dedicated to her?'

The woman stilled her broom. Though her gaze was as innocent as a lamb's, the soft words carried a barb. 'St. Asella was walled up alive.'

2

In the deepening twilight, tall trees seemed a grim backdrop to swollen grave mounds and a stone circle. As their little group neared the gap in the wall of trees that promised to be a trail, Ivar looked back over the clearing. He had never seen a stone circle in such perfect repair, each stone upright and all the lintels intact. It looked as if it had been built, or repaired, in recent months. Only the great stone at the center lay flat. His companions paused as dusk settled over them and a breeze sighed through the forest. The grave mounds seemed to exert a spell, luring them back. Ivar simply could not move, as though dead hands gripped his feet and held him tight. A twig snapped, breaking their silence.

'Do you think we're really near Herford Monastery?' asked Ermanrich, voice squeaking.

'As long as we're well away from that Quman army, then I don't care where we are.' Ivar knew he sounded braver than he felt as daylight faded. A wolf howled in the distance, answered by a second, and everyone grabbed for their weapons. 'Where's Baldwin?'

'He was right behind you,' said Ermanrich.

'He didn't wait.' The younger Lion, Dedi, pointed toward the trees. 'He went to look at the path.'

'Why didn't you stop him?' demanded Ivar.

Ermanrich gave him a look. 'When has Baldwin ever listened to any of us?'

'Nay, Ivar, don't be angry at Dedi.' Sigfrid laid a gentle, but restraining, hand on Ivar's arm. 'Ermanrich's only speaking the truth, which you know as well as we do.'

'Damned fool. Why couldn't he wait?' But Baldwin never listened, he just pretended to.

'He probably ran off because he thought he saw Margrave Judith come looking for him,' joked Ermanrich nervously.

'Why should a margrave like Judith come looking for the likes of *him*?' asked Dedi with a snort of disbelief.

'Hush!' said Hathumod abruptly. 'Listen!'

The sound of thrashing came from the trees. Baldwin burst out of the forest, arms flailing.

'A lion!' He hadn't run more than ten steps into the clearing when he tripped and fell.

They hurried over to calm him down, but as they swarmed around him, he jumped to his feet with a look of terror on his beautiful face. 'I found an old hovel over at a rock out-cropping, not far from here, but when I stuck my head inside, I heard a cough behind me. I turned around and there was a lion up on the rocks!'

'A Lion?' demanded Gerulf. 'From which cohort?'

'Nay, a lion. A beast. Quite tawny and as hungry looking as you please. A second one came to stand beside the first.'

Gerulf snorted. 'I'll thank you not to pull my leg, Son. There aren't any lions in the north except them as you might find in the regnant's menagerie. Lions live in the southern lands.'

'I know what I saw.'

'If it was a hungry lion, then why didn't it eat you up?' asked Dedi with a laugh. 'Or was it too busy admiring your pretty face?'

Ivar jumped between Baldwin and Dedi just as Baldwin drew his arm back for a punch. 'Baldwin can't help the way he looks. No need to tease him for it. It's getting dark anyway. I don't care to spend a night here inside this stone circle with those barrows as our guardians. Do any of you?'

No one did, not even Sigfrid, whose powerful faith made him hardest to frighten.

'Anything might happen here among the stones and graves,' said Ermanrich. 'I'd rather face the lions.'

'We'll let you go first,' said Hathumod dryly to her cousin, 'for then they'll have a good meal and won't need to eat any of the rest of us.'

'There's the path.' Gerulf pointed toward the gap.

'I'd hate to take any path with darkness coming on and wolves howling nearby,' said Ivar.

'Not to mention the lions,' said Dedi.

'You'll see,' muttered Baldwin.

'How big is this hovel?' Gerulf nodded toward Ivar to show he agreed that they shouldn't try to go far lest they lose them-selves in the night.

'One man could sit inside it, but not comfortably,' said Baldwin. 'But right below where I saw the lions the out-cropping cuts in and makes a bit of an overhang.'

'That might serve as shelter,' said Gerulf, 'enough for one night. We can follow the path in the morning.'

'You don't believe me!' Baldwin looked from face to face. 'None of you believe me! Ivar?'

Drops of rain brushed Ivar's face. A gust of wind, heralding stronger rain to come, rattled through the trees. 'It might have been wolves,' he said reluctantly. Seeing Baldwin's indignant expression, he quickly went on. 'Or lions. I'd hate to fight them out in the open. We've weapons enough to fight off ravening beasts as long as we have a good stout wall at our back.'

'There you are, Son!' replied Gerulf cheerfully. 'If we can get a fire going, then a good overhang will serve us better whether wolves or lions or even a guivre itself comes a-courting. Better anyway than standing out here and getting soaking wet. You'd have made a good Lion, lad.'

'I would have been no Lion,' said Ivar, stung by this statement. 'I'd have been a Dragon, if my father who is count up in the North Mark would have let me ride with them instead of putting me into the church.'

'I pray you, my lord,' said Gerulf hastily. 'I meant no offense.'

The momentary embarrassment, the realization that although their group had escaped the Quman as comrades they were, in fact, quite unequal in station, held them motionless until rain drove them into action. They slogged through what remained of the grassy clearing, sheltering their heads against the rain as best they could, keeping the torches dry. Luckily, the track ran straight and true through the trees. They took not more than one hundred steps on a downhill slope before they stumbled out onto a rocky outcropping. Cliffs rose above and below, staggered like the shoulders of a hulking beast. Rain washed over them with a fresh gust of wind, and they stumbled into such shelter as the overhang afforded. In the last of the fading light, Ivar saw a tiny hovel built of sticks standing off to one side, out in the rain, but truly, as Baldwin had reported, it hadn't enough space even for one man to lie down in.

'Come, there's plenty of sticks here to build a fire that'll last the entire night, and they're not too wet yet,' said Gerulf, then added: 'If you will, my lords and lady.'

They gathered up fuel as quickly as they could and lit a fire just as it really got too dark to see. After some discussion, they settled on watches: Gerulf and Hathumod to begin, followed by Dedi and Ermanrich, and Ivar and Sigfrid last. Baldwin had already bundled himself up in his cloak and lain down to sleep in the deepest, driest crack of the overhang. They set out torches within easy reach, in case they needed them as weapons against marauding beasts, and settled down for the night.

Ivar lay down next to Baldwin. He dozed off at once and was startled awake much later by the sound of Hathumod's voice, as soft as the brush of rabbit fur across his skin but rather more persistent.

'Nay, friend Gerulf, it isn't a heresy at all, although the church may have said so.'

'I beg your pardon, Lady Hathumod, but why should the church mothers lie? Why would the holy women who have worn the robes and seal of the skopos each in her turn be party to such a deception?'

'Some simply were ignorant. They were taught as we were and knew no better. But truly, I do not know why the ancient mothers who wrote in the early days concealed the truth. They were the heretics, and the Enemy spoke through them. But now the truth is unveiled and shines brightly for all to see. I have witnessed miracles—'

Ivar had heard similar words from the lips of Lady Tallia, whose tortured body and zealous gaze had thrown all of them onto the path of heresy back in Quedlinhame. As he drifted back into sleep, he marveled that Hathumod, despite her undistinguished voice and unremarkable bearing, could sound so persuasive.

A foot nudged him, and when he shifted to turn his back to the summons, it nudged him again.

'Nay, nay,' he muttered, thinking himself back at Quedlinhame, 'it can't be time for Vigils already, is it?'

'So it might be,' whispered Ermanrich cheerfully, 'although with the clouds overhead I can't see the stars to tell what hour it is. It's your turn for watch.'

Ivar groaned. He hurt everywhere. Even his fingers throbbed, but when he rose, crouching, and closed his hand over his spear, the grip felt funny. Memory jolted him awake. He'd lost two fingers in the battle. Maybe the Quman were already on their trail, ready to cut off his head. He straightened and promptly banged his head on the rock above.

'Hush,' hissed Ermanrich. 'No need to go swearing like that. We've seen nothing on our watch and nothing was seen on the first watch either. I think Baldwin's lions must have been scared off by his handsome face.'

'God Above.' Ivar stepped out past Ermanrich. A rush of cold night air swept his cheeks. He'd been breathing in smoke from the fire all night, and his lungs ached with soot. Outside, the rain had stopped, but he still couldn't see any stars. 'I'd forgotten how much I hated rising for prayers in the middle of the night.'

'Where's your purity of faith? Don't you remember the miracles?'

'They never took place at Vigils.'

Sigfrid stood next to the fire, rocking back and forth with eyes closed as he murmured prayers. Ivar fed a stick to the fire and rubbed his hands near the flames to warm them. Ermanrich and Dedi settled down on the ground to sleep.

Ivar didn't like to interrupt Sigfrid at his prayers, so he stood quietly at watch. Neither did he want to pray. He had learned all those prayers in the church of his childhood and youth, the church of his mothers and grandmothers. But after witnessing the miracle of the phoenix and the miracle of Lady Tallia's bloody wounds, he knew the church had lied to him. Perhaps Sigfrid and Hathumod could still pray, changing the words so they echoed the truth that had been hidden for so long. But prayer seemed to Ivar like an illusionary feast, pretty to look at and delectable to smell but tasting like ashes when you went to gobble it down.

Perhaps he had suffered so many betrayals and setbacks

because he had himself believed what was false. Yet others believed what they had been taught, and they hadn't suffered as he had. Nay, truly, his trials must have been a test of his resolve. Maybe he had been granted leave to witness the miracles because he had resisted Liath's blandishments. She had tempted him, but he had escaped her. Even if he did still dream of her, here on a rainy night lost in a distant country, wondering what was to become of them all.

If it hadn't been for Liath, maybe his father would have let him join the Dragons. But of course, then he would have been killed at Gent by the Eika along with the rest of the Dragons; all but that damned Prince Sanglant, who everyone knew had been enchanted by his inhuman mother so that he couldn't ever be killed.

Looked at that way, maybe Liath had saved him from death. Or maybe it wasn't Liath at all. Maybe God had saved him, so that he and his friends could work Her will. God had saved them from the Quman, hadn't She? God had transported them by a miracle from the eastern borderlands to the very heart of Wendar. God had turned summer to autumn, and healed their wounds, and by these signs had revealed their task: It was up to them to tell the truth of the blessed Daisan's death to every soul they encountered. God had given the truth into their hands and saved them from sure death in order to see what they would make of these gifts.

The shape ghosted past at the limit of the fire's light.

Startled, he dropped his spear. As he bent to pick it up, he noticed a second shape, then a third.

'Hsst, Sigfrid! Wolves!'

As if their name, spoken out loud, summoned them, the wolves moved closer. Lean and sleek, they eyed the sleeping party hungrily. The leader yawned, displaying sharp teeth. As he gathered breath into his lungs to shout the alarm, Ivar counted two, then four, then eight of the beasts, poised to leap, ready to kill.

They scattered, vanishing into the night.

The shout caught in his throat, choking him, as a lion paced into the circle of the fire's light and lifted its glossy golden head to gaze at him. It had huge shoulders and power-ful flanks, and when it yawned, its teeth sparked in the fire-light like the points of daggers.

A choking stutter came from his throat. For a space during which he might have gulped in one breath or taken a thou-sand, he stared at it, and it at him, as calm in its power as God's judgment.

Then he remembered that he had to wake the others before they were ripped into pieces and made into a feast.

Something touched him, and he jumped, but he still could-n't find his voice, and anyway, it was only Sigfrid.

'Nay, Ivar,' he said in his gentle voice. 'They're protect-ing us.' His small hand weighed like a boulder on Ivar's fore-arm.

He didn't dare move, because the lion hadn't attacked yet. As he watched, too stunned to do anything, a second lion paced majestically into the fire's light. This one had a coat so light that it seemed silver. It, too, stopped and stared with a gaze so intelligent that at once he knew it could see right down into his soul. It knew all his secrets, every least bitter and petty thought he had ever entertained, every ill he had wished on another, every greedy urge he had fulfilled. It knew the depths of his unseemly passion for Liath and how he had allowed lust to smother his decent affection for Hanna, who had never turned away from him, even when he had treated her badly. It recognized how far he had fallen into debauch-ery among Prince Ekkehard and his cronies. But it also saw his efforts to preach the truth of the sacrifice and redemption of the blessed Daisan to the city folk in Gent and to the vil-lage folk in the marchlands. It saw how he had aided his friends on the battlefield and helped the wounded Lions to safety. It witnessed, through him, the glorious flight of the phoenix, and for these things it forgave him his sins.

'W-why should they protect us?' he stammered when he found his voice.

'Lions are God's creatures,' said Sigfrid. 'They're waiting here.'

'Waiting for what?'

'I don't know.'

Rain spattered down and ceased. The lions paced back and forth, obliterating the tracks of the wolves. Their steady movement, weaving in and out but never coming close, made him so sleepy that he swayed on his feet, started awake, then drifted off again.

And found that it was dawn. Light stained the east, and from this outcropping he saw forest falling away into a deep cleft rank with trees and rising again into wooded hills. To the south he saw the edge of a tidy clearing that suggested a settlement, perhaps the fields of Herford Monastery.

Sigfrid had found a spring in the rocks and drank deeply as the others woke, stretched, and came to slake their thirst. Ivar walked forward, but the ground betrayed no trace of what he had seen in the night. He saw no prints of wolf and certainly nothing like the massive paw prints that lions of such a size ought to have left behind them as evidence of their passage.

Gerulf came up to him. 'I see you've noticed it as well. That looks to me like the monastic estate. We'd best strike out at once, so we don't have to spend another night in the forest.'

'Alas, Lord Baldwin,' Dedi was saying back by the spring as Baldwin staggered up, still half asleep but no less handsome for looking quite rumpled, 'it was quiet enough this night, although your stout friend Ermanrich quite bent my ear the whole time we were on watch with so many astounding tales that I don't know what to think.' He paused, as a thief might pause to listen before grabbing the jewels out of their resting place in a nest of silk. 'I fear your lions chose not to pay us a call, eh?'

There was a scuffle, broken up by Hathumod with a sharp whack to each of their behinds with a stick.

Gerulf grabbed Dedi and hauled him aside. 'You'll be polite, Nephew! This man's a lord.'

Dedi muttered a comment under his breath.

'I did too see lions!' retorted Baldwin. 'No one *ever* believes me.'

Ivar examined the ground again but the only prints he saw
were his own boots. 'It's said that the Enemy brings strange
visions at night,' he said.

'So may God, my lord,' replied Gerulf, 'but it's hard for
mortal man to tell the difference between the one and the
other. Saw you anything on your watch?'

Ivar didn't have the courage to speak of what he'd seen,
nor did Sigfrid mention it.

IX

A GRAVE CRIME

1

In the city of Darre, one saw the years laid bare on every street. Near the river, laundresses hung out clothing to dry on fallen columns from a temple once dedicated to the goddess of love. Competing hospices for pilgrims filled three-storied apartment houses near the monumental baths built in the time of the Emperor Tianathano. Cattle and goats grazed in the vast arena where horses had raced. The vast brick marketplace erected during the reign of the Empress Thaissania, she of the Mask, had been abandoned in favor of an ever-changing collection of makeshift stalls set up within the shelter of colonnaded temples that fronted the main avenues, which had themselves been built to honor gods whose names Hanna did not recognize, although Liath might have.

The four-tiered aqueducts built by ancient Dariyan engineers still brought water into the city from the hills; under their arches beggars sheltered from the sun. Itinerant cobblers repaired shoes on the marble steps of palaces, now empty, and whores sported where emperors had enjoyed other kinds of feasts. But with half the buildings in the city deserted, no one lived in hovels; every woman there might bide with a spacious and only slightly damaged roof above her head, even if she starved. The Dariyans had built their city so that it would last until the end of time. Maybe it would.

It seemed impossible that so many people could live all together in one place. Hanna could not fathom what the city must have looked like in the days, hundreds of years past, when every building had its purpose and the half-breed citizens of the old empire, proud and resolute, crowded the streets.

'I beg pardon.' She paused beside a merchant's stall in the shadow of a colonnade near the baths; this enterprising fellow sold copper medallions which displayed the images of saints. 'I have lost my way. Which road leads to the west gate?'

She had learned enough Aostan in the months she had been here to serve her in situations such as this; understanding the natives when they replied was trickier. This man was used to dealing with foreigners. He looked her over, gaze lingering on her pale braids, then studied her companion, Rufus, whose hair was as startlingly red as hers was pale blonde. He spat on the ground and with a gap-toothed grimace pointed to the right where the avenue forked.

'Not much for words, was he?' commented Rufus as they trudged on, keeping to the late afternoon shade.

'I don't think he liked us.' The glaring heat made an oven of the city. She was sweating so much that she had given up wiping it away. Her tunic stuck to her back, and a line of sticky sweat had formed where her hat pressed against her forehead.

'None of them do. They think we're barbarians. They think we're stealing their grain and their chickens.'

They paused to gawk at the huge bulk of the amphitheater, known colloquially as the Ring, looming to the left as they followed the avenue east. The river lay behind them, and when Hanna turned, the broad brim of her hat shading her eyes, she could look up at the hill on which lay the two palaces, side by side, skopos and regnant, elaborate new constructions grown up on top of whatever ancient temple had once graced that hill. 'The upper city,' the folk who lived there called it, in distinction from the rest of Darre.

'I don't think there're this many buildings in all of Wendar and Varre.'

'Maybe so.'

'I'm glad you came with me,' she added. 'I'd hate to walk down here without a companion. I hear there are at least ten murders every night.'

'So they say, and half of them northerners killed out of spite. I don't know if it's true.'

'I wouldn't leave the safety of the palace after dusk if I were alone, that's certain. Safety in numbers, I suppose.'

They came to the sprawling market for foodstuffs, situated close to the walls so it would be easier for vegetables and fruits from the fields to be carted in each day. Chickens squawked in cages next to thrushes and pigeons. Greengrocers presided over offerings of apples and figs, quince, lovage, onions, and the familiar mounds of turnips. Lush bundles of red peonies and white lilies were offered for sale next to bowls of mustard seeds and stacks of dried plums. One entire section encompassed a herb and spice market; the heady scents made Hanna's head swim as they passed.

Yet few people seemed to be buying. The longest line lay ahead outside the old law courts where, by the mercy of the skopos, grain and olive oil were handed out to the poor each Hefensday. Women in patched clothing waited restlessly in line, peering ahead to see if they would make it to the gate before the allotment for this week had run out. Even the children stood with tired patience, too hungry to run and play, dazzled by the sun beating down on their heads. A trio of boys, their clothes ragged and their upper lips stained with snot, shouted nasty oaths at the two Eagles.

'Wendish dogs!'

'They're eating all our food! Pigs!'

'Their mother was a sow!'

Hanna picked up their pace. Many more folk waited sullenly in pockets of shade or leaned against the marble facings of the grand old buildings, half-fallen into disrepair.

Guardsmen lined the length of the colonnade, keeping an eye on a score of young toughs loitering on the steps of an old temple on the other side of the avenue. Murmured oaths could be guessed at, nothing more; some played at dice. A few spat in the direction of the street, but it was hard to tell whether they meant to insult Hanna and Rufus, or the city guards.

'Seems a few want for nothing,' said Rufus, 'and the rest are in want.'

'I've heard it said the war is draining the regnant's coffers. The palace servants told me it's worse now than it's ever been. They hate us because it's our king leading the war.'

'Won't it be best for Aosta once all the foreigners are driven out, and the nobles all bend their knee to one regnant?'

'I hope so,' she said fiercely, for wasn't that why she had turned her back on Hathui and ridden this far? Because she had faith in King Henry?

A man stumbled out into the street and collided with Hanna. His hands groped her chest as he murmured, 'Wendish whore!' His breath stank.

She shoved him off with a grunt as Rufus, startled, turned around to see four young toughs headed their way with ugly grins on their faces. The city guards watched passively.

Hanna grabbed Rufus' arm and tugged him onward. 'There are the gates!'

It was said that no gate in Darre did not have four churches built nearby upon the ruins of the old imperial temples. There were six within sight of the western gate, all but one simple structures of brick that could scarcely hold more than fifty worshipers. The sixth was a domed temple, cleared of pagan statues and rededicated to St. Mark the Warrior; his sword of righteousness, which grants strength to the believer, was painted in bright colors above the portico. But which was the church they sought?

'They're getting closer!' gasped Rufus.

A pair of fraters hurried up the steps of St. Mark's. Closer by, a trio of clerics in the modest robes of novices walked past; the shortest of the young women glanced her way.

'I beg you, my lady—'

The novices seemed neither to hear nor understand her.

'Oh, shit,' swore Rufus. 'They've got knives.'

'Run for it.'

'Eagle!'

Carried on a litter by four men, a presbyter appeared out of the crowd. The four toughs veered off. Hanna knelt; Rufus dropped to both knees. The stone burned hot into her knee through the cloth of her leggings.

'Your Excellency,' she murmured breathlessly, heart still pounding with fear. 'We are honored at your notice.'

She recognized Brother Petrus. Bland and powerful, he had received her when she had first arrived in Darre and listened patiently and with aristocratic reserve to her message. She had not seen him since that day, when he had assured her that the matter would be brought to the king's attention just as soon as Henry returned from the south, but that it was too dangerous for her to ride south herself.

'Do you come often into the lower city?' he asked in the tone of a man who is surprised to see a heathen worshiping at the Hearth of God in Unity.

'Nay, Your Excellency. I am not accustomed to its size. There are so many streets and alleys, and so many people.'

'True enough.' He looked toward the law courts, where the crowd gathered to receive grain and food was growing ever more restless as the day came toward its end. Many still stood empty-handed. 'So many people, and not all of them with God's best interests at heart. It is best to be careful. Even some of your own Wendish folk agitate in the shadows, weaving intrigue among the innocent and the gullible.'

'I am sorry to hear that my countryfolk are so wicked, Your Excellency.'

'As would any person be who trusts in God. There is one woman in particular, a servant who calls herself Aurea, who is no better than a goad on the flail wielded by the Enemy. Beware of those who bear false tales out of turn in the hope of stirring up trouble.'

Because her head was bent in respectful obeisance, the brim of the hat concealed her expression. Strange that he should mention Aurea, to whom she had spoken up in the attic only two days before.

'Have you spoken to this woman, Daughter?'

'I have. I am always happy to find those within the palace who speak my own tongue, Your Excellency, those who are my countryfolk.'

'Did she speak aught of conspiracies and treachery?'

Only of clerics hidden like rats in the dungeon. Eyes that could see through walls, and traveling Eagles. But perhaps Hanna was making a conspiracy where none existed. Perhaps the woman had hoped for nothing more with her tales than an appreciative audience. Brother Petrus could not know that Hanna had spoken to Hathui over a year ago in the southern forests of Wendar. He did not know what she knew.

Faced with her silence, he went on. 'I hope you will come to me, Daughter, if there is anything you wish me to hear. You need only to ask for me at the skopos' palace. You Wendish Eagles are said to see all kinds of things that the rest of us cannot. I know you are held to be loyal without measure to your king.'

He spoke a word in Aostan, and his servants carried him on.

She glanced around as she rose to make sure no suspicious souls approached them, but the young toughs had vanished into the crowd. His words chilled her. Hadn't Aurea spoken almost exactly those same words: 'an Eagle might see all kinds of things'? Was it a slip of the tongue or simply a chance similarity of phrase? Did he mean it as a warning?

'I don't like it,' remarked Rufus, 'when those high and mighty church folk know who I am. Where I come from, the old folks used to say that it's better to be a pig foraging in the woods with hunger in your gut and no one to know your name than a fat-bellied rooster strutting in the farmyard and all eyes on you when feasting time comes around.'

'He saved us from a fight.'

'True enough. Never turn your back on small blessings.'

Nearby, the three clerics had paused while one among their number shook a stone out of her shoe.

'Come, now, Sister Heriburg,' said one of her companions tartly in clear Wendish. 'We shan't get a place to sit in St. Asella's chapel if you do not hurry. You know how crowded it gets when Brother Fortunatus gives his sermon.'

'I beg pardon, Sisters. We are Wendish Eagles, servants of the king, come to worship at St. Asella's. May we accompany you there?'

'Any true servant of King Henry is welcome to keep company with those of us who are loyal clerics in his schola,' said the tall one in the same tart voice she had just used to scold her companion.

'I thank you, my lady,' replied Hanna politely. 'We will keep company with you gladly. I am called Hanna, and this is Rufus.'

These were highborn girls, unaccustomed to chatting idly with commoners; the quiet one looked alarmed at the introduction of names, and the other two hesitated before hurrying on with Hanna and Rufus at their heels.

'You are clerics in King Henry's schola, my lady?' Hanna prompted, an imp of mischief directing her tongue. She wanted to see how they would respond. 'Did you march here with the king?'

'We have lived in Darre for over two years now,' said the tall one as they passed the portico of St. Mark's and turned left down a side street. A tower marked an old church built on a more ancient foundation. Inside, a half dozen slits in the walls illuminated the interior. Two clerics lit sconces in the wall as these patches of sunlight faded.

There were benches set in the nave, most filled with sundry folk speaking Wendish. Their companions moved to the front to sit with their clerical brethren. Hanna squeezed in beside Rufus toward the back, resting her floppy hat on her knees.

She saw no sign of Aurea. Had she misunderstood the woman? The whitewashed walls of the small church whispered no answers; it did not even have painted windows, only slits to let in air, although the thick stone kept the interior cool. She was no longer sweating. Two clerics ascended toward the choir along the nave, lighting vesper lamps set on tripods at the end of each row of benches. At the front, a deacon entered the rounded choir from the sanctuary and approached the altar, where she raised her hands in the blessing as she began to sing the liturgy.

'Blessed is the Country of the Mother and Father of Life, and of the Holy Word revealed within the Circle of Unity, now and ever and unto ages of ages.'

'Amen,' Hanna murmured, the service sliding smoothly into her thoughts and her lips moving in the responses without a need for her to think.

'In peace let us pray to our Lord and Lady.'

'Lord have mercy. Lady have mercy.' Yet how did Ivar pray, if he were even still alive? How did heretics pray? Her gaze was caught by the flame burning beside her, a flickering golden glow, restless but strong, that hissed as if whispering secrets. Were those tiny wings in the heart of the flame? Were those shadows moving within the curtain of flame that danced before her? Beyond the veil of fire, she saw onto another place.

Six men and a woman make their way along a deserted track through broken woodland as afternoon creeps toward evening. Briefly the sun shines, but then a shower passes over their party, driven northward by a strong southerly wind. The wind blows back the hood of one of the men. She recognizes his red hair first before anything, and after that the lineaments of his face.

It is Ivar. Joy chokes her. Is it possible he still lives?

Heat burns her face as she leans closer, trying to get his attention.

'Hanna? You'll burn yourself!'

She broke free of the vision to find herself in the church, blinking dry eyes, tears wicked away by the flame. The lamp hissed and flickered, but it was an ordinary flame, just like all the others that lit the nave.

'For healthful seasons, for the abundance of the fruits of the earth in a time of want, and for peace in this country, let us pray.'

'Hanna?' Rufus had hold of her arm in a painfully tight

grasp. 'Are you feeling faint? I thought you would fall into the lamp.'

'Nay.' Her tongue felt swollen, and she was dizzy, both heartsick and elated. 'Eagle's Sight.'

He flushed, easy to see with that complexion, and dipped his head shamefacedly. 'I know what they say, and what some of the others claim, but I've never seen any vision in fire or water.' He hesitated, realized he still clutched her arm, and let go as though she were poison. His expression had a dark stain on it, and his lips were twisted down. 'What about you?'

She shook her head too quickly. 'Just shadows in the flames. Like now. Just shadows.'

'Blessed are the humble and patient, for the grace of God shall descend upon them at the end of days. Blessed are the pure in heart, for their glory will shine forever.'

'Amen,' she and Rufus said in unison with the rest of the congregation.

Believing Ivar might yet be alive was almost worse than resigning herself to his death.

A cleric came forward to deliver the Hefensday lesson. The man looked vaguely familiar, but probably that was only because of his beardless face and the cut of his hair, trimmed and shaven in the manner of a male cleric who has put aside the duties of a man of the world, husbanding and warring and sowing, for the cares of the Hearth. He waited a moment for folk to shift on the hard benches, for silence to open a space for listening. The stone walls muted all sound; she could not hear a single thing from outside, as though they were no longer in Darre but translated to holy space, sundered from the world.

'I pray you, sisters and brothers, take heed of the lesson that God utters on this day, the feast day dedicated to St. Dominica.'

The words of the liturgy were familiar to her; she knew what the prayers meant even when she did not recognize every single word. But the startling change – that he was speaking in Wendish – struck her so hard after so many months in Aosta hearing a foreign language day in and day out, that it took her a moment to follow what he was saying.

'So it happened that one day after the rains the beloved child walked out among the hills. As she walked along the stream's edge below the overhanging cliff, the rocks came loose and fell down upon her, burying her.

'Her powerful companions howled and cried out in vain! The lion roared and the bull bellowed and the great eagle screamed, but they could not find the child beneath the vast expanse of rubble.

'The humble wren, least of birds, flew to the top of the pile of rocks and sang, "Hush!" When all at last quieted, they heard the small voice of the child, crying. She was still alive underneath the rock.

'How the lion roared and the bull bellowed and the great eagle screamed! But despite their powerful voices, and their biting claws, and all the strength of their limbs, they could not shift the rock.

'The blind mole peeked out from the earth and said, "I can dig a hole to the trapped child, and through this hole she can crawl to safety."

'"But how long will it take?" objected the wise owl. "Surely the child will die before a creature as small and weak as you can dig a tunnel large enough for her to creep through!"

'The lion roared, and the bull bellowed, and the great eagle screamed, but all their powerful voices joined together could not feed the child trapped beneath the rock.

'The small brown field mouse called her sisters and brothers, her cousins, and all her kin. They slipped between cracks in the rock and carried in bits of bread and acorn cups of water to the trapped child, and in this way kept her alive for seven days while the patient mole dug a hole deep through the earth broad enough for the child to escape.

'And the lion and the bull and the great eagle remained silent, when they saw that it was the work of their humble brethren that saved the child.'

Hanna rested her head on clasped hands. Strange that he should seem to be speaking intimately a message meant for her ears. Looking up, she noticed the three young clerics seated on the foremost bench. As though her gaze were a greeting, the tall one glanced back. Hadn't this young woman called one of her companions 'Sister Heriburg,' the same name mentioned in passing by the servant woman, Aurea?

'They know her,' she murmured.

'I beg pardon?' whispered Rufus.

'Nay, nothing,' she demurred, but in her gut she knew. They wanted her to see them and to hear this lesson about the work of the humble and the small. The knowledge coursed up through the soles of her feet, making her unsteady. It almost seemed the lamp beside her was swaying.

Ivar's sister Rosvita *was* alive, buried in the dungeon because she had witnessed what the powerful wanted kept secret. Hathui had told the truth.

A rumble hummed up from the ground, a grinding roar like a distant avalanche. The lamp swung on its chains as the feet of the tripod skipped along stone. A woman sobbed out loud. Under Hanna's rump, the bench rocked as though shoved.

Rufus swore. 'Damn! Not another one!'

Voices rose in agitation and fear. People bolted for the door, and by the time Hanna realized that the rumbling and rocking had stopped, the church had half cleared out. Yet from outside, through the open doors, she still heard a hue and cry. By the Hearth, the cleric who had been preaching stepped aside to talk to the three young clerics; they looked drawn and anxious as they listened to the growing clamor. A distant horn sounded the call to arms.

A woman hurried back in through the doors, followed by a dozen companions.

'Shut the doors!' she cried in Wendish. 'There's a riot! They say they're going to kill every Wendishman they can find!' Folk rushed to the doors, shutting them and stacking benches as a barrier. 'Ai, Lady! It was the breadline! All those folk went wild.'

The door shuddered as a weight hit it from the outside, causing the left door to creak, shift, and crack open.

'Help us!' shrieked one of the men up front. With several

companions he slammed the opening door shut.

Hanna ran forward with Rufus and set her shoulder to the doors. Blows vibrated through her body as she leaned hard against the wood. Through the wood she heard the screaming of men and women, their words incomprehensible because of rage and the heady wildness of a mob inflamed by hunger and fear. Incomprehensible because it was a foreign tongue, not her own. An ax blow shook the door, followed by a second.

'We'll never hold out! They'll kill us all!'

A babble of voices rose within the heart of the church as the assembled worshipers wept, moaned, and wailed.

'I pray you!' cried the cleric who had spoken the lesson. 'Do not despair. Do not panic. God will protect us.'

'They only have one ax,' shouted Hanna between blows, 'or else they'd be chopping more quickly. Is there another way out of the church? Or another way in that we should be guarding?'

'Oh, God,' wailed an unseen soul in the sobbing crowd. 'The deacon's sanctuary has a door to the alley!'

Too late. An unholy shriek cut through the wailing. The deacon who had led the service staggered out from the low archway that led back to the sanctuary. When she fell forward onto her knees, they all saw the knife stuck in her back.

'Use the benches!' shouted Hanna as the door shook. The mob had evidently given up pushing from outside and was now waiting for the ax wielder to destroy the door. 'Pick them up and use them as shields. Throw them. Two can lift one.'

Her muscles throbbed already, bruised under the assault. The door shuddered again. Splinters, like dust, spit from the wood. How soon would the ax cut through? It was only a matter of time. Yet if they left the door to face the new assault, they would be hit from two sides.

No one moved. Two ragged men burst from the archway. The leader stumbled over the deacon and went down hard, cursing as his companion tripped over him.

'Rufus!' Hanna leaped away from the door with Rufus right behind her and ran toward the altar. 'Grab a bench!' she shouted to the paralyzed clerics, who stared as the two toughs got up and hoisted broken chair legs like clubs. She grabbed an end of a bench as Rufus hoisted the other end.

'Out of the way.' The male cleric shoved the three young women aside.

'Heave!'

Hanna and Rufus launched the bench as the two toughs ran forward. It slammed into them, knocking them backward to the floor. She heard a bone snap. One screamed. The other, falling hard, cracked the back of his head on the stone and went limp.

She grabbed the chair leg out of his hand. Rufus tugged the bloody knife out of the deacon's back. The tall cleric had gone over to the deacon's side and with commendable composure had got hold of her ankles to drag her aside, leaving a trail of blood.

'More will come in that way,' said Hanna. 'I'm surprised they haven't already.' She turned to the cleric who had given the lesson. 'Can the sanctuary door be fixed closed?'

'Yes. I'll show you.'

'Is there nothing you can use for a weapon?'

'I cannot fight in such a manner,' he said quietly, but he picked up the holy lamp that lit the Hearth and jerked the altar cloth off the Hearth with such a tug that the precious silver vessels fell clattering to the floor, holy wine and pure water splashing onto the stone and running along cracks to mingle with the deacon's blood. 'This will shield me somewhat. Sister Heriburg,' he added, handing the lamp to the stoutest of the young clerics, 'you must see that these criminals do not escape or harm anyone else.'

'How can I?'

'You must.' To Hanna and Rufus: 'This way.'

Hanna had never stood in any choir, never ventured beyond the Hearth into any sanctuary where deacons and clerics meditated in silence and communed with God. In such places deacons slept, and the church housed its store of precious vestments and vessels for the service. She caught a closer glimpse of the two faded tapestries hanging on the choir walls, then ducked under the arch with the cleric and Rufus behind

her, the club upraised to ward off blows. Two steps took them
down into a low, square room, drably furnished with a simple
cot, a chair, a table, and a chest. Two burning lamps hung
peaceably from iron tripods. The table lay upended, torn pages
of a prayer book strewn along the floor in among broken fragments of a smashed chair. The chest lay open, and a young
man with dirty hair and dirtier clothing pawed through it so
eagerly that he did not see Hanna and the others come up
behind him. It was impossible to tell from this angle if he had
a knife. Alarmingly, there was no one else in sight, although
the door that led outside, cut under an even lower arch, stood
ajar.

All this she took in before the youth looked up. With a
startled grimace, lips pulled back like a dog baring its teeth,
he groped at his belt.

'The door,' cried Hanna, jumping forward. She brought
the chair leg down on his head as a knife flashed in his hand.
He dropped like a stone. The knife fell between a pair of
holy books he'd discarded on the floor in his haste to find
treasure.

Distantly, through the open door, she heard a second horn
call followed by shouts of triumph and fear.

With a thud, the side door slammed into place, muffling
the sounds from outside. Grunting with effort, Rufus dropped
a bar into place. Through the archway that led back into the
church, Hanna heard an odd scuffling sound. The steady
drone of weeping and wailing drowned out the noise of the
crowd pounding at the front doors.

'Why isn't there such a bar for the church doors?' she asked
as the three of them stared first at each other and then at the
youth lying unconscious on the floor.

'The door leading to God's Hearth must always remain
open,' said the cleric, 'and there is always a cleric or deacon
awake to tend the lamps by the Hearth. But thieves may sneak
in through the side door, seeking silver and silk while God's
servant rests here in solitude. What do we do with this one?'

This one had warts on his nose and hands and pustulant
sores along his lower lip. His stink made her cough. His wrists

were as thin as sticks. Hunger had worn shadows under his eyes. Drool snaked down from his slack mouth into his fledgling beard.

'Is there rope?' Rufus was grinning a little, sweating and excited. 'We've got to tie him up.'

The youth moaned. They heard a shout and the slap of footsteps, and one of the young novices burst into the room.

'The king has returned! He's at the gates. The mob is running away. We're saved, Brother Fortunatus!'

They were all too tense to relax even at such hopeful news, and Brother Fortunatus gave Hanna such a look as an escaped slave might give to his companion just before the chains are clapped back on them.

'For now, Sister Gerwita.' He nodded at the moaning youth. 'Drag him outside and let him go. I would not hand any poor soul over to the justice of the city guard.'

'But—' Rufus began.

'Nay,' said Fortunatus. 'He still had his knife on him, so he's not likely the one who assaulted Deacon Anselva. His only crime is poverty, and he stole nothing, after all. The other two must face justice for what they did to the deacon.'

Cheers broke out from the church, echoing through the archway. Hanna grabbed the youth's ankles and dragged him out the door after Fortunatus unbarred and opened it.

Although twilight hadn't yet faded into full darkness, the walls leaned so closely together in the alley that she had to pick her way by feel, stepping more than once into piles of noxious refuse. The stink was overwhelming. She shoved the boy up against the wall of the church. He stirred, retching. She stumbled back to the open door. Looking up the alley, she saw the thoroughfare beyond – torches and lamps lighting a magnificent procession. A roar of noise echoed among the buildings, the ring of hooves on paved streets, shouting and cheering and an undercurrent of jeering in soft counterpoint amid the clamor. Smoke stung her nostrils. The peal of the fire bell summoned the city guard.

When she slipped back inside, bending to get under the lintel without banging her head, Rufus barred the door behind her as she checked the soles of her sandals in the lamplight to make sure she wasn't tracking in anything awful.

They took both of the lamps as they returned to the choir. The front doors had been thrown open. Most of the worshipers had flocked outside, but a dozen waited by the doors, too cautious to venture out. The walls looked different; holding high her lamp, Hanna realized they were bare. The two tapestries lay on the floor, rolled up tight around the two criminals' bodies; it was odd to see them squirming so. The tall cleric and the one called Gerwita huddled by the Hearth, whispering to Brother Fortunatus, who still held the altar cloth. The third knelt beside the wounded deacon, holding a lion-shaped lamp in one hand. With a pad of cloth torn from her own robe she applied pressure to the wound on the deacon's back. Blood stained the prone woman's white garment.

Hanna bent down beside her. 'Sister Heriburg, will the deacon live?'

She had a bland, amiable face but a glance that hit like the sight of black storm clouds in winter. 'I pray she will. It is in God's hands now.'

Rufus had gone to the doors to examine the damage done by the ax. Here in the silence of the choir they were alone except for the muffled groans and panicked curses coming from the men bundled up in the tapestries. They had only two lights. Another five or six burned along the nave, but most of the remaining lamps had been taken forward to the doors by worshipers, making a veil of light that shrouded the night scene beyond.

'Are you loyal to Henry, Eagle?' asked Brother Fortunatus, coming up behind her.

'Yes. That is why I came.'

'From Princess Theophanu.'

Although she had not met this man in the months she had loitered in the regnal palace, she knew that her arrival had surely been gossiped about from the lowest halls to the highest. 'I rode here at the behest of Princess Theophanu to bring a message to her father, the king.'

'Was there no Eagle who came to Theophanu in the time you were with her?'

She rose stiffly. Her legs ached from the effort she'd spent bracing; her bruised shoulder throbbed. Even her fingers hurt from gripping the chair leg so tightly before she'd hit the thief. The two women now flanked Brother Fortunatus: the tall one, still nameless, and timid Gerwita. They hardly looked like a foul cabal of conspirators. Wasn't it possible that Henry had enemies who might seek to entrap the ones most loyal to him? If Hathui had told the truth, those who now controlled Henry would seek to eliminate anyone, even a common, powerless Eagle, who might act against them.

Anything might be possible.

From outside, the roar of acclamation rose to a high pitch as some notable – perhaps Henry and Adelheid themselves – approached down the thoroughfare.

'No Eagle came to Theophanu while I was with Her Highness, but I met one of my comrades north of the mountains who had come from Aosta. She rode one way, and I another. Where she is now I do not know.' The memory of Hathui's expression, at the end of their conversation so many months ago, made her throat tighten. Yet for all the bitterness that curdled in her when she thought of Sanglant and Bulkezu, she could not wish Hathui ill. 'I pray she is well.'

The cheering swelled at the porch of the church.

'Beware—' Fortunatus broke off as Rufus called to her and the people gathered at the doors cried out in thanksgiving as they knelt with heads bowed. A tall, elegant figure moved forward through the glow of lamplight like an angel advancing out of the darkness to lead the benighted to salvation.

Only this was not an angel.

She knew him even before she saw him clearly. No person who had seen him could ever forget him and especially not when he was burnished, as now, by the light of a dozen lamps and the heartfelt acclaim of people who had been rescued from certain death by his timely arrival. A fire burned in her heart, and she took a few steps forward before she remembered what he had done to Liath. She scarcely heard the whispers and footfalls behind her as Hugh entered the church.

Presbyter Hugh, they called him here. Everyone talked about him, but it was easy to ignore talk. Talk did not have golden hair, a handsome face, and a graceful form.

'Is this where it happened?' he asked with outraged concern. He caught sight of Rufus. 'An Eagle! I thank God you survived. Lady have mercy! Look how they tried to chop their way in through the door.'

It was impossible not to be moved by that beautiful voice, both resonant and soothing. Impossible not to be lulled, until the moment when he looked up, directly *at* her.

She stood frozen halfway down the nave, forgetting how she had walked so far, drawn as though by a tether line being reeled in.

He saw her.

He *knew* her.

'He always knows.' Liath had cried, long ago in Heart's Rest. And he had known that day. He had returned to stop Hanna from speaking with her friend. He wanted no comfort given to the one he had made his slave.

Just like Bulkezu.

Such a shudder of misgiving passed through Hanna's body that the lamp trembled in her hand. He smiled gently, and she remembered the way he had looked at her that day in Heart's Rest in the gloom of the chapel: as if he were measuring her to decide if she posed a threat to him.

He had dismissed her then. She was only a common girl. He might recognize her face, because of her link to Liath, but she doubted he remembered anything else about her.

It was better when they didn't know your name.

'We heard news of an Eagle come from Princess Theophanu,' he said, walking forward. She remembered to kneel; she found another bruise that way, on her right knee, that she'd gotten without knowing. He paused beside her without looking at her, because he was examining the choir with a mild expression of surprise. 'Are you the last one here?'

Rufus stood behind him, looking puzzled as he, too, stared

at the choir and the writhing tapestries. She turned her head. The four clerics were gone.

'The other clerics—' Rufus began.

'—fled with the rest, in fear of their lives,' she interrupted. 'We are all that is left. Your Excellency, if I may rise, there is an injured deacon and the two criminals who assaulted her. She is gravely injured.'

Hugh knelt beside the deacon, lifting the bloodstained pad of cloth from the wound. He frowned and set fingers carefully along the curve of her throat, and shook his head. 'She is dead. May God have mercy on her soul.' After murmuring a blessing, he looked up. 'Do you know her name?'

'I do not, Your Excellency,' she lied. 'My comrade and I came here to St. Asella's today because we were told we might hear the lesson delivered in Wendish, which our souls craved to hear after so many months in a foreign land.'

'Ah.' He dabbed a smear of blood off his forefinger onto the deacon's robe and rose. 'Eagle.' He indicated Rufus. 'Certain of the king's soldiers wait outside. See that these criminals are taken away to the regnant's dungeon. I will send clerics from the queen's schola to take away this poor deacon's body and prepare it for burial.'

At the Hearth he studied the holy lamp set on the bare stone floor, the scattered vessels, and the altar cloth spilled carelessly over them. 'A grave crime,' he said as he picked up the altar cloth and the vessels and set all to rights, smoothing the gold-trimmed cloth down over the Hearth and placing holy lamp and precious vessels in the precise arrangement on its surface, reflecting the glory of the Chamber of Light, which awaits all faithful souls.

'It is a grave crime to assault and conspire against those who serve God and the regnant.' His gaze marked her, who was waiting only for his permission to go. He had beautiful eyes, a fine, dazzling light blue, but in their depths she saw a splinter of ice. 'Isn't it, Hanna?'

'Your Excellency.' It was all she could say.

'You will accompany me. Their majesties King Henry and Queen Adelheid will wish to hear your report. And so will I.'

2

Herford Monastery had the slightly run-down look of an estate that has been neglected by an incompetent steward, but as Ivar and his companions approached the main gate, they saw scaffolding around the church tower and men laboring on its ladders and platforms, whitewashing the walls. Beyond the low double palisade that fenced off the monastic buildings from the surrounding estate, a group of lay brothers bound new thatch on the roof of the monks' dormitory. Outside these walls men sawed and hammered, constructing benches and tables, while a trio of laborers built a kiln with bricks.

The gatekeeper had big hands, a big nose, and a relentlessly cheerful disposition once he realized he had visitors of noble lineage. 'Come in, come in, friends. We'll be glad to hear tidings from the east.' He called to a scrawny boy climbing in an apple tree. 'Tell the guest-master I'm bringing visitors up.'

The child raced ahead. They followed more slowly, since the gatekeeper had a pronounced limp. His infirmity had not weakened his tongue. 'The old abbot died last year, may he rest peacefully in God's hands. Father Ortulfus has come new to us this spring, and though I do not like to speak ill of the dead, I will say that he has been setting things right, for I fear the monastery got run down. Father Ortulfus has even sent to Darre to see if a craftsman can be found to repair the unicorn fountain, which I'm sure you have heard of.'

'I fear we have not—' began Ivar, but the gatekeeper chattered on as he directed them to a side gate that opened into an enclosure surrounded by a high fence and populated by a tidy herb garden, a gravel courtyard, and three square log blockhouses, each one freshly plastered.

'Nay? You'll see it soon enough. Here my lady must retire, for women aren't allowed within the monastery walls. Father Ortulfus has brought his cousin to preside over the guesthouse and with her a few servingwomen to ensure the comfort of any ladies who may come by in traveling parties or with the king's progress. Alas, under Father Bardo's abbacy I fear that women were let walk as they wished in the monastery itself, but that shan't be happening now.'

A pretty young woman with a fair complexion and an almost insipidly sweet smile emerged from one of the cottages. 'What have you brought us, Brother Felicitus?' She couldn't have been more than fourteen. 'We haven't had a visitor in ages, although I fear, my lady, that you look in need of a bath.'

She clapped her hands. Three equally young women rushed out in her wake, followed at a more stately pace by an elderly matron who had the visage of a guard dog, ready to strike first and growl later.

'I am Lady Beatrix,' continued the first girl. 'Cousin of Father Ortulfus. He's my guardian now that my parents are dead, and he's brought me here until— Oh!'

'Oh!' echoed her young companions.

They had seen Baldwin.

'Best you be getting on, Brother Felicitus,' said the matron threateningly, setting herself between her charges and temptation.

Hathumod stepped forward with a martial gleam in her eye. 'I thank you for your welcome, Lady Beatrix. I am Hathumod. My grandmother was a count in the marchlands. I was first a novice at Quedlinhame—'

'How come you here, then, my lady?' interrupted Lady Beatrix, although she hadn't taken her gaze off Baldwin, who stared soulfully at a table set under an awning and laden with wine, bread, and cheese. 'Who are your companions?'

'I pray you, friends.' Brother Felicitus cleared his throat for emphasis. 'Let us retire to a more appropriate place.'

'I'm so hungry,' said Baldwin plaintively. 'We haven't eaten for two days.'

Lady Beatrix dashed to the table and brought Baldwin an entire loaf of white bread, still smelling of the oven.

'I thank you,' he said, turning the full force of his limpid gaze on her innocent face. Ivar thought she might swoon, or perhaps he was the one who was dizzy because the bread smelled so good and he was really so desperately hungry.

'Come, come.' Brother Felicitus herded his charges toward the gate. 'Let us not linger here, but if you will come with me I will see that you are fed.'

As they retreated, Hathumod began to speak. 'How I came here is a long tale. If you have the patience for it, it will change you utterly.'

'No tale can be too long if it is also exciting,' retorted Beatrix, 'for we bide unGodly quiet here. We get so few visitors—'

'She's very young,' said Brother Felicitus as he closed the gate, cutting them off from the women's enclosure. The men followed him through a gate in the log fence marking out monastic ground from the unhallowed buildings set up between the inner and outer fence. 'But her parents are dead, her elder brother rode east with Princess Sapientia, and her elder sister died at the battle to recover Gent. Duchess Liutgard is her distant kinswoman, but the duchess has been called south by the king on his great expedition to Aosta, so it fell to her cousin Ortulfus to give her guidance.' Having established his abbot's noble credentials, he felt free to eye Baldwin distrustfully, as if he feared Baldwin intended to lure poor young Lady Beatrix into a life of debauchery. Baldwin was too busy tearing up the loaf into four equal portions to notice.

'I feel sure Father Ortulfus is a Godly man,' said Ivar.

'So he is. Here is the laborers' dormitory.' Felicitus indicated a long hall with a porch set outside the inner wall. 'Those who are servants of the abbot, or of the king—' He nodded at the two Lions. '—reside here. Our circatore, Brother Lallo, will take care of you. Here he comes.'

Brother Lallo was brawny and immaculately groomed. For a circatore – the monk set in charge over the manual laborers – his hands were remarkably clean.

'Can they work?' he demanded, looking Gerulf and Dedi over and not appearing to like what he saw. They were all unkempt. 'I've a full house these days, for it's troubled times as you know, Brother Felicitus. I wish you would have consulted me first—'

'And risked sending them down the road to Oerbeck where they'll get no more than a thin broth for their supper? We are still the king's monastery, Brother, and God's house, and have an obligation to travelers.'

'And vagabonds, evidently!' replied Brother Lallo sourly. 'At least they don't have dogs with them! Come this way, then. You're stout-looking fellows, I'll give you that.'

'We are Lions in the king's service,' said Gerulf, with real annoyance.

Lallo blinked. 'Why aren't you with the king?'

Dedi seemed about to speak, but Gerulf signed him to silence. 'That is truly a long tale, and a cursed strange one, for I've seen such things as few would believe—' He broke off, rubbing his throat. 'Ach, well. My throat's too dry to talk much.'

'Come, come, then,' said Lallo eagerly. 'We can find you mead. There'll be porridge and apples for supper. A long tale would be welcome here.'

As Gerulf and Dedi walked off to the laborers' dormitory, Baldwin gave Ivar, Ermanrich, and Sigfrid their share of the bread. Ivar wolfed his down before they reached the inner gate, but all it did was make him hungrier.

At the inner gate Brother Felicitus handed them over to the rotund guest-master, who saw them washed and fitted with clean robes appropriate to their status and brought them to the abbot's table just in time for the evening's feast.

Father Ortulfus was young, vigorous, and handsome. He had a sarcastic eye but a gleam of humor in his expression as he rose to welcome his guests. The dozen monks seated at the abbot's table gaped at Baldwin, who had cleaned up nicely.

'My spies brought news of your arrival. There are places for you on these humble benches.'

Since all the furniture in the abbot's dining room was elaborately carved and painted, as befit the son of a noble house, Ivar merely smiled. 'You are most gracious, Father Ortulfus. We have traveled a most strange road. I am Ivar—'

'—son of Count Harl of the North Mark and his late wife, Lady Herlinda,' finished Ortulfus. 'Before I became abbot, I had the honor of being a member of Biscop Constance's schola. I will not soon forget the trial of Hugh of Austra before an assembled council in Autun. Nor, I suppose, will you, Brother Ivar.'

Ivar knew his fair complexion branded him, since his blushes could never be hidden. His cheeks burned. 'Nay, I suppose I will not.'

Baldwin had already found a seat next to a slender monk of aristocratic bearing whose expression was, alas, not at all pure as he offered to share his platter, on which lay a steaming and handsomely spiced whole chicken. Ermanrich and Sigfrid held back at the door, waiting for Ivar's reaction.

'God knows Father Hugh was arrogant,' said Ortulfus as his retinue of monastic officials and highly placed brother monks watched avidly. 'I suppose it comes of being the son of a margrave.' He glanced at Baldwin before smiling mordantly at Ivar. 'I admit, Brother Ivar, that I wasn't sorry to see you stand against Father Hugh, even if it was only because that sorcerer they spoke of had enchanted you as well.'

'Perhaps she did,' retorted Ivar, stung and flattered at the same time, 'or perhaps Hugh was lying. I could tell you—'

'And I trust you will,' interrupted the abbot smoothly, 'but I beg you to take drink and food first, for you look famished. When Biscop Constance raised me to the abbacy of Herford Monastery, she strictly enjoined me to see that travelers were always well cared for. Will you not share a platter with me, Brother Ivar?'

No one could refuse such an honor. In this way, the four visitors were separated from each other and each given to one of the abbot's officials to entertain. Wine flowed freely. The

abbot did not stint when it came time to eat. The savory
chicken was all Ivar could have hoped for, and it was suc-
ceeded by a clear broth to cleanse the palate, after which the
meat course arrived, a side of roasted beef so heavy it took
two servants to carry the platter. Three types of pudding followed the meat, each one richer than what came before, and
there were also apples, pears, plums, cherries, and the sticky
honey cakes common to feast days.

As the meal wore on, Ivar realized that this astounding
repast was, indeed, in honor of a saint's day. A young monk
with a face so undistinguished that one hesitated to look twice
at him sang most sweetly various hymns in praise of St.
Ingrith, she who was patron of weavers and benefactor to
every person who has faced down and wrestled with an unexpected setback.

The battle against the Quman had been fought in late
Aogoste. The feast day of St. Ingrith was celebrated in late
Setentre, almost a full month after the equinox. Impossibly,
in the two days since they had escaped the Quman, over one
month had passed here at Herford Monastery. Impossibly,
they had traveled from the eastern borderlands all the way to
the heart of Wendar by walking into – and out of – a barrow.

'You said you had a strange tale to tell us,' said Father
Ortulfus. 'I confess myself prey to the sin of curiosity, for I'm
thinking that your handsome companion is the infamous
young bridegroom of Margrave Judith, the same lad who vanished the night after Hugh of Austra's trial.'

Although he hadn't appeared to be paying attention to anything but his food, Baldwin leaped to his feet, ready to bolt.
'I won't go back to her!'

Ortulfus laughed in surprise. 'Truly, you will not. Can it
be you don't know that she was killed in a battle against the
Quman three years ago?'

The sickly sweet scent of plum wine made Ivar queasy.
The infirmarian burped. The singer faltered and fell silent,
and every man there turned to watch the abbot and his guest.

'I don't understand what you're saying,' said Ivar, pushing away his cup of plum wine. 'We saw Margrave Judith lead

her troops into battle against the Quman not one month ago, under the command of Princess Sapientia and Prince Bayan.'

The monks at table set down spoons and knives as they glanced nervously, or meaningfully, toward Father Ortulfus. Ivar studied them. Each man wore robes and a sigil to identify his place within the monastic order. The abbot wore an ivory Circle of Unity incised with perfectly articulated scenes in miniature from the life of the blessed Daisan. Beside him sat the rotund guest-master with his cloak pinned by a brooch in the shape of a wine barrel, signifying hospitality. The abbot's trusted second-in-command, the prior, wore a dozen keys of all shapes and sizes on a gold chain around his neck. The infirmarian had his caduceus, the cellarer his silver spoon, the chief scribe his pen, the novice master a stylus, and the sacrist a little golden vessel representing the oil used to light the holy altar. Even the servants, tending the braziers set in each corner to warm the room, wore brooches of bronze wire twisted into brooms, although with their burly shoulders and military bearing they looked as if they had only recently come from fighting in the wars.

'My friend,' said Father Ortulfus, measuring his words, 'Prince Bayan has been dead these two years, killed at the battle of the Veser River. It's a long road from the marchlands here to Herford, one that can scarcely have been traversed in a month even by such stout fellows as you.' He moved his wine cup a hand's width to the right.

A servingman entered, bent to whisper in the sacrist's ear, and stood back to wait. With a nod of apology, the sacrist rose.

'I pray you, Father, we've run out of oil for the Hearth lamp.'

'Go on.'

The sacrist left, closing the door behind him.

Father Ortulfus went on. 'After the trial at Autun, the court supposed that you had escaped Margrave Judith's clutches with the aid of Prince Ekkehard, whose preference for Lord Baldwin had become, shall we say, well known. When we heard that Prince Ekkehard had married the new margrave,

Gerberga, those of us who remembered the trial assumed that the marriage was in some measure payment for his earlier theft of Judith's young husband. So you must imagine that your appearance here, at this late date, raises more questions than it answers.'

'Do sit down,' said Baldwin's companion with an unctuous smile. 'Won't you have more honey cake?'

Baldwin stubbornly remained standing.

'You need not fear that any of us are loyal to the kinfolk of Margrave Judith,' added Father Ortulfus. 'We are all first and foremost servants of our most gracious and magnificent biscop and duke, Constance.'

Both Ermanrich and Sigfrid looked at Ivar.

Ivar rose slowly. 'Baldwin, I pray you. Sit down.' With a pretty frown, Baldwin sat. 'Is this some trick, Father Ortulfus? We have traveled far and by strange paths, and we have witnessed miracles, not least of which was that God delivered us from the Quman. We have been given by God the obligation to bring the truth to those of you who still linger in darkness, for it has come to us to know that the church has taught a falsehood these many years. For God so loved the world that She gave to us Her only Son, that He should take upon himself the measure of our sins.'

Ermanrich took up the litany. 'He came before the Empress Thaissania, she of the Mask, and He would not bow down before her, for He knew that only God is worthy of worship. The empress had him flayed, as they did do to criminals in those days, and His heart was cut out and thrown into the courtyard, where it was torn into a hundred pieces by the dogs. Aren't we, ourselves, those dogs?'

'I knew it!' thundered the prior. 'Such babblings as we've heard from vagabonds this past year could not have sprung fully grown out of nowhere. Here's the plague's root!'

'"A novice poisoned by heresy."' The abbot had elegant fury to spare. His disdain and disgust were a well-honed weapon. 'So you were accused when you came forward at the trial of Hugh of Austra, Brother Ivar. Do you and your companions deny that the Mother and Father of Life brought forth the universe through the Word? Do you still profess this vile heresy of the Redemption?'

'It isn't heresy! The king's own sister, who is abbess at Quedlinhame, ordered Sigfrid's tongue cut off as punishment because he kept speaking the truth. Yet he speaks with a purer voice than you or I, because of the miracle, when the phoenix rose out of the fire. Why would God have restored his voice if he spoke only falsehoods?'

'It was the sign of the blessed Daisan.' Sigfrid's expression shone as he remembered that awesome moment when the phoenix's wings had unfurled and it had risen in glory into the dawn, leaving a trail of flowers in its wake. 'For the blessed Daisan also rose from death to become Life for us all.'

'You are still polluted,' said Father Ortulfus. 'If you will walk with God, then walk in silence and free your heart from the Enemy's grasp. Let there be no more of these tales, which spread like a plague upon the Earth!'

Too late Ivar recognized the servants for what they were: retired soldiers. Even the abbot had the bearing of a man who had fought in a battle or two as part of the biscop's military host. They were many, and Ivar and his friends were few.

'But there *was* a phoenix,' objected Baldwin. 'I *hate* it when people don't believe me.'

'Where did this miracle take place?' demanded the prior.

'In the borderlands, some days east of Gent,' said Ivar.

'A conveniently long distance from here,' said the abbot. 'Have you any other witnesses?'

'The villagers saw it,' said Ermanrich.

'The villagers are not here, my friend. What of the Lions who accompany you? Or Lady Hathumod?'

'Prince Ekkehard saw it, as did all of his companions,' said Baldwin.

'Prince Ekkehard abides far to the east as well, and is now married to Margrave Gerberga—'

'He does not!' retorted Baldwin, who was never more indignant than when he was utterly sure of his ground. 'He's abbot of St. Perpetua's in Gent. He can't be married. And he was just at the battle with us. I saw him cut down!'

'It's said Prince Ekkehard survived many things, including battles, captivity, and his own treasonous actions. I think your account must be confused, Brother Baldwin.'

'It is *not*!'

'Baldwin.' Ivar had a bad feeling that he was missing something very important. 'Father Ortulfus, you must forgive us if we seemed confused. It seems to me that only a few nights have passed since I saw both Margrave Judith and Prince Bayan alive. It seems an ill omen when I hear you speak as if they're dead.'

'Ivar!' Sigfrid's whisper was like the murmuring of ghosts on the wind. Sigfrid had thought of something that the rest had not.

'What is it?'

'The year,' said Sigfrid diffidently.

'The year?'

'What year is it?'

'Any fool knows that it's – um – what year is it, Sigfrid?'

The prior made to speak, but Father Ortulfus silenced him simply by lifting a hand. 'Go on, Brother Sigfrid,' said the abbot more kindly than before, although his sudden gentleness made Ivar unaccountably nervous. 'What year is it?'

'The year of our Lord and Lady, seven hundred and thirty,' answered Sigfrid quietly, but he had a sad little frown on his delicate face.

The door set into the wall behind the abbot's seat opened. 'My lord abbot,' said a brother, leaning his head in. 'The brothers have assembled and are waiting for you.'

It was time for prayer.

'It *was* a miracle,' said Sigfrid stubbornly. Despite his small size and unprepossessing appearance, he had both the intelligence and strength of faith to speak with an authority that made others listen. 'Ask if you will at Quedlinhame, for they will remember clearly enough when they cut out my tongue. How, then, can I speak now, if not by a miracle?'

'A difficult question to answer,' agreed Ortulfus, rising from his chair. His officials stood as well, leaving only Baldwin, Sigfrid, and Ermanrich on their benches. 'Be sure

I will write to Mother Scholastica for her account. But it will take many weeks or even months to get a reply, and I must decide what to do with you in the meantime. In truth, like any pestilence, heresy spreads quickly unless it is burned out.'

The monks blocked the doors, and while the chief of scribes hadn't the ready stance of a fighter, the others looked able to hold their own in a scrap.

They were trapped.

'You are three years too late,' added Father Ortulfus. 'This is the autumn of the year seven hundred and thirty-three since the Proclamation of the Holy Word by the blessed Daisan.'

Three years.

Sigfrid swayed, and Ermanrich made a squeak, nothing more, as his eyes widened in shock and his mouth dropped open with an 'o' of surprise and disbelief. No one knew better than Ivar how well Sigfrid attended to his studies. Sigfrid hadn't been wrong.

'What three years?' demanded Baldwin.

Ivar felt the grasp of that ancient queen who had appeared to him in the barrow, clutching him by the throat, squeezing the life from him, her hands cold as the grave. Magic had caught them in its grip, and now they were paying the price. They had escaped the Quman, but not at the cost of two nights. Not even at the cost of a month.

'Three years,' he whispered.

'Maybe we were asleep,' said Ermanrich, who for once had no joke to make, 'like that Lord Berthold we saw under the barrow.'

Monks murmured in surprise and alarm, and a startled servant, hearing that name, scurried out the door.

'It's a lie!' cried the prior, a bluff, soldierly looking man. 'They're liars as well as heretics! I was here the day Margrave Villam's son disappeared up in the stone crown among the barrows. He hasn't been seen since, and those tunnels were searched for any trace of the young lord.'

'We did see them!' protested Baldwin. 'I don't know why none of you believe anything we say!'

'I'll have silence,' said Father Ortulfus, his voice like the crack of a whip.

Cold air eddied in through the open door, disturbing the warm currents off the braziers. A misting rain darkened the flagstone pathways in the courtyard, seen beyond the brother waiting patiently in the doorway. In the center of the courtyard stood an elaborate fountain depicting four stone unicorns rearing back on their hind legs. A hedge of cypress hid the colonnade on the opposite side of the courtyard, but several stout monks loitered there. The abbot had left no escape route unguarded.

'My lord abbot,' said the servant again. 'The brothers are waiting for you to lead Vespers.'

'Come, then,' said Father Ortulfus grimly. 'Let us pray all of us together, for surely in this hour of trouble and confusion we have need of God's guidance.'

X

THE DEPTHS
OF HIS GAZE

1

'The Eagle, Your Majesty, recently come from Princess Theophanu at Osterburg.'

All morning every person in the palace had done nothing but talk about the triumphal procession of Henry and Adelheid into the city yesterday evening. With each hour the story grew in the telling: how the king had single-handedly quelled the riots, how the queen's mercy had saved children from death, how malcontents had thrown down their staves at the sight of Presbyter Hugh. God had smiled on the righteous in their campaigns in Aosta. They had won a great victory over the Jinna bandits outside the town of Otiorno. Although the Arethousan usurpers in southern Aosta still clung to power, the authority of Henry and Adelheid in northern and middle Aosta could now be called decisive.

Yet despite these epic feats, the scene confronting Hanna seemed strikingly domestic in its intimate charm. King Henry sat at a table in a private chamber, staring at the chessboard across which he and Duchess Liutgard of Fesse battled, ivory against black. Hanna knelt, grateful for the cushion of carpet beneath her knee. Because the king did not look up from his game immediately, she had time to study the room and its occupants.

The king looked little older than when she had seen him last. Had it really been three years since she had left his court at Autun bound for the east with a company of Lions? Much of that time seemed like a blur to her, passed in captivity or in illness. She had been on the road a long time.

About half of the royal garden was visible through an open window. A dark-haired child played in that garden, followed by a veritable swarm of attendants. Even at this distance Hanna heard her shrieks of delight as her nursemaids tried to catch her while she ran excitedly along the twisting pathways of a floral labyrinth, stumbling on unsteady feet but always climbing gamely up with a new burst of energy.

Mathilda, child of Henry and Adelheid, was the anointed heir to the kingdoms of Wendar and Varre and to the kingdom of Aosta. She was not much more than two years of age, but every one spoke of her as the child who would be empress in the years to come. No one spoke of Henry's children by Sophia at all, except muttered comments about the untrustworthiness of Arethousans bearing gifts. And soon Mathilda would not be sole child of Henry and Adelheid.

Adelheid reclined on a couch, and by the shape of the queen's belly Hanna judged her about midway through a second pregnancy. While a singer accompanied herself on a lute, the queen chatted in a desultory way with white-haired Duke Burchard and half a dozen noble courtiers. Adelheid had such a graceful way of using her hands to punctuate her speech, like birds or ribbons, that Hanna did not realize she was staring at the queen until she heard her own name spoken.

'Hanna! The king will hear your report now.'

Henry moved his castle to threaten Liutgard's biscop before turning.

'What did you say, Father Hugh?' With narrowed eyes, he examined Hanna, resting his chin on a cupped hand. Rings glinted on his fingers, set with gemstones, a banded cabochon of onyx, polished sapphire, and a waxy red carnelian. No spark of recognition lit his face, but perhaps he had already seen and noted her as she came in.

'Your Majesty.' Was there any hint, in his expression, in his carriage, in his tone, that Hathui's accusation had been true? She saw nothing damning. He seemed entirely himself, the regnant robed in dignity and luck. 'Your daughter, Her Most Royal Highness Princess Theophanu, sent me with an urgent message.' She bent her head, letting the words unfold that she had memorized over a year ago and kept fresh each day, awaiting this moment. '"To my lord father, His Glorious Majesty Henry, king of Wendar and Varre, I, his loyal daughter Theophanu, send heartfelt prayers for his health, his well-being, and his wisdom. I pray you, my lord king, let my pleading words awaken compassion in your heart for the troubled state of your kingdom."'

The litany of afflictions rolled easily off Hanna's tongue. Internal strife in Wendar and Varre. The Salian civil war spilled over into Varingia and Wayland. Famine and plague, flooding and hailstorms. A plague of heresy and the destruction wrought by the Quman invasion, under the command of Bulkezu, who had gone so far as to take Prince Ekkehard prisoner and with flattering words and rich presents turn him against his own countryfolk. The town of Echstatt burned and the palace at Augensburg still a ruin, where crows feasted on the corpses of Bulkezu's hapless prisoners. A rot spreading among the rye, poisoning the grain and any who ate it. A two-headed calf born alive. Tallia pregnant by Conrad, and the duke celebrating Penitire in Mainni as if he were a king. Biscop Constance's silence from Autun. The death of Duchess Rotrudis followed by plotting and quarreling among her unworthy heirs. Prince Bayan dead in battle against the invaders, and Princess Sapientia ridden east with Sanglant, who had taken over her army and made it his own. The traitor, Prince Ekkehard, promised to Margrave Gerberga.

Hugh made a stifled exclamation.

'*Margrave* Gerberga?' Henry sounded surprised, or perhaps puzzled.

'Judith was killed in battle three years ago against the Quman, who rode under the command of the same Bulkezu whom Prince Bayan and Prince Sanglant defeated at the Veser.' No need to regale them with the story of how Judith's head had survived as an ornament hanging from Bulkezu's belt. 'Her daughter Gerberga inherited Olsatia and Austra.'

'The margrave has taken a grave step by marrying Ekkehard, Your Majesty,' said Liutgard, speaking now that Hanna had already been interrupted. 'No person vowed to the church may be forced into marriage vows. Wasn't Ekkehard promised to the monastery?'

'Indeed,' said Hugh. Did he mourn the death of his mother? Or did he already know she was dead? 'Ekkehard was invested as abbot of St. Perpetua's in Gent. It was your own wish that he be offered to the church, Your Majesty. Do not forget the incident with Lord Baldwin. You did not give permission for Prince Ekkehard to be released from his vows and ride to war, much less be allowed to marry.'

'This is rebellion.' Henry caught hold of a captured black dragon and squeezed it until his knuckles turned white. 'My own sons and daughter have turned against me.'

'Princess Sapientia may only be Sanglant's pawn,' said Hugh.

'It seems likely,' said Liutgard, glancing toward Duke Burchard who, with the rest of the folk in the chamber, had drawn closer to listen. 'Sanglant has the stronger personality, if indeed it is true this is rebellion and not some other business. If the Quman invaded, then perhaps he has pursued the remnants of their army east to make sure they do not threaten Wendar again.'

'My God,' murmured Burchard. Contemplating the ruin the Quman had made of Avaria, he looked as frail as a withered stick blown about in storm winds. 'I should have been there to defend my people. Did the Quman meet no resistance at all? Were there none left to fight them?'

Hanna dared look at him directly, hearing shame in his voice. And oughtn't he be ashamed? He had not met his obligations to protect his own people. 'No one, my lord duke, except the common folk who died defending the land and their families. I don't know how many of the noble lords rode south with you to Aosta. Those who remained in Avaria paid off the Quman so they would go away. Lord Hedo's son abandoned his post to join the quarrel in Saony. I don't know what happened to him.'

'That's enough,' murmured Hugh.

She flinched, expecting a blow. It did not come. Her knee hurt where it pressed into the carpet, not so thick after all; not thick enough to protect her from the obstinacy of the marble floor.

'There is more to my message.'

Henry rose, cutting her off. 'I have heard enough.'

Even Liutgard looked surprised. No one ever cut off an Eagle's message.

Ever.

'Adelheid.' The king held out his hand, making ready to leave, and as he turned, Hanna looked up full into his face.

She saw his eyes clearly.

She had never forgotten the complex brown of his eyes, veined with yellow and an incandescent leaf-green. He had beautiful eyes, worthy of a regnant, deep, powerful, and compelling.

His eyes had changed.

She could still see the brown or at least the memory of that pigmentation. But the deep color had faded, washed into a watery, pale blue substance that writhed in the depths of his gaze like a wild thing imprisoned and straining against the bonds that held it within its cage.

With a shudder she swayed and caught herself on a hand. The emerald ring he had given her shone on her middle finger: an oiled, milky-green stone set in a gold band studded with garnets. She had sworn to bear witness for the king who had gifted her with that ring. But she was no longer sure the man standing here was the same man to whom she had given her loyalty, and for whom she had suffered and survived as a prisoner all those months.

'Your Majesty.'

Henry brushed past her. His companions and attendants followed him to the covered terrace that looked out over garden and maze.

'Papa! Papa!' Princess Mathilda shrieked in the distance, galloping to greet him.

A handful of worried looking men and women, all Wendish, remained behind.

'I would hear the rest of your message, Eagle,' said Duke Burchard, leaning on a cane as he stepped forward.

'I beg your pardon, my lord duke.' Hugh moved smoothly up beside her. He had not left her alone since they had departed St. Asella's the night before; she had even slept on a pallet in his bedchamber, beside his other servants. 'I am commanded to take down the Eagle's message in writing to deliver to King Henry when he has more leisure to contemplate Princess Theophanu's words. If you wish to interview this Eagle, you will have to wait until I have finished with her. I pray you will forgive me this inconvenience. Your distress is evident.'

Duke Burchard's lips tightened. He glanced at Duchess Liutgard. These signs were too fragile to stand up to scrutiny, and perhaps they were only the trembling quirks of an aging man.

'I know you are the king's obedient servant, Your Honor,' Burchard said at last. 'I pray that after you have taken the Eagle's statement you will allow one of your servants to escort her to my suite, so I may interview her. It appears she has firsthand knowledge of the Quman invasion.'

'So it does,' replied Hugh with a lift to his voice that made Hanna rise to her feet, as in a sparring contest. She was still waiting for the blow. He gestured to her to follow the servant who hovered always at Hugh's heels, carrying a satchel.

She glanced back as they left the chamber in time to see Burchard, looking after her, beckon to Liutgard. The two heads, one hoary and aged and the other young and bright, leaned together as the duke of Avaria and the duchess of Fesse bent close in intimate conversation. The door closed, cutting them off, and Hanna felt rushed along as Hugh led his retinue at a brisk pace under shaded porticos and out across the blistering hot courtyard that separated the regnal palace from the one where the skopos dwelled.

Too late, Hanna realized the direction they were heading. Shading her eyes did little to soften the sun's glare or the nagging fear that crawled in her belly. Her knee still hurt. They crossed under the shadow of a vast arch and passed more sedately along corridors inhabited only by the occasional scuff of a cleric's sandals on swept stone. Open windows offered glimpses onto bright gardens, golden and sere after summer's dryness, where the spray of fountains made rainbows in the air. She felt the breath of that moistened air as they passed, swiftly fading, the merest touch.

Where was Hugh taking her?

The golden halo of his hair was no less brilliant than the sun's light. His carriage was graceful, his attitude humble without false modesty, and each glimpse of his face reminded her of whispered tales of innocent children half asleep at their prayers catching sight of angels.

This was no dream.

Elderly presbyters bowed their heads respectfully as Hugh passed, and he paused to greet them with such unassuming sincerity that it was impossible to fault him for pride or self-aggrandizement. It was hard to imagine him in his humble frater's robes disdainfully leading services in the rustic church at Heart's Rest for a congregation of half-pagan and thoroughly common northern folk whom he obviously despised. Even Count Harl had seemed crude beside Hugh's elegance, and Hugh had not deigned to hide his scorn for Harl and Ivar and their rough northern kin. Yet to see Hugh here was to see a man so different in all ways that she felt dizzy, as though she were seeing double.

This man did not seem the same arrogant frater who had abused Liath, been outmaneuvered by Wolfhere, and who had left Heart's Rest in a fury. The one she had admired so foolishly because of the beauty of his form and the cleanness of his hands.

Perhaps he'd had a change of heart. Perhaps God had

healed him. Perhaps his beauty now masked nothing more than a heartfelt and pure desire to serve God and the king.

Did the outer form match the inner heart? Or was Hathui right?

If she had not seen a difference in the king's eyes, then her memory had played her false. If she had, then an aery daimone infested him, hidden within his mortal form and glimpsed only through the window made by his eyes.

Because she had never been in the skopos' palace before, because it was such a warren of rooms and branching corridors, she was lost by the time they halted in front of a set of double doors. Gilded with gold leaf hammered over a relief carved into the wood itself, the doors displayed scenes from the Ekstasis of the blessed Daisan, who prayed and fasted for seven days as his soul ascended through the seven spheres to the threshold of the Chamber of Light.

Guards outfitted in the gold tabards representing the glory of the skopos, God's representative on Earth, opened the doors to admit them into a hall striped with light from a succession of tall windows. At the far end of the hall stood a dais and a single chair and behind it a mural depicting the Translatus of the blessed Daisan, when he was taken bodily up into the Chamber of Light by the Lord and Lady, who are God in Unity; the Earth lay beneath his feet. The mural filled the entire wall, broken only at the far right by a curtain dyed the deep blue of lapis lazuli and worked into the design of the painting as the depths of the sea.

Otherwise, the hall was empty.

Hugh spoke to one of the guards, and the man hurried off down the corridor. Then Hugh walked into the hall, his footsteps echoing through the space as he crossed from shadow to light to shadow to light, Hanna and his servant behind him. The second guard remained at the open door.

They stopped at the foot of the steps, and there they waited, in silence.

In silence, Hanna studied the floor, strips of marble and porphyry set into expanding and contracting spirals. The ceiling arched high above, dimly perceived, each span glittering with intricate mosaics. Even the single chair had its fascination, the dark wood grain inlaid with ivory rosettes and geometric patterns made of gems mounted in gold. She had never seen so many amethysts in her life.

The servant coughed, clearing his throat. Hugh had closed his eyes, as though praying. But she didn't like to look at him. Looking at him reminded her of Bulkezu.

'Is there any man handsomer than you?' she had asked Bulkezu.

'One. I saw him in a dream.'

This could be a dream, except that from outside, through the windows, she heard the sound of a gardener raking dirt.

Better to be a pig starving in the forest than a fat rooster strutting in the farmyard when feasting time comes. She had once envied Liath for attracting Hugh's attentions. She knew better now.

Bells tinkled as a cleric stepped through the curtain and held it aside for a woman to pass. The lady wore a white robe overlaid with an embroidered silk stole falling over both shoulders, its fringed ends sweeping the floor. A gold torque shone at the woman's throat, and on her head, almost concealing her pale hair, she wore a golden cap. A huge black hound padded at her heels, growling softly as it lifted its head.

Hanna sank to her knees. She had never thought she would stand before the skopos, the most powerful person on Earth, closest to God Themselves. She bowed her head and clasped her hands so tightly that her knuckles turned white. Her bruised knee was already hurting, but she dared not look up into the face of the Holy Mother.

'Brother Hugh.' The skopos' voice was neither soft nor loud. It did not ring sharply, yet neither did it carry a tone of merciful compassion. 'You may approach.'

Hugh ascended the steps and knelt before her to kiss her ring. When he stepped back, she sat. The hound lay over her feet and rested its head on massive paws, but it gazed at Hanna as at an enemy, ready for her to bolt or to attack, so that it might have the pleasure of rending her limb from limb and gnawing on her bones.

Hadn't she seen this hound before, or one very like it?

'Who is this Eagle?' asked the skopos.

'She is called Hanna, Holy Mother. She comes from the North Mark of Wendar. In earlier years she called herself a friend to Liathano. She has recently ridden south bearing a message from Princess Theophanu, nothing we have not heard before except that she herself spoke with Prince Sanglant many months ago. He is now ridden east with a portion of the army that defeated the Quman.'

'To what end does he ride east, Eagle?'

Dared she speak the truth?

'I am only an Eagle, Holy Mother,' she said, surprised she had enough breath to form audible words. *I am only a pig, hiding in the forest.* 'For many months I was held captive by Prince Bulkezu of the Pechanek tribe, the leader of the Quman army. When Prince Sanglant and Prince Bayan defeated Bulkezu at the Veser River, they freed me. Prince Sanglant sent me west to bring news of his victory to his father.'

There was so much else she could say, but in the end, it came down to this: Did she hate Sanglant for sparing Bulkezu more than she feared the power of those who might have ensorcelled the king? Even if Hugh had done what Hathui accused him of, did that mean that the Holy Mother was involved? She didn't know whom could she trust or who was most dangerous.

'Your Excellency,' began Hugh, 'this Eagle brought news about Prince Sanglant and the folk who travel with him. I think it worthwhile to question her closely about—'

A movement by the skopos, glimpsed by Hanna but not really seen, stopped him.

'Are you one of those who bears the Eagle's Sight?'

The question surprised her. 'Yes, Holy Mother.'

'Who taught you?'

'An Eagle called Wolfhere, Holy Mother.'

'Wolfhere.' A complex hint of emotion colored her voice. 'When did you last see Wolfhere?'

'He rides with Prince Sanglant, Holy Mother.'

'So he did.'

That delicate place between her shoulder blades prickled,

as though an archer stood at the far doors with bow raised and an arrow sighted at her back.

Did, which meant not any longer. Whose side was Wolfhere on?

The earth lurched sideways beneath her. The hound barked once before settling beneath the throne. A grinding noise shuddered through the palace and faded as quickly as it had come, draining away to silence. The sound of raking stopped, leaving nothing but faint echoes, more a memory of the sound than the sound itself.

Hugh coughed. 'They're coming more frequently.'

'God are angry that we have not acted more swiftly and decisively to drive out the Arethousan interlopers. Sister Abelia, bring the brazier. Fan the coals into flame.' The cleric nodded and went out behind the curtain.

'It won't work,' said Hugh curtly.

'Do you think not, Brother Hugh?'

'If I could not, then how can she?'

'It may be so, but we must leave no avenue untrod. It will take months, even years, to locate and rebuild the lost crowns. My envoys have heard stories of an intact crown by the sea in Dalmiaka, but the Arethousan despots who rule there refuse to let them travel to that place. On every side we are thwarted. We are too few, and our enemies too many. Sister Venia is missing and St. Ekatarina's Convent closed up and apparently abandoned. We must have seven when the time comes, aided by tempestari so we can be assured of clear skies. I need my daughter.'

'Is it wise to speak so freely, Holy Mother?'

'To you, Brother Hugh? You have joined our Order willingly, and with a clear purpose. Is there some reason I should not trust you?'

'I meant before this Eagle, Holy Mother.'

'The Eagle? She is only a servant.'

'Even servants have tongues, Holy Mother.'

Hanna kept her head down, but she *felt* the touch of that devastating gaze. So might a fly feel before being swatted. So might a fly, holding still, be passed over as being of too little account to bother with when there were more annoying pests to exterminate.

'If my daughter trusted her, that bond may yet link them.'

The cleric returned and set a brazier on the step in front of Hanna, then stepped back to work a small bellows so coals shimmered and flames licked along their length.

'Watch carefully and learn, Sister Abelia,' said the skopos before turning her gaze on Hanna. 'Use your Eagle's Sight to seek the one you know as Liathano.'

One did not say 'No' to the skopos.

She leaned forward, hearing the hound's menacing growl at her movement and the command of the skopos, calling the dog to heel. It was hard to concentrate, knowing how nearby that fierce creature bided. It hadn't seemed so menacing when Lord Alain had commanded it. Without meaning to, she recognized it. She had last seen this hound, and Lord Alain, when she had watched King Henry pluck the county of Lavas out of Alain's hands and give it over to Lord Geoffrey and his young daughter.

A Lavas hound.

No person who had ever seen the Lavas hounds could mistake them for any other dog. How had the skopos acquired this one? Hanna had last seen Alain on the field of battle with the Lions. Hadn't he died there?

Her gaze fell forward through the veil of fire.

The only way he can bear his sorrow is to keep silence and let work soothe his soul into a stupor. There is plenty of work for a pair of able hands on a well-run estate in the autumn: pressing apples for cider, rhetting flax, splitting and sawing, cutting straw to repair roofs. He binds wood with trimmings from flax and soaks the bundles in beeswax and resin for the torches needed to light the winter months. His hands know how to do the work. Just as well, because his head seems stuffed with wool, hazy, clouded, distant.

'Did you live by the sea?' asks Brother Lallo, stopping beside him where he sits on the porch of the laborers' dormitory. The hounds lie docilely at his feet. 'You have a knack

for plaiting and net-making.'

Vaguely surprised – what was he thinking about just then? – he notices that he is weaving willow rods into a kiddle that the fishermen will place in the river to catch fish. 'I beg your pardon, Brother?'

'The Enemy is pleased with feet that wander off the path of good works! Keep your thoughts here with us. I asked you, did you live by the sea?'

To remember the sea makes him recall Adica and that long voyage, towed by the merfolk, when they had stared into the watery depths and seen the vast whorl of a city unfold beneath, strange and wonderful. All dead now.

Pain drowns him. Grief makes him mute. It is a kind of madness.

Maybe it was all a dream.

Lallo tugged at his own ear with a frown. 'You're a hard nut to crack. Enough of this. It's time for prayer, Brothers.' He shepherds his charges to church for Vespers.

Alain sets down the half-woven kiddle and follows with the others. Dusk has a way of sliding over the monastery, catching him in twilight unawares. Maybe he has been walking in twilight for a long time and never noticed it. Sorrow and Rage pad alongside. Despite their fearsome aspect, they behave as meekly as lambs. No man here fears them, and the monks willingly give him scraps with which to feed them. Each hound eats as much as one man, and they provide no labor for the benefit of the monastery, so he works doubly hard – when he doesn't forget himself and fall into that dreaming stupor. He wants to earn the hounds' portion as well as his own.

The hounds sit obediently outside the church. He goes in with the others.

As they file through the transept and thence into the dark nave, he notices the Brother Sacrist hurrying into the church with more oil for the lamps burning at the five altars. The lamps flicker, wicks running dry, but as he takes his place with the other laborers at the back of the nave, as he murmurs reflexive words of prayer, the sacrist makes a startled exclamation and halts halfway down the aisle. A side door opens. The elegant abbot enters in company with the prior as well as certain nobly-cut figures unknown to him. Have these visitors been here before? Were they here yesterday? One is a remarkably beautiful young man, unnaturally handsome and strangely familiar, who smiles and nods whenever Father Ortulfus speaks without making any reply himself. His redheaded companion answers the abbot's queries.

The lamps at the main altar and the seven stations dedicated to the disciplas burn strongly. Brother Sacrist hesitates in confusion but when Father Ortulfus lifts his voice in the opening chant, he slips into his place at the front with the other monastic officials, setting the unused pot of oil at his feet.

Father Ortulfus has a reedy voice, not full but true. 'Blessed is the Country of the Mother and Father of Life, and of the Holy Word revealed within the Circle of Unity, now and ever and unto ages of ages.'

The liturgy slides by as smoothly as water pours down a rock. The abbot marks the stations of the service by moving from lamp to lamp in a complicated pattern that, were he attached to thread, might weave truth into the stone. Praying, Father Ortulfus seems agitated, distracted by a gnawing annoyance that causes his mouth to slip down into a fierce frown when he forgets himself. When he returns to the altar to deliver his homily, his indignation takes flower as he scolds the congregation with quotations from the Holy Verses.

'"I have heard such things often before, you who make trouble, all of you, with every breath." It is the Enemy who makes you so stubborn in argument, who makes your speech trouble the hearts of the simple man and the credulous woman. "Can it be that God have thrown us into the clutches of malefactors, have left us at the mercy of those who are given over unto wickedness?" If you will walk with God, then walk in silence and free your heart from the Enemy's grasp. Let there be no more of these tales, which spread like a plague upon the Earth!'

The stone columns absorb this castigation in aloof silence.

Carved flowers crown each column, and on this flowery support rest ceiling vaults ornamented with vines. High up on the wall above the central altar stand the stucco figures of martyrs, each displaying a crown of sainthood. Their grave faces do not move; they cannot, of course, they are only representations, and yet their steady gaze pierces to his heart.

Dead. Dead. Dead.

All dead.

Mice live in the nave. He has coaxed a few out of their hiding places when, late at night before Nocturns, he can't sleep and wanders like a shade from one place to another within the compound, rootless and lost. They shelter in his hands, so small and helpless and warm, giving him trifling comfort. Is that their scritching now?

He has had keen hearing ever since the day he bound himself to the Eika prince now known as Stronghand. He hears not the clitter of mice on wood but a human gasp and the scrabbling of fingers on another's arm, seeking attention. Looking to the right, he catches sight of two men wearing the mended but clean tabards of Lions.

They stare at him in shocked amazement, mouths open, prayer forgotten. They are no longer listening to the abbot's homily – any more than he is – as it thunders to a close and as the prayer for forgiveness swells up among the gathered monks, novices, laborers, and visitors.

They stare at him as though they recognize him.

The high halls reel around him. The vaulted ceiling shudders, and vines writhe. Distantly, he hears Rage whimper.

Isn't that the young Lion called Dedi, who won a tunic off poor, foolish Folquin one night, gambling at dice? The older man called himself the boy's uncle, and probably he was. Yet they died in the east long ago. Is this church a gathering place for dead souls caught in purgatory, like him?

Why isn't Adica here with him?

He doubles over as men all around him drop to their knees in prayer, but he can no longer see or hear as he fights hot tears. Grief cuts into his belly. Claws are shredding his heart in two.

All he can do is sag forward beside the other laborers and hang on as the fit drowns him.

'Who is that young man she sees?'

The words dragged Hanna back as questions crowded her mind. *How is it that he still lives? What grieves him?*

Nay, she must concentrate. It seemed so long ago that she had last seen Liath, in disgrace at the palace at Werlida when she had married Sanglant against the wish of King Henry. She had ridden off secretly one night, never to return, but Hanna still saw her clearly, tall, a little too slender as if she never quite had enough to eat, her hair caught back in a braid, her eyes a fiery blue, as brilliant as the stars. In Heart's Rest no one had ever believed Liath and her father to be anything except nobly born, brought down in the world by fortune's wheel. But Liath had never treated Hanna differently by reason of birth. Liath had seen her as another soul, equal in the sight of God.

Ai, God. Where was Liath now?

Fire flared brightly among the coals before dying back as abruptly as if an icy wind smothered them.

She sank back onto her heels, sweating and trembling. Tears streaked her face. Was she crying for Liath, for Alain, or for herself? She wiped her nose.

'Nothing,' said Hugh. 'As I told you, Liath no longer walks on Earth.'

'Who is that young man she saw?' the skopos asked again.

'He looks familiar. . . . Nay, I do not know him.'

'He was attended by hounds who might have been littermates to the one who guards me. Is this one not a descendant of Taillefer's famous hounds? Why do I see its kinfolk at the side of a common boy? Eagle, what man was that you saw in the flames?'

How could she lie to a sorcerer so powerful that she could see into the vision formed by Hanna's own Eagle's Sight? 'His name is Alain, Holy Mother. He was heir to Count Lavastine until—'

'Lavastine!'

Hanna winced at the sharp tone, but that slight movement alerted the hound, which scrabbled out from under the throne to loom over her. The growl that rumbled in its throat was so low as to be almost inaudible. She shrank back. With only a word's command, it would rip her face off.

'Lavastine.' The word was whispered with the calculation of a general about to embark on a holy campaign. 'Sister Abelia, you will leave tomorrow to seek out Brother Severus. I want the one called Alain found and brought to me.'

'Yes, Holy Mother.'

The skopos rose and left the room with her attendant. The hound click-clacked after her; its nails needed filing. Hanna wondered, wildly, idly, who dared groom it.

'Do you know where Liath is, Hanna?' asked Hugh once the curtain had fallen into place behind the skopos and her attendant. 'Have you seen her in the flames?'

'I have not, Your Excellency.'

'Do you know what happened to her, Hanna?'

'I have heard the tale Prince Sanglant tells – that fiery daimones stole her.'

'Do you believe it?'

She fixed her gaze on the mural. The temblor had shaken open a crack that split the plaster base right through the blessed Daisan's left foot. 'For what reason would Prince Sanglant lie, Your Excellency?'

'Indeed, for what reason?'

A glance told her everything she needed to know: he was not Bulkezu, who savored the battle of wills. He was not even looking at her; he had dismissed her already. The monster Bulkezu had seen her as a person of some account, almost as a peer, because she was the luck of a Kerayit shaman. Because she dared stand up to him. To Hugh she was only a servant. He recalled her name because of her bond with Liath. She did not matter to him at all; only Liath did, then and now.

Which gave her a measure of freedom she had never had with Bulkezu.

'Prince Sanglant is no poet, Your Excellency. It is poets

who make up tales to confuse and beguile their listeners. I do not think he could have concocted a false trail to lead his enemies astray. That is not his way.'

He gave a slight noise in assent. 'No, he is not an educated man. There is a child as well. Does she live still?'

'When I last saw the prince, she did.'

'Does she look like her mother?'

Strange that a cold draft should twist through the hall, chilling her neck. 'In some manner, Your Excellency. She resembles both her mother and father. She is very young still.'

'Very young still,' he agreed, as if to himself, as if he had forgotten Hanna was there, 'and soft, as youth is soft and malleable. It is too bad Brother Marcus failed. Still, there may yet be a way. . . .'

She braced herself, expecting more questions.

None came.

He had forgotten her already. She shifted her weight to her heels to take some of the pressure off her knees. Outside, the raking started up again. As Hugh's silence dragged on, she began to count the strokes.

She had reached four and ninety when Hugh spoke.

'Yes. That is the way to do it.' He walked toward the doors, paused, turned back. 'Come, Hanna. You must make your report and a cleric will write it down.'

'Your Excellency.' She stood. 'It is an Eagle's duty to report to the regnant directly.'

He waited in a stripe of sunlight. 'Your loyalty is commendable. But it will not be possible for you to give your report to the king today. He will be far too busy to see you.'

'Then I will wait. It is by the regnant's own command that we Eagles report to him alone, when we come to his court. I dare not go against the king's express command, Your Excellency. Pray do not ask me to go back on the oath I swore to King Henry.'

The quirk of anger twitched on his lips, and he clenched his right hand, the one he had most often struck Liath with. But this was not the reckless, arrogant young frater who had suffered the indignity of ministering to the half-pagan common folk of the North Mark with barely concealed contempt. This man had a presbyter's rank, the respect of his peers, the love of the common-born Aostans, and an unknown wealth of power made palatable by his modest demeanor and undeniable beauty. He spoke easily with the Holy Mother herself and stood at the right hand of the king and queen who would soon be emperor and empress.

'Nay, nor should you,' he said at last with perfect amiability. 'Your oath to the king is what gives an Eagle honor. You were taken prisoner by the Quman alongside Prince Ekkehard, I believe?'

'I was, Your Excellency.'

'Then how are we to know that you did not turn traitor against your countryfolk as well, if this tale of Prince Ekkehard's treachery is true? How can we be sure that any of these stories you bring to us are truth, and not lies? Do you support the rightful king? Or do you support those who rebel against him?'

God, what a fool she had been to think she could outmaneuver him.

He smiled sadly. The light pouring over him made him gleam, a living saint. 'So it is, Eagle, that the king must consider you a traitor as well. You know how he feels about Wolfhere, whom he banished on less account than this. How can he treat a traitor otherwise? How can he even bear to speak to one of his own Eagles if he believes that Eagle has betrayed him together with his dearest children?' Although he had not moved, he seemed to have grown even more imposing, a power which, like the sun, may bring light to those trapped in darkness – or death to those caught out under its punishing brilliance.

'I will do what I can to see that you are not imprisoned outright for treason, Hanna. I have done that much for you already. The dungeons here are not healthy. The rats grow large. Yet if you do not cooperate with me, then there is nothing I can do, no case I can make before the king. If that happens, I do not know what will happen to you then. Do you understand?'

2

Gasping, he came to himself as everyone around him rose. The service had ended. The two Lions no longer sat on the benches to his right. Maybe he had only hallucinated them. He was dreaming, confusing past and present.

Only Adica seemed real – she, and the bronze armband bound around his upper right arm that he could not pull off.

'F-friend.' Iso had a limp and a stutter. Abandoned by his parents, he had been a laborer at the monastery for half of his life. Although he didn't act any older than sixteen, he looked aged by pain and grief and an unfilled childhood hunger. 'It's a-uh-it's a-uh-a hurt one. Come.' He had bony fingers that no amount of porridge could fatten up, and with these he tugged at Alain's sleeve as the laborers waited for the monks to file out before them. The abbot sailed out with a fine stern expression on his face and his guests quite red with consternation behind him, but Iso kept pulling on him and his quiet pleading dragged Alain out of his distraction.

'I'll come.' He let Iso lead him out of the church and, with the hounds following, to the stables.

Iso didn't have many teeth left, which was why he could only take porridge and other soft foods. Sometimes his remaining teeth hurt him; one did tonight. Alain knew it because now and again Iso brushed at the lower side of his right jaw as though to chase away a fly, and a tear moistened his right eye, slipping down to be replaced by another. Iso never complained about pain. Maybe he didn't have the words to, and anyway it was probably the only existence he knew. Perhaps he had never experienced a day in the course of his entire life without physical pain of some kind nagging him, the twisted agony of his misshapen hip, the withered ruin of his left hand, burned and scarred over long ago, the nasty scars on his back.

Yet for all the pain Iso lived with, and maybe because of it, he hated to see animals suffer. More than once he had taken a rake from a furious cat when he'd saved a mouse from its clutches, or risked being bitten by a wounded, starving dog at the forest's edge when he offered it a scrap to eat.

The beech woods had been so heavily harvested in the vicinity of the estate that the nearby woodland was dominated by seedlings and luxuriant shrubs. The hounds smelled a threat in the undergrowth beyond the stable, and they bristled, curling back their muzzles as they growled. Twigs rattled as a creature shifted position. It sounded big. The twilight gloom amplified the sense of hugeness.

Alain gripped Iso's shoulder, holding him back. The smell of iron tickled his nostrils, and a taste like fear coated his mouth. Although he saw only the suggestion of the shape where young beech trees struggled with honeysuckle and sedge for a footing, his skin crawled.

In the east, a waning gibbous moon, just two days past full, was rising.

'Th–they'll kill it if th–they f-find it.' Tears slipped from Iso's chin to wet the back of Alain's hand.

'Hush now.' Alain signed to the hounds and they sat obediently, although they didn't like it. Cautiously, he stepped forward to part the brush.

The creature lying under the shadow of sedge flicked its head around, and where its amber gaze touched him, torpor gripped his limbs. Iso whimpered. Sorrow yipped. The creature was as big as a pony, with a sheeny glamour. It scrabbled at the earth with its taloned feet. Leaves sprayed everywhere. It had the head of an eagle with the body of a dragon, and a whiplike tail that thrashed against the bole of the sedge behind it. Awkwardly, it heaved itself backward. It was meant to fly, but its wings were still down, not yet true feathers.

'What i–i–is it?' whispered Iso. 'M–my feet feel so slow.'

'It's a guivre.' Its hideous shape should have frightened him. 'It's a hatchling.' The torpor wore off. It hadn't the full

force of an adult's stare, that would pin a man to the ground.
The nestling stabbed forward with a stubborn 'awk' but
couldn't reach him because it dragged one leg under its body.
It feared him more than he feared it and what it would become.
'It can't even fly yet. Do you see the wings? They don't have
their feathers yet. It should still be in the nest.'

'I–it's a m–monster. Th–they'll kill it if they f-find it.'

'So they will.'

Maybe they should. One shout would bring an army and
with staves, shovels, and hoes they could hammer it to death,
staving in its skull. But it was so young, and it was free, not
chained and brutalized like the one that had killed Agius. In
its own way it was beautiful, gleaming along its scaly skin
where the last glow of sunlight and the silvery spill of moonlight mingled to dapple its flanks. Only God knew how it had
come to be here.

Then he saw the wound that had crippled it, opening the
left thigh clean to the bone.

'Iso, get me combed flax and a scrap of linen soaked in
cinquefoil. Do it quickly, friend. Don't let anyone see you.'

Iso mumbled the words back to himself, repeating them.
He had a hard time remembering things. He lurched away
with a rolling gait, for on top of everything else, he had one
leg shorter than the other.

Alain eased into the brush and crouched as the hatchling
hissed at him to no avail. It couldn't reach him, nor could it
retreat. Leaves spun in an eddy of wind, fluttering to the
ground as the breeze faltered. Distantly, voices raised in the
service of Compline, the last prayer of the day. The monks'
song wound in counterpoint to his own voice as he spoke
softly to the hatchling. He spoke to it of Adica, of the marvels he had seen when he walked as one dead in the land
where she lived. He spoke to it of dragons rising majestically
into the heavens and of the lion queens on whose tawny backs
he and his companions had ridden. He spoke of creatures
glimpsed in dark ravines and deep grottos and of the merfolk
and their glorious undersea city.

Guivres were unthinking beasts, of course, but the hatchling listened in that way in which half-wild creatures allow themselves to be soothed by a peaceful voice. The hounds lay in perfect silence, heads resting on their forelegs and eyes bright.

Iso returned with his hands full. The young guivre kept its amber gaze fixed on Alain but remained still as he pulled the lips of the wound together, pressing linen over the cut, and bound it with flax tightly enough to hold but not so tight that it cut into flesh.

'Harm none of humankind,' he said to it, 'but take what you must to survive among the beasts of the forest, for they are your rightful prey. May God watch over you.'

As he backed into the spreading arch of a hazel, the hatchling came to life. It spread its wings and, beating them, rattled branches as though calling thunder. Sorrow and Rage barked, and the creature lurched away into the forest, using its wings to help power it along since it couldn't rise into the air. With a great deal of noise, it vanished from sight.

Behind, the last hymn reached its final cadence. Services were over. This was the time of day when the worshipers returned to their final tasks before making ready for bed.

Iso hopped anxiously from foot to foot. 'Th–they'll hear and th–they'll come.' He wasn't frightened of the beast but of what Brother Lallo might do to him for missing Compline.

A stone's throw away, the stables remained oddly quiet, although now was the usual time for laborers who had no cot in the dormitory to make a final check on any animals stabled within before finding themselves a place to sleep in the hayloft. For a long time Alain couldn't bring himself to move away from the forest's edge, although he knew he ought to get Iso back to the dormitory. Instead, he listened to the progress of the beast and after a while couldn't hear any least tremor of its passing. Would it grow into a fearsome adult, preying on humankind? Had he spared it only to doom his own kind to its hunger?

He remembered the poor guivre held captive by Lady Sabella, tormented by starvation and disease, fed dying men and, in the end, used by her as ruthlessly as she used the rest of her allies. He could not regret saving one after having killed another.

Sighing, he turned away from the forest and walked back to the dormitories with Iso hobbling, gasping and whispering, at his side. It would be hard for Iso to keep silent about the guivre, but who would believe him?

Alain laughed softly. Maybe disbelief could be a form of freedom. For the first time since he stumbled out of the stone circle with the memory of Adica's death crushing him, he felt a lightness in his heart, a breath of healing.

As they passed the stables, they almost ran into old Mangod, who had labored here for more years than Alain had been alive. Like Iso, he was a cripple with a withered arm that, once broken, never set right. When he lost his farmstead to his sister's son, he retired to the monastery.

He had an excitable voice and a way of hopping from leg to leg like a child needing to pee. 'Have ye heard?' he asked in his western accent. 'There come some holy monks this morning to the abbot, and a couple of king's soldiers. They say they've seen sleepers under the hill with the look of old Villam's son, the lad who got lost up among the stones a few years back. Terrible strong magic, they say. And a revelation, too, to share with us brothers.'

His words made Alain nervous; they pricked like pins and needles in a foot that's fallen asleep. As he and Iso walked up past the stables, he saw most of the day laborers clustered on the porch although they would normally be in their cots by now. A dozen of the monks stood among their number, straining forward, and at one corner of the porch huddled six pale-robed novices who had escaped from the novices' compound where they were supposed to live and sleep in isolation until the day they took their final vows.

'"His heart was cut out of him! Where his heart's blood fell and touched the soil, there bloomed roses."'

'Th-that's a woman!' stammered Iso as they pressed forward into the crowd gathered on the dormitory porch.

The guivre's eye could not have struck such sluggish fear into Alain as did her voice. He knew that voice.

'"But by his suffering, by his sacrifice, he redeemed us from our sins. Our salvation comes through that redemption. For though he died, he lived again. So did God in Her wisdom redeem him, for was he not Her only Son?"'

'Heresy,' murmured a monk standing at Alain's elbow. 'This one comes from the east, from the Arethousans.'

'All liars, the Arethousans,' whispered his companion. 'Still, I want to hear her.'

'Do not let others frighten you. Do not let them tell you that the words I speak are heresy. It is the church that has concealed the truth from us—'

'To what purpose?' An older monk stepped forward. 'Were the ancient mothers dupes and fools, to be taken in by a lie? Do you mean to say they were schemers and deceivers who conspired to damn us all by hiding the truth of the blessed Daisan's true nature and his final days on earth? You haven't convinced me with this wild talk!'

Alain pressed through the crowd until he was able to see the speaker. It was Hathumod. Somehow she had escaped the battle in the east and reached Herford. He hung back. He didn't want her to see him.

A frown creased her rabbitlike face as she examined the scoffer. She appeared the most innocuous of interlocutors. No one could look more sincere than she did. 'Brother Sigfrid will answer you,' she replied.

Four young men stood beside her: the handsome blond and the redhead whom Alain had seen at services, as well as a stout fellow who resembled Hathumod and a slight young man no larger than Iso though apparently sound in all his limbs. The two Lions, Dedi and Gerulf, stood behind them, arms crossed as they surveyed the crowd with practiced vigilance. As Dedi glanced his way, Alain ducked down behind the shoulder of one of his fellow laborers, and when he glanced up, the slight young man had climbed up on a bench to address the crowd. He was dressed in a tattered monk's robe, but despite his disreputable appearance, he responded in a voice both rich and sweet.

'Truly, Brother, I dare not set myself higher than the Holy

Mothers out of whose words flowered our most sovereign and holy church. Yet you and I both know how few of their writings have come down to us, and how many have been lost. What might the ancient mothers say to us now, were they here and able to speak freely? What fragments have we been left to read, despite the best efforts of our brethren, brothers and sisters who copied and recopied the most holy texts? Has it always been the most holy who have worked in the scriptoria? In whose interest has it been to conceal this truth?'

'That's so! That's so!' one monk muttered, maybe reflecting on old grievances.

Another said, loudly, 'In whose interest is it to spread this heresy?'

The laborers merely stared, mouths agape. Several fingered the wooden Circles hanging at their chests.

'Heretics are burned,' said Sigfrid. 'They gain no benefit from preaching the truth. When the split with the Arethousan patriarch came in the year 407, over the doctrine of separation, those in power in the holy Church may have feared losing the staff by which they ruled. They may have wished to crush for all time any discussion of the divine nature of the blessed Daisan.'

'The blessed Daisan does not partake of God's divine nature!' cried one of the novices, a hound belling at a scent. 'The blessed Daisan is just like us!'

'Can it be that the blessed Daisan partakes nothing of God's substance?' demanded Sigfrid. 'Can the Son be unlike the Mother? Are they not of the same nature? Would God reveal Her Holy Word to one who was stained by darkness, as are all of us who live in the world? Nay, friend, Son and Mother are of like substance, and the Son comes directly out of the Mother's essence—'

Brother Lallo's roar came out of the twilight like that of a chained lion prodded and poked until it lashes out. 'What manner of heretical babble is this? These poor foolish men are my charges. Who are you to corrupt them?'

He lumbered up onto the porch, striking to each side with his staff. The laborers scattered before him. His gaze lit on poor Iso, and he grabbed the lad and shook him until the boy's teeth slammed together. Iso began to cry. 'Must we throw you out for disobedience?'

The other laborers scattered into the night. The poor novices fell all over themselves trying not to be seen, but their master came running in Brother Lallo's wake, his face flushed with anger. Other torches bobbed, a flood tide of monks rushing to investigate the commotion. The abbot and several of his officials hurried up the steps onto the porch.

'You have abused my hospitality by preaching to these poor half-wits!' cried Father Ortulfus as he glared at Hathumod and her companions. 'Are you oath breakers as well as heretics, that you take our bread and then throw it in our faces by breaking the rules by which we govern this monastery?' Son of a noble house, he had aristocratic bearing and elegant fury to spare, and his disdain was a well-honed weapon.

The frail Sigfrid did not back down. His friends moved forward around the bench, Lions forming a shield wall to meet an implacable enemy. 'God enjoins us to speak the truth, Father. It would be a sin for us to remain silent. I do not fear your anger, because I know that God holds us in Her hands.'

'So be it.' Father Ortulfus beckoned to his burly prior. 'Prior Ratbold will escort you to Autun, where Biscop Constance can deal with you. The punishment for heresy is death.'

The red-haired one stepped forward with the calm of a man who has faced battle and not faltered. 'We won't go to Autun. We'll leave here peacefully, but we won't be made prisoners.'

'Leave to spread your wicked lies throughout the countryside?' Father Ortulfus shook his head. 'I cannot allow it.' Behind him, Prior Ratbold signaled to certain brawny monks half hidden in the shadows. Iso trembled like a captured fawn in Lallo's grasp as the abbot went on. 'You will be taken to Autun and placed under the biscop's authority—'

'I won't go to Autun!' cried the handsome one petulantly. All at once, Alain remembered him: the pretty young trophy husband taken by Margrave Judith and paraded through the king's progress in the same fashion she would have displayed a young stallion offered for stud. 'We won't go, and you can't make us!'

The mood shifted as violently as wind turns and gusts in a storm. The novices were dragged away bodily by the master and his helpers. Ratbold's assistants raised staffs, ready to charge. Dedi picked up the bench, bracing himself, and his uncle drew his eating knife while the young nobleman fell back behind their redheaded leader.

Alain could not bear to see any more. He stepped into the breach between the two groups. 'I pray you, do not desecrate this ground with fighting.' Words came unbidden as he turned to face Father Ortulfus. 'These men rode with Prince Ekkehard. This woman serves God with devotion and a pure heart. These Lions are loyal soldiers of the king. They fought a battle in the east, in the army of Princess Sapientia and Prince Bayan, and deserve more of a hearing than this!'

Father Ortulfus was so surprised to hear a common laborer scold him that he could not speak.

Hathumod shrieked and flung herself forward to kneel at Alain's feet. 'My lord!' She grabbed his hand to kiss it. Horrified, he stepped back to escape her. 'My lord, how have you come here? How have you escaped that terrible battle? I pray you, give us your blessing!'

Her obeisance hurt, an old wound scraped raw.

'Nay, I pray you,' he said desperately. 'Stand up, Hathumod. Do not kneel there.'

'What would you have us do, my lord?' she asked. 'We will do as you command.'

Father Ortulfus stared in stunned silence with his officials clustered in like stupefaction around him. At the forest's edge, an owl hooted. Wings beat hard back in the woodland, and for an instant Alain thought the guivre had returned, causing them all to ossify into stone. The owl hooted again. The moon's light had crept up the east-facing porch, sliding up Hathumod's arms to gild her face until she looked waxy and half-dead.

'Biscop Constance is a fair woman. She will not judge you rashly,' he said.

'But what of our case, my lord? You walked with Brother Agius before his martyrdom. You heard him speak.'

'Brother Agius was a troubled man.' It was the only answer Alain could give. 'I cannot say if he was right or wrong, nor can any of you. Do not imperil your souls by bringing violence to this peaceful place, I beg you. Go to Autun. If your cause is just, the biscop will listen to you.'

'I don't want to go to Autun!' objected Margrave Judith's young husband.

'Shut up, Baldwin,' said the redheaded youth. 'They've got twenty stout men with staves, and we've only got knives. We can hardly preach the truth if we're dead.'

'We have nothing to fear,' said Sigfrid, 'since we walk with the truth. Remember the phoenix, Baldwin. Do not lose faith.'

'I have not lost faith, my lord,' cried Hathumod. She reached up boldly and touched his cheek where the blemish stained his skin, then flushed and pulled her hand away. She fumbled at her sleeve and thrust an old rusted nail into his hand. 'I have not forgotten that God tested us by offering us a broken vessel in place of the whole one. I still have the nail.'

Surely the guivre had returned, its baleful glare in full force, because he could not move. The nail burned his skin. He had rid himself of both promises and burdens, but what he had given away to the centaur shaman had returned to haunt and plague him. Would he never be free of Tallia's sin? Was it possible he loved her still? Was his memory of happiness with Adica only a delirium, caught in the mind of a wounded man?

He refused to surrender to the chains that once bound him.

'This is no longer mine.' He pressed the nail into Hathumod's pale fingers. 'I am not what you think I am. I am bound to this monastery now—'

'Who are you?' demanded the abbot. 'You came to us raving about the end times and yet stand here like a lord born into a noble house.'

'He was a Lion,' said Dedi, speaking for the first time.

'Nay, he was a count,' said Hathumod. 'It was wickedness and the greed of others that brought him low! I know what he truly is, for I have seen that which follows in his wake!'

'He's a laborer born and bred,' objected Brother Lallo. 'I've seen the calluses on his hands. He knows plaiting and weaving as would any child born to a family who work along the sea lanes.'

'These cannot all be true.' Father Ortulfus' irritation scalded his tone.

'I am no one, Father.' He could not keep the bitterness from his voice, although he knew bitterness was a sin. He must not blame God for the happiness he had shared with Adica; too well he understood how brief life, and happiness, were. 'I am just a bastard born to a whore and an unknown father.'

'Yet those fearsome hounds follow you as meekly as lambs. One might say you had bewitched them.'

'Say what you will,' said Alain. 'God alone know the truth of what I am. What kin my mother was born to I cannot say, only that she died a pauper and a whore.'

Hathumod whimpered, the kind of bleat a small animal might make when caught in a falcon's claws.

'What are you now?' Father Ortulfus' intent gaze might have been that of the falcon.

'I am grateful to be a common laborer, working in peace at this monastery.'

The sacrist appeared out of the clot of officials who had fallen back at the first sign of violence.

'Think of the oil, Father!' he whispered so loudly that all heard.

The abbot bit his lip, hesitating, then gestured for the sacrist to step back before he addressed Alain again.

'Is it your intention to declare yourself as a converso? To work for a year and a day at this place and then, when that year and a day have passed, to devote your life to God as a monk?'

The night was so still and restful, chill without the biting cold that would come with winter, that its tranquil presence spread a glamour over them, washing away the tensions that had threatened to erupt moments before. The evening breeze touched Alain's face and spilled peace through his soul. He remembered the breath of healing that passed over his heart after the guivre vanished into the wood. Was it a presentiment?

The man who raised him, his foster father Henri, pledged him to the church in return for the right to foster him. Didn't he turn away from that vow when he pledged himself to the Lady of Battles? All she had brought him was death.

Nay, love, too. He would not be dishonest. For all the pain it brought him, he would never disavow his love for Lavastine, for Adica, and even for Tallia, who had turned her back on him. For his faithful hounds, who followed him.

It was time to return to the vow first made, although he was only an infant when it was spoken over him.

'Truly,' he said, meeting the abbot's avaricious gaze, 'I will labor here for a year and a day, and then enter the monastery as a monk, devoting my life to God, as it should have been all along.'

'So be it.' Father Ortulfus turned to Prior Ratbold. 'Escort our visitors to cells. There's still the matter of Lord Berthold to investigate. We'll send a party up to the barrows in the morning. I will interview them further after we've seen if there's any truth to their claim.'

'What if we can't find them again?' objected handsome Baldwin. 'I don't want to go back to those nasty barrows. They scared me.'

Hathumod turned on him angrily. Her tear-stained face glittered under the moon's light. 'You'll hush now, Baldwin! I've had enough of your whining! No matter what happens next, no harm will come to us, will it, Lord Alain?'

He did not know the future. Yet in his heart he did not fear for them. They were not wicked liars, probably only mistaken in their belief, desperate for the passion brought to them by Agius' tortured vision.

'No harm will come to you,' he agreed. 'Father Ortulfus is a good man. He will listen carefully to what you have to say, as long as you are honest.'

As soon as Prior Ratbold escorted the visitors away, the laborers crept back onto the porch and into the dormitory, slipping away to their cots in the hope no one would notice. Father Ortulfus did not leave immediately. His attendants lingered beside him as the moon rose higher still, bathing the forest's edge in its gray-silver light. From here, on the porch, they could not see the other buildings of Herford Monastery, only a corner of the stables, the spindly outlines of apple and pear trees, and the fenced-off garden, fallow at this season except for a rank stand of rosemary.

The sacrist approached Alain, bobbing nervously. He wore a good linen robe, befitting his rank, under a knee-length wool tunic trimmed with fur. 'There is a cell free for your use, Brother, set apart from the rest as befits your position among us, but with a good rope bed, a rug, and other small courtesies.'

Alain regarded him with surprise. 'Nay, Brother, what would I want such courtesies for? I will labor among my brethren here until I have fulfilled my vow. A cot in the dormitory is good enough for me.'

Father Ortulfus watched him but said nothing. He and his attendants departed quietly. Alain stood on the porch listening, and after a while he heard the muffled sound of weeping. He walked into the dormitory to find Iso facedown on the coarse hemp-cloth cot, trying to stifle his sobs.

Kneeling beside the youth, Alain rested a hand on his bony back. 'All has been set right.'

Iso struggled to speak. Fear made his stammer worse. 'B-but th-they'll th-throw me out. I h-h-have nowhere to g-g-go.'

'Nay, friend, no one will disturb you. You'll stay here, where you belong.'

As Iso calmed, Alain became aware of many listening ears, those of the other day laborers, poor men, some crippled, some slow of wit, some merely down on their luck or seeking the assurance of a meal every day, who served the monastery with labor day in and day out, although few of these men would ever be allowed to take the vows of a monk. It was so quiet in the dormitory that a mouse could be heard skittering along the eaves. It was so quiet that the moon seemed to be holding its breath. The wind did not sigh in the rafters, nor could he hear the night breeze moving through the trees outside. Rage grunted and settled down beside Alain's cot. It was too dark to see her as anything but shadow. Sorrow stood by the door, as still as though he had been turned to stone.

'Go to sleep now, Iso,' he said. 'Let everyone rest. There is work to do tomorrow. Don't let your hearts be troubled.'

They did shift and settle, they did go to sleep at last, although Alain lay wakeful for a long time before sleep claimed him. Memories drifted in clouds, obscure and troubling. He still felt the touch of the nail against his skin, like poison, and for a long time he saw Sorrow standing vigilant in the open door.

XI
SIGNS AND PORTENTS

1

She had once been a captive in hardship. Now she suffered as a captive in luxury. The food was better, and she slept on a comfortable pallet at night in a spacious suite among the devoted servants of Presbyter Hugh. She never saw anyone murdered for sport or out of boredom and neglect, but otherwise the two conditions contrasted little. Twice, a servant of Duke Burchard approached one of Hugh's stewards, asking that the duke be allowed to interview her himself; after the second refusal, the man did not come again. Hugh allowed no one to talk to her, not even the other Eagles. Seven Eagles besides herself attended Henry at court, including Rufus, but they slept and ate in other quarters to which she was never allowed access. Nor was she sent out with any messages, as her comrades were, riding out to various places in Aosta, north to Karrone, and even one to Salia.

She wore no chains, but she had no freedom of movement. Of course it was preferable to be a prisoner without the misery she had endured under the Quman, even if she had been subjected to far less than the hapless folk forced to follow, and die, in the army's train.

Of course it was preferable.

That didn't make it palatable.

If Hugh suspected that she had seen Hathui and heard her accusations, he never let on. Maybe he didn't think so. Maybe if he thought so, she would be dead by now. In fact, he paid no attention to her at all once she had given an account of her travels and travails to him while a cleric busily wrote it all down. He had questioned her; she had replied. She hadn't said everything she knew, but perhaps she had said enough. She could not tell if he suspected her of disloyalty or treason. Anyone as unrelentingly benevolent as Hugh could not, as far as she was concerned, be trusted.

And yet.

Small acts of charity softened the path he trod every day. He did not fear to walk into the grimmer parts of the city, where folk lived in the meanest conditions: beggars, itinerant cobblers, and whole families whose work seemed to consist of gleaning from sewers and garbage pits. In a city brimming with poverty, he turned no beggar away without offering the poor man bread and a coin. Laborers were hired out of his own purse to work on the walls and reconstruct buildings damaged in the mild earthquake. Now and again he redeemed captives brought to the market for sale into service as domestic slaves, those who professed to be Daisanites. Each week he led a service at the servants' chapel to which any person working in the palace, high or low, might seek entry; no other presbyter deigned to humble himself in such a way when there were clerics aplenty available to minister to the lowborn.

No one at court spoke against him. Nor did any whisper of any unseemly connection between the beautiful presbyter and the young queen reach Hanna's ears. As days passed, Hanna saw herself that Hugh was never alone with Queen Adelheid. Never. It was so marked that she supposed it was done deliberately.

In any case, the queen was pregnant. A second child would seal Adelheid's grip on the imperial throne. Through all this, Hugh stood at the king's right hand.

So it was today, on the feast day dedicated to All Souls,

the twelfth day of Octumbre. The king received visitors in the royal hall with his court gathered around him. Hanna waited to the right of the throne, standing against the wall, watching as Hugh intercepted each supplicant before allowing them to ascend the dais and kneel before the king and queen.

No information reached Henry that did not pass Hugh first. He controlled what the king knew and how the king made decisions. Hugh's influence remained subtle, but pervasive. Was it possible that no one else saw as clearly as she did?

But looking over these courtiers who chatted as they waited in attendance, bright in their fine clothing and precious jewels and baubles, she saw no suspicion in their bearing or their gaze. A wind had dispelled the heat wave that had lingered, according to the natives, unusually long into the autumn season, so it was no hardship to pass the afternoon in gossip and splendor as petitioners came and went, most of them artisans and guildsmen fashioning the many trappings and the great feast that would accompany the coronation.

Now that the king had begun his inevitable transition into emperor, none of the nobles had the kind of companionable intimacy she had seen them once share with Henry back in the days when Margrave Villam and Sister Rosvita had counseled the king. Had Henry become proud? Would the crown soon to grace his head exalt him far above those who had once been his peers?

She wondered if she had dreamed that flash of blue in Henry's eyes. Perhaps Hathui had betrayed the king and tried to drag Hanna into the conspiracy. Perhaps her own loyalty to Liath had disoriented her, complicated by the familiar tangle of envy, love, fidelity, and a tiny spark of resentment. Yet Liath had left her and the Eagles behind. Why should she cling to a friendship that had likely meant far more to Hanna than it ever had to Liath?

She could not shake constancy. She understood better now the fears and weaknesses that had driven Liath. Whatever had happened in the past, she could not abandon the memory of the fellowship and harmony they had shared.

She had a sudden, odd feeling that someone was looking at her. Turning her head, she caught sight of a cleric sitting among a dozen others at a table to one side of the king's throne. These members of the king's schola were at work writing down the names and pledges of each of the artisans, making a careful record of the great undertaking they had now all embarked on which would culminate in the first Emperor since the days of Taillefer, one hundred years before.

One man had paused in his writing to look at her: Brother Fortunatus, who had given the sermon at St. Asella's. He did not look away immediately when their gazes met. He studied her, frowning slightly, serious; he had a gaunt-looking face, as if he had once been a lot heavier and healthier and happier with the extra weight. No doubt he wondered why she walked among Hugh's entourage. No doubt he wondered if she had betrayed him.

A courtier approached the king to introduce three aged clerics, residents of the famous institution of the learned St. Melania of Kellai. They had studied the Holy Verses and with careful prognostications had several well-omened dates to suggest for the coronation itself. The king and queen listened as the scholars argued over the relative benefits of a coronation held on the feast day of St. Peter the Discipla, which was also Candlemass, or that of St. Eulalia, two days later, whose attendance at the birth of the blessed Daisan would bring her saintly approval to the birth of a new empire.

Beside Hanna, two of Hugh's clerics were chatting softly in counterpoint to the discussion going on publicly before the king.

'Nay, but the arguments for holding the coronation on the twenty-second day of Novarian are very strong, if we speak only of the stars.'

'They'll say no such thing publicly! People still fear mathematici.'

'That won't last. The Holy Mother herself did the calculations. It was she who said that when Jedu moves from the Lion into the Dragon, it would be well for the king to crown himself from the lesser beast into the greater.'

'But I've heard others argue that we had better look to a conjunction with the Crown of Stars, for that signifies the empire, and thus would command better success. Erekes will reach conjunction with the Crown on the eleventh of Askulavre.'

'Erekes is fleeting. Would that not cause the reign of the new emperor to be fleeting?'

'Life is fleeting, Brother. Yet doesn't Somorhas come into conjunction with the Crown soon after? And linger there for many days, into Fevrua?'

'Because she goes into retrograde. That can scarcely bode well. Yet on the first of Sormas, she touches the Child's Torc, signifying heaven's blessing on the rule of Earth's regnants.'

They would argue endlessly. Hugh's private schola, his coterie of clerics and church-folk, was riddled with women and men professing to understand the teachings of the mathematici, magic outlawed by a church council a hundred years ago but come back into favor with the blessing of the new skopos, herself an adept of the sorcerous arts.

Brother Fortunatus was not the only one watching her: so did Duchess Liutgard, with narrowed eyes, as if wondering why an Eagle had sought refuge under Hugh's wing – or why Hugh had confined an Eagle within the cage of his faithful retinue.

She dropped her gaze to stare at her feet and the honest pair of boots covering them. She had followed the trail set before her by the will of others for too long. Maybe it was time to branch off on a path of her own making.

2

The door into the chamber where he was confined for the night, separate from the others, stood so low that Ivar had to crawl to get inside. With a blanket wrapped around him, he

huddled on the stone platform that served as a bed, unable
to sleep, stricken with wretched cramps from the rich food.

Why did the righteous suffer and the wicked thrive? Ivar
could not imagine Hugh spending even one single night in
discomfort. No doubt he lay in a fine luxurious bed waited
on by servants. Had he a woman in the bed with him? Yet
the image wouldn't rise. Hugh had never shown interest in
any woman in Heart's Rest, not until Liath. Maybe Hugh
lusted just as most men did but knew how to control himself.

Anger writhed in his gut at the thought of Hugh until
finally he staggered over to the bucket placed in the corner
and vomited the remains of his dinner. When he sagged back
onto the hard bed, he felt a little better. He must not let
despair and hatred control him. He could not let the memory
of Liath torment him. He had to figure out how to get his
companions out of this prison, and he could not do so if he
let jealousy and fear and hate consume him. He had always
acted so impulsively before. Unbidden, the memory of his
elder half sister, Rosvita, came to his mind. She would never
have found herself in such an awkward circumstance. She
would never be so stupid as to be thrown into a prison cell
for some rash action or thoughtless words. How many times
as a child had he heard her held up as a paragon of shrewd-
ness and composure? He had to try to be like her. He had to
set aside his passions and *think*.

How could three years have passed in the space of two
nights?

In the morning, the prior came with a party of men and
took away Gerulf as well as Baldwin, whose indignant complaining could be heard through the heavy door. Later, a servant brought venison, bread, and leftover pudding, but Ivar
couldn't bear to touch anything but the bread. Wine didn't
quench his thirst, but a diet of bread and wine eased the ache
in his bowels.

The day passed with excruciating slowness. The afternoon
service of Nones had come and gone when, at last, all seven
of them were brought under guard to the abbot's office. Ivar

needed only one look at the expression on Baldwin's and Gerulf's faces.

'Nothing, my lord abbot,' said the prior. 'We entered each of the mounds and found a passageway in to a central chamber. Villam's men did the same thing five years ago when the lad first disappeared. The chambers lie empty. We saw no tunnels or stairs leading farther into the ground, nor did we find any trace of Lord Berthold or his companions.'

The abbot regarded Ivar as he toyed with an ornament: a deer carved from ivory, so cunningly wrought that each least detail, ears, flared eyes, nostrils, the tufts of hair on its legs, had been suggested by the artisan's skill. A servant came in with a covered bucket to add charcoal to the brazier.

'Truly, it puzzles me that Lord Ivar and his companions should make such a claim when they must have known how easily it would be disproved. They do not strike me as fools – well, perhaps with one exception. Still, this matter goes beyond my jurisdiction. Only the biscop's court can judge cases of heresy, and whether these tales are true. A phoenix rising from the ashes, healing the lame and the ill. Three years passing in the space of two nights. A two months' journey overland accomplished by walking into and out of a barrow, through a labyrinth of chambers buried far beneath the old grave mounds.'

'Sorcery!' exclaimed the prior. 'Like those stories we've heard of bandits who eat the souls of their captives.'

'Hush!' scolded Ortulfus. 'Speak no ill gossip lest you bring the sickness back on yourself. Lord Ivar, at Hugh of Austra's trial you yourself admitted to consorting with a woman condemned and outlawed for the crime of sorcery. How am I to judge? I must send all of you to Autun.'

'I don't want to go back to Autun!' cried Baldwin. 'And you didn't tell them about the lions!'

'Ai, God,' said Gerulf impatiently, forgetting his station as a humble Lion, 'his ravings won't help our case any.'

'Nay, hold,' said the prior suddenly. 'What lions?'

'The lions on that rock outcropping,' said Baldwin irritably. 'The one by that tiny old shelter.'

Father Ortulfus set down the deer. His expression grew pensive, even troubled. The sacrist whispered furtively to the chief scribe, and the cellarer rubbed his hands together nervously while the prior plucked at his keys.

They knew something. Here lay the opportunity.

'I saw the lions, too,' Ivar said at once. 'They came at night while I was on watch with Sigfrid. They drove off a pack of wolves and kept watch over us where we sheltered under an overhang near by the hovel.'

The abbot wavered.

They had struck on the one thing that might convince him.

'You never said you saw the lions!' exclaimed Baldwin indignantly. 'You let everyone think I was a maniac!'

That quickly, Father Ortulfus' support slipped away. Picking up the deer, he surveyed his prisoners with a sigh of derision. 'Convenient that you recall just now to mention that you saw lions, Lord Ivar.'

'But I did see them,' Ivar insisted, hearing his voice grow shrill. It was so hard to stay calm when disaster stared them in the face. God have mercy! Mother Scholastica had cut out Sigfrid's *tongue* for speaking heresy. What would Biscop Constance do to them?

'Why did you not mention it to your companions?' Ortulfus went on. 'To see a lion in this part of the world would be an unexpected event, would it not? Did you see a lion, Lord Ermanrich? Lady Hathumod? Gerulf? Dedi?'

One by one, reluctantly, they shook their heads.

'Why did you say nothing?' repeated Ortulfus.

'I – I – it seemed like a dream to me. In the morning, I didn't see any tracks, so I thought perhaps I had dreamed about lions only because of what Baldwin had said.'

'And you, Brother Sigfrid?' Father Ortulfus' tone was the more damning for being so composed.

'There were lions, my lord abbot, but unless you see them with your own eyes, you cannot understand that they exist.'

'So be it. Suspected on the grounds of heresy and sorcery. Biscop Constance must judge this matter, for I cannot. Prior Ratbold, make ready a party to escort them to Autun for trial.'

3

'I went to St. Asella's once,' Hanna admitted as she ate supper that evening with the other Wendish servants in Hugh's retinue. 'Do you go often?'

'Indeed, we do,' said Margret the seamstress. Normally she had a piece of embroidery or mending on her lap. It was strange to see her clever hands engaged in any other activity, even so commonplace a one as spooning leek and turnip stew into her mouth. 'My lord Hugh is most generous, as you know, and gives us one morning a week to attend Vespers at St. Asella's.'

'You're not frightened at going down into the lower city so late? The Aostans don't love the Wendish.'

'They do not love us,' said Vindicadus the scribe, 'but they'll be ruled by us no matter what they wish.' He glanced at Margret.

The seamstress brushed a tendril of graying hair out of her eyes. 'We walk down in daylight. That is safe enough. By the time evening song is over, we are all together. We walk back to the palace as a troop. None bother us, even if a few throw curses our way.'

'I wonder if I might come with you. It gladdened my heart to hear a lesson given in Wendish. My ears grow weary of hearing Aostan, if you'll pardon me for saying so.'

'No need to ask our pardon, but you must ask the steward.' 'Vindicadus' wasn't the name given him by his mother. He came of low birth from a village in western Avaria but had learned to read and write regardless and been allowed to take the cleric's tonsure in a frontier monastery in Austra, where his talents (and, it was rumored, his pretty face and pleasing figure) had come to the attention of Margrave Judith.

He had evidently flowered young and faded quickly, for although a well enough looking man he had gone to fat, and it wasn't clear to Hanna by what chain of events he had ended up in Darre. Hugh used him to make copies of any royal cartularies and capitularies which might be of interest to the skopos and to run errands.

The next day the steward said there was no objection to such an expedition as long as Hanna remained with Margret and Vindicadus. The holy presbyter was a generous lord and favored those of his servants who obeyed him and did right by God.

So she found herself the following evening, as the service of Vespers began, sitting toward the back of the nave in St. Asella's, watching and waiting while Margret and Vindicadus bent their heads in prayer.

'May the Mother and Father of Life have mercy upon us—'

Two male clerics led the service this day, but she saw Fortunatus and the three young women standing at the rear of the choir. Was that Aurea, the servant woman, sitting on the third bench? Even with lamps burning along the aisle, it was hard to tell because the drape of her shawl concealed her face.

'In peace let us pray to Our Lord and Lady.'

The soothing words melded with the whispered gossip of the group of women on the back bench, more interested in chatting about their day than about saving their everlasting souls. It was hard to concentrate on prayers. There were so many distractions, thoughts flickering in and out of her mind as she struggled to quiet the tumble of ideas that fell one over the other. She became aware of a mild rumbling in her stomach, the gift of the strongly-flavored leek stew, three days old, she had eaten this afternoon. She covered her mouth to burp as the two clerics paced out the stations marking the blessed Daisan's life and ministry as he brought the Holy Word to the faithful.

She felt queasy, actually, a little shaky, as though the stew had turned bad. She shut her eyes, but the nausea didn't go away. The bench rocked back. The ground jerked so hard that she slammed into Margret. She fell forward, banging her knee on the bench in front of her.

A scream split the drone of the service as the ground pitched back the other way, grinding and howling. A brick fell square in the middle of the aisle. A tripod teetered, tipped, and spilled fire along the aisle. People leaped to their feet shouting and crying out in fear as Hanna stared uncomprehendingly at the spilled oil, fire running along the stone floor of the church, racing like wildfire. Bricks rained down. Dust smothered the lamps.

Chaos erupted. People bolted for the doors, yelling, as a second tripod tipped over. Fire caught the hem of a man's tunic.

The ground had stopped shaking, but another brick fell smack onto the head of a woman clawing her way past others. She fell and was jerked up by her terrified companion. A man slammed into Hanna and shoved her aside.

'Down!' shouted Hanna, dragging Margret down beside her, using the benches as shields, cowering under them. Vindicadus had vanished. A brick hit the wooden bench right above her head and shattered into two, one half falling on each side. Dust coated her face. Screams deafened her. She saw a man tumble, crushed by the panicked crowd.

'We've got to get out of here!' cried Margret.

'Not that way!' It was hard to be heard with oily smoke filling her lungs when she sucked in air to speak. She kept her hand on Margret's sleeve as she coughed. 'There's another way out past the Hearth!'

They clambered under and over tumbled benches, some standing miraculously upright, others pitched over on their sides, but when they reached the aisle, Margret fled toward the doors. Hanna stumbled through the acrid smoke and streaming dust to fetch up against the Hearth.

'Eagle!' A man's voice. 'This way!'

Her eyes wept tears, and she had to cover her nose and mouth with her sleeve in order to breathe. A firm hand propelled her forward. She tripped on rubble, went down hard on her bruised knee, and fell flat as a body slammed into her. Other hands plucked her to safety, and they stumbled out into open air. The alley was littered with debris and fallen masonry. They picked their way over mounds of bricks, slipping, staggering, hands scraped raw and clothing torn as they reached the spot where the alley opened onto the avenue. There they huddled together, a forlorn group of eight wretched, terrified souls.

Clouds of dust blotted out the twilight sky and the first stars and billowed like fog down the street. Smoke poured skyward as fires took heart from the confusion to run wild. Everywhere men and women stampeded along the streets without purpose, running, shouting, many seeking a gate out of the city. It was hard to tell anything with dust choking their view.

'Oh, God! Look!'

Hanna's neck hurt, but with a grunt of pain she turned. Wind had blown a gap in the dust.

The domed temple dedicated to St. Marcus the Warrior had caved in. Dust rose in clouds, drifting lazily into the sky. Moans and screams from folk trapped within the mound of rubble made a horrible chorus. A distant horn blew. Drums beat from the palace; the upper city was visible in snatches through dust and smoke. The sun bled a deep red as its rim dropped below the horizon. It looked as if the heavens, too, were burning.

Brother Fortunatus stood beside her, weeping tears of fright, or compassion, or pain.

'What did you mean,' she asked suddenly, 'when you preached the parable of the child buried beneath a landslide?'

His face was streaked with dust and a smear of blood, and his eyes seemed startlingly white in contrast, like those of a spooked horse. 'Are you Presbyter Hugh's spy?'

'I am a King's Eagle, Brother. But on my journey south to Aosta, I met one of my fellow Eagles, a woman called Hathui—'

He sank to his knees. Around him, his companions exclaimed while drums resounded and horns rang. Distantly she heard a troop of horse pounding along an unseen street. No one regarded them. A brick fell from the wall of St. Asella's, shattering where it hit the ground not a body's length from them.

'We are desperate, Eagle.' Fortunatus clasped her hands as though he were a supplicant and she the regnant. 'Sister Rosvita has been imprisoned in the dungeon of the skopos for over two years. I pray you, help us rescue her.'

'How can it be that the king has allowed this to happen? She is his most trusted counselor. Did she turn against him?'

'Never! That night we heard only Hathui's frightened testimony. She told us that the queen and the presbyter had conspired to control the king with sorcery, with a daimone. Sister Rosvita went away with the Eagle to seek Margrave Villam and the king. She must have seen the truth. Why else would they have imprisoned her?'

'Why not kill her, then?'

'I have often wondered, but I think—'

'Look!' cried Sister Heriburg.

Cavalry advanced down the crowded avenue like ghosts advancing through fog. The soldiers pressed forward through the panicked mob, who threw bricks and screamed abuse at them.

'There will never be a better time,' said Hanna, scanning the chaos. 'They'll need every guard in the city to restore order, to dig out the injured, to protect the king and queen and the Holy Mother herself. If we go now, perhaps we can save her. Who is with me?'

'I am with you!' cried Fortunatus, rising to his feet. 'Nor need I vouch for my companions.' He gestured to the rest of their party.

'I am with you!'

'And I!'

'I will never desert Sister Rosvita!'

'God bless you, Eagle.' Aurea wiped blood from her cheek with her scarf as she wept.

They all cried out, these soft, educated, nobly-born clerics. How much hardship had they ever faced, three girls freshly come from the convent? The two young men looked no more worldly. Only Fortunatus and Aurea seemed constructed of sterner stuff, less likely to shatter if a cataclysm wrenched them. But they had all endured in Darre for two years, fiercely protective of their imprisoned mentor.

Hanna admired their loyalty.

She could not believe that Sister Rosvita would ever turn against the king, just as she herself would never turn against the king. But if the king were no longer in control of himself, then she must do what she could to fight those who had made him a captive in his own body.

'We must hurry, while they're still in confusion. Where does this alley lead if we go the other way? Can we get to the palace by back streets? We'll need lamps.'

Fortunatus braved the church and returned with three miraculously unbroken lamps and a jar of oil. They made their way back toward the palace, keeping off the main avenues where they were most likely to meet soldiers. The destruction, although extensive, wasn't as bad as that terrible collapse of the dome of St. Marcus. Yet they still had to pick their way over waves of rubble. They still heard the screams of the trapped, the crushed, and those who feared a loved one might have perished. Dust made them cough, so they fixed cloth over their faces to protect themselves. Their clothing was filthy, their faces blackened by soot, ash, and the clogging, stinging dust.

The main ramp leading up to the palaces was choked with traffic as courtiers and servants fled. A fire had broken out in one wing of the regnant's palace. It was not easy to push against the flow of bodies frantically flooding away, but by the gates the crush worked to their advantage as they slipped past the guards undetected.

They pressed through the agitated crowd and into the relative quiet of a niche where travelers could water their thirsty mounts. A leering medusa face came into sudden focus as Hanna raised her lantern. The shaking earth had cracked its hair, and a chunk of the bowl had fallen to the ground. Water dripped uneasily from a loose pipe.

'Do you know how to find Sister Rosvita?' Hanna asked.

'I do,' said Fortunatus.

'Then you and I, and you two, will seek her.' She pointed to the young men, who identified themselves as Jerome and Jehan. 'Sisters, you must brave the chaos. We'll need horses, mules, some kind of wagon or cart in case Sister Rosvita is too weak to ride. Blankets. Provisions, if they're easily come by. Weapons. I use a staff, and a bow. A sword, in dire straits. Knives would be better than nothing.'

'None of us are fighters,' said Fortunatus.

'Make way! Make way for His Honor!'

Hanna glanced out into the dusty courtyard, but the haze and the fitful movement of the torches made it impossible to see what noble courtier or presbyter fled the palace. Perhaps the king had already seen his young queen to safety. Perhaps Henry waited in a smoky hall, unable to make any decision unless another voice spoke in his ear.

She could not dwell on such things. She could, perhaps, save one person tonight. She could not save the entire world.

Aurea and the young women left to seek mounts and a wagon. Fortunatus led them through the servants' corridors into the palace of the skopos, to the ancient gate where corpses had, in olden days, been hauled down to the river.

Here, by this gate, a set of steps cut down into the foundation of the palace. No guards barred their path. They crept down the stairs cautiously. A rumble rattled under their feet, and they stopped, pressing against the walls, fearing that the masonry walls might collapse and bury them. Jerome moaned in fear.

The old palace seemed stable enough. Downward they went on stone stairs rubbed smooth by the passage of many feet, down into chambers cut out of bedrock. As they descended, the air cleared, becoming free of the clinging dust that abraded their lungs. They stumbled into the guards' room. Everyone had fled, leaving a scarred bench and a table with dice and stones scattered heedlessly over the top. A wooden platter bore a half-eaten loaf of bread and a crumb of cheese. Two mugs had overturned, spilling ale over the tabletop, slowly drying up. A single helm molded of leather lay on the floor.

But not everyone could flee. Echoing down the two tunnels that cut deeper into the rock, where cells were hewn to house the prisoners, rose cries for help, prayers, and even one poor soul's maniacal laughter.

'This way,' said Fortunatus, hurrying down one of the tunnels.

'What about the other prisoners?' asked Jehan. He and Jerome scuttled along like nervous dogs, shoulders hunched.

'Heretics, malefici, and worse,' called Fortunatus. 'We dare not let any of them go.'

'I pray you, guardsman! Let me out!'

'Is the world coming to an end?'

'Have mercy! Have mercy!'

'There is no God but Fire!'

The cries resonated. Although muffled by the thick stone walls, the pleas pierced her heart. Would these captive souls be left to die?

She bent to pick up the helm. A rat scurried out of it, running over her fingers, and she shrieked and jumped back, cursing, and slammed into the wall. For an instant, sucking in air that would not come, she thought she would asphyxiate. The walls closed around her, dizzying in the feeble glow of the lamp she still gripped. The air smelled sour. Another tremor might cause the entire palace to fall in on top of them.

They would be buried alive.

'Get hold of yourself!' She kicked over the helm and cautiously picked it up, shook it. No rats. She set it on the table before venturing three steps into the low tunnel that ran opposite the one down which Fortunatus had vanished. She heard, behind her, the scrape of a bar being lifted off a door, heard close by the scritch of hands, or claws, on the walls, a madman's chitter, all singsong. The flame wavered in an eddy of air.

Voices.

'—deserting your post!'

'Nay, Sergeant! What does it matter if God chooses them

to die? I can't bear to remain down there where it's all dark. The walls will cave in. I'm afraid, Sergeant. Don't make me go! Don't make me go!'

She ran back into the guardroom. The guards had fled with their weapons. Grabbing the helm, she fastened it over her head, then tested the weight of the bench. If a humble bench could serve as a weapon one time, then it would surely serve again. Mercifully, this was a lighter bench than the long bench she and Rufus had hoisted in St. Asella's. She hoped Rufus and the other Eagles were all out of the city on the king's business. She prayed the king was safe.

Up the stairs, the shimmer of a lamp chased away the darkness. She slipped into shadow by the arched opening, the bench braced against her knees, upright. Her arms burned at the weight. Her heart raced.

Distantly, as through a fog, she heard Fortunatus' voice. 'Come, Sister Rosvita. We are here to rescue you.'

'Brother Fortunatus?' So changed was that voice, more like a frog's croak than a woman's speech, that Hanna would never have recognized it. But it was not without strength. She sounded weak but not weak-minded, frail but not beaten.

How could anyone survive for two years in such a pit? You might as well be flung into the Abyss.

'I'll whip you forward if I must!' cried the sergeant. 'What are we to say to the skopos if—'

Shadows spilled onto the floor before her feet. She heaved up the bench. The two soldiers lurched into view just as Jehan and Jerome appeared at the mouth of the tunnel with a body carried between them and Fortunatus bringing up the rear.

She brought the bench down hard on the soldiers' heads before they had time to utter a word. The sergeant went down hard, caught by the full weight of the bench. The soldier staggered forward two steps before his knees buckled under him, but even so he caught himself on his hands and, on hands and knees, retched.

No mercy.

She slammed the bench down on him again, and he fell flat. Blood pooled from his nose. Hanna set down the bench and stripped them of their weapons and belts: a stout spear, a short sword, and two knives.

'No time to get their armor. We've got to lock them up.'

The soldier still wasn't knocked out, but he could only whimper and struggle weakly as she rolled him into the open cell where Rosvita had been confined.

'I pray you, mercy!' he sobbed as he clawed at the ground, trying to get up, but his legs wouldn't hold him. Blood and vomit smeared his face and the front of his tunic. The sergeant was a dead weight, and Fortunatus had some trouble shifting him, but together they dragged him down the tunnel and, after shoving aside the pleading, weeping soldier, hauled the door shut and dropped the bar into place.

'Oh, God.' A wave of dizziness so overset her that she stumbled and caught herself on the wall, hearing the moans, the cries, beseeching, begging.

'We must go,' said Fortunatus.

It was a nightmare, as though she had fallen into the pit where the souls of all of the people Bulkezu had murdered were trapped forever within stone, never to be free, never to ascend to the Chamber of Light. She was leaving them all behind. She was abandoning them.

'Jehan and Jerome have carried Sister Rosvita up! Anyone might come! There's nothing we can do for these people!'

'We could let them go.'

'Who knows what terrible crimes they have committed? Why else would the skopos have confined them here? Did you not hear the apostate crying out the Oath made by the fire worshipers?'

'What if they are unjustly imprisoned, as Sister Rosvita was?'

'We dare not take that chance. What if even one of them is mad and tries to stop us? We must escape with Sister Rosvita before more people come. I assure you that the skopos, Presbyter Hugh, and the queen herself will not rest until they find her, once they know she is gone. I pray you, Eagle.'

'I'm sorry,' she whispered, knowing none of the prisoners could hear her although she heard them, their voices rising with despair and panic. 'God, forgive me.'

They took the last oil lamp, leaving the dungeons in a foul darkness.

A strange power afflicted her limbs, so that she raced up the steps and yet was not winded when they reached the top. The air reeked of dust and hot ash, scalding her lungs. By the Dead Man's Gate they found Aurea and two of the young sisters waiting with a mule, a broken-backed nag of a mare, and a handcart in which the young brothers had already laid Sister Rosvita most tenderly, cushioning her on a blanket and covering her with another. The young women fussed and whispered, unwilling to let go of Rosvita's hands, chafing them, kissing them. Aurea had hold of the mounts. She wept silent tears, so overcome with emotion that her face had settled into a grimace as she stared fixedly into the darkness toward the main portion of the palace. The sound of soldiers marching, of a horn and drums, assailed them. Were the soldiers leaving the palace to march down into the city by the main gate, or were they returning in force to garrison the palace? Hanna could not tell. Lights moved on the narrow path that led down to the riverside.

'Fortunatus.' That croak of a voice had gained power. 'What has happened? Why am I here?'

Dry-eyed, Fortunatus kissed Rosvita's hands fervently. 'God brought about a miracle, Sister.' He was distracted by the sound of hurried footfalls, the slap of sandals. 'Where is Heriburg?' he demanded.

'She *would* go off!' cried one of the girls aggrievedly.

There she came, laden with books. 'I have your *History*, Sister!' she cried as she caught sight of them. 'I knew you would not rest easy if we had to leave it behind. We must hurry. A whole troop of soldiers is marching in.'

'The books!' Rosvita lay back in the cart, exhausted.

Heriburg thrust the books in and around the cleric's legs and Hanna pulled the blanket over her completely, concealing her.

'Come,' Hanna said. 'We'll take turns with the cart. Let any who question us be told that we're rescuing books and cartularies from the king's schola.'

It took four of them to negotiate the cart down the steep path, but they had better luck along the avenue that led directly to the western gate. None of the buildings on this stretch had collapsed, although they still had to negotiate the many people milling along the roadway, too afraid to go back inside to fetch their belongings yet unwilling to leave the city without their worldly possessions. A few shouted curses at them, as though the Wendish had brought the disaster down on the city. One man threw a stone that cut an ugly gash on Aurea's cheek.

They kept their heads down after that, and Hanna was glad they weren't leaving by the eastern gate, where anti-Wendish sentiment seemed more volatile. The roar of sound, shouting, wailing, drums, a booming crash that reverberated and collapsed at last into a long rumbling echo, the bleating of goats and the barking of frantic dogs, drove them on.

When they came to the gates, there were indeed guardsmen, but they trundled past in the safety of a mob of complaining, crying women, laundresses by their garb and talk, laden with bedding and dripping garments.

'May God have mercy,' murmured Fortunatus as they cleared the wall.

They had escaped.

They pushed on, looking fearfully from one side to the other, afraid that someone might recognize them and call to them, but no one did. They walked, switching off at the hand cart, trudging along the road with thousands of refugees. Everywhere, in the fields and along the open pastureland that surrounded the city, people had halted in exhaustion. No one dared to spend the rest of the night under a roof.

All this Hanna saw in glimpses, shapes lost in darkness. Dust swathed the sky behind them, veiling half the sky. It was, horribly, a new moon, so dark that the eerie glow of dozens of fires within the city walls, darkened and intensified by the pall of dust, made the place glow like a furnace, the forge of the ancient gods who had once ruled here. Maybe they had returned to wreak their vengeance at last. Maybe God had punished the interlopers.

She took a turn at the cart, pushing until she thought her

hands would fall off, teeth gritted as she followed the bobbing lamp held by Jehan. No one had ridden the mounts yet.
Without saying as much, they all agreed to save the strength
of the poor beasts for later. None of them ate. Hanna wasn't
sure if they had provisions, even water. Her throat ached.

The night wore on endlessly as they took turns pushing the
cart and, later, spelling themselves with a ride on the mule.
Soon they left the refugees behind and made their solitary way
along the deserted road. After a time, the ground sloped up.
They had reached the foothills. Pausing partway up the first
slope to catch their breath, they all turned to look back the
way they had come. Fortunatus pulled the blanket back so that
Sister Rosvita could see and held a lamp aloft beside her.

Darre was burning, not just the city itself but the plain all
around, the glow of bonfires where people camped out and,
closer in to the walls, lines of funeral pyres. Most strangely,
to the southwest, in the mountains, the air was spitting sparks.
She shuddered. The earth rumbled and stilled beneath her
feet.

'Where do we go?' asked Fortunatus. 'We can't cross the
Alfar Mountains this late in the year.'

Silence greeted his words. Even Hanna did not know what
to suggest. She and Fortunatus had led them this far, but they
had come to the end of a rope spun from impulsiveness,
courage, and loyalty. Once Hugh discovered in what direction they had fled, he would pursue them.

She shivered as a cold wind drifted down from the highlands.

Rosvita stirred, stretching her limbs. 'Listen,' she said in
her croak of a voice. 'Listen.'

They listened, but they heard only the night wind. Even
the noise of the city had fallen behind them.

'We must go where they cannot follow, and pray that we
will be given shelter.' With some effort she raised herself on
her elbows. Her hair had gone utterly white, startling even
through the grime of the dungeon. 'We must go to the
Convent of St. Ekatarina. Mother Obligatia helped us once
before. If she still lives, I pray that she will aid us again.'

4

On that morning when Hathumod and her companions left Herford Monastery, the whispering hadn't gone away with them. For days and weeks after they left, as autumn lingered and winter gathered its strength, their heretical words endured like a ghostly presence among the inhabitants of the monastery and estate. Doubt haunted the monks and the laborers. Many scoffed, but others whispered of signs and miracles, of a phoenix, of lions, and of seven innocent and holy sleepers lost beneath a hill.

Although Father Ortulfus delivered more than one furious sermon on the dangers of heresy, even he could be found at odd intervals consulting books in the library or standing lost in contemplation at the edge of the forest, seeming to stare, as Sorrow had that night, at an unseen threat – or toward a promise.

XII

A CALF IN WINTER'S SLAUGHTERHOUSE

1

It was a dreary ride in horrible cold weather from Herford Monastery to Autun. Ivar lost count of the passing days as their escort prodded them grimly along. Once they were forced to spend a week locked up in a freezing outbuilding at a convent because ice floes made a river crossing impassable. Once Prior Ratbold came down with such a bad fever that they had to bide in the stables at an isolated monastic estate while the prior thrashed in delirium, but by the fifth day he sweated out whatever evil humors plagued him and within two weeks felt strong enough to set out again. No one else got sick.

At Dibenvanger Cloister, Sigfrid almost got his tongue out a second time when he squeezed through a gap between boards – he was the only one small enough to fit – and sneaked into the novices' house to preach for the whole evening before Prior Ratbold noticed he was missing.

'A fox among the chickens!' the furious prior roared. 'The only way to stop him is to make sure he can't speak!'

The mild-mannered abbot of Dibenvanger Cloister dissuaded Ratbold from any violent acts and sent them on their way the next morning, but not before coming himself at dawn to counsel the wayward prisoners.

'Do not despair, friends,' he said quietly. 'You are not alone.'

These mysterious words lifted Ivar's spirits as the days wore on.

Yet when at last they descended into the Rhowne Valley, a fit of melancholy swept over him. The painful anticipation wore him out. How would Biscop Constance rule at their trial? Would she be lenient or severe? Would they face excommunication? Even death? It seemed impossible to hold onto resolve through bad times as well as good.

The Rhowne Valley was rich country, well populated with prosperous holdings and verdant estates. Even blanketed by snow the roads and fields had a tidy look to them, well traveled and well tended. Biscop Constance shepherded a thriving flock.

A bell hung under a thatched awning by the ferry crossing. Prior Ratbold rang the bell. The rest of them dismounted and led the horses around to keep them warm while, on the other side, the ferryman emerged from his cottage, surveyed their distant party, went back into his house, and came out a while later to haul the ferry across by a cable strung over the broad river.

It took three crossings to get them all across. While he waited, Ivar brooded.

Gerulf and Dedi went over with the first load. The two Lions had developed a friendly banter with the monks who were their guards; three of the monks had been in the Lions before they'd retired from war and the world and dedicated their lives to the church. Despite their misgivings about the heretical charges set on Gerulf's and Dedi's heads, they still respected former comrades. It was its own form of kinship, based not on family ties but on shared service to the king. They'd fought, seen comrades fall, suffered and marched and remained faithful.

Prior Ratbold, a younger son of a noble house, had no such

reason to treat his charges kindly. His family had no connection to any of theirs, and their families weren't important enough to matter to him. To Ratbold, they were sinful heretics, nothing else.

Maybe Ivar's sister Rosvita could have helped him, had she wished to, but she wasn't here. And his father had long since contrived to get rid of him. The old familiar desolation washed over him as he clutched the railing of the ferry in the last group to go across. Brownish-green waters swirled beyond his boots. A big branch thudded against the side of the ferry, rocking them and disturbing the horses, before the river's grip carried it on.

Everyone had deserted him. His father had never cared for him, not really, and he'd been an infant when his mother had died. To his brothers and sisters, he was a nuisance, the red-haired baby who got in their way. Hanna had ridden away to become an Eagle. Liath had tempted him and then abandoned him for the embrace of a prince. Yet his life had been good before Hugh had come to Heart's Rest. He had a memory of how much he had once hated Hugh, a feeling like holding a burning blade in your hand. Hate had felt good once. Now his hate streamed away with the river's water, flowing down-river to the sea.

If he threw himself in the river, no one would miss him. Not even Hugh would care. Hugh probably didn't even remember his name.

The river tugged at the ferry as it tugged at his heart. He saw figures in the water, water nymphs calling to him and stretching out their arms as they beckoned and wept. *Come to us,* they said as their bodies undulated through choppy wavelets. *Come to us.* A cold grave, but a peaceful one. He tightened his grip on the railing and leaned far over, giddy with despair. The water looked so comforting. So final.

'Are you crazy?' Baldwin grabbed Ivar's shoulder, jerking him back. 'You might fall over and drown, and then what would I do? You're not even paying attention to what I was saying! Can you see it, there? That's the tower of the biscop's palace of Autun.'

Ivar's eyes were too blurred with tears to see. Ermanrich appeared on his other side, setting a steadying hand on his elbow. 'Yes, I see it, Baldwin,' he said, without letting go of Ivar.

'Don't you see, Ivar?' demanded Baldwin impatiently. The river wind streamed through his pale hair; color blushed his fair cheeks. If the water nymphs were mourning and wailing, it was probably because they'd just realized they'd never get their hands on any creature as handsome as Baldwin. 'The biscop's banner isn't flying over the palace. She's not there! And if she's not there, she can't hold a trial!'

To the ferryman's disgust, the others crowded over to stand alongside Ivar. The ferry pitched like an ungainly horse, and water spilled onto the boards and seeped away.

'Where do you think the biscop has gone?' Hathumod asked.

'She's duke of Arconia as well as biscop of Autun,' said Ermanrich. 'She'll have duties elsewhere in the duchy, not just in Autun. When I was a novice at Firsebarg, I saw her one time when she rode by on her progress.'

He glanced at their guards, standing at the opposite railing to make a counterbalance. The ferryman and his assistant pulled mightily, dragging them along while the current did its best to wash them downriver.

'Biscop Constance is a fair-minded noblewoman,' Ermanrich went on more quietly. 'I've never heard any but a respectful word spoken of her, even where it couldn't be heard. She'll be a fair judge.'

'If there can be a fair judge,' muttered Ivar.

'You must trust in God, Ivar,' scolded Sigfrid. 'Hasn't She watched over us all along?'

Baldwin leaned against Ivar, folded a warm hand over one of Ivar's cold ones, and bent his head close. 'Of course she has.' His voice caressed like a gentle kiss. 'We'd be dead two or three times over if it wasn't for God. I'd still be married to Margrave Judith.'

Who had died three years ago. It didn't seem right, or possible that so much time could have passed. Had Father

Ortulfus lied to them as a cruel jest?

'Ivar, what do you think will happen if Biscop Constance isn't there?' asked Ermanrich expectantly. The others echoed his question: shy Hathumod, frail Sigfrid, even Baldwin, although Baldwin didn't speak, only batted his gorgeous eyelashes in attractive confusion.

They waited for him to speak. They looked to him for answers. Why on God's earth did they think *he* had any answers, when he couldn't even fathom his own heart? Yet they expected him to lead them. They counted on him.

They needed him.

'There!' Baldwin pointed. 'Now do you see it?'

Ivar glimpsed a stone tower among trees, lost as the ferry pulled laboriously in to shore. The banner flying from that tower didn't look like Biscop Constance's white-and-gold standard.

Before disembarking, Ivar paused to study the flowing river. Had he only dreamed the water nymphs? Certainly he now saw nothing except water streaming past, its melodious song singing in his ears. Their horses were brought, they mounted, and rode on. Where they came out of the trees, Autun rose before them, its main ramparts clambering along a defensible hill and more recent settlements sprawled below the old walls along the river, each ringed by a palisade. The biscop's palace stood between a timber-and-stone cathedral and the old duke's tower, a squat watch post built entirely out of stone in the time of the Dariyan Empire. Above these magnificent edifices, on the highest portion of the hill, lay Taillefer's famous palace and the splendid octagon chapel where his earthly remains were interred in a marble tomb.

The banner flying from the biscop's palace displayed the green guivre, wings unfolded and red tower gripped in its left talon, that marked the presence of the duke of Arconia.

'Strange,' murmured Prior Ratbold. 'Why isn't the biscop's banner flying at its side, as it ought to?'

They waited at the main gates while the Autun guards sent for a captain from the citadel, a man called Ulric. He had a grim face and a cynical eye, and orders from his superiors.

'Heretics, is it?' he asked wearily, as if he'd heard this tiresome refrain a hundred times already that day. 'Come all the way from Herford Monastery, have you? Isn't that in the duchy of Fesse?'

'So it is, Captain,' agreed Ratbold, 'but you might recall Father Ortulfus was but recently a member of the biscop's schola. That's why he was given the abbacy at Herford when it fell vacant.'

'Ah, yes, so he was.' Ulric grimaced in much the same way as might a man commanded to eat maggots. 'I'll take these prisoners from you, Prior, and see that they are housed as they deserve. You may return on your way.'

'Without even a night's shelter and a hot meal for our pains?' Anyone would have been outraged at this insult, and Prior Ratbold was not the most sweet-tempered of men. 'I can't believe we'd be turned away after a journey of four weeks' time, standing in muck to our ankles and likely snow coming on.' The monks muttered among themselves, shocked by such a breach of the customs of hospitality. 'Where are we to stay this night?'

'The ferryman has lodging enough to house you.'

As Ratbold began to protest again, Ulric quite unexpectedly grabbed the prior by his robe and pulled him close. Only Ivar was close enough to overhear the captain's soft words. 'Listen, friend. I'd advise you strongly to turn right round and get on your way before anyone takes notice of who your master is. You're just lucky it was me on duty this afternoon, or you'd be marching to a nice locked cell at this very moment. Do you understand me?'

'B-b-but—' For once, Prior Ratbold lost his power of speech.

Ulric let him go and watched with narrowed eyes and a bitter frown as Ratbold hurriedly got his party turned around and headed south, away from the city. The captain had the patience of a saint. Only when an orchard and a dip in the road hid their backs from his sight did he turn to regard his prisoners.

'Bring in the heretics,' he said caustically to his guardsmen. 'What's seven more in our lady's service?'

They were taken to a low room in the barracks loft, the kind of prison that soldiers accused of a crime like petty theft or fistfighting would be thrown into. Here they languished for four days, measured by the light coming and going in the smoke hole. Food and drink arrived at regular intervals. Their slops bucket was emptied twice a day. They had no fire but plenty of straw for padding and although it was cold enough that Ivar was always shivering, the heat from below made it bearable. In fact, judging by the noise and activity, there seemed to be an awful lot of soldiers gathered in Autun, as many as if the king dwelled here. In the dim light they couldn't tell what was going on. They could only listen and pray.

On the fifth morning the trap was flung open, admitting a roil of smoke and a summons. One by one they climbed down the ladder. The awkwardness of their descent on a rickety ladder made them vulnerable, as did a dozen sour-looking guards waiting below. Impossible to make an escape in these circumstances.

'They'll need a wash before they're taken in to see Her Most Excellent Highness.' Captain Ulric paused in front of Baldwin, scratching his beard as he looked the young man up and down. 'See that this one is given clean clothes. One of you can trim his hair and beard, but don't let him or any of his comrades handle the razor.'

'Going for a bonus, Captain?' jested one of the guards, a slender young man with pale hair.

'Shut up, Erkanwulf. I do what I must to protect my position and the men under my command. If I can gain Her Ladyship's favor, so be it. Now move along.'

'Something doesn't feel right,' whispered Ermanrich, before getting a hard tap on his behind from the haft of a halberd.

'No talking,' said the one called Erkanwulf. Like his captain, he had a surly expression as though he'd eaten something disagreeable.

Ivar glanced at Gerulf, but the old Lion just shrugged.

Something wasn't right here, but it was impossible to know what it was except for the unusual concentration of soldiers, visible as the prisoners were marched through the barracks, out through the busy courtyard, and over to the famous palace baths.

In these stone halls, built long ago by Dariyan engineers, Emperor Taillefer had held court while luxuriating in the waters. His poets had sung of the curative powers of the baths, and more than one tapestry woven in those times depicted Taillefer at his ease among his courtiers in the baths or reclining at dinner on couches as the ancient Dariyans were said to do. The great emperor had restored the glory of the old Dariyan Empire for a brief and brilliant span.

Yet his Holy Dariyan Empire had collapsed when he had died. No one after him had been strong enough to hold it together.

A pair of elderly women had charge of the baths at this hour. Not even they, crones both, were immune to Baldwin's staggering beauty, and by the time they were done with him, he looked better than he had in weeks with his hair neatly cut in the style favored by the royal princes and his beard trimmed to show off the handsome line of his jaw. A guard brought him a clean wool tunic, simple in cut and color but more than adequate compared to their travel-stained gear. Even Gerulf whistled admiringly.

'God above,' swore Dedi, as if he couldn't help himself. 'I'm glad my Fridesuenda never got a look at him. She'd have forgotten I ever existed.'

Baldwin looked ready to weep, like a calf just realizing that it's about to be led off to the slaughterhouse. Ivar set a hand on Baldwin's shoulder. 'Just stick by me.'

'You won't abandon me, will you, Ivar?'

'Of course not, Baldwin. I'll never abandon you. Never.'

Baldwin's bright-eyed gaze made Ivar uncomfortable, and even a little aroused. What had Ivar ever done to deserve Baldwin's loyalty? Well, a few things, maybe, that he blushed to recall now. Those months they'd spent drinking and carousing and whoring with Prince Ekkehard were not ones he cared to dwell on; it was as if they'd been stricken by a plague of lechery and greed that had burned away anything good in them until they were merely rutting husks. But it hadn't been all bad. He didn't regret the intimacy he'd shared with Baldwin, because that at least had arisen from genuine love.

Love.

Ai, God. Why hadn't he seen it before, when it had been staring him in the face all along? Baldwin stood there in all his beauty, so delectable that with only a little effort he could have just about any woman, and a few of the men, at his feet with a smile. But it was Ivar he gazed at trustingly, Ivar he clung to, Ivar he followed through thick and thin.

He loves me.

Captain Ulric arrived and, with a curse, surveyed Baldwin, Ivar, and the silence that had fallen between them. 'Please don't tell me he can't get it up for women.'

'He's a novice, sworn to the church,' retorted Ivar angrily, hastily removing his hand from Baldwin's shoulder. But he knew a blush flowered in his face. His complexion always betrayed him.

The guards snickered until Ulric shut them up with a curt command. 'Move them along. Her Most Excellent Highness doesn't like to be kept waiting.'

From the baths to Taillefer's palace was a climb up a flight of stairs carved into the rock. A light snow fell, white flakes spinning down to dust rocks and rooftops, but not a single flake touched them because of the walkway built over the stairs so that the emperor could walk to and from his baths without getting rained on. Slender stone pillars supported a timber roof. Each pillar had been carved in the shape of an animal: dragons, griffins, eagles, and guivres accompanied their climb. Once Ivar came abreast of a noble phoenix, but when he paused to touch its painted feathers, Erkanwulf prodded him in the back with the butt of his spear.

'Move along, just as Captain said.'

By chance he had ended up behind Baldwin, and as he climbed he could not take his gaze away from the curl of Baldwin's hair against the trim of his tunic, or the way glimpses

of his neck, still moist from the baths, revealed themselves as
Baldwin's tunic shifted on his shoulders to the rhythm of his
climb up the stairs. Did Baldwin really love him? Or was he
just the only thing Baldwin had to hold on to?

A gate carved with Dariyan rosettes admitted them to the
palace compound. Guards stood watch here, too. They were
everywhere; a wasps' swarm of guards inhabited Autun, all
of them agitated and tense. Their party emerged into a courtyard bounded by a stone colonnade on one side and a stout
rampart on the other. Opposite, Ivar saw the octagon chapel
with its stone buttresses flaring out from each corner. He had
once been allowed to pray inside the glorious chapel, kneeling in front of the stone effigy marking Taillefer's resting
place. He remembered that stern and noble visage and, most
of all, the precious crown held in carved hands, a gold crown
with seven points, each point adorned with a precious gem.

But he scarcely had time to gape at the exterior of the
chapel before he was hustled away down the colonnade and
into the great hall. In this hall he had tried to intervene in
the trial of Liath and Hugh. How miserable his failure had
been. He'd got a beating for his trouble, Liath had been
excommunicated, and Hugh had been sent south to stand trial
before the skopos. No doubt that bastard Hugh had by now
charmed his way into the Holy Mother's good graces. And
for all Ivar knew, Liath was dead.

He couldn't hate a dead woman. Was Hanna dead, too?
Tears started up in his eyes as he stared around at the tapes-
tried walls, the high ceiling above, half lost in gloom, and the
lamps hung from brackets on every pillar and beam. Those
hundred blazing flames threw off enough heat to warm the
room.

It was strange to stand here again. He seemed doomed to
come to grief in this hall. Baldwin caught his hand and
squeezed it, then let go as the others were pushed up beside
them.

Three princely chairs sat on the dais. Two were unoccu-
pied. Soldiers, courtiers, servants, and hangers-on chattered
casually among themselves as, on the dais, a noble prince sat

in judgment. She was a robust, handsome lady of middle years, probably past any hope of bearing children, wearing a gold coronet on her brow and the richly embroidered clothing of a prince who might at any moment ride out to war. Ivar had only time to catch the glint of the gold torque at her neck, signifying her royal blood, before he was prodded forward. A dozen strides brought them to a halt in front of the dais steps. The butt of a spear jabbed Ivar so hard in the back of his knee that he lost his balance. Reflexively, he knelt, dropping hard, just as his companions did around him.

Captain Ulric stepped to one side, the better to display his prisoners. 'Another party of heretics brought to the gate, Your Highness.'

'Lord save us,' whispered Gerulf, who was kneeling so closely behind Ivar that one of his knees had ridden uncomfortably up on Ivar's toes. 'What's that traitor doing sitting in the seat of judgment?'

2

They followed the defile by the light of a full moon. The play of shadows across the rock and the daunting silence made the landscape ominous, but they had to keep going.

'Not much farther now.'

Hanna had a hard time understanding their guide; the Aostan spoken in Darre seemed to have little to do with the language spoken in this God-forsaken region, although they were supposedly the same tongue.

'I recognize the path,' said Fortunatus. He held the reins of the mule on which Sister Rosvita rode.

'I do not, except as snatches of a dream,' replied Rosvita.

'You were very ill last time we came this way.'

'Journey in haste, repent in leisure,' she agreed, glancing back down the narrow track the way they had come. They were hemmed in by rock faces sculpted by God's hands into terrible visages that glowered over them. 'We seem fated to travel here with enemies at our heels.'

Hanna also looked back along the trail. It was too dark to see anything beyond their line of march: the three girls behind her, then Jerome and Jehan leading a goat, and, last, the servant woman, Aurea, with Hanna's staff gripped in her hands. In daylight, the dust of a large troop of horsemen would give away the position of those who followed them, but at night they had to rely on other stratagems. She fingered the amulet of protection she wore around her neck. Woven by Heriburg from fennel and the withered flowers of noble white, these were all that had allowed them to come so far without being spied out by the Holy Mother and her council of sorcerers.

Jehan coughed, echoed by Ruoda, a hacking cough that rose from her chest. Sickness dogged them, too.

'Here.' The old guide halted, whistling softly. A thrown pebble snapped on the track in front of him, and in its wake a boy scrambled out of the rocks. The child had the family nose, beaked and noble if overlarge on such a small face, and the wiry build common to the countryfolk in this desolate region.

The boy babbled too swiftly for Hanna to catch more than a few words, but Rosvita listened intently before turning to the others, who crowded up behind her.

'The child says that there are twenty horsemen an hour or more behind us, led by a lord so handsome that some in the village wonder if he might be an angel and we the demons he's been sent by God to pursue.'

'How did they find us?' demanded Heriburg. 'We should have remained hidden from them. We have the amulets, and we used every means of misdirection.'

'Yet these were evidently not enough.' Rosvita lifted a hand to silence her. 'Perhaps they picked up our trail at the village. It no longer matters. We must hurry if we hope to reach the convent before they catch us.'

They kept going. They had very little left except their determination. At the last village they had traded the handcart in exchange for the old man's services as a guide. It was the only thing of worth they had left. The mare had gone lame and they had sold the mule for food. The last of the coins brought by Fortunatus had gone days ago to buy a milking goat, grain, and wine. They had nothing now except the clothes and cloaks on their backs, the precious books, Hanna's staff, bow, quiver, and knife, and three eating knives shared out between the rest of them. Even the blankets had been traded for quinces, porridge, and a stock of dried fish, now eaten.

The moon set behind the western highlands as dawn lit the eastern hills. In this half light, as inconstant as hope, they cut to the right along the gully and found themselves on a flat field running up to the base of a vast cone of upthrust rock that loomed like the hammer of God before them.

Stumps of trees and patches of dry scrub gave the ground a leprous appearance. No birds sang. Where the valley broadened, it snaked back around either side of the huge outcropping, but the steep hills on either side quickly closed back in. Shadows still filled the valley. There was no sign of life.

'My God,' said Hanna. She thought her legs would give out. 'Are you sure someone lives up there?'

'I am sure.'

Dismounting to stand at the foot of the cliff, Rosvita shouted out. No one answered.

She shouted again. They waited. Wind teased the rock. Above, a pale scrap fluttered where a narrow ledge stuck out from the cliff face, but Hanna could not quite make out what it was. No one answered. There was no way up that precipitous slope.

The guide glanced repeatedly toward the gully, expecting the troop of horsemen to burst free at any moment. At last he edged away from them and, with a nervous burst of speed, jogged back the way they had come.

'Let him go,' said Rosvita as Aurea started after him, brandishing the staff. 'He drove a fair bargain, and gave us what we asked for.'

'And no doubt had his kinfolk betray us to the ones pursuing us, for an equal price,' said Aurea bitterly.

'I hope he got a better bargain than the one we gave him,' said Fortunatus. 'The axle on that cart had already broken once and it was ready to crack for good and all.'

'One of you must have a stronger voice than I,' said Rosvita. 'We must all shout together.'

They did so, but there was still no answer.

Day lightened around them, although they remained in the rock's shadow.

'How are we supposed to climb up there?' Hanna asked.

'There were rope ladders before,' said Fortunatus, squinting at the glint of sun as it crested the eastern hills. He pointed to the fluttering scrap Hanna had noticed before. 'That's one there, you can see the corner of it, but it's been pulled up.'

'There must be someone still up there,' said Rosvita. 'If they had all left, the ladders would be down.'

'Oh, God, I'm afraid,' said Gerwita, beginning to cry. 'What will they do to us if they catch us?'

'I'll climb,' said Hanna. 'If I can reach that ledge, then at least we can get up that far, out of their reach.'

'Not out of reach of their bows,' said Fortunatus.

Rosvita had a serious gaze, one that Hanna had come to trust in the last weeks. 'It will be risky to climb, Eagle. We might hide farther down into the ravine and hope our pursuers turn away, thinking we have escaped them.'

'We might. But I don't think it would work.'

'The north face can be climbed,' said Fortunatus. 'Lord John Ironhead sent soldiers that way. Don't you recall that they were killed by the daimone?'

'Yes, poor souls. May God have mercy on them.'

'We're trapped, aren't we?' said Aurea. 'No matter what we do. For even if we can get up there, we haven't enough people to hold off an attack if they choose to send soldiers up after us on this north face you speak of.'

'We shall see,' said Rosvita. 'One can set traps of one's own in such precarious circumstances. They cannot besiege us forever. And there is one other chance. . . .' She trailed off, looked at Hanna again, a searching gaze, and nodded.

'I'll go,' said Hanna. None of the clerics were hardy enough, in truth, nor had they the strength to haul Rosvita up the cliff, and despite how much strength Sister Rosvita had gained in the last weeks of their flight, she had not the strength to climb a rugged rock face.

Fortunatus led Hanna around the base of the huge outcropping to the north face. It took a while; the outcropping was huge, and beyond the level field where olive trees had once grown, the ground became rugged enough that they had to slow down in order to pick their way through fallen rocks and shallow gullies. She was sweating by the time Fortunatus halted, out of breath, and wordlessly gestured to the rock face above them. She studied its contours and ledges as well as the message written by the way burnet and scraggly pine had taken root in crevices and ledges along the face.

'Here,' she said, stripping off her gloves and handing them over. She took rope, her knife, and a skin half full of bitter ale, leaving the rest of her gear with Fortunatus.

'I'll wait until I see you're safely at the top. Then I'll return to the others.'

She picked her way over scree to the place where she had chosen to begin. The climb wasn't as difficult as she'd feared, as long as she didn't look down. Her fingers and hands began to hurt; that she had expected. But her shoulders ached, too, the soles of her feet, her thighs, any muscle she had to tense in order to hold on. She learned to brush dust from any handhold before surrendering her weight; she was less likely to slip if no grains slid under her fingers. At times she wedged her knees into hollows and shelves into the rock, and once or twice was able to lean into the rock face because of a shift in its slope, giving hands and feet a rest. Yet at such moments, given a chance to reflect, she decided that an enemy lurking above could easily send her plunging to her death by rolling rocks onto her from above.

But no one did.

No horsemen came riding out of the gully. No movement stirred above as she fought her way up the cliff, resting wherever she could but never for long. Human assailants were not the only danger she faced; the scree at the base of the slope was testament to that. One of her fingers began to bleed, stinging each time she used it to grip. The day remained quiet, disturbed by only a light breeze. The sun warmed her shoulders although the air remained chill.

Sister Rosvita had a plan. They had to delay their pursuit, that was all. As long as she believed that, she had the strength to go on. As long as she did not look down.

The steep-sided face gave way to a gentler slope slippery with loose rock. After a terrifying slip that almost sent her hurtling back over the cliff, she swept clean spaces for her feet as she crept forward until the ground leveled off and she entered a forest of rock pinnacles. She stumbled across a broad path and hesitated, not sure which way to turn. At last she simply began walking in one direction and within twenty steps the pinnacles gave way to a flat summit crowned by a stone circle.

The sight stunned her. She had never seen a stone crown in such good repair, but the upright stones seemed ominous rather than magnificent, a secret key to a place better left unexplored. The wind bit through her tunic, now soaked with sweat from her exertions. Sun glittered on an oval patch of sand situated about three steps in front of the closest archway, which had been created by an imposing lintel stone bridging the gap between two of the standing stones. From this angle, she could not tell if there were eight or nine uprights. White glinted on the stony ground. She took several steps before stumbling to a stop. A sour taste rose in the back of her throat. Broken skeletons lay strewn within and around the circle of stones, the remains of a dozen people at least. One lay not two bodies' lengths from her, picked clean, bones tumbled by wind and rain, decaying tunic pinned by rock and ribs, a bit of fabric caught like a tongue between the gaping jaw. Trembling, she drew the Circle of Unity at her breast to ward off its restless spirit.

No living creature waited here. She retreated, backtracking past the spot where she had come across the path, and followed it down. The trail cut along the rock face with cliff to one side and open air on the other. She kept a hand on the rock to steady herself. Only once did she look out over the chasm of empty air. Were those tiny figures Rosvita and the others? Her knees buckled, and a wave of dizziness staggered her. She remained kneeling until her body stopped shaking. After that she kept her eyes on the path. The wind teased her hair. Although the sun was high, it gave no warmth.

In time the path broadened to become a terrace whose far entrance was a cave's mouth. She hesitated at the entry. A dank smell wafted from the depths, but there was light enough to see. She entered cautiously, finding herself in a low cave lit by openings along one wall that gave way onto narrow terraces. One cave opened onto another, this also with a terrace formed beyond. Animals had been kept here; heaps of scorched and broken bones littered the cavern. It grew darker, her steps more hesitant. She climbed over a low wall, its sides stippled with small squares hewn through the barrier like arrow slits. These were not natural. Whoever built this place expected to be attacked, and to have to defend themselves.

Beyond this wall she found herself creeping down a tunnel into the heart of the massive stone outcropping. Cunning shafts cut through the stone angled sunlight onto her path, giving her enough light to see.

Even so, the next barrier almost killed her. She felt a breath of air brush her face first; then she marked the ground, murky with shadow, shrieked, and sat back, catching herself before she tumbled over the lip of a chasm.

Panting, she sat there, listening to her breath and the silence of stone. She groped for and found a pebble, dropped it down the shaft. Counted. At 'eight' the barest *snick* echoed up from the depths.

'Oh, God,' she murmured. She found another pebble and tossed it across the chasm. *Snick.* It wasn't far, but it was definitely too far to jump. A broad plank rested on the ground on the other side, a makeshift bridge.

Sister Rosvita was right. Perhaps the holy nuns and lay sisters who had once lived here were dead now, but in any case, they hadn't departed. Some had remained, to live or to die within the rock.

'Sisters,' she called. 'I pray you, heed my call. I seek Mother

Obligatia or any of the holy sisters under her care. I come on behalf of Sister Rosvita—'

There came that sharp *snick* again, a pebble smacking against rock. As her eyes adjusted she saw past the chasm and the plank: the tunnel ended in a stone wall. Even if she found a way to cross the pit, the path was a dead end.

There was no way in.

Their flight had been in vain.

Tears flowed, choking her. She had failed Rosvita and the others. They would become prisoners again, at the mercy of folk so powerful that they could ensorcell the king. Their pursuers might already have captured Rosvita and the others while she searched for a path to freedom.

It had all been for nothing.

How long she sat there, stunned and exhausted, she was not sure, only that she was too discouraged to move.

Snick. Another pebble, although she'd not thrown anything.

A bodiless voice whispered out of the darkness.

'*Who are you?*'

She jumped to her feet, leaping back from the chasm.

There was no one there. No one in sight. Only silence.

Snick.

The voice had spoken in Aostan, so she replied as well as she could after so many months in Darre. 'I am called Hanna. Here I come with Sister Rosvita and her companions. We flee her enemies. I pray you, help us.'

'*Who is Sister Rosvita?*'

She gritted her teeth in frustration, until she realized that the question might be a test. 'She is a cleric from Wendar. She is counselor to King Henry. She protected and counseled the king, but she made enemies, whom she now flees. I pray you, we do not have time.'

'*How may one know Sister Rosvita? What is her life's work?*'

'To serve the king as well as she is able!' cried Hanna, exasperated.

Snick.

Think as a cleric thought, as a churchwoman might think. Act as Sister Heriburg had acted, when they had fled from

Darre in the aftermath of the earthquake.

'A book! A history of the princes of Wendar. She has it with her still!'

Snick.

A grinding noise reverberated in the enclosed space. The blank wall beyond the ditch shifted and rolled to open a gap through which a slight figure slipped. Hanna faced across the pit an emaciated, corpse-white woman wearing the tattered robes of a nun, her sleeves pushed back to reveal wiry arms. She shoved the plank out across the chasm, balancing it deftly until the far end rested on Hanna's side.

'I am called Sister Hilaria. We live hidden deep within the rock now, since the day the daimone attacked us. It takes all of our strength to guard our prisoner and nurse our Holy Mother. We have turned our backs on the outside world. It was the pebble that alerted me while I was fetching water. I came at once to investigate. Follow me, friend. If we are to save Sister Rosvita, we must hurry.'

3

Gerulf's traitor surveyed them with princely dignity and a keen gaze, although her eyes flared when she caught sight of Baldwin, kneeling to Ivar's right. But a prince of her stature could not be cowed even by Baldwin's singular loveliness. 'You have been brought to Autun accused of heresy and implicated in matters of sorcery. Yet you have nothing to fear from me. The truth is welcome here in Arconia.'

She paused, expecting a response; perhaps she was curious to see who would emerge as the leader. Ivar waited, too, until he realized that the rest were waiting for him to speak.

'Your Highness,' he said, stumbling over the words. 'I – I am Ivar, son of Count Harl and Lady Herlinda of the North Mark—'

'I know who you are.' She gave an amused grunt. 'I haven't forgotten the trial of Judith of Austra's bastard son Hugh a few years back, nor your part in it. It was one of the few entertaining days I had during my confinement here in Autun. I believe you must be related to Sister Rosvita, my brother Henry's favored cleric. Ah!' She looked up expectantly as a big man strode up onto the dais, attended by a handsome, shapely girl of eleven or twelve years of age. She had dark skin but unexpectedly light golden-brown hair, a contrast that reminded him bitterly of Liath although there was otherwise no resemblance.

'My lord duke,' said Captain Ulric with rather more warmth than he'd shown to the lady. 'My lady Ælfwyn.'

'God Above!' swore the duke as he sank down into the left-hand chair, leaving the middle seat empty. The girl stood behind him, holding onto the back of the chair while she examined the prisoners with bold intensity. 'So this is the infamous bridegroom who escaped Judith's clutches!' A pair of brindle hounds swarmed up after him, licking his hands before collapsing worshipfully at his feet.

'No wonder the margrave was so furious,' mused the lady prince. She had a strong face. Her silver hair had been braided and dressed with ribbons, but she wore it uncovered in the manner of an unmarried maiden or a soldier. She gestured toward Ivar. 'Come, Lord Ivar, you were speaking before Duke Conrad arrived. Go on.'

Conrad the Black could not be mistaken for any other man in the kingdom. And although Henry had many sisters, only two were older than he was: his bastard half sister Alberada, who served as biscop in the east, and the woman who had already contested his authority once by leading a rebellion against him.

'My lady Sabella,' said Ivar, inclining his head to show respect. 'We are not heretics. It is the church which has concealed the truth. Can it be possible you have heard and accepted the true Word of God and the truth of the blessed Daisan's sacrifice and redemption?'

Her attention had wandered back to Baldwin. 'If report is

true,' she said absently, 'you were all novices at Quedlinhame.'

'So we were, Your Highness, but we were punished for preaching the true Word. We escaped those who tormented us. Now we walk as best we can to spread the true Word to all those who live in the night of lies and deceit.'

'Then let them preach,' said Conrad impatiently as he rubbed the head of one of his hounds. He glanced up to mark his daughter, and her serious expression immediately melted into a charming grin, a comrade marking her best companion in her battle against the world. He winked merrily at her before turning back to address Sabella. 'Let them preach. We were just about to ride out to hunt when you sent for me.'

'Let us preach?' breathed Sigfrid, forgetting that Ivar was their spokesman.

'Let you preach,' said Sabella with a smile obviously intended for Baldwin. 'Here in Varre, all are welcome to preach according to their knowledge of the sacrifice and redemption.'

Baldwin seemed struck dumb.

'We are?' squeaked Ermanrich, as Hathumod sighed happily.

'Yes, yes, you are,' said Conrad, tapping a foot on the floor as he lounged back in the chair. His hounds whined and thumped their tails anxiously, catching his mood. 'If there's no other business that needs my attention, Cousin, then I'll go.'

'Nay, nay, Cousin. Wait a moment, if you please. You see there behind our novices two fighting men, who report has it are Lions, deserted from my brother.'

'Deserters?' Conrad straightened. 'I've never heard of Lions deserting their regnant. What complaint have you against King Henry?'

'No complaint!' declared Gerulf stoutly. 'Nor have we deserted. We marched east to fight the Quman and came temporarily under Prince Bayan's command.'

'Yet you are not in the east now,' observed Conrad. 'How goes the campaign there?'

Gerulf glanced at Ivar, unsure how to respond, but Ivar

motioned him forward to stand before Conrad as a messenger. 'We have no more recent news than you do, my lord duke. Prince Bayan and Princess Sapientia met the Quman begh Bulkezu on the field of battle beyond the eastern borderlands, and it went badly for them. The Quman are many, and we are few. The Wendish forces desperately need reinforcements or the Quman will overrun the marchlands. That is all we know.'

'Yet two years ago Prince Sanglant defeated this same Prince Bulkezu outside Osterburg, on the Veser River,' commented Conrad. 'Or so we heard. Rumor says Prince Sanglant rode east after the battle, to what purpose I cannot say.'

'I hear he means to rebel against Henry,' said Sabella. 'Yet how can it be called rebellion when Henry is more interested in his Aostan queen and her lands than in those he claims already to rule?'

'We've had no news since the battle Prince Bayan and Princess Sapientia lost to the Quman,' said Ivar.

'Let it be said plainly,' said Conrad. 'Henry has married the Aostan queen and remains in Aosta to restore Adelheid's throne to her, and to play his own games with his dream of Taillefer's empire. If he chooses to turn his back on his own lands, then he must not be surprised if others choose to rule for him here.'

No sudden death knell tolled from Taillefer's chapel. No hush dropped like the stench of the grave over the assembly. These words surprised no one except the seven prisoners who had so recently come into town.

'You're rebelling against King Henry's authority,' said Ivar, knowing he sounded idiotic.

'Nay, child,' said Sabella. 'Henry abandoned us. We are simply caring for those he left behind. I pray you, consider what it means to you that Conrad and I now serve as regents in the kingdom of Varre. You may preach freely. None shall attempt to stop you, excommunicate you, or punish you. Is that not more than you could have expected under Henry's rule?'

Gerulf muttered angry words under his breath, and Ivar

calmed the old Lion by laying a hand on his arm. 'Truly, it is more than we expected. We expected to be brought to trial before Biscop Constance on the charge of heresy.'

'Biscop Constance no longer rules here,' said Sabella, while Conrad shifted restlessly. 'You are safe from her.'

It was too much to take in all at once. Could it actually be possible that they had found a refuge where they could serve God in peace? 'Who do you rule as regent for, if not King Henry?'

'Ah.' The exclamation had no joy in it, nor even as much respectful anticipation as she'd shown when Conrad made his entrance. Conrad rose. Sabella did not. 'I am glad you saw fit to interrupt your prayers, Daughter.'

Many times Ivar had glimpsed her holy presence through the gap in the fence in the novices' courtyard in Quedlinhame. There she had dressed in sackcloth and ashes. Now she was arrayed in queenly robes made rich with gold thread embroidered in the shape of leaping roes. *She* it was who had brought the truth to them all. Her wheat-colored hair shone with health, and her thin face had filled out. Even her fingers, once nothing more than skin stretched over bone, had fat on them.

As she moved to touch Duke Conrad's hand in a gesture of anxious affection, one could see why she was noticeably plumper than she had been at Quedlinhame when she had scourged her earthly body with fasting and hair shirts in order to prove her holiness.

Lady Tallia was far gone in pregnancy.

Hathumod leaped to her feet with a wild look on her normally mild face. 'Liar! Fraud! I saw the nail you abused yourself with. I know with what lies the Enemy tempted you, and how you turned your back on the very one who showed you honor. And now this! *This*! You betrayed every holy promise you made to him—'

Ermanrich grabbed his cousin and wrestled her down, although she fought him, so in the grip of this unlooked-for frenzy that she seemed unaware of everything around her. It was already too late.

Tallia shrieked hysterically, hiccuping cries interspersed

with bleating moans that made Ivar want to slap her if only it would shut her up.

'For God's sake,' said Sabella, 'control yourself, Tallia.'

'I can't! I don't care! I won't have her here. She betrayed me when I needed her! She abandoned me! Everything she says is a lie. She's an evil, wicked woman—'

Conrad rose with the massive grace of a bull and slapped Tallia right across the face. His young daughter winced at the sound, but her lips pulled tight with satisfaction. Tallia stopped screaming so quickly that Ivar flinched, thinking she might drop dead on the spot, but instead she started sniveling. Conrad put an arm around her.

'Hush, Tallia.' He sounded as disgusted as might a man who, receiving a prized pup from the regnant, discovers that it has a habit of peeing in the bed. 'Calm down. What is it you wish?'

Tallia shuddered and, finally, gazed up into his face with a look as abjectly worshipful as that of his hounds. Remarkably, after all that wailing and moaning, her eyes were dry. 'She's an evil, wicked woman.' Ivar recalled her voice so clearly from Quedlinhame. Who else spoke in such pure and monotonously zealous tones? That voice, the stigmata that had miraculously appeared on her hands, and the miracle of the rose; these had whipped him into the arms of heresy. But it was her voice more than anything that had driven like a spike into his heart. 'An evil, wicked, *wicked* woman.'

'So you said,' observed Conrad. 'What's that to do with us?'

'She lied about the nail!' shrieked Hathumod, breaking free of Ermanrich's grip. 'God never came to her and tore her hands. She did it to herself! She's the broken vessel that the Enemy cast down upon this Earth to harm God's holy messenger—!' Then Ermanrich had her again, this time with Dedi's help, because she was writhing and fighting and ready to fall into a frothing fit. Ivar had never imagined that Hathumod, soft little rabbit that she resembled, could contain so much fury. And he had a bad feeling that it was unwise to insult a great prince's daughter so publicly.

'Take that madwoman out of here,' said Sabella coolly. 'I won't have my court disturbed in this way.'

'Nay, let me go with her,' pleaded Ermanrich. 'She's my cousin. There's no harm in her—'

'Go!' commanded Sabella. 'Ai, God! Take the others, too.'

'Kill them!' shrieked Tallia, cowering in the shelter of Conrad's massive arm. 'Kill them! Just kill them!' She began to sob, and as the guards jerked Ivar roughly away, he heard her mutter, 'No one must ever know.'

'An execution might serve to keep the troops in line, those who aren't sure of their loyalty,' remarked Sabella.

'Stop there at once!' barked Conrad.

Captain Ulric halted the line of prisoners. He had the look of a good soldier, the kind who doesn't make mistakes because he's slack. His men regarded Conrad with respect as the duke continued speaking. 'I will not be party to slaughtering two innocent Lions. I hate wasting good soldiers.'

'And indeed,' remarked Sabella as she studied Baldwin, 'it would be a shame to put an end to such beauty.'

'I haven't seen his "end,"' said Conrad, laughing now as his arm tightened warningly around Tallia, 'but I'm sure you'd find it to your taste, Cousin.'

'So I might.' Sabella's smile made Ivar shiver. 'What of the others?'

'You must kill them. You must!' sobbed Tallia. She lifted her pale gaze to her husband's dark face. 'You know how much I love you, Conrad. Wouldn't you do it for me?'

She faltered. Maybe she was just smart enough not to want an answer to that question. Her thin lips curved down in a cunning frown as she shook off his arm and stepped forward.

'Am I not queen here, Mother?' Her eyes took on a feverish glaze as she spread her hands over her belly. 'That's what you promised me. That I would be queen and my children rule over a realm where all people have to believe in the Holy Word of the Redeemer. I'll order the execution done if you are too squeamish to do so! Guards! Guards! Take that woman and her companions away and execute them, at my order! Now!'

Conrad shrugged, unwilling to interfere. Sabella lifted a hand as if to give permission.

Baldwin sprang forward, pushed past the guards, and threw himself on the steps at Sabella's feet. 'I beg you,' he cried, turning the full force of his cornflower-blue eyes on her. 'If you kill them, I'll hate you forever. You can whip a stubborn horse and still not make it run. But if you spare their lives, then I'll do whatever you ask.'

Sabella blinked, stunned either by his extraordinary beauty or else by the complete idiocy of his impulsive gesture. 'Whatever I ask?'

Conrad swore appreciatively. 'Now there's an offer that makes me look forward to a hard ride out in the fields.'

'Guards! Do as I command!' Tallia's voice cracked into a whine.

'Shut up,' said Sabella without looking at her daughter. She could not keep her gaze from Baldwin's delectable form.

'B-but you said that I was to be queen—' protested Tallia.

'Inter them at Queen's Grave,' said Conrad. 'Think of what a welcome their heresy will receive there.'

Sabella didn't turn her head to acknowledge the duke's words. She looked, if anything, dumbfounded at the events which had landed Baldwin in her lap.

'Perhaps you'd better haul him up to your chambers and just have done with it,' Conrad finished with a snort of laughter.

'Nay, Cousin, that would be your style, not mine,' Sabella replied. 'I like to savor a well-spiced dish, not bolt it down like a dog. It's a good thing that Judith is dead, or we might come to blows over this handsome morsel.'

'You're not *listening* to me!' cried Tallia. 'I *said* I wanted them killed.'

'Go along, Tallia, back to your prayers,' replied her mother. 'You must rest and keep up your strength.'

'But—'

'Daughter, there's no escape from Queen's Grave, so you needn't fear for your honor or whatever it is you're babbling about. For God's sake, Conrad, take her away.'

'Come, Tallia,' Conrad said firmly, but it was his big hand closing on her frail wrist that forced her to move. He dragged her away without a backward glance, chatting amiably with his daughter as they left the hall.

Ivar felt dizzy, and beside him Sigfrid moaned, Hathumod sobbed softly, Ermanrich trembled, and Gerulf and Dedi stood rigid, awaiting events, glancing at every entrance as if seeking escape. Baldwin did not look at any of them. He was already alone, kneeling before Lady Sabella.

'Captain, remove the prisoners. Detail an escort to take that woman and those three youths to Queen's Grave. Conrad may do as he wishes with the Lions.'

Gerulf laid a hand on Dedi's arm as if to reassure him, or restrain him, but the younger Lion did not respond. He seemed too stunned.

'As you wish, Your Highness,' responded Captain Ulric with toneless obedience.

'I'll see you're rewarded for bringing Lord Baldwin to my attention, Captain,' Sabella added.

'You are most gracious, Your Highness.' Ulric gestured toward his prisoners. 'Move on. Move!'

What could Ivar do? There knelt Baldwin, turning at last to stare after him with tears in his eyes. All this time Ivar had believed that because Baldwin was so damned handsome he couldn't truly care for anything but his own pretty face. There was no doubt now of Baldwin's feelings. Baldwin had sacrificed himself to save Ivar and the others.

Would I have done the same, risk everything, throw all caution to the winds, for Baldwin? Or would I have treated him as Liath treated me?

Shame made him flush. Baldwin winced, seeing Ivar betrayed by his fair complexion.

'Go on, man,' said Erkanwulf. 'There's nothing you can do.'

Prodded by a spear, Ivar staggered forward as Baldwin turned away, shoulders heaving with a sob. No choice but to abandon him. Just as he had been abandoned by Liath at Quedlinhame.

XIII
AFTER DARKNESS

1

Sister Hilaria used flint, iron, and a scrap of dried mushroom to light a lamp. As the fire caught, she wiped away tears. 'I am not accustomed to the smell any longer,' she said apologetically. Holding up the lamp, she indicated that Hanna should roll the stone back into place. 'Then none can follow you.'

The stone that blocked the path was so precisely balanced that it ground easily into place and Hanna turned, dusting off her hands, to regard her new companion. The nun was still blinking because of the wavering flame.

'I know these paths so well that I no longer use light. We conserve our meager oil in this way. Still, it will go more quickly for you if we have light. Follow closely.'

The floor ran smoothly under her feet, although she kept one hand tracing the wall as she walked behind Hilaria, trying not to bump into her. The nun gave off a strong scent like overripe yeast, not entirely displeasing. The lamplight chased shadows around them, but it did little to dispel the gloom. Tunnels branched away on either side, some ascending and some descending. Passing one opening, Hanna caught a

distinct whiff of rotten eggs. As she stopped, recoiling from
the strong smell, a will-o'-the-wisp shifted in the nether darkness, a flash of pale lightness like the glimmer of eyes.

'Sister!' She grabbed hold of the nun's arm. 'I saw something down that tunnel.'

The nun's smile was mysterious but untroubled. 'We are
not alone.'

She hurried on. Hanna followed despite creeping shivers.
Blackness closed in behind them. It was better not to look
behind, in case something was sneaking up on her, but she
looked anyway. She saw nothing but swallowing darkness.

'Are we safe? Where do those tunnels lead?'

'Into the depths of the earth. We stand atop a labyrinth,
friend, whose heart lies beyond our knowledge. So much has
been lost to us, who wander in darkness.' Was Hilaria speaking of the little community of nuns, or of humankind? It was
hard to tell. 'Do not fear. The creatures that abide in the earth
have done no harm to us. I wish I could say the same of our
human brethren.'

They came to a ramp that opened onto a cavern broad
enough that Hanna felt a change in the air. Their frail flame
barely lit the darkness. She saw neither ceiling nor floor, only
the suggestion of an open area wide enough to house monsters, or a manor house and its outbuildings.

'Is this where you live?'

'No. But we harbored an army here once. This way.'

The light formed a halo around them as they crossed the
wide cavern, coming to a corridor that struck into the rock.
Their footfalls echoed in whispers. They rounded a corner and
came to another blocked passageway. Hanna set her weight to
push aside the great wheel stone, but it did not budge as easily
as the other one. At last she got it moving, and with a grinding grumble it rolled into a recess cut in the rock.

'Hold.' Hilaria squeezed through the gap. 'Now let it block
the path again.'

'We won't return this way?'

'No. We'll return by a different path.'

They crossed a ditch dug into the rock that reminded

Hanna of a channel where rainwater might run off, and as they toiled up a steep ramp Hanna realized that she could see the walls. Hilaria pinched out the flame. A chamber hewn from rock greeted her astonished gaze. Ventilation shafts cut through the rock let in light, revealing what had once been a kitchen with hearths, a single heavy table, and half a dozen large, open, but empty barrels.

'Quickly.' Hilaria walked so swiftly through the chamber that Hanna scarcely had time to glance around.

Light shone bright and welcoming as they moved into the rock-hewn chambers that had once housed the convent dedicated to St. Ekatarina. Being good nuns, the sisters had not abandoned the outer rooms precipitously. Except for a thick coating of dust, the dormitory, the chapel, the library, and the refectory remained in perfect order. Benches in the chapel, lecterns and stools in the library, table and benches in the eating hall, two looms, all were set in order; before fleeing, the nuns had taken the time to tidy up. Luminous frescoes adorned the walls, and the tale they told caught Hanna's interest: strangely-garbed folk walked through archways of light woven in stone crowns.

'This way!'

Hanna shook herself before following Hilaria out into the hard sunlight on a terrace. A shout rang up from below, but the nun did not answer, instead shifting a heavy white canvas cover that concealed a rolled-up rope ladder. A shove sent it tumbling down the cliff face.

'I pray you, go quickly. Do you see the dust?'

Where the open ground folded away into hills, a gully cut up through the highlands. This was the path they had walked to reach here. No mountains, these, but rather hills so ancient that all that remained were their dry backs and rugged terrain. Little rain had fallen over the winter. Now the dry path betrayed their pursuers. Dust puffed and billowed, marking the advance of their enemy.

'God help us,' she murmured. 'They're close.'

'Go,' said Sister Hilaria. 'Below you will find a steep staircase. At its base there is a second ladder. Cast it down. And

once more descend another set of steps cut into the rock, to
where there is a third ladder, the longest. They must climb
to safety.'

Hanna scraped her knuckles more than once in her haste.
The ladder gave her less trouble than the steep steps, where
she felt she was hanging in midair, ready to tumble off.
Coming to a lower ledge, she uncovered another rope ladder
and rolled it over the side, cursing when it tangled. Below,
her companions had fallen silent. As she swung over the side
to start climbing down, she saw their upturned faces. They
clustered at the foot of the towering rock. No need to call out:
they understood what was happening.

Her elbows ached by the time she got down the next set
of steps and ladders, where she found a broader ledge – wide
enough to hold a brace of baskets shoved under an overhanging
shelter. A broken winch had been abandoned in pieces. The
rocks that pinned down the corner of the canvas covering the
ladder had been knocked astray by the wind, and it was this
white flap they had seen fluttering.

Below, Gerwita wept.

A horseman appeared at the gap where the gully gave out
onto open ground. With a shout, the man turned and disappeared back the way he had come.

Hanna grabbed the ladder and flung it over the side. It
unrolled with a hiss, rattling down the stone face. Aurea
grabbed the base and yanked it down.

'Go!' shouted Hanna. 'Bring my quiver and arrows up
first!'

Their lack of baggage helped them. Heriburg started up
first, the heaviest pouch of books slung over her shoulders,
with Jehan behind her with the quiver and arrows on his back.

The rope struts on the ledge jerked and strained as the
clerics climbed. Hanna heard Fortunatus' voice rising. 'Nay,
Sister Rosvita! You must go now. Better we be taken than
you be lost.'

'Sister!' Hanna shouted down. 'Don't argue! Come quickly!'

She marked the dust cloud, but at this angle it was lost
behind the hills. She had no way of telling how close their

pursuers were, and if that first horseman had been their lead rider or a scout ranging far out in front of the main force.

Soon she heard Heriburg's ragged breathing. As soon as the young cleric's head and shoulders appeared, Hanna grabbed her under the armpits and helped her up onto the ledge. Heriburg crawled forward and rested on hands and knees before struggling to her feet and measuring the pitch of the staircase angling up the cliff. With a grimace, she started up.

Jehan rolled onto the ledge and stood. 'I fear Gerwita is not strong enough to get up so many ladders,' he said.

Hanna grabbed one of the large baskets to test the strength of the rope and the security of the hook hammered into the stone, where the rope was anchored. ''Ware below!' she shouted before heaving the basket over the side and together she and Jehan paid out line until it rested on the ground. Rosvita was halfway up the ladder, Jerome behind her to steady her. Below, Fortunatus helped Gerwita into the basket. Aurea cut loose the goat.

With Jehan's help, it was not as difficult as Hanna had feared to haul her up; the girl had grown frail during their escape and weighed no more than a child. By the time they had her hauled up on the ledge, Rosvita and Jerome, too, had collapsed panting on the narrow terrace, and Ruoda and Fortunatus were most of the way up the ladder with Aurea just beginning to climb. The servingwoman had rigged her belt to bind Hanna's staff onto her back, but the staff impeded her progress. Every time she shifted her shoulders, it banged against the rock face.

'Look!' Jerome pointed toward the gully.

First one horseman, then five, spilled out of the ravine onto the open ground. As they fanned out, twenty more appeared. One rider bore a banner aloft which displayed a silver Circle of Unity sewn onto a field of gules. Beside him rode a man wearing a red cloak.

'A presbyter,' gasped Jerome.

Rosvita raised her head to look but it was obvious that small movement exhausted her. Her skin had drained of all color; her lips seemed almost blue.

'Keep going,' said Hanna.

Heriburg and Jehan had reached the second ledge. A moment later, a basket slithered down the cliff to land beside Hanna.

'Sister Rosvita must go in the basket,' said Gerwita, her voice no more than a whisper. 'I'll climb.'

Rosvita did not protest as Hanna and Jerome helped her into the basket. Once the basket began to move, bumping up along the rock, Hanna strung her bow and knelt with an arrow held loosely between her fingers.

'Are you good with that bow?' asked Jerome diffidently.

'Not very good,' she admitted. 'I don't wish to kill anyone, only to encourage them to keep their distance long enough for us to get to the top.'

'If you could climb the north face, so can they.'

'Once they find it. Once they think to do so. We'll have a little time.'

'For what?'

She smiled at him. Like the other clerics, he was young – not much younger than she was herself, in truth – rather sweet and a little unworldly, a lad who had grown up in the schola and spent his life writing and reading and praying. Not for him the tidal waves that afflicted the common folk, who had few defenses against famine, war, drought, and pestilence. No cleric was immune to these terrors, of course, but the church offered protection and stability that a common farmer or landsman could only pray for and rarely received.

'For Sister Rosvita to save us.'

The answer contented him; they all believed in Rosvita that much. He headed up the steps, following Gerwita.

A head appeared to her right.

'Brother Fortunatus!' Even she was astonished how pleased she was to see him. With his good nature and sharp humor unimpaired over the months of their harrowing journey, he had wormed his way into her affections. But she did not move to help him as he swung over the edge and turned around to assist Ruoda, who was wheezing audibly, face red, nose oozing yellow snot.

'Go on,' he said to Ruoda. 'Go up and help the others. I'll follow.'

Aurea was only halfway up the ladder.

As the horsemen advanced across the open field, past the stumps of olive trees, a second score of riders emerged from the gully. No need to guess who commanded them. Even at this distance, unable to make out features or even, really, hair color, Hanna knew that the man in the red cloak was Hugh. She knew it as though he stood beside her, whispering in her ear.

Hanna. You know it is best if you wait for us. Do not think you can escape. You have been led astray by the Enemy, but we are merciful—

'Not to Liath,' she muttered, nocking an arrow.

She sighted on the approaching horsemen, measuring their path, leading with the bow, waiting. Waiting. The staff thrust up abruptly into her view. As Fortunatus heaved Aurea up and over onto the ledge, the first rider got within arrow shot. Hanna loosed the arrow.

It skittered along the ground just in front of the riders, causing them to rein back.

'Pull up the ladder!' she cried as she readied a second arrow. She had only a dozen arrows left. Fortunatus and Aurea reeled up the ladder and cast it against the baskets while the riders huddled out of arrow shot, unwilling to expose themselves further.

'Go! Go!' she cried. 'I'll cover you.'

The rest of the party, led by the presbyter, closed with the five scouts. Fortunatus and Aurea scrambled up the staircase while Hanna waited. Now, at last, she could protect the innocent. She had stood aside for months while the Quman slaughtered her countryfolk and done nothing. She had never risked herself. She had never been able to act. But she could now, and she would.

She was no longer afraid.

Hugh and the others halted beside the scouts to confer. The longer it took them to decide what to do, the more time Rosvita and her companions had to escape. Hanna waited, bow drawn.

Yet surely Hugh understood their predicament as well. He did not dither. When he broke away from the main party, she heard the cries of his companions, calling him back, but he raised a hand to silence them and rode forward alone.

She loosed a second arrow, aiming for the ground at his mount's feet. The horse shied, but Hugh reined it calmly back and kept coming. She saw him clearly. The sun's light, as it sank toward the western hills, bathed him in its rich gold. The world might have been created in order to display him. He was beautiful.

But so was Bulkezu.

She readied a third arrow and drew the bowstring.

'Leave us, I beg you, my lord,' she called down.

He reined the horse up below, an easy shot, yet she could not make herself take it. She could not kill a man in cold blood. Would it have been easier if he were not so handsome?

'I pray you, Eagle, do nothing hasty,' he called. 'Where is Sister Rosvita? If I can speak with her, then surely we may come to an agreement.'

From far above, Rosvita called down, her voice faint and raspy, but audible. 'I know what you are, Father Hugh. I know what you have done. I fear we are enemies now. Forgive me, but there can be no negotiation.'

He sighed as might a mother faced with a stubborn child who, having done wrong, will not admit his fault. 'You cannot escape, Sister Rosvita. Better to surrender now, I think.' He shaded his eyes to survey the setting sun. There was perhaps an hour of daylight left. 'If you refuse, I will be forced to besiege you and your party. I know it is possible to climb the north face.'

'Why not let her go, my lord?' Hanna asked. 'What harm? If you wanted her dead, you had plenty of time to see it done when she was a prisoner.'

Hugh smiled softly. 'I do not want her dead, Eagle.'

Hanna shuddered. How simple it would be to shoot him full in the chest. *I do not want him dead.* Was it sorcery that stayed her hand and clouded her mind? Or only the memory of a naive girl's infatuation? *I was that girl once.*

Rosvita knew the truth about King Henry and the daimone that infested him; she had witnessed the death of Villam at Hugh's hand. But Hugh had not killed her when he could easily have done so.

He is deeper than I am.

Yet Hanna knew that if she could not kill him, then she had to run with the others and pray that Sister Rosvita could outwit Hugh. Rosvita was the only person who could. Not even Liath could stand against Hugh; he had abused her too badly.

Just as Bulkezu abused me.

I am no different than Liath. I have to learn to stand firm despite what I have suffered – and I haven't even suffered the worst.

The other riders remained beyond arrow shot. She rose, unstrung her bow, and climbed the steep steps carved into the rock face. She resisted the urge to look down, although she heard the sound of horses moving, hooves rapping on the earth, men calling out each to the others. Any soldier who sought to impale her with an arrow would find her an easy target, clinging to the rock well within range of their bows.

No one shot. She reached the next ledge to find Fortunatus waiting for her. Aurea and Ruoda struggled up the second ladder, on their way to the next ledge. The basket bobbed against the wall somewhat above and to the side of Aurea, and it scraped and jostled the rock as it was hauled upward. She could not see Rosvita from this angle but was happy enough to catch her breath, leaning her weight against the cliff, as she watched the basket rise away from her.

'We'll not be rid of them easily,' said Fortunatus with a grin. He was red in the face from the exertion of climbing but his usual wry humor lightened his expression. 'Look.'

The servants below had begun to set up a traveling camp.

'Why does Lord Hugh not wish to kill Sister Rosvita?' Hanna asked. 'Can she not convict him if she testifies against him?'

'If any court would believe her.'

'Then what does it matter to him if she lives or dies? Better to kill her and have done with the threat.'

'So you would think,' he agreed, glancing up at the basket, now nearing the next ledge where anxious faces peered down, awaiting its safe arrival. 'Were I in Hugh's place, I would have disposed of her as soon as I could. Perhaps it was not Hugh's choice that she remain among the living. Perhaps the skopos stayed his hand.'

'Do you think so?'

'I am only a simple cleric. I cannot presume to guess the thoughts of the Holy Mother or her favored presbyters. They are as far above me as . . . an eagle above the humble wren.'

'I would take you more for a starling, Brother. They fly in a flock. Wrens are more solitary, are they not?'

'We will be an evening's tidbit for the eagle below if we do not fly, my friend.'

She insisted he go first. By now they were high enough that any archer might have trouble finding his mark. None tried. Hugh's servants finished setting up camp as afternoon faded. One of them caught the goat while a score of soldiers took torches and fanned out to set up sentry posts around the base of the huge rock.

In the morning they would climb, as she had done. Then her party would be well and truly trapped, no better than Rosvita in her dungeon cell.

By the time Hanna reached the uppermost ledge, Sister Hilaria had already conducted the first arrivals within the safety of the convent walls.

'Well done,' Hilaria said as Hanna heaved herself over the lip and lay flat on stone, aching, out of breath, and greasy with sweat. Her heart hammered against the ground. A spasm stabbed through her right hand, and she lay there gritting her teeth as a wave of pain convulsed her hand and forearm.

After a while she could bend her fingers. Hilaria remained standing beside her, and Hanna rolled over onto her back, heaved herself up to sit, and stared blearily out over the gulf of air. A hammer rang on metal as an unseen servant drove a stake into the soil. She recognized the steady rhythm, the way the pitch flattened when the hammer didn't hit quite head on. The sun had melted to a glowing reddish-gold ball, streaming pink and orange along the hills. In the east, the hills darkened, color leached out as twilight fell.

'They can't climb at night,' said Hilaria. 'We must hurry. If Sister Rosvita can do what she suggests, then tonight is our only chance. I pray Mother Obligatia is strong enough.'

'What does she mean to do?' asked Hanna, climbing to her feet, but Hilaria had already hurried inside and Hanna could only follow, aching all over, as Hugh set in his siege.

2

As they pressed forward into the interior rooms of the abandoned empty convent, a sense of serenity settled over Rosvita as might a cloak thrown over her shoulders. The dimness reminded her of the two years she had spent in the cell beneath the skopos' palace, yet here, she knew, she was at last entirely free. She had chosen her path, for good or for ill, and she had taken responsibility for those who followed her and looked to her for leadership.

King Henry remained a prisoner. She might never have the power to free him, but she had to try. If Hugh caught her and delivered her to Anne, all this would be in vain.

As the light grew dim, Gerwita clutched Rosvita's hand, whimpering. 'I'm frightened,' she said in a low voice.

They paused on a landing. Ahead lay the kitchens, but Sister Hilaria indicated the stairs that led down to the well.

'This way.'

'Do we not go on to that great cavern where Queen Adelheid and Princess Theophanu and their attendants sheltered?' Rosvita asked.

'Not today.' Hilaria set down the lamp she carried and, striking flint to stone, caught a spark on a scrap of dried mushroom. This tiny flame, coaxed along, lit the wick.

'Is everyone here?' she asked as she lifted the lamp to survey their party. 'Follow me.'

As they edged down the steep stairs, their path lit only by that one flame, Gerwita clung to the back of Rosvita's robes. She had borne up bravely enough in the weeks after they had escaped from Darre, but the final push to the convent had drained her, and now the poor girl wept incessantly. The others shuffled along flat-footed, feeling their way down the steps. The ceiling entombed them, although for a mercy they could easily walk upright, nor had they to squeeze through any narrow passages. Ruoda coughed; she had succumbed to a stubborn grippe two weeks ago that had taken root in her lungs. Like the others, she needed to rest. They all needed to rest. They had been on the run for forty days, hounded and scared. It was no way to recover one's strength. That they had held out this long amazed her.

'Sister Rosvita!'

A ghostly shape appeared at the edge of the flame's halo. It took Rosvita two breaths to recognize Sister Diocletia, the weaver, standing below them on the steps. Like Hilaria, she had become emaciated, and her skin had a deadly pallor, as white as mushrooms. But her smile had the same patient warmth Rosvita remembered.

'I pray you bring us good tidings, Sister Rosvita,' continued Diocletia. 'We have been sorely tried. I fear we are on our last strength.'

'I beg you, tell me what has happened to all of you. Why have you abandoned the convent? Where is Mother Obligatia?'

Hilaria and Diocletia exchanged a glance. They had been the best natured and strongest of the nuns, and even now, as fragile and worn through as they looked, Rosvita sensed a powerful will shared between them.

'We're taking you to her now,' said Hilaria finally.

They continued down, far down, until Rosvita lost count of the stairs and grew accustomed to stepping over the lip carved at the edge of each one, a fringe of stone that kept the foot from slipping on the descent. The stone was very cold to the touch but not wet. The footfalls of the others echoed around her, muffled by rock; she heard their breathing, but no one spoke. The light did little to dispel the darkness. She could touch solid stone on either side; otherwise they might as well have been descending into the Pit. Had the church mothers been mistaken all along, teaching that the sinful fell, bodiless and helpless, for eternity through a cloud of stinging aether? It was perhaps more reasonable to suggest that each erring soul carved her own path down the steep slope of the Abyss, trudging into eternal damnation. Sin itself was the punishment, turning away from what was right.

She was about to throw herself into the camp of the Enemy, making her no different than Queen Adelheid, who had led them here the first time. Who could have guessed that Adelheid would prove so treacherous toward her husband? Yet fear, as much as treachery, might have impelled her. She might have succumbed to Hugh's poisoned words or the skopos' influence. She might only have done what she thought necessary to secure a throne for her infant child and surety for her own preeminent position among the princes of the land.

Perhaps Adelheid had stepped into the Pit while doing what she thought was right.

As I must.

Rosvita knew what she had to do to save her companions from their pursuers. But that didn't make it right.

Her feet slipped on loose pebbles. She grabbed Gerwita's hand to balance herself, heard Fortunatus, toward the back of the party, murmur a warning to the one who walked behind him.

They came to the bottom of the stairs where curving walls rose on every side into blackness. The well was dry except for a sheen of water caught in a hollow beyond Hilaria, but it wasn't empty. At the center of the space a hole pierced the rock; a sturdy wooden ladder poked up out of the depths.

'How much farther?' gasped Gerwita.

'Not far,' said Diocletia kindly. She turned to take hold of the ladder, easing herself onto the rungs. 'Follow me. Sister Hilaria will come last.'

Rosvita went second. The rungs were worn smooth by much use. At first, rock scraped against her back, but after six rungs the space opened up and after another seven she set foot on stone. A hand grasped her elbow.

'Stand aside,' said Diocletia. 'We must all stand here together before we go on.'

One by one the others descended the ladder, rungs creaking beneath their weight, feet scuffing on stone when they reached the bottom. One by one, they edged cautiously past Rosvita into the blackness. It was so profoundly silent that she could distinguish each person's breathing: Gerwita's shallow and moist with tears; Jerome's quick and nervous; Heriburg's steady and even. Ruoda coughed wetly, echoed by Jehan's dry cough. The Eagle shifted, rattling the arrows remaining in her quiver. Aurea probed the floor by tapping it with the staff: *rap rap rap.*

'Ai!' cursed Fortunatus. 'You hit my toe.'

Everyone chuckled anxiously.

Above, Hilaria doused the lamp, so even that whisper of light was lost to them. The rungs creaked again; feet scuffed the ground.

'Are we all here?' It was impossible to mistake Diocletia's high, raspy voice for the lower tones of her companion.

'We are all here,' answered Hilaria.

It was too dark for Rosvita to see her hand in front of her nose. The earth had swallowed them.

'Where are we going?' whispered the Eagle from the right.

'Deeper,' said Hilaria.

'How can we go deeper?' asked Gerwita in a trembling voice. Her fingers brushed Rosvita's hand and fixed on it, forefinger and thumb wrapping tightly around the older woman's wrist as a child might cling to its mother.

A scraping rumble shuddered through the room. A kiss of dry air, faintly sulfurous, brushed Rosvita's face.

'Take hold each to another's hand,' said Diocletia, 'and speak your name, so that we know that we have not left anyone behind.'

Someone giggled nervously, but Rosvita did not recognize

the laugh. After some fumbling, each person spoke, some softly, others with more strength. When Hilaria spoke last of all, Rosvita felt a tug on her hand and she followed Diocletia grimly into such blackness as seemed impossible to fathom or endure. Behind her, Gerwita choked back sobs.

'Hush, Daughter,' murmured Rosvita, squeezing her hand. 'We are in good company. They will not let us come to harm.'

For an eternity they moved through a darkness that had direction and space only because now and again the flow of air would shift and faint scents or stinks touch them before fading away: rotten eggs, yeast, the sting of an iron forge, lichen and, strangely, salt water. Mercifully, the floor remained level. No one tripped or ran into anything, although they could not see their own feet much less any landmark around them.

Soon, a steady, labored wheezing drifted into audibility, like a blacksmith's bellows or a man stricken by lung fever struggling to breathe.

'So might a sleeping dragon sound,' said Fortunatus out of the darkness, 'as some poor deluded treasure hunter crept up on it.'

Hilaria laughed. 'So might it, indeed, had we such a creature hidden in this labyrinth. It is no dragon, Brother, but something stranger and more unexpected.'

The faintest brush of color limned the walls, shading blackness into a rainbow of subtle grays. The tunnel down which they walked split at a crossroads, branching off in five directions, but Diocletia led them toward the light, toward the whistling wheeze.

'God save us,' said Gerwita faintly, pressing up behind Rosvita as the tunnel opened into a cavern no larger than a village church, the rock walls marked with odd striations, ribbons of color painted onto the rock.

Here, the nuns had constructed a crude living quarters. Four pallets lay along one wall, three neatly made with feather bedding and one heaped up untidily. At the single table and bench a thin woman wearing tattered nun's robes sat fretfully twisting her hands; she did not look up as they entered. Three medium-sized chests, enough to store clothing or a small library of scrolls, sat beneath the table. A dozen assorted pots and amphorae lined the far wall, half lost in shadow, although Rosvita found it remarkable that she could see at all. Two oil lamps rested on a rock shelf in the cavern wall, but neither one was lit.

'What is making the light?' Hanna murmured.

'What is making that noise?' asked Fortunatus.

The untidy pallet stirred, like a beast coming alive. 'Have they come safely?'

'God be praised!' Rosvita rushed heedlessly across the cavern to kneel beside the pallet. 'Mother Obligatia! God is merciful! You are still alive.'

'Sister Rosvita!' A painfully thin hand emerged, shaking, from under a blanket. Rosvita grasped it, careful to hold lightly so that she might not crush those ancient bones. 'I had prayed to see you again, but I confess I did not hope that God would bless us so. We are prisoners here, but against what enemy we do not know. Have you come to rescue us?'

Rosvita laughed bitterly. Obligatia looked so ill that it was impossible to understand how someone so frail could still live except through stubbornness, a sense of duty, or the simple inability to give up hope. Age had worn her skin to a dry fragility; a touch might crumble it to dust.

The others ventured cautiously into the cavern, spreading out so they wouldn't feel cramped, glancing around nervously, looking for the source of the light and that constant wheezing whistle. Sister Diocletia leaned down beside the seated woman and spoke to her in an undertone. It was Sister Petra, the librarian and scribe. She looked so changed, as though half of her soul had fled, leaving the rest behind in a broken vessel.

'Pray tell me what has transpired, Mother Obligatia. Why have you fled the convent? Where are the others?'

'There are things we never dreamed of that still walk the Earth although they are mercifully hidden to our sight most of the time. Pray that it remain so. We have seen—' That strong voice faltered. Her body was weak, but her gaze remained sharp and solid, fixed on Rosvita. 'We have seen terrible things, Sister.'

'Look!' said Hanna from the other side of the cavern. 'It's the lichen that gives off a glow.'

'I have gone over the events so many times that I begin to feel as though I have lived through them a hundred times or more. Yet first, Sister Rosvita, tell me. We sent poor Paloma, that good girl, to Darre to seek you. Did she ever find you there?'

'God have mercy on her. She found us, but she was murdered. We had no way to send word to you. Nor do we know who killed her, or why. We can only guess.'

The sigh that escaped Mother Obligatia's lips whispered out like an echo to the rhythmic wheeze that serenaded them: *schwoo schwhaa schwoo schwhaa.* 'I feared as much. I knew she would not abandon us. I pray she rests at peace in the Chamber of Light with Our Mother and Father of Life.' She murmured a prayer, and Rosvita joined her, the words falling easily from her tongue. How many times had she said the prayer over the dead?

Too many.

'After that a cleric came. She sought access to our library, saying she came from the schola in Darre to examine old chronicles. We had no reason to distrust her.'

'You do not think she came to study old chronicles in the library?' Rosvita asked, rearranging the bolster that allowed the old woman to lie somewhat propped up. Obligatia grunted in pain as Rosvita helped her sit up.

'The good sisters move me frequently,' she said, 'yet still I have sores from being bedridden. Yet is it not a just punishment for my blindness?'

'Your blindness?'

'She called herself Sister Venia.'

Heriburg and Fortunatus had crept forward to listen.

'I recall no such cleric,' said Heriburg.

'The name seems passing familiar,' said Fortunatus. 'There are so many clerics in the palace schola, but I believe a woman who went by that name served the skopos.'

Obligatia's lips pulled up, but not in a smile. 'I know she did not. She came to kill us. She murdered poor Sister Lucida and used her warm blood to summon a creature that had no earthly form or substance and a stench like iron. This *thing* she sent to kill us, or to kill me, I suppose, although the only one it killed was Sister Sindula. It consumed Sindula as though it were fire, leaving only her scorched bones. May God have mercy on her.' A frail hand sketched the Circle of Unity in the air. 'Yet I believe I was Sister Venia's target all along. They know who I am, and they will stop at nothing to murder me.'

'So be it. I have no kind words in which to tell you this, Mother Obligatia. I found out what happened to your daughter.'

Obligatia shut her eyes. A tear squeezed out from the closed lids, sliding down to dissolve in the whorl of one ear. 'My daughter,' she said softly. 'Even after so many years, I still grieve for what I lost.'

How did one speak, in the face of such sorrow, knowing that the next words would only compound sadness? She had to go on. Without the truth being laid bare, they had no hope of winning free.

'Your daughter is now the skopos. She is called Anne, and she is a mathematici, a powerful sorcerer.'

'My daughter.' The words brushed the air as might a feather, a tickle, ephemeral. Obligatia was silent for a long time, but she wept no more tears. 'Then it is my daughter who wishes to make sure I am dead.'

Rosvita looked up to see Fortunatus' dear face close by, pale with concern. 'We should have listened to Prince Sanglant. He warned us against Anne and her cabal of sorcerers before we traveled south to Aosta. We did not heed him.'

'How could we have guessed?' said Fortunatus. 'Do not blame yourself, Sister.'

'Now that they have raised Taillefer's granddaughter to a position worthy of her eminence, she fears what I know,' said Obligatia. 'What I am.'

'Perhaps,' said Rosvita. 'But do not think others elevated

Anne. She raised herself. When Holy Mother Clementia died, may she rest at peace in the Chamber of Light, Anne came before the king and queen and displayed her power to them. In this way, she seduced them into supporting her election as skopos. She told him—' She recalled the words as clearly as if they had been spoken an hour ago. That was the price she paid for her prodigious memory: that every painful moment she had ever endured might be relived with awful clarity at unlooked for and unwelcome intervals. 'She said, "Without my aid, you will have no empire to rule."'

'You have a powerful memory, Sister.'

'I spent two years in the dungeon of the skopos. I had time to meditate, to pray, and to read back through my book of memory.'

Yet this time had allowed her to complete, in her mind, her long neglected *History*. It had allowed her to master the skill that might allow them to escape their current predicament.

The wheeze sucked in and out, and by now she recognized on her skin the slight pressure in and suction out of air that accompanied the sound, not a breeze but more like the action of a bellows shifting the air. The temperature within this cavern remained cool, yet not as cold as the chill night would be outside. Fearing for their lives, they remained in more comfort than Hugh's men. The irony made her smile.

'I had another child,' said Obligatia into their silence. 'Another child.' She faltered, her voice trembling as badly as her hands. She groped down the blanket that covered her slight body until she found Rosvita's hand and clutched it tightly. 'What became of Bernard? I saw him—'

'You saw him?'

'Nay, nay, I saw him in his child.'

'You saw his child?'

Sister Hilaria returned with a bucket of water, which she set down beside the abbess. Kneeling next to the pallet, she dipped a linen cloth into the water and bathed the old woman's forehead and throat. 'You are tiring her, Sister Rosvita,' she scolded.

'So I must, if we are to survive this. What do you mean, Mother? How could you have seen his child? If this man is the one I think he is, he had no child.'

Hilaria looked up sharply. 'She does not lie.'

'Nor do I mean to say she does—'

'Hear me first,' said Mother Obligatia gently. 'When the demon came for us, we knew we would all die. It consumed Sister Sindula as easily as we breathe, and nothing we could do would stop it from devouring us as well. But there appeared out of the air a daimone. I do not believe it was an angel. It was a woman with wings of flame, yet one who bore an earthly bow and arrow. It was she who pierced the creature with her dart and banished it from Earth. It was she who warned us to bind the sorcerer who had attacked us. It was she—'

She began to weep quietly, unable to go on in the face of overwhelming grief. Hilaria dabbed cooling water on her forehead, murmuring words of comfort.

Rosvita burned. Shame afflicted her, to witness this woman's sorrow and yet exult in it. She was so close. In her heart, in her bones, she understood that she had suffered in the dungeon, risked everything, to arrive at this moment.

'She saved our lives. Yet I knew her. I knew her.' Obligatia pushed the damp cloth away from her forehead. 'I pray you, Hilaria. I will not die in this hour.' By the set line of her frail jaw and the stubborn and fixed nature of her gaze, Rosvita saw it was this memory that had kept her alive for so long. She had recovered the strength of her voice; she had mastered her sadness, as must all those who live to a great age, for otherwise they would have died of grief long ago.

'I saw her, Sister Rosvita. I saw Bernard's child. I saw him in her face. I do not know what she is, where she came from, or where she went. Can you explain what happened?'

The others had gathered close by to listen, struck dumb, it seemed, by the intensity of Obligatia's testimony and her question.

But not every one of them.

'You saw Liath.' The Eagle pressed forward to stand beside Rosvita, towering there with her robust figure and her pale, northern coloring, her hair as colorless as snow. 'I've seen her, too, these past two or three years, glimpses of her but nothing more than that. She had wings of flame. I thought they were visions, hallucinations. But now I have to believe that what Prince Sanglant said is true. She was taken away, up into the heavens, by fiery daimones.'

'I do not forget how we heard her voice manifest out of a whirlpool of air,' said Fortunatus grimly. 'That day when Prince Sanglant returned to the king's progress. That day when we saw that he had allowed his daughter to be suckled by a daimone.'

'When did that happen?' Hanna demanded of Fortunatus.

'Before he rode east. Before you met up with him.'

'Yes,' she agreed thoughtfully. 'That would make sense. It would fit with what you and Sister Rosvita have told me of your own history, and conclusions.'

'Liath is Anne's daughter,' Rosvita said, as if hitting the nail hard enough would drive it into impenetrable rock. 'How can she be the daughter of Anne, yet look like Bernard, if the story Prince Sanglant told us is true? If only one of her parents is human?'

'It could be true if Holy Mother Anne is the one who is lying,' said Hanna.

For a moment there was silence, except for the wheeze, and Gerwita's sniffling, and Ruoda's cough.

If the Holy Mother were lying.

Hanna went on, her tone like ice. 'Why shouldn't she lie? If she needed Liath, and everyone who knew her, to believe that Liath was descended from Emperor Taillefer? I knew Bernard. He loved his daughter. *And they looked alike.* Even though she was burned brown on her skin, any fool could see they were father and daughter, just as a puppy or foal may bear the markings of its sire.'

'My grandchild,' murmured Obligatia. 'Can it be true? Bernard had a daughter? Can it be true?' How cruel the look of hope on her face. 'Does he live still, my son?'

Hanna knelt beside the pallet. She was not a beautiful woman, more strong than handsome, yet her expression became so suffused with compassion that it shone from her in the manner of all true beauty, born of the inner heart and not the outer seeming. 'I am sorry, Mother. He died years ago trying to save his daughter from those who pursued her. I saw his dead body.'

'My son.' The words trailed into nothing, but Obligatia did not weep. Perhaps she had no more strength for weeping.

'He was a good man, with no more frailties than any one of us suffer, and many virtues. He helped others until there was nothing left for himself. But he feared those who sought to find him and Liath. He did the best he could. He loved her.'

Schwoo schwaa schwoo schwaa.

Had they fallen under a spell? To Rosvita, it seemed they had. No one moved or spoke.

Only Mother Obligatia was strong enough to break that spell. She had survived too long to be overmastered.

'Why does my daughter wish to kill me, Sister Rosvita?'

Rosvita glanced at Fortunatus, at Hanna, but they only shook their heads. 'I do not know. I can only guess. She has not given up. A presbyter of noble birth waits below the rock. Tomorrow at dawn he will send soldiers up the north face to capture us.'

'He cannot reach us here.'

'How can we sustain ourselves, trapped within the stone with no source of food or drink? How have you survived these past two years?'

'Where is Teuda?' Obligatia asked.

'She is coming, Mother,' replied Hilaria. 'She has seen to the prisoner, and gathered enough bread for everyone.'

'Help me stand,' said Obligatia.

With both Rosvita and Hilaria to support her, the old abbess was able to rise. She insisted on being helped to the bench, although the effort clearly taxed her. Sister Petra, still squeezing her hands anxiously and murmuring in an undertone, fell silent when Obligatia patted her soothingly on the arm as one might a nervous hound.

'Sister Petra has not been well since that awful day,' said

Obligatia without apparent irony, considering her own weakened condition. Yet her expression had such clarity and strength of will that Rosvita could not help but contrast the old woman's energy and evident sanity with the bewildered gaze of Petra as she stared at the shadows, mouth moving but no words coming out. 'Sister Carita died soon after we fled here, may her spirit rest at peace in the Chamber of Light. Hilaria, Diocletia, and Teuda have remained rocks.'

'God granted us strength,' said Diocletia, who had risen in order to give Obligatia room to sit on the bench. 'We serve you as faithfully in this life as we will serve God in the next, Mother.'

Obligatia bowed her head, aware of the burden of their loyalty. Rosvita, looking up, saw her own dear companions gazing at her with that same dreadful and wonderful steadfastness. Like Lavastine's hounds, they had chosen with their hearts and now could never be swayed.

'Pray God we are worthy of their loyalty,' she murmured to herself, but Obligatia's hearing had not suffered.

'Amen,' the old woman whispered. She braced her hands on the table and with an effort pushed herself up to stand as Rosvita hurried to steady her with a hand under her elbow. 'In this way I maintain my strength. My task on this Earth is not finished. I have a few more things left to do.'

'Here is Teuda.' Diocletia hurried to a passageway that struck into the rock opposite the tunnel through which they had entered. She met there the lay sister whom Rosvita recalled as a gardener. Teuda carried a large clay pitcher filled with water and a basket, which she set on the table. It was filled with white cakes shaped like small loafs of bread but formed of a substance Rosvita did not recognize. It had no smell. Obligatia led the blessing over drink and food, sat, and indicated that Teuda should pass the bread around. When Rosvita bit into the cake handed to her, she discovered it had no taste as well as no scent, its consistency firm but not hard, with some give when you pressed on it without being spongy.

'What is it?' asked Hanna, too suspicious to eat.

'We call it bread,' said Teuda. 'Do not turn your nose up

at it, my friend. It comes to us as a gift. Without it, we would all have died of starvation months ago.'

'A gift from whom?' asked Hanna, unappeased. 'Sister Hilaria said there are creatures that bide in the earth. Has this something to do with them?'

As with one thought, Teuda, Hilaria, and Diocletia looked at Mother Obligatia. Only poor Sister Petra did not respond; she nibbled at her cake as might a mouse, glancing up frequently at the shadows as though expecting a cat to spring.

'I heard a tale once,' said Ruoda, who had been silent for so long because of the grippe that afflicted her, who had struggled to keep moving although she was feverish and ill. 'I heard it said that the wealth of the Salian kings comes from a deep mine that strikes far into the earth, where lies a treasure-house of gold. Or iron. No man can suffer the deep shafts and live, so they say. They say that the Salians have made slaves of a kind of creature lower than humankind but above the common beasts, who burrow in the earth and seek silver and gold.'

Obligatia nodded. 'Long ago, creatures carved this labyrinth out of the rock. It runs deep. We have explored only a tiny portion of it. Paloma used to bring rolls of string down and unravel them behind her, so she could find her way back, yet even she discovered merely how much lay beyond our knowledge. What cunning and skill they must have had to construct such a vast network!'

'Do you mean to say that all this, and more, is not natural? That it was hewn from the rock?'

'Just as the convent was, yet even there the founding sisters merely expanded on what already existed. This labyrinth is, we believe, but the top layer of the onion. We will never know the truth.'

Gerwita began to weep again, her nerves stretched so fine that any least brush set them jangling.

'Pray go on!' said Rosvita. 'What mystery lies beneath the rock? Truly, I stand amazed.'

Eating the bread had restored Obligatia enough that she could sit straighter and sip at the metallic-tasting water Teuda poured into a wooden cup.

'After the creature that murdered Sister Sindula was killed, we sought out and bound Sister Venia. No need to take her to trial. She was found in the midst of her sin, with Sister Lucida's corpse and the traces of her sorcery nearby. Yet what could we do? It was obvious we were in danger. If we let her go, she could strike again. She might return to those who sent her and seek additional help. Yet neither could I bring myself to kill her, even to save ourselves. I felt we had no choice but to keep her as a prisoner, with us, so that she might not work her mischief again. Yet if she did not return with a report to those who had sent her, surely they would send others to seek her out. And in time they did. Where could we flee and gain refuge? Whom could we trust? In the end, we retreated. I would not suffer those in my charge to be harmed.'

'If you had given yourself up to those who sought you, then those in your charge might have continued their lives undisturbed,' said Hanna suddenly. 'Did you even consider it?'

Teuda was a big-boned woman and not as thin as the others; she placed herself before Hanna, fists set on hips and chin thrust out in a challenge. 'By what right do you speak to our Holy Mother so disrespectfully?'

Obligatia smiled. A leopard might smile so, before it gobbled up its unsuspecting prey. 'Nay, let her speak. It is a fair question. Why not give myself up to save them?'

'As if such villains wouldn't have killed us anyway!'

'Hush, Teuda. Yet that is indeed the first reason. Why should I believe they would not pinch off all the loose ends, those who knew I existed, who knew my secret. If they would not hesitate to kill me, why hesitate to kill those under my charge? Who will notice if a handful of isolated nuns vanish? Few know of our existence. We matter to no one.'

'You would matter to Liath, if it were true that you were her grandmother. Ai, God, she has prayed so often for some knowledge of her family. . . .' Hanna trailed off, wise enough to be humble in the face of this woman who had suffered so much and survived despite everything.

'So you have the other answer. I am selfish, child. If

Bernard's daughter still lives, if there is any hope I might yet clasp her hand in mine, see his dear face in hers, and kiss her as one kinswoman to another, then I will do so.'

To Rosvita's surprise, Hanna knelt and bowed her head. 'Forgive me, Mother. I have misjudged you.'

'There is nothing to forgive, child—'

Gerwita collapsed to her knees and began to sob noisily. 'I have sinned!' she cried, words garbled by gusts of weeping. 'I have betrayed you! God forgive me.' She grabbed for the eating knife left out on the table after Teuda had cut up the cakes. Fortunatus got hold of her wrist; Hanna leaped forward and pulled the knife from her grasp before she could plunge it into her own abdomen.

'Flee!' she sobbed hopelessly. 'No matter where you hide, he will find you. You cannot imagine his power.'

The force of her wailing and crying racked her body; she jerked back and forth like a woman trying to expel a demon, and all that soft, placid, neat exterior, the calm, reserved novice, dissolved into a woman torn by pain and guilt.

For a drawn-out time, measureless, everyone stared at her, too shocked to speak.

But Rosvita recognized the dismay curling up her toes, into her limbs, suffusing her; it scrabbled at her heart, long-fingered dread, like the rats in the dungeon that never ceased to gnaw even and especially on the living who had become too numbed to feel and too weak to fight back.

'Hugh,' she said at last.

Gerwita sobbed, curled up with her body against her thighs and her head hitting the floor repeatedly.

'Restrain her,' said Rosvita. 'Do not let her harm herself.'

'She betrayed us!' cried Heriburg. 'We would have escaped. There had to be some reason they found our trail, despite everything. She betrayed us!'

'Heriburg! Leave off!'

Heriburg snapped her mouth shut, but she stepped back to grasp Ruoda's hand tightly as together the two young women glared furiously at their longtime companion.

If a look could kill as easily as a dagger—

Rosvita knelt beside Gerwita. At her touch, Gerwita jerked sideways away from her and wailed and shrieked like a woman mourning the death of her only child.

'Gerwita! Hush! Listen to me, and grant me silence!'

It took a space for Gerwita to calm down, to swallow her sobs, to lie still, face hidden, in silence.

'Look at me.'

Gerwita lifted her head. She had scraped her forehead on the stone; blood trickled into her eyes.

'Did you betray us willingly? For money? Preferment? Out of desire?'

Tears streamed down Gerwita's round face. At first she seemed unable to speak, but finally she choked out words. 'N-nay, Sister Rosvita. I would never betray you willingly, not for anything. B-but he threatened my family. I have a younger brother who is a novice at St. Galle's, a great honor for our family for we are not of the first rank. He said he feared that harm would come to him, if I did not heed him and aid him. I believed him, Sister. I believed he could harm my brother.'

'Why did you not come to me with this tale at the time?'

'B-because you were in the dungeon!' she cried, outraged and furious and humiliated. 'How could you have helped me?'

'What did he want from you in exchange? He can't have known that an earthquake would strike Darre. He can't have guessed that it would provide the opportunity for my escape.'

She hid her face in her hands, ashamed. Rosvita could barely make out her muffled words. 'He wanted to know what you knew, how much you knew, about the Holy Mother, Anne. The skopos. I–I told him.' She wept again, choking and coughing on the sobs. 'God forgive me. I told him everything.'

Fortunatus began to chuckle, then laughed outright.

Outraged, Heriburg slapped him across the face.

'Child!' Obligatia's voice rang like a hammer.

'Nay, nay, give me silence for a moment,' said Rosvita, rising. Fortunatus' cheek was red, but the slap had not discomposed him; he still smiled with his usual sly irony, fond of finding a friendly joke in the weaknesses of others. 'Brother Fortunatus is right. Gerwita, you did not betray me at all. I think, Daughter, that you may have saved my life.'

'How?' said several of them at once, disbelieving.

Gerwita was too startled to protest.

'Why didn't Hugh have me killed? I saw him murder Villam. I know he is a maleficus, that he used condemned sorcery to imprison King Henry by insinuating a captured daimone – the very one that had been trapped in the stone crown at the height of this rock – into the king's corpus. Why didn't he kill me? My testimony, which is worth something, I believe, could and would condemn him in front of an ecclesiastical court.'

Silence from the rest of them, waiting, tense, confused.

Only Fortunatus understood.

'Because he means to use me to protect himself against Anne. Holy Mother Anne does not know how much I know about her past. She does not know that I know the secret of her birth, of her incestuous marriage. That her mother still lives.'

'Her incestuous marriage—?' Obligatia whispered faintly, slumping.

'I pray you, Mother. Let me explain later. I think you need not be ashamed of your son's behavior. Yet think. Hugh knows what I know, because of what Gerwita told him. If I am alive, then he holds a weapon to use against Anne, if need be.'

'Why would he want to harm the Holy Mother?' asked Aurea.

'Because he is an ambitious man. That is his weakness, as Fortunatus has seen.'

'I do not think Presbyter Hugh so simple as to have only one reason for anything he does,' added Fortunatus. 'There may be other reasons he has left you alive, Sister Rosvita.'

Hanna spoke harshly. 'Perhaps only to let you know that he holds the power of life and death over you. There are a few creatures in this world who hunger for that kind of power.'

'So there are,' agreed Rosvita. 'But he does not have me

yet, and I do not mean for him to capture me at all.'

She turned to regard Mother Obligatia, who simply nodded, as if she expected the speech that would come next.

'You must trust me, Mother. Where is your prisoner?'

'Not far from here, safely interred. She no longer speaks to us, but I think her still sane.'

'And the creatures from whom you have received your bread – what of them?'

'They are not ours. Soon after we fled into the depths, we found one wounded, and did our best to heal it. After that, one among their number led us to a spring deep beneath the rock beside which one could harvest this bread – although it is no true bread. On this nourishment we have subsisted.'

'Leave your prisoner behind. Free her if need be. I agree that it would sit ill with a good conscience to murder her when she is helpless. Let others judge her and bring her to trial for her sins. We do not have time. Gather up what you must. We will carry you, Mother.'

'Ah,' said Obligatia, nothing more.

'But the rock is surrounded,' protested Gerwita. 'How can we escape?'

'I have had two years to meditate, to pray, and to remember all that I have seen and heard. My memory is good, and I have had many days to contemplate the spell woven by Hugh of Austra when we escaped Lord John with the queen. Now I must know, Mother – have you studied the lore of the mathematici all these years? Have you the knowledge to make the proper calculations?'

The secret, long hoarded, proved difficult for Obligatia to give up, but at last she nodded. 'The abbesses of St. Ekatarina's have studied the murals left on the walls. They have taken down the accounts of travelers. This knowledge they have passed down to each new abbess in turn – to me, last of all. Yet I and my predecessors have never discovered the incantations that open the stones.'

'I know them.' Rosvita gestured to her companions, all of them waiting, all of them hopeful, all of them trusting.

This was the burden of leadership.

'If you are willing to aid us, Mother,' she continued, 'we will go now. It was a clear day when we arrived. We must pray that it has remained clear and unclouded. This night is our last chance. If we do not escape tonight, we will be trapped for good.'

3

After darkness came light.

Antonia, once biscop of Mainni, had endured her captivity in silence, but that did not mean she had not planned out in explicit detail the punishment she, and God, would inflict on her tormenters once she was free.

She had prayed, and she had meditated.

In a way, God had rewarded her for her diligence and loyalty by allowing her this respite, as interminable though it had seemed, in which she had had the leisure to ponder the sinful nature of the world and the myriad ways in which most of its creatures, humankind first among them, had gone astray.

At least the beasts of the water, field, and sky were simple and therefore innocent. Perhaps some children were innocent, although she doubted it. The claws of the Enemy dug deep and swiftly. How many slights had she herself suffered as a child from her kinfolk, even from the smallest among them? Of course, they had each one earned their just reward in the end, but she had never forgotten the lesson she had learned.

In the end, only the innocent could be free from fear, and the evident fact that almost every person, adult or child, woman or man, suffered and feared obviously meant that they were all guilty. Had they been innocent, God would have had no reason to punish them.

These ruminations comforted her, yet even so at times she succumbed to the sin of anger at those who had thrown her in harm's way and abused her trust. In truth, she had recognized all along that Sister Anne was not as holy as she seemed, being afflicted with the sin of overweening pride. Anne must have known into what danger she had sent Antonia. She must have known that the nuns of this isolated, impoverished, and pathetic little convent possessed unexpected powers to confront and bind sorcery; if they had not, they could not have called up a winged daimone of fire to battle and banish the galla. Antonia had not failed in her quest. She had been betrayed by the one who sent her. No doubt Anne feared her because of Antonia's greater righteousness.

Always it proved to be so, that the wicked envied the pure.

Yet God again had rewarded her. Anne likely thought her dead and when, in the fullness of time, God freed her, she would be able to strike when and where Anne least expected her. She had enjoyed the many, many hours, or days, or weeks – impossible to keep track of the passing calendar when buried alive in this black pit – during which she had contemplated the defeat of vice by virtue and her final triumph over Anne and her minions.

She must only be patient.

She was an old woman, and getting no younger, yet she knew in her heart that God would not abandon her. God would not deny her the final victory granted to the just.

After darkness came light.

A glimmer of light flickered above her where the hole opened in the ceiling of her pit. The light announced mealtime, such as it was: a bucket of water and a tray of a bland, chewy substance that must not, she supposed, be scorned, since it had kept her alive.

As the light strengthened, shading black into a murky gray, she lifted her gaze to track its approach. She had to keep her eyes strong for that day when the sun again shone on her. She heard whispered voices, caught scraps of words. Was that a man's baritone, sliding in and around the lighter tones of a woman? Surely not. She had hoped never to fall into madness, but perhaps God had chosen a new way to test her.

She waited for the rope to lower down with its precious

burden of food and drink – it was the one moment they were vulnerable, and she enjoyed their apprehension, an almost tangible smell drifting down to her.

Something scraped on the rock above. Twin spears stabbed down through the hole, and she was actually so startled that she scrambled back to avoid their thrust.

As the spears thudded onto the floor, she realized her mistake: it was a ladder. The voices faded, retreating, taking the light with them. They had left neither water nor bread.

What did this mean?

It was not her place to question God's will. She rose, tying the worn blanket they had given her around her midriff like a belt. She had been careful to exercise her body, walking circuits of the oval pit, keeping herself as clean as she could through judicious use of the water for bathing and for her necessarium a much smaller hole that plunged so deep into the earth that she could not smell the stink of her own refuse.

The rungs held her weight easily, but she wasn't sure if the ladder would slip as she climbed with no one to hold it in place. Yet how else to ascend? Carefully she climbed, and when she heaved herself over the lip, she lay there for the space of several breaths, stunned by the change in the air and the coursing exultation that freedom sent through her body.

She had no time to waste.

Why had they freed her?

She rose, edging carefully away from the pit, and found the wall by touch. A faint glow permeated the air; she followed it, cautious with each step, not sure what traps might have been laid. The passageway ran smooth and straight. Lichen grew in patches on the wall, and it was these plants that emitted the steady, if fragile, light, which was accompanied by a wheeze like the rattling breath of a sleeping giant.

The passageway turned sharply to the left, debouching into a cavern the size of a humble village church. The remains of habitation littered it: four crude pallets, a table and bench, several chests and amphorae. These did not interest her. An oil lamp sat unlit on the table accompanied by a leather pouch pregnant with water, its sides glossy and damp, and a linen cloth unfolded around several loaves of the bread.

They had fled, abandoning her.

Well. She could expect no better behavior from the guilty, yet their sinfulness might not be the sole reason they had left.

Something had driven them out.

Despite the eerie glow, the dimness and the constant wheezing whistle made her nervous. She shuddered; a shiver like the touch of the Enemy crept down her spine. Pebbles rattled behind her.

Creatures skulked in the rock. She had heard them while in captivity; she did not doubt the testimony of her weakened eyes now. Better to flee while she had the strength.

Tying up the food, she slung it and the pouch over a shoulder and picked up the lamp. Because her hands trembled, it took her several attempts to snap sparks from flint and catch a flame to the wick. Once the lamp burned, she hurried into the farther passageway, shading her eyes as best she could against its brilliance.

Was that the sound of footfalls behind her? Who followed? Had the others hidden, hoping to see her go?

God had mercy upon her. Although the passageway stretched on interminably, it dared not deceive her with twists and turns. Now and again she passed an opening out of which wafted distinct smells: the sea, rotten eggs, frankincense, rising bread, and the familiar iron tang that accompanied the galla. But these small passageways were either too low to admit a human form easily or set too high in the passage wall for any mortal woman or man to consider climbing up into them. Only one path led in the right direction; that was God's plan, after all.

Soon she found traces of those who preceded her: a worn leather strap; a stain of spilled water, not yet dry; a discarded scrap of parchment which she rolled up and tucked into her sleeve. Noises echoed around her: whispers and hisses, two snaps like rocks dropped from a height, a high-pitched giggle, the skittering of feet. Once she heard a horse's whinny, so strange a sound that she faltered, wondering if she had begun to hallucinate: first a man's voice, then that of a horse.

No matter.

The passage ended abruptly in a wall of rock, but to the left a narrow opening gave into a broad, circular chamber whose carpet was covered with puddles of water in the hollows and a floor of damp pebbles on the higher ground. The smell of the air changed, laden with moisture. She entered, careful where she put her feet. Near the center of the chamber a ladder thrust up and out a hole.

Whispers teased her. Standing here, even with the burning lamp to guide her, made her uncomfortable. She crossed quickly to the ladder and with some difficulty held the lamp in one hand while she steadied herself with the other, taking the rungs one at a time.

Her head had just reached the level of the base of the hole when echoes murmured and stretched around her. It took a moment for her to understand that she heard, ahead of her, voices belonging to those who had climbed this ladder before her. Yet those voices mingled and resonated with whispers below.

Snick.

The sound startled her. She looked down.

Pale shapes scuttled into the chamber below. As ghastly white as lepers afflicted with a rash of silvery-white scales, the creatures balked as if the light hurt them. They had no eyes, only bulges on their faces like giant, moist egg sacs, but it was not only this deformity that made them grotesque and misshapen, *wrong*, the broken vessels from which the Enemy had attempted to create a mockery of angels. Their heads were too big for their bodies. Scabrous pustules grew on their twisted limbs. Some wore charms and amulets dangling at their necks; these ornaments chimed softly as they clamored each against the others in a wordless music as incomprehensible as their animal muttering.

They shuffled closer, clawed hands grasping and clicking at the air, seeking prey.

She scrambled up the final rungs, shoved the lamp safely onto the floor before her, flung herself over the lip of the hole, and dragged the ladder up behind her. God had not freed her only to allow her to fall into the hands of such creatures.

Panting, she sidled away from the hole. Could they leap? Fly? Dig? She hoped she had trapped them below, banished them within the depths of the rock.

Picking up the lamp, she hurried up a stairwell carved into the rock. Ahead she heard the faint voices and footfalls of the ones who had gone before her. Even had she been tempted to hurry, to catch them, she could not. Soon enough she had to stop, bent double as her sides heaved and she fought to catch her breath. Only after some time could she start up again, and each time she took fewer steps before she had to stop and rest – yet each time God gave her the will and the strength to continue.

She had keen hearing, honed during this time that sight had been denied her. Aided by a good sense of direction and a nose for misdirection, she followed the trail of her captors through winding passages, along the side of caverns that smelled of horses, past desiccated midden heaps and, at last, out under the blinding brilliance of a nearly full moon hanging just above the horizon in a cloudless night sky. She could barely endure its light and had to rest, after extinguishing the lamp, to fight off nausea.

After a while she felt able to continue, although her eyes hurt. As she walked, the night air swirled against her with such a bewildering miasma of scents that she staggered sideways, halting at the brink of a cliff. The path cut up along the shoulder of the vast rock that housed the convent where she had journeyed so long ago. The moon sank behind dark hills.

Dawn was coming and, with it, the sun.

Sparks and threads of light winked into existence at the topmost crown of the great rock.

Sorcery! She recognized the handiwork of a mathematicus, weaving starlight into a stone crown. Only Anne and her minions knew these well-guarded secrets. Had they betrayed her twice?

Astonished and deeply dismayed, she limped onward as quickly as she could, although her feet ached and her back burned and her eyes still stung. Lamp, water pouch, and bundle she dropped behind her; they seemed of little account now, and they weighed so heavily as she grew tired.

The path led her through a grove of rock pinnacles before vanishing on a flat summit crowned by a stone circle. There they stood, the miscreants, the very ones who had cast her into the pit. Yet surely her eyes had suffered after so long in the dark, for it seemed to her that there were twice the number that had inhabited the convent when she had first come. Three of their number were certainly male. Two held between them a pallet, where lay the very woman Antonia had been sent to eliminate.

Was Mother Obligatia the one whose power had thwarted Antonia's galla? Or had Anne betrayed Antonia by teaching the secrets of the mathematici to someone else?

Obligatia gestured to a woman who arranged small stones on a patch of oval sand the color of moonlight. Rising, that woman chanted in a clear, authoritative voice.

'Matthias guide me, Mark protect me, Johanna free me, Lucia aid me, Marian purify me, Peter heal me, Thecla be my witness always, that the Lady shall be my shield and the Lord shall be my sword.' Using a polished walking stick, she traced lines between the stones, and with each line in the sand a line of light threaded down from the heavens to catch in the stones. 'May the blessing of God be on our heads. God reign forever, world without end.'

The others were too intent on her sorcery to notice Antonia, and yet she was herself too exhausted from her climb to act. The woman worked quickly as the night sky lightened imperceptibly with the coming of day, weaving threads where Mother Obligatia directed her.

Shouts rang up from behind, startling Antonia so badly that she staggered back against rocks and sank down, too worn even to stand.

'Hurry!' cried one of the assembled clerics, a very young woman now breaking down into sobs, while another hushed the crying girl sharply.

The woman sang while using the staff to weave the threads

into a new pattern woven in and out between the monoliths. The web of light thrummed, pulsing as to the dance of an unseen spider tangled in its own weaving. Light blossomed into an archway surmounting the nearest lintel.

'Now!' cried the woman. The light of the weaving limned her gaunt profile.

Antonia knew her: a noble cleric from the north country of Wendar, a notable counselor to King Henry. What was Sister Rosvita doing here? Why was she not in Darre with the king and his court? Why did she look so old?

'Stop them!'

A man's voice rang out from within the forest of rock pinnacles behind her

'Go!' shouted one among the clerics, a young woman with the pale hair common to the northern barbarians only recently come into the Circle of Unity. She wore an Eagle's cloak; her face, glimpsed briefly, seemed vaguely familiar. Antonia set her jaw and with an effort clambered to her feet, but it was too late. Behind, she heard the shouts of men rushing across rocky ground, feet crackling on stone. Ahead, the clerics hurried through the gleaming archway, the first two carrying Mother Obligatia. One by one the rest vanished.

'Rosvita!'

To Antonia's amazement, Hugh of Austra emerged from the pinnacles, furious, disheveled, and outwitted, a score of soldiers crowding up behind him and exclaiming aloud in terror and wonder.

Rosvita glanced back last of all, pausing on the threshold of the glittering archway. She marked the man who, out of breath and flushed with anger, now stood beside Antonia, but she neither smiled nor frowned; she simply looked, measuring him, noting Antonia for the first time without any outward evidence of surprise.

The crown of light faded.

Sister Rosvita turned, stepped through, and was gone.

The crown disintegrated into a thousand spitting sparks that drifted to the ground like so many fireflies winking on and off.

'Damn!' swore Hugh. His hands were dirty, his golden hair wild in disarray; he wore a layman's tunic and hose, and these were scuffed and even ripped at one knee, as though he had been climbing, no better than the common soldiers massed behind him. Yet despite this he remained beautiful, almost radiant in his fury as the sun rose in pitiless splendor behind him.

She lifted a ragged sleeve to cover her eyes. The light gave her a vile headache, and spots of shadow and light flashed and whirled in her vision.

'I pray you, Presbyter Hugh,' she said, pleased to discover that her voice worked, calm and in command, 'I have been a prisoner here, cast into a pit of darkness. I would be most grateful if you would escort me back to my rightful place.'

Her words like a hook yanked him back to himself. He brushed away a smudge of dirt on his cheek.

After a pause he spoke, now completely in control of himself, all that blazing emotion tucked away. 'You must be Sister Venia. Holy Mother Anne thought you irretrievably lost, Sister, but I am heartened to find you whole and safe.' He glanced heavenward before offering her the support of his arm. 'Come. Let us retreat to the shade. I pray you tell me what happened, and why you did not return to Darre.'

He found her a decent place to sit and made sure that a soldier padded the rock with several tunics to make a comfortable seat. He sent soldiers to reconnoiter. Meanwhile, wine was offered to her, a subtle vintage that cleansed her palate.

With these assurances to strengthen her, she was able to tell her story, careful to let no hint of her anger at Anne color her words. Hugh was surely well placed in Anne's councils by now; she could only guess at his loyalties.

'So you are free, after two years in captivity,' he said wonderingly, laughing. 'In exchange for Sister Rosvita, it seems. A clever irony.'

'Was Rosvita also a captive?'

'She was. She . . .' He frowned as he glanced toward the stone circle, mostly hidden by the pinnacles that surrounded them. 'She discovered things too dangerous for her to know. Holy Mother Anne, Queen Adelheid, and myself had to take action to help King Henry, who came under the influence of bad advisers, Rosvita among them.'

The comment surprised her. Antonia had never hesitated to dispose of those who threatened her. 'You did not simply eliminate her?'

His smile would have broken the heart of any maid, soft and sad as that of a gentle lover thwarted in his plans by the arrival of a nobler suitor. 'You are a woman, Sister Venia, and thereby fashioned out of stronger metal. I am sentimental, as men are. I admire Sister Rosvita too much to deal so arbitrarily with her. I had hoped for another solution.'

She did not believe him, but the words sounded nice. He knew how to evoke sympathy while hiding his true motives.

'A solution may yet be offered to those who are both patient and pure of heart, Father Hugh.'

He laughed again, sweetly this time. 'I fear I am not pure of heart, Sister Venia. I struggle with temptation as does every human soul.'

No need to remind him of her own virtue; it usually irritated people, none of whom liked to be reminded of the select few upon whom God had showered Their favor.

He hesitated before speaking again, this time with an odd tremor in his voice. 'Tell me what else you recall of this fiery daimone borne up on wings of flame. How is it she banished the galla? By what signs were you sure it was a woman?'

She had not forgotten what drove him. A man's weaknesses were the harness under which he could be put to work.

'I saw her only through what senses are granted to the galla, who come from another plane of existence. She was bright and powerful, most certainly a woman. You must not doubt me.'

'I do not. Yet did she speak?'

'If she spoke, I could not hear her. Yet Mother Obligatia spoke, when she saw her.'

'The abbess also saw this apparition?'

'Indeed she did. She recognized her.'

'Recognized her?'

'She called her "Bernard" before realizing her mistake, that it was no man who stood before her but rather a creature with a woman's form.'

'Bernard,' he mused. 'But of course there was a striking resemblance between father and daughter. Yet if that is true, then how—?'

'You are puzzled by something, Brother Hugh.'

He started as might a child who looks up to find himself discovered in the midst of secret mischief. 'Nay, Sister. I am only wondering whether I seek a mule or a hinny.'

She chuckled. 'You are speaking of Liath. Do you suspect that she is not in truth Anne's child?'

Turning, he looked away as though to hide his face and what it might reveal, but when he turned back his expression remained bland, veiled. Only a certain tightening of the skin about his eyes betrayed his intense interest. 'It is difficult to know what to think.'

'The world is full of mysteries,' she agreed, watching him closely. 'I trust that Anne will reward her supporters with that which they desire most, whatever my own feelings. Or at least, were I in her position, it is what I would do.'

'Would you?'

'Oh, I would. God reward us all in the end with that we desire most. It is the fate of most people not to understand their desire until they have been swept into the Abyss – but upon reflection they can see that their entire lives were simply one long dialogue with the evil inclination. Yet there are a few who remain clear-sighted and who serve God and receive what they deserve in the end.'

'We must all hope to ascend to the Chamber of Light,' he said with a pious nod, 'else we will suffer eternity with God's face turned away from us.'

'Is that what you wish, Father Hugh?'

He trembled. The movement was slight but noticeable to a woman so long immured in the pit that she had come to rely on hearing, touch, and breath to capture any nuance of life and being around her.

'Or would you risk everything only to possess her?'

He could not answer.

She smiled and rested a comforting hand on his fists where they were clenched in his lap. With his gaze lowered humbly, he displayed his profile to advantage; even in the shade his hair shone as though the sunlight were caught in it. It was difficult to imagine how any young woman could resist him.

'Anne will never give her to you. But I will.'

He flushed, but he did not look up at her. 'That is a bold promise. How do you capture a woman who is only half humankind? How do you intend to defy Anne?'

'Anne need not know that I still live. If she believes that I died here, then she has no reason to guard herself against me. I mean no harm to Anne. She has set herself a great and worthy task. There is no one else who can accomplish it except her—'

'And those who aid her, the Seven Sleepers. Of whom you are, or were, once a part.'

'It is true I learned much during my time among the Seven Sleepers. I also learned that when they weave a powerful spell, the weakest among them dies. The spell exacts its price for the power they draw down.'

That she had startled him was obvious from the way he looked at her, leaned forward with hands pressing on the rock. Evidently he had never considered this striking and unfortunate possibility. 'Is this true? The cauda draconis is struck dead?'

'I have suffered in the pit for two years, Father Hugh, but those two years have given me time to ponder much that mystified me before. Surely I will be accounted weakest among the Seven Sleepers now. Anne gathers and manipulates the power of the sorceries we weave, but she does not risk herself. That is why she needs a cauda draconis, although in truth I proved stronger than she expected, I suppose, since it was poor foolish Zoë who died.'

'Are you not willing to die in order to enact God's will on Earth?'

'Certainly I am. But I am not convinced that Holy Mother Anne knows everything, that she knows or understands all of

God's will. I come of royal stock in my own right. I served faithfully as biscop in the north before I was myself betrayed and cast aside. I have certain magics of my own and, as I said, I have been granted a very long time to meditate, pray, and think.'

She smiled as he settled back. She had set wheels turning, made promises, exposed herself. He would now, of course, feel that he stood in a stronger position than she did, and that would make him reckless.

'So you see, Father Hugh, I am at your mercy now. You may arrest me for disloyalty and turn me over to Anne, thus insinuating yourself into her good graces.'

He was too elegant and well bred to protest that such a deed would be beneath him. The presbyters in the service of the skopos bought, sold, and betrayed each other at every opportunity in order to curry favor or gain a better position within the skopos' court.

'Or you can escort me elsewhere, somewhere isolated but civilized, where I might recuperate.'

'Anne is a powerful sorcerer,' he objected. 'She could obliterate either of us should her anger be turned against us. Indeed, she might at this very moment be spying upon us, since she has mastered the Eagle's Sight.'

Antonia drew an amulet, now withered and fragile, out from under her tattered and filthy robe. 'If you have not protected yourself against farseeing, Father Hugh, then you are not as wise as you seem.'

He touched a hand to his chest but revealed nothing. 'Or I might encourage you, Sister Venia, and escort you to a private villa where you can recover your strength – only to turn you over to Anne later, when it serves my cause best.'

'So you might. But I think that Anne will never give you Liath, and I think Liath is what you most desire.'

Feet scraped on pebbles as one of the soldiers approached, pausing out of earshot. He inclined his head obediently as he waited to be beckoned forward.

'What is it, Gerbert?' Hugh asked genially.

'The boys have found a way through to the old convent,

my lord. We need not climb back the way we came but can descend by way of the ladders they have on the other side.'

'And the convent?'

'Deserted, my lord. No one has lived there for a long time. It seems everyone fled, or has died. There were bones.'

Hugh rose. 'Pray bring four men and a chair or pallet on which to carry Sister Venia. I will investigate the convent myself, but I think it likely we will leave tomorrow. Have Cook prepare broth and porridge for our guest, something gentle on the stomach.'

'Yes, my lord.' The man departed.

Hugh did not sit down. He seemed pensive, even unsure. He was tempted but fearful, avaricious but restrained by caution, like a half grown colt deciding whether to bolt through the open gate of its familiar corral for the wide open woodland beyond.

The rising sun had altered the shadows, and light began to creep up the stone on which she sat. Her eyes still hurt, but the pain was becoming bearable, slowly receding.

'I know a place,' Hugh said at last, and offered her his hand.

XIV

THE APPROACHING STORM

1

In the Kerayit language, Breschius told him, there were multiple words for the manifold gradations of cold. Not cold enough to freeze broth. Lambs must be covered cold. So cold that bronze water jars burst.

Cold enough to turn dragon's fire to ice.

It was now cold enough to freeze piss, Sanglant reflected as he staggered back into the frail shelter of his tent. With three lit braziers set around the walls, the inside of the tent had warmed just enough that he could peel off the bulky furs that did not keep him warm outside in the Wendish winter. Malbert hung the furs from the cross braces. The prince was still bundled in the clothing that he would normally wear outside in the Wendish winter. His face ached from the cold blast.

'How do these people endure it?' he demanded of the two dozen people crammed shivering in the tent.

'I'm not cold,' said Blessing. 'Come see the letters I wrote, Papa. I hope you like them.' She sat cross-legged on a feather bed on the opposite side of the tent and, indeed, wore nothing more than an ordinary wool tunic with her cloak thrown casually over her legs. Heribert knelt beside her. Fingers white with cold, he picked up the wax tablet on which he was teaching her to form letters.

'My lord prince.' A woman dressed in the fashion of the Quman slaves stepped out of the crowd, dropping to one knee. 'Her Most Glorious Highness, Princess Sapientia, commands that you attend her. At once.'

The thought of going back out into the cold was enough to make a strong man weep with frustration, nor did he like the tone that Sapientia, after months on the road in the company of the Pechanek Quman, was taking with him. But this was no time to pick petty fights.

He gestured for Malbert to help him back on with the furs. 'Hathui. Breschius.'

Frater and Eagle bundled themselves up, and Hathui grabbed a lantern.

'What about my letters? Aren't you going to look at my letters!'

'I will tomorrow, little one.'

'I want to go!'

'You may not.'

'You can't stop me! I'll go out whether you want me to or not!'

'You will not, Blessing. You are too valuable a hostage. I cannot trust the Pechanek. If they get hold of you, then I will be forced to trade Bulkezu in order to get you back, and then the Quman will have no reason to guide us to the eastern lands where we can hunt griffins.'

'I want to hunt griffins!' she cried, shifting ground. She would never admit she was wrong.

'When you are old enough.'

'I'm old enough now!'

'Your Highness,' said Heribert gently, 'you are not even a woman yet. Nor have you trained with arms for more than a few months, and in such limited circumstances because of this God-forsaken winter.'

'You never looked at my letters! You hate me!' Blessing

flung herself facedown on the feather bed and sobbed noisily. Her attendants fussed over her, trying to soothe her.

It was a relief to step outside into the cruel slap of winter.

'Is not the young princess old enough to be married, my lord prince?' asked the slave, falling into step beside Sanglant. She had a deadly way of looking sideways at a man, but he wasn't sure if she meant to be provocative.

'She is not yet a woman.'

'She might still be betrothed and sent into the care of her husband's family so that she would understand their ways.'

'In what land were you born?'

'In Avitania, my lord prince.'

'Salian, then.'

'That explains it,' muttered Hathui.

Sanglant chuckled, sensing an undercurrent of hostility between the two women, who only ever met in such formal situations. 'We have different customs. How came you to serve a Quman master?'

'I was sold to an Arethousan merchant, my lord prince, and taken into the east to the estate of a noble family. There I was captured by a Quman raiding party.' She spoke the words with no sign of anger or grief.

'You learned Wendish from a good teacher.'

She glanced at Hathui. 'Brother Zacharias was what he was.'

'A slave like you!' retorted Hathui angrily.

The slave nodded, choosing not to argue. Probably she had long since given up any notions of argument. She was a stolid woman in all ways, except for that amorous gaze, an open window in an otherwise shuttered-up house. She endured the cold without complaint, although she wore less clothing than he himself did: heavy felt trousers and tunic and a skin coat with the fur side turned in and wrapped tightly around her torso, all of which concealed the lush figure he recalled noticing in warmer days. Because she had the patience of a woman who has served a harsh master for many years and expects no release, she said nothing as he took his time making a spiral walk out of his own encampment, which was curled tightly around the two central tents.

At the entrance to the tent placed beside his own, he stopped to speak to the guards.

'How's the prisoner, Anshelm?'

'Quiet, my lord prince.'

'It's a change.'

'Truly, it is, my lord prince. Barely a peep out of him since those Quman came. I never thought to see him wetting his leggings like a frightened boy, but I admit it gives me pleasure still to think on it.'

Sergeant Cobbo pushed through the entrance flap. 'I heard voices.' He bowed his head. 'My lord prince.'

Sanglant glimpsed the figure within, so heavily weighted with chains that it was a miracle the prisoner could sit upright, but sit upright he did. Before the flap cut off his view, Sanglant felt the force of Bulkezu's gaze like the nip of a cold wind biting his face.

Quiet, but not broken.

'We was just talking of the prisoner, Sergeant,' said Anshelm. 'Think he lost his voice when he caught sight of his mum?'

Cobbo laughed. 'Never did I think to see the day that beast would get his own back! How it made me laugh to see him humbled!'

Unlike his soldiers, Sanglant gained no pleasure from Bulkezu's humiliation and fear; he recalled his own too well. 'Stay alert.' He nodded and went on.

The camp was laid out in concentric rings, the tents set in uneven ranks so as to break up the blowing wind as much as possible. He paused at each tent to inquire after the soldiers within. Certain companies always had the privilege of being set up within the inner ring. When the healer came out to greet him, the man wheezed as the cold air hit his lungs.

'Whew! Each night I think it can't get any colder. Then it does!'

'How many are sick this evening?'

'Not more than twenty. Chustaffus was the worst of them yesterday, but he seems better today. These Quman witches have a brew that brings the fever down and clears out the lungs. After the first two, poor lads, we've not lost a single man to the lung fever, which I count a miracle. Chuf's a strong fellow. I don't fear for him now.'

Sanglant nodded and went on.

Resuelto and the remaining Wendish horses – about a third of the stock had died – had to be stabled at great inconvenience in shelters.

'Nay, it's true,' said the stable master while Sanglant groomed the gelding and, when he was done, fetched from his pocket the last of the apples they'd brought from Sordaia. It was withered, skin all loose, but Resuelto gobbled it up and slobbered on his shoulder, hoping for more.

'We'll lose another tonight,' continued the stable master. 'Colic. They can't take the weather, poor beasts. I'm nursing along six that are foundering, but two of those won't last. The weak ones aren't much to eat, either, with so little flesh left on their bones.'

'I never thought to eat so much horseflesh,' said Sanglant wearily. Even sturdy Resuelto had suffered, losing the flesh that would give him some protection against the cold. Sanglant prayed that they had survived the worst of the winter, yet although Breschius and Heribert had counted off the days and assured him that the new year *had* come and that it was by rights spring, he had no idea how long this crushing cold might last.

The stable master's hands were seamed with work and hatched with white scars. He sniffed, wiped his nose. 'Never stops running,' he said, then waved toward the crowd of horses. 'I hope the meat doesn't turn us into geldings like the ones we're eating!'

'They're keeping up their spirits,' said Breschius when they left, continuing along the second ring of tents.

'So they are. Here, now, Ditmar. Berro. How fares it with you this night?'

'Well enough, my lord prince.'

'We're dicing, my lord.'

'Nay, we're dreaming of decent women, my lord. Those

Quman women are the ugliest creatures I've ever laid eyes on! They don't have noses!'

'I saw one who was as handsome a maid as any Wendish girl! That was back before it got so cold.'

'And where is she now? Bundled up in furs, most like, and oiled up with stinking grease like her mother!'

The slave woman stood back and said nothing.

So it went, tent by tent. His soldiers greeted him cheerfully despite the searing cold and the interminable journey eastward across the bleakest land he had ever laid eyes on. The men had stitched together smaller tents into larger ones, crudely strung up but strong enough to withstand the howling winds and able to house more all together and thus keep everyone warmer through the terrible nights.

He had placed his most experienced, strongest men along the outer rim of the encampment together with the steppe horses who suffered the cold and could dig through the drifting snow to find grass, twigs, or tree bark. Like Quman women, Quman horses were as ugly as any he had seen, but they were tough.

He lifted a hand to greet four sentries huddled in what shelter curtains of felt provided against the cutting wind, which thrummed merrily against the cloth. The covered lamp Breschius held rocked as the wind caught it square on.

'My lord prince! It's cold to be out tonight.'

'How do you fare?' he asked them.

'We're having a pissing contest, to see whose piss can reach the ground without freezing.'

'Sibold left his sword out too long, so it froze off. Now he'll never get a wife!'

'A few sticks bound together will serve him well enough, won't they, Surly?'

'I hope so, since that's more than you have, Lewenhardt!'

'Hush now, you men.' Captain Fulk emerged from the tent, having heard voices. 'You lot go in, you've been out long enough.'

With groans of relief, the four men hurried inside. Ice splintered off the tent flap as they jostled it, raining down on the snow-covered ground in a crystalline spray.

'How do the men fare, Captain?'

'Well enough.'

'Provisions?'

Fulk frowned at four soldiers moaning and chafing their gloved hands as they edged outside to replace the ones just come off watch. The men greeted the prince warmly and, stamping feet and rubbing arms, squinted into the darkness toward the fires that marked the Quman encampment, an arrow's flight from theirs. Over in the nomad camp a man was singing, voice rising and falling in a nasal whine; despite the skirl of the wind, Sanglant was able to pick out a few words – man, woman, river, ice, drowning, death. If the Pechanek Quman knew any happy songs, he had yet to hear them.

'We're down to the last two barrels of salted fish eggs, my lord prince.'

'Thank God.'

'I can't stand the taste of it either. Poor man's food, as Brother Breschius told us, but it will go hard on us unless we reach a place we can obtain food in greater quantities than what we have available to us now. We'll have to start eating horse every day, slaughter the weak ones.'

'Or drink their blood, as the Quman do.'

'I pray we never do such a barbaric thing, my lord. Their milk wine is bad enough.'

'Do you think so? It isn't so bad.'

Breschius moved up beside him to stare out at the gap of land between the two encampments. Snow dusted down, swirling on the ever-present wind, but Breschius squinted into the darkness as though seeking something that lay beyond Sanglant's sight. Briefly the prince heard the tinkle of delicate chimes, fading and vanishing below the whine of the wind.

'Do you know where we are, Brother, or when we can expect to find better shelter and a good supply of food?'

Breschius shook his head, looking distressed.

'Do you know?' Sanglant asked the slave.

She shrugged, looking away from him. 'These are not

questions I can answer, my lord prince.'

'Have you remembered your name yet?' he demanded, irritated by her placidity. At least Zacharias had hated and reviled his captors.

'You may call me what you wish, my lord prince. Whatever you require, I am bound to agree to, so the mothers have said.'

Her lips were so red, full and shapely. Was she hinting that he might ask her into his bed? Or pleading with him in the only way she had, short of outright defiance of her masters, to beware what he asked of her? Was she begging for freedom?

'The wind would be worse,' said Breschius suddenly, 'but you can see how the slope protects us from the brunt of it.'

'It's difficult to imagine it being worse,' said Hathui.

Fulk drew the Circle at his breast. 'May God have pity on us. I'll be glad to see spring, my lord prince.'

'It is spring in Wendar,' said Breschius, 'but when the winter cold blows off and warmer weather comes, then the travel will get worse since it rains all day.'

'And in summer you boil,' said Hathui.

Sanglant laughed. 'A fine place to make your home. Come,' he said to the slave, 'grab the rope.'

Each afternoon when they stopped to set up camp, a Quman boy strung up a rope between the two camps in case of blizzard. Because the ground was frozen, they could not drive in a post on which to fasten their end of the rope, so Gyasi and his nephews had volunteered to act as post wardens and gatekeepers. They strung the rope from the small felt tent in which they sheltered each night. Sanglant ducked under the awning that protected the entrance of their tent, slung at an angle to cut off the prevailing wind. The old shaman crouched at the threshold, eyes closed. Behind him, glimpsed through a slitlike opening, Sanglant saw the twisting flame of a lamp and dark shapes clustered around it. An owl hooted nearby, calling out of the night, and Gyasi raised hands to his mouth and answered it.

'Great lord,' he said without opening his eyes. 'Be warned. Storm comes.'

'Worse than this? Is there any threat to my people?'

'I am still listening.'

Captain Fulk followed him under the awning.

'Captain, send word along the line for the men to make sure everything is secure.'

'Yes, my lord prince. Do you desire an escort?'

Sanglant glanced back toward the slave, who was, he gauged, out of earshot. He spoke quietly. 'We still have Bulkezu. If I show weakness or anything they interpret as fear, the Pechanek may feel free to attack.'

'They might take you prisoner, my lord prince, and then we would have to bargain for your release.'

'We have sworn oaths, an agreement.'

'People are tricky,' Gyasi said, still without opening his eyes. 'One man may promise life to his brother and after this stab him in the back.'

'What protection should I take?'

One of the nephews eased out from between the slitlike entrance. He dropped to one knee before Sanglant in the gesture of obedience common to the Quman, then slipped out into the night with his bow case bobbing on his back.

Because of the way the light cast shadows, Sanglant could not see Gyasi's face distinctly, but he knew when the shaman opened his eyes. That stare could be sensed even when it could not be seen, as a man can feel the glare of the sun on his back or the appraisal of an interested woman.

'We protect you, great lord. Bulkezu had one time a brother who is like me a shaman. Now he is dead.'

'He is the one whose magic killed Prince Bayan.'

Gyasi shrugged. Bayan's fate held little interest for him. 'Many seasons ago I am driven out of the tribe like a sick woman with no sons to protect her. My cousins know I hold no love for them in my heart after they have beaten me with sticks and burned my tent. No shaman walks with the Pechanek tribe who is so powerful that he can walk the shaman's path beside me. Do not fear them. They fear me. If they kill you, I will eat their flesh and grind up their bones to feed the dogs.'

Sanglant laughed. 'Then I shall walk into their camp without fear. I'll go alone, Fulk, with Breschius and Hathui. They
can't kill me in any case, even if they try, and it's better if
they continue to fear me because I do not fear them.'

'I do not like this, my lord prince.'

'I have made up my mind.'

Fulk nodded unhappily. He was the most valuable of captains: a good man in all ways, including knowing when his
protests might receive a hearing and when it was better to
shut up.

Gyasi shut his eyes, humming in a singsong voice as though
he had forgotten them.

Sanglant stepped out into the full blast of the wind and
took hold of the rope. As they trudged across the open
ground, the lamp sputtered and went out despite its glass
casing, but with a hand on the rope it was possible to move
with reasonable certainty across the uneven ground. A dark
figure ghosted past – one of Gyasi's nephews, scouting the
perimeter. They and their uncle guarded the camp at night
and slept by day on horseback. The cold never seemed to
bother them.

Was it wise to leave his life in their hands? Or was he
becoming more reckless? This long journey chafed him,
thrown on the mercy of others without being able to choose
direction or speed. Once upon a time he had ridden at his
father's behest and never questioned, but he had lost the habit
of obedience; he could no longer bear to be ruled by another,
and he knew that he put himself at risk every time he pushed
at the boundaries of what seemed possible.

He had forged out into a wilderness of his own making.
He did not know what he would find at the end of his journey.

Before the winter, he could have smelled the stink of the
Quman camp long before he reached it, but ice and snow had
their mercies. Sooner than he expected, he came to the end
of the rope, which was tethered to a slender line hung with
tiny bells that encircled the entire Quman camp. The bells
chimed in counterpoint to the whine and thrum of the wind

among the tents. Only as the sentry stepped back to let him pass, ducking under the line, did he catch a hint of the familiar rank stench of rancid grease compounded with offal, sweat, and farting horses.

The Quman laid out their tents in a curving windbreak behind which most of the herd sheltered and a handful of dung fires burned. Men squatted around them, although he couldn't imagine how they did not freeze to death. He had already lost feeling in his toes, and his fingers stung as though he had rubbed them with ice. Although common sense and his own observations argued against it, maybe it was true that they weren't fully human. How else to explain their unnatural resistance to cold?

The tent of the mothers was constructed of white felt, spanning two wagons, the fabric blending into the snow swirling around it. Its entrance was turned to the south, away from the prevailing wind. Two sentries stepped aside to let him climb the steps that led into the interior.

'Beware the threshold,' murmured Breschius as Sanglant ducked through the opening.

Inside, smoke hazed the air, sated with a sour-sweet incense that did not cover the nauseating stink of rancid oil. Two musicians sat beside the center pole of the tent; one tuned a spiked fiddle while the other arranged a collection of rattles and scraps of bark around a pipe. Although several braziers placed up on tripod legs made it pleasantly warm, here where they need not lie down directly on the frozen ground, the sight of the little pipe chilled him with the cold breath of memory: Bloodheart had tormented him with such an instrument, a bone flute carved from the remains of one of Sanglant's own men.

Six men sat cross-legged on rugs and pillows near the musicians, all of them seated on the left-hand side of the circular tent. One was young and effortlessly handsome with features that resembled a younger Bulkezu. He rested his hand on a pair of wings constructed out of griffin feathers and, like the others, faced the right side of the tent where the three mothers of Bulkezu sat upright on two couches. The stiff posture of the men reminded him of Bulkezu, wrapped in chains but sitting bolt upright.

In contrast, Sapientia reclined at her ease beside the youngest of the mothers. A slave girl massaged the Wendish princess' bare feet.

'Brother!' she cried without sitting up to greet him properly. 'I expected you sooner!'

The three mothers of Bulkezu did not greet him. Although one was a maid, one middle-aged, and one an enormously fat crone, they looked mightily similar, as if they were three ages of the same woman in three different bodies. Had one of the older two actually spawned Bulkezu, giving birth to him out of her own womb?

He did not know, nor did he have Zacharias here to interpret their customs and speech for him. Sapientia and her new allies had him at a disadvantage.

The slave woman from Salia crossed to stand behind the mothers' couch. Indeed, only slaves remained standing. He caught the eye of the griffin warrior. With the merest tightening of one eye, as though he wished to grin but dared not, the young man tossed him a pillow embroidered with a red-and-gold griffin. Sanglant sank down cross-legged, mirroring the casual pose of the other men. Hathui hunkered down beside the entrance. Breschius bowed his head, still holding the lamp, and remained standing.

'The mothers of Bulkezu are displeased,' said Sapientia. She sipped at a bowl half full of the fermented milk they quaffed like ale, and after she was done, handed it to a black-haired girl no more than ten or twelve years of age.

The mothers of Bulkezu watched him. They never blinked. They might have been carved in stone: maid, mother, crone, implacable and morose.

'We are traveling too slowly,' continued Sapientia. 'We have to spend too much time setting up and taking down camp each day because you insist that your army uses the big tents. They want to know why the western soldiers are such weaklings.'

'These western soldiers defeated their great begh and their powerful army.'

'Under Bayan's leadership! With the aid of Ungrians, who have left us.'

'I won the battle, Sapientia, however bravely Bayan fought. Bulkezu remains my prisoner.'

'Only because you betrayed me.'

'Because you are the strongest piece on the chessboard. No other has as much weight as Bulkezu, to achieve our ends. You agreed to this yourself.'

'Maybe you tell yourself I agreed to deliver myself to the Pechanek as a hostage. If you do, you are lying. You coerced me. I had no choice.'

Drink and anger brought her emotions to the surface where, like a broad path through the forest, her thoughts were easily traced: consternation, pride, frustrated anger, shame.

'But that doesn't mean I am helpless, Brother. I am honored here as I deserve. If I were commanding the army, we would not suffer these troubles. You should have got rid of all our horses. The steppe horses are better. You're only slowing us down by having to kill so many. What a waste of horseflesh! You'll lose the entire army before we reach the hunting grounds!'

'We have lost five men out of eight hundred.'

'Winter isn't over yet!'

'Where are your Wendish attendants, Sister? I have not seen Brigida or Everelda in many days, nor any of your servingwomen.'

She changed color, flushed face bleaching to white. Her hands trembled as she took the shallow bowl from the slave girl, swallowed a healthy draught, lowered the bowl, looked at him, lifted the bowl again, and drained it.

The slave woman leaned forward to whisper into the ear of the crone, and the old woman lifted a hand in a gesture of command. The fiddle player set his instrument vertically on its spike and sawed a drone on its string. All the Quman in the tent listened intently as, after an interminable prelude featuring only that drone, the other musician began to sing in a high-pitched, nasal voice.

Although he had made some effort to learn the rudiments

of the Quman tongue, Sanglant found it difficult to pick out individual words: eyes, spear, griffin, and the ubiquitous references to death and rivers, usually together. Now and again, to break the monotony of a song whose melody did not seem to span more than five notes, the man lifted a scrap of birch bark to his lips and imitated the calls of birds.

His thoughts wandered.

When had he come to despise his poor sister? He regarded her surreptitiously through the hazy air. She had been so sweet when she was a little girl tagging after him, passionate in her likes and dislikes. Envy had soured her.

Perhaps he had hoped that the Quman would solve the problem she represented for him. She was difficult, light-minded, easily led, and, despite her name, had no head for wisdom. Bayan might have made something of her, but Bayan was dead. King Henry was ensorcelled, and no other noble in the kingdom had the authority to make a marriage for her, except Sapientia herself.

Rash vows make weak alliances, so the saying went.

Hadn't he rashly sworn to marry Liath?

It was almost satisfying to press such needles of recrimination against himself.

Yet down that tangled path he hesitated to walk for the thousandth time. Every helpless night of longing, thinking of her, every memory of how when they were together they seemed never to speak the same language, every glimpse of the bright spark that lay at the heart of flame veiled inside her, brought home the foolish impulsiveness of what they had done.

How had they come to be so stupid?

He could not regret it.

The Salian slave woman knelt beside him. He had not noticed her cross the rugs, but now he was painfully aware of the swell of her breasts concealed beneath her felt jacket, brushing against his arm.

'This is the story of the ancestor of the Quman people.' Her expressive voice flowed counterpoint to the monotonous tune.

'Is it a lengthy tale?'

'No. It only takes five nights to tell. Listen!'

The song rose and fell like waves on a shore, but now two slaves – a girl on the women's side and a man on the men's side – brought around a ceramic pipe with steam bubbling in its belly; a smoky odor drifted up from its bowels. Sapientia sucked greedily at the pipe before it was transferred down the row of mothers, the fierce-eyed girl, the powerful matron, the dour crone. The Quman warriors each took their turn on the pipe reserved for the men. When Sanglant's turn came, he inhaled cautiously. The smoke tasted sweet on his tongue, but it bit afterward deep into the lungs like a burrowing worm swollen and heavy with dreams.

He felt as if he were rising off the carpet, but it was some other part of him that, shifting, loosened from the cord binding it to the earth.

He hunted alone in the tall grass, flayed by a winter wind that had a malicious soul which hoped to devour his flesh until only his bones remained scattered on the steppe. The wind was his enemy.

In the way of dreams, he came unexpectedly upon a shoreline where he saw himself in the cold blue waters: but he wore a face not like his own, with eyes shaped like almonds, with a mustache, with short black hair crowned by a white foxskin hat.

If I am not myself, then who am I?

There came from the grass behind him a hooting cry of challenge: the griffin that stalked him just as he stalked it. Into the grass they ran, fighting the wind, tumbling and clashing, until he pinned her to the earth, and she became a woman clad in burnished iron skin struggling beneath him. He entered her, and in her rapture she transformed back into a griffin, but she was already his. He had tamed her. He had made her pregnant with his seed.

That night to mark his triumph he shot burning arrows into the sky, each one blossoming into a star.

Thus were the Quman people born of the mating of man and griffin.

He turned his head as the firelight glinted off the skin of the slave woman, giving her eyes an iron gleam, shading her skin until it shone like metal, silvery and strong. Was she a griffin, stalking him in her human form? He smelled her musk, but whether it was witchcraft sewn around her body to capture him or only the immemorial mystery of man drawn to woman and woman to man, he could not tell.

She turned, and with the twist of her body the light shifted. A man ducked out through the entrance flap. A gust of pungent smoke swirled.

He floated on the haze, staring down at Sapientia asleep on her couch, snoring softly as the mothers of Bulkezu sucked at their pipes and watched his empty body without expression.

The griffin warrior ran a finger along the sharp quill of one of the feathers that made up his wings, which were laid out beside him. Down that trickle of blood Sanglant's thoughts drifted up through the smoke hole until he hovered above the camp, seeing tents like a flock of mushrooms battered by snow and wind. He smelled the blizzard coming. A solitary figure picked its way up the long slope below which they had set out their camps, but he flew higher still as effortlessly as an eagle catching the updraft under her wings.

A blizzard was coming, hard and powerful, as implacable as the stone-faced mothers and their hatred for the man who had defeated the son of their tribe.

The wind breathed ice through his spirit. The ancient hills bent under the weight of the storm.

Something was waiting farther away even than the approaching storm. He could not see it, but he felt it along his skin, a prickling like sparks in the frigid air.

Down a long distance, he heard an owl's faint call of warning.

Something is coming.

He fell hard through the shivering night air, back into the prison of his body, jerked upright as he came back to himself. Lips brushed his ear. The Salian woman leaned against him, overcome by the lassitude brought on by the drug, moaning under her breath with such a perfume of desire that he at once, all of him, came alive with shamefully intense arousal, hot and strong.

His hands strayed to the laces fastening her jacket. He felt the promise of her skin so close, only the thin layer of clothing separating her from him, all of it easily discarded. She pressed eagerly against him. He followed the movement, gaze sliding down the length of her body to the sensuous curve of her bare feet, but the twisting patterns in the rug caught his eye, seducing him along their unfolding paths. While the slave woman nibbled gently at his ear, he followed this other trail with his gaze until he ran up against the cold stare of the mothers.

They were waiting for him to bare the chink in his armor. They were waiting for him to lose face, even if it meant sending their slave to couple with him publicly as a bitch in heat seduces any nearby dog.

Every man has his weakness.

He pulled away, scrambling to his feet. The musician still sang as his companion bowed that infuriating drone on and on. 'He heard thunder in the air. Tarkan heard the thunder of wings, these wings which were beating as the hunter approached. Now the heavens were full of the sound as the great creature approached.'

Was that thunder, or the boom of wind against the tents?

Abruptly, the musicians ceased, bringing silence.

The griffin warrior leaned forward to blow along the length of his iron wings; the tone that sang so softly from them was sweet and deadly.

It did not sing alone against the rising wind.

Sanglant stepped to the entrance. Hathui stood beside him as he lifted the flap and listened.

'Something is coming,' he said.

2

'Anna! Wake up!'

A hand pinched Anna's forearm.

'Anna! Wake up!'

'Ouch!' She sat up to find Blessing crouching on the pallet they shared. The girl's breath misted in the air. Lying back down, Anna pulled quilt and furs up to her neck, shivering.

'Anna!' The girl's voice was a hoarse whisper. Around them, the prince's courtiers slept hard, some snoring, some whistling in their sleep, others still and silent as the dead. 'Something's coming. I've got to go out and see what it is.'

'Your Highness!'

'Don't call out! I command you.'

Already dressed, Blessing moved fast. She had an almost supernatural sheen to her, apparent only when it was dark – a faint suggestion not of light but of *being*, as though her soul could be glimpsed as a shimmer beneath the surface of her skin. By the time these muddy thoughts made sense to Anna, the entrance flap had stirred and Blessing had slipped outside into the deadly night.

She drew in a breath to shout for help.

Stopped.

The last time they had let Blessing slip away, Prince Sanglant had whipped Thiemo and Matto and threatened to cast her out should she fail in her duty a second time. She still remembered the way his switch had cut into the dirt, the way grit thrown up by the force of his anger had lodged in her teeth. He would banish her and Thiemo and Matto out into the killing winter night.

Terror made her stutter out a bleat. Her voice choked off as if a hand throttled her. Shaking, she groped for her third tunic, her cloak, and furs, fumbling and clumsy as she struggled into them and fastened pins and brooches.

Thiemo and Matto had been banished to the far side of the large tent, forced by the prince to share a pallet so they would learn to tolerate each other, but the merciless cold and the seemingly endless journey had done more than this punishment to dull their anger. She crept between the pallets and sleeping figures to reach them, shaking them awake.

'Hurry! The princess is gone missing.'

She reached the entrance without mishap. The slap of the night air was cruel. It hurt to breathe, but she pushed out past the guards, scanned the dark camp, and turned on them.

'Where is the princess?' Her eyeballs hurt, stung by air so cold it seemed likely to freeze them in their sockets.

'The princess?' That was Den's gravelly voice, though she couldn't make out his features. 'Anna, you must be sleepwalking. I've not seen the princess out here. She's in her bed, and warm, unlike us. You'd best go back in.'

The moan of the wind shifted, rising in pitch. The tent shuddered, the entire frame bending under a blast. Snow spun out of the heavens and, abruptly, came down in streaming waves of dense white. Shouts, and frightened whinnies from the horses, broke out all through camp.

'God protect us!' shouted Den's companion, Johannes.

A blinding curtain of snow driven on a gale obliterated their view of the nearby tents. The wind roared. Thiemo and Matto stumbled out of the tent. Inside, a babble of voices raised in alarm as the tent rocked in the wind.

Thiemo yelled, but she couldn't make out his words over the scream of the wind. She huddled miserably under the scant shelter provided by the tent's awning.

'. . . Princess Blessing!' Matto shouted, his words torn away by the wind.

'Where is she?' shrieked Thiemo.

Heribert appeared at the entrance, holding a lamp that blazed long enough for her to see his frightened face. A gust of wind rattled the tent and actually lifted her off her feet as the men around her cried aloud. The lamp flame snapped out. A groan and crash splintered the air as the tent next to them – the one that held the prisoner – keeled over under the force of the wind. Its felt walls flew; poles snapped in two, their shards spun away. Soldiers scrambled to grab hold of the covering, but they could not stand upright.

Snow swept down. She could no longer see Den or Johannes. The icy grip of the wind blistered her face and stiffened her fingers. Her toes went numb.

She was yanked back into the safety of the tent – if it could be called safety, with the entire structure creaking under the assault of the storm. Men gripped the tent poles in a desperate attempt to hold it down. Thiemo was yelling at her, his hand fastened so tightly on her wrist that his grasp burned, but she couldn't hear him over the roaring wind. Heribert had fallen to his knees beside the feather bed where Blessing was supposed to be sleeping.

'She's gone!' screamed Anna. 'She'll die!'

She jerked her arm out of Thiemo's grasp and pushed out through the entrance flap before he could stop her.

She flung herself forward into the blizzard, stumbled when a hand clasped her boot and dragged her into drifting snow. It was no hand; it was a tangle of rope. Her fingers were so cold she could scarcely unwrap the rope from around her ankle, and with every precious, passing moment the cold bit deeper into her bones. It was hard to stand, but the wind pressed her forward as she floundered through the remains of the collapsed tent. Twice she collided with soldiers crawling over the fallen walls. They shouted at her and grabbed at her, but she eluded them. She had to keep going. She had to find Blessing.

She tripped over a fallen pole and fell into a nest of scalding serpents that writhed around her, tongues biting through her gloves to pierce her skin. She cried out, terrified, until she realized these were not snakes but cold iron.

A chain writhed down over her head unexpectedly. It dug into her eye before scoring her cheek and nestling like a viper at the curve of her neck. A force more powerful than the wind jerked her back into a solid wall. The chain choked her. She threw her head back, trying to get air. Snow dusted her lips and eyes; she swallowed, struggling against a powerful grip.

'Give it up, or I will kill you.'

Bulkezu's voice had the ability to penetrate the howling winds where none other could. His icy grip squeezed off the useless scream rising in her throat. He pushed her down on top of the chains and knelt on top of her chest, his weight forcing her into the rough metal links. Although the pain drove like knives into her spine and back, terror made her mute.

This is how I will die.

Snow blowing into her face made tears come to her eyes; her legs burned as the cold melted through her clothing to scald her skin, a cold so intense that it burned like heat. His hand curled around her throat, pushing *just so* at the soft belly of her neck. She gagged, choking, coughing, drowning. Figures swam into view through the wall of snow, hanging back when they saw that the prisoner had taken his own captive.

Stalemate. She had watched the prince play chess many times; she had sat silently while Brother Heribert tried to teach an impatient Blessing the basic strategy of the game.

'Lions can be sacrificed,' he would tell her, *'to advance the other pieces.'*

With her peripheral vision she glimpsed a suggestion of cautious movement to either side, but to move her head even slightly caused Bulkezu to probe for a more painful place to squeeze. She whimpered; his lips creased upward in a smile, although he did not look down at her.

She lay still as her body grew numb from terror and cold, as Bulkezu's hand twitched, once, twice, a third time, on her neck as if reacting to a sight she could not see. He darted forward, then fell back with one knee grinding hard into her abdomen. He had ripped a spear away from one of the prince's soldiers. Which one had thrust at him, risking her life?

She was only a Lion. The prince would sacrifice her rather than lose Bulkezu.

Tears turned to ice on her cheek. She could no longer feel her lips or her fingers or her toes. How could she have been so stupid? If she hadn't panicked, if she had kept her head and asked for help, she wouldn't lie here at his mercy.

If Blessing hadn't run away.

The loathing and rage hit with as much force as the storm: *I hate her, the spoiled brat. I don't care if she's dead!*

'Anna! Anna! You let her go, you ugly monster!'

Shouts broke the stalemate.

'Catch her!'

'Stay back, Your Highness!'

'She got my knife!'

'Grab her, you fool!'

The spear's haft slapped against her head as Bulkezu twirled it, getting a better grip to meet a new attack. There was a scuffle, roars of anger from the soldiers, and a body hit Anna across the chest so hard that the wind was knocked out of her. The weight of that small body caused the chains to bite into her shoulder blades. She coughed out a mewling cry of pain as her vision hazed. Blood dribbled down around her ear, freezing. Her eye would not open.

Blessing had tried to rescue her.

Shouts reached her faintly, a distant swarm of movement felt more than heard. Bulkezu straddled both Anna and the second body as he braced for a new attack. When he laughed, high-pitched and gleeful, the sound cut across the screaming pitch of the wind.

'Free me, prince of dogs,' cried Bulkezu triumphantly. 'Or I kill her.'

Blessing whimpered in pain.

Prince Sanglant's voice reached her over the buffeting wind, a ringing tenor that easily pierced the clamor of battle. Anger and thwarted frustration made him sound hoarse – but then, he always sounded like that.

'Let her go free, and I'll let you go free when we reach the hunting grounds of the griffins.'

Bulkezu laughed again. 'To be hunted down by my own tribe?'

'Very well,' shouted Sanglant. 'I'll throw down my weapons and trade myself for her—'

'Your daughter is a far more valuable hostage than you would be. Free me, or I kill her. But I will take her with me, so that you will keep my tribe from hunting me.'

Why had Blessing charged in against a foe she could not hope to defeat? Now she was unconscious, wounded, and Bulkezu's prisoner.

'Take me as your hostage and my soldiers will see that your tribe does not hunt you. I can make no bargain with my daughter's life—'

The wind roared, obliterating the sound of the prince's voice as a wave of white swept over them. She could no longer see Bulkezu through frozen eyes and the howling white fog of the blizzard.

This was the end.

Something smooth and silken brushed her lips.

The stinging blast of the snow and ice faded under an entirely unexpected surge of warm wind. White flower petals swirled over her like a cloud of butterflies. Ice melted on her face, making runnels down her cheek as petals tickled her mouth and eyes. This was no natural wind—

Sorcery!

The soldiers cried out in alarm and surprise at the shower of petals and the shock of the wind's abrupt change.

'Hai!' Bulkezu shouted. A weight hit him, throwing him off her. Within the streaming petals two men fought – Sanglant and Bulkezu – wrestling and rolling. The chains writhed around her, scraping over her legs, burning her arms. Snow that had been caught beneath chains sprayed and scattered.

'Get the princess!' cried Matto.

'Anna! Anna!' Thiemo yelled, running toward her.

She was trapped in a tangle of spitting, biting iron. She got to her knees, but a hand grabbed her ankle and jerked her hard so she fell forward while being dragged backward. Iron ripped up the skin on her cheek. She screamed. Bulkezu threw her on top of Blessing's prone body. Anna's swollen eye was crammed into the slush, a muck of snow and petals and mud that covered the ground, but she could see the awful scene unfolding a hand's breadth from her face.

Bulkezu grabbed Blessing's hair and twisted the princess' head back. A knife blade pressed against the vulnerable skin at her throat. The prince cursed violently but helplessly.

Bulkezu laughed that giggling, mad chuckle that would, surely, sour milk and curdle eggs in the nest; she hadn't heard it for months. She began to weep.

The soldiers beyond had gone deadly silent as petals spun down.

'Now we are both trapped,' said Bulkezu. 'Only a Kerayit witchwoman or her mistress can raise a wind like this.' He laughed again. 'Free me. I am still fast enough to kill the girl and strong enough to kill her even if you wound me first. My freedom. Or your daughter's life.'

A crowd of men gathered around them, holding back as if a fence caught them up short. The blade biting into Blessing's skin raised a trickle of blood although the girl remained limp.

Was she already dead?

Beyond, the camp had dissolved into chaos: horses trumpeting in fright, men shouting and cursing, a thin voice wailing in agony.

A horn call rising in strength: the call to arms.

Petals streamed everywhere as the warm wind drowned them.

'My lord prince! Come quickly!'

'My lord! My lord! An army approaches!'

'We've been ambushed!'

'Horsemen, my lord prince!'

'So be it.' Sanglant's was not a voice that hid emotion often, but she could not tell if fury, frustration, fear, or cold raging bitterness ruled him now.

'Your sister, Princess Sapientia, my lord—'

'Not now, Breschius. Captain Fulk, I want spears to the fore, braced to face down a cavalry charge.'

'Yes, my lord prince.'

An object hit Anna hard on the head, slid down her nose, and fell into snow and petals. It was a key.

'Let the hunt begin, Bulkezu. If you harm her, you will suffer tenfold what she suffered.'

Bulkezu's weight shifted painfully on her back as he grabbed the key off the ground. The knife pricked Blessing under the jaw as he shifted. Chains clattered down. He took hold of the back of Blessing's tunic and hoisted her up, holding her tight with the knife still at her throat.

'If you want her to live, girl,' he said to Anna without looking down at her, 'then you will accompany us because I cannot be bothered to care for her.'

Blessing had risked her own life. Anna could do no less.

She pushed up to her feet, swaying and dizzy. Blood stippled the churned snow and muck and stained the iron links of the chain. Men scattered around them, running to the boundary of the camp with weapons in hand. Grooms fought down maddened horses as petals drifted in clouds through the air. Mud spattered everywhere as the warm wind melted snow, as feet ground moisture into grass and dirt.

Anna staggered after Bulkezu through the clamor and chaos. No one heeded them, although perhaps it only seemed so because she could not see very well. He had no trouble keeping Blessing held tight with one arm while brandishing the spear with the other; he had remained strong even after months of captivity.

Men formed up around the perimeter, tense but ready, their spears and shields a fragile line of defense.

'Let him through! Let him through!' shouted Matto ahead of them. 'God curse you! Make a way through for him, or he'll kill them both!'

Bulkezu carried the princess past the line of men formed up along the outer perimeter of the camp. He paused long enough to sling the girl over his back, a shield against arrows, and plunged forward up the slope with knife and spear in hand, silent but breathing hard. Snow turned to sludge under his feet as a last few petals spun down around them. In the east, light rose as dawn threatened.

Blessing woke at last, kicking at the backs of his knees.

'Quiet, worm!'

The iron edge of his voice subdued her.

He will kill us, thought Anna, too stunned to weep. Was

it better to struggle and die fighting or to follow quietly in the hope they might escape?

Though he labored, he did not slow. They crested the hill as the rim of the sun splintered the horizon. In a broad valley below, a river meandered through towering grass that shimmered like gold. The lowland ended abruptly at the foot of steep crags jutting up along the eastern horizon. A petal brushed her cheek; another settled on Blessing's upturned rump. Wind carried the scent of grass and of spring. Snow melted into dirty mounds, the icy remains of winter; spring had swept in.

On its wings, off to both left and right, an army of mounted men approached with bows and spears held ready. They weren't Quman – they didn't wear wings – but there was something misshapen about them nevertheless that Anna could not discern with one swollen eye and her back and arms on fire with pain.

Bulkezu had seen the soldiers, too, had heard the thunder of their approach across the ground.

'Witches!' He spat on the ground before forging down a slope made slippery by melting snow and the sheen of fresh mud churned up under his footsteps. He stumbled once, swearing as he fell to one knee, but his grip on the girl did not falter. He was unbelievably strong. His hands were chains, as unyielding as iron. He had tucked the knife into a boot where Blessing could not reach it, but Anna wondered if she herself could grab for it. Yet he still carried the spear. If he killed her, then Blessing would be at his mercy.

As they descended the slope, the grass rose from knee-high at the crest to thigh-high as the ground leveled off. The pale sea cut off her view of everything except the ragged summits of the crags. He waded into this ocean, the grass reaching his waist, his chest, and soon higher than a horse's head.

She had heard that the griffins roamed in the lands where the grass grew as tall as houses.

Maybe that was how she would die: Bulkezu would stake her out and use her as a lure for the griffin he meant to kill so he could build himself new wings. Grass stung her face, whipping against her, focusing her thoughts as she jolted along.

I will not die. I will not let Blessing die.

There had to be a way to escape. He said nothing, just trudged at a steady pace.

'Please,' Blessing said at last. 'If you put me down, I'll walk.'

He stopped, dropped her, and waited without speaking, breathing hard, while the princess winced and, cautiously, pushed up to stand.

'Anna?' she croaked.

'I am here, Your Highness.' Her shoulders throbbed; her eye ached and her cheek stung. She saw the sky as patches of blue and white, clear sky and clouds, glimpsed through the waving stalks above her. It was impossible to know what direction they walked in; she could no longer see even the eastern crags. Only the trail Bulkezu had left, beaten down by his weight, betrayed their path, and even so the grass was springing back up behind them.

Soon they would be utterly lost.

'Go.' He poked Blessing with the spear.

The two captives led the way, walking side by side. It was exhausting work trampling the grass, pushing through with arms raised. Vegetal dust matted her hair and formed a layer of grit on her lips. Soon she was sweating although it was warm only in contrast to the killing cold they had survived.

Twice she veered sideways, thinking to lead them back around in a circle in the direction of camp, but he poked Blessing each time hard enough to make the girl cry out, so Anna had to fall back in line. He was herding them like beasts in the direction he wanted them to go.

Once Blessing tried to outrun him, hoping his long captivity would make him slow, but he caught up, slammed her across the back with the haft of his spear, and waited silently as she groaned and struggled back to her feet with Anna's help.

He, too, seemed exhausted, but there was in his expression

a look of such cold determination that Anna knew he would never falter. His gaze met hers. He had beautiful eyes; even his face, scarred as it was, remained handsome – if one could admire such swarthy features. But he measured her as a man measures his horses, wondering which is healthiest and which he might need to kill for food on a hard journey.

'Come, Your Highness,' she said.

Wincing, weeping silently, Blessing took Anna's hand and went without a word.

In time, the sun rose above the grass and tracked across the sky. She was sweating in earnest, dressed in her winter clothing, but dared take nothing off. If this warm spell was only a sorcerous spell, how soon would winter blast back in to kill them? For how long could a witch alter the weather? How far did the spell's reach extend? They might easily walk right out of this warm cocoon into the blizzard. Surely a weather witch, no matter how powerful, could not wipe away a storm of such power. Yet there was nothing she could do about that. She staggered on, concentrating on each single step as the only thing that mattered in the world. Blessing did not speak, only trudged.

As long as they kept moving, he would not kill them.

A high scream pierced the heavens, an eerie cry that lingered on and on and chilled her to the heart.

'Go!' said Bulkezu, although she had speeded up at the cry.

Was *he* frightened?

Almost she turned to examine his expression, but she dared not. It was wounded animals that were most likely to maul you. The cry rose again, off to the left this time, not behind them, echoed by a second voice to the right.

'We're being hunted,' whispered Blessing, squeezing her hand.

Bulkezu jabbed her with the haft. 'Go! Go!'

She heard the murmur of running water just before the ground broke away precipitously and she slid and stumbled down a steep, short slope. Breaking out of the thick grass, she rolled on the gravelly shore of a river not more than a strong man's spear toss across, nothing like as deep and wide as the Veser River at Gent. East across the river, visible from this shore because of the lay of the ground, clouds roiled over the crags. A veil sheeted down from the cloud cover. She smelled the chill scent of streaming snow. The blizzard did indeed still churn above the mountains, reaching north and south like gigantic arms to encircle them where they rested in the heart of a spell. The sun shone above as merrily as it might on any fine spring day.

Bulkezu cursed wickedly, standing at the brink, not going forward into the current although the river looked fordable. She crouched to splash water on her face. Its touch stung, so sharp a pain especially on her bruises and cuts that she whimpered, trying to hold the sound in so he wouldn't know how scared she was. That was the lesson she and Matthias had learned in Gent: never let your fear rule you. Those ruled by fear died.

The wailing cry cut through the air again, closer now, followed by an answer off to the right and, abruptly, a third yipping wail behind them.

A rider galloped toward them along the shore of the river. Anna blinked, thinking the sun or her injuries had addled her mind: the creature had only one head, yet it was obviously human. Wasn't it?

'Pray God,' she murmured, drawing the Circle of Unity at her breast, waiting for Bulkezu to force them out into the water. 'Lord and Lady protect us.'

'Anna! It's centaurs! I heard them coming!'

Bulkezu broke to the right, but as Blessing bolted for the slope, he whirled back, grabbed her, and slammed her against his body, holding his knife to her throat.

Three horsemen came out of the grass, bows drawn and arrows fixed, aiming right at Blessing's chest. Anna's heart thudded madly.

They were not horsemen.

They were not human.

They were women – that was obvious, for they went bare-breasted – but at their hips their human form flowed away and became beasts. Women with the bodies of horses.

Centaurs.

Bulkezu did not move nor did his knife waver.

One of the centaurs, a cream-colored mare with dark hair on her woman's head, spoke to him in words Anna could not understand. Still he did not move, although he was surrounded.

'They told you to let us go!' shouted Blessing indignantly, squirming in his grasp. 'I hate you, you smelly bag of grease!'

He released her. The centaurs backed up, still with their arrows trained on him, but they did not move as he bolted away upriver, running east toward the crags.

'I told you something was coming, Anna! No one ever believes me!'

Anna staggered. The sun made the swaying grass into a green-gold haze, impossible to focus on. A cloud of white butterflies rose up from the shoreline of the river, light winking with each beat of their dazzling wings. A distant call rose, high-pitched, melding with the song of the river. Far above, a graceful shape emerged out of the vanguard of the new storm sweeping in from the east.

'Look!' shrieked Blessing. 'Look there!'

Its iron wings flashed and glittered, catching the sun's light. It wore an eagle's proud head and a lion's strong body, with a snake's tail lashing as it flew. If it saw them, it ignored them; perhaps they were beneath its notice. Certainly it was too far away for any of the centaur women to shoot at it.

'I *knew* we'd reached the hunting grounds! Now we can hunt!'

Anna's knees gave out, but she did not hit the ground. Strong arms caught her, and she was lifted as easily as a grown woman hoists a weary infant and thrown across the back of the cream-colored mare.

She clutched at the creature's mane to drag herself upright. This was neither mare nor woman. Creatures out of legend had rescued them. Bulkezu had not raped and murdered them. They were free. Laughing, crying, she could not speak to thank them, but she had no need to do so since Blessing had already begun asking questions, demanding to know more about the griffins and the river and the storm of butterflies.

Someday Anna would go home to Gent and tell the tale of her adventures. Matthias would never believe her.

That thought only made her cry more.

3

'Centaurs!' breathed Captain Fulk. Like the rest of the men, he stared in astonishment at the inhuman army – perhaps five hundred strong – that approached their hastily-drawn line.

'Let the men remain in formation,' said Sanglant, 'but do not act unless I give you a signal. Or if I fall.'

'My lord prince!'

'I know what I'm doing. Breschius, accompany me.'

He sheathed his sword and stepped out in front of the line of soldiers drawn up along the slope with the camp behind them. They had a terrible position, downslope, where the weight of the centaur charge would press them backward into the wreckage of their camp, scattered, frightened horses, tangled ropes, twisted and fallen canvas everywhere . . . yet such a ruin gave dismounted soldiers an advantage over four-legged opponents.

Breschius and Hathui fell in behind him as he trudged up the slope toward the creatures advancing at a walk over the crest. Behind, men called out, calming horses, seeking armor, trading weapons, strengthening their line in case the worst happened. He had only his red cloak to shield him should they attack – that, and his mother's curse. 'Are these the sorcerers we seek, Breschius?'

'We must hope so, my lord prince. The Bwr people have little mercy for our kind.'

'Be sure I am remembering the history of the Dariyan

Empire and their fate at the hands of a Bwr army so long ago. Yet in the old tales it is always said that the Bwr people came not only to plunder and capture slaves, but because they hated the empire itself. Why would the centaur people hate the Dariyans so much?'

'Poets entertain by embroidering fancy patterns on plain cloth. I think bloodlust and greed suffice to explain the Bwr invasion that destroyed the Dariyan Empire. After all, they are more like to the beasts than we are. Yet if these meant to attack, they could have done so under cover of the storm when we were helpless.'

'So I am also thinking.' Grass whispered against his legs as he followed the scars left by Bulkezu's passage up the hill, pockets of snow melting into slush that made for slippery going. 'Do you think there are weather witches among them who brought the storm?'

'Truly, it is said the centaurs of old taught weather magic to the Kerayit shamans, my lord prince. They might have sent the blizzard before them, or overwhelmed it with this spring wind.'

'The Quman are retreating, my lord prince,' said Hathui. 'They are abandoning their tents and fleeing.'

'Keep your eye on them in case they attack us from the rear.' He dared not shift his attention away from his new adversaries as he and his companions came into bow range. He had to try to turn these inhuman creatures into his allies, but he wasn't at all sure they would believe his stories of distant conspiracies and a vast cataclysm.

And what of Blessing? What she might suffer at the Quman chieftain's hands . . . He dared not think of her if he was to command effectively.

Although it was hot only in contrast to the appalling cold they had just suffered, Sanglant sweated under the blaze of an unexpectedly bright sun. He paused to catch his breath and wipe his brow. Ahead, the massed line of the centaurs came to a halt. He noticed for the first time that although they carried bows and wicked-looking spears, they wore no armor.

'God help us,' he breathed, half laughing, 'can it be that

they are *all* females? Are there no stallions among them? Nor even geldings?'

'Beware, my lord prince,' said Breschius. 'One comes to meet us.'

'What of the Quman, Hathui?' He kept his gaze fixed on the silver-gray centaur now picking her way down the slope, stepping with precise neatness through pale winter grass.

'They seem truly to be running, my lord prince. I would guess that they did not expect to meet up with the ones we face now.'

'They are wise to be fearful,' commented Breschius, but his voice seemed steady enough for a man approaching, unarmed, an army that might prove foe as easily as friend. Sanglant glanced at the frater's right arm, which ended in a stump, but although Breschius, too, was sweating, he did not seem afraid. Sanglant waited, more impressed than he cared to admit, as the centaur halted a body's length from him, surveying him as closely as he examined her.

She was old. Strands of glossy black hid within her fine silver coat and the coarse braids of her human hair, which fell past her hips. She wore no clothing of any kind except a quiver across her back and a leather glove covering one hand and wrist. Once all her coat and her woman's hair had been black, a fine contrast to the creamy color of her woman's skin. Now faded green-and-gold paint striped her human torso, even her breasts, which sagged as did those of crones well past their childbearing years. It was hard to read age on her face, for she did not possess the exact lineaments of a human face but something like and yet unlike, kin to him and yet utterly different. The expression of her eyes seemed touched by ancient pain and hard-won wisdom. Like a virtuous biscop, she wore holiness like a mantle on her shoulders. She looked older than any creature, human or otherwise, he had ever seen.

He inclined his head respectfully. 'I give you greetings, Holy One,' he said, using the Kerayit title which, Breschius had taught him, was used to address the most senior of their shamans.

She returned his scrutiny with her own appraisal. 'I do not

know you, although you have the look of my old enemy. Yet you are not the one I seek, the one I hoped for. Has he not returned?'

'I do not know what person you speak of.'

'Do you not? Is he not known in your country?'

Already she had lost him. 'Who is your old enemy, Holy One?'

'Humankind once called them the Cursed Ones, but the language you speak now is different from the language you spoke when you were young.'

'I have always spoken Wendish, even as a child,' he began, but he faltered. 'You are not speaking of me.' When *who* was young? He felt as though he teetered on the edge of an abyss whose depths he could not plumb. 'How old are you, Holy One?'

She smiled, something of warmth and blessed approval in her expression. 'You see keenly, you who are son of two bloods, for I smell both humankind and the blood of my old enemy in you. What are you called?'

'I am Sanglant, son of Henry, king of Wendar and Varre.'

'This "Henry" is your mother? Is king among her people?'

'Henry is my father.'

Her surprise startled him. Although he could not be sure that he could interpret her expressions as though she were a human woman, she seemed taken aback at the word 'father,' as though it were ill-mannered or even a little coarse to mention such a word. But she recovered quickly.

'You are bred out of a stallion of the human line, then. Who is your mother?'

'My mother no longer walks on Earth. She is one of the Aoi, the Lost Ones.'

'You have more the look of the Ashioi than of humankind. You are therefore a prince twice over in the manner of your people, for your mother must be a shaman of great power. I have seen her – or the one who must be her, since in all the time of their exile only one among them has negotiated the crossroads where worlds and time meet. She alone has set foot upon the earth they yearn for.'

'You know of their exile?'

Her smile now was less friendly, even bitter. 'I helped bring it about, Prince Sanglant. Do you not know the story?'

'I know no story of the Aoi exile that includes mention of your people, Holy One. I would gladly hear your tale.'

'So you may, in time.'

A spike of anger kicked through him; he was not accustomed to being spoken to so dismissively. She seemed unaware of his annoyance, however, and continued talking.

'First I need to understand what has brought you here, in the company of those vermin who call themselves children of the griffin.'

He looked over his shoulder. The Quman had fled, leaving their tents and half their wagons, but none of their horses. The dust of their passage formed a cloud that obscured their flight, or perhaps that was only one of their shamans raising a veil to hide them.

He turned back. 'How is it you speak Wendish, Holy One? Have you met one among my people before?'

'I survived the bite of a snake and now carry its magic in my blood.' She tossed her head as might a restless horse. 'Such things are not important. If you were come to attack us, surely you would have done so by now, Prince Sanglant. Nor would you have approached us alone, with these two unarmed companions, if you did not wish to speak with us. What do you want? Why have you traveled so far?'

'To meet you,' he said, 'for it is known that among the Kerayit tribe, who are your allies, there live powerful sorcerers. I seek powerful sorcerers and the feathers of griffins.'

'You have ridden a long way, seeking that which you are unlikely to obtain. What is your ambition, Prince Sanglant? What manner of man are you, who desires what he cannot have?'

He laughed, because the pain never left him and now had scarred him afresh. 'I have already lost what I cared most for. Twice over. What I seek now I do not desire for my own use, but only for duty's sake – that duty which I was born to because I am the son of the king. I owe my people protection and well-being. Do not believe, I pray you, that because you live so very far from the cities and lands ruled by my people that you are therefore safe from those among them who can work magic.'

'The seven died, and their line died out too quickly. Only the Kerayit remember the ancient knowledge.'

'Do you mean the Seven Sleepers? They live still, and they have uncovered a working of great power which they mean to weave again in order to cast the Lost Ones back into the aether.' Was that impatience in her expression? She stamped her back leg, and he had an odd instinct that, had she been able to, she would have lain her ears back in annoyance and snapped at him as does a mare bored with a stallion who is bothering her. 'If you would only let me explain the story to you in full, I pray you—'

'I know the story, as you cannot. I know what is coming, Prince Sanglant, as you cannot.'

'Many will die—'

'Yes. Many will die. They always do. The Ashioi were our enemies once. We banded together with humankind to war against them. But in the end it is your people who crippled us and brought us low. It is your people who threaten us now, the Quman, the Sazdakh, the Jinna, the Arethousans, these Daisanites who bring their words that make us sick. We chose the wrong enemy. Or perhaps our fate was already sealed.'

'I am not your enemy!'

'I could argue that you are my enemy twice over. Still, I will be willing to speak with you as if you were a female, Prince Sanglant, but only when you have proved your fitness to lead.'

The words angered him, but he replied as evenly as he could. 'How may I do that?'

'Have you not already spoken of it? Males prove their fitness in the same fashion, whether human or horse. They exist to breed, and to protect the herd when brute force is needed. There is a beast loose in the grass—'

'You have seen him?' Hope shone briefly. Anger sparked, blazing hot and strong. 'He has taken my daughter captive!'

'Destroy the beast that stalks in the grass,' she repeated. 'Then I will speak to you again.'

'Will you not help me save my daughter?'

She raised an arm. A huge owl glided in to perch on the centaur's glove. Breschius gasped out loud. The centaur leaned closer to the owl, but even with his keen hearing, Sanglant made out only a rustling as soft as downy feathers rubbed together. She launched the owl back into the air, and it flew away over the ranks of the centaurs, quickly lost to sight.

She examined Sanglant again. 'Hunt, Prince Sanglant. If you return, then we will negotiate.'

With a flick of her tail, she sidestepped, turned, and walked up the hill to her army.

Hathui had got a spear from Captain Fulk and now hastened up the slope to bring it to Sanglant. He unfastened his cloak and turned it inside out, hiding the bright red cloth and exposing the pale fox-fur lining, which blended better with the grass.

'My lord prince.' Hathui handed him the spear, the best balanced of those he possessed. Fulk had chosen well, of course. 'I beg you, my lord prince, go carefully. We are all of us – all of Wendar and Varre – lost if you are lost to us.'

'I am lost if I let a man like that kidnap and despoil my daughter.'

'He wants you to follow him. Surely he must kill another griffin, and defeat you, in order to restore his honor and position. Princess Blessing is merely bait.'

'So I hope,' said Sanglant as he surveyed the sky and the slope of the hill. 'That will make it easier to find him.'

'Shall I attend you, my lord prince?'

'Nay. Repair camp. Find a more sheltered spot, if you can. Fortify yourselves against unexpected attack, from whatever quarter. Take what you need from what the Quman abandoned. Do not forget that they may creep back and ambush you, but I think that Gyasi can warn you if they approach.'

'If we can trust him,' said Hathui.

'I trust that he seeks revenge against those who wronged

him. Watch him, but do not ignore what he has to say.'

'As you wish, my lord prince,' said Breschius.

'What if Bulkezu's tribe claims him?' asked Hathui.

'They fled before they could collect on their bargain, taking my sister with them. No matter.'

He hefted the spear. Storm clouds piled up to the east where a line of crags erupted out of the high plateau. He smelled the tempest on the west wind. Out in the grasslands, up in the highest lands beyond the reach of the centaur witch, winter still ruled.

Its chilly blast could not possibly be as savage as his anger.

'Bulkezu is a dead man now.'

4

For a moment only, as she crossed through the heart of the burning stone, she kept hold of Alain and his hounds. Then the weight of the world below ripped them out of her grasp, and she spun, between the worlds, balance lost, the Earth turning beneath her as she fell back into the world she had left behind days ago. She glimpsed the winking glimmer of the crown of stars, laid out across the land, but the turning spheres caught her in their rotation, propelling her away from the lands she knew. The heavy elements of earth and water dragged her down as her wings disintegrated, their aetherical substance too fragile to exist in the world below.

As she passed from the aether into the net of the solid world, she fell through a nether world, betwixt and between, neither grounded in the world below nor afloat in the aether like the Ashioi homeland. She glimpsed a band of shadowy figures on the march, outfitted with spears and bows, children and dogs, both male and females armed and ready. They wore clothing like to that worn by the Lost Ones, and the young man leading them looked strangely familiar to her although she knew she had never seen him before. He looked a little like Sanglant.

He glanced up, sensing her, but he could not see her. 'Soon!' he called to the people following him. 'We have not much longer to wait. Make haste! Make ready!'

She reached for him, seeking an answer to this mystery, but tumbled past, drawn by a force she could not measure and could not see. Eastward as the land lay, as the world spun, helpless against that great dragging weight, she was pulled far off course as by a grasping hand. What linked her to Earth, calling her back?

Was it Sanglant? The baby?

An instant she had to pray before she fell into a screaming blizzard, the cold so bitter that she could not take in a breath of air because her lungs froze and her face burned and her courage splintered, cracked, and shattered.

Cold.

She was numb with cold. She would never be warm again. Hugh would come, with his lamp, and lead her back into the church where he had made her his slave. She whimpered. God Above, let her imprisonment not happen again.

All this passed through her mind as swiftly as a rock drops from hand to ground. Then, as stinging snow bit into her skin and the wind screamed against her, she fought up to her knees, defying the storm.

She was not that girl any longer. She was no longer defenseless and alone. She had walked the spheres. She had found her mother's kin. She had made peace with her father's memory and his struggles. She had unlocked the door behind which Da had sealed her power.

Hugh no longer ruled her.

But cold could still kill.

The howl of the storm deafened her and she could not see more than a stone's toss in any direction, blinded by snow. She knelt in grass bent earthward by the wind's force; it, too, gave no shelter, but within its fibrous stems lived fire.

Downwind, she called fire out of the grass. Flames licked upward, burning fiercely in an arc of brightness, and she

pressed as close to the fire as she dared, careful of her cloak
and clothing. The blaze warmed her for a time, difficult to
count how long she stood there shivering, but the blizzard
beat against fire and bit by bit smothered the flames until they
wavered, receded, and died.

The wind screamed, scattering the ashes. She tugged her
cloak more tightly around her shoulders. Already, through
her gloves, her fingers grew numb. Her ears hurt. Cold seared
her.

Again she called fire, this time in a wider swath.

As the flames sprang to life in a semicircle around her, a
hunched figure emerged from the blizzard, approaching her
at a run. It was a man; that much she could see. He carried
a spear.

She drew her knife and waited. No use shooting arrows in
this wind. The heat of the fire melted the snow around her;
icy water pooled at her feet, soaking her boots. The man halted
a prudent distance from her, measuring her as she measured
him. Although the clothing he wore appeared scarcely heavier than her own, he did not seem on the verge of death by
freezing. He was, oddly enough, smiling as he surveyed her.
Ice rimed his black hair, and he had a startling and massive
scar across one cheek that marred his features but did not,
quite, make him ugly. Otherwise he appeared as might any
man caught out in such a storm: wary, freezing, desperate,
and respectful of the fire burning at her back.

'I saw the fire,' he shouted, words almost inaudible under
the scream of the wind. 'Are you the one called Liathano? I
did not think to find you in this country.'

She had never seen this man before. Or had she? Memory
nagged at her, but she had no time for the luxury of caution.
Questions must come later. Already she could not feel her
feet, and the hot flames were losing their battle against the
storm, dying down around her despite their initial fury.
Against the blizzard, even fire could not triumph. By his coloring and the cast of his features, this man was one of the steppe
tribesmen. Although barbarians, they knew this country as no
other humans did.

'Do you know where we can find shelter?' she cried, pitching her voice to be heard above the wind.

He laughed, a mad and rather disturbing cackle. 'Here there is no shelter but that found where griffins nest.'

'So be it,' she said, 'for I will certainly die out here without shelter but may yet survive hidden within a griffin's nest.'

He gestured with his spear. Within this storm, all directions looked the same to her. 'Come,' he said.

Bracing herself against the wind, she followed him.

XV

A HAPLESS FLY

1

In the great hall that had once belonged to the queen of Alba, Stronghand held court as winter winds blew a chill rain across the courtyard outside, visible through open doors.

'Bring the prisoners forward.'

A captain herded the captives up before the dais, adults and children all together, a pack of ragged fugitives. They had been living no better than animals out in the woods when a patrol had stumbled across their stick hovels and crude tents and rounded them up. Winter had rendered them too weak to fight and now the presence of his dogs, eager to kill, made them too scared to run away.

They huddled together in such a trembling mass that it was difficult to distinguish one from another. Their clothes hung in tatters; their emaciated bodies gave them the look of cattle better slaughtered for soup bones than left out to graze winter pastures, where they would only die and their carcasses be gnawed by wolves.

But these Alban folk had not died, or at least not all of them had. Daily his troops captured such refugees, folk who had escaped the fall of the city or who had fled the nearby farms which had once fed the town. While his strike forces searched and harried the countryside beyond the reach of the Temes River, he had a different task.

He beckoned to his interpreter, a Hessi merchant's son named Yeshu. Like a well-trained dog, he approached without fear.

'Discover what manner of people these are,' he told him.

The Hessi merchants taught their children many languages, the better to follow the trade routes. Yeshu spoke his tortured mother tongue as well as Alban, Wendish, and Salian.

'They are artisans, my lord, so they say,' he replied after an interrogation of the eldest woman. 'According to their report, they fled the city and hid in the forest lands. Half of them have died so far this winter, so they claim.'

'What kind of artisans?'

'Carpenters and turners, my lord.'

He glanced around the great hall, crudely refurbished after the battle fought last autumn but in need of good craftsmen to restore it. 'Are they kin to each other? Of one tribe?'

'Out of two clans and three houses, my lord.' He wore a cap out of which black locks straggled. His dusky skin stood in marked contrast to the fair-skinned, light-haired Albans. 'This is what they tell me: They came together in their flight because some of their kinfolk married between them, as is the custom of Alban artisans.'

'Woodworkers,' he mused, looking them over. They were a sorry lot, and many might still die no matter what mercy he showed them, but that they had survived for so long and stuck together in numbers, to protect themselves, suggested intelligence and practicality. A tool may look worn and almost broken yet may still be fixable. Useful.

There was more than one way to conquer a country.

'Let them be given grain and such salt as they need for the remainder of the winter. They will be left in peace to ply their trade as long as they reestablish themselves in their home and put themselves to such tasks as they are accustomed to. They will give me labor in exchange for my protection. This hall needs rebuilding. The doors do not shut properly. What tithe did the queen require of them?'

Another conversation ensued. The youth could bargain; since Stronghand could understand what Yeshu was saying to the Alban prisoners he understood that the elders of their house, despite the seeming hopelessness of their condition, hoped to convince the lad that the Alban queen took less of a tithe than he knew she normally did based on the testimony of other prisoners and the Hessi merchants with whom he had established trading relationships.

'Enough,' he said at last, in Wendish. Even the Hessi lad did not yet suspect that he understood the Alban speech. In truth, he was surprised he understood it at all, but ever since the return of Alain, the speech of all creatures seemed eerily open to him, as though the all-encompassing wisdom and sight of the OldMothers had infested his mortal, crippled blood. 'If they argue, then they do not wish to tell the truth. One day in three will be their tithe. If they are faithful, they can earn the privilege that those loyal to my rule enjoy of one in six. Tell them to return to their home and rebuild.'

This mercy they had not expected. Weeping and wailing, they threw themselves down before him to offer obeisance, but he knew he could not trust them. To show his displeasure he chose the healthiest looking child from their group to send to Mother Ursuline at Rikin Fjord as an acolyte. He cared little for the quarrels between the gods of the Alban tree sorcerers and the circle god esteemed by the Wendish, but the adherents of the circle god were more useful to him, especially while the tree sorcerers remained his adversaries.

As the prisoners were herded away, he stroked the wooden circle that he wore around his neck. While he mused, his councillors maintained a respectful silence: the chieftains of Hakonin, Vitningsey, Jatharin, and Isa, Papa Otto, and Samiel, the Hessi merchant he had appointed as his steward because he knew how to read, write, and figure numbers.

'Woodworkers can also build a bridge upstream, where the

river narrows. That will make our task easier. When spring comes, and they have finished the hall, let them work one day out of four on this task.'

'Yes, my lord.'

Out in the courtyard, a scouting party jogged into view.

'Let them through.'

His herald — one of his littermates — called them up.

The captain among them — one of Hakonin's sons — gave the report: they had ridden south and west following the winding course of the Temes River. One fortlet they had burned, three skirmishes fought with no men killed. There were two substantial towns, both fortified although, in truth, they could be taken with a sufficiently large force. Of the Alban queen they had seen no sign.

Stronghand turned to his councillors. 'Of the eight parties sent out, six have returned. None have found any trace of the queen. We await news from the north.'

'We should strike now at the towns we can plunder,' said Vitningsey's chief, called Dogkiller.

'We should strike where our blows will have the most effect and not waste ourselves seeking treasure,' said Hakonin's chief, called Flint.

'These prisoners are a burden,' continued Dogkiller. 'If we killed them, we would be free to seek farther afield for their queen and their riches. What do you say, Ironclaw?'

'I say nothing,' said Isa's chieftain. 'I am still waiting to see whether Rikin's son flies, or falls.'

Jatharin's chief remained silent, as he usually did.

Stronghand nodded at Papa Otto, who had learned over time that his master preferred his counsel to his silence. 'If you defeat the Alban queen, then you can become ruler in her stead. But as long as she or any of her lineage remain alive and free and allied with the tree sorcerers, the Alban people will fight behind her banner and for her heathen gods. Strike at their gods, and you will win Alba.'

'Kill the Alban people, and there will be no one left to fight you,' said Dogkiller.

Papa Otto shook his head. 'Kill the Alban people and the

land will become wasteland, worth less to you than the good crops farmers can grow to feed artisans and soldiers.'

Stronghand rose, surveying the court he had gathered around him: councillors, RockChildren eager to gain glory and gold, human men willing to serve a better master than the one they had left behind, slaves, prisoners, and the doubters, like Ironclaw, who were waiting for him to falter so that they could wrest from him what he had so far gained.

But even Ironclaw, who was wiser than most, did not fully understand Stronghand's purpose and methods.

'We will wait until we have heard from the north. Our forces will continue to sweep the countryside until all the land three days' walk on every side of Hefenfelthe is under our control. Burn what you must, but build where you can. A burned house is not a strong house; it cannot hold off rain, storm, and wind. Let the priests of the circle god follow in your wake and walk among the Alban folk.'

So it would be done. He sat, shaking his staff; it clacked softly, bells chiming, as he beckoned to his herald.

'Bring the next group forward. Are there any farmers among them?'

There were.

Satisfied, he sent this starving and pathetic group back to their farms with seed corn and enough grain to last through winter and early spring. He dispensed justice while morning passed, the rain stopped, and the sky cleared, although the wind still cut wickedly into the hall, leaving the humans shivering. The carpenters would have much to repair.

Recently more and more prisoners had fallen into his hands, not all unwillingly. It was easy enough to let rumor do its work for him and to allow Alban scouts sent from parties hiding in the woodlands to penetrate the lines of defense around Hefenfelthe and see for themselves the increasing activity in the city. To see their countryfolk hard at work, fed, and alive.

2

Queen's Grave.

The words had an ominous sound, but the rolling hills and countryside they walked through with their escort before and behind them seemed pretty enough to Ivar despite the winter chill.

'Pretty enough for a graveyard,' said Ermanrich, observing the leafless orchard trees and the shriveled gardens of the most recent village they passed by. Folk came out of their houses to watch them pass, but said nothing. They whispered, gesturing to the banner that marked this party as Lady Sabella's men-at-arms.

'They don't like us,' whispered Hathumod.

'Or they don't like Lady Sabella,' muttered Ivar. 'Don't despair.'

'Not yet, anyway,' said Ermanrich.

'Look,' said Sigfrid, pointing down the road. 'That's a palisade. It looks like a fort.'

As they came closer to a prominent ridgeline, they saw where the log wall closed in a narrow valley's mouth. A makeshift camp with barracks, tents, and a small number of cottages lay outside the palisade beside a stream. A few men loitered there, staring – soldiers by the look of them. A woman came to the door of one of the cottages, pulling a tunic on over her grimy shift, and grinned as they marched past.

'Hey, there! Handsome!' It wasn't clear whether she was talking to the prisoners or their escort. A man emerged beside her, slapped her on the bottom, and went out, whistling.

'What's this?' he called to his fellows. 'A new crop of sparrows to clap into the cage? A brace of lads and a boy! That'll put the cats in among the pigeons!' He whooped.

A surly captain met them at the gates, herded them inside, and sent their escort packing without even offering them ale to wet their throats before setting off again into the chilly day on their way back to Autun.

'We were ten days on the road!' protested young Erkanwulf, who'd been given charge of the expedition by Captain Ulric. 'Can't we at least spend the night and dry our clothes before heading back?'

'Get!' snarled the captain. 'No one's allowed to bide here except those guards assigned to my command. That's by order of Her Highness, Lady Sabella.'

Erkanwulf scowled, glanced at the prisoners, and with a shrug of frustration ordered his men to depart.

'That's that, then,' said the captain, closing the gates so as to leave the four of them on one side and the captain and his guardsmen on the other.

'Hey!' called Ivar from inside the palisade, where they'd been abandoned. 'What about us?'

The bar slammed into place. They were locked in. He turned. They stood at one end of a well-tended valley with several fields, a pasture dotted with sheep, an orchard, a stream, and a compound of buildings.

'This is a very old convent, an early foundation,' said Sigfrid, studying the layout of the buildings. 'Do you see? It's laid out in the old style.'

'What old style?' asked Ermanrich.

'Before the reforms of St. Benedicta and the elaborate plans of the Brothers of St. Galle created a new ideal for the construction and layout of monastic foundations. Quedlinhame and Herford were laid out in the new style. This isn't. Perhaps this was a villa in the time of the old Dariyan Empire, refurbished as a convent. But I think it's more likely the architect built it in imitation of Dariyan villas. Not all the details are right. See how the drains—'

'Why would you build a villa to be a prison?' asked Hathumod.

'Hush,' said Ivar.

A very pretty girl approached them, eyeing them warily.

'Who are you?' she demanded. 'We got no message saying anyone was coming. What do you want?'

Ivar stepped forward. 'We've been sent here by Lady Sabella to join your convent.'

'Have you?' She tossed her head; the movement made her scarf slip halfway back on her head. She had black curls so astonishingly lustrous that all three youths stared at them, then remembered that they were novices and she a holy nun, sworn to the service of God. She snorted, smiling at their discomfiture. Hathumod stared at her admiringly. 'Come.'

The main compound was built as a square with an inner courtyard placed in the center. Guards stood watch at double doors, but the black-haired girl ignored them, opened one door, and ushered her charges into the suite of rooms beyond.

'Your Grace! Biscop Constance!' She had a piercing voice and was not afraid to use it. 'We have new sheep. Do you think they're spies for the usurper?'

A silver-haired woman sat at a writing desk, an older lady by the hunch of her shoulders and the color of her hair. Ivar looked around the chamber hoping to see the biscop, whom he remembered well from the trial at Autun – young and glorious and handsome as befitted a daughter of the royal house. An elderly nun came into the room, stopped, and frowned.

'Sister Bona!' said the nun, chiding the girl who had led them in. 'You must ask permission before you come charging in here—'

'Nay, let her be,' said the woman at the desk. Laboriously, favoring one shoulder and one leg, she turned. 'Give me my staff, if you will.'

Ivar gasped.

Biscop Constance smiled wryly. She was still a handsome woman, vibrant with command, but she had aged thirty years. When she rose, when Bona leaped forward to help her, Ivar saw why. She could barely walk. She had sustained some kind of massive injuries, although he dared not ask how.

'Sit, I pray you,' she said patiently to her visitors. Bona helped her to the biscop's chair and Ivar, Sigfrid, Ermanrich, and Hathumod hastily knelt before her. She offered them her hand to kiss. They did so.

'They're spies!' insisted Bona.

'Are they? I'm not so sure I think they are. Sabella has never been a subtle chess player. I remember you, Ivar. You are son of Count Harl out of the North Mark. You gave testimony at the trial of Hugh of Austra. I admired your foolhardiness and your passion for justice, although you by no means helped yourself that day. Indeed, as I recall, you vanished soon afterward and were presumed dead or lost or absconded together with Prince Ekkehard, my nephew.'

He bowed his head in shame. 'The last, Your Grace. It is nothing to boast about.'

'Bona, bring wine and something to eat.'

Bona flounced out but returned quickly with a tray. Half a dozen others arrived just as they had finishing telling the biscop their names and lineages. Constance chuckled to see her nuns crowd into the room.

'You see, my friends, you are a nine days' wonder. We live very quietly here at St. Asella's.'

'I thought this place was called Queen's Grave,' said Ivar.

'So it is. It was founded by the saintly queen Gertruda. She lived centuries ago. Her story is told in the chronicles of those times, that written by St. Gregoria of Tur. She was married against her wishes to a cruel king who was no proper Daisanite. In fact, he was a pagan or a heretic, as it suited him and his political needs of the moment. When he died, poisoned by a former wife, I think, Gertruda fled to this valley and founded the convent in honor of St. Asella.'

'Who walled herself up alive,' said Sigfrid, nodding to show he understood the lesson.

Constance smiled. 'You have studied well, Brother Sigfrid. We need another scholar in our ranks, for my schola has grown thin this past year.' The pain never left her; that was clear enough. But she possessed a quiet determination that would not let pain or defeat break her. She had retained a sense of humor, a subdued appreciation of irony. 'Queen Gertruda took vows as a nun to escape the marriage her grasping relatives wished to force her into. In her cunning she created a refuge for other women, and a very few men, who also sought to escape forced marriage and instead devote themselves to God.'

'It's too bad Baldwin didn't know about this place,' muttered Ermanrich.

Ivar frowned. Shame flared and turned to anger. 'He did!'

'Ah!' said Constance. 'There's a story there. Well, then. You have an audience, for we hear nothing and see nothing. That is the fate of those interred in Queen's Grave – to be buried alive. We would like to find out what goes on in the world outside. Tell us your tale, I pray you.'

3

In early spring, Alain stood knee-deep in muddy water, wielding a shovel. He and a dozen of his lay brothers drained a strip of marshland, extending the land and channeling away the standing water. The slap of watery earth tossed onto the margin made a soothing rhythm as the men alongside him sang.

> 'Out into the four corners of the world
> walked the blessed ones.
> Sing again their stories.'

The tales of the early saints made a good chorus for working, because the verses could be added to as long as the lay brothers could recall saints to sing about. The afternoon passed quickly.

Rage and Sorrow waited farther up the slope as Alain bent, thrust the edge of his shovel into the muck, and cast mud and dripping tangles of vegetation onto the growing shoreline. The hounds usually dozed all afternoon while he worked, but now Rage, growling softly, rose to her feet and shifted her attention away from him, scenting the wind. Brother Iso was bundling reeds to hold the margin; he lifted a hand to shade his eyes against the sun as he squinted westward. It was unusually mild for this time of year, warm enough that they only needed to wear their cloaks at night.

'Caught one!' shouted Brother Lallo, displaying a wriggling eel.

The other men cheered, laughing as the eel slipped out of Lallo's wet grasp and vanished with a plop into waters muddied by their digging.

'S-s-smoke,' said Iso, pointing.

A thread spun heavenward southwest above the span of skeletal forest whose branches had not yet leafed out in green.

'Is it the monastery?' asked one of the brothers, frightened. 'Is there a fire?'

'Too far.' Lallo measured the thread of smoke, the trees, and the sky. 'It must be from one of the steadings.'

'D-d-do you think i-it's bandits?' stammered Iso, because he had heard tales of bandits and foul magics all winter and often cried at night before sleeping, fearful of what his dreams and the dark hours might bring.

Sorrow rose, too, and like Rage stared steadily westward. He barked once.

Two brothers emerged from the trees and hurried around the verge of cultivated land, avoiding sinks where the mire of winter hadn't yet been chased away by sun and heat. This past winter there had been little snow but too much rain. Fields of winter spelt and rye wrested years ago from the marshlands surrounding the monastic estate had to be dug out again to save the crops.

'Brothers! Ah! There is Brother Alain! Father Ortulfus is asking for you, Brother. Pray come with me.'

One stayed behind to take Alain's place while he walked back to the monastery with the other, the hounds trotting behind.

'What news, Egbert?'

'Nothing good. You see that smoke? That's from Farmer Hosed's steading. One of their sheep was brought 'round here a few days past because of trouble with its lambs—'

'I remember that.'

'Yes. Now there's rumor that he's got murrain at the steading. What if our sheep caught it here?'

Alain drew the Circle. 'God pray they do not. Poor man!'

'If it hasn't already spread . . . God help us! We could lose all our livestock!'

'Nay, Brother. Pray for the afflicted, but do not beg for trouble. You don't know yet that his sheep are ill, nor that our livestock will become so.'

Brother Egbert looked at him sidelong, then drew the Circle of Unity at his breast and mumbled a prayer under his breath. 'Wise words, Brother. I will endeavor to accept God's will.'

Father Ortulfus awaited them beside the low fence that ringed the monastic buildings. Sheep and lambs grazed on lea land, and beyond their pasturage lay broken woodland where the forest had been cut back for firewood and timber. Prior Ratbold stood among the small herd of milk cows, checking their muzzles and hooves.

'You have heard the news, Brother Alain?' asked Father Ortulfus.

'I have, Father.'

He nodded crisply, not one to waste words. 'You will accompany Prior Ratbold to the steading. If it is a murrain, the law must be obeyed. The farmer must pen all the animals in. When they're dead, he must burn them, and after stake their heads up as a marker of the plague.'

'Why send me, Father? I grew up on the shore. I know fishing better than sheepherding.'

'Go with him,' said Ortulfus in a tone that discouraged argument. 'Do what you can.'

Ratbold returned, shaking his head. 'The brown cow does have a limp, Father, but it's too early to tell what's caused it. It could be the mud, nothing more.' He brushed dirt off his hands as he acknowledged Alain. 'No sense in waiting, Brother. Are you ready to go?'

They set off with ale in a skin and a hank of bread and cheese for their supper so that they did not trespass upon the afflicted farmer's troubled resources. It was an hour's walk to the southernmost steading of those that had grown up in the shadow of the security offered by a monastery held under the king's protection. All the farmers around here brought tithes to Father Ortulfus twice a year, salt, honey, chicks, firewood, and occasionally a child when too many mouths overburdened scant harvests. A portion of the grain they brought in to be ground at the mill was reserved for the monastery's store-house, set aside for lean years.

Last summer's harvest had sufficed, despite rumors of rot and drought ruining crops both south and west of Herford's lands. This spring the untimely heat dazzled. Flowers bloomed early; trees budded; green shoots poked up along the banks of sodden ditches. The road was all mud, so they walked on the verge, slogging through knee-high tansy and bur-geoning thistles that Alain beat down with a staff to make an easier passage for the hounds and the prior. The slap of the stick came easily to him, rousing memories of skirmishes fought months or years ago.

It might as well have been a lifetime past. All that he had loved was utterly gone and could never be regained.

'You are troubled, Brother,' said Ratbold in his blunt way.

Alain wiped away a tear. Ratbold had a reputation as a surly man, impatient and rude to those he disdained, and per-haps it was true that the prior castigated ones who seemed like fools to him. But never once in the months Alain had abided at Herford had Ratbold rebuked or belittled Brother Iso or any of the lay brothers who might be termed 'simple.'

'I am only thinking of what I lost, Prior, my poor wife who is dead.'

Ratbold made no reply, waiting for Alain to go on. The sun gilded a profusion of violets crowded along the edge of the track, mingling with a golden scattering of coltsfoot, har-binger of spring.

'I am content to be here, for I believe this is where God mean me to be, but I still grieve when I think of her. She would have known a cure for the murrain.'

'Would she now? Do any know such a thing except witches and sorcerers?'

'Do you see those violets? A syrup cooked down from the flowers is a remedy for a child's cough. A compress can soothe a headache. Coltsfoot dried and burned can soothe a cough as well. This and much more I learned from her.'

'Any herb-wife knows such lore. So does Brother Infirmarian. That does not make a witch.'

'She had great power, alas. That is why she died.'

'Ah. The cataclysm you spoke of when first you came to us.'

'I know none of you believe me,' said Alain wearily, 'and I do not see how I can stop what has been set in motion. If I knew, I would act, but I have nowhere to go, no one who will listen—'

Rage yipped like a startled puppy, plunging into the under-brush, and Sorrow barked once and followed. Branches thrashed and rattled, marking their trail.

'A rabbit,' suggested Ratbold.

Alain halted and leaned on his staff. 'It's more like they're frightened.'

'Those hounds, frightened!' Ratbold snorted, then cocked his head to one side. 'Listen!'

From down the road came the noise of a troop of riders in procession, the jingle of harness, the rumble of cartwheels, and a faint snatch of a hymn. The two men waited as a cavalcade rolled into view, a dozen caparisoned horses fit for a noble lady accompanied by three carts and twenty soldiers outfitted with halberds and bearing a distinctive banner: a gold Circle of Unity on a black field.

'These come from the skopos!' whispered Ratbold. His staff, forgotten, tipped and fell into a swath of violets.

The fine and noble clerics leading the procession took no notice of two rumpled brothers standing humbly at the side of the road. The passing carts sprayed mud all over them as Ratbold stared, too astonished to speak, and Alain watched. There was something familiar about the lean, elderly cleric riding at the fore. Why had the hounds run off like that?

The procession moved quickly along the road and out of sight.

'Clerics from the skopos herself! How exalted they appeared! Such fine mounts they rode! Did you see the embroidery on the saddle blankets!' Ratbold was so beside himself with excitement that he was flushed. 'Do you think they mean to take guest privileges at Herford?'

'They can scarcely be going anywhere else on this road.'

The underbrush rustled as Rage and Sorrow reemerged, hindquarters waggling madly as they begged forgiveness. Alain rubbed their heads and patted their shoulders as Ratbold got hold of himself and picked up his staff.

'Well, now, Brother Alain. We've an errand to run!'

The hounds proved eager to journey on in the opposite direction of the procession, and although Alain glanced back, he could not divine what had spooked them.

Farmer Hosed was desperately pleasant when he greeted them beside the log fence that ringed the clearing he and his family had hacked out of the woodland. The fire was out of sight behind a row of healthy apple trees backed by a thick hedge. Its smell burned in Alain's nostrils.

'Come in, Brothers! There's a bit of cider left over from the autumn. It's a little sharp, but it will still wet your throat. No need to have come so far. We've everything well in hand. There's nothing here to see. Nothing. Nothing.'

A group of children of varying ages stared mournfully at them, keeping their distance from the hounds. The eldest was a girl; after she offered each man a wooden cup filled with sharp cider, she stared at them with a hopeless gaze, hands wrapped tight in her apron. She had warts all across the fingers of her left hand and her left cheek had a blistery rash. All of the younger siblings bore a similar rash.

'My good wife died two year ago, leaving me with all these young ones. There's no wife to be had in these parts, all of them married and none old enough to wed for a good number of years. There was a widow last year, but she died of that flux that took off my youngest. I kept a man in to help me, an easterner, but he was no good. He took all of his things and six eggs yesterday morning and abandoned us. I suppose

it's him who spread tales.' He was skittish, but it wasn't the
hounds that scared him; he glanced once in their direction
and then not again.

'Can we see the herd, friend?' asked Ratbold. 'The good
abbot has asked us to do what we can.'

The farmer looked ready to cry as he led them past his
cottage, which was split into living quarters and a wintering
stable for his livestock. The penned-in area beside the stable
lay calf-deep in mud from the winter rains, but no sheep sheltered there now. They continued past the garden and the hen-
house to a meadow where a bright-eyed dog and an older boy
kept watch over the flock: three ewes and four lambs. The
hounds ventured forward cautiously to view the other dog,
who eyed them from a distance, growling softly but not leaving his station at guard over the sheep.

'It's just the mud,' the farmer insisted. 'That's what made
them go lame. That's why I brought them out here, to get
their hooves out of the mud. It's only two I had to slaughter.
I burned them, just to make sure, because I knew folk would
talk. These others, they were right as rain this morning.'

Ratbold cursed. Two of the ewes were lying down and the
third was limping badly. The lambs seemed unnaturally quiet
where they lay beside their mothers, not romping, making no
reaction at all as strangers walked up beside them.

Ratbold caught up to the limping ewe and grabbed a leg,
cupping its hoof in one strong hand. 'It's the murrain, all
right,' he said. 'The blisters are hard to see. Here, all round
where the horn joins the skin. Here in the cleft. Can you feel
how hot the hoof is?'

The other ewes showed no blisters, although they refused
to rise, gathering their hind legs far forward and going no farther up than a half crouch.

'Ai, God!' The farmer hovered restlessly at Ratbold's back,
struggling to hold back tears. 'Is there any hope for it?'

'It's breaking the king's law to hide the murrain,' said
Ratbold. 'You must pen in all your animals and burn them
after they die, put their skulls up on stakes as a warning—'

The farmer's first sound was a wordless, despairing cry,

followed by a burst of sobs and lamentation. 'My good sheep! My good sheep! What will happen to us?'

Behind, the children began to blubber and weep. It was a cataclysm for this family, who would lose their flock and all the wool, lambs, meat, and cheese it brought them. The steading lay on the slope of hills with a dense clay soil; this marginal land was suitable for pasturage and a garden and not much else but still close enough to gain a substantial benefit from proximity to the monastery and its adjoining farms.

'Let me bathe their hooves,' said Alain. 'Maybe some good will come of that. Have you wound-heal or sicklewort?'

The farmer could barely speak through his tears. 'Nay. Nothing of that sort, Brother. I've never heard of such things. Is there any cure for the murrain?'

'You know there is not,' said Ratbold. 'Now pray leave us, for Brother Alain and I must discuss what to do next.'

Weeping, the farmer retreated to the huddle of his children, watching helplessly as Ratbold scolded Alain.

'Brother Alain, it is a sin to raise false hopes. There is no cure. He'll lose his entire flock.'

'I pray that he does not!'

'Once it strikes a herd, it strikes them all. This is truly the Enemy's feast. All we can hope for is to kill this plague here so it doesn't spread to the other steadings and the monastery.'

'Father Ortulfus said I should do what I can. *Has* anyone tried a bath of herb water, or an ointment?'

'Do you suppose they have not? If there was any healing that would banish the murrain, it would have been found by now. Do what you wish, but it will make no difference. We'll have to pen in the animals and stay here to watch over them. We can't trust him to follow the law. He knew it was the murrain – and was hoping to hide it. When the animals are dead, we'll see them burned and then return to the monastery. That is the only way.'

'May I bathe their feet in any case, Prior? No harm will come to me, and it may ease their suffering.'

'It's foolhardy—!' began Ratbold, but checked himself as if a voice too quiet for Alain to hear chided him. 'Nay. Do as you wish, Brother Alain.'

'Coltsfoot may work as well,' mused Alain. Three of the children had sores around their lips, although he had never heard of murrain striking people. Yet the children, too, might benefit from Adica's herb-craft, a mash to heal sores and ease rashes, an ointment to banish warts or soothe the eyes. Adica was gone, and his life with her had been obliterated in the white heat of the terrible spell she and her fellows had raised to destroy their enemies, but what he had learned from her would not perish as long as he lived and could pass the knowl-edge on.

The girl and the two youngest children trailed after him, keeping their distance from the hounds, as he gathered colts-foot and violets. He showed the girl what he was doing, let her assist him. The flowers he boiled down into a syrup, the leaves mashed into a fresh poultice.

It was dusk by the time he sank onto a stool in the meadow and washed the hooves of the sheep. The animals were too ill to fight him, although the blisters seemed no worse than they had looked earlier.

'Will they get better?' asked the girl, crouching beside him. He had painted her warts with oil of gentian; purple dots speckled her hand, and a greenish plaster coated her cheek. She smelled medicinal, like a child who had rolled in the wild spring greening.

'I pray they will, but it's in God's hands now. I'll sit up and watch over them.'

The children were exhausted with grief and fear and went to their beds without complaining. The farmer insisted on spending the night outside with his precious sheep.

'I'll sit the first watch with him,' Alain said to Ratbold.

The prior nodded. Because the night was fair, Ratbold rolled himself up in a blanket under the shelter of the nearby trees, but the farmer sat meekly on the ground, all vigor gone out of him.

After a long silence, the man said, 'Is it hopeless? Will your herb-craft cure them? I am ruined. . . .'

'I do not know.'

He was helpless, as he had told Prior Ratbold. It had been easy to remain at the monastery as the season changed; the round of work never ceased; the hunger of his fellow lay brothers for companionship and comfort never ended. The destitute and desperate always found their way to the gates, those who could. Those who could not suffered where they were. There was nothing he could do. He hadn't even been able to save Adica.

He, too, sheltered a blight on his soul. He, too, was penned in, waiting only to die. He was imprisoned and might bide on Earth for long years, if God were not merciful, long years remembering Adica's sweetness and the light she brought with her, that was her essence. The smell of meadow flowers.

It would have been better to walk in company with her down the path that leads to the Other Side.

Yet how could he bear to leave the world, which was so beautiful? Even here, on this deathwatch, the night blossomed around him. A nightjar churred. The hazy cloak of air thrown across the sky hid half the stars and pricked the others into unexpected brilliance. Sounds unfolded beneath the canopy of trees barely stirred by a lazy breeze: the breathing of the ewes, the skittering of a mouse, the ticking of a bug, the distant tumble of a stream. The shadow of a bat swooped past; an owl cooed. Grass tickled his fingers where his hand lay slack on the ground, and he felt a tiny body creeping into the shelter of his hand as an owl glided past, seen swiftly and then gone into the trees. A minuscule tongue tested his skin. He sat very still so as not to scare the mouse away. The wind rustled in the branches and the grass swayed and whispered, playing along his wrist and hand, telling him a story of lands far away, lost to him once. . . .

The last patrol to return brings the long-awaited news. North lie fens where the tree sorcerers hide their secrets and where the Alban queen has fled to rebuild her power. On an island isolated in the middle of that wasteland of water and reeds rests a stone crown. But the marshland swallows strangers foolish enough to venture in without a guide.

'We will find a guide,' says Stronghand, indicating that they should go on with their report.

Hefenfelthe is only one among the queen's many strong-holds. Other hill forts guard the tracks that lead north through hostile territory now swarming with Alban war bands and a growing Alban army, called together to resist the invader. If the Eika army marches, it will meet with heavy resistance. They will have to fight every step of the way, and that is even before they reach the impassable southern margin of the fens.

'I do not fear the Albans,' he says to his soldiers, 'nor do you. Yet fighting along the roads is not the only way to conquer a country. I respect the dangers posed by the marsh, but I do not think it impassable. Is there no river we can sail up? Does the water in these fenlands not drain into the sea?'

The fens drain northward; this much the scouts observed, but they did not scout the fens themselves or journey north beyond them once they confirmed the rumors of the queen's sighting. Other voices chime in with their own observations. Eika have raided sporadically along the Alban coast for gen-erations, and it is well known that a great wash of water domi-nates the middle northern coast. Yet how many rivers spill into this drainage none know, nor have any Eika navigated those channels. They might sail up a hundred rivers and streams and still not find what they are looking for in such a maze of waterways and bog.

'We can send scouts,' he says, 'but we cannot wait for their report. The Alban queen cannot be given enough time to con-solidate her position. We must march overland and strike them from the south, through the fens.'

Ironclaw shakes his head. 'Did you not hear what they said? The Albans will fight us every step of the way through country they know like their own hand. They are dogs, loyal to their queen. They will bite and nip at us all the way.'

'Do you fear them?'

'No! No! No!' protests Ironclaw, seeing he has lost face by expressing caution. 'We are stronger, but we lack numbers. The Albans will never lay down their arms.'

'Will they not? Is Hefenfelthe not alive with Albans working in the forge, rebuilding this tower, and plowing the fields?'

He glances at Papa Otto, who bides quietly among his advisers. He has never forgotten the words Otto spoke to him long ago in a tent shelter beneath a bitter winter wind driving ice along the rock face of a cove. That day seems long ago to him now, back in the days before Fifth Son of the Fifth Litter took the name Stronghand, before he became chieftain over Rikin tribe and defeated his enemies at Kjalmarsfjord. Long ago, but no less vivid in his mind's eye.

'I have no choice but to serve you,' the slave Otto had said. Hate had burned in his expression, but he had been helpless to act against the master he loathed and despised.

Stronghand lifts his head to scent the spring wind. His dogs lie in a restless mass around him; they stir and wiggle and yip, eager to run. Most of his troops are eager to run. Victory at Hefenfelthe has not tested them, only sharpened their zeal. They chafe at their restraints.

Yet it remains true that the Eika are few, while humans are many. But the Albans, like the Eika and all their human brethren, keep slaves, war captives, the destitute, the unfortunate, the weak, and the helpless. The ones born into servitude.

The ones who hate their masters.

'We will march,' says Stronghand, raising his staff. Wind moans in the bone flutes and rattles beads and finger-bone chimes. 'We have other allies, who do not yet know they are waiting for us.'

A tickle against his fingers woke him, and he started up.

Stronghand would help him! It came clear as suddenly as a blast of light banishes darkness when fire catches tinder and blazes up. Memories burned into his mind's eye made sense as they had not before, when he could neither think nor make sense of the nightmare he had glimpsed through the heart of the spell woven by Adica and the others. The Eika were born that long ago day, created out of the supernatural melding of humans, great standing stones, and dragon's blood.

Stronghand would listen, and believe.

He was halfway up before he remembered to check under his feet. The mouse was gone. He rubbed his eyes as he glanced up to gauge the position of the stars. How long had he slept? How soon could he act?

'Brother Alain!' Ratbold stumbled up from his crude bower at the edge of the woodland, scratching his stubbled chin and looking mightily irritated. 'You did not wake me! Where are the sheep?' He halted as Rage growled at him, startled by his aggressive movement toward Alain.

The disk of the newly reborn sun gilded the eastern tree-tops with a tender clove-pink glow. The fog that weighed down Alain's soul dissolved as though the rising sun were burning it off.

'God curse him!' Ratbold strode to the center of the meadow; only prior and lay brother stood where the sheep had suffered. Flat patches of grass betrayed where the stricken sheep had lain in their illness. They hadn't gone far, or long ago. 'That damned man has stolen his sheep away!'

'Wait, Prior. I hear them.'

Hidden by the trees, the farmer was laughing, calling out. 'Come along! Come along now! Look how they walk!'

Farmer, children, and lambs gamboled into the clearing, the ewes trotting among them under the supervision of the steadfast dog. Ratbold was too astonished to scold them. He rushed over, ignoring the yapping sheepdog, and brusquely examined the hooves and mouths of the ewes. The lambs scattered as he moved among them. The children and the dog rushed around, dog barking, children screaming with delight, as they chased the lambs back from the woodland edge. Light clouds scudded in from the east, shadowing the sun; a shower misted the scene, moving off as quickly as it arrived, and the sun came out from behind the clouds.

'Impossible,' cried Ratbold, checking each of the ewes in turn.

'I said it was not the murrain!' shouted the farmer triumphantly. 'Just a fungus. A rot. Cured now! Cured! Once I got them out of the mud.'

'Impossible,' repeated Ratbold.

But true.

Ratbold insisted they remain at the steading two more days to make sure the disease did not reoccur. He believed in the murrain, and he feared that without his supervision the outbreak would spread.

Alain chafed, eager to return to Herford, but he recognized the farmer's needs as well. No need to wait fruitlessly when so many spring chores needed doing. Because of the threat of murrain, the local oxherd would not bring his oxen for plowing, so they had to laboriously turn over the earth for the garden by hand. For three days they worked, sweating despite the cool weather, and in the evenings Alain told the children stories and taught the two eldest a little from his meager store of herb-craft, so they might add to their larder and soothe simple illnesses that afflicted them. Three days passed and the sheep showed not the slightest sign of lameness, blistering, or sores. The children's rashes healed.

It was with a lightened heart that he set out at last beside Ratbold.

'Why did you not wake me that night?' Ratbold asked when they reached the main track and turned toward home.

'I fell asleep, Prior. I pray, grant me your pardon. I meant to wake you.'

'Nay, never mind it. You need no pardon from me.' Ratbold remained distracted as they strode along. He wielded his staff like a weapon, whacking off the heads of thistles as they walked. 'That night I dreamed I stood in a high hall waiting for the king to hear my case.'

'The king? Not the abbot?'

'Nay, the king, for I was dressed in the garb of a soldier, as I once was in the king's service.'

It seemed long ago that Alain had himself stood before the king. Henry had ruled against him, had disinherited him and stripped him of the county gifted to him by a dying Lavastine, but had shown mercy by granting him a position in his own humble Lions. Alain uncovered no anger in his own heart, remembering that day. He only hoped that Lord Geoffrey was proving to be a good steward over Lavas county, that his daughter, and heir, would prove as wise a count as Lavastine had been in his time. That he had failed Lavastine pained him; only that.

'What case did you bring before the king in your dream?'

'I know not.' Ratbold's habitual frown was set as strongly as ever on his face although his disapproval in this instance seemed turned on himself. 'All I did was wait my turn, like a man standing on the knife edge of the Abyss who knows not whether he is meant to fall into the pit or rise to the Chamber of Light. Then I woke. You know what happened next. I should have known. I should have trusted in God.'

They walked for a while without speaking. The peace of the morning sank over them. Here along the track they might have been the only two people in the wide world, alone except for the robins and a flock of honking geese flying north. Birds sang out of the depths of the forest, but the trees were silent, untouched by wind. Water dripped from branches. Shallow pools lay in perfect stillness in basins and ruts cutting across the wheeled track. The hounds padded along with ears raised, listening, alert, pausing now and again to lap up water.

'Why do you stay at Herford Monastery, Brother?' Ratbold asked at last.

'You took me in when I was desperate and alone. Isn't that reason enough? But I cannot stay any longer. I know where I must go next. I must find the one who will believe my tale and help me.'

'Alas,' murmured Ratbold. 'So we are served for our lack of faith.'

'What do you mean? I, too, had a dream that night, Prior. Do not blame yourself or the others. Why should you? How can it be that any sane man could believe the story I told you when first I came? I can scarcely believe it myself, although I lived through it. Yet I know it is true, and that I must act — I don't know how, or what I can do. Perhaps nothing. But I must act. I must try. I cannot bear any longer only to stand and wait.'

Ratbold missed a step, staggering, but righted himself as Alain paused to help him. 'Let me go with you, Brother.'

'Go with me?' The request astounded him because it was so unexpected.

'I will serve you—'

'What can you mean? Father Ortulfus depends on you, Prior Ratbold. He can't administer the monastery without your help. I must go alone. I mean to journey into lands held by the Eika.'

'The Eika! Will you become a missionary?'

Alain laughed as a tiny frog hopped out of one of the standing pools and vanished under a tangle of blackberry vines. For months now he had been paralyzed by grief, unable to feel or think or move, but that morning with the sheep when he had passed from sleep into waking had brought blood back to his limbs, warmth to his skin, feeling to his heart, painful but blessedly welcome.

Adica was gone. He had lost her.

But he still had a task to complete.

'I don't know. I only know I must reach the one called Stronghand, whom I see in my dreams.'

Ratbold turned his face away and touched his hidden cheek with one finger as if to wipe away a tear. 'So be it, Brother. There is no one here who can stop you.'

No one.

When they reached the monastery, they were brought to Father Ortulfus' study where the good father entertained exalted guests, the same clerics who had passed them three days before, taking no notice of two humble monks standing alongside the road.

The eldest of the clerics was a lean man called Severus whose ascetic face suggested that he had passed many long nights on his knees in prayer after long days of solitary scholarly study. He refused to speak Wendish, using only Dariyan.

'Had we known, we might have taken him then and gone on our way more quickly. These delays are a trouble to us. I have come all the way from southern Salia, leaving my assistants behind me to oversee the work necessary there. I am on my way to Alba.'

He looked Alain over, mouth tight, expression doubtful. 'This one? This is the man we were sent to recover?' He shook his head, but his skeptical gaze touched the hounds sitting faithfully on either side of the door. Not even Father Ortulfus forbade the hounds any chamber they wished to enter. All of them had discovered that if the hounds were let be, they behaved peaceably enough. 'Are these his hounds?'

'They are mine,' Alain replied. 'Who has sent you, Brother?'

'You are bold, speaking before you are spoken to.'

'I beg your pardon, Brother, but it is obvious that I have been spoken of without my knowledge. Prior Ratbold and I are only just returned from a distant steading where we have watched over sheep suspected of carrying the murrain.'

The other clerics shuddered, wringing hands, whispering.

'Yes, there is a murrain abroad in the lands south of here,' said Father Ortulfus, 'so these good clerics report. They passed skulls set on posts and whole steadings burned out. It's a terrible plague, although some say it's the work of soul-murdering bandits. But I have not yet heard your report, Brother. Prior Ratbold, what of Farmer Hosed?'

'He burned two of the sheep.' Ratbold glanced at Alain, then at the clerics, before returning his gaze to the abbot. 'But the others . . . the other ewes and the lambs.' He hesitated, unwilling to speak further in the presence of strangers.

'Go on.'

Words came raggedly. 'There is no murrain on our lands.'

Ortulfus had no experience concealing his feelings and thoughts; born of an ancient and noble lineage, placed in a position of power at a youthful age, he had never learned to school his expressions. His look now, staring first with dis-belief at Ratbold before shifting to regard Alain, betrayed his innermost heart.

The intensity of Ortulfus' gaze startled Alain. *They do not want to give me up.* At Lavas he had been cast out; no one had wanted him, although he had been accepted by the Lions because of the king's imprimatur and, he hoped, his own hard work. Adica and her village had taken him in as one of their own, but he had been deposited there by a shaman of great power and terrible wisdom. Here at Herford he had been accepted out of charity; he had believed himself suffered more than loved.

Had he misunderstood the good brothers? What man would smile sadly as Ortulfus did now, as if searching for a question to an answer he already knew?

'Brother Alain, these honorable clerics come from the skopos in Darre. It is their wish that you journey to Darre to meet with the skopos.'

Their wish, Ortulfus said, but in his tone Alain heard otherwise.

Their command.

'Why would the skopos wish to meet with me?'

'We do not ask,' said Brother Severus coldly. 'We only obey. We will leave in the morning.'

Ortulfus gestured to Ratbold and his other attendants, indicating that they should go about their business, see about supper, return to their work. 'You may go, Brother Alain, and make any preparations necessary.'

Alain considered objecting. That powerful compulsion to seek Stronghand still rode him, yet the pragmatic voice of Aunt Bel whispered in his mind.

If it is true that Stronghand is in Alba, how will you cross the sea with no goods or coin to trade for your passage?

He was a pauper, living on the sufferance of the church. Surely the skopos had a powerful reason to seek him out. Perhaps she had knowledge of the magical forces that had cast him here. He would make her heed him. Once her belief was secured, all others must believe him as well.

'I will go then, Father, with your blessing.'

Ortulfus shook his head, that tight, ironic smile still caught on his lips. 'You have my blessing, Brother Alain. I pray you, think as well of us as you can.'

'How could I think otherwise? You took me in when I was mad with grief. You have sheltered me. I pray none of you come to any harm.'

Father Ortulfus steadied himself on a chair, lowering his gaze humbly. His eyes brimmed with tears.

There was nothing else to say. Alain whistled the hounds to order and left the chamber, but as he walked away he heard them speaking still.

'He is not what I expected,' said Brother Severus, voice carrying, perhaps, farther than he meant it to.

'Nay, Your Excellency,' retorted Father Ortulfus boldly. 'It is not for us to judge.'

Iso wept. 'Let m-m-me come with you, B-brother. I am alone here.'

'You are not alone. The others will look after you.'

He grieved to leave Iso, who was so frail, so crippled, so trusting. He had abandoned Lackling to his fate, all unknowing; now it seemed doubly criminal to leave Iso behind, but the boy could not sustain the rigors of a long journey, nor did Alain trust the supercilious clerics who served the skopos to be patient with anyone who might impede their progress. They seemed an impatient group to him as he joined them in the cold breath of dawn with dew glimmering on every blade of grass. Cattle and sheep grazed placidly in their pastures. No trace of the murrain had blighted the monastic herds, Ratbold had told him last night, but the prior had spoken the words in the way a man relays information that his listener already knows.

With Father Ortulfus at their head, all of the lay brothers and monks gathered beside the gate to see him off. Even Brother Lallo cried. Iso trembled as he wept. The entire crowd of them remained watching at the gate, silent except for poor Iso's convulsive sobs, as the cavalcade lumbered away. Alain kept looking back over his shoulder, lifting his hand a second time, a third, a fourth, to convey his fare-you-wells. A few raised hands in answer. The sun rose behind them, and as the road curved he lost sight of the monastery first in the glare of the sun pushing up above the forest and at last as the bend in the road concealed it irrevocably.

XVI

AN ARROW IN
THE HEART

1

Sheltered by a makeshift awning, Blessing sat unnaturally still, legs crossed, hands on her knees, and watched the centaurs confer. The woman–horses ranged in a circle, hindquarters out and torsos in. They spoke in voices both human and mareish, words punctuated by snorts, flicks of their tails, and the stamping of hooves. They remained at the crest of the slope while sentries surveyed the land on all sides. The prince's forces lay out of sight, although threads of smoke from their campfires marked the sky.

The centaurs had not returned them to the prince's camp.

Blessing's silence made Anna nervous. She had never seen the princess go for so long without saying *something*.

Had the centaur shaman bewitched the girl?

'Honored One? I see if your cuts heal?'

A fair number of actual people traveled with the centaur army, all of them congregating around a cheerfully painted wagon whose occupant Anna never, ever saw. The healer was one of these humans, although she was odd in her own right with dark eyes outlined with kohl and strangely large hands and feet. She wore a woman's felt jacket, a skirt split for riding with leather trousers beneath, and a tall felt headdress decorated with bronze spirals and prancing deer. Her voice, if rather low, was soothing, and her hands, probing Anna's injuries, were gentle.

'How do you come to speak Wendish?' Anna asked.

The healer smiled. Bells tied to her headdress tinkled as she nodded. 'We prepare for this meeting. For this reason, some learn the speech of your people. The Holy One sees the day to come and the day already walking past.'

Could the shaman see into the future? How much power did she have? Yet Anna could not say she felt particularly nervous as the healer fed her gruel and a sharp, fermented milk before leaving her and Blessing alone. The milk made her head spin. She became unusually aware of her hands, her lips, her elbows, the red-and-orange carpet on which they sat, the ragged clouds overhead in a pale blue sky which, to the east, faded to a stormy gray. She smelled winter, but it didn't touch them.

Blessing refused both gruel and milk. Tears streaked her face, but she kept silent, all her fear and uncertainty held in. Anna's heart broke to see her so bereft. She was so young, despite her size, no more than three or four years of age, still a baby for all that her body had matured rapidly. Although the girl looked twelve or so, she had neither experience nor maturity.

No wonder her father feared for her. He must have known it was only a matter of time before she got herself into trouble beyond his ability to fix. It was a miracle that the centaurs had rescued them from Bulkezu, and even now they were still in grave danger even if the centaurs seemed calm and polite.

It was no wonder Blessing feared the centaurs. She had never lived under the hand of any authority except that of her doting father. Then Bulkezu had abducted her most violently, and now she was held prisoner by these strange creatures.

Blessing hadn't learned the lesson of Gent. She didn't know

that sometimes you had to bide your time and hunker down in such shelter as you could find, because you no longer had any control over the storm blowing around you.

The old one, the shaman, tossed her head abruptly, backed out of the council circle, and walked over to them.

Blessing stood and stepped forward, her little face creased with determination, her eyes black with anger.

'When are you going to take me back to my—'

She jerked and spun sideways as though a giant's hand twisted her around. Her hands clutched at her throat, and her eyes rolled skyward. Light winked, flashed, in the corner of Anna's eye – barely seen and gone as quickly.

Blessing screamed. 'I hear her! I hear her! She came back! She's all on fire!' She fell limp to the ground.

'Blessing!' Anna shook the girl, chafed her hands, but she did not respond although she was breathing and her eyes were open. A shadow covered the princess' face, and Anna looked up to find the shaman looming over them. 'What did you *do?*' she cried, then fell silent as the shaman's gaze touched her.

The centaur said nothing, only gazed at Blessing, coolly appraising. Her face, despite its human shape, had an uncanny appearance, maybe only the luminous shine of her eyes or perhaps the oddly disturbing horn color of her skin and the contrasting gold-and-green-painted stripes across her torso.

It had to be a spell.

Slowly, Anna got up, although it still hurt to move. She was bruised and cut and aching, but it was incontrovertibly true that the centaurs had saved her and the princess from Bulkezu. For all their terrible strangeness, they didn't look insane.

'Who came back?' demanded Anna rudely, forgetting prudence and courtesy. 'Who is on fire?'

The shaman scented the air, facing east. 'A powerful force has entered the land.'

Blessing could not speak, but Anna had not lost her tongue. Not anymore.

'What are you going to do with us? Where is Prince Sanglant? Why can't we go back to our people? What have you done to Princess Blessing?'

The shaman examined Anna as though the young woman were a particularly loathsome grub that she might, upon examination, decide to squish. That look was spell enough. Anna ducked her head. Maybe the end would come swiftly, a bolt of lightning called down from the heavens to burn her to ash.

'I have done nothing to Princess Blessing except spare her the brutal mercies of the beast who stalks in the grass. What affliction besets her, I do not know.'

'There are healers in the prince's camp—'

'This is not an earthly affliction. There is nothing we can do.'

'There has to be something!'

'Does there?' The tone made Anna flinch, but no blow landed. 'The storm blows itself out. A warm wind will finish it, and the first flowers of spring will bloom. We will wait. I will not interfere with the hunt.'

Anna wiped her eyes and knelt beside Blessing, clasping her hands over the girl's heart. Blessing's chest rose and fell in a steady rhythm, but her eyes remained open, blind and unresponsive.

'What do you do?' asked the shaman curiously.

'The only thing left me to do. I'm going to pray.'

2

When you have seen the world end and you are lost in a storm of ice, all you can do is fight forward toward an unseen and even unknowable destination.

Wind battered her. The ground became rocky as they began to climb. The stranger leading her dropped in and out of sight, screened by a blast of snow one moment only to be revealed as the wind shifted. His unbound hair whipped and curled in the gale like writhing snakes. Hunched over, he trudged up the steep slope into the teeth of the wind and did not look back to see if she were following.

Where else would she go?

They walked forever until her hands and feet were numb and she could not feel the weight of her bow on her back. Her cheeks burned. Twice she slipped and stumbled as loose rocks, unseen under the blowing snow, rolled away beneath her feet. Each time she cursed as she hit knees, once an elbow. The wind screamed down off the height, pummeling her; a pebble gouged a cut below her eye, the blood wicked away by the blast of the gale.

He vanished. She stumbled over rubbish, tripped, hit the ground knees first and found herself scrabbling among bones, but her hands were so numb that she couldn't feel to get her balance. He hauled her up and shoved her forward into the shelter of a lopsided hut crazily woven of sticks and grass. An old and threatening scent pervaded the air, but at least the cutting wind had lessened enough that she could hear him speak in perfectly grammatical but clearly accented Wendish.

'If you light fire, we live.'

Out of the wind, she began shivering all down the length of her body. It was hard to concentrate, even to think of her own name much less remember how to call fire in such a dangerous place, with dry vegetation all around them ready to burst into an inferno.

He nudged a pile of debris on the ground which she recognized belatedly as a fire pit stacked with dried dung. As she knelt, her knees popped and creaked like those of an elder. A finger bone slipped under her knee and rolled away into the fire pit. What manner of predator devoured human flesh yet built nests like a bird?

She already knew the answer.

Although it was difficult to coordinate her movements with her hands numb and aching, she pulled off one glove and rested her fingers on the lowermost layer of dung. Out on the open ground, she had called fire indiscriminately; here, she must probe as with a needle, sewing finest silk, so as not to engulf herself in her own conflagration.

Fire caught in the fuel and licked upward as she sat back

hard, out of breath. It was so cold. So cold.

'Where have you come from?' asked the man.

With an effort, she lifted her head. He crouched down opposite her, eyeing her with an intelligent if disturbingly intent gaze across the waxing fire. His hair had settled, not snakes at all but long, thick, black hair furiously tangled by the wind. It made her think of Sanglant – who had never tired of combing out her hair, the one thing he could sit still for, who was always needing to pace, to walk, to move.

Ai, God, where was Sanglant now? Where was their daughter? She had prayed that the force of her longing for them might drag her back close to them, but now she despaired. What reason had they to be wandering in this wasteland? She didn't have time to seek them out, because time and tide and the infallible turning of the stars would not wait. How could she get back to them knowing that she might be driven onward on a path that would not intersect with theirs for days or months or even years? She did not know how long she had been absent from this world. She did not know how much time she had left until the great conjunction.

'Tell me first,' she said carefully, 'who you are.'

'If I were your enemy, you would already be dead.'

She laughed because, as he spoke, the tenor of his face reminded her of Cat Mask. She touched her sword, Lucian's friend, to reassure herself that it still hung faithfully at her belt. 'Perhaps. It is possible that you are not capable of killing me. It is possible that you would not wish to.'

'It is possible that you are now my hostage.'

'It is possible that you are mine.'

He laughed, an echo of hers, but his voice cracked and she had an uneasy feeling that he was hiding something profound, not just his identity and his purpose here but a deeper secret, like a fire smoldering beneath peat that may burst out unexpectedly to scorch the digging hand.

'I am no one, just a man in search of griffin wings.'

'And this –' She gestured. '– is a griffin's nest?'

'Yes.'

'Then you are in the right place to meet the fate you desire.'

He laughed again, that disquieting cackle. 'Are *you?* Where have you come from? What do you seek?'

She said nothing.

He brushed a hand along the curve of his throat. The casual movement unsettled her. Not meaning to, she touched the gold torque she wore, which she no longer had the right to wear.

'Only the lineage of the regnant wears the ring of gold at their neck,' he said. 'Who is your father?'

'A humble man with neither king nor queen in his ancestry. How is it you speak Wendish? Are you a merchant?'

'I am nothing, nameless and purposeless, until I have griffin wings.'

'Then what will you be?'

'That depends on whether I defeat my enemy. He also wears a gold ring at his neck.'

She flushed, feeling heat on her skin, the racing of her heart. Henry might be fighting the easterners. It was too much to hope that this man knew the whereabouts of Sanglant, and she dared not reveal knowledge he could use against her.

'How will griffin wings defeat your enemy?'

'The feathers of griffins are proof against magic. Maybe even proof against yours, Liathano.'

He was, probably, a little mad, and certainly he played this as a game, shifting ground, casting straw into his opponent's eyes. This man was not her friend. It was still difficult to gauge whether he was her enemy. She changed her tactics.

'How do you know my name?'

The fire snapped as he regarded her, tilting his head to one side, listening. She heard only the howl of the wind and the whispering rustle of the outermost layers of the giant nest.

'I have been seeking you because yours is a name of great power. Because you burned down a palace. Fire is a weapon.'

'Then you must know that you can't hope to kill me, or take me prisoner. Fire is a weapon that not even griffin feathers can defeat.'

'You have already served your purpose. Listen.'

She listened. But all she could hear was the wind.

He gripped his spear across his body and without warning dashed outside. She jumped up just as the entire nest
shuddered. Sticks and debris rained down on her. A broken
eggshell, disturbingly large, dropped from the ceiling and
shattered into tiny pieces at her feet. The low opening quivered as though probed. A beast screamed shrilly outside. A
vast shape moved beyond the entrance and before she could
find shelter – not that there was any crevice or cove to crawl
into – a huge tufted eagle's head thrust in through the opening. Snowflakes glittered on its beak. Its throat feathers had
an iron gleam and its eyes the look of amber, but it rested its
bulk on a lion's tawny paw, made sharp with cruel talons.

The griffin had come home.

3

Sanglant had never had cause to consider the limits of his
mother's curse. His wounds never festered, only healed. The
grippes and agues that afflicted others never touched him. He
could not die in battle or intrigue, only watch as his allies and
enemies succumbed.

Now, some hours after fording the shallow river, he
huddled in his cloak while the freezing gale tore at him, chilling him to the bone. Walking had warmed his wet feet and
boots, but every time he stopped they stiffened and burned.
Storm, he reflected, is neither male nor female. Cold is no
disease but merely a state.

Maybe Bulkezu wouldn't need to kill him, only get the
credit for it afterward when he dragged in Sanglant's frozen
corpse.

Yet Sanglant could do nothing else but hunt him down.
At first, traveling east across Ungria and through the steppe,
duty had driven him. Now hate and rage impelled him.

Bulkezu had stolen his daughter.

To even think about it made his head cloud with fury, made him want to shriek and rend like a maddened dog.

But he was a man, and he would only defeat Bulkezu and recover his daughter if he thought and acted like a man.

How did a man hunt a griffin?

Seek them in their lair.

As he did himself, child of human and Aoi, griffins partook of different essences: eagle, lion, and snake. Lions prowled the plains, so lore said, and eagles loved rivers and mountains, often preferring open country. Before the storm closed in around him, he had got a good look at the landscape that lay east, where a river wound through a broad, grassy valley that ended abruptly in the steep slopes of rocky crags.

He heaved himself up to his feet and headed east into the wind. The cold raged around him, but he trudged onward. As the day faded, the gray sky turned to a deep blue-gray shadow and the high crags became a black wall. The snow trailed off, leaving frozen ground swept clean by the wind. The temperature did not rise, nor did it fall.

Through the night he walked on, never varying his pace. His voice was lost; no words formed in his head. Thoughts existed in their raw, inhuman, natural form as he turned his senses outward, seeking, listening, smelling.

The night spoke to his ears: 'There is nothing before you, nothing behind.' The earth spoke on his feet as the thin crust of soil was crushed beneath each step: 'This is a hard land. Beware.' The cold spoke through his skin: 'I come from the mountain, from the sky, from the cold worlds beyond. Join me, and I will carry you away.'

The wind spoke most clearly, bringing scent as he neared the eastern heights. A deer, injured, bleeding, lay down to die. A winter-starved wolf and its mate circled in for the feast. A lone eagle dove in the turbulent winds, investigating a blast of heat high up on the westernmost outcropping of the crags.

Fire.

A blaze tore at the wind high above him, directly east. A campfire, or a bonfire. A signal.

To this conflagration Sanglant listened, thwarted in his

quest when the wind shifted and whispered other secrets, as if knowing he sought signs of human life, teased forward when it changed direction and blew down from the east once again. As the night drew on, the cold winter gale subsided into a drowsy breeze hinting of spring, blown up from the south along the ridgeline. He began to lose the scent.

He walked more quickly. The ground shifted subtly upward, then steepened, until he had to pick his route up the slope using his spear as a staff to steady his way. He smelled and listened to the lay of the ground more than saw it; his eyesight was not particularly keen at night, so the curl of the breeze against the land revealed the trail. Late into the night, with the scent of dawn in the air and the clouds shredding into patches through which stars shone, he caught sight of a flicker of light high up among the rocks.

The waning moon breached the clouds, its light casting a silver sheen over the rocks, and with this lamp to guide him he made a track through fallen rocks, careful not to slip and betray himself with a loud sound.

He thought the campfire far away and was not prepared to hear its steady roar so close by, a trick perhaps of the echoing rock face of the crags above him. Behind, the valley lay in darkness, as unfathomable as the sea. He paused to catch his breath, shut his eyes to listen for the scrape of a foot on the rock that would give away the presence of his enemy.

He could not smell him, but an itch between his shoulders, along his palms, a whisper in his mind, told him that Bulkezu was close. Smoke tickled his nose.

He edged forward along an outcropping and negotiated a scatter of boulders fallen from the crags above. Beyond this obstacle a hollow widened out of the mountainside, forming a sheltered niche where griffins had built a gigantic nest out of branches, grass, reeds, bones, scraps of cloth, and a litter of iron feathers woven together.

The huge nest blazed up into the night sky. A griffin crouched in the space between the burning nest and the far edge of the hollow, where the mountainside split away into a cliff face. It was a magnificent creature, bigger than an ox, with gleaming iron wings and a pale-silver coat, its eagle's head raised as it stared at a single figure standing a stone's toss away from it. The slender human had retreated up on a tumble of rocks. Facing each other, at a stalemate, neither griffin nor the foe it hunted moved. The fire sparked and roared.

He tightened his grip on his spear as a faint rose glow brushed the eastern horizon beyond the line of crags. The griffin shifted position, lashing its snake's tail, ready to spring. The last glint of the setting moon's light washed the mountainside in silver and revealed the form and face of the person standing up on the rocks.

Liath.

He was dreaming. Bulkezu had cast a spell over him.

Moonlight gilded her hair to a pale glamour. Her face had not changed at all in the intervening years, and it seemed the spark of blue fire in her eyes blazed so brightly that he could believe he actually saw a flicker of fire reflected there, although certainly he was too far away to see the details of her face. Fire consumed the nest, smoke and flame billowing heavenward, and a faint shimmer of golden-orange-red light danced like an aurora around her as well, making her shine as invisible fire limned her body.

She was as beautiful as he remembered her, but she was something else now – powerful in a discomforting way like the blast of heat from a well-stoked hearth that prevents the blacksmith from approaching too closely.

She did not see him.

The hem of her cloak lifted as wind caught it, swirling it around her knees. She had braced herself on the rock, bow bent with an arrow ready to fly, yet she did not loose it. The griffin did not spring, although its tail whipped along the ground, stirring up a misty cloud of dust.

He stared, stupefied at the unanticipated sight of her. Where had she been all this time? Why had she never sought him out?

Ai, God. A single arrow was no match for a griffin.

He broke forward – and in that instant death brushed his shoulders. Turning and ducking in the same motion, he just missed being caught in the face by a spear point thrust out from the rocky shadows behind him. His enemy had crept up while he gaped, dumbfounded and witless, at his lost wife. He tripped, rocks slipping under his boots, and threw up his spear barely in time to knock away Bulkezu's second thrust. Falling hard, he lost control of the spear, which rolled into the rocks. Bulkezu leaped forward with his own spear and planted himself before the prince, legs braced, hands sliding and then tightening on the haft as he spun the weapon a quarter circle and raised it for the final, downward thrust.

Time slowed, as it often did for Sanglant in battle, when the world around him shrank until only he and the enemy he fought remained in focus. He grabbed for his knife, but his belt had twisted in the fall and the sheath was caught beneath his hip.

Could a man cursed as he was survive a thrust through the heart?

Bulkezu shouted – a word, a battle cry, a curse – his scarred face lit with triumph as he laughed madly and tightened his hands to drive home the blow.

The arrow blossomed to the left center of his torso, in the heart.

Sanglant flung himself hard to the right over the rugged ground as Bulkezu toppled forward, a surprised look on his face. Even so, the prince's legs got tangled in the corpse, and as he struggled to free himself, the griffin cried shrilly behind him. A cloud of dust and a battering ram of sharp wind, the gust made by its wings, slowed him as he grabbed the spear out of Bulkezu's hands and ran forward, half blinded by the stinging particles of earth blown up into the air, the grit pummeling his face.

It was too late.

The griffin had launched itself into the air and as he watched helplessly, too far away even to cast his spear, the beast lifted Liath off the rock, her shoulders caught in its talons. She had a new arrow half drawn from her quiver, but as the griffin carried her upward, she lost hold of it and it fell to clatter in among the tumble of rocks where she had been standing.

Cursing, he watched the great creature fly heavily west-ward out over the plain as the sun crested the heights behind him. Dawn came and with it a warm breeze off the crags. He was sweating freely now from both exertion and the change in temperature. Mist rose out of the valley, shrouding the lowlands in gloom, and into this haze of white the griffin and Liath vanished.

'Blessing!' he shouted. 'Anna!'

There was no answer. An animal scrabbled through the rocks. A flock of early swifts circled over the nearest crag, swooping for insects.

Bulkezu's corpse lay among the stones. Wind whispered in the arrow's flighting where it protruded from his chest. Amazingly, there was no blood.

He called again, listened, but heard nothing except the wind moaning along the heights, the crackle of the dying fire, and the scratching of that damned animal. Briefly, it popped up into view – a rabbitlike creature with small ears. As abruptly it disappeared, bolting for cover. An owl ghosted into view and settled on a nearby rock. It appeared to study first him and then the burning nest before launching itself into the air again and flying away westward. He recognized the shaman's familiar. Through the owl's senses she saw all; perhaps she knew all. Yet she refused to aid him.

Swearing like a madman, he groped among the rocks until he found the arrow Liath had dropped wedged in a crevice. He wrenched it free and stood staring at it. He was staggered, his mind empty. The sight of Liath had utterly stunned him, who had always before acted swiftly and decisively in battle.

Slowly, in the way a sleeping man wakes up bewildered at his surroundings and takes in only one small detail at a time, he really looked carefully at the object he held in one hand. He had fletched this very arrow for her back in Verna. He recognized the goose feathers, taken from the same wing, and the horsehair from Resuelto used to secure the plume.

How could it be that after three years she still had this arrow? Had she lived all this time in no danger, a life of ease? Why was she here on the steppes? How had she got here?

Why had she never sought him out in all this time?

He wept without shame, as a man weeps when powerful emotion overcomes him. Anger, fear, loss, lust, duty, honor, frustration all tangled within his breast, a maze without end or beginning.

Grimly, he walked back to Bulkezu's body, but there was no sign on the dead man's boots, sleeves, or trousers of where he had trod other than fragments of steppe grass and slivers of rock and dust. He had no blood on his hands.

The arrow that had killed him was a mate to the one the prince held in his hand. He rolled Bulkezu up on his side and pushed the arrow through and out the back. Bits of flesh and heart clung to the point. Blood oozed sluggishly from the body, spilling over the rocks. The nest, still burning, crashed in on itself, wings of ash puffing up into the air to be dissipated by the wind.

A griffin's cry echoed along the crags. He stared out over the valley but saw no movement except the blanket of mist unraveling into drifts and patches and fingers of white. The brilliant sun rose higher into the sky, heralding a glorious new day.

4

She and her mate had fed well the day before. They had tracked a deer for two suns before bringing it to earth beside the headwater of the lesser flowing water. That the deer was unexpectedly plump despite the season had been the first good luck of their northerly journey. The flight from the wintering mountains had been hard because bitter cold still raged all along the route to the nesting grounds. Snow and rough winds lingered unseasonably late this year.

Late snow made her nervous and wakeful as she curled in last year's nest, beside her mate. The threads that wove the great nest of the world were disturbed by a shuddering touch so distant that it was barely tangible. She felt like a hapless fly settling down to rest on a dew-sparkled, innocent-seeming hair and feeling the brush of a spider's foot at the very edge of its complicated web. Maybe the late snow was part of that disturbance. Maybe the nesting season would be disrupted by these unseen forces. Maybe the hatchlings, if there were any, would suffer and die.

Even the Horse Tribe was on the move, gathered from the four winds into a confluence of herds. That by itself would make any creature uneasy.

Now, a sound that was not a sound, a touch that was not a touch, a spark that was not precisely anything seen with the eye, troubled the air and caught her attention. Because she was wakeful, she smelled the exhalation of shrouded fire that swept along the hidden ways, those thrumming lines of force that wove the great nest of the world into one piece. At once, sensing the faint convulsion, her mate lifted his head. He was a little smaller than she, of course, not as strong, but clever and resourceful and never quarrelsome, as many males could be.

'Go,' she told him in the language used by the griffins, not words precisely but comprised of small movements, scratching in the dirt, scents, and the rumbling pattern of her song. 'We are come north too early. Go south along the greater flowing water to the sunning stone. I will meet you there.'

It was a short journey, but it would get him out of the way and keep him safe. He took flight, and she waited a moment, marking his path as he beat southwest toward the winding trail of the water where it cut through the hunting grounds. Once he was well away, she flicked her tufted ears, flexing her claws, as she sought that chance-felt disarrangement in the normally calm surface of the great nest of the world. Was the shrouded fire already gone, or still wandering on Earth?

There!

She marked it as she would a banked fire smoldering beneath a snow-covered slope. It moved across the lowlands, where the blizzard smothered the landscape. From the crag's edge she launched herself out into the air and fought the gale winds as she plunged into the storm. The swirl and roar of the wind delighted her, although it proved a distraction from the hunt. She dove through the turbulence, banked, rose, and dove again above the valley floor and along the rim where the high crags thrust out of the plateau. Here the winds made merry, roiled by the meeting of lowlands and high crags, and it was sheer pleasure to fly.

By the time she recalled her purpose in hunting she had lost the trail. A hint of a warm front blowing in from the east clouded the exhalation of fire that had teased her. She felt it still, a constant but frail feather touch singing within the threads that bound the great nest of the world, but somehow it had moved up into the crags now, half swallowed by the deafness of stone. The cold wind still blew hard, but she tasted flower petals in the air.

Circling back to the nest with flurries of snow spinning around her head, she came upon the intruder unexpectedly. The man darted out from the nest and thrust for her exposed underbelly, but he had miscalculated his distance. She landed and lunged for him, yet he slipped past her, as agile and slippery as a weasel, into the shelter of the rocks. The momentum of her lunge slammed her into the nest, which shuddered, but held, as it had held for years under the onslaught of storms.

She screamed her rage, furious at losing him. His scent, curdling in the air, maddened her: he was a killer. A very few among humankind stalked in griffin country, murdering her kin. Of those few, most died at the hands of her cousins. This one bore the stink of success twice over.

Why was he here yet again? Was it not enough that he had slaughtered and profaned two of her kinfolk? Had he also desecrated the nest?

She ducked down and stuck her head inside the nest, the musty-cold familiarity tainted by the lingering stink of his killer's touch. No hatchling could thrive here, not now. By his presence alone he had poisoned the nest.

He had not been alone. A second creature had taken shelter within the cavernous nest. She looked, and was blinded.

The veil that shrouded aetherical fire had little utility at such short range. No ordinary earthly creature gave off such a refulgence. This daimone blazed with an aura of fire. She shrank back, fearful of its terrible power, and bent her head to show respect. Low in her throat she sang a song of courtesy and esteem, and a soft whimper of appeasement.

'Beware!' cried the fire daimone, leaping sideways.

A spear point stabbed into her hindquarters, and she whipped her tail to dislodge the point. The killer danced away with spear still in hand. He was laughing.

She pounced, but the light was dim. Humankind suffered and navigated the night better than she could. Stones rattled down as the daimone-creature bolted out of the nest and clambered up the untidy fall of rocks that rested uneasily to one side of the hollow.

The griffin circled the hollow, but the killer had vanished into the darkness. Above, braced on the rocks, the daimone-woman drew forth a bow and bent it, an arrow set against the string, ready to fly. The bow had an aetherical flicker, flashes of a blue aura clinging to its curved outline. The wood core was yew, but the virtue inherent in the bow derived from the strips of bone glued to the core: not ram's horn, but griffin bone. The essence of a dead griffin's stolen potency and a remnant of its numinous soul welled up from those strips to infuse the entire bow with an enchanted power, sealed and bound by the yew core. Yet no stench of 'murderer' permeated the daimone-woman. Although she wielded the bow, she had not tainted her hands killing any griffin.

Hadn't she cried out a warning? Didn't that make her an ally?

Wasn't her heart of fire beautiful?

All lay quiet except for the moaning wind, yet only a careless hatchling would consider the killer gone for good. She lowered her head to peer for markings in the dirt that would reveal his path, but could make out nothing. It was too dark to see. A step whispered on the ground, the merest scuff of a foot on dirt.

'Hai!' shouted the daimone-woman.

The griffin shied sideways just as the spear was thrust out of the shadows, but although she swiped at the dark shape brushing past, she could not see him well enough to strike him.

The daimone-woman cursed. Attuned to the great nest of the world and the threads that construct it, the griffin felt the creature waken the sleeping sparks of fire that resided in the sticks and branches and dried matter out of which she and her mate had built their nest over the years.

Fire woke.

The nest erupted into flame.

Exposed, the killer stood rooted in the light. The griffin lunged. He fled back into the night as an arrow chased him, clattering on the rocks. Heat from the fire melted the snow in the hollow and sent rivulets streaming down the slope that plummeted westward into the valley.

They waited for a long while as the nest burned. The daimone-woman readied a second arrow, her entire body tense as she scanned the darkness for any sign of movement.

Nothing.

The griffin stalked the perimeter of the hollow, tail lashing, but the night shadows blinded her, and while her sight was keen and her aetherical sensitivity vivid, her other senses were not particularly strong. She flexed her wings. Up on the rocks, the daimone-woman seemed to be flexing as well, as if she struggled to unfurl invisible wings of her own, but despite her straining she could not defeat the weight of earth that, in the world below, dampened and shrouded the power of aether. She seemed reluctant to leave the shelter of the rocks, yet at the same time immensely restless, eager to depart.

The griffin paced, seeking signs left by the killer, but she found nothing. She grew drowsy, being a creature of day, and finally settled down near the blazing nest, her thoughts drifting. They would have to rebuild the nest, but it had been despoiled in any case and at least now they could use this same nesting ground rather than seek a new one. Fire purified. The heat soothed her as snow spun slowly to earth, flakes dissolving in waves of heat and smoke.

Too late, she heard a shout. She heaved up as a figure

burst out of the night into the hollow. A second man lunged after the first. The two scuffled in the rocks, but the second man had already got the jump on the first; he knocked away the other's weapon and, with a shriek of triumph, went for the kill.

The daimone-woman shot.

Her arrow pierced the heart of the killer. He toppled, his corpse tangling with the body of the living one – another hunter, this one with magic woven through his bones and flesh.

The griffin saw no reason to wait for the living one to choose his course, not protected as he was by sorcery. The night put her at too much of a disadvantage. She launched herself upward and snatched the daimone-woman away to safety. She was no heavier than a mountain deer. Below, the second hunter shouted after them, but she banked down into the lowland mist and flew a steady course for the sunning stone.

If the hunter dared pursue her, she would be waiting.

Meanwhile, she had saved a friend from the depredations of barbaric humans. The daimone-woman remained wisely still, not fighting against the grip of the claws. From this height, a fall would kill. She flew higher, seeking the trail of the greater flowing water whose course would lead her to the sunning stone. A warm wind lifted off the crags. Were those few droplets of moisture rolling down her claws the last remnant of snow or the breath of the heavy lowland mist rising to greet her? What noise was it that the female made? If only they had speech in common, they might thank each other for the help they had given, each to the other, this cold night.

5

Sanglant appeared out of the darkness as though hunting her. The sight of him surprised her so profoundly that she didn't see her enemy's stealthy approach. What was Sanglant doing out in this God-forsaken wasteland? Had his presence drawn her as she fell back into the world below? And if he were here, then where was Blessing?

These thoughts distracted her. Too late, she saw the other man leap out of the darkness and strike down Sanglant.

She drew. She shot. Seeker of Hearts did not fail her. But before she could do more than grab another arrow, the griffin took flight. Talons fastened on her shoulders and hauled her upward. She kicked once, and it tightened its grip. Pain shot through her flesh. The arrow slipped out of her hands, and she almost lost the bow.

No aetherical flame could burn in the world below, or at least, she had not strength enough to call it forth. She tried again, concentrating on the unfurling glory of the flames, but nothing came. She was earth-bound, a thing of flesh, and all that was fire was shrouded and chained by the hand of the world below. Even if she fought free, she would plunge to her death because she could no longer fly. She was a prisoner, caged by the weight of the Earth.

She wept, as much from the pain of the griffin's grip as from frustration.

As the sun came up behind them, the mist burned away, revealing a broad valley lush with grass. A river sparkled as the sun's light lanced across it. Hills rose to the west, and behind them, eastward, lay the ridgeline of crags. The sight of this glorious landscape wiped away her tears.

How had the world come to be so beautiful?

Her mother, caged by a spell, had been given no choice but to remain on Earth and, in time, be subsumed into the earthly substance of the child she gestated in her aetherical womb.

Liath had chosen to return. She had wanted to return.

They followed the river's winding southwestern course and the griffin dipped little by little until they skimmed close above waters swollen by snowmelt. Rocks broke the current at erratic intervals; minnows flashed and scattered below the surface. A deer bolted from grassy cover along the verge and leaped into the high grass beyond. A golden eagle clutched a spar and, still and silent, watched them as they passed by. Her boots brushed the cold water. The gurgling noise of the river rose to her ears.

Just as they reached the bank, the griffin released her and she tumbled to the grassy slope, almost slipping back into the water because she only had one free hand. Catching herself, she dug a knee into the dirt and grabbed a fistful of exposed roots. She scrabbled upward and threw herself panting into the grass, shaken but not harmed. Her bow rested crookedly on the ground beside her. Above, the griffin shrieked, its cry ringing in the air.

She clambered to her feet, brushing off her knees, and drew her short sword for protection. Eventually she discovered a long rock half concealed by grass where the river curved around a headland. Climbing it gave her a vantage point to survey the land.

Grass rolled out in all directions, so high that along the horizon she saw only the humped curve of the western hills and the ragged heights of the crags looming over them to the east. The sun had just cleared the eastern ridgeline. A few last tendrils of mist coiled alongside the riverbank as if caught in the bushes fed by the river water.

The golden eagle winged downstream on the trail of the griffin, saw her, banked, and flew away westward. A moment later an owl glided into view and settled onto a hillock about an arrow's shot from her position. It was huge, with mottled plumage and bold ear tufts.

'I know you,' called Liath. 'What do you want? Where am I?'

It winked at her, big eyes closing and opening over amber irises and pinprick pupils. Then it flew away.

A low 'chuff' sounded behind her. Startled, she turned, slipping on the curve of the rock, and caught herself. Froze. A silvery-hued griffin stalked up behind her. It was smaller than the one she had saved from the steppe hunter's spear. Staring at this powerful and humbling beast, she wondered if she had been foolish to intervene.

Perhaps that warning she had called out – the words

surprised from her by the speed of the hunter's movement behind the griffin and her own distrust of his motives, the way he had abandoned her just as the griffin arrived – had set in motion the events that led her here, with a griffin a stone's toss away looking ready to gulp her down whole.

It settled back on its haunches and examined her with interest, as might a dog scrutinize a human whom it suspected of harboring treats.

Beyond it, far enough away that it appeared half the size of the second one, the first griffin paced, stamping down the tall grass to reveal a low stone outcropping set where the land dipped in a broad hollow like a shallow bowl. The river burbled past behind them. Out of sight, a bird called out with a frantic 'peewit' and, when she turned, she saw its tumbling flight over the pale expanse of grass.

Although she did not move, she felt herself falling. Tumbling.

Memory washed over her, triggered by the sight of that wide, flat stone, of the waving grass, and of the griffins, one darkly iron in hue and the other as lustrous as silver.

Through the reflection of the mirrored armor worn by the angel of war she had suffered a vision. She had endured a memory that was no memory but a horrible premonition of the time to come. Was it not said by the ancient philosophers that in the aether, far beyond the bounds of earth, the angels and their kinfolk can see both backward and forward in time?

If she remained still, her feathers would blend into the pale grass and only the keenest eye could observe her. Sanglant was intent on her mate, a silver-hued griffin asleep on the sunning stone. The prince's spear was poised as he prepared to strike. His eyes calculated his next move, as did hers. She would not let him kill her mate.

She pounced. He spun to meet her, but the shaft of his spear shattered as her weight bore him to the ground. His knee jabbed into her belly, and he tensed to fight her off, grabbing desperately for her throat, palms scored with cuts as he clawed for purchase at her iron feathers.

She struck at his vulnerable eyes.

Dead.

The female griffin had killed Sanglant.

Here, by this stone.

Here, with these griffins, through whose eyes she had seen the whole. She had saved the very creature who would strike the deathblow.

'Ai, God,' she whispered. If she killed them, then they could not kill Sanglant. She sheathed her sword and fumbled for her bow, set an arrow to the string, and bent it. But the bow swung wildly in her hand, tugging her off the mark. However many times she pulled it back to aim at the breast of the nearer beast, it jerked away. She could not draw on either griffin. Seeker of Hearts would not slay them. Was there some virtue in the griffins that made it impossible to kill them? Or was it the sorcerous heart of the bow that twisted away from inflicting harm on the beasts?

To fight them with only a short sword was absurd, and suicidal.

'Think, you fool,' she muttered as the silver-hued griffin watched her with an almost comical amiability, as if her struggle with the bow amused and interested it. It made no move to assault her.

They do not stalk me.

These fearsome creatures had not attacked her. The larger ducked its head as hounds do to invite play.

In the sphere of Jedu, she had experienced the unfolding scene through the eyes of the griffin. Now, she stood in that very place, alive and present. Sanglant lived; she had seen him herself. Therefore, he had not yet met his fate at the sunning stone. He would follow the griffin.

She pulled the hood of her cloak over her head to ward off the glare of the sun and, with her short sword resting over her thighs, settled down against the vantage stone to wait for him.

6

As the fog lifted, Sanglant clambered down the slopes of the crags. Sometimes he scraped his hands and once, badly, his knees, but the discomfort only fueled his anger and frustration and urgency. The griffin had taken Liath. Bulkezu was dead and could not be forced to tell him what he had done with Blessing. And now he must hunt griffins in the midst of a wilderness whose landscape was utterly unfamiliar to him, nothing like the fields and woodland and hills he had grown up in.

He called out as he went and took numerous side trips to investigate hollows and overhangs, but he found no sign of Blessing or Anna nor even of Bulkezu's passage. When he reached the valley, a little before midday, he struck out for the river.

His hearing and keen sense of taste and smell served him well; despite the bewildering lack of direction once he waded through the high grass, the scent of flowing water and the alteration in vegetation along the river as it wound through the valley guided him. Stunted fir trees grew along the banks, and it was in one of these copses that he halted late in the afternoon. He slid down the chalky slope that gave way where the ground formed a lip above the river itself, forming a bluff face not much more than an arm's length high but crumbling and dangerous because of soft earth and the erosion caused by the snow melt that had swelled the river's banks. As he crouched down with water swirling around his toes, he drank his fill and considered his situation. The cold water was like a slap as he splashed it on his face and washed the worst grime off his hands. He was light-headed; hunger gnawed in his belly, but he had no more food and only the river water for his thirst and, at least, a waterskin to carry it in. His daughter was missing and possibly dead. His wife—

A griffin screamed. The shrill call reverberated from upriver.

He waited, but the call did not come again.

Liath, at least, he had a hope of finding. He used his spear to lever himself up the bluff, grasped the tough roots of a straggling bush, and scrambled up to catch his breath in the copse of fir. The sky overhead remained gloriously clear, the hard blue dome of the heavens dappled with streaming clouds like dissolving gossamer wings. He ripped up a handful of clover and ate the fresh leaves, knowing that these might provide him with some strength. He picked what he could find for later, rolling them into a bundle tied up with stems of grass and tucking them away into a sleeve. The rest of the foliage was unknown to him, and he dared not experiment. He could not afford any retching sickness brought on by poisonous plants. Last, he checked his weapons – the knife and the spear, good iron.

He had survived a year of captivity by Bloodheart. He would survive this, and he would find his daughter whether she was alive or dead. Best not to consider that, if she were dead, he could never avenge her. He had not been granted the immense satisfaction of killing Bulkezu himself.

He hiked upstream along the river, watching the sky and the billow of the grass as the wind moved across it. The day's shadows drew long as the sun sank toward the golden curve of the western hills. The frosty sliver of the waxing moon crept above the dark crags. A harrier glided close to the river's bank. A startled grouse rustled away into a taller stand of grass. Following its path, he almost stepped on an abandoned nest, half of it scattered by winter's storms. He knelt, but it was too early for eggs.

Hunched low and unable to see over the grass, he heard the beating of wings and so kept still just as mice freeze when the shadow of a hawk passes overhead. A silver griffin – not the one that had carried off Liath – flew upriver not a stone's throw from his hiding place. He waited until the noise of its wings had faded, then followed its trail. By keeping to the tallest stands of grass, the occasional screen of shrubs or a narrow rank of such trees as could survive alongside the river, he kept out of sight. Where the river made a broad bend, the slope of the land rose on the riverside but fell gently away to the east to form a hollow.

The ground had been worn away to expose a wide, flat rock. The silver griffin lay draped along the warm stone, sunning itself with its head resting on its paws and its wings folded back over its body. Its tail flicked up and down, up and down, as though its bodily repose concealed a restless heart.

A scan of the landscape revealed only grass, the spearlike tops of a trio of lonesome fir trees, and a scattering of gray rock outcrops thrust up here and there throughout the grass. He heard no birdsong, only the sigh of the wind. He was alone with the griffin. He took a step, and a second, as he shifted his grip on the spear and edged sideways.

His keen hearing saved him – that, and the unwieldy mass of the second griffin.

The scrape of its footfall rang out like a scream in the silence. He spun, throwing up the spear to protect himself, but her body bore him to the ground and the spear shattered under the force of her swiping claw. She was immense. He jabbed his knee up into her belly. That beaked head slewed around to get a better look at him. He clawed desperately at her throat, but each time he closed his hand, each time he scrabbled for purchase at her neck as he tried to squirm away out from under her, her feathers cut him. Blood streamed from his hands from a score of fine incisions. She reared back her head and struck.

He jerked sideways, but not far enough. Pain ripped through his chest and his vision hazed. His bleeding hands flexed impotently as they sought any kind of weapon to grip, but their feeble grasp closed on nothing, only air, and even that weak movement sent waves of pain flooding through his body until he could neither think nor move. He could not even see. Agony blinded him. He could only wait for the deathblow.

He could only wait.

A flash of heat and fire exploded around him. Had the griffin struck again? Was this the pain of dying? Or was he already dead, ascending through the spheres toward the cold bright eternity of the Chamber of Light?

I don't want to die.

I'm not ready.

Pain, and this billowing heat that washed over him in unending waves, tore away his thoughts.

The shadow of the griffin moved off him. The sun's blazing light scalded his face and made him blink.

Liath stood over him, golden-brown hair fallen all untidy over her shoulders. It needed combing. He loved to comb her hair. That steady stroke in the lush thickness of her hair was one of the few things that could soothe the restlessness that ate at him.

'Pray God I am not too late,' the vision of Liath said, although she could not possibly be kneeling beside him. She had abandoned him four years ago, left him and the child without a word. He had a lot of things to say to her, hoarded up over the months, some of them festering and rancid and others painful and sweet.

An actual physical body blocked the stabbing of light that tormented him. A touch brushed his brow.

'Sanglant, I pray you, answer me if you can.'

Her lips touched his parted mouth. It was like water to a parched man, giving him strength for the fight ahead.

Never let it be said that he did not fight until his last breath.

'You will never kill me,' he said to Bloodheart. Some days, those were the only words he remembered how to say.

'He lives.' A fire burned behind her, or perhaps it was the setting sun streaming golden light across grass troubled by the wind. A knife flashed, but he could not struggle against the killing blow. He was paralyzed, staring at the knife in her hand. She cut away his tunic from his torso and bared his flesh to the air. So much color leached from her face that she looked gray when she saw what lay beneath the cloth.

'I was too slow,' she said. 'Too late.'

A few solitary raindrops splashed on his cheek, although he saw no clouds in the darkening expanse above. Nearby, a griffin shrieked its chilling call.

'Beware,' he whispered, trying to warn his benefactor, who had taken Liath's shape. Pain made him hallucinate. 'The griffin stalks. Her feathers . . .'

'Hush,' she said. 'Rest.'

'Griffin feathers cut the threads of magic.'

She sat back, surprised, her expression an odd combination of fear and startled, joyous revelation.

'Griffin feathers cut the threads of magic!' she repeated. Blue fire sparked in her eyes, the wink of fire caught and contained in her deepest heart. That spark blinded him, sent him falling and spinning although he lay supine on the ground.

He has wings, or must have, because he rises above the earth and above his body, above the grass like a dragon launching itself into flight, a little slowly, somewhat ponderous, but determined and powerful. He sees a man lying on the ground, his torso horribly slashed. His dragon's vision is so keen that he can actually see the heart beating in that torn cavity, pulsing and darkly red. Blood spills over shoulder and arm, staining the cloth of his tunic, staining the grass and the soil. A beautiful woman kneels beside the body. Although she looks exactly as Liath looked three years before, she must be a witch able to conceal herself in the form of another. Yet she speaks with Liath's voice and moves with Liath's nervous grace and stares up defiantly as an owl glides into view and comes to rest a body's length from the two humans.

Behind, griffins prowl like sentries, circling at a distance just beyond a scorching ring of fire now burning down to ash. The griffins are such magnificent creatures that his attention wanders away from the woman and man and the peculiar circle of dying flame. The larger griffin is darker in color, and its wing feathers boast the gleam of good iron. The other has a more silver cast and a smaller stature, but its feathers look just as wickedly sharp. The feathers glint where the light of the setting sun catches in them. As the silver one turns to pace back toward the sunning stone, it flexes its wings and several loose feathers shake free as a bird might molt. They do not precisely drift on the wind toward the ground as would a common bird feather, but neither are they as heavy as iron, and so fall straight down as would a sword or knife. A living griffin would provide an endless although not plentiful supply of its feathers while a dead one provides one set of feathers only. One could husband griffins as a farmer husbands geese, he supposes as he, too, drifts on the wind, thoughts shredding into insubstantial bits.

'I need help,' says the woman to the owl, although it is strange to think of a person talking to an owl, who is after all only a dumb animal. 'I have no power against such a wound. I am helpless. I pray you, aid me now, if you can.'

A hand jostled him. The pain jolted him into awareness, and for a moment he was sorry that he was looking out of his own eyes up at the woman he loved most in the whole world.

'Liath?' he whispered.

Tears streaked her face. 'My love,' she said.

Pain swallowed him, and the world went away.

XVII
THE BROKEN THREAD

1

At the end of the second day's journey their party took shelter with a minor lordling on a minor estate that barely had room for their entire company to sleep in the hall and stables. Lord Arno greeted them by name; the clerics had stopped this way traveling north toward Herford. Although the road north and a rutted track leading west remained clear, a barricade made up of handcarts, a wagon, and felled logs had been thrown up across the road where it continued southward. The barrier was manned by a dozen field hands armed with staffs sharpened to a point, a single metal-tipped spear, shovels, and scythes.

Over a meager supper of tart cider, roasted chicken, and spring greens, the lady of the house took it upon herself to warn them.

'Go not down the southern road, Your Excellencies.' She looked exhausted, face pale, eyes dark with strain, and she rested trembling hands on her pregnant belly as she glanced at her husband, who was, it transpired, lame from a wound taken in the battle of the guivre, fought near Kassel.

'The western road will serve you better,' the lame man

added. 'You will not ride more than ten days out of your way. It is safer.' As he spoke, he gripped the arms of his chair so hard that his knuckles turned white.

'I must turn west, as I have already suffered unreasonable delay,' said Brother Severus, 'but their road lies south to Darre.'

'I pray you, do not go that way, Your Excellency. All the farms are blighted with the murrain. We've heard that not one farm in ten has sheep, cattle, or pigs left to them. We turned back two families yesterday. They were trying to escape north with their flocks. We pray morning, noon, and night that our own herd has not caught the contagion.'

'Yet you let us pass these six days past. I saw no barricade then.'

'The blight had not come so far north, Your Excellency.' The lord called for more cider and apologized for the fourth time that there was no more wine to be had. The long hall in which they feasted was only scarcely longer and wider than Aunt Bel's house in Osna village. Although the floor was swept clean, the tapestries on the wall had a shabby look about them and all the children, huddled under the eaves on straw mattresses, had runny noses. 'We only blocked the road three days past. We've heard rumors that bandits have come into the countryside as well. We've heard dreadful stories—'

'Speak no more of it,' said Severus, turning back to his food. He examined the gamy chicken with a prim frown. 'My companions will continue south. God protect the righteous.'

Husband and wife glanced at each other, but there was nothing they could do. Simple country lords could no more change the chosen path of the skopos' own clerics than they could prevent the tide from coming in.

Brother Ildoin was the youngest of Severus' clerics, a slight young man with a blemished face, an amiable if often inattentive expression, and two fingers on his left hand permanently twisted from a childhood accident. He had not yet had every last drop of compassion wrung out of his soul, although it certainly seemed to Alain that Severus had burned any such wasteful and inconvenient sentiments out of his own heart.

'We have no livestock with us,' Ildoin said to the lady, 'only horses. Horses do not take up the contagion, so you are safe from us as will be those we seek shelter with in the days to come.'

With that their hosts had to be content.

In the morning Severus took a dozen men as attendants and rode west, leaving his factor, by name of Arcod, Brother Ildoin, and ten rough-looking clerics who seemed as much at ease with a spear as with a holy book to escort Alain on the southerly route.

'Where is Brother Severus going?' Alain asked Ildoin as they left the besieged manor house behind. 'I thought he meant to return to Darre, too.'

Ildoin had a way of lifting his chin, like a man recoiling from a sharp blow, when he was surprised by any comment or unexpected sight. 'Brother Severus is a great and holy man, one of the intimate counselors of the skopos herself, may she remain hale and hearty and live many long years under God's protection. We do not question him! However, he is a *powerful* man in more ways than that of intrigue and wise counsel—'

'Brother Ildoin!' Arcod drew up beside them. 'Idle chatter is a breeding ground for the Enemy's maggots. We will ride in silence, or sing Godly hymns, if you please.'

Alain was content to ride in silence. They made a peaceable caravan with the pack mules ambling along in the middle of their group and the hounds padding alertly to either side of him. It was a lovely spring day, the sky strewn with broken clouds. At first, birdsong accompanied them and a skeane of geese honked past above. But as the morning passed, Alain noticed that the joyous noise gave way to an uneasy hush. Midmorning they passed an abandoned hamlet, where a scatter of huts lay empty beside the road. A thread of smoke drifted heavenward a short distance off the road; otherwise there was no sign of life.

'Should we investigate?' Alain asked.

'No,' said Arcod. 'It's none of our business. Our business is to take you to the skopos.'

They hadn't gone much farther through open woodland before a second clearing opened before them. Judging by the well-thatched longhouse, fenced-in garden plot, rubbish pit, and three pit houses, a prosperous farming family had once lived here. Stakes lined the roadside, four posts staggered on either side of the track, set there as a warning. On each stake a sheep's skull was affixed, glaringly white against the lush green eruption of spring growth all around. Some of the skulls had a bit of flesh left, but most had been picked clean by carrion crows still flocking among the buildings. Here, too, they saw no movement, heard no welcoming hails, but the porch of the longhouse was swept clean as though its occupants had only recently departed.

The clouds drew in darkly. A chill wind blew up from the south as a mist began to fall, trailing off at intervals only to spatter down once again, inconstant and irritating.

'Another one!' shouted the cleric riding at the front of their party. He'd been chosen for this duty because he could speak Wendish. 'Ho! Well met! Are there any folk living here?'

As they rode into a new clearing, they saw a scattering of huts, an empty chicken coop, a small roofed paddock, a trough half full of water, and an abandoned plow sledge. Four stakes pounded into the ground at the four corners of the paddock bore animal skulls, one sheep, two horned cattle, and something that looked remarkably like a dog with a patch of skin and pale fur hanging from the muzzle. Dried plants had been woven into the eye sockets, and a tangle of tiny carved wooden figures dangled down from the gaping jaw on a leather strip.

Rage barked once. Sorrow whined.

'Some witch has sullied her hands with magic workings and amulets,' said Arcod. 'No wonder they were struck down by God's anger.'

'Do you think so?' asked Alain. 'Perhaps they were only trying to protect themselves.'

'Then they should have called for a deacon or a frater, not this unholy weaving and binding.'

Their party did not tarry but rode past nervously. There was not even a carrion crow in sight. Alain heard no birds at all. Once the clearing lay behind them, Ildoin looked back at Arcod, who was riding at the back of the group, before judging it safe to speak to Alain.

'I'm glad your hounds are with us. It fair gives me the creeps, it's so dead and quiet here. I wonder where all the farming folk have gone.'

'Fled, most like,' said Alain. 'Gone to find kinfolk who will take them in. If anyone will take them in. Didn't you pass this way just a fortnight ago?'

'In rain and wind,' agreed Ildoin, scratching his stubbly chin. Like the other clerics, he was letting his beard grow rather than struggle to keep it shaven on the march. 'We were housed and fed hospitably enough. By Vespers we should come to a little river where there's a village. They put us up for one night. When we came north, the murrain hadn't reached them, although we brought them rumor of it from what we'd seen on our journey south of the river.'

'I wonder where the birds have flown,' said Alain, 'and what they're so afraid of that they've stopped singing.'

The village had a tiny wood church, a mill, and six houses in addition to the dock where a ferryboat was tied up, but it had no people and not even dogs or chickens. Every door had a wreath of plants and carved amulets hanging above the threshold, but these protective measures had not spared the inhabitants. There was no sign of any living thing.

They hurried through the commons and down to the riverside. The hounds were skittish, sniffing the air as though they sensed danger but could not place its locus. The sturdy ferry rope should have ridden taut between the deeply driven posts on either side of the narrow river, but it had been cut. The near end flapped in the current, dancing in water running high with spring rain and distant snow melt. Alain dismounted and drew the cut line up to shore. The end had frayed with the beating it had taken in the river, leaving a sodden mass of splitting rope in his hands. To cross the river they would have to row, or swim. He examined the silent village while Arcod sent two pairs of men to reconnoiter. The hounds would not sit.

Rage growled low in her throat. Sorrow whined nervously.

'There's a trench dug out there.' Ildoin pointed to a patch-work of fields beyond the outermost house. 'It looks fresh.'

'Mayhap there's a shovel to be found—' said Alain.

'No need to probe so closely,' said Arcod. 'You and I and the lad will go. The rest can stay here to watch over the horses.'

Leaving the other clerics in the road, Alain, Ildoin, and Arcod walked out across four unplowed fields laid down in long strips, to the fifth field, which was still stubbled with the remains of last autumn's wheat. The smell hit before they got close enough to see what the long mound of fresh dirt concealed. The stench of burned flesh was made worse by the stink of putrefaction. Ildoin gagged as all color washed out of his face. Arcod covered his nose with the tip of his sleeve.

'Rage! Come!' Alain commanded, but she sat down at the edge of the field and whined, head cocked in the direction of the men waiting by the horses.

'It *is* the murrain,' said Arcod as Sorrow got the top layer of dirt dug away. The smell of burned flesh billowed up from the trench. Sorrow nosed among the tangled, scorched legs of sheep with strips of skin still hanging from bone. The poor sick creatures had been burned in haste and buried before the job was properly finished. But the hound scratched, seeking another scent that teased and eluded him. As the dirt spilled down on either side, maggots swarmed out of the earth, a writhing mass of them that scattered to safety and vanished back into the disturbed earth. At the sight of them, Ildoin staggered back, fell to his knees, and vomited onto the ground.

Sorrow uncovered a boot. It still had a foot in it. Sorrow nosed at it, then gripped the leather toe in his teeth and threw it sideways. It tumbled over to reveal a gaping putrid wound where the foot had been hacked off at the ankle. Bile churned in Alain's stomach, but he forced himself to probe for the rest of the body. No person deserved to be thrown out like rubbish.

'God help us,' said Arcod, looking stricken and white. He hung back, unwilling to get any closer.

'I can dig better if you would give me your staff,' said

Alain. 'I don't really want to dig for the rest of the corpse with my bare hands.'

Arcod seemed not to have heard him. 'What manner of brute chops up a man as if he were a cow?' He was shaking so hard that his death grip on the staff was the only thing keeping him upright.

Ildoin was still retching, hands gripped over his stomach as he moaned. He stared at the mutilated foot. 'Oh, God.'

Rage barked and with a nasty growl padded back toward the village before stopping short, hackles raised.

Alain rose, suddenly alert. 'I pray you, Brother Arcod. Such brutes might still be lurking nearby. We should leave this place. Now.'

'Now!'

The strange voice came from a distance, muffled but imperative.

'Who calls?' Arcod started around to stare back toward the village, raising his staff.

Too late.

An arrow buried its point in the neck of one of the clerics waiting on the road. He fell backward in a graceful curve that bent, and bent, time drawn out so that one breath seemed to hold for an hour or a year, and then his body collapsed all at once to hit the ground limp and dead. The other men shouted and grabbed for staves and short swords, but the bandits had the advantage of surprise and cover.

The whistle of arrows made a horrifying accompaniment to one who stood so far away as a helpless witness to the massacre. It happened so fast. A second man went down as he turned to see what the shouting was about. A third tried to mount but had five arrows in his back before he settled into the saddle. Two clerics ducked behind horses and tugged on the reins, running toward the river, but a swarm of men, a score at least, tumbled out of the mill and the church to pursue them. Others took aim from the tower and the upper story of the mill.

A pair of bandits standing on the road gestured toward the three men stranded out by the incriminating trench.

'Where are the rest of our brothers?' gasped Ildoin. 'We heard no cry of alarm.'

'They're dead or captured.' Alain ripped the staff out of Arcod's hands, who stood like a fish out of water, mouth agape, stunned. 'Take Brother Ildoin and run for the trees. Get back to the manor. Alert the lord, let him send out men at arms—'

Arcod did not move. Six men brandishing weapons headed at a trot toward Alain and his companions.

'Go! Someone must live to tell the tale! Go!'

'What of you, Brother Alain?'

'I'll try to give you time to escape.'

Still, Arcod hesitated.

Alain shoved him toward the trees. 'Go!'

One staggering step led to another, and a third. Arcod caught Ildoin's sleeve and yanked him up.

'Run, Brother!' he wept. 'Run!'

They tripped and stumbled over the trench and sprinted across the fields toward the woods. Alain hadn't the luxury to watch them go, to make sure they reached the woodland and weren't killed by some other lurking bandits. He had to face the enemy.

One of the clerics made it out onto the dock before being cut down. Miraculously, only one of the horses was injured. Now, having won the valuable mounts and pack animals, the company of bandits seemed to lose their sense of purpose. One man, swathed in a cloak, kept bending down over the fresh corpses with a flask in his hand. The others milled about stripping the bodies and emptying the saddlebags – except for the six men who loped across the fields toward Alain.

He steadied the staff in both hands and whistled the hounds up next to him. Against archery, the hounds would perish. But he knew they would never abandon him, and after all this time he doubted they would outlive him. It was strange to feel so calm.

He had to give the others enough of a head start.

'Down.' Whining, Rage and Sorrow lay down on either side of him. 'I pray you, Lord of Mercy, Lady of Justice, let my comrades escape.'

He lifted the staff and held it horizontally above his head, gripping the haft with both hands, to show he meant no threat to them. The bandits slowed, and two put arrows to the strings of their bows, but he could see that besides these two bows the men carried the crudest of weapons – staffs sharpened to a point at one end, spears tipped with stone blades.

'Well met, brothers!' he cried. 'Thank the Lord and Lady that you have rescued me from these prating clerics!'

He took two steps forward before giving the hounds a second command. 'Stay.'

He kept walking.

The six men stopped, four of them bunched and the other two – with the bows – hanging to either side as flankers.

'I pray you will let me join your brotherhood,' Alain continued as he approached them, staff still held above his head, his pace measured and his voice clear. 'I have longed to escape my life of servitude to the church.'

'Come no closer!'

He could not tell which spoke, although at this distance their ragged garb and pinched faces were easily visible. One – no more than a lad by the look of his skinny legs and narrow hips – ran back to the village while the others kept weapons raised.

'Come no closer,' repeated the leader among them, a dark-haired man wearing a torn tunic, filthy leggings, and bearing the scars of shackles on his wrists. He had warts on his nose. 'Wait there, or we'll shoot you.'

'Truly, you're right to trust no man. It's a hard world, as I've seen myself. It seems that those who have, hoard to themselves, and the rest of us are left to fight over the bones.'

Some of the men nodded in agreement; the leader kicked the one nearest him. 'Stop that, you dolt. We'll see what Father Benignus has to say. He is the master of life and death.'

Said so flatly, in the tone of a man weary beyond measure who has seen such things that he no longer doubts the power of evil, the statement made Alain shiver. There was about these men a choking miasma that could not be seen or heard or smelled but only *felt*, and not only because they had blood on their hands from their most recent killing.

'Is he so?' Alain knew he had to stay calm in order to convince them that he was a fugitive eager to join their company. 'I'm always happy to make the acquaintance of a man with power.'

'Here he comes,' said the leader. He scratched at his nose, and then his fingers found other work tugging at his straggly beard and twining the wispy hair between his fingers. Father Benignus rode a fine mare fitted out with well-made bridle and saddle but his clothing was no richer than that worn by his band of cutthroats except for the handsome leather gloves that concealed his hands and a gray cloak tied around his shoulders. His cleric's robe, cut away for riding, was stained with blood and other, unidentifiable substances, the long sleeves were frayed, and the hem was ragged. The boots on his feet had the scuffs and discoloration of ill use or, perhaps, leather buried and disinterred after too many days beneath the dirt. He wore a broad-brimmed hat that shaded his face although it wasn't sunny enough to warrant such a covering. A gauzy veil, like that worn by beekeepers, had been sewn to the curve of the brim, and its filmy drape made it impossible for Alain see his face.

He pulled up but did not dismount as the leader spoke to him in a voice too low for Alain to hear. This mysterious creature might have him struck down with a single word, yet Alain faced him without any sense of fear although certainly a sickly air clung to Father Benignus rather like a halo reversed that emanates with the stink of evil rather than goodness. He tossed the staff to the ground. Behind him, the hounds did not move, awaiting his command.

'Your face is familiar to me,' said Father Benignus finally, addressing Alain. His voice was a soft, slurred tenor. 'What is your name? Where are you from?'

'I am called Alain. I come from Osna village, a free town under the protection of the counts of Lavas.'

'The hounds,' said Benignus. The twitch of his shoulders suggested surprised recognition. As he raised his head to examine Rage and Sorrow, Alain caught a glimpse of a pale, mottled face, but as quickly the veil slipped back into place. 'I have seen those hounds before in the company of a lad who was a prisoner of Biscop Antonia. He was a companion to the heretic frater who was called Brother Agius. Are you that boy?'

'I am that one.'

Although two men had arrows trained on him, his hands were steady. If he died, he would cross to the Other Side where Adica was waiting for him there where the meadow flowers bloom. But his mantle of calm was beginning to burn away under the itch of curiosity.

'What are you, Father Benignus? How is it that our paths have crossed before?'

'You will not recognize me. I was cursed, used ill by those powerful enough to discard me when I was of no more use to them. Their indifference and greed scarred me. But I have not forgotten what they taught me. Thus you find me here.' He gestured toward the dead village, the silent woodland, the fresh trench, and the men who, done with their scavenging, made ready to ride with their newfound gains. 'I journey now in better and more honest company than I found myself with before among the most noble courtiers and holy church-folk, back when I believed that the Lord and Lady would protect me from evil. Bartholomew says you were a prisoner of these clerics. Is that true?'

Alain smiled. 'If it were not true, would I say so now? You have me at your mercy.'

The noise the other man made was difficult to interpret, especially since Alain could not see his expression.

'Bring him,' said Father Benignus to Bartholomew. 'But kill him, and the hounds, if he tries to escape.'

2

The wound ought to have killed him, but he still breathed. His chest rose and fell in a shallow, erratic rhythm. In that first awful moment she had actually been able to see shattered ribs and the dark fist of his heart pulsing, but already the jagged tear filmed over as the body knit itself together. The wound was so raw and so deep that she feared touching it would only break it open, but she cut strips from his tunic in any case to make a pad and lightly cover the gash. She washed around the wound with river water, but the cold shock did not revive him.

Finally, she risked stepping away to gather sticks and rushes from the brush that grew alongside the river. She hadn't got far when she heard the heavy tread of one of the griffins, and she dashed back to Sanglant just in time to find the female griffin stalking close, lifting a claw to rend his helpless body in two. She leaped between them, raising her sword.

'Mine!' she cried. 'He is mine! Don't touch him!'

The griffin huffed in surprise and retreated. Two feathers shook loose from its wings as it backed away, and these she grabbed and tucked into her quiver. The fire she had first called hadn't entirely died away. Bits of burned grass spun in the air. A fine ash settled on her clothing and hair before the last of it was dissipated by the wind.

At last her hands stopped shaking enough that she could bind rushes and grass and twigs into little torches. After she laid a sixth torch beside her, she seated herself next to Sanglant. The griffins prowled at the edge of her vision.

When she concentrated, emptying her mind of all that distracted it – and that was quite a bit – she could believe that she saw the glamour of the spell woven into his flesh and blood and bones. His mother had bound a great working into his body to protect him from harm and to grant him unnatural powers of healing. Now, as in the past, he would suffer agony because of it, but he would also, probably, survive as he had survived a half dozen times before from fatal wounds taken in battle. In the realm of Jedu she had lived through death a dozen times, dealt at his hands. She had seen him struck down.

Yet this was not the reunion she had expected.

The sun set. The sky turned red-orange and darkened to

a hazy purple before the first stars appeared with the waxing quarter moon already near the zenith. A few clouds concealed patches of the sky, but she could see most of the span of the heavens, the most beautiful sight in all of creation. Had it only been seven or eight days since she had left Verna, torn away by her kinfolk? Yet what she had seen of the landscape surrounding her tallied in no way with any place she had ever visited – and she had traveled more widely than most: Aosta, Kartiako, Aquila, Salia, Varre, and Wendar. According to her father's lore, broad grasslands lay east beyond the border counties, many months' ride into the wilderness. Sanglant could not possibly have traveled so far in seven or eight days.

She settled back with a hand resting lightly on his throat to track the beating of his heart and so that she might, now and again, brush her fingers over his beloved lips.

The brilliance of the night sky staggered her. The River of Souls streamed across the western quadrant of the sky, dense with light. How could she have forgotten this stunning beauty? The sight of it never failed to quiet her soul.

Bright Somorhas hung low on the western horizon but sank quickly after the sun, leaving fiery Seirios as the first star that stayed visible as dusk deepened to night. She searched the heavens for clues.

It was spring, certainly, with the Dragon rearing up in the east and the Child lying down to sleep in the west. Aturna stood in the Lion, close to zenith, the only other wandering star visible to her, but there were many of the heavens' most brilliant stars fixed up in the sky: the yellowish glare of the Guivre's Eye; the bright head of the elder Sister; the bluish Eye of the Dragon; Rijil, the Hunter's brightly-shod foot, and Vulneris, the red wound on his shoulder.

She brushed her hand over Sanglant's shoulder and brought her fingers to her lips, tasting the blood. He lay frighteningly silent, not even murmuring as he was wont to do in sleep. Blood oozed but not with that same horrible gush she had seen when she first reached him.

Her helplessness wore at her as a constant ache, but she possessed no healing magic. She carried no cache of herbs for a poultice. She was not strong enough to carry him and had no horse. In the morning, when she could see, she would attempt to build a sledge to drag him.

Where could she take him?

The stars continued on their appointed rounds as the night spun onward. Where was she? *When* was she?

The Sapphire and the Diamond skated low along the northern horizon, and in the south, although the Bow and Arrow were visible, the Huntress who wielded them was not. She was about as far north as she had been in Wendar and likely a little farther south than Heart's Rest. North and south were easy to calculate because of the altitude of the individual stars.

She sat with her mortally wounded husband in the midst of a vast wilderness, guarded by griffins, as the night wind played in her hair and whispered through the grass. The moon sank westward, followed by Aturna, the Red Mage. New constellations rose and with them the planets Jedu and Mok. The Angel of War gleamed balefully in the Serpent while the Empress of Bounty journeyed with the Unicorn.

Where had Mok stood, when last Liath walked on Earth?

It hadn't been so long ago, after all, only seven or eight days, that she had last stared up at the glorious sky.

She searched into her city of memory, up through the seven gates that corresponded to the seven spheres, until she reached the crown of the hill where lay the observatory. Here, in nooks and crannies, she stored all her observations, marked with figures and images so she could recall each detail.

Mok's path was easy to find and to recall, a golden alcove in which a robust woman presided from a throne, surrounded by cornucopia, sheaves of wheat, fatted calves and, on the domed ceiling of the alcove, sigils representing each of the Houses of the Night. Seven or eight or ten days ago, in Verna, she had marked the constellation of the Dragon with a tiny shining sheaf of wheat to indicate Mok's progress.

Because Mok took about one year to travel through each House, that meant that the planet had in the intervening time journeyed through the Scales, the Serpent, and the Archer before reaching the Unicorn, spending about one year in each.

Four years.

Could she have been gone so long?

The heavens could not lie because, as the blessed Daisan had written, they had no liberty to govern themselves. Subject to the Lord and Lady's immutable laws, they did what they were ordered to do and nothing else.

Four years, give or take six months. Would her daughter recognize her? Did Blessing even remember that she had a mother?

A worse thought intruded, as rot insinuates itself beneath the clean surface of a house, weakening the foundations and posts: Had Sanglant thought her dead, and remarried?

I have been gone too long.

In a year and a half at most, Mok would travel through the Unicorn and the Healer and touch the far boundary of the Healer.

When Erekes walks backward. When Bright Somorhas, walking backward, reenters the Serpent. When Jedu and Aturna enter the House of the Dragon. When Mok, retracing her steps, poises on the cusp between the Healer and the Penitent. On this same day, when the Crown of Stars crowns the heavens.

On that day, in less than eighteen months, when the Crown of Stars crowned the heavens, the way would be open for Anne to weave a great spell to cast the Aoi land back out into the aether, to create a second cataclysm. Unless Liath intervened.

Stopping Anne came before any other consideration. Even her husband's life. Even her own happiness.

'I will not leave you again,' she whispered, but Sanglant could not hear her.

At dawn, Sanglant stirred without opening his eyes or seeming aware of his surroundings. He was hot to the touch but not gray with impending death. As the promise of the sun brightened the eastern sky, limning the crags with its pale glow, the griffins sank down on the sunning stone. She knew they were awake because of the way their lively tails flicked up and down.

She rose to stretch out her limbs, but at the movement the

larger griffin startled up, staring eastward past the river. The second followed her lead. Liath, too, turned.

She had only seen centaurs in her dreams, majestic creatures more wild than civilized but immensely powerful and full of magic. There were not many of them – not more than a dozen – but as they approached, she stared in amazement and only belatedly thought to free an arrow from the quiver and draw her bow.

After marking her position, they turned downriver and disappeared from view. A little later she heard the rumble of hooves and saw them clearly in the light of the new sun spreading gold across the grass. The griffins padded restlessly back and forth on the sunning stone as though eager to retreat but unwilling to desert her.

How had she won their loyalty? She could not guess.

Respectful of the drawn bow she held, the herd came to a halt out of range of arrow shot. They were all female; they wore no garments, only paint to decorate their torsos, and the shapely curve of their woman-bodies was impossible to miss. Two of the centaurs hauled a wagon between them, bar and tongue fashioned so that they might draw it without using their hands.

A silver-gray centaur trotted forward alone, bearing no weapon except a quiver of arrows slung across her back. It was a brave thing to do, considering the proximity of the griffins. She held no strung bow in her hands as she halted at the edge of the burned area. She had no way to defend herself if they sprang.

Now that she was closer, Liath realized that she was not gray as much as ancient, her coat faded because of her immense age as a crone's black hair turns to silver. Green-and-gold stripes half covered the horn-colored skin of her woman's body. Her eyes bore an inhuman luminosity. There was, too, something oddly familiar about her, a tugging sense of connection, as though they had met before.

One of the griffins gave a shrill cry as an owl skimmed in over the river. The centaur lifted an arm to receive the bird on a forearm sheathed in leather.

Liath lowered her bow.

'Well met,' she called in Wendish, not sure if the other one could understand her language, 'if you are friend to us. I am called Liathano in the speech of humankind. I pray you, we are in grave need of your help if you are willing to give it.'

The centaur approached with stately dignity across the burned out area. Ash puffed where she placed her hooves. Once she had to sidestep to avoid a hot spot, not yet burned out.

'You are Liathano,' she said. 'Known as Bright One.'

'How do you know me?'

'I walk within the paths marked out by the burning stone, which is the gateway between the worlds. I cannot ascend into the spheres because I cannot leave Earth, but I have seen the traces of your passage. I have glimpsed you. I know your name, because it is the same as my own.'

'I have an Arethousan name,' protested Liath. 'How can our names be the same?'

A spark flared in the city of memory, recalling to her mind memories she had seen in the heart of the burning stone when, for an instant, she could see time, past, present, and future as a single vast landscape stretching out on all sides.

A centaur woman parts the reeds at the shore of a shallow lake. Her coat has the dense shimmer of the night sky, and her black woman's hair falls past her waist. A coarse, pale mane, the only contrast to her black coat, runs down her spine, braided with beads and the bones of mice.

'Look! she cries. 'See what we wrought!'

She looses an arrow.

'Li'at'dano!' Words stuck as though caught by thorns.

Years ago, a humble frater by name of Bernard had named his daughter after an ancient centaur shaman written of in the chronicles of the Arethousans, who had witnessed and survived the Bwr attack on the Dariyan Empire. Some called her undying. All called her powerful beyond human ken.

'"Liathano,"' she repeated stupidly, in the softened consonants of the western tongue. It was too difficult to believe and yet it stood smack in front of her. 'How can you still be alive?'

The centaur lifted her arm to release the owl, which flew away to find a resting place in the shrubs along the river's bank.

'I am not human, nor even half human, as you are. We are another kind entirely, born out of the world before humankind walked here. That is why your people fear us, and hunt us, and war against us, all except the Kerayit tribe, whom we nurture as our daughters. I am not like you, Bright One.'

'No. You are not.'

She was legend made flesh. It was impossible that any creature might live so long, generations upon generations, yet she knew in the core of her, the heart of fire that had once belonged to her mother, that it was true.

'You made the cataclysm,' Liath said.

'I do not possess the power of working and binding.'

'You taught the seven who wove it.'

'It is true that I encouraged those who devised and wove the great spell. None of us understood what we would unleash. I regret what I did.'

'Do you regret it enough that you would be willing to stand aside and see your old enemies return to the world below? The land where the Ashioi dwell was torn from Earth. That you know. I have set foot in the exiled land. It is returning to the place it came from. And it should. It must. I came back to stop the Seven Sleepers. They wish to weave a second spell atop the first and cast the Ashioi back into the aether. If you intend to aid them, or hinder me, then we are enemies.'

The old shaman indicated Sanglant, whose eyes had not opened. He showed no sign of consciousness; he wasn't aware the centaurs had arrived or that this conversation was taking place. 'Is it not rash to provoke me when I have the means to save this man? You may be throwing away his life.'

Because he lay so still, it was easy to admire the handsome lines of his face and the clean lines of his limbs. He had not lost any of his strength or beauty. He did not look as though four years had passed although perhaps there were wrinkles at the corners of his eyes, the product of worry and strain. Those hands had stroked her once; those lips had kissed her in a most satisfactory manner, and would again, she prayed.

He was only one man. Lives would be lost no matter what happened, but a second cataclysm would affect unimaginable numbers, would wipe out entire villages and towns and, as she had seen, perhaps whole civilizations. In the heart of the burning stone she had witnessed the cataclysm as it had ripped the heart out of uncannily beautiful cities built by creatures not of humankind yet somehow like them in their clever industriousness: the goblins and the merfolk. They existed as legends, stories told about beasts not as dumb as cattle yet animals still. But maybe the stories weren't true; maybe humankind had forgotten the truth or hidden it so as to hide the shame of what it had done all unwittingly.

'I love him, but his is only one life. I would sacrifice my own life to save his, but I will not sacrifice the world. I will save as much as I can and see justice done. On this, I am determined.'

A sliver of a smile cracked that aged face. It was not an expression of amusement, yet neither did it mock. 'You are an arrow loosed, Bright One. I wonder if you can be turned aside.' She ducked her head as a sign of respect, although not of submission. At last she closed the gap between them, and Liath had consciously to stop herself from taking a step back because of the weird aura of her presence, her very appearance, and because like any horse she loomed larger than one expected. She was big, and could crush a human skull with one good kick.

But she stretched out her hand and offered Liath an arrow from the quiver slung over her own back.

'We are not enemies, Bright One. This arrow I will give you, in addition to my aid in bringing this human to safety. There is a child held for safekeeping in my camp whom he has sired.'

'My daughter?' The bow slipped from slack hands to fall to the ground, the arrow click clacking down on top of it. 'Blessing? How came she to you?' All the questions she had

kept fettered ever since she had first seen Sanglant broke free.
'What was Sanglant doing here, hunting griffins? How did he
get here? Is he alone? Exiled? How far are we from Wendar?
How fares my daughter? Was she with her father all along?
How came she into your care? What grievance had that man
who attacked Sanglant? How can we return to the west?'

Li'at'dano chuckled. 'You are still young, I see. You spill
over like the floodwaters.' She bent, picked up bow and both
arrows, and gave them to Liath. 'Let us return to the encampment. Once there I shall answer your questions.'

3

The odd thing was that the healer who attended him was
dressed as a woman but resembled – and smelled like – a man.
He was giddy with pain, and therefore, he supposed, unable
to make sense of the world properly. The sky had gone a
peculiar shade of dirty white that did not resemble clouds,
and it had an unfortunate tendency to sag down and billow
up. The effect made bile rise into his throat, and the nasty
taste of it only intensified the way pain splintered into a thousand pieces and drove deeper into flesh and bone.

Sometimes the mercy of death was preferable to living.

Yet.

Never let it be said that he did not fight until his last breath.

He tried to speak her name but could get no voiced breath
past his lips.

'He moves,' said the healer, speaking to someone unseen.
'See you his finger, this twitch? Fetch the Bright One.'

A shadow skimmed the curved wall of the sky, distorted
by corners and angles, and abruptly he recognized his surroundings: he lay inside a tent. He sensed a smaller body lying
asleep near to his, but as the flap of the tent lifted a line of
light flashed, waking every point of pain.

He gasped out loud. Agony shattered his thoughts.

'Sanglant.'

Her voice startled him out of the stupor of pain. This time he could speak.

'Liath? Where have you been? You abandoned us.'

She was crying softly. 'I was taken away by my kinfolk, but I had no wings to fly with. I could not follow them nor return to you. But now I have walked the spheres, love. Now I've come back to you and our child.'

'Ah,' he said.

The light faded. He fell into darkness.

And woke.

He hurt everywhere, but the pain no longer was excruciating; it was only a terrible throbbing ache that radiated throughout his body. Air thrummed against the walls of the tent in a complex melody that rose and fell depending on the strength of the wind and minute shifts of its direction, although in general it seemed to be coming from the southeast.

He heard Liath's voice.

'I can see nothing. I have little knowledge of healing. I do not understand why she should have fallen into this stupor. What can *I* do to wake her?'

'Look more closely, Bright One.' The shaman's inhuman voice stirred unexpected feelings in his breast – irritation that she had dismissed him so easily, fear for his lost daughter, determination to hunt down Bulkezu.

Bulkezu was dead.

But not by Sanglant's hand.

A strange scent tickled his nostrils, a light stinging heat that was both sweet and hot and yet not really a smell at all. It was the taste and touch of sorcery.

Liath caught in her breath in the way a woman might, prodded to ecstasy. 'I see it! It's a pale thread, *there*. She is still linked to the daimone that suckled her, who returned to the sphere of Erekes.'

'Nay, as you see, the thread is broken.'

'So it is, God help us. As long as I walked the spheres, the thread between them remained unbroken. But when I crossed back into the world below . . . think of a man on the shore and one in a boat on the river who remain in contact by both holding onto a rope. If that rope is cut, the one on the river will be borne away by the current.'

'She has drunk the milk of the aether and it has changed her. She has not grown in the fashion of a child of Earth, not if she was born only four years ago.'

'She's grown so quickly.'

'In body, but not in mind. Now that thread of unearthly sustenance is cut off. She lies adrift, betwixt and between this world and the one above.'

'What can we do?'

'Ah. You have asked me a question I cannot answer. I have not walked the spheres, nor can any reach the ladder who are mired in Earth.'

'How came my father by such knowledge, then, that he could teach me and that I could use that knowledge to climb?'

The shaman chuckled. Something about the comradely wryness of her response aggravated Sanglant in the same way a constantly buzzing mosquito makes it difficult to sleep. The centaur had not treated *him* with such respect. He was not accustomed to being treated as anything lower than a king's son, a prince of the realm, and captain of a powerful army. He was not accustomed to being expected to *prove* himself to another's satisfaction.

'Liath!' he said, emphatically, and found he could sit up. The movement dizzied him. Pain stabbed in his chest. He clutched the pallet he sat on and waited for the agony to quiet, as it did. He recalled the process of healing well enough. He had gone through this torment more than once. It would swell and ebb in stages until he was as good as before.

He touched his damaged throat, the voice that had never entirely healed.

Or almost as good as before.

It was still better than being dead.

'Sanglant!' Liath had braided her hair back, and her face was clean. It shone with joy. She grasped his hands.

'A powerful spell,' remarked the shaman, behind her. Her mare's body filled half the space of the tent, and she loomed ominously over the raised pallet that rested on the ground before her. A slight shape lay curled up on the pallet. It was Blessing, unhurt but utterly slack. Normally Blessing slept with her hands closed into fists, tucked up against her chin; now she lay like a corpse.

'What have you done to my daughter?' he demanded.

Liath recoiled slightly, a movement checked immediately but not so quickly that he didn't notice that her first instinct had been to pull away from his anger.

'Has she cast a spell on her?'

'Nay, love, she's done nothing.'

'Then why does she lie there like a body that's had its soul torn from it?'

'I pray you, Sanglant, do not speak such ill-omened words! Blessing fell into this stupor at about the same time I fell to Earth, or so we believe. She spoke, she said that she heard me and that I was all on fire. Ai, God.' The words were spoken regretfully. 'She's so big. Has it really been four years?'

'Three years! Four years! I'm no cleric to keep track. To me it seemed like an eternity, falling into the pit, but perhaps you suffered less hardship separated from me than I did from you!'

She took a step back, surprised by his anger, as was he. But it just kept boiling up, and boiling up, and he couldn't stop it.

'How do you know this creature is not our enemy? She refused to help me find Blessing. Now I find Blessing *here*, in her clutches. How can you know that *she* did not injure our daughter?'

'Her people *rescued* Blessing from this man called Bulkezu. Blessing's own servant Anna told me the story. Anna? Anna!'

'She is gone to fetch water, Bright One,' said the healer. Sanglant had not noticed her, but she sat by the entrance on a cushion, hands folded in her lap.

'Anna could have been bewitched—'

'She seemed a practical enough girl to me. Here now, love.' Liath eased up beside him and set her hands on his shoulders. He knew her expressions intimately; he saw that she was concerned, even apprehensive, and – surely – treating him as if he were a flustered hound that needed to be calmed before it could be settled for the night in its kennel. 'You're not healed yet. You should lie down and rest.'

'Why are you taking their side against me?'

That offended her, and she stiffened, shoulders going rigid as her chin lifted. 'I take no one's side. I am as much a prisoner, or a guest, of the Horse people as you are. As our daughter is. I have little more than a year to plan a great undertaking. I will ally with whom I must in order to stop Anne from bringing down upon us a cataclysm of such terrible strength and breadth that – God Above, Sanglant! You know what I speak of! You were at Verna. Why are you arguing with me?'

For the instant it takes to draw in a breath, a shimmering aura of flame trembled around her as though she were about to flower with wings of flame. *This* Liath had a terrible power. She was somehow the same woman who had vanished from Verna and yet now something else entirely, a creature not quite human and not quite the beautiful, graceful, scholarly, yet fragile woman he had married. The one he had saved from Hugh, from Henry's wrath, from life as a fugitive.

The one who had needed him.

This Liath had killed Bulkezu with a single shot and driven off a pair of griffins with a blazing ring of fire. She spoke with the ancient centaur shaman as with an equal. She stared at him now forthrightly, her gaze a challenge.

'I don't know you,' he said.

XVIII
GRIM'S DIKE

1

The country north of Hefenfelthe was rich and sweet, as green as any land Stronghand had ever seen, laced with fordable rivers and manifold streams, and so gentle that it placed few obstacles in the path of his army. Spring brought frequent showers, but although it rained one day out of three, they made good time and met with occasional, if stiff, resistance as they marched north on the trail of the queen. Mostly they found abandoned villages and empty byres.

'The scouts have returned!' called Tenth Son, who marched with the vanguard.

Human outriders called down the line of march and the army creaked to a halt at a stagger as word reached the ranks behind. The van had come to the top of one of those gentle, if long, slopes that allowed Stronghand to survey the line of his army where it snaked back along the ancient Dariyan road. The paved road made their passage swift, although it exposed them to attacks from the surrounding woodland.

The RockChildren marched in even ranks, five abreast, each unit bearing the standard representing their tribe. Rikin's brothers were given pride of place at the front and the rear, while Hakonin guarded the wagons with their precious siege engines, supplies, extra weapons, treasure and loot, and the ironworks that could be set up as forges in a semipermanent camp. Like rowing, pulling the wagons strengthened a warrior on those days when there wasn't any fighting to be had. The other tribes took their places in the order of march according to the honor they had earned in the last battle or skirmish, a shifting dance of bragging rights that kept the soldiers eager. Even the human levies were permitted to compete, and in truth their presence made his own people fight harder. None wished to be an object of ridicule by having killed fewer of the enemy or gathered less loot than the Soft Ones.

'There they are,' said Tenth Son on the seventh day out of Hefenfelthe, as the sun neared the zenith.

Stronghand moved up to the front with Hakonin's chief, Papa Otto, and the young Hessi interpreter beside him. The scouts approached at a gallop along the road. Eight had been sent out. Only five were returning.

Outriders cantered forward to meet them and soon a dozen soldiers pulled up in front of the vanguard. The five scouts dismounted. Their mounts went eagerly to the human grooms who would walk and cool down the blown horses. Only horses bred on the fjords ever really became used to the smell of the RockChildren.

One of the scouts stepped forward to give his report; the gripping beast pattern decorating his torso marked him as a Hakonin son.

'A substantial force moves northeast off to the west of us. They fly the banner of the queen's stag and one of a white boar. They'll soon cross this road. If they get ahead of us we've worse to face ahead. There are fortifications lying across our path, a line of ditches and embankments. The land narrows. There are steep wooded hills to one side and marsh to the other, but a corridor down the middle. That's where the fortifications lie.'

'Are they newly built?' asked Stronghand.

'They're old.'

Stronghand gestured. Word was passed down to the thirtieth rank, where Alban volunteers marched.

'You trust these turncoats?' asked the Hakonin scout. By the markings on the scout's shoulder, Stronghand identified him as First Son of a Thirteenth Litter.

'These are not turncoats, First Son. They had no coats to turn. They were slaves. Now they seek honor and position in my army because they had none before nor any chance to try.'

'Yet they are soft.' First Son bared his teeth to show the flash of jewels, earned in Stronghand's battles. He was sharp, and bold, and independent. Worth watching, for good or for ill.

'They may be,' agreed Stronghand. 'They have yet to prove themselves.'

A pair of men, one young and one gray, trotted up. Both had knowledge of this country, so they claimed.

'What are you called?' asked Stronghand, because he knew that with humankind, names give power and knowing the name of another brings power to the one who names.

The older man spoke with an odd accent. 'I am named Ediki. That is my true name, though my master called me Wulf in the manner of his people. I was born in the fen country. When I was a lad, the Alban lord of Weorod captured me and sold me as a slave into the great city. We're close by the manor and lands of Weorod now. This lad goes by the name Erling. His mother was my kinswoman. She was taken away even before I was, but he was born and raised in the city. From her, he knows a bit of lore.'

'I will call you the name you were born with, Ediki. Tell him of the fortifications.'

Ediki listened intently, nodding all the while, as First Son spoke and Yeshu translated. 'Yes, that's right where the lord of Weorod makes his home. The earthworks are called Grim's Dike and the Imps. Built in my grandmother's grandmother's time by the winter queen of Lindale, called Aelfroth. Her brothers warred against her out of the western highlands. She built earth walls to hold them back.'

Erling scratched the slave brand that scarred his cheek,

whether because it itched or because he was nervous, Strong-hand could not tell. Unlike Ediki, he wasn't small and dark but had the height and fairness common among the tall, blond Albans. 'My mam said that Grim's Dike was built by the old southerns, the iron soldiers, them who called themselves Dariyans and once ruled this land before the Albans came. She said it was built to stop the Albans who was then invading.'

Ediki shrugged. 'If it were, it didn't hold them back, did it? Maybe the lad's right. Maybe I am.'

'When the Albans invaded? You are not an Alban?'

'The fair ones? No. They are latecomers, those. We are the true people. This is our land from the first days. The Albans are no friends of ours.' He looked up at Stronghand. With his broad chest and burly shoulders and coal black hair, tied back with a strip of leather, Ediki looked more like a bog spirit than a man, but his gaze was keen and his hands steady. If he feared the RockChildren, he knew how to hide it. 'Lord, only the queen's uncle has the right to fly the sigil of the boar. If this high lord and his army reach Grim and the Imps first, we'll fight hard and ugly to get past them, I'm thinking. The lord of Weorod will have fighting men as well, to support him. If the high lord reinforces the queen – then she'll be as strong as she can be.'

Stronghand nodded. 'Therefore we must reach the forti-fications first and set our own positions.'

'There's a small force holding them already,' added First Son. 'This lord of Weorod the slave speaks of.'

Stronghand grinned, baring his teeth in a challenge. '"The slave" is a slave no more but a soldier in my army. Speed is what matters now. We'll march at double time, hit them in force front on while First Son leads his Hakonin brothers around through the forest to flank them. If he can.'

First Son grinned in response, accepting the challenge.

The two Imps were smaller ramparts placed to hold the low ground between the forest, their angle and position but-tressed by the tangle of streams that interlaced this country, but whatever band was holding Grim's Dike hadn't the manpower to hold these westerly ramparts as well, so it was an easy task to swarm over them and march east as the afternoon progressed.

'Will we leave men to hold the lesser dikes?' asked Tenth Brother.

Stronghand shook his head. 'No. We'll see the worth of our Alban allies proved today. Let everyone advance.'

The sun lay behind them. Their shadows drew long and longer as they spread into battle order and advanced at a trot on the last great rampart. Grim's Dike was grim indeed, the ramparts cunningly positioned to stretch across grassy heath with, according to Ediki, one end thrust into thick oak and ash woods and the other dabbling its toes in lowland marsh. From the vantage afforded by their approach, however, Grim's Dike stretched out to either side far beyond what a man could see, a formidable obstacle with the great ditch gaping before them and the embankment rising high above. Ediki reckoned it at least two leagues in length. Behind it lay Weorod, where Ediki had been captured as a young man and sold into slavery in the distant city. Threads of smoke curled up from fires in that manor – hearth fires, perhaps, or forges as the Albans prepared for war.

First Son and his strike troop had already vanished into the forest as Stronghand raised his standard to signal the attack, nothing more complicated than a straightforward assault against massively inferior forces. He allowed Vitningsey to lead the charge and placed himself in the second rank. In silence they bent low and ran with the dogs loping beside them. These soldiers were limber and strong, so it was easy for them to leap down into the ditch and no difficult feat to scramble up the steep-sided embankment; they raised their shields to cover their heads as arrows and javelins rained down on them, but even such weapons as got through did little damage to their tough skin. The Albans guarding the rampart boasted bronze and stone weapons but evidently no steel, and while steel or iron could cleave the hide of one of his warriors, not much else would.

The defenders were few enough that it was hopeless in any

case. He clambered up the embankment and kicked aside a bloody body as the first wave went over the top and, in silence, did their work. Only the screams of hapless men and the battering of spear and ax against shields and flesh accompanied the keening of the wind. As he reached the top, troubled by nothing more than a single arrow rolling down the slope past him, he saw both the battle unfolding and the landscape beyond. Within the haze made by the sun's slanting rays casting gold across the heath he glimpsed a distant cluster of buildings, ringed by a low stockade and surrounded by fields and pasture. Tiny figures fled the estate with nothing more than what they could carry. Below, the remaining Alban defenders, not more than three score, formed into tight groups, shields held firm as those who had survived the initial assault attempted to regroup and retreat. They were determined, but they could not last long.

Far behind, he heard a horn blast.

The Alban lord and his army were approaching quickly.

For his plan to work, he needed control of the dike at once.

First Son's force burst out of the trees and hit the Alban defenders from the rear, just as he had intended. The Alban shield wall collapsed and the dogs went to work finishing off the wounded. Around him, his army flowed over the rampart and down like floodwaters breaching an embankment. Ten hundreds, as Alain would say, in the way that the Wendish ordered men. He needed no exact count to understand that while he had a large army, he had been forced to leave a second group as large to garrison Hefenfelthe and the surrounding countryside. Forty ships had sailed north so that he might have reinforcements massed to come in off the sea – if he could reach the sea. From the embankment he had a better view of the countryside to the northeast where the land sank into a flat marshy ground that seemed to go on forever, treeless, open, and utterly bleak. He saw no shelter for his army, no way to approach with stealth, no cover at all.

Yet out there in those trackless fens, the queen of Alba sheltered.

'My lord, we are ready.' Out of breath, Ediki stopped beside him with the two-score volunteers, First Son's turncoats, the men who had once been slaves. They were tough, but the run and the climb had winded them. Were they strong enough to do what he needed?

'You know what risk you run,' he said. 'You know what will happen if you fail?'

'We know, my lord. We know what you have promised us. It is worth the risk. We have no love for those who ground us down.' Ediki spat on the corpse that lay next to Stronghand's feet, a blond youth not so very old; his chin had been smashed in by an ax-blow, but it was the spear thrust that had disemboweled him that had killed him. 'They are not even my kinfolk – these ones. They came from over the sea.'

'Just as we did,' said Stronghand.

'No offense meant, my lord,' said Ediki as the other Albans murmured. A few of them, like Ediki, were short and stocky, with dark hair and brown eyes, but the rest had the height and pale coloring of the Albans. 'But it was the Albans who drove my ancestors into the hills and the marsh in the long ago days.'

'They raped my mother,' Erling said suddenly in the way of a man meaning to prove himself by displaying his anger. 'I'm a bastard, and a slave woman's son. You are the only *man*—' He hesitated as if seeing Stronghand for the first time. After so much time spent among humankind, Stronghand knew what disturbed them most about his appearance: the claws thrust out from the backs of his bony hands; the scaled copper of his flesh; his black slit eyes, the braid of coarse white hair, and the jewels that flashed when he bared his teeth. So like a man and yet not a man. Erling recovered himself and floundered onward. '—the only *lord* who has offered me anything but chains and the bite of his whip.'

'So I am,' Stronghand agreed. 'And so I promised. Let the slave become the master, and the master become the slave.'

Half a dozen of his soldiers hurried up from below, carrying mail and bloody tunics and open-faced helms taken off the dead men. 'Put on what you can,' said Stronghand, 'and take your places. We haven't much time.'

His army had all crossed over the dike and arrayed

themselves according to his plan, a third kneeling in staggered ranks just below the crest, a third running back to invest the palisade and manor house, and the others split onto either flank. An entire hundred crept back into the forest under First Son's command, backtracking.

He knelt beside Ediki, letting the old man conceal him with one of the rectangular Alban shields. His Alban volunteers now wore the outward garb of the men who had once defended the dike.

Two banners bobbed into view, fluttering with the sun's light streaming across them: the queen's stag and its attendant boar. No wolf's head glittered among the host, but a man rode at the forefront wearing a helm ornamented with the tusks and snout of a boar. His army came in good order, well disciplined and confident. He estimated there were five or six hundreds of them, enough to inflict real damage if it came to a pitched fight. They could see from the dirt churned up by the passage of the Eika army that a large force had moved across this ground ahead of them.

Erling stepped forward and waved his arms. 'Make haste!' he shouted. 'Brothers, move quickly! My lord, I pray you, beware! A small pack of the beasts are hiding in the forest the better to ambush you, to scare you off and make you think they've taken the dike. The rest have swung up along the dike toward the fens. We held them off, but we haven't long before they attack again.'

The other Alban volunteers moved up alongside him, an easy target for arrows if the Alban host distrusted their tale. It took courage to place themselves so nakedly in the line of fire.

'Make haste!' they cried. 'Make haste! We need reinforcements!'

For an instant, for a year, for the space of ten breaths, Stronghand wondered if the Alban lord with his boar's head helmet would take the bait.

Then First Son played his hand – axes and spears clattered against shields to create a host of noise rising out of the woodland. These Albans didn't yet understand that the RockChildren attacked in silence.

The lord shouted a command; his banner dipped and rose to signal the advance, and the host broke forward at a run, making haste, and their tight formation came undone as one man outpaced another, as they raced for the safety of the ramparts.

Stronghand bared his teeth. Behind, he felt as much as heard the murmur of his army tightening their grips on their weapons.

When the first of the Albans came over the top, awkward as they climbed and winded and thinking that their brothers awaited them, they hadn't a chance.

In the end, after the slaughter and with the sun sliding down beneath the western horizon, they took the boar's head alive. He was a man of indeterminate years, lean, hard, and cunning by the look of him, not easy to subdue. He was too proud to curse at his fate and too clever to waste his breath begging for mercy or modesty when Stronghand's soldiers stripped him. He wore luxurious garb under his chain mail, a padded tunic chased with gold thread, the gold armbands worn by Alban lords, a pair of gold necklaces, and silver rings and bracelets, a rich haul by any measure. In his time he had survived three wounds, long since healed, but on this day only his right hand was bleeding from a stroke that had knocked his gauntlet off. His shield was almost hacked in two, but it had fared better than the four young men who had died in a last attempt to break him out of the battle and escape toward the fens.

The Alban volunteers gathered to look him over. They had the look of starving dogs waiting to feed but held back by the chains of fear – because they feared this scarred and battle-hardened nobleman who stood stripped to his shift before them, barefoot, unarmed, and entirely at their mercy. Nonetheless Stronghand could smell their fear, a perfume as rank as old meat.

'The young should not die to save the old,' observed Ediki solemnly as he examined the four corpses sprawled at the foot of the noble lord.

'I am the queen's uncle, called Eadig, Earl of the middle

country and Lord of Wyscan,' said the noble to Stronghand, as if Ediki had not spoken. He took no notice of the former slaves. 'What ransom will you take for me, raider? How may I ransom those of my soldiers who still live?'

Stronghand raised both hands, palms up, in a gesture he had seen used among humankind. 'Your fate is not mine to judge. I have promised certain of my lords that they may enslave any man among the survivors.'

Eadig's arrogant gaze skipped over the branded faces of Ediki and the others, ranged farther afield to encompass the Eika now looting the dead or settling down for the night's bivouac within the safety of the palisaded manor. 'You have lords among you? I thought you were like the wild dogs who hunt in packs and devour everything they meet.'

'Then you do not understand us. Yet what we are should not concern you. You have lords among your own kind, Eadig, for you were once one among them. Now, here are others. I name them for you, because you must know at whose hands you will suffer mercy, or justice. Here is Lord Ediki of Weorod—'

'Eadwulf is lord of Weorod!' cried the nobleman indignantly. 'My cousin's niece married him five years past!'

'Eadwulf is dead or soon will be. It is no concern of mine. This man standing here at my right hand is Lord Ediki of Weorod. Here is his kinsman, Lord Erling of – What lands do you claim?'

Erling laughed, reckless with triumph. 'South of Hefenfelthe lies Briden Manor. My mother is buried there. It lies under the authority of Lady Ealhflaed.'

'Very well, Lord Erling, you are now lord of Briden Manor. As for these others—'

But as he turned toward them to discover what claims the other men would make, Eadig stepped forward with the fearless manner of a man accustomed to ruling and to being obeyed. His tone was sour and scornful and he trembled, as tense as a dog straining against a leash.

'You have no authority to steal the inheritance of those who came legally into possession of these lands!'

'Have I not?' Stronghand asked curiously. 'I have the right granted me by force of arms. Can you say otherwise?'

'It goes against nature for slaves to take the place of free men and claim to rule as masters over those who are rightfully lords by law and divine favor!'

Stronghand closed with him, unsheathing his claws a handbreadth from the earl's face. Eadig's expression changed utterly; his eyes flicked nervously to the corpses littering the ramparts and field and his nostrils flared in a pallid face, but he did not retreat.

'In truth, your objection puzzles me,' said Stronghand, turning his left hand the better to display his wicked claws. 'You ruled over them. Fortune's wheel turned, and now you have lost both law and divine favor. How does this go against nature? One day a wolf may flourish, hunting down the sheep, and the next he may be pinioned by the spears of the sheepherders.'

'Call me a slave, but I will still be earl of the middle country.'

Stronghand grinned, baring his teeth. 'Erling, kneel.'

Erling did so, one knee in the dirt, face lifted obediently to look upon the one who ruled him.

'I name you earl of the middle country and lord of Wyscan.'

Eadig sputtered, but Stronghand brushed his chin with the tip of his claws and the man fell silent.

'"E-arl?"' Erling stammered. 'I never thought – a manor, my lord, but to be titled an earl—'

'I am in need of loyal men to rule, Erling. You are one of them. I consider it no easy task. I expect you to become a responsible steward of these lands. The riches of Alba are not to be squandered. There are other men who desire what you have now been given. Serve me well and you will prosper. Serve me ill, and you will die.'

'Y-yes, my lord.' The young man had gone so white that his slave brand burned red against the pallor of his skin. His companions stared at him, whispering among themselves and beginning to eye each other as if wondering who might gain the greatest prize from their generous benefactor.

'Not all of you will serve me well,' remarked Stronghand.

'Such is the nature of humankind, I have observed. But I rule in this land, and those I have raised up I can bring down.'

'Only for as long as you live.' Eadig spat in Stronghand's face. 'You cannot defeat the queen and her council, nor can you pray for the gods' favor.'

'Let me kill him for you!' cried Erling, leaping up.

Stronghand did not mind the spittle. It was as inconsequential as rain even though he knew that to humankind it was a mortal insult. 'Lord Ediki, does this nameless slave serve us better alive or dead?'

Ediki considered the question with a serious frown, as it deserved. 'Living, my lord, but crippled. If he is blind, then he can no longer lead slaves in revolt or bear arms against us.'

'Very well. See that his eyes are put out, Lord Erling. Best that he survive the operation. Lord Ediki, walk with me. We'll need torches.'

Torches were brought. They climbed back up onto the ramparts, careful to step over the cooling bodies of the dead Alban soldiers. There were so many of them. Eadig's screams cut through the air and for an instant Stronghand smelled the sour stink of burning flesh, but he did not look back.

Two score of Eika soldiers carrying torches to light their way attended them as they walked. The smooth path that topped the rampart was divided here and there by a stockade or a jumble of branches piled up to make a barrier. In time, as the night crept on and the moon touched the zenith, they reached the northern end of the barrier. The moon's light was so strong that he could survey the landscape, all pale silver and coarse shadows. To his left, mixed forest land swept away to the south and west, but northeast the land sank and leveled off into a sheet of pewter. What he smelled off the wasteland was indescribable – sweet, heady, with the barest sting of salt.

'The fens,' said Stronghand. 'The queen waits for us out there.'

'You'll be lost if you march the army in there without a guide,' said Ediki. 'Lost, and dead. Spirits live there, the souls of men who drowned.'

'You lived in this land as a boy.'

'So I did, but I've lost much of the lore I knew then. And the waters will have changed. The safe paths will have shifted.'

'The queen found her way to safety.'

'So she did, my lord. She keeps allies and slaves, just as you do. But I know those who may still help us. I have kinfolk who do not love the Alban queen. Give me time, and I will find them.'

'How much time? The longer she eludes me, the stronger she gets. You cannot remain Lord of Weorod if the queen of Alba regains what she has lost.'

Ediki grinned, easy to see in the moonlight. He had strong, straight teeth for a man of his years; he hadn't lost even one, remarkable considering the many healed stripes Stronghand had seen on his back the day Ediki had joined up with his army.

'Before the moon is full again, my lord, I promise you, I will find you a guide into the fens. But the queen is powerful and her sorcerers are dangerous, as my kinfolk discovered to their sorrow back in the days when we were still free, and rulers of this country. Long ago.'

Stronghand glanced toward Tenth Son, standing close enough to hear every word. His littermate shook the standard, and the bones and beads rang, clacking together.

'I do not fear the tree sorcerers, nor should you. We are strong, we who were born in the north. Your kin will rule again in this land if they are among those who serve me well and faithfully. Show me how to find the queen. That is the first task I set you and your tribe.'

Ediki bowed his graying head as a sign of obedience and understanding, but he looked pensive and content. The days of traveling and fighting had not wearied him. 'It is a small task compared to the years I struggled to hold my head high although I was a slave.'

Moonlight shivered on the waters. The beauty of the half-seen landscape and the quiet night washed over Stronghand as if on a rising tide, enveloping him. It was so still. The countryside was a mystery to him, a trackless wasteland of water and reeds that was, despite everything, a place of numinous wonder. Did the spirits of drowned men cause the waters to shine, or was that only a glamour of the moon? Lights flickered and sparked and died among the shadows, among the sedge beds and stands of reeds, each flare like a candle lit for a moment before being extinguished.

Like life, he thought. His own life would be a bright, brief flame that might split the darkness for as long as lightning kindled the heavens, but no more. Even the moon's glow could only reach so far into the ceaseless tide of years.

'What are those lights?' he asked Ediki. 'They burn for an instant and then they're gone.'

The lord of Weorod smiled sadly, but his expression was clean and joyful as he gazed over the landscape of his childhood.

'Those are the souls of the men we killed today. They're seeking the gateway that leads to the other side, to the land of the dead, where the meadow flowers bloom.'

2

Ediki steered the canoe down a side channel into a labyrinth of sedge and reed. Islets like the rounded backs of whales humped up out of the shallow waters, covered with grass or low-lying brush willow, white with flowers. Through this maze they glided, Ediki kneeling at the stern of the canoe and his nephew Elafi at the stem.

They had found Elafi ten days after the assault on Grim's Dike, and it had taken all of Ediki's persuasive powers to convince the young man that he was who he said he was. In the end, Stronghand had agreed to come alone to meet the refugees in the marsh. It was the only way Elafi would agree to guide them into the marshland.

The sun was just coming up as the crescent moon set. The

last stars faded as the sky slowly brightened, and the soft breath of a dawn breeze lifting off the waters whispered through the reeds like the murmuring of the drowned.

'We're here, Uncle,' said Elafi, grinning back at Ediki. 'You're a little slow and sloppy, but you steer like a man who grew up in the fens.'

Here proved to be nothing more interesting than a broad hummock of sedge and reeds shouldering out of the waters, but Stronghand smelled that people camped here. The canoe slid up onto a muddy shore where the reeds had been cut back; otherwise it was impossible to see that the islet was inhabited.

'There she is,' said Elafi unnecessarily as a short, middle-aged woman pressed through the reeds and halted on the beach, mud squishing between her toes as she stared at them, face alight with joy.

'Manda!' Ediki clambered from the boat, but in his haste the boat tipped and sloshed, and he splashed up to the woman, laughing, and she grabbed him and hugged him fiercely as she wept.

'Brother. Brother. I thought you were lost to us.'

Elafi gestured to Stronghand to climb out of the canoe; together, they pulled the boat up onto the shore and stowed it where it could not be seen. There were a half dozen crude boats hidden among the reeds. He took his standard and his spear and followed the young man up to the camp where Ediki was now greeting every person from the eldest to the youngest.

This was a camp of fugitives, about a score, half of them children. The sturdiest shelter consisted of a lean-to built of sticks covered by a roof woven of reeds, their clothing was little more than grass skirts and cloaks, cunningly braided together, and they had only one cooking pot among them as well as baskets and sharpened sticks fashioned into spears or fishing forks. Yet there was plenty of food: plucked ducks and coots, skinned voles and hares, gutted perch, roach, and pickerel as well as a bounty of slippery eels, and blossoms and young leaves from the spring flowering.

A lad approached them, bearing a bronze cup.

'Will you drink, Honored One?' he asked boldly.

Stronghand regarded the cup gravely. The liquid steaming within did not smell at all appetizing. Ediki hurried back with his sister beside him.

'My kinfolk offer you guest rights,' he said. 'I pray you, my lord. Drink.'

He let his grin flash, knowing that they tested him. He took the cup from the youth and raised it.

'I come alone to offer an alliance to you,' he said, and drank half. The brew went down easier than he had imagined, laced with an aftertaste that puckered his tongue so sharply he almost laughed in surprise. Instead, he held out what was left.

Ediki's sister stepped forward. 'I am Manda, grandmother of this clan. I give you welcome. I dreamed of you, dragon-man.'

She was not lean and muscled like a warrior; she was stocky, even plump, despite the obvious hardships she and her clan had suffered, and she had the same coarse black hair – cut short – as Ediki had, although hers had less gray in it. She looked like an ordinary woman in all ways, if one only looked on the surface. But in her stance he saw authority and in the way the others deferred to her, holding back until she had spoken, he saw leadership. She was a honed spear forged in a time of trouble. She had weight, and heft, and her surety was like the sharpened edge of a killing blade.

'I have dreams,' she continued, by way of explanation. 'I dreamed a man was coming who wasn't a man, and he sailed in on a ship that wasn't a ship but a dragon born of wood. The goddess told me that this man who wasn't a man would bring my brother back to me, although he was lost to us long years ago. The goddess told me that I might offer him the cup held between allies.' She took the bronze cup from him and drank the rest, wincing at its bite, almost grinning, as he had.

She whistled between strong teeth. The waiting boy took the cup from her and retreated, leaving her to speak with Stronghand alone. Even Ediki walked back into the clutter of the camp. Several of his kinfolk clung to him, still amazed by his existence, but no one spoke; they only watched as the negotiations began.

'What do you want, stranger?'

'I want your help to track down the queen of Alba and kill her, and to destroy the power of her tree sorcerers. When that is done, I will rule Alba and reward those who aided me.'

The sun rose. Light shone on the waters. A flight of geese flew low overhead, honking so loudly that Manda waited until they had passed before she resumed speaking.

'Their power you can never destroy. Their magic is very strong. It defeated us, my people's claims to this land long ago, my clan and I not so many moons ago. The queen and her army drove us off the holy island where we have lived as caretakers back into the dawn of time. My mam was caretaker there. The right to the land and honor of the guardianship came from her mam before her and hers before her, back into oldest times. There's enough land to grow a small crop of grain and keep a big flock of sheep and a gaggle of geese. That's all gone. You see how they drove us off.'

She indicated the makeshift camp, the crude shelters, the open campfires, the ragged children. They had not escaped with much. But they did not seem hungry and desperate.

'You come with an army,' she said. 'Will you attack them?'

'Should I?' he asked.

'Overland? No. You will all die in the fens.'

'What if we sail in from the sea?'

'It will be hard to sail to this place from the sea. It's shallow. The tree sorcerers will raise a mist to confound you.'

'Our ships can sail in shallow water. The sorcerers' magic will not disturb us. But we don't know the path that will lead us from the sea to these islands.'

To his surprise, she shrugged. 'Even I don't know what rivers lead to the wash and how they tangle in the fens. There are some who live on the seacoast who know, but it is these clans who guided the queen to the holy island. They will not help you. They are in league with the Albans.'

'Without help, our ships will get lost in the marshlands, won't they?'

She cupped her hands over her mouth and gave a 'courlee' call. A second cry answered from a distance, out among the reedbeds and mires. 'That's my other child, called Ki. My sister's daughter – now mine. You can't see her, and so can't the white-hairs. To hunt in the fens you need a guide.'

'I need guides for my army, and I need a caretaker for the holy island.'

Her smile flashed like lightning, quickly seen and quickly gone, but her expression remained solemn. 'Give me back the holy claim that my clan was charged with in the long ago days, and I will help you. But if you promise me, and cheat me, then you will fare no better than the queen. I have dreams, stranger. There is power in dreams.'

He nodded, acknowledging her blunt wisdom, and the naked threat in her words. 'I know the worth of my allies.' He drew a finger around the contours of the wooden Circle hanging at his chest as he gazed out over the fens. From deep within this labyrinth the Alban queen might strike at will against his garrisons. From this shelter within the fenlands she might hold on for months or for years, a worm in his side. Alba would not be his until she was dead, her heirs executed, and her tree sorcerers shorn of their power.

Manda licked her lips as if tasting the last of the brew. 'Show your trust, stranger. Let my children guide you out into the fens. They will show you the holy island and the queen's camp, and you can judge for yourself if the fight is worth it.'

XIX

A PRISONER OF POWER

1

This reunion was not going as she had expected. Sanglant's anger was palpable, and because Liath simply had no idea how to respond, she turned around and left the tent. His hostility and Blessing's illness were too much to take in at once.

The shaman followed her outside, herding her toward the crest where they could see the landscape spread below them.

'Why do you allow this male to speak to you so disrespectfully?' she asked.

'He is my husband!'

'He is not like you,' said the shaman reasonably as they strolled up the hill.

Grass pulled along Liath's thighs. The sun shone down. There was not a single scrap of cloud in the heavens. She had never seen a sky so vast, hills tumbling away on either side and the blue dome stretching away to the ends of the earth.

'No,' she agreed at last. He was no scholar; he was not bookish or thoughtful, not educated, not restful, a man interested more in action than in words. A good soldier, an excellent captain, and a loyal prince. Hugh had taunted him with the title 'prince of dogs,' after his year as Bloodheart's captive, and there was something to the name. But she did not know what he was now. He had lived for *four years* without her, years which to her had seemed scarcely more than a week. 'I don't know how he has changed while I walked the spheres.'

'It is best to set aside a pura which has become unpredictable and dangerous.'

'That isn't our custom. He needs time to recover from his wound.' *From his anger.*

The shaman flicked back her ears. Reaching the crest, they turned to look down at the centaur encampment settled near the base of a hollow.

'How can I save my daughter?' Liath asked.

'She did not die when the thread was severed. That must give us hope that she may yet recover.'

'She must eat and drink in order to live.'

'It may be possible to sustain her for a time by means of sorcery.'

'My father said that a cocoon changes a caterpillar to a butterfly. It's a magical binding in and of itself. Would sorcery change her?'

'I do not know. But if we cannot wake her, it may be the only way to keep her alive until we discover how to heal her.'

Liath sighed.

To the east the land fell away into the valley; the distant river winked at them, light dazzling on the flowing water as it cut through the grass in giant curves. Farther east, the crags shone where the afternoon sunlight played across them, catching glints of color. To the west the sun blinded, but if she squinted she made out a countryside of hills rumpled up like the ridges in a furrowed blanket.

'Is that smoke rising?' she asked, pointing to threads of gray curling up into the sky.

The shaman had no need to narrow her eyes to see what Liath indicated. 'Prince Sanglant's army camps there.'

'He has an army with him? Where did he get an army?

How long does it take to travel from here back to Wendar?'

'Many months of travel, I would imagine.'

'He brought an army so far with him? How can that be possible? He must have suffered many losses, of men and animals both.'

'I do not know. It is not a subject we discussed.'

'No,' said Liath, wondering what Li'at'dano *had* discussed with Sanglant or if she had discussed anything. 'We must send word to his people that we are here. Why did he leave his army and go out into the grass alone?'

'To stalk the beast.'

'The griffins?'

'Nay. The man. The killer. But griffins as well. He seeks griffin feathers and sorcerers to combat these "Seven Sleepers" you also have spoken of. He hoped to find both here in the grasslands.'

'Did he?'

'He found you, and he found me and those under my tutelage. As for the griffins—' She gestured toward the sky where one or both of the griffins circled, never content to let Liath out of their sight. 'There they are.'

They walked down into the centaurs' encampment. The layout had a subtle warp to it: the largest of the round felt tents lay in the center while the rest radiated out from it in a spiral pattern. The centaurs traveled light; despite their numbers she counted only twenty tents, ten of which lay in the outermost ring like a protecting corral although it wasn't apparent that the centaurs wished to keep anyone out, or in, except wolves.

The centaurs had brought a number of their Kerayit allies with them, including the healer who attended Sanglant, and two dozen wagons, most of which were rigged to be pulled by oxen while only two were constructed to allow centaurs themselves to haul the vehicle. Most of the wagons sat along the outermost ring to provide a barrier, but one, gaudily painted and built like a tiny cottage on wheels, sat next to the centralmost tent where Blessing slept and Sanglant healed.

There were horses, too – real horses, but they were kept separate, watched over by both centaurs and their human allies. Nearby, some men sheared sheep, collecting greasy wool in huge leather pouches.

As Liath and the shaman came into camp, centaurs surveyed Liath curiously but did not approach. A few coltish centaur children followed their dams, and half a dozen colts did as well, nudging at the teats of the centaur females. All of the adult centaurs carried bows slung over their backs and a quiver full of arrows.

A trio of human women cooked mutton stew in an iron kettle slung over a campfire; another polished jesses and leather hoods for goshawks while her companion mended a cage; a pair beat wool while next to them others poured boiling water over beaten wool in preparation for making the felt with which they covered their tents and made their rugs and some of their clothing. Five men were engaged in churning milk in a skin vat; the milk bubbled. Its tart scent stung Liath's nostrils. Suddenly she realized how hungry she was.

'Come,' said the shaman. 'There is one more you must meet, because we two will not be enough to defeat those who oppose us.'

'We are allies, then? You have not said so before this.'

'If we were not allies, you would not walk beside me, nor I beside you. I am not foolish enough to set myself and my people against one whom even the griffins fear. You are not like the other humans, Bright One. Your father has given you the form worn by those born into the tribe of humankind, but your heart and your soul had their birth in the heavens.'

'It is true I do not stand easily in either world, here or there. It is hard to choose. I cannot have both.'

'Then you have chosen.' They halted in front of the painted wagon. 'Here lives my apprentice. She has met her luck, so now she must remain hidden from the sight of those who are not her family or her slaves. But you, I think, exist beyond such earthly prohibitions. You and she must meet. Go in.'

'I do not wish to break any prohibitions if it means harm may come to another.'

Li'at'dano had a horsey way of laughing, more like a snort. 'The harm comes not to Sorgatani but to the one afflicted by her power. I believe you are powerful enough to be safe.'

Liath laughed. A queer sense of exhilaration filled her. 'Then I pray you are right.'

She felt no fear, only curiosity, as she mounted the steps that took her up to the high bed of the wagon. Before she could scratch on the door, it opened, sliding sideways along the wall, and she stepped over the threshold as she ducked inside.

She expected to feel closed in, but magic was at work here; it tingled right down to her bones. The inside of the wagon was considerably larger than the outside. There was no other way to account for the spacious chamber that greeted her astonished gaze, which resembled the interior of a round tent. The corners of the space were lost in shadow and possibly did not properly exist. Walls fluttered in the breeze, sagging gently in and out, although she could have sworn that, out-side, they were constructed of wood planks. Above, spokes supported the round felt roof, radiating out from a central pole that, set straight up, pierced a smoke hole. Definitely, absolutely, she had seen no central pole sticking out of the wagon's roof. The heavens glimpsed through the smoke hole had a gray shimmer shot through with shifting sparks, not the hard blue shine of the open sky.

On the left-hand side of the tent sat a boxed-in bed with a chest resting at its foot. A colorful felt blanket ornately dec-orated with bright animals – a golden phoenix, a silver grif-fin, a red deer – spread tautly across the mattress, tucked in on all sides. A layer of rugs and two cushions completed the furnishings, because the rest of that left side of the tent lay empty; it was uninhabited. An altar stood in front of her, beyond the center pole, containing a golden cup filled to the brim with oil with the surface lit and burning, a mirror with handle inlaid with gold and pearls, a silver handbell, and a stoppered flask. Beside the altar table squatted a portable stove. Coals glowed within this brazier, and a bronze bucket sat on a slab of rock beside it, filled with ash, smoking slightly.

A young woman crouched beside the brazier with an iron ash shovel gripped in her right hand; she stared up at Liath as one might gape at a bull that comes crashing into church in the middle of prayers. A second woman, much older, stood next to a high bench; she paused in the act of pouring a white liquid into cups. She held a beautiful double-spouted silver ewer, the necks, heads, and open mouths of camels forming the spouts.

'You are called Bright One because you shine.'

Liath looked around for the source of the voice.

The third person in the room sat on a broad couch. Her figure was veiled by a gauzy net of finest translucent silk that tented the wide couch, strung up on posts set into the four corners. Next to this couch-bed stood a tall chest cunningly worked into a shelf fitted with large and small drawers, each one lovingly painted with antlered deer and arrogant rams. Beside it a beautiful saddle was set up on a wooden tree, its side skirts brushing the carpet; the silver ornaments that decorated the frame and seat winked in the smoky light. A bridle had been thrown carelessly across the cantle.

'Drink with me.' Her voice was light and airy but firm. She gestured for Liath to move forward. Liath's footsteps made no sound on carpets laid over a woven grass mat. As she approached, the other woman swept aside the gauze veil so that Liath could sit on an embroidered cushion at the opposite end of the couch.

Liath had never had trouble seeing in dim light, but the breath of sorcery hazed her vision; she could not get a clear look at the other woman's face although she sat little more than an arm's length from her. She wore a robe woven of golden silk. Her ornaments gleamed in the dim light: a tall headdress stamped with gold from which hung streamers of beads and gold lacework, and earrings curved like reed boats dangling fish from a dozen lines which brushed her shoulders. Whenever she shifted, the earrings chimed softly and the gold lacework rustled.

The older servant, too, rang: she wore anklets and wristlets sewn with tiny bells and silver earrings that danced and sang when she moved. She carried the silver ewer over and poured them each a cup of the heady brew, stinging and sharp, from the camel's mouth. When Liath drank, it went right to her head.

'You are the one who bears the name of my teacher,' said the other woman.

'In my own tongue I call myself Liathano.'

The other woman tried this several times but could not produce the softer consonants, so in the end she laughed, amused at her efforts.

Liath laughed with her, warming to her lack of arrogance. 'You are called Sorgatani.'

'So I am. I, too, am named after one who came before me. Because she died the year I was born, her name and her soul passed into me.'

'Do the souls of your people not ascend to the River of Light?'

'They remain on Earth. Souls endure many lives. We are born again and again into the world below. Do your people not know this truth also?'

Liath shook her head. 'I have seen many things recently that have made the world above and the world below look very different to my eyes. Yet it's true my people do not believe as you do. The Lord and Lady bide in the Chamber of Light, which exists beyond the world above. It is there that our souls ascend after we die, to live in peace and harmony with God.'

'That is very strange,' said Sorgatani. She was silent, then broke into delighted laughter. 'What do your souls do in this chamber of light? Do they dance? Do they eat? Do they find pleasure in the bed? Do they ride and hunt?'

A churchwoman might have been offended by such a questions, but to Liath they suggested a mind with an affinity to her own.

'There is some disagreement among the church mothers on this point, actually. Some say that only our souls can exist within the Chamber of Light, that we will dissolve into the eternal bliss that is the presence of God. Others say that our bodies will be fully resurrected, that we will exist bodily in the Chamber of Light but without any taint of the darkness that gives rise to the evil inclination. The Enemy will have no foothold in the Chamber of Light.'

'If your bodies are resurrected, then what do you eat? Who feeds this vast tribe?'

'God are the food on which blessedness is fed.'

'Isn't God consumed, then?'

'No. God has no material substance, not like we do.'

'I admit I am puzzled. Who is this enemy?'

'Darkness and corruption.'

'But darkness and corruption are everywhere. They are part of Earth. How can any place exist that does not contain all that is? Does this "enemy" cause humankind to do evil things?'

'No, not at all. We live our lives according to free will. Darkness came into the world, but it is up to us to choose that which is good, or that which is evil. If God had made it otherwise, that we could not choose evil, then we would be slaves, "an instrument in the hand of Them who set us in motion," to quote the blessed Daisan.'

'Then who is responsible for evil?'

'Darkness rose from the depths and corrupted the four pure elements.'

'Surely this is impossible. The world has always existed as it was created in the days long ago by the Great God. Darkness was part of creation, not the foundation of evil.'

'Then who do you think is responsible for evil?'

'There are many spirits abroad in the world above and the world below, and some of them are mischievous or even malign. They plague us with sickness and bad luck, so we must protect ourselves against them.'

'What of the evil that people do to each other?'

'Are there not answers enough for this? Greed, lust, anger, envy, fear. Do these not turn to evil when they fester in the hearts of humankind?'

Liath laughed. 'I cannot argue otherwise. This drink has made my tongue loose and a little clumsy. I have not eaten for many days.'

'No guest of our tribe goes hungry!'

Sorgatani clapped her hands. The younger servant brought a wooden tray and set it down in front of Liath. Three enamel bowls contained yogurt, dumplings stewed in fat, and a hot barley porridge. The two servants moved away, bells settling and stilling as they sat beside the threshold with heads bowed. Sorgatani averted her gaze while Liath ate, forcing herself not to gulp down the meal. When she had finished, the servant removed the tray.

'I ask your pardon if my questions have caused offense,' said Sorgatani. 'You are my guest. We do not know each other.'

'Nay, do not apologize. As the blessed Daisan wrote, "It is an excellent thing that a person knows how to formulate questions."'

The older servant refilled Liath's cup, and she drank, savoring the aftertaste flavored like milk of almonds. The fermented drink flooded her limbs with warmth and made the heavens, glimpsed through the smoke hole, spin slowly, as a sphere rotates around its axis. She and Sorgatani were the axis, surely, and the whole world was spinning around them, or they were spinning; it was hard to tell.

'How is it that you speak Wendish so well?'

Sorgatani downed a second cup as well. 'Humans are born with luck that leads them either into ill fortune or good fortune throughout their life. We who are shamans among my people have so much power within us that we have no room for luck to be born into our body, so our luck is born into the body of another. My luck was born in the body of a woman of the Wendish tribe. Because I see her in my dreams, I understand and speak her language.'

'This is a thing I have never heard of before. Is it common for the luck of a Kerayit shaman to be born into a foreigner?'

'Our luck is born where fate decrees, and where our path lies. It is my fate that my path lies west, intertwined with that of your people. I think you know her, because she speaks of you in her dreams. She is called Hanna—'

'Hanna!' Liath had not seen Hanna since Werlida, when

she had fled Henry's wrath with Sanglant. 'Do you know where she is? Better yet, I'll search. Is there a fire I can look into?'

Sorgatani lifted a hand, and the older servant brought the silver cup over on the tray, now cleared of bowls. She set it down before Liath and retreated.

Liath passed a hand over the shimmering surface of flame, as smooth as water licked by ripples of fire. With ease, she drove a path through the flame and sought Hanna.

Only the coruscating blue-white flicker of the burning stone met her seeking gaze, as if Hanna were caught within the gateway, wandering the ancients paths woven between the stone crowns.

'How can this be?' she whispered.

Shadows danced, and faded, making her dizzy, and she found herself back in Sorgatani's tent. The oil in the cup had all burned up to reveal, in the bottom, an astonishing wheel of horses' heads, spinning like a pinwheel, one galloping after the next, until she realized that she was staring at a pattern beaten into the silver. She took her hands off the cup. The jangling of tiny bells announced the arrival of the older servant, and the cup was removed.

'She does not walk on Earth,' said Liath, surprised to find she could still speak. The effort had tired her, and the question of Hanna's fate weighed on her, an impossibly heavy burden. Hanna was her northern star, the one sure stable point in a tumultuous world. 'I pray she is not dead.'

'She walks the crowns,' said Sorgatani carelessly, as if to walk the crowns was no greater a feat than a morning's stroll down to the river.

'Who but the Seven Sleepers knows the secret of the crowns?'

'A woman, I think, whom Hanna saved from a deep pit, which you call a dungeon. Now they walk the crowns to escape those who pursue them. She is safe.'

'What woman?'

'I do not know how you call her. Your names are puzzling and difficult to pronounce.'

Liath squelched her frustration. This was no time to irritate her allies. 'Do you have any way of knowing for how long she is safe?'

'Only the Holy One can see both ways through time. She can see across great distances and pierce the veil of time through the heart of the burning stone. Can you not as well?'

'I can see through fire, but not into the heart of the crowns. I saw glimpses of past and future when I crossed through the burning stone, but that sight is closed to me here on Earth.'

'Then what does it mean, to "see through fire"?'

'It is a gift known to those who have taken Eagle's vows in my country, to see folk and places through fire. The Eagles are messengers for the regnant. In this way they can be also the regnant's eyes and ears.'

'Can you teach me this sorcery? Or is it forbidden?' Her tone dropped wistfully. 'There is so much I wish to learn, but there is much that is forbidden to me. We live under the tutelage of the Horse people. They have always been our allies and our mothers, our guardians.' She shifted sideways on the couch, smoothing out a lump in the embroidered cushion she sat on, moving a little closer to Liath. 'I know I am impatient. Some days I hope that my fate leads me westward where I can see new things.'

'Are you a prisoner?'

As if a muffling blanket had dropped down around them, the hiss of burning oil became the only sound. Liath could not even hear the breathing of the two servants. Of the camp outside, surely audible through the walls, she heard nothing. It was as if magic had torn them away from normal intercourse with the world and thrust them into the heart of a maze, where sight and sound altered and warped until they might stand a spear's length from their companions and yet be utterly separated from them by a wall of stone or a veil of sorcery.

'I am a prisoner of my power.' Sorgatani spoke in the same matter-of-fact tone with which the steward of an estate proclaimed which cattle were marked out for the Novarian slaughter. 'The Horse people are immune, as are my blood kin and the other shamans. Those who serve me are bound to me by magic so that they do not suffer in my presence.'

'Nothing has happened to me.'

'You, like me, possess a soul that was passed on to you from another being. Mine came from my aunt. Yours came from a creature born of fire.'

'Have you seen with your own eyes the fate suffered by ordinary humans who are brought into the presence of one of your kind?'

'Nay. This lore I had from my teacher.'

'Has it been tested? If you have not seen it for yourself, how do you know it is true and not just a superstition?'

Sorgatani laughed bitterly. 'What if it is true, Liat-ano? Am I to walk into a camp of strangers with no care that I may bring death down upon people I do not know? We tell stories, in our tribe, of how a Kerayit shaman destroyed an entire tribe, one who warred against us, by walking through their camp at midday. Every soul there died, and their tribe vanished from Earth and memory. I dare not risk it. I seek knowledge, not death. I am not a warrior.'

'I am no warrior either, although at times I must fight. After everything I have seen, I wish it were not to a war that I have returned, for there is so much to learn and to study. This war seems like a desert to me, a barren wasteland. But still, it must be crossed.'

'You speak as if with my own heart.' Sorgatani's earrings chimed as she shifted on her cushion. Her words seemed freighted with reticence, the speech of a woman shy of speaking her deepest feelings because she had never had a close companion before, only the comradeship of duty, the tutelage of one more powerful than she, and the inevitability of the isolated life that she would inherit when she came fully into her powers.

Power frightened those who did not possess it, and well it might when it resided in the flesh of an otherwise ordinary woman.

'You must be lonely,' said Liath. The bitterness of the solitude she had suffered with her father as they lived as fugitives all those years was as fresh now as it had been when she had lived through it. It was impossible to trust when you were always running. It was hard to clasp hands with people soon to be left behind, never to be met again. Her years in Heart's Rest had been Da's last gift to her, and giving that precious respite to her, granting her the time to develop affectionate bonds with Hanna and Ivar, had killed him. He had given his enemies time to catch up with him, because he wanted to make his daughter happy.

Impulsively, Liath reached out. 'We are alike, you and I. We might be sisters.' She grasped the other woman's dark hand.

A spark burst where their skin touched. A report like the clap of thunder deafened her as she recoiled. The servants leaped up, bells jangling, but Liath nursed her hand and, when tears stopped stinging and she had enough courage, turned it over to examine it. Red blisters bubbled on her palm. They burned like sin.

'I pray you, forgive me!'

'Nay, you must forgive *me.*' Sorgatani sounded near tears. She cracked an order at the servants, and the older one hurried to the chest and brought out a tiny leather bottle. Bowing low before Liath, she produced a salve and, when Liath held out her burned hand, smoothed the sweet-smelling paste over the burned skin.

'I should have warned you not to touch me,' continued Sorgatani. 'I should not have let you sit so close. If I could wish one thing it would be that you do not abandon me, now that you know the truth. You see how it is.'

'I see how it is,' said Liath, wonderingly, lifting her gaze. The sting had dissipated the sorcerous veil that disguised the Kerayit girl's features. She could now see Sorgatani clearly – a beautiful, almond-eyed woman no older than herself, with black hair neatly confined in braids, an oval face broad at the cheekbones, and a lovely dark complexion. 'I see you. I could not see you clearly before.'

Sorgatani stared back, taking her measure, and they both smiled and, in unison, glanced down. Liath blew on her palm.

The cooling touch of her breath and of the salve eased the pain.

'May no person touch you? Can you never have a husband?'

'No Kerayit woman will ever have a husband. That is the law. We are the daughters of the Horse people. Just as they have no husbands, so do I and my sisters have no husband. There was one of us who married many years ago – it was allowed because he was her luck. When he died, the luck passed into the body of her son. They are both dead now, mother and son. Such is fate.'

'Do you live always alone, confined in this wagon?' Such a fate seemed so ghastly to Liath that she struggled to hide the pity in her tone. Sorgatani deserved better than pity.

'We have puras, who mate with us and bring us pleasure and give us company. You have a pura, do you not? The prince who hunted in the grass.'

'He is my husband,' she said, amazed that her voice emerged so evenly despite the turbulence of her thoughts. *He is my beloved husband, but I scarcely know him.*

'Oh! You are allowed husbands in the western lands, are you not? It is a custom common among barbarian women. If you don't want your husband anymore, then perhaps I might have him as my pura, if you are willing to trade him to me. It is true I get lonely.'

What an idiot she had been to think that walking away from Sanglant's anger would make the trouble go away. Over the years Sanglant had, perhaps, come to believe she would never return; maybe he had mourned her loss and, then, been blindsided by her reappearance. On top of that he was horribly wounded. The servant girl, Anna, had told her of his devotion to Blessing and how he had agonized over their daughter's unnatural maturation. Anna had spoken a very little bit of their journey east, but only Li'at'dano's words had brought home to Liath what a massive undertaking it was to lead a western army so far into the wilderness. Sanglant understood the threat Anne and the others posed; he was not afraid to face them down.

'He is still my husband, although we have been apart for

so long. Have you no men in your own tribe whom you desire?'

Sorgatani's shrug had an eloquent lift. 'How is your hand?' she said instead. 'Will it heal? Have I scarred you?'

Liath turned up her hands to expose the lighter skin of her palms. 'It's gone already,' she said, surprised to find it so. The merest sting, like the probing of a bee, and a sheeny pink flush shading the skin were all that betrayed which hand had touched Sorgatani.

'You *are* very powerful! I hope we can become allies.'

'I hope we can become friends.'

Sorgatani's smile was, like a rare flower, beautiful and precious and bright.

Hammering blows stuttered against the door. The entire structure shuddered. In a cacophony of bells, the younger servant leaped up and slid the door sideways enough to peer through. Torchlight flashed through that gap. Outside, amazingly, night had fallen although Liath had no sense of so much time elapsing while she conversed with Sorgatani.

'Bright One!' The shaman's powerful voice had the force of an avalanche. Even Sorgatani, unwittingly, trembled.

'Come quickly, Bright One! Prince Sanglant is missing. He has taken the child.'

2

Pain made his head throb, and he knew that pain of such intensity, touching every point in his body, did not help him think straight. But he would not remain a prisoner in the centaur camp any longer. If he had no help from his wife in making his escape, so be it. He had survived four years without her. He had managed all that time. He could manage now.

'My lord prince! You shouldn't try to stand, my lord!'

It was astonishing how much agony it cost him to stand. 'My clothes, Anna.'

Dressing was child's work, yet he grimaced as he pulled his wool tunic on over his under-tunic. He could not bend to bind on his leggings, so he sat on the chest and let Anna lace up his boots.

'Where is my spear?'

They had left his gear on the carpet next to his pallet, which suggested that he was not, precisely, a captive, but he ignored these distracting thoughts as he buckled his sword over his back, wincing, and threw his cloak over everything, pushed back on the left shoulder so he could draw his sword. Every time he moved, he felt a thousand daggers pricking him in each muscle; hot fire ran up his tendons. His chest ached horribly; each breath hurt.

'It's here, my lord.'

'Are you strong enough to carry Blessing?'

'I think so, my lord. But—'

'Pick her up.'

'Her Highness Liathano has not returned yet, my lord. She went out with the shaman—'

'Anna!'

She knelt beside Blessing, got her arms around the girl, and heaved her up. Blessing wasn't that much smaller than Anna but she was light, and Anna was strong and stubborn. She draped the unconscious Blessing over her shoulders like a sack of grain. Sanglant got a good grip on the spear. The extra weight of the sword across his back seemed like the hand of a giant, pressing him down, but he refused to give in to weakness.

The healer sat placidly by the door, watching his struggles without speaking, her kohl-lined eyes intent with curiosity and her broad face as expressionless as uncarved stone. As Sanglant reached the threshold, the healer rose.

'You are not healed,' she said in her gruff voice. 'Not wise to walk.'

'I am returning to my army.'

He stepped out into the camp, leaning on the spear to support himself, and paused there, fighting to catch his breath, as Anna negotiated the threshold with Blessing and halted beside him. Twilight had descended, but the waxing moon gave off enough light that they might walk through the night grass with a reasonable certainty that they could mark their way.

The healer followed them. She was not much taller than Anna but considerably broader through the shoulders. She held a cured sheep's bladder and a leather flask.

'Are you going to try to stop me?' asked Sanglant, feeling dangerous because his head reeled and the moon shone overly bright and the ground had a disconcerting sway to it.

'Nay, lord. I receive the duty to heal you. I follow you.'

'Don't try to stop me.' Stubbornness was all the strength he had, that and this coiling, burning anger that drove him. Liath had abandoned him, stolen his victories, and chatted companionably with the creature who had kidnapped his daughter and refused to help him rescue the child from Bulkezu.

Something in this train of thought didn't make sense, but he wanted to recover under the supervision of those he trusted – he did not want to be beholden to these uncanny creatures and their human companions.

He wanted allies who treated him with respect.

'They're more like slaves, if you ask me,' he said to no one, or to Anna, as he hobbled through the grass toward the western ridge somewhere beyond which his army camped. The pain of healing had drawn his nerves so fine that he distilled the thread of his army's campfires from out of the strong scents that surrounded him in the centaur encampment: boiled wool, blood, fermented milk, horse.

'Who is, my lord prince?' she asked, huffing as she walked.

Not many walked abroad through camp now it was dark and those who did made no attempt to stop him. Though he staggered frequently, he possessed sword and spear, even if he needed the spear's aid to walk. Tents loomed as obstacles but proved easy to walk around although the extra distance took its toll.

After an eternity they reached the edge of camp. He surveyed the long slope ahead and wondered how any person could reach the top.

'Will you have drink?' asked the healer solicitously, holding out the sheep's bladder.

It contained drugged wine, no doubt.

'No,' he said, although he was desperately thirsty. He glanced back to survey the camp. A group of centaurs gathered a spear's throw away. They consulted together but made no move to come after him. One carried a lamp. Its light played over their torsos, illuminating the curve of their breasts, the drape of bead necklaces, a pair of coarse, auburn braids hanging over the shoulder of one and reaching to that place where woman hips flowed away into a mare's body.

That long hair reminded him of Liath, the way her braids would fall over her shoulders and sway along her backside as she walked.

Where had Liath gone? Why had she barged out after those few reasonable things he had said to her? Why hadn't she returned? No doubt she had more in common with the shaman. Liath had changed so profoundly; she was not the person he had married. It was like meeting a stranger who wears familiar clothing – or an old companion who can no longer speak a common language.

'Where are all the male centaurs?' he asked suddenly. 'Don't they ride to war? Or do they wait in the wilderness and let the mares do battle for them?'

The healer waited, obviously expecting him to answer his own question. When Sanglant said nothing more, she spoke as if to a particularly slow child. 'No male Horse people walk on Earth.'

'They're all crippled? Dead? Gelded?'

'No males,' repeated the healer helpfully. 'Only horses.' She gestured toward the distant herds, mostly lost to sight on the opposite side of the encampment.

Sanglant shook his head irritably. He hated when things made no sense, but it wasn't worth arguing about now. He started up the slope.

They made it to the top, one exceedingly slow step after the next, before Anna had to stop to rest, and he was grateful for the break although he dared not sit down for fear he would never get up again. She knelt and set Blessing down on the grass.

'I'll carry her,' he said to Anna, who was clearly winded, breath rasping as she bent over double, clutching her sides.

Blessing had not stirred. Her eyes remained open, but she did not see anything around her. She did not react to sound or touch. All she did was breathe.

He had failed her. He hadn't protected her after all.

'I can carry,' said the healer.

'It would be good,' whispered Anna, sides heaving.

He knew he hadn't the strength, and that just made him angrier.

But eventually Liath and the shaman would return to the tent, and they would come after him. He would not be hauled ignominiously back to captivity like an injured dog.

'Very well.'

The healer squatted, got arms under and around Blessing's slender body, and lifted her easily. Maybe it was the way her shoulders flexed under the felt jacket or the way her narrow hips fell in a line with her shoulders, or maybe it was the broad splay of her hands.

Maybe he was delirious and, like madmen, saw glimpses of truth beneath the falsehoods worn by the world.

The healer was a man, but a man dressed as a woman.

Sanglant shook his head and with teeth gritted against the pain set out again. No matter. He was hallucinating, or the Kerayit were stranger than he thought. It made no difference.

'Camp is—?' he asked, because the wind shifted and he lost the scent.

'That way.' Anna rose with a hand pressed into her ribs. 'I saw the smoke. I know where we're going.'

Downhill was harder than up because each footfall jolted him from heel to skull. He plodded along grimly. He *would* reach the camp, and there he would rest, and he would not leave his daughter's side until she recovered, or she died.

Ai, God. What if she *were* dying?

Nay, the Lord of Mercy could not be so cruel. And yet, why not? The Lady of Justice could not be so arbitrary, and yet, why not?

He slogged on while the moon reached zenith and began

to sink, occluded now and again by streaming clouds. The passage of those clouds along the heavens made him dizzy, as though he were spinning, and it made him recall that infuriating conversation he had once had with Liath years ago now, when they had sheltered at Verna.

There, too, she had dwelt easy among her sorcerous companions, who had accepted her as one of their own while treating him as an outsider. The way she had chatted with the shaman had triggered those old feelings of being an interloper, less important to her life than the weaving and binding of magic woven into her soul.

She had been shooting arrows into the sky to determine if it were Earth or the spheres which rotated. These questions she asked at first had made no sense, and yet in a corner of his mind he could hallucinate – he could visualize – the Earth as a sphere turning endlessly as the heavens rested in eternal repose around it, or perhaps it was the Earth which rested unmoving while the other spheres rotated, spheres nested inside spheres and all spinning at a different rate and speed and direction.

Was it the turning Earth that made him reel? Or exhaustion and his injuries? The wound on his chest had opened up; a sticky oozing of blood pasted his tunic to his skin, sliding and ripping as it began to dry or got wet all over again. No ordinary man could ever have walked so short a time after having his chest half ripped away, but ordinary men weren't cursed as he was.

He concentrated on setting one foot after the next, heel pressing into the ground and the foot rolling forward across the arch and onto the ball to begin the cycle again. Amazing how this most commonplace of movements might prove so daunting, so absorbing, so difficult. Even the curl of wind on his cheek carried extraordinary significance. How far had that wind traveled? Did wind have a home or did it simply travel around and around the Earth? Perhaps it was the wind that caused the Earth to turn, or perhaps the Earth's turning caused the wind.

He was dizzy, obviously. Why else would his mind stray

along such tortured and unexpected paths? The tang of smoking fires caught his attention. They were now closer to his army's camp than they were to the centaur encampment; he could separate out the disparate smells in the same way a discerning man can savor on his palate the blend of spices from a rich dish.

They might actually make it.

A shadow covered the moon but slid away quickly. The healer cried out in fear and dropped to her – his? – knees clutching Blessing close against her – his – body to shield her.

Anna screamed.

The silver griffin flew over them, banked awkwardly, and with wings beating hard came to rest in front of them. It lifted its massive eagle's head, turning it to one side for a better look first with one eye and then with the other. Its eyes gleamed like tiny suns. As its claws raked the ground, its tail lashed wickedly against the grass, scattering a cloud of chaff.

Anna whimpered. The healer did not move. The creature sank low on its haunches, ready to pounce.

He was too weak to kill it.

As he sagged forward, scarcely able to hold himself up on the spear, all he had left were his wits.

A griffin is one part eagle, one part lion, and one part snake, so the poets said. Lions were wild beasts and snakes were vermin, but eagles like all birds of prey had long lived in a measure of harmony beside humankind as hunting birds.

He dropped the spear, unpinned his cloak, and swept it off his shoulders in one smooth motion that took all his strength. The wound in his chest tore open. Adrenaline kept him going as he swung the cloak high up and over the griffin's head and, with the beast momentarily distracted by the fluttering cloth, leaped in against its shoulder and yanked the cloak down over its head, covering its eyes. And tensed, waiting for its violent reaction.

Hooded, and thus blinded, the griffin went utterly still.

'Go on,' he said hoarsely. Blood trickled down his abdomen. Sweat sheened his neck. 'Go, Anna. Go to camp and bring help. Bring rope, the strongest in camp. Bring fine cord, horsehair or gut, and needles stout enough to pierce this thick cloak. Take Blessing and go. Now!'

Anna slapped the healer on the arm and took off. The poor Kerayit hesitated, torn by duty, but the griffin terrified him; having been given permission, he abandoned Sanglant and trotted after Anna with Blessing safe in his arms.

Sanglant hung there, hands gripping the cloak closed below that massive, cruel beak, and took it one breath at a time. If he could keep the griffin hooded through this breath, drawn painfully in and let out with even greater agony tearing through his chest, then he could do it through the next one, and the next, and the next. He could hang on here until help came.

Wind whispered through the grass. The stars spun overhead, or maybe it was only his own head spinning, but he kept hanging on. Although the griffin stayed still, there remained shifts and tensions in the griffin's body just as there would in a horse held tight under its rider's hands: a twitch in one shoulder, a tufted ear laid back and flicked up, a shudder of restless muscles held in check.

He talked to the griffin the way he talked to Resuelto, hoping it would become accustomed to his voice, hoping that the time would pass and give him a chance to survive. Hoping that he could think of something other than the pain that had ignited deep in his chest, so hot and violent that he feared he would pass out like a snuffed flame. But he kept his voice steady and soothing nevertheless.

'What sort of beast are you? Where do your kind come from? Why did God make you? You are a strong, handsome fellow, are you not? You remind me of my gelding Resuelto, who is as strong and beautiful as you and loyal in the bargain, a fine horse. A good companion. Are you like a horse who may respond to good treatment? Or are you so wild that you will kill me as soon as you get the chance?'

As long as he kept the cloak tight over the griffin's eyes, as long as it couldn't see, it did not fight him. The play of the moon's light across its pale hindquarters fascinated him, yet a miracle also were its folded wings and the place around its shoulders where lion's body became an eagle's head. The twinkling of the stars seemed to reflect in the iron feathers, so edged, so dangerous, so close to his hands and body but not *quite* touching him because he was protected by the griffin's unexpected docility.

He waited, weak but stubborn, holding on. The moon reached the western hills; soon there would not be enough light to see more than suggestions of shapes. But he had never relied mostly on eyesight. He listened to the murmur of the wind through the grass, the melodic rubbing of the griffin's feathers where the breeze ruffled them, the scrabble of tiny claws through the grass where a mouse or rabbit foraged. He heard a distant shout, hushed by another voice.

They came prudently, moving swiftly but not recklessly, with Fulk in the lead and others close behind. Torches lit the night, and the crackle and hiss of flames and the pitchy scent of their smoke made the griffin uneasy.

'Hush, now,' he said, wishing he could stroke it, but if he touched the head and neck feathers, they would cut his hands, and he dared not shift enough to reach the tawny shoulder for fear of letting the cloak slip.

'My lord prince!' Fulk called to him from a safe distance.

An awed whisper, many voices murmuring at one time, rose from the troop. They did not rush forward, being well trained as well as practical, so although certainly the griffin smelled and heard and sensed their arrival they did not panic him. Not yet.

'Quietly, Captain. Come forward with the strongest thread you have, a canvas needle, and strong rope. We'll sew this cloak tightly over its head and lead it in to camp. It's kin to an eagle. No reason we can't jess it and train it.'

Silence greeted his words just as they would the utterances of the insane, but Captain Fulk came forward nevertheless. His legs hissed through the grass and his footfalls clipped along steadily, a man who did not lose his nerve even in the worst situations. A man I can trust, thought Sanglant, who dared not turn to watch Fulk's approach because his hands were numb and if he shifted the griffin might realize that a single strong jerk of its head would free it from the cloak.

Fulk was accompanied by some damn fool bearing a hissing torch that made the griffin shudder down the length of its body, but the man veered off downwind, crouched, and held the torch in such a way that it illuminated the scene so that Fulk would be able to see what he was doing.

'I pray you, Captain, work quickly. Sew it tightly and jess the beast's forelegs with just enough play so it can creep. We'll use the rest of the rope as a leash.'

'Yes, my lord prince.'

Captain Fulk was a most excellent soldier. He did what he was told and did not flinch or cower. Sanglant edged backward just enough to allow Fulk room to duck in under the griffin's head, where he started stitching the edges of the cloak together, working efficiently and with a remarkably steady hand. From this angle Sanglant was barely able to see over the beast's shoulder to the man reckless enough to accompany Fulk with the torch.

It was Sibold. Of course.

The young soldier was grinning madly. 'I see you found your griffin, my lord prince. I told them you would.'

XX

A STRONG POTION

1

Bartholomew assigned a burly oaf, called Stinker by the other men, to be Alain's jailer. He was big, and he did stink, and he had a nasty mouth on him, always cursing and muttering.

'You call me what the rest do and I'll bite your shitty little ears off,' said Stinker as they walked through the village, heading south. He kicked one of the dead clerics to show how tough he was, but otherwise the corpses were left lying as Father Benignus ordered them to move out.

'Bet you wish you had a big cock, like I do.'

Alain glanced at Bartholomew, who walked behind him, scratching his chin anxiously, but the man looked away, ashamed.

'I'm a big man, you cocksucker,' added Stinker, 'which is what you must have been if you rode with those pissing clerics. They're lying in their own piss and blood now, aren't they? Hate them, I do. I hate everyone.'

'Why?' asked Alain.

Stinker made a move to strike him, but Sorrow growled and the big man backed off while the bandits around them snickered.

'You wanna take me?' shouted Stinker. 'What about you, Red?' With his staff, he poked a youth whose cheek and chin were stained with a huge red birthmark. 'You making fun of me, Dog-ears?' He spat at the feet of a second man. 'You wanna make something of it?'

'You wanna get your teeth knocked out?' snarled Dog-Ears, tugging on the lobe of his remaining ear. 'We're just waiting. You say the word, Stinker.'

'Shut your mouths,' snapped Bartholomew. 'You know what happened to the last two men what got in a fight. You know how Father Benignus don't like that. You know what he'll do.'

That shut them up.

They walked south through the woodland until it was too dark to see and then wrapped themselves in their cloaks on the damp ground. A dozen men – about half the group – remained on watch, nervous and fearful. Alain allowed them to loop a rope around his wrists and tie him loosely to a tree trunk, and he leaned there, dozing, as the night passed. Mist pattered down through the branches, wetting his face. No owls hooted. He heard no sounds of life at all, only the intermittent shush of rain. As far as he could tell, Father Benignus spent the night huddled on his horse, never once dismounting.

At dawn, as the bandits rose groaning and made ready to depart with their captured horses and the clothing, food, and gear they'd stripped from the dead clerics, Alain caught Bartholomew by the arm and whispered in his ear.

'Does the holy father always stay on his horse? How does he pee?'

'Shut up.' Bartholomew yanked on the ropes. 'You're not dead, but you will be if you don't keep your mouth shut.'

Rage growled softly, enough to make Bartholomew start back as he eyed the huge hound, but she did not lunge. It was only a warning.

'Keep that dog off us,' warned Batholomew, moving away. 'Hey, you, Stinker! Get up here with your prisoner.'

'Hush.' Alain stroked Rage's head, and Sorrow nosed in as well, wanting attention.

Stinker kept his distance from the hounds. No one spoke

as they set off. They all seemed to know where they were going.

It was a miserable slog through the hilly countryside with a drizzle filtering down through beech and oak forest. Many of the trees hadn't reached their full foliage so, with no leaves to catch the mizzle, all the deer trails were churned to mud by those who walked at the front. Now and again an unexpected puddle lying athwart the track ambushed their steps until all of them, whether barefoot or shod, had sopping wet feet. Rain dripped from branches and misted down from the heavens until their shoulders were sodden and their hair slicked against heads and necks.

They reached their encampment about midday.

From the trail Alain glimpsed no hint of any campsite but there was an increasing restlessness in the hounds, who lifted their heads to sniff the air and made several darting forays into the undergrowth before he called them sharply to heel. Just before they broke free of the forest, he caught the scent of smoke, but because the wind was blowing at their backs, it faded away and he didn't smell the campfires until they came right out of the forest and could see them. There wasn't much of a clearing except where trees had been cut back. One ancient and vast trunk marked where a huge old oak tree had been cut down, although the stump was now weathered and brown with age. Where the trail ended and a cluster of ragged tents and makeshift hovels spread out through the clearing, he stopped short and stared.

At the far edge of the clearing, seven rugged stone pillars erupted out of the ground like uplifted scales along the back of a dragon buried in the earth. This craggy ridgeline rose starkly above the trees, a jumbled mass of natural rock pale in color and pockmarked by openings, steps, niches, overhangs, and what looked like windows carved into the upper reaches of the little crags.

The broken line of rocks reminded him of the Dragonback Ridge on Osna Sound.

He had seen dragons falling from the sky in that last vision of Adica's world, just before he was ripped away from her. An unexpectedly sharp stab of grief pierced him and, gasping, he dropped to his knees and covered his face with his hands.

'Hey, boy, move your sorry butt!'

A foot slammed into his hip, but the pain made barely any impression. Nor did Bartholomew's voice, sounding so distant, leagues away.

'Leave it, Stinker. Go on. I'll make sure he sticks here.'

Stinker's reek moved away, subsumed in the smoke and clatter of the camp, but these distractions dissolved as Alain struggled to make sense of his grief and of the world it had left him in.

Were these really dragons, stricken by magic to become stone and fallen to earth as the great sundering ripped through the world?

He pressed his palms into the mud and with the hounds growling at any who came close, he bent his head, shut his eyes, and listened through his hands.

He sought blindly for some echo that might reveal the presence of a monstrous dragon petrified into stone. Was that murmur the memory of its respiration? Or was it only the wind rustling in the trees? He heard as from a distance the sound of the bandits slogging past and their sarcastic comments, directed at his kneeling form, but he thrust that distraction aside and sought farther down, deeper into the earth. Was that faint thrum the heartbeat of the Earth singing through the ley lines that bound all of world together? These threads drew him like a clear straight path through an otherwise impassable forest, and he felt his awareness hurtling outward, away from his body. Voices called to him through the stone.

Who. Are. You? What. Have. You. Seen? Help. Us.

He could not reach them. He was not strong enough. He sought the one he needed to find if only he could call to him across the vast gulf of distance that separated them.

Stronghand.

There!

The thread splintered into light and became vision.

He skims across a world that is only water and sky, gray above and gray below, but after a moment he realizes that sedge beds and clumps of reeds break up the monotony of the expanse of dark water although he sees no break in the cloud cover above. Tufts of greenery mark islands. Birds flock everywhere, wings flashing in constant motion. The noise of their honking and shrilling and piping and whistling drowns the stealthy stroke of paddles dipped in and out of the water. He leans over the edge of the canoe to stare down into the murky waters, and sees himself.

He is Stronghand. His teeth flash as he grins; jewels wink in the reflecting waters. Beneath the surface fish teem. He could reach right down and catch eels with his hands. Here, in this seemingly desolate place, he has found riches.

'Keep low,' says the girl. 'We're close.'

The chattering chorus of birds covers the sound of their approach, although in truth the canoe parts the waters with no more sound than a duck dabbles, and both of his youthful guides know the secret of paddling silently as they dip and turn the oars. The boat slides into a dense cloud of reeds, and the girl slips over the side into knee-deep water and wades ashore.

Ki looks different than her cousin, not short and dark but half a hand taller, with the blonde hair and pale blue eyes common among the Albans. For the hunt today, she has streaked mud through her hair.

Half hidden among the vegetation, she gestures for him to follow. He slips over the side of the dugout, careful not to jostle his standard, which lies along the keel. Elafi leans against the opposite board so the boat won't heel or slosh.

The water parts around his legs as he wades after Ki as silently as possible, although to his ears he sounds like a fish thrashing in shallow water as it seeks the safety of the depths. Mud sucks around his feet. Bent low, he kneels on the shore beside a nest made of grasses that shelters four tiny eggs within its woven bowl. Ki picks one out, casually cracks it open, and swallows the slippery mass of half-formed bird.

The girl hands him a second egg. 'Take half, leave half.'

None among his kind eat eggs; it is taboo.

As he hands the egg out to Elafi, in the canoe, Ki speaks

again. 'From here, you can see the holy island.'

They creep up a low embankment, moving slowly so as not to startle birds into flight. Buntings perch on the tops of swaying reeds, but they do not take wing, unwilling to abandon their nests to these slow crawling beasts.

The birds are right to fear us, he thinks. *They have no means by which to fight back.*

Ki parts the reeds and beckons. He pads up beside her and gazes across a last glittery stretch of open waters. Three islands rise from the marsh, two of them low, buttressed by earth embankments thrown up around their perimeters that serve both as dikes and as fortifications, and the third a fully natural island set high enough that the tidal wash and the spring and summer floods cannot swamp it. There are so many armed men on the islands that the land is covered with them like swarming locusts. Tents lie higgledy-piggledy on the lower islands although some training grounds have been left bare, where men practice their swordcraft. Even from this distance he can hear the slap and ring of blows struck and countered as they prepare for war. A longhouse and three attendant huts hold pride of place on one of the islands but they were clearly built long ago, not newly raised. A golden banner marked with the image of a white stag flies from the thatched roof of the longhouse.

The Alban queen is here.

He can smell her. Her power and the magic of her tree sorcerers has a scent as sharp as smoke.

'Look!' whispers Ki, pointing.

The low summit of the third island bristles with teeth – or so he thinks until he realizes that a stone crown rises from the hill. All of the undergrowth has been ruthlessly cut back away from the circle of stones, and men labor with ropes and levers and earth ramps to raise a fallen monolith into position.

'What goes on there?'

She shakes her head in dismay. 'When our family watched over the holy place, we left it in peace. No good will come of this, I am thinking. They'll stir up the old spirits. Men have come from over the sea.'

'Ones like me?'

'Nay, not like you,' she says boldly. 'None of you dragon-men. You would not touch the holy place, I am thinking. These are circle priests who have come from the east lands across the sea. Elafi saw there was a fight between the circle priests and the tree priests, for the queen's favor.'

'How saw he this?'

'There's a place to come up close without being seen, right up inside the crown. Only our family knows about it, because we got the secret from the grandmothers.'

'Can you take me?'

Ki has a pup's grin, full of sharp teeth and playful expectation. 'Not till the dark of the moon. It isn't safe otherwise.'

Out of the still waters a majestic heron takes flight, wings wide as it glides low over them with its head tucked back on its shoulders and its legs dangling low, brushing the reeds. Its shadow covers them briefly.

Ki murmurs a blessing or a spell and ducks her head. 'It's a sign of the goddess' favor,' she whispers.

Perhaps.

The gods seem fickle to Stronghand, offering favor or withdrawing it according to unknown and unpredictable whims. The RockChildren have never been burdened by meddling gods. They are masters of their own destiny.

But still, only a fool casts dirt in clean water when he is thirsty.

'If your goddess smiles on us, then truly we will meet with success.'

'What do you mean to do?'

He looks up at the gray sky. He smells a change in the weather, the wet taste of the east wind. A misting rain approaches. He can actually see the shadow of its passage over the pools and dark waters as it nears them.

'We will wait until the dark of the moon,' he says. 'Then you will show me this secret place inside the crown.'

The girl is sharper than most of his advisers. She has never lived under the heel of a lord who holds over her the threat of life and death. That is why she is not afraid to question him. That is why she does not fear taking him out into the fens. 'And then?'

Stronghand bares his teeth, a startling flash that, for an instant, takes the youth aback. Maybe, for the first time, she understands the threat he poses. Ki's hand tightens on her knife, but she does not move at all, only stares back at him, eye for eye.

'I would like to know who these circle priests are, and what they are doing to the stone crown. Once I discover that, I will know what to do next. I have dreams, too.'

Ki pinches her lips together, eyes drawn tight. 'Dreams are dangerous, my lord. My mother says that dreams have killed men and brought low those who were once queens and those who wished to rule after them.'

The rain front washes over them, hissing in the waters. Through the curtain of rain it is hard to see farther than a spear cast; the islands lie obscure and veiled, but he feels the presence of the stone crown as a throb deep in his bones. A shout carries over the waters. A cheer.

A stone has been raised, and sunk in place.

'Dangerous,' he agrees, 'but it is more dangerous still to ignore them.'

That humming whisper vanished, and Alain found himself back in the dirt with mud slipping through his fingers and his knees cold and wet. The deep awareness that lived in the core of the stone was overwhelmed by the noise of the waiting camp: the scrape of a grindstone milling grain to flour, the steady stroke of a hammer, clucking chickens and complaining goats, a shout of excitement as the newcomers met their allies. The sound of a woman's weeping.

He blinked, trying to shake off the flood of sounds and images, but he could not shake his vision.

Long ago he had dreamed of the WiseMothers, seen through Stronghand's eyes, and in those dreams they had spoken of a great weaving that bound the Earth together. They knew of the great cataclysm because it had created them. The eldest among them were impossibly old.

Sorrow and Rage whined, licking his face, as he sat back on his heels. The WiseMothers, in their slow and patient way, also sought to mitigate the furious storm that was coming. The stone crowns were the key. If he could reach Stronghand and the WiseMothers, then maybe, for once, he could act. His knowledge might aid them. Adica's death would not have been in vain if by having witnessed he could save others.

A horse halted beside him.

'Are you praying?' asked Father Benignus.

He shook mud off his hands before wiping them on his leggings.

'We should all pray, Father,' he said, rising. 'A storm is coming.'

The veil that concealed the man's face shuddered as Benignus shifted his seat in the way an exhausted man fears sliding off into the mire. Yet he did not dismount. He lifted a gloved hand and indicated that Alain should follow him.

Bartholomew had waited at Alain's side all this time, and he trudged alongside, keeping an arm's length from the hounds.

Alain surveyed the camp. Including the new arrivals, perhaps three score souls sheltered here, although fully a third of them did not bide here of their own free will. They were the ones whose feet were bound so tightly with rope, as a horse is hobbled, that they could only shuffle as they went along on their errands carrying water, milking goats, and grinding grain. All of these captives were women, and there were no children in camp except for some infants bundled against their mothers' hips and three filthy toddlers sitting on their naked backsides in the mud and squalling like stuck pigs. Stinker, passing the children, swore loudly, slapped one hard, grabbed a second and shook it, and then for good measure slapped the young woman who came running to quiet their terrified shrieks.

'Bitch! These screeching brats can be sold as easily as their sisters and brothers if you sluts can't keep their mouths shut!'

The rope on Alain's wrists had been little more than a

show of docility. He shook it free now and ran over to place himself between the cringing woman and the stinking, scarred man, who looked eager to crack her across the face a second time. Maybe he was just waiting for an excuse.

'What manner of creature are you,' Alain demanded, 'who is such a coward that he must show his strength by bullying those so much weaker than he is?'

Heads turned. Dog-Ears guffawed outright and was kicked by his companion, Red. Bartholomew said a few words too softly for Alain to make out. The captive women around the camp went as still as if they'd been touched by a guivre's eye, and although none of them looked toward him he was immediately and intensely aware that they all knew exactly what was going on.

'You ass-licking bastard!' roared Stinker, who had the fight he'd been wanting. He lunged.

Sorrow leaped at him, but Stinker had already anticipated an attack, shifting sideways, and thwacked the hound on the side of the head with his staff, laying the poor beast out. Rage bolted back, yipping but not fleeing, and she kept her distance from the staff as she circled with a dog's measure, looking for an opening. Alain stood his ground, not even raising his arms to fend off the blow. The woman dropped to the ground behind him with a cry of fear and despair.

Father Benignus turned. A gust of wind rattled the trees.

'Eloie! Eloie! Isabaoth!' He lifted a hand and crushed something in his fist.

Stinker jerked up short an arm's length from Alain. His scream cut the air, and his face contorted into a rictus of agony as he twitched and danced, slapping himself silly and groaning and shrieking. His leggings soaked with piss, followed by the stink of his bowels as he voided them, and he gibbered and coughed up blood and finally, mercifully, collapsed in a stinking heap on the earth at Alain's feet.

Silence settled over the camp. The wind died.

One of the toddlers hiccuped a sob before being hustled away by the woman, herself sniffling and choking down tears. The other two children trotted after her on their scrawny legs.

Hobbled women scooped them up and stood trembling, eyes lowered.

Sorrow whined and, with a grunt, padded gingerly over to Alain, who stroked him carefully and found the hardening bruise where the staff had struck him along the shoulder. Rage, still growling softly, loped up to stand beside him.

Stinker had fallen onto his back. The coarse burlap rags he wore had a fist-sized hole burned through the cloth. Alain knelt by the dead man's shoulders and reached toward the frayed burn.

'Don't touch it!' gasped Bartholomew. 'Only Father Benignus is allowed—' He faltered and glanced up to where Father Benignus sat silent, shoulders bowed as if from exhaustion. Ducking his head, he waited for a blow.

No one moved.

Alain peeled away burned tunic from weeping flesh. Stinker wore an amulet around his neck, and it was this crude binding that had erupted into flame and scorched his skin. He stank, indeed, and not just from the pulpy mess he had voided in his death throes. He had been burned from the inside out.

Alain rose and straddled the corpse, lifting his chin as he looked at Father Benignus. 'Is this justice?'

Bartholomew made a strangled noise. What had passed for silence before deepened into a dreadful anticipatory pause, the moment before the executioner's ax falls.

'What is justice?' replied Father Benignus in a voice so weary it might be called cruel.

He shook the reins and guided his horse forward, halting beside the corpse. With a stick, he fished for the amulet, hooked it, and yanked it hard enough to break the thong that held it around Stinker's neck. Flipping up the stick, he caught the amulet in his hand and rode his horse toward a wagon covered with a tent to make a kind of house on wheels.

'Bartholomew, bring him. I want no more interruptions.'

'Yes, Father Benignus,' whispered Bartholomew, scratching his warty nose. He did not look at Alain; he sidestepped Stinker's corpse and shied anxiously away from Sorrow's growl. 'Come, then, you fool,' he muttered in a low voice. 'Can't you see how dangerous it is to keep the good father waiting?'

'Who are these women?' Alain demanded, not moving.

'Fair winnings.'

'No better than slaves, fettered so. What happened to their children?'

'You ask too many questions. If you're stupid enough, you'll ask Father Benignus, not me. I'm just a poor man.'

'Even a poor man is made in God's image, is he not? Is this right, what you do?'

Bartholomew had begun to shake, and by the sheen of sweat on his face and the pallor under his scruffy beard Alain suddenly realized that the man was terrified. He twisted the cloth of his tunic between his fingers, right over a slight bulge in the fabric where he, too, wore an amulet.

Alain shook his head. 'I am sorry to see any man suffer so, but surely you and the others had committed grave crimes. I see the residue of them everywhere. I pray you, friend, give some thought to the fate of your soul.'

'Here's the wagon,' muttered Bartholomew. 'Wait outside.'

Father Benignus had handed the reins of his horse off to a stammering youth, who held its bridle while the hooded man swung awkwardly from the saddle to the bed of the wagon and, bending double, vanished inside the shelter.

'Stay!' Rage and Sorrow sat beside the wagon, but they looked ready to spring into action. As Alain scrambled up onto the tailgate, he heard the startled murmurs of the bandits in camp. Everyone was watching, as wolves watched an injured elk, waiting for its thrashing to subside enough that they can dart in to tear out its throat.

He ducked in after Father Benignus.

'I knew you would come.' Father Benignus had his back to Alain as he lit a candle and dropped the amulet into a bowl filled with a clear liquid. It hissed, and the liquid boiled and subsided, leaching a strong vinegar smell. 'The others fear me, as they should. You should, too.'

The tent vaulted just high enough that he could stand upright in the center of the wagon. The flame flickered uneasily as the man unwrapped the veil and took off his broad-brimmed hat. He had long, greasy hair that might once have been blond. That much Alain glimpsed in the dim light before Benignus turned to face him and sank down on a narrow bed, exhausted.

He was horribly disfigured. Lesions had eaten away half his face, exposing bone. His eyes wept pus, and sores had long since eaten his ears.

'Are you a leper?' Alain shuddered. Leprosy passed from one man to another by means of contamination. It would strike any man. It was God's worst punishment. Yet having come so far Alain would not retreat.

Because Father Benignus had no lips it seemed that he smiled all the time, a skeleton's grimace. His teeth were good, strong and white; he was only missing two.

'I am no leper.' Benignus said mockingly in his soft voice. 'I am least among men, but no leper. I am the one so easily forgotten even by those who used and discarded me. So easily forgotten by pawns and biscops alike, for you were only a pawn, as I was, weren't you? Although Father Agius kept you close. Did he pollute you with his heresy?'

Alain recognized his voice, even distorted as it was by his affliction. He remembered pale blue eyes.

'I know who you are. I called you Brother Willibrod once. You were a cleric in the retinue of Biscop Antonia. She set you and the others to binding and working. You made the amulets that protected Lady Sabella's forces from the spell laid on humankind by the glance of the guivre's eye. They hoped to win the battle against King Henry.'

'But Father Agius killed the guivre! All our work for nothing! So we were abandoned, all of us who had poisoned ourselves doing God's work! All but Heribert, who never soiled himself with binding and working! We were left to the mercy of the sisters of St. Benigna who locked us in an attic and left us to die!' Willibrod shook all over, then gagged, and reached for a flask hung from a nail pounded into the frame onto which the tent's fabric had been nailed. His palsied hand could not grip the leather flask.

Alain stepped forward, unhooked the flask, and took out

the stopper. Willibrod drank nothing stronger than vinegar, apparently, tinged with a scent so sharp it gave Alain a headache. He handed the flask to the other man. Even so, Willibrod could not hold it because he trembled so violently, and the flask tipped out of his hands and spilled onto the floorboards.

Gasping and choking, Willibrod cried out in pain as liquid pooled over the wood and began to soak in. He flung himself onto the floor and writhed there, licking it up like a frantic dog.

Alain dropped down beside him.

'Don't touch me!' Willibrod jerked back from Alain's hand only to slam into the bed's wooden frame, but the impact had no effect on him.

'I pray you, Brother. Let me.' Alain salvaged the flask; perhaps a third of it had leaked out. The liquid stung his fingers and he winced at its touch.

Willibrod yanked the flask out of his hand and set it to his lips, gulping desperately while Alain hastily wiped his fingers on his leggings. The vinegar was raising blisters on his skin.

'What are you poisoning yourself with?' He blew on his hand, but blisters kept popping up where the liquid had burned him.

Willibrod lowered the flask. His hands had stopped shaking, but his face was as ghastly as ever, his mouth caught in its eternal grimace. 'The distillation of life,' he whispered, eyes lolling back like one drugged. 'The souls of dying men. It makes a strong potion.'

Had the pain of his affliction driven him insane? Yet the expression in his eyes had an awful clarity, the look of a man who knows he has done something so horrible that he can never atone for it.

'Kill me,' Willibrod begged hoarsely, voice barely audible.

The aroma of the vinegar and the putrid smell of sores and lesions stifled, as choking as smoke. Alain coughed, fighting for breath, and took a step closer to the other man just as a shudder passed through Willibrod's frame, a palsy that made his body jerk and tremble. Alain bent to hold him down, but before he could touch him, Willibrod's eyes shifted; the stark agony of his gaze dulled and his expression changed in the same manner that the sky changes color when a cloud covers the sun.

'Stand back!' The stink of his breath startled Alain badly – it was like the stench that rises off the battlefield, attracting carrion crows. It was the reek of decay and despair, yet he spoke like a triumphant general. 'Do not touch me! Why have you come here?'

Outside, Rage barked twice, then fell silent.

Alain stepped backward to touch the entrance flap. 'You are not Willibrod any longer.'

'Willibrod died in the attic under the care of the sisters of St. Benigna. Life did not leave him entirely, but he died nevertheless.' That death's-head grin did not falter. 'Now I am Father Benignus, taking my revenge on the world.'

'You are taking your revenge on folk who never did you any wrong. Folk who had nothing to do with the pain inflicted on you by Biscop Antonia and Lady Sabella. The evil done to you does not justify the evil you do to innocent others.'

'What makes you think I believe in right and wrong any longer? How did God reward my loyalty or the faithful service of my fellow clerics? Now I have power, and I will use it as the whim takes me. I do not serve either God or the Enemy. I serve only myself.' The potion had renewed him. He rose, looking vigorous and unexpectedly powerful, if no less hideous. 'Are you with me, Brother Alain? Or do you prefer to die and let your soul feed mine?'

2

Liath swept through the entrance and stopped short. It wasn't only the run from Sorgatani's wagon that made her heart race. What she saw made her tremble with anger and apprehension. The tent lay empty, its disarray evidence of the hasty departure of Sanglant and his retinue. He was gone, gone, gone. How could he be so stupid?

A bowllike lamp placed on a closed chest kindled with the force of her feelings. Flame sheeted the surface of the oil.

When she spoke, her voice shook. 'He'll have gone back to his army.'

'So we believe.' The shaman did not venture past the threshold, only ducked her head down to examine the interior. Behind her, the misty late night haze dissipated as dawn's twilight lightened the sky.

'You *saw* him go?'

'I did not, but others did.'

'They didn't stop him?'

The oil burned so fiercely that she reached with her mind's eye and shuttered it as one might shutter a window. Just like that, the flames died. Smoke curled up, vanished, and left a faint scent. She crossed to look down into the lamp. That brief flare had scarcely affected the level of the oil in the shallow lamp bowl. In Sorgatani's wagon, while searching for Hanna, an entire bowl of oil had been consumed. She had imagined innocently, foolishly, that the force of her seeing had eaten up the oil quickly but now she realized that she had drifted within that gateway for far longer than she had guessed. She had searched for Hanna all night while Sanglant gathered up his daughter and his servant and staggered back to those he trusted.

She kicked the pallet he had lain on. It felt good to have something to hit.

'We'll have to go after him,' she said, gathering up her weapons, which she had left on the ground between Blessing's pallet and the tent wall.

'Why must you go?' asked Li'at'dano as Liath came outside. The centaur shaman seemed honestly puzzled. 'We are allies, you and I. There is much to be done if we are to combat these Seven Sleepers. We have a long journey ahead of us, unless you can weave the crowns.'

'I'm going after my husband,' said Liath as she adjusted the weight of her sword and the angle of her quiver.

'He is only a male. You can find another mate when it is time for you to breed again.'

'Not one like him!' The comment gave her pause. She swept her gaze over the encampment. 'Why are there no male centaurs among you? There are both men and women among your Kerayit allies, but I see no males among your kind at all.'

Li'at'dano blinked. For a moment Liath feared she had insulted the shaman. Although her features looked very like those worn by humankind, there was a subtle difference in the way expressions played across her face that betrayed her essential otherness.

She is like me but not like me, thought Liath. *I cannot assume that she thinks as I do, or that our goals match exactly. We are allies, not sisters.*

'I pray you,' she said aloud, wishing she had asked Sorgatani more questions about the centaurs. With Sorgatani, she had felt so entirely comfortable; she had felt that no comment might be misconstrued, only explained or expanded on. She had felt understood, in harmony. 'I pray you, I mean no insult if I have spoken of something that you consider taboo.'

'We are as we are, and as you see,' said Li'at'dano finally. 'That you are otherwise is a mystery to us. It is the great weakness of humankind.'

'I don't understand you, but I ask you, forgive me if I behave in any manner that goes against your ways. I must go after my husband. If there are any who will accompany me, I would appreciate an escort. I do not know where his camp lies.'

'You have an escort already.' Li'at'dano pointed toward the western slope. 'The beast fears and desires your heart of fire.'

The griffin paced on the grassy hillside, keeping well out of range of the centaur bows. The rising sun gilded her feathers and she shone, her wing feathers shimmering as the light played across them, her beauty all the more striking because she was so huge and so dangerous and wild. Her tail lashed the grass; she was disturbed and anxious.

'God help me,' murmured Liath. Yet there was no way but to go past her, not if she wanted to follow Sanglant.

'West and north,' added Li'at'dano helpfully. 'You can see the smoke of their campfires. Do not make us wait long. We must move quickly. The wheel of the heaven turns no matter what we do here on Earth.'

'I know.' She turned back to meet the shaman's gaze, which appeared to her cold and steady but not hostile, simply quite another thing from the look of humankind. 'I could have remained with my kinfolk, beyond the heavens,' she said at last. 'I could have turned my back on humankind entirely, but I did not. These are the chains that bind me to Earth. I cannot escape them now, nor do I wish to.'

Li'at'dano nodded, an acknowledgment but not, precisely, comprehension. 'It is not our way. I will not interfere with your customs, because you are not mine to command. Go quickly.'

Go quickly.

Suddenly the fear that something awful had happened to Sanglant and her daughter overwhelmed her. She had journeyed so far; what if she lost him now?

As soon as the griffin saw Liath coming, she padded away, tail beating the grass like a whip. Liath followed her; no question that the beast knew where she was going, and Liath saw traces of a trail – not an actual path cut through the landscape but the evidence left by the passage of a small party some time earlier: broken stems of grass, beads of blood dried on glossy leaves, a spot where someone had lain down to rest. These minute signs reassured her, but they made her wonder.

'Why do you lead me?' she asked aloud. 'Why does this path interest you? What do you seek?'

The griffin swung its huge head around to stare at her, its amber gaze unwinking. It ducked its head down and with a shudder unfolded its wings to flash in the sun like a host of swords before furling them along its body. They moved on at a brisk pace. Liath had to run to keep up with the griffin's strides.

She began to suspect the worst when, soon after, they reached a place where the ground was churned up by the trampling of many feet, where the soil had been ripped up by the force of claws digging into the ground.

Sanglant had, after all, been hunting griffins. Yet he was far too weak to kill one. There wasn't enough blood, only drops visible here and there. If he had been torn to pieces by the griffin, then it had not taken place here, and if he had slaughtered the griffin, a field of gore would have marked their struggle.

Her breath came in ragged gasps as she sprinted, seeing the smoke of their campfires just over the next rise.

The griffin bounded to the crest of the hill and paused there, shining in the midmorning sun to scream its rage as a challenge. Adrenaline hammered through her as she bolted forward, hoping she had not come too late. When she crested the rise and saw the unexpectedly large camp laid out in an orderly fashion below her, when she saw – and how could she miss it? – what Sanglant had done, she began to laugh or else, surely, she would have cried.

3

'There's a griffin on the hill, my lord prince!' Even Captain Fulk, pushed to his limit, could sound frightened sometimes. 'God Above! And a woman walking with it. She has a bow.' The hesitation that followed these words was so heavy that Fulk's astonishment seemed audible. 'Lord have mercy!'

'My lord prince,' said Heribert softly. Joyfully. 'It is Liath.'

Sanglant had never known it could hurt to open your eyes, but it did. Everything hurt. Breathing hurt. The sunlight hurt, but he looked anyway at the dazzle of light on the eastern slope. It was hard to see anything with the sun so bright and the beast that paced there so very large and fierce-looking, its wings gleaming ominously as it stretched them wide.

It screamed a challenge. Horses whinnied in fear, and he heard men shouting. In response to that cry the silver griffin strained and fought against the ropes and chains that bound it, but the soldiers had done their work well. One rope snapped, but the others, and the chains thrown over its deadly wings, held. Surly darted in to grab the thrashing rope and with the help of several of his fellows tied it down. No one got hurt this time, although it had been a different outcome hours ago when they had walked the hobbled, hooded griffin into camp and staked it down.

'What do we do, my lord prince?' asked Fulk, still nervous. Horses stamped and whinnied, not liking the approach of the griffin one bit despite the calming work of their grooms.

That griffin did indeed look fearsome. Its iron tang drifted on the breeze. It had, no doubt, come to rescue its mate. But what on earth was Liath doing walking beside it as though it were her obedient hound?

'Where is Lewenhardt? We'll need every archer. Spearmen set in a perimeter, in staggered ranks. Double the guard on the horses if you haven't already.'

He rested on a couch his soldiers had dragged out into the center of camp so that he could lie close – but not too close – beside his captured griffin and talk to it, when he didn't doze off. It had to become accustomed to him.

He gritted his teeth and made an attempt to stand, but he did not have the strength. Hathui and Fulk and Breschius moved to help him, but he waved them away impatiently.

'Let her come to me. I need not move.'

I cannot move.

'My lord.' They glanced at each other; if thoughts were words, he would have heard an earful, but they remained mercifully silent.

Liath started down the hill toward them while the griffin remained on the hill. Maybe it had intelligence enough to be wary of the soldiers forming up throughout camp, faces grim and weapons ready. Maybe she commanded it with words alone. Maybe she had that much power.

'Do you wish for shade, my lord prince?' asked Hathui.

'No,' he said, because the sun's warmth – such as it was so early in the spring – soaked into his skin in a healing fashion, as though light itself could knit him back together again.

His retinue gathered beside him, keeping well back from the hooded griffin. It had not liked entering the camp; the scent of horses stirred its blood, and Sibold had taken a gash to his shoulder and several men had been clawed, but in the end they had secured it without loss of life. Blinded by the cloak, it had submitted. Now it stirred again, knowing its mate was close. But that hood still constrained it. It hated and feared blindness.

It was his, now, and he did not intend to lose it. Not even to his wife.

She walked into camp, armed and glorious, and approached him, halting a body's length from the couch on which he lay. He found himself distracted by that long snake of a braid falling over her shoulder and across one breast, all the way down past her waist. He remembered the way the tip of that golden-brown braid swayed along her backside when she walked.

'Prince Sanglant,' she said in the formal manner, jolting him back to the cold, cruel present.

Two could play that game.

'I am Prince Sanglant.' *In case you have forgotten.*

Her expression did not change, but her chin lifted, so he knew she had taken the blow. Yet she went on in the same vein.

'I am come to make an alliance with you. You marched east seeking griffins and sorcerers. I see that you have captured your griffin. What of the second part of your quest?'

'I believe I can train a griffin to eat from my hands and come at my call. Are sorcerers as obedient?'

Anger sparked in her eyes – really sparked; it was uncanny how the blue fire of her irises flashed as though it burned.

'May we speak privately?' she asked finally.

He had enough strength to lift a hand. Fulk chased off the onlookers and finally only Fulk, Hathui, Breschius, and

Heribert were left in attendance, hovering close, anxious and pale.

'I listen,' Sanglant said, in the formal manner.

'Where is our daughter?'

'With me, under my care and that of her loyal attendants who have served her faithfully for four long years, never leaving her side and even risking their own lives to keep her safe.' He read how the blow landed by the tightening of her lips and the twitch of her shoulder, but she did not reel or stagger.

'She suffers from a malady that cannot be healed by any ordinary physician. She will die if she is not protected by sorcery until we understand how we might heal her.'

'She has not died yet. I believe it was your return that injured her.'

'Sanglant!' Yet she hesitated. She thought, hard and deeply, although her expression gave away nothing. His attendants stared at her, amazed at her presence; amazed, perhaps, by this negotiation that was more like the maneuvering of rival families than the reunion of intimate partners.

Heribert seemed ready to speak, but Sanglant caught his gaze and, with a sharp sigh, Heribert shifted from one foot to the other and kept his mouth shut.

'Sanglant.' Again she hesitated, but only to gather her voice, to speak softly enough that even those standing nearby might not hear her words. 'Why do you speak to me as though we are enemies?'

He did not care what others heard. He wanted witnesses. 'Enemies? Worse than enemies! You abandoned me! Just left me behind in Verna. Your daughter is enchanted, spelled in a way no one here can comprehend, but you were not here to combat it. Now maybe she will die. I was left behind with all else. For four years! I thought you vowed to be faithful to me, but you proved no different than my mother. Husband and child, abandoned without thought.'

It was so good to fight back. He wanted his words to hurt her, and they did. He saw her face go gray; he saw her hands curl and her entire body quiver.

She was not without weapons of her own.

'Your mother was never married to King Henry.'

'That's right! She'd made no pledge to him! She had no obligation to uphold! But you did! Why did you leave us? Why did you wait so long to return?'

Now she was really angry; she shone with it. 'I did not abandon you! I was taken from Verna by my kinfolk. I never asked to go with them. When I could not follow them higher up into the heavens, I found myself in your mother's land, where I learned all that Anne says is true, and worse besides, that her understanding of the truth is twisted by her own fanaticism. But now I have walked the spheres. I have seen through the gateway of the burning stone into the ancient past. I know what destruction awaits us if Anne weaves the spell a second time.'

She had really worked herself up. Her voice rang as if above the din of battle, carrying over the camp so that the griffin quieted and every soul stopped and turned.

'I did not leave you for four years. In the lands of the Ashioi, time does not run by the same measure it does here. There is an old sorcerer still alive there who lived in the days of the great cataclysm when his people and their land were torn from Earth. He is your *grandfather*, Sanglant. Still alive, although by our measure he would have lived – ai, God – twenty centuries or more. Yet he seems no older than an elder who boasts seventy years. When I walked in that far country, when I ascended the mage's ladder and walked the spheres, it seemed to *me* that no more than seven days had passed. It seemed that I left Verna only a handful of days ago. I could not have returned sooner! I did everything I could. I suffered, and I learned, and I placed myself in danger, and I have grasped the heart of the power that is within me. Maybe I am the only one here who can stop Anne. Maybe that duty, that obligation, has been forced upon me. Maybe that obligation has to come first. Maybe the lives of untold countless thousands and tens of thousands have to count for more than one life, even the life and happiness of my beloved husband. I am sorry that four years passed for you! I would not wish for it to have happened in this way, but there was nothing I could have done differently. I could have stayed there, with my kinfolk, in a place much better and brighter than this one! But I chose to return to you. To Blessing. To Earth. To my father's home. And I surely expected to come back to a better welcome than this!'

In the absolute stunned silence that followed this declamation a rolling rumbling *whoosh* of flame erupted along the ridge, causing the big griffin to take wing and circle away to a safer resting place. Grass sizzled and soldiers cried aloud. Smoke poured heavenward as Liath looked up, startled, and saw the spreading fury of the fires. With an intent gaze, attention shifting entirely and horribly *away* from him, she frowned. The fires snuffed out, just like that. Smoke puffed; ash sprinkled down over the camp and drifted away on the wind.

Sanglant had become suffused with an entirely unexpected – or foredoomed – flush of arousal just looking at her, being close enough really to smell the perfume of her. His anger made his senses that much more on edge and her presence that much more intimate, although they did not touch. She was so beautiful, not in the common way but in the remembered way, when he had dreamed of her those nights in Gent, when he had woken up beside her those nights in Verna and been astonished and delighted and utterly famished, starving for the touch of her skin, her hands, her lips.

Maybe he couldn't walk yet, but he had strength enough to move his arms. He caught her around the back of the neck, where skin and hair met at the nape. Just that touch made him drunk with ecstasy. He pulled her head toward him and kissed her. And kissed her.

And kissed her.

Her warmth melted him like the sun's fire, as though desire itself could knit him back together again.

'My lord prince! The griffin!'

He released Liath as she pulled away from him, jumping to her feet. Her cheeks were flushed and her eyes bright, as passionate as he was. But behind her, the griffin stalked through the line of tents. Men cowered, but the beast did not strike. Fulk stepped forward, spear raised, but Liath intercepted him.

'Don't move!' she said sharply.

Heribert had gone gray-white, like curdled milk, and Hathui tensed, her mouth a grimace, as she prepared herself for death. Only Breschius stared in outright awe, gaze lit with wonder, as the griffin swung its head to examine him. The frater looked ready to die at that moment, as long as he was slain by something so terribly beautiful.

Then the creature moved past him and loomed over Sanglant.

'Don't move,' said Liath, but of course he could not move even had he meant to kill it. An iron reek rolled off it like the heat of the forge, soaking him to the bones. He had to close his eyes; his face was sweating.

'Now what?' he asked, cracking open his eyes. He almost laughed. He was entirely helpless; it could take his head off, and even his mother's curse could not save him then. Yet he could not keep his gaze away from his wife's form, glimpsed beyond that massive eagle's head. He knew what lay beneath Liath's tunic; he saw the curve of her hips, the swell of her breasts, and frankly after all this time the griffin seemed rather more a distraction than a danger. At this moment. At this instant. Maybe it wouldn't be so bad to die if you expired in the arms of the one you loved best.

The griffin huffed, a wheezing cough, and the silver griffin uttered a yelping call in answer.

'Do you wish to free her mate?' Liath asked.

'No,' he said defiantly. 'I need griffin feathers. A live beast serves me as well or better than a dead one. I claim him.'

'So does she.' She, too, was laughing – although not aloud. Her expression sang with it. She didn't fear the griffins, and more importantly she still desired him.

The griffin lowered its head until that deadly beak hovered an arm's length from his face, seeking his scent or an understanding of his essence.

'Do you still love me?' he asked, thinking that he might

die before he could take another breath. He had to know.

Now she did laugh. 'I swore an oath to never love any man but you, Sanglant, so it scarcely matters, does it? I bound myself. I will never be free of you.'

'Thank God.'

The griffin huffed again, a noise that shuddered through its body, and lifted its head, then sat down on its haunches like a watchdog. The audible gasps of the soldiers and his attendants flowed around him like the murmur of a rising wind. An iron feather shook free and drifted down to slice through the grass beside his couch. He reached and found that if he grasped the quill and kept his fingers away from the feathered vane and edges, he did not cut himself.

'I couldn't even kill Bulkezu,' he said in a low voice, staring at the feather. The anger wasn't gone, only swallowed. 'I need this griffin, or you may as well lead the army yourself.'

She grimaced as a shadow covered her face. 'I am no leader. I am no regnant.'

'You are Taillefer's heir!'

'I am not!' she cried triumphantly. 'Anne is not my mother. I am not the child of any human woman. Do not burden me with Taillefer's legacy. I am rid of it.'

He let go of the feather and shut his eyes as a spasm of pain twisted through his chest. After a while, he could speak again.

'If you are not Anne's child – if you are not Taillefer's great grandchild. What of Blessing, then? What of her claims?'

'You are the child of a regnant, Sanglant. Blessing is Henry's granddaughter. Isn't that claim enough?'

No.

For all this time he had paraded Blessing in front of his allies as the rightful heir of Taillefer. To discover the claim wasn't true silenced him.

The griffin settled down to rest her eagle's head on her forelegs. She closed her eyes and huffed once more, the strength of that sound rippling through her shoulders and tawny haunches. Her tail slapped the ground, and stilled.

'I am not even Anne's daughter,' she repeated so softly

that he heard her only because of his unnaturally keen hearing. 'I am the bastard child of my father, Bernard, and a captive fire daimone. It's true Da was born into a noble house, but it is the most minor of lineages.'

'You said once that Sturm was your kinsman.'

'So Wolfhere told me. I believe it to be true. But Wolfhere lied to me about Anne, so maybe he lied to me about that as well.'

'Ai, God,' whispered Sanglant as the tide of adrenaline and arousal ebbed, leaving him drained and exhausted and in so very much pain. 'How can we know what is true and what is the lie? How can we choose the right path?'

'Griffins and sorcerers.' Her gaze flicked toward the dozing griffin, and he saw in her expression that she wasn't quite as fearless as he thought – the creature made her nervous even though she believed it would not hurt her. 'You have been walking on the right path all along. You have what you marched so far to get. Together we can turn back to the west and fight Anne.'

'We will need a powerful army to defeat our enemies.'

'I cannot bring you an army.'

'Nor do I ask you to,' he said irritably. 'I boast a talisman better than griffin wings. I know how to raise an army. First, we must call a council . . .' Yet he was so weak he could not sit up. 'I need two days to heal.'

'The heavens revolve regardless of our hurts. We must move swiftly.'

'I must have two days! I cannot—' He coughed, grimaced, and only her hands pressing on his shoulders stopped him from thrashing and thereby breaking open the wound. He grasped her fingers and with eyes shut just breathed, lips pinched together and his entire face knotted up as he waited for the agony to subside.

'My lord prince. Liath, what is wrong?'

'Bring him something to drink, I pray you, Heribert. Wine, if you have it.'

'We have nothing but this nasty fermented mare's milk.'

'That will do. It will ease the pain.'

She eased her weight off his shoulder and brushed fingers caressingly along one cheek. He got hold of her braid and twisted it around his hand, letting its feel distract him, breathing out the pain with each breath until, piece by piece, he could relax.

'Blessing,' he said at last, when he could speak. 'What of Blessing?'

'It is no form of sorcery I understand. Perhaps Da wrote of it in his book, but I don't have his book anymore.'

'Hugh has your father's book.'

'Hugh is another danger,' she agreed. 'I will go back to Li'at'dano. I will convey to her your wish for a council. I will ask her to do what she can to protect Blessing.'

'Can we trust them? They destroyed the old empire. They feared and hated them. They fear humankind now.'

'I trust Li'at'dano.'

'Do you trust her with your daughter's life?'

'Do you trust me with it, Sanglant?'

'Ah!' It was an unexpected stab, a knife in the dark. The words came hard, after all that had passed, but he said them. 'Do what you must.'

4

'No.'

The stink of Willibrod's sorcery filled the tent and made Alain's eyes run, yet he wept with sadness and disgust as well. Reaching behind his own back, he found the coarse cloth of the tent, the flap that covered the entrance, and gripped it. 'I will not join you. And you will not kill me. You have no power over me.'

'I have power,' whispered Willibrod.

'The power to turn men's hearts so they eat at themselves and succumb to the worst that is in them. The power to make others suffer. The power to prey on the weak. I am not weak.'

'You are alone.' Willibrod took a step toward him, but Alain held his ground and jerked the flap aside to let light stream in.

Willibrod shrieked, staggering backward. He groped for the hat and veil while, outside, Rage and Sorrow began such a clamor of barking that the folk who had crept close to listen scattered in fear.

'Can you bear the touch of the sun? Or the touch of the earth? You are vulnerable, Willibrod. By abusing your power you have forged the weapon that will kill you.'

Willibrod was still whimpering in pain as he struggled to settle the veil over his face. Alain stepped sideways out of the tent and stood on the lowered tailgate of the wagon. Rage lunged toward Bartholomew and a gang of five other men who had sidled forward, and they bolted back to a safe distance. Red hefted his staff to protect himself, but the hound danced out of his range.

'Father Benignus is not master over life and death!' Alain pitched his voice to carry, knowing that the fear the bandits felt in the presence of Willibrod worked to his advantage. Anger made him reckless. 'He can hurt you only as long as you wear the amulets he gave you.'

'They protect us against death!' shouted Bartholomew. 'No man wearing the amulet has died in battle.'

'Against what implacable enemy have you fought? Poor peasants? Frightened children? Folk who have no better weapons than their shovels and hoes? Would you fare as well against armed men? Because armed men will come soon. The levy of Lord Arno will ride, alerted by my companions. How will you survive against trained men-at-arms?'

The wagon rocked under his feet, and he jumped off the tailgate and landed on the earth.

'Will Father Benignus protect you? He cannot even protect himself! Has light touched his skin since the day he first gathered you together? Have his feet touched this earth? He fears light and earth, because he is not a strong man but a weak one. He needs you for one purpose only, to bring him souls to drink to keep his husk alive for one day longer. In the end, he will eat your souls, too, because his hunger rules him.'

He had them now. A score whispered, backing away, as Willibrod pushed past the entrance flap. The maleficus was once again veiled and gloved with not a speck of skin showing. Women cowered against the stone ridge.

'Kill him,' said Willibrod. 'The man who kills him can have his choice among the women tonight.'

Alain took a step toward the gathered men. Theirs were a bleak line of faces, some worn and weary, some merely fashioned, like untrained dogs, to jerk where each least instinct pulled them.

'Is this the reward he gives you? That you can force women who get no pleasure from the act and will hate you afterward?'

'What care we if they hate us,' cried Dog-Ears, 'if we get the pleasure in doing them? I was a slave in a lord's steading and there were no women for me there and never would be. Now at least I've something I hadn't before.'

'I have a good wool cloak, and a silver necklace,' said Red. 'I never had such things before!'

'Enough to eat, and meat to share!'

The rest muttered in agreement. These were outlaws and outcasts, slaves and servants, homeless day laborers, the ones who, like Willibrod, were used and discarded according to the whim of the folk who had power over them. Why should they care if they gave way to the evil inclination? They had no hope anyway. Lord Arno's men would kill them like vermin, so they took what was offered by Willibrod since it was a feast compared to the leavings that had been cast in the dirt before them in their previous lives.

He could not sway them with this argument.

Bartholomew set arrow to string. Red and Dog-Ears took threatening steps toward Alain, staffs raised, hesitant only because of the growling hounds. Their amulets dangled at their chests.

Their amulets.

That stink of vinegar held the key.

'Do you know how Father Benignus sustains himself?' Alain cried.

'Kill him!' shrieked Willibrod from the wagon.

'It may be true that none of you die when you attack the poor and the helpless. But you fight among yourselves, and Father Benignus punishes those who break the peace. And when that man dies, his soul is captured by the amulet. When *this man*—' He gestured toward Willibrod. '—takes that amulet, he soaks it in water and drinks that man's soul. It gives him life for another day or another week. He feeds on you now. He drew you together only to use you. He bears no love for you. He cares nothing for any hardships you may have once suffered, nor does he care what cruelties you inflict upon others. He lives for no reason except his own hunger. In the end, he will kill you all.'

'Kill him!' shouted Willibrod, but the bandits held still, whispering each to his fellow, fingering the amulets, lowering their bows.

'Or I will kill you!' shrieked Willibrod. 'Eloie! Eloie! Isaba—'

Bartholomew let the arrow fly.

It ripped through the tattered robes. Willibrod spun backward and slammed into the tent. Canvas ripped as the frame splintered, but he flailed and righted himself, still standing despite the arrow protruding from the center of his chest. He raised his hand to call down the curse.

'Eloie! Eloie!'

Sorrow leaped and got his leg in her jaws. The force of her bite overbalanced him. He staggered. With a horrible shriek he tottered, spun his arms, and lost his footing. His robes fluttered and his veil streamed open; he fell and hit the ground hard as Sorrow, yelping in pain, scrambled backward, shaking her head from side to side as though she had been stung. She buried her muzzle in the dirt.

Silence followed, hard and heavy. No sound of birds, no murmur of wind in the trees, no noise at all broke the unnatural hush.

Willibrod did not move. Around the camp, voices whimpered in fear. An infant squalled and was hushed by its terrified mother.

'Ai, God,' said one of the men.

His voice shattered the spell that held Alain. He knelt beside Willibrod and plucked at his robes. The body beneath shifted, clacked, and rattled. What was left of him? Although Alain sniffed, he smelled nothing like the stench of putrefaction, only a hint of that vinegary tang. Bracing himself against the awful sight he might see, he lifted away the veil and hat to reveal a grinning skull, jaw agape.

Willibrod was gone. Only his skeleton remained, darkening where sunlight soaked into pale bone.

Rage leaped, growling furiously, and Sorrow lunged.

Too late Alain sprang up. A staff smacked into the side of his head. He went down in a heap, hands and legs nerveless, paralyzed by the blow, while all around him he heard the snarling battle of the hounds, outnumbered, and the screams and cries of the bandits, closing in.

'Go,' he murmured, commanding the hounds, but he had no voice. His head was on fire, and the rest of him was numb.

Why had he turned his back? Even for that one moment, thinking that all of them were shocked by Willibrod's death and disintegration; even that one moment had been too long. Anger and grief boiled up. What had he done to his faithful hounds? Better that they run and save themselves. He stirred, fighting to get up, to protect them, to save them.

A second blow cracked into his back, and a third exploded in pain at the base of his neck, this flare of agony followed by a long, hazy slide as he was caught in the current of a sparkling river flowing toward the sea. Now and again he bobbed to the surface, hearing voices but seeing only a misty dark fog.

'He knows what we are! He knows what we've done! I say we kill him!'

'Kill him! Finish him off!'

'Nay! Hold, there, Red! Put down your knife!' That was Bartholomew, speaking quickly. 'What profit is in it for us if we kill him?'

'We must be rid of him!' That was Dog-Ears. 'This Lord Arno will be after us soon enough, if what this cursed one says is true. We'll have to abandon camp. We'll have to run, even split up. I say we kill him.'

'Kill him! Kill him!'

'We could gain coin and bread if we sell him at the slave market with the women. He's strong and healthy. He'll bring a good price from the Salian merchants.'

Where were Rage and Sorrow? He could not see, nor could he hear any trace of them. Ai, God, were they dead? Had the bandits killed them? He had been careless, such a fool, to turn his back even for a moment.

The current caught him and dragged him under.

XXI

TRUST

1

Sanglant slid from wakefulness to sleep so imperceptibly that the transition happened while she blinked. Heribert tucked blankets in around him as Liath beckoned to Hathui.

'I pray you, give me a report of what has transpired while I have been gone.'

'Have you a day for the telling?'

Liath smiled wryly. 'I have not. Tell me what is most important. I can learn the rest later. Come, you can speak to me while I sit with my daughter.'

'I'll stay with Prince Sanglant,' said Heribert.

Liath found Blessing attended by an old man whose naked torso was entirely tattooed with intertwined animals. His eyes widened when he saw her, and he backed away respectfully, humming in his reedy voice. The sound shuddered up and down her spine like the wandering of an unfinished spell, seeking an entrance.

Others bowed, acknowledging her: the Kerayit healer and a trio of anxious Wendish attendants – the young woman with the peculiar skin color called Anna, a youth by name of Matto, and a young lord named Thiemo who seemed sweet on Anna and annoyed with Matto, although he and the other youth were of an age and might surely otherwise be expected to be friendly companions.

They are not so much younger than I am, thought Liath, but she felt immeasurably older. She had traveled so far that at times she felt as if she had aged one hundred years in the space of a few days. Still, as she stood over the pallet on which Blessing lay, she could not imagine being old enough to be the mother of a child who appeared to be twelve or so years of age.

Nor was she. Blessing was barely four years old; it was only the aetherical link to Jerna that had accelerated her growth. Would her little girl burn brightly and live only a brief span? She might soon be older than her parents, tottering around in her second childhood and losing her memory of what had passed for a life.

It was too painful to consider.

'What is your name? What are you?' Liath asked the old man.

He nodded. 'I am Gyasi. I am shaman of Kirshat tribe. I owe my life to this one.' He indicated Blessing. 'So I serve her.'

'Have you any sorcery that can wake her?'

He clicked his tongue against the roof of his mouth, lifting his chin – a negative response. 'This is powerful spell. I know not. I am helpless.'

She stared down at her child, fallen so far away from her. Anna worked a comb through the girl's thick hair, and Liath wondered idly if it wouldn't be more practical simply to cut it short. Was her daughter vain of her hair? She did not even know such a small, intimate detail. She knew nothing of her, not really.

Blessing was a stranger.

'Hathui, I pray you,' she said, voice choked with tears. 'Tell me the tale of the years I have been gone.'

The sun had reached the zenith by the time she emerged from the tent. Sanglant still slept. The griffin napped beside its mate, content to doze in the noonday sun. The soldiers had moved the skittish horses upwind. As they went about their tasks, the men circled warily around the griffins. They kept their distance from Liath as well.

They all treat me as though I'm something dangerous.

She called Captain Fulk to her and asked him to have Resuelto saddled. 'I will ride back to the centaur camp.'

'How many do you wish to escort you, Your Highness?' he asked.

'No escort. Heribert, you'll stay with Sanglant?'

'So I have been doing these four years,' he said, but he kept looking over at the griffins. 'Is it safe, my lady? Will they attack us once you are gone?'

'I hope not.'

'Are you sure you'll have no escort, my lady?' asked Captain Fulk. 'See there.'

He gestured toward a tent shaped differently than the Wendish campaign tents – a mushroomlike felt shelter lying low to the ground, more a bulge than a tent. Three stocky young Quman men loitered under the angled awning, gazes fixed on the griffins, but after a moment Liath saw that Fulk was pointing toward two men standing in the shadow cast by the tent. They edged forward rather like starving beggar children might creep toward a forgotten crust of bread left lying on the roadside, trying very hard not to draw attention to themselves or the crust. They wore threadbare robes cut differently from those in the west and their red caps came to a curling point.

'What are two Jinna men doing here?'

'They were among the slaves your daughter freed from the ship. We offered them their freedom, but there's none here who can speak to them. I don't know if they stay because they don't know they are free or if they've nowhere else to go. They're good with horses. They do their share of work. We've no complaints of their service, even though they're heathens.'

The two young men dashed forward. Fulk leaped out, drawing his sword.

'Hold, Captain!' It had been a long time since Liath had spoken Jinna; she could read it better than speak it, but the basic words did not elude her. 'Honored sirs, it is better if you approach with prudence.'

The two men threw themselves down bellies to the ground and dipped their foreheads three times to the earth before rising to their knees and extending their hands, palms up and open.

'What means this?' asked Fulk, astonished.

Their postures looked uncomfortably like those of slaves offering submission to a master.

'What do you mean by this, honored sirs?' she asked, echoing Fulk's amazement.

One raised his head. He steepled his fingers and, hiding his eyes behind the 'v' made by his hands, replied.

'Do not disdain your servants, Bright One. Let us serve you, who walk on Earth and speak with human speech. We recognize you as one of the holy messengers of Astareos.'

'What are they saying?' asked Fulk as a number of Sanglant's soldiers gathered at a distance to watch. There was nothing to do in camp except stare at the terrifying griffins; these men welcomed a new source of entertainment.

Liath had forgotten how much she hated being the center of attention of any crowd; and all of Wendish court life was crowds. One could not be a prince without a retinue. No noble lady had ever traveled alone with just her father, making her way through the world.

One of the Jinna spoke. 'If we have displeased you, if we have sinned by calling attention to your presence, Bright One, speak only the word and we miserable worms will slit our throats.'

'No,' she said hastily. 'Do not hurt yourselves. I am surprised, that is all. No matter.' That was the first phrase one learned in Jinna, a word so useful and so complex that it could not be properly translated into Wendish. *No matter.*

'What is your wish, Bright One? We are your servants.'

She did not want a retinue. She had never become accustomed to one. But as she glanced around the camp, seeing the shining bulk of the griffins, the herds, the tents, the patient army of men and women who had followed Sanglant across the wilderness simply because he had asked them to, she knew that what she wished for most – solitude – was to be denied her.

Duty came first.

'Obey this man, as you have been doing,' she said at last, resigned to her fate. 'He is called Captain Fulk. He is a good man. I must go to the camp of the Horse people. When I return, you may serve me.'

They wept with gratitude.

She could have wept, with frustration, but she didn't have time. She didn't need the burden of their belief that she was something she was not.

'I pray you, my lady, what do they want?' asked Fulk again, too eaten up by curiosity to take heed of her sour expression.

'The Jinna worship Astareos, the fire god,' she said at last. 'It is no secret that, like Prince Sanglant, I am only half human. By some magic known to the Jinna, they must see my mother's soul in me. They think I am an angel.'

'I will agree to attend a council,' said Li'at'dano when Liath returned to the centaur encampment to begin the second phase of her campaign, 'but I am not accustomed to the presence of males who claim to speak with authority. They are emotional and unstable. I grant you that a stallion may be a handsome creature, but all he is good for is fighting and breeding. Still, because I have known a few human and Ashioi males who have – what shall I say? – been able to think with the same rigor and intellect as a woman, I will allow all those you mention to join the council. In exchange—'

This was the part of negotiation Liath hated most: all the stipulations and exceptions and claims and demands.

'—the child will be given into the care of my people. She will be well cared for, bound around with magic so that she cannot suffer or weaken.'

'And when she wakes?'

'*If* she wakes.'

'What if I give her to you only to discover that she is being held as a hostage? What if we succeed – as we must succeed

– in defeating Anne, only to find Blessing used as a weapon held at our throats, to make us agree to whatever conditions you demand?'

'Desperate times call for desperate measures. You must trust me, Daughter. Are you not my namesake?'

Liath laughed angrily. 'This is no argument.'

Li'at'dano inclined her head in agreement. 'This is no argument, that is true. *This* is the argument: Already she grows weak. In three or four more days, without a cloak of protection, she will die.'

Liath set her booted foot on the stairs that led up to Sorgatani's door and paused there to survey the horse herds that accompanied the centaurs and their Kerayit allies. These horses were nothing like the stocky beasts that now made up fully half of the mounts in Sanglant's army – the herds bred by the centaurs were powerful and cleanly built, with long, slender legs and big heads. The Kerayit used oxen to pull their carts, but both men and women rode their lovely horses. Right now the members of the tribe labored about the necessary tasks of living while they waited for Li'at'dano's command to move on, women and men together although working at different tasks. Among the herds she saw mares and geldings and the stallions – the best among the males, the ones left intact. There were foals, from yearling colts down to one lanky, awkward newborn, and foals among the centaurs as well, although not so many of those and all of them female.

It troubled her.

She rapped on the door. The younger servant admitted her.

Sorgatani knelt beside the brazier minding a tiny pot, set over the coals, in which herbs withered and smoked. The scent shot straight up Liath's nostrils and gave her a headache behind her eyes. She waved a hand back and forth in front of her face to dispel the smoke while Sorgatani chuckled.

'You should see your face!' The young Kerayit woman rose, gave the bronze spoon she held to the older servant, and sat down on the broad bed. 'Sit beside me. There isn't as much smoke over here.'

Indeed, a fair amount of the smoke spiraled up and out the smoke hole, through which Liath still saw that same gray shimmer, neither day nor night. In the world above, nothing changed. That surety lent a little peace to her anxious thoughts. She sat beside Sorgatani.

'I did not expect to see you back so soon, Liath.'

'Here I am.' She smiled. 'I am come to negotiate, but I'm discovering how little I like it. When I traveled with my father, just he and I all those years, we made a decision and acted. We had no one else to placate or argue with or persuade.'

'You lived and traveled alone, without kinfolk or tribe? Without herds? With no servants or companions? No cousins or aunts? Had you no mothers?'

'I had no mother.'

'No mothers!' The confession shocked Sorgatani, but she recovered quickly. 'I am seeing there hangs a tale from those words.'

'So there does. If you travel with us west, to fight our enemies, then I can tell you that tale at length.'

Sorgatani had a lively, expressive face and the bright eyes common to people who love life. It was as much this vitality that made her beautiful as the actual pleasing composition of her individual features.

'Is this how you open your negotiations? You are too blunt. You must begin by discussing the season, and whether a spring storm will drive away the warmth and how much it will rain before summer. Then you go on with complimenting my lineage, my herds, and the clothing my servants wear. We share the tales of our grandmothers. That is just to begin. The day after next you may come finally to the point of your visit. Meanwhile, I must entertain you as befits a guest.'

She beckoned. The younger servant padded forward to offer them both steaming cups of dried leaves steeped in hot water.

'What is this?' asked Liath. The brew had a minty smell, heady and tantalizing.

'We call it *khey*. I do not know if there is a word for it in your language.'

'I don't think so.' Liath sipped, and sighed. 'That is good.' She drank again before settling back to regard Sorgatani. 'Can I be blunt? We must move quickly. It will take many months to travel back to the west. We haven't much time left. It will be difficult—'

'You intend to travel by land all the way back west. That might take years! The west is very far away.'

'How else are we to go?'

'Oh!' said Sorgatani. 'Oh.' She fiddled with her earrings – today she wore tiny golden pigs dangling on delicate chains. 'If nothing has been said to you, then I do not have permission to speak.'

'Must you have permission to speak?'

'We are the daughters of the Horse people, given into their hands many generations ago. As daughters, it is our duty and obligation to obey our mothers.'

'Your "mothers." But not your fathers. Where are all the male centaurs?'

Sorgatani stared at her blankly, hand dropping away from the tiny pigs. Liath might as well have said, 'Where are all the talking dogs who rule as dukes among you?'

'Do they kill them?' Liath pressed.

'Do they kill who?'

'Do they kill the colts?'

'Of course they don't kill the colts! No good herdsman does so. The choicest ones are held aside to be puras, and the rest are gelded. Geldings make sturdy and reliable mounts. We can trade them, too, since we're known for the quality of our horseflesh. We trade along the oasis road. They prize our horses and pay well for them in silk, gold, spices, and *khey*, these leaves you drink.'

'Sorgatani. Where are the male Horse people?'

Sorgatani set down her cup and clapped her hands. The younger servant brought a tray of candied fruits, which she offered to Liath before taking some for herself. They were both sweet and spicy, tingling on her tongue as she waited.

'I see what you are asking,' Sorgatani said after she had savored an apricot and a pair of peach slices crusted with sugar. She licked her lips for the last grains of sugar. 'They are with the herds.'

'With the herds?'

'Yes. Of course they never leave the herds.'

Liath drained her *khey*, pursing her lips at the sweet aftertaste. 'What about the old stories of the Bwr assault on the Dariyan Empire? Their great general was Azaril the Cruel.'

Sorgatani nodded gravely. 'It's true she earned her name, and in the end the Horse people suffered because of her ambitions. They never recovered their strength after losing so many in her campaigns.'

'But Azaril was a male, wasn't he? He took female prisoners hostage and forced them to marry him. There's a famous story about a saint—'

She faltered as Sorgatani chuckled.

'Is it said so, in the tales made by your people? Perhaps they saw what they believed must be true. I can only tell you what I know. Not all of the Kerayit tribes live beside the Horse people. We have grown more numerous than them. The remnants of the Horse people have retreated to their most ancient pasturelands as their strength wanes. I was sent away from my tribe to be the apprentice of the Holy One, so now I have lived among them and know some truths about their kind.'

Liath could guess the rest: the centaurs had left their males behind to guard what was most precious, their homeland and the core of the herds. It seemed obvious now, but Sorgatani's expression made her think there were things left unsaid.

'Are you glad to study with the Holy One?'

'It is the greatest honor. She is eldest among the Horse people. She is a powerful shaman.'

'Do you ever wish you could go home to your tribe?'

Sorgatani shrugged, saying nothing, although a tear glistened on her cheek.

2

At sunset Liath rode back into the Wendish camp. Her Jinna servants ran up. One took Resuelto; the other offered stew and mare's milk while deftly opening a camp chair so she could sit.

'Where is Prince Sanglant?' she asked as Captain Fulk hurried up to her.

'He sleeps within the shelter of the tent, my lady.'

'My daughter?'

He frowned, the gesture furrowing a shadow between his brows. 'The same, my lady. The healer has certain arts. She has managed to sit Princess Blessing upright and work a bit of broth and honey down her throat.'

'Showed she no sign of waking?'

'None, my lady.'

The griffins gleamed in the darkness, their wings faintly luminescent. With their heads set on their foreclaws they seemed to be slumbering.

'Have the griffins eaten anything? If they become hungry, they'll become more dangerous.'

'Prince Sanglant has already seen to that, my lady.' Fulk's tone held a hint of reproach. 'Two deer were brought in this afternoon.'

'Ah.' She should have known Sanglant, even as injured as he was, would not forget.

She ate mechanically, knowing she must eat to keep up her strength. The stew was hot but its flavor bland. Only the fermented mare's milk had bite enough to make an impression. Captain Fulk and the servant hovered, and the Jinna man took everything away when she was finished.

'Have you aught you wish to say to me, Captain?' she asked.

'My lady,' he said. That was all.

He walked with her to the tent where her husband and daughter slept. She did not know him – she could not tell whether he wished to speak and kept quiet because he feared her or whether he was content with circumstances as they stood. This was Sanglant's army, Sanglant's people, all of them loyal to Sanglant. She was simply not accustomed to moving within a mass of hundreds of people – as many as a thousand, she guessed, measuring the circumference of the camp. Sanglant lived and breathed this life; it was the one he knew best and loved most. He had never been happy in the isolation of Verna.

Even inside the tent there were a dozen souls present, half of them asleep and the rest chatting idly or finishing up their work before snuffing the flame from the precious oil lamps. They glanced at her but said nothing as she set down her weapons and her cloak. She knelt beside Blessing and stroked the child's lank hair, matted from being pressed against the mattress, but although her daughter breathed, she was unconscious to the world. The Kerayit healer sat at the foot of the bed.

Liath took off her boots, and lay down beside Sanglant. There was just room enough on the traveling pallet to squeeze in beside him. The warmth of his body was a comfort to her. Because she had only left him a few days ago, by her reckoning, she had never got used to sleeping alone after those long months at Verna sleeping always beside him.

He slept deeply, his breath steady and his body still. He did not stir as she rested her head alongside his shoulder. He was warm and solid, and he smelled good.

She woke at dawn to see one of her Jinna servants curled up at the foot of the pallet like a faithful dog. The other crouched at the entrance, keeping watch as attendants moved in and out of the tent.

She sat up. Sanglant appeared not to have moved at all during the night. His color was better, his breathing slow and restful. She beckoned the healer and together they inspected the wound on his chest. The Kerayit shook her head, whistling sharply through her teeth as if she did not like what she saw.

'It looks as if it is healing,' whispered Liath, not wanting to wake Sanglant.

'Yes,' agreed the healer with a frown. 'Is not natural, to heal quick. The wound must kill him. But it not kill.'

What kind of sorcery did Sanglant's mother possess that she could knit magic into her son's body? That was a question Liath had never asked Eldest Uncle, and perhaps even he could not answer her. He had not walked the spheres, but his daughter had. She had surpassed her father in power, if not in wisdom. Liath, too, had gained greatly in power by walking the spheres, but the power she had gained came really more in self-knowledge than in any heightened sorcerous strength. If anything, her ignorance seemed clearer to her now; the gulf between what she had seen and what she truly understood yawned as perilous as the Abyss.

'I will sit with my daughter,' she said when Fulk knelt to ask what commands she had for the army. 'Let any who wish to speak with me wait outside, and I will come to them. Send Hathui to the centaur camp to convey this message: tomorrow morning we will ride out to a meeting place midway between this camp and that of the centaurs. There we can hold our council of war.'

Fulk regarded her unsmiling. She could not read him at all, though he did not seem to be a surly or uncommunicative sort. He struck her as exactly what he was: the kind of man you wanted at your back in a fight. Assuming he was on your side.

He nodded, rose to leave, but turned back briefly. 'I will see that Argent and Domina are fed, my lady.'

'Argent and Domina?'

'The griffins, my lady. The prince named them.'

Was he mocking her? Or sharing a joke?

She could only incline her head to show her approval.

She cradled Blessing's head in her lap while Sanglant slept soundly beside them. In the child's narrow face she sought desperately the memory of the infant Blessing had been. The chubby cheeks were gone, and it was difficult to trace a resemblance to father or mother because of the slackness that muddied her features. The girl's color had faded to a sickly gray and her black hair tangled lifelessly. Her lips were as bloodless as those of a corpse. The healer squeezed a little honey and broth down her throat by slipping a hollow reed into her mouth and pinching fluid through, but such meager nourishment could only stave off the inevitable.

I gave up four years of her life, the only time she may have.

She wept silently but no great fist of grief gripped her chest; no wrenching sobs, no moans of sorrow. *Do I not love her?* If she loved her more, would she feel a fiercer grief? Yet the child's slight weight seemed more comfort than sorrow. She mourned what she had lost, but she knew she could have done nothing else. The fire daimones had taken her without her own volition; once she found herself in the country of the Ashioi, she had comprehended the full weight of obligation. Duty might be cruel, but it was necessary.

Had she not made the sacrifice, Anne would win without a struggle. Anne had been willing to sacrifice Blessing to begin with; perhaps Jerna's gift had been to gain Blessing four years of life with a doting father. Anne might still win, and Blessing might die, but Blessing would have died anyway without Jerna's nourishment, and Anne had not triumphed yet.

Within the interstices of the burning stone lay many paths, some taken in the past, some branching into the present, and some only possibilities that would vanish when no foot took passage there. It was a madman's game to second-guess oneself.

But it would have been nice to watch the child grow, to see her face animated, to hear her talk and laugh and sing, to feel her little arms thrown around her mother's waist, as children did, and the warmth of her cheek pressed against her mother's face. It would have been nice to soothe her tears and kiss her small hurts.

It had all just happened so fast – a handful of days like a coil of rope on one side that had been stretched out to its full extent on the other. The years had burned through her hands without her even realizing they had passed.

The dim tent made a fitting bower as the hours passed. Blessing's attendants woke and went about their business, but they were inclined to murmur among themselves and approach her with questions and requests and at least four times Fulk himself came in to ask her to meet with one person or another outside the tent who had a niggling concern that for some reason they felt obliged to bring to her attention. Couldn't they just do what needed doing and leave her alone?

Heribert sat beside her for a time, the only person who knew how to bide in silence. He held Blessing's limp hand and wept silently. Outside, the soldiers followed their round of work, although once she heard a griffin's shriek and hard after that the sounds of crunching and tearing as the creatures set to work on a meal.

After some time, the sleeping Jinna woke and traded places with his companion, who crawled over to Liath.

'What is your will, Bright One? May this miserable worm bring you food?'

'What is your name?'

'Whatever name you wish to call me, Bright One.'

'I wish to call you by the same name your comrade addresses you by.'

'He calls me "brother," Bright One.'

She smiled. 'Are you brothers in truth, then?'

'We are, Bright One.'

'Was it your father or mother who named you at your birth?'

He recoiled slightly. 'It would be against God to name a baby before it lives through three summers and can speak like a human being.'

'Then what name were you given when it was time to give you a name?'

He glanced up at her and as quickly averted his gaze. Like his brother, he was not nearly as tall as the average Wendishman. He had a complexion darker than her own and eyes so brown they were almost black, with thick lashes and heavy black eyebrows. She did not know how long he had been a slave, but something in the way he and his brother persistently insisted on serving her had a certain irritating charm.

'My child name was Mosquito, Bright One, and my brother was called Gnat. We bothered our aunts greatly, and so won these names from them. But when we were sent to the men's house to be sealed by fire—' He brushed the mark branded across his brow. '—we were given our men's names, which I may speak aloud to no woman, not even one of God's messengers.'

'Then I will have to call you Mosquito and Gnat, after the fashion of your aunts.'

'That would be well, Bright One.'

She chuckled, but her amusement only pleased him.

'I will take broth and heated water.' She consulted with the healer. 'These herbs can be steeped in water, so that I may wash my daughter.'

All was done as she wished, but the tincture rubbed over her skin made no difference to Blessing's deteriorating condition. Sanglant slept all day, and Liath was driven outside in the afternoon to get fresh air, to survey the restless griffins and their nervous keepers, to walk for a while along the hills outside camp so that she might have solitude. The big griffin – Domina – paced a stone's toss behind. Grass raked along its legs, and now and again the touch of its feathers sent sliced stalks fluttering into the breeze, spinning and tumbling. Only its threatening presence kept Mosquito and Gnat at a distance; they seemed eager to stick as close as the bugs their aunts had named them after.

All these tents, soldiers, comradeship, and the seemingly incessant desire of every person there to chat about the most inane subjects, never leaving a person free simply to ponder without interruption, was driving her crazy. How did Sanglant endure it? How did anyone?

So much needed to be done as they prepared their counterattack against Anne, and she needed time to think. There was no paper to be had, so that she might make calculations, a tremendously difficult task even for a mathematicus and practically impossible if it had to be done all in the head, even for a person trained in the art of memory. How did one get anything done with these constant interruptions?

'Liath!' Hathui this time, returned from her errand. Only belatedly did she recall that Liath, once her comrade among the Eagles, was now something entirely else. 'My lady! If you will.'

'What news, Hathui? You need stand on no ceremony for me.'

'Do I not? You are changed, Liath.'

'So I have been told,' retorted Liath a little bitterly. 'What news?'

'This. That the centaurs will meet us just after dawn.'

Liath looked out across the encampment with its circle of tents, makeshift corrals made by rope strung into fences between squares of wagons, and a stretch of empty ground around the slumbering griffin. Farther out and well upwind of the griffins, soldiers kept a tight check on grazing horses, taken out in shifts so as to minimize the likelihood that the griffin would decide to steal a snack from among them. There were so many people, more than had lived in the neighborhood of Heart's Rest, certainly, and all of them loitering or working or gossiping or drilling. It was a king's progress, for wasn't Sanglant king among them in all but name?

'Tomorrow, then,' said Liath, exhausted at the sight of such a large gathering.

'Will we ride west at last? I fear we may already be too late for King Henry.' Hathui's gaze was steady. She expected bad news but did not fear to hear it. She had taken three scars to the face in the years since Liath had seen her last and walked with a limp. Her injuries had not dimmed her strong spirit, yet Liath glimpsed vulnerability in her expression.

'You are Henry's loyal Eagle, are you not, Hathui?'

Pride sparked in her face. She lifted her chin. 'I am.'

'Then I'll tell you truly. I just don't know. I've heard your tale, and I think it likely that his keepers must keep him alive until Princess Mathilda is older. It's even possible they don't actually wish to kill him, only to control him.' Despite his twisted nature, Hugh had never seemed to Liath like a man who reveled in death. He would choke you until you yielded, but he would not gleefully spill blood. He liked things tidier and more elegantly disposed. 'That's all we can hope for.'

'What of you, Liath? You gave up your Eagle's badge to follow Prince Sanglant, yet now the prince has rebelled against his father. It was said you were the great granddaughter of Emperor Taillefer, yet now you deny it. What are you, then? King Henry's subject? Or do you also count yourself a rebel?'

Liath shook her head. 'My fight goes so far beyond the regnant's authority that I cannot really consider his well-being as I make my plans. If we do not stop Sister Anne, then we may all die. What does his lineage and mine and yours matter then? Isn't it true that in the Chamber of Light, before God, we all stand as equals? It may be we will find out.'

'And what then?' Hathui's face and lips were chapped from months of battering by cold and icy wind, yet the sunshine of the last few days had burned her hawk's nose, now peeling. If it hurt, she seemed not to notice it. She had suffered worse, no doubt.

No, Hathui wasn't afraid of the truth. She could face down anything.

'What then?' Liath echoed. 'I have walked the spheres. I have seen things I cannot describe, though when I close my eyes I can still see them as vividly as ever I did when I faced them. A daimone of glinting ice barring my path. A sea of burning water that ate through the flesh of my hand. A golden paradise rotten with illusion and false hope. Wheels that spun and burned. A rainbow stairway that led up into the highest reach of the heavens. My mother's death. And more besides, far more.'

Hathui nodded. Liath had not spoken in detail of her journey, not even to Sanglant, but the Eagle understood its momentous import. The wind stirred the grass around them. The sun sank westward and the lazy warmth of its glow melted into her skin.

'I have seen a crown of stars laid out across the land, spanning Taillefer's empire and far beyond. In ancient times seven sorcerers wove a vast spell to sunder the land. I do not believe that these seven wielded such power because they came of

noble bloodlines. I believe they possessed hard-won knowledge, they possessed determination, they possessed courage.
They feared and hated their enemy so much that they were
willing to risk anything and everything to rid themselves of
them. They were willing to die. And to kill.'

Willing to die, and to take friend and foe with them into
death. One of these victims she had known.

By unknown sorcery, Alain had come to inhabit the ancient
past. What did he know of the great spell woven there? He
might possess valuable secrets, crucial knowledge, if only she
could find him.

'And then?' Hathui coaxed.

'And then?' The comment left her scrambling to remember what she had been speaking about. 'Only this. Why do
God grant each one of us souls? Is the soul of King Henry
weightier than yours? Or does each woman and man bear a
burden of equal worth? If King Henry can save us, then I will
follow him gladly. But if he cannot, then I see no need to
follow him blindly only because he is the son of a king.'

'These are dangerous words.'

'Are they? Or are they practical ones? Sister Anne *is* the
granddaughter of the Emperor Taillefer, but that does not
mean we must do what she wishes us to do only because of
her grandfather's imperial throne.' Examining Hathui's wary
expression, Liath shook her head, dismayed. 'Nay, you yourself, Hathui, are worth far more than she is.'

The griffin huffed behind them, and Hathui started, then
sidestepped nervously, keeping her gaze half on the griffin
and half on Liath as if she were not sure who posed the worst
threat.

Would it always be like this? Liath knew her journey had
changed her, and now she wondered if she could ever again
live easily among humankind.

Sanglant was awake when she returned to the tent, and not
just awake but up and moving with only a trace of the stiffness one expected in a man who had so recently suffered such
grave injuries. In fact, he was sitting on a bench and eating,

careful not to bolt his food but clearly starving. When she swept past the entrance flap of the tent, he looked up immediately, set down his spoon with a sharp rap on the camp table, and stood.

She had forgotten the way every action in any chamber he inhabited danced about the center – which was him. He did not clamor for attention; he just possessed the king's luck, the regnant's glamour, that brought all gazes to him whether they intended to look that way or not.

'Liath,' he said. That was all. What he didn't say needed no words. He stared at her. Devouring her with his gaze, as the poets said. He didn't even need to touch her.

Two unlit lamps caught flame.

She flushed, bent her mind to their fires, and snipped them off.

He laughed and, satisfied, sat back down and took up his spoon.

'My lord prince.' Captain Fulk entered with a young soldier behind him.

'What is it?' Sanglant saw the second man and beckoned him closer. 'What news, Lewenhardt? Were you on watch?'

'I was, my lord prince. Gyasi returns with two-score companions, half of them winged and the others women or boys. They'll be here within the hour.'

'Very well. Place my best chair outside with an honor guard. Let it face west. Call all the captains. I will receive them there.'

He was sitting on a bench cleverly fastened together so that it could be broken into easily transportable sections. He looked at Liath and slid to one side, making room for her.

When she sat, he gave her his spoon so she could share his stew. The smell, however bland and greasy, made her stomach growl and her mouth water, and she set to work, all the time so very aware of him beside her, every least shift of movement as he adjusted his posture or set weight on an elbow or nudged his foot up against hers. She had forgotten how big he was, something more, really, than just muscle and height and the breadth of his shoulders. This was the glorious prince she had fallen in love with at Gent — miraculously recovered from his mortal wounds and fully in charge of the army that followed at his heels very like a well-trained and adoring hound.

For the next hour the flood of petitioners did not abate. No complaint was too trivial to address; no soldier too humble to be refused entrance; no decision too weighty, since he evidently had the gift of knowing exactly whether it needed immediate resolution or time for thinking over.

A horse must be put down, but its meat and gristle could be added to the stewpot, its hair and sinews used for stringing bows and strengthening rope, its hide scraped, its hooves boiled down. Two men had quarreled, and a knife had been drawn and one of them stabbed, although not fatally, but Sanglant simply assigned them to different units and forbade them from speaking.

'Shouldn't an example be set so other men don't pick fights?' Liath whispered.

Although his foot lay hard against hers, he was careful not to touch or look at her in view of the men waiting their turn to address him.

'This is the time for a soft hand, not a firm one,' he murmured so quietly that only she, and Heribert standing behind him, might hear. 'No one will say so aloud, but it is a lovers' quarrel. My army has marched a long way without the comfort of women. Such things will happen. I won't punish them for seeking relief.' He shifted restlessly and pulled his foot away from hers, as though it burned. But then he spoiled it by grinning, although he was not looking at her.

That grin had the force of a hundred caresses. She got very hot, but she was ready; she guarded the force of her desire, not wanting to light the tent on fire. She could control it — more or less. Yet holding it in only made her want him more.

Captain Fulk stuck his head in. 'My lord prince.'

Quickly he armed himself. He paused only to kiss Blessing before he went outside with Liath. There, a dozen captains and noble companions waited.

'Who's this fine heifer?' demanded a big man dressed in

the embroidered tunic and fur-lined cloak of a nobleman. He leered at her as he looked her up and down, and she knew that she had seen him before, but she could not place him. 'Can I have her when you're done?'

Sanglant stopped dead and turned. A hush choked off the conversations between the gathered crowd as everyone stilled. There are some things that have no physical body and yet can be felt as strongly as the slam of a rock into one's head.

'What did you say about my wife, Wichman?' he asked so pleasantly that Wichman went ghastly pale and took a step away from him, although Sanglant had not moved, not even his little finger.

Liath recognized him now – Duchess Rotrudis' reckless son, who had harried Gent for months and taken Mistress Gisela's poor niece into his bed against her will. Sanglant's interference irritated her; did he think her helpless? Yet she did not know how to respond. She possessed no skill at crossing words like swords. She had power, but so did a spear – and it was the person who wielded it who gave it direction and aim.

She fumed as Wichman retreated, as the other captains and nobles came forward to greet Sanglant and exclaim over his return to strength. To meet her warily or pleasantly, depending on their nature. She had to learn who they were, but names and titles spat at her in such quick succession that while all the names stuck she could not recall which name matched which face.

'And this is Lady Bertha, my strong right hand,' Sanglant said last of all. 'She is the second daughter of Margrave Judith.'

That caught Liath's attention.

'You are Hugh's sister,' she said, not having meant to speak any such words.

'So my mother told me.' Bertha looked nothing like Hugh, having no particular elegance and less beauty, but she appeared tough and competent. 'So he claimed, since it gave him the advantage of our support when he needed it. I might have wished otherwise, since I always detested him.' She smiled mockingly as Liath schooled her expression, for she had never expected to hear Hugh spoken of so slightingly by his own kinfolk. 'Have I offended you? Perhaps you held him in some affection.'

Sanglant glanced at her, but she shook her head, aware of the way his shoulders tensed as he waited for her reply.

'I did not. I am only surprised.'

'My mother spoiled him, and he only a bastard. Why should my sisters and I not resent him? Well, so be it. According to this good Eagle, he has earned his just reward and luxuriates in a position of great power and influence with many a noble lady begging for admittance to his holy bed-chamber. It was ever so with him, and he always put them off, like dangling meat before a starving dog and then pulling it away before it could taste it. He liked them to beg. And they did.'

Sanglant was looking stormy, and while Bertha's sentiments might appeal, Liath did not find the noblewoman's manner particularly sympathetic. But she did not know how to change the subject.

Heribert stepped forward. 'They are coming, my lord prince.'

Bertha looked past Liath, and laughed. 'Not as many as you wished, eh?'

Sanglant seated himself in the chair. 'That depends on what they have to say.' The others ranged around him, falling into obviously familiar patterns but leaving Liath unsure how to position herself. Where did she fit in?

She had felt so strong, walking the spheres, but there she had been acting alone. Here, maybe she would never fit into the tightly woven army that Sanglant led. She stared at the sun's fiery trail, a golden-pink layer sprawled out along the western hills. Ai, God, how cleverly Sanglant had placed himself: it seemed as if the sun set in order to do him obeisance.

Gyasi appeared at the head of a score of riders who pointed at the hooded griffin, exclaiming among themselves. They bore two banners, one marked with three slashes and the other

with a crescent moon. Sanglant shifted in his chair, hand restless on his hilt of his sword, as Gyasi dismounted and led six
of the Quman forward: four winged warriors and two women
wearing impossibly tall conical hats ornamented with beads
and gold. The two barbarian women were burdened with more
jewelry even than Sorgatani, as if the weight of their gold
determined how important they were.

As they advanced, Liath slipped sideways, out of the crowd.
Wichman glanced at her as she slid past him, and he recoiled,
bumping into Brother Breschius, who constituted the other
half of Sanglant's schola.

'I pray you, Brother, attend me,' Liath said softly, and
Breschius obediently walked with her a stone's toss away from
the rest. They halted near a group of soldiers come to stare
and to keep their prince safe from the interlopers. 'What do
you know of these Quman?'

'Little enough.'

'What do those markings mean?'

'It is the mark of a snow leopard's claw, the device of the
Pechanek tribe. They are the ones who abandoned us the day
we met the Horse people. The other—' He shrugged helplessly. '—I do not know. Brother Zacharias would have. He
knew a great deal, for he had lived as a slave in the Pechanek
tribe.'

'I know no Brother Zacharias. Where is he now?'

'He fled with Wolfhere when we were in Sordaia.'

'I heard a little of this tale. Is it certain that Wolfhere
betrayed Prince Sanglant?'

Breschius shrugged. 'Who can know? Both he and
Zacharias are gone in the company of a small, dark man, a
powerful sorcerer, so Gyasi says. That's all I know. I was with
Prince Sanglant at the palace of the exalted Lady Eudokia. I
did not witness the incident. Only Brother Robert did, who
was Lady Bertha's healer. The poor man died a few months
ago of the lung fever. It is a miracle that Prince Sanglant kept
so many of us alive. Yet perhaps not a miracle at all. He has
the regnant's luck.'

So he did, as he allowed the Quman representatives to

kneel before him. The griffin cowed them; he had been right about that.

'How came you to his service, Brother? I do not recall you from King Henry's progress.'

'I am not Wendish, my lady. I was born in Karrone but sent early to a marchland monastery. That is how I come to speak Wendish. I lost my hand in the service of the God, for I set out to bring the light of the Unities to those who live in darkness. It's a convoluted tale, but this much may help you make sense of it. I was a slave among the Kerayit, taken to be a pura by one of their shamans.'

Astonished, she looked at him more closely, but no mystery clung to him. He seemed calm, and confident, a middle-aged man with handsome enough features that, she supposed, might attract the attention of a lonely young woman doomed to isolation. Of course, he had been young then.

'You do not live among the Kerayit now.'

Breschius' smile was leavened by regret, an old sorrow never quite recovered from. 'She died, and I came into the service of Prince Bayan. When he died, I swore to follow Prince Sanglant.'

'Why?'

'Can you not see why, my lady? Look at these Quman. They come to ally themselves with the man who defeated their greatest leader, the man who led the army that devastated their ranks. They see it, too. They will not resist him.'

Yet not every creature that encountered Sanglant succumbed to his charisma. Li'at'dano had not.

'Tell me this, then, Brother, since you lived among the Kerayit. Why do their males remain among the herds?'

'I beg your pardon?'

'Why is it only the female centaurs rode out to meet us?'

'Ah. Yes. That puzzled me as well, for the Kerayit I traveled with had little intercourse with the Horse people. But I learned the truth eventually. The Horse people are not like us. They are only female.'

'How can they only be female? What does that mean?'

'It means just that. They are only female.'

'How can they breed, then?'

'They have puras, do they not? The stallions. Only the female foals breed true. The males are all colts.'

An eerie whistling rose from the ranks of the Quman riders, and the hooded griffin tugged at its chains. It lifted its blinded head and screamed as the whistling grew more shrill. Sanglant stood and strode across the flattened grass as, above, Domina appeared in the sky, circling. The last rays of the sun flashing in her iron wing feathers. The whistling ceased as the Quman fled to their horses and cowered when her shadow passed over them. But Sanglant moved in within range of the silver griffin, and before Liath could cry out a warning, he grabbed hold of the rope that bound the hood around its neck and yanked its head down.

'Fulk!' he shouted. 'Bring me meat!'

There they stood, he and the griffin, engaged in a battle of wills as its mate shrilled an anxious cry and, at last, beat down to land in a flurry of wings while men shouted and dashed for safety. It infuriated Liath that he would put himself in danger so soon, but she clenched her hands and endured, teeth gritted and heart hammering madly. She knew better than to interfere. Some idiotically brave soldier ran over to the prince carrying a satchel; the young man had an arm already bound up in a sling, but that did not deter him. He even had a stupid grin on his face, relishing the danger, and would have stuck close if Sanglant had not ordered him to stand away.

Under the gaze of every soul there and with Domina poised tensely but still so close beside him that in a single pounce she could bury him under her claws, he fed the meat to Argent. The griffin ate neatly out of his hands, although certainly he was careful to keep his fingers clear of its vicious beak.

'The Quman follow those who wear the wings of a griffin, and now he means to tame one, not just kill it,' murmured Breschius admiringly beside her. The cleric was as much a fool as the rest of them! Yet it was true that Sanglant was a magnificent sight, uncowed by the griffin, master of his fate. 'Now these who are here will bear this tale back to their tribes.'

3

At long last the crowd dispersed, all but the two dozen attendants who swarmed in and around his tent, and she found herself seated on the pallet with her boots off and Sanglant wide awake beside her, the barest smile illuminated on his face and the rest of him shadowed.

'I pray you, Heribert,' he said softly, 'put that lamp out.'

Heribert rolled his eyes, but he rose from the pile of furs he slept on, licked his fingers, reached up to the lamp hanging from a cross pole, and pinched out the flame.

Sanglant sighed heavily.

A hundred thoughts skittered across Liath's mind, and died.

All at once he enveloped her with his arms and let his weight carry her down onto the pallet, and there he lay with his body half on her and a leg crossing hers at the knee.

'You can't know,' he murmured. 'You can't know. Not one day went by that I did not think of you. And mourn for you. And curse you. And want you. You can't know how much I have been wanting you.'

By the feel of him pressed up against her, she had a pretty good idea. She wriggled a little, and his grip on her tightened so very gratifyingly as they kissed again and he eased a hand up under her tunic to brush the contours of her ribs.

Then someone coughed.

'I can't,' she whispered, going rigid in his arms.

He tensed. 'You *can't*?' Anger tightened his voice. Whenever they spoke, his anger swam close to the surface, waiting to strike.

Yet this was no battle against *him*.

'There are so many people in here,' she whispered. A dozen

or more, many of them still stirring as they settled down. That cough was likely an honest clearing of the throat, but it had startled her out of her passion nevertheless.

She felt his attention flash away from her. His fingers rapped a beat on her ribs as he puzzled over her words.

'They're sleeping,' he whispered in reply.

'They're not! Not all of them.'

'Then they soon will be.'

'And if they don't?'

'They'll pretend to sleep.'

It was nothing to him, who had spent his entire life in just such a mob, never truly alone, never knowing privacy and certainly never craving it. The only time he'd known solitude was as Bloodheart's prisoner, and even then he had been surrounded by Eika dogs, his pack; surely he'd been driven half mad because of his isolation.

'I just can't,' she repeated, not sure if he could ever understand her. The press of them all around was too much. She could not ignore it. She could not endure it.

'I can stand this no longer,' he said hoarsely, in echo of her thoughts. 'I don't care where, but I do care when. And if I don't do this now, I swear to you, Liath, I am going to die of frustration.'

He grabbed her cloak, her hand, tugged her up to her feet, and said, commandingly, to the tent at large, 'No one follow us!'

Heribert began to chuckle, and then half the tent did as well. She was burning with embarrassment, but Sanglant took no notice because he never did. He dragged her out of the tent, and by the time he had ordered off half a dozen startled but swiftly amused guards, she was laughing, too, running with him out into the grass in her bare feet. She had left her belt behind, so the hem of her tunic lapped her calves.

When they reached the crest of the hill, she tripped him and they rolled, tumbling, wrestling, giggling, until the slope of the ground shifted and they came to rest where the ground cupped into a man-sized hollow. He kissed her so long and hard that she got dizzy. There was grass in her hair and up and down her sleeves and between her toes, and for a miracle the grass distracted him more than it did her. He cursed as he brushed himself off, and he shook out the cape and settled it over a swath of grass. After trampling the cloth to make a flat resting place, he drew her down.

She unbuckled his belt, suddenly intent on her task, on wanting to caress him, to feel his skin naked and pressed against her own, but he caught her hand in one of his.

'Nay, not yet. Not yet.' He kissed her knuckles before clasping her to him. 'Ai, God. Let me savor it.'

They lay there for a while. She closed her eyes and let the chill spring breeze kiss her face. Nothing could make her feel cold now, with her arms wrapped around him and his around her. He breathed, as silent as the brilliant stars that blazed above them.

'Liath,' he said after a long time, 'do you still love me?'

'You asked me this before. Weren't you content with my answer the first time?'

'You don't ask whether I still love you.'

Annoyance flashed, as brief as a falling star that streaked the night sky, and then she laughed and rolled up on top of him, trapping him beneath her.

'Do you still love me, Sanglant? I know you still desire me, that is obvious enough, but desire isn't always love.'

'I still love you,' he said, the laughter gone out of him, 'but I don't know you. Are you still Liath under all these clothes? Are you still Liath under your skin? Are you still Liath at all, or a succubus come to plague me? Will you abandon me again?'

'Never willingly,' she whispered.

He shook his head brusquely; she felt the movement as much as saw it. Although her night vision was keen, sight mattered much less now than touch, than smell, than the taste of his despair and anger and the elixir of his arousal.

'I do not fear death. I only fear madness. I have cursed you for four years for abandoning me, because anger was the only thing that kept me from despair. I know that we have undertaken a great battle. I know that circumstances may force one of us to travel along a separate road from the other for a time, a short time, I pray. But I will have you pledge to me now what you pledged to me in Ferse village, our mutual consent made legal and binding by the act of consummation and the exchange of morning gifts. If we can have no marriage, then let it be done with. I can suffer and go on alone if I know this is the end. But I cannot love you this much and always wonder if you will leave me again as unthinkingly as my mother abandoned my father. As she abandoned me.'

The wind tickled her neck. A chill ran down her spine, and she shivered. The agony in his tone was awful to hear but Sanglant was not a subtle man. What he felt, he expressed. He knew no other way. He could be no other way.

'There,' he said, his voice a scrape. 'I've said it. You know how badly I want you, Liath. God know how desperately I have dreamed of you by day and by night. Worst it was, by night. I have kept concubines briefly, or gone without, but whichever it was, it never made any difference. I could never stop thinking of you and wondering if you ever intended to come back to me, if you really cared for me and the child. Or if you were dead. There were days, God help me, when I thought it would be simpler if you were just dead, for then I would know that you had not meant to leave me behind. That you still loved me truly. Not that you made a rash vow once when you thought I was safely dead, or spoke a pledge in a rush of infatuation and desire for me, but that it was the wish of your heart despite anything else the world and the heavens offered you. That you want me that much. As much as I want you.'

He gripped her wrists, pinning her hands to the ground on either side of his body.

'I must know, Liath. I must know.'

She wept silent tears, burned out of her by the force of his pain and his honesty. After a while she was able to speak past the quaver that kept strangling her words.

'I possessed wings made of flame. *Wings.* My kinfolk welcomed me into my mother's home, a city encompassed by aetherical fire. It is the most beautiful place I have ever seen. A river of fire flowed there, and I followed its current into both past and future. The ladder of the mages was laid plain. I glimpsed the mysterious heart of the cosmos. Nothing was closed to me. Nothing. Not even my own heart. Because that is what I fear most.'

'Your heart?' His gaze remained fixed on her, dark and terrible. The breeze swept strands of his black hair across his face, their movement too dim for mortal eyes to see – but not for hers. She knew now what she was, and what she was not.

'Just . . . just . . .' Each word was a struggle. The truth was so hard. 'Being brave enough to trust. To love. Being brave enough not to hide. I don't know—' Emotion choked her, and she shut her eyes to contain it, as if it might explode out through her gaze. Grains of fire trembled everywhere around her, in the grass, in the earth, in the wind itself, the seeds of a devastating conflagration. She dared not let them loose.

He lifted a hand to touch her chin. The caress of his fingers was like water, cooling, calming.

'I'm not like you,' she said, 'so open. So honest and true.'

'So mad,' he muttered.

She smiled. The salty liquid of her tears tickled her lips. 'So mad. And so strong.'

'Am I?'

'You are. I don't know if I can love fully and truly. Da and I lived apart from the world for so long. We hid ourselves away. We veiled ourselves from the sight of those who hunted us. When Hugh took me as his slave, I built an even higher wall to protect myself. It was easier that way; it was the only way I knew. But even when you came, though I let you in, that wall held firm. I was used to the wall. I felt safe with it to protect me. And then. When I ascended into the heavens, I saw everything I had ever wanted.'

She tilted her head back and through a blur of tears gazed at the beauty of the sky so shot through with stars that it seemed to hold as much light as darkness.

He was silent. He did not move except to release her wrists.

'I could have abandoned the world below to its fate. I could have left all this behind. Forever. Anne and her sleepers, Henry and his wars, everyone and all of it. Hanna and Ivar.

You and the baby. I could have joined my mother's kinfolk and cast off this flesh. But I had to know. I couldn't leave you behind because I've never really known you. I don't know if I can want you as much as you want me. I don't even know how much that is. But I have to try. That's why I came back.'

The stars burned in the night sky. Did her kinfolk journey there, so high above? They had not mourned her leaving; the span of a human lifetime meant little to them. They had simply looked into her heart and let her go.

She cupped his face in her hands. 'Look into my heart, Sanglant.'

'Ai, God,' he murmured, like a man who has received his deathblow, but he gazed at her face, searching.

Poised there, she waited as the wind rustled in the grass and a nightjar churred. In the distance an owl hooted.

'Fire,' he whispered hoarsely, as though stricken by wonder; but then, his voice always sounded like that. 'Fire is the heart of you.'

He reared up, almost dislodging her from his lap, and crushed her in an embrace so tight that for a moment she could not breathe. 'I am not waiting any longer,' he added, half laughing and all out of breath, so vibrantly alive and awake and aware that his presence swallowed everything else, the heavens, the world, sound, and light.

Well. Everything except the grass tickling the sole of her left foot.

But when she kissed him, when he kissed her, that distraction, too, vanished.

4

Except for the presence of the daimone-woman, she could have made easy work of the hunter now sprawled, sleeping, on the grass, vulnerable and alone away from his tribe. Yet she had killed him once already, hadn't she? Hadn't that stab been enough to kill an elk or a bear?

He had recovered because of the magic woven into his bones.

There was more to this hunter than could be seen and smelled on his skin. He had captured her mate and proved his dominance over him. For her to kill the hunter now would be an affront to the dance of the males, who owned as their birthright the measure of their dance, each of them competing with the others for right of place.

So.

She could abandon her mate, or she could follow the hunter and the daimone-creature, who claimed the hunter as mate just as she had many seasons ago claimed hers.

Wind rippled in the grass, singing softly in her feathers. The aetherical tides waxed and waned in every season, but the threads that bound the world were digging new channels; this she sensed. The world was in flux.

With her nest destroyed there could be no hatchlings this year. It would take an entire season to restore the nesting grounds, and she did not want to abandon her mate. Perhaps it was better to abandon the old ways for one season, to strike out into new territory, to follow the paths made by the thrumming lines of force as they wove into new patterns.

For as long as her mate remained a captive, she would follow the hunter.

Why not?

XXII

A NEW SHIP

1

'They know we are here,' said Stronghand to his assembled chieftains and councillors in the hall at Weorod, where Lord Ediki sat on the lord's seat and presided over the servants and slaves who brought meat and drink around to each member of the gathering. 'Yesterday, according to our allies, two Alban ships brought reinforcements to the island.'

Rain drummed on the roof. Under the eaves at each side of the hall, children and dogs huddled, watching. Some had been slaves, others the children of those who ruled here before, but Ediki had commanded that each one be given opportunity to prove themselves no matter their birth. It was the way of the Eika, their new masters, so Lord Ediki proclaimed, as well as the ancient way followed by his ancestors.

'We have no ships on this shore,' said Dogkiller. 'How can we invade across the waters? It would be death to wade.'

'We must scout the waterways that empty into the sea,' said Flint. 'Then our ships can sail in and attack from the north.'

'Scouts we will have and in plenty,' agreed Stronghand, surveying his company as he waited for Yeshu to finish translating into Alban. He himself spoke first in his own language and then in Wendish, but although he understood Alba well, he still stumbled over speaking it. 'Manda, head-woman of the Eel tribe, has put fourteen boats and twenty-four skilled guides at our disposal. I need volunteers to search north.'

About three score men – RockChildren and human alike – had crowded into the hall to listen and, as Stronghand had expected, half of them lifted their voices, clamoring to go. They were the ones who sought honor and glory and riches, who gazed on Lord Ediki's new holdings with envy, or who simply craved the danger.

Stronghand lifted a hand, and the voices stilled.

'Two men will go in each boat. A gold nomia to every man who reaches the sea and our ships. For every ship guided back through the fens to our position here, I will give another nomia.'

They were eager to start out, despite the dreary weather. As the company dispersed, he took Tenth Son outside. Many score soldiers had gathered to hear the council tidings, and they dispersed in groups, heading back to their tents and bivouacs or to make ready for guard duty. Tents had been thrown up within Weorod's stockade while the rest lay scattered between the stockade and the dike, using wagons and recently dug ditches to create barriers in case they were attacked unexpect-edly. Everyone was waiting for the next assault, with varying degrees of patience. As long as the queen lived, she ruled.

Stronghand ducked under the shelter of an empty byre and stood there with Tenth Son as rain drizzled down around them, leaking through the thatched roof, which was not yet repaired after the winter. Although the stalls had been cleaned out, clumps of manure pebbled the floor, and the smell of animal and dung clung to the earth.

'I will take two brothers with me, but I wish you to remain behind, not because I do *not* trust you, but because I do.'

Tenth Son nodded, accepting the statement – however startling it might be, since the RockChildren never spoke of trust between themselves.

'The standard stays with me. If I fall, then it will be of no use to anyone else. The magic is tied to my life.'

'Yes,' agreed Tenth Son. 'If you fall, this army will splinter into a thousand spears, each one striking at the others. Why do you not wait for the ships?'

'If I wait for the ships, then the queen will know I am coming. If I go now, she will not expect a visitor. I will see this crown for myself. I must know what it is they hope to accomplish there. In my dreams . . .'

He trailed off. He rarely spoke of his dreams because RockChildren did not dream, but he knew that many secrets lay half revealed in the dreams he shared with Alain, more precious than gems and gold.

'What will you do when you get there?' asked Tenth Son.

'I don't yet know,' he admitted. While most RockChildren would see the answer as weakness, Tenth Son could understand improvisation as a strength.

The rain let up as the gray afternoon darkened toward an early twilight. Clouds hung low and heavy. A child laughed. Nearby, Elafi and Ki squatted on the ground beside a small wicker cage. They had wished to see Stronghand's camp and the size of his army, and had explored and poked around for much of the day, but now they turned to their own preparations for this night's journey. Strangely, they were tying scraps of candles to the feet of two squawking pigeons. From the camp he heard the ring of a hammer beating out iron, but it was his companion who interested him most right now.

'Why do you follow me?' he asked finally.

Because they were littermates, Tenth Son was very like to Stronghand in looks, but although he, too, was rather more slender than most RockChildren, he had a hand's height advantage over Stronghand and more bulk through the shoulders and chest. He was bigger and stronger, as most RockChildren were, but strength wasn't everything.

'I am not as clever as you are, Brother,' Tenth Son said at last, 'but I am clever enough to know that my fortunes rise with yours and will fall with yours. Hakonin and the other chieftains will not march behind my standard. If you die, I am nothing.'

'What is it you want? You have been loyal to me in the manner of humankind. I would reward you, if that is what you wish.'

Tenth Son bared his teeth. Like all warriors, he wore jewels drilled into his teeth to advertise his prowess. 'Can you give me anything I ask for?'

'No. I cannot give you the moon or the sun. I cannot give you life beyond the one you are fated to live. I cannot make you anything but what you are.'

Tenth Son nodded, satisfied with the answer. Against the gray afternoon backdrop, his braided hair gleamed as white as bone. 'Those things I do not want. I want what even the slaves among the humans possess. I want a name.'

Later, as they glided through the water of the fens, Stronghand brooded.

A name.

For generations the WiseMothers had hoarded names like gold and allowed only the chieftains of each tribe to take a name. The lowest slave among humankind bore a name; why not his own kind? Did the WiseMothers consider their grandsons lower than slaves? Or had there never been any reason for names among creatures who gave little more thought to their lives than did the dogs that followed at their heels?

Did the two Rikin warriors who accompanied him desire names, too, or was it only Tenth Son who had caught the fever?

'You are thoughtful, my lord,' said Ki.

She and Elafi paddled as quietly as ducks as the twilight gloom settled over them. Even the pigeons, confined in a cage placed at Ki's feet in the belly of the canoe, remained silent. Reeds shushed along the boat, parting before the prow as they cut through a mire lying just northwest of the island where queen and crown waited. Here, near that island where her army sheltered, the birds had been hunted out, so they had the water to themselves and their progress flushed no betraying clatter of wings. From this direction the high face of the island looked as if it had been cut away by the swipe of a dragon's tail to leave a steep embankment as tall as two ship's masts set one atop the other. At the height could be seen the shoulders of two stones thrusting up into the slate-gray sky, fading from view as the light dimmed.

'Hush,' said Elafi as he guided the boat alongside a low bank and under the sprawling branches of a willow. Strong-hand ducked as branches scraped overhead and along the sides.

'Hush,' repeated Elafi.

The greenery hid the land around them, but they still had ears.

'Did you hear something?' A woman's voice, speaking in the Alban tongue, floated on the air.

'Nay, I can't hear nothing for the slithering of these eels.' Her companion was an aggrieved man.

'Here, now, set down that basket and have a look round.'

'I will not! I'll never get this thing heaved back up, it's that heavy.'

'Do it anyway, you fool! You've heard the news as well as I have, that the savages have come and burned Weorod Holding and killed our good queen's uncle and brother over there by Grim's Dike. They might be anywhere, skulking like serpents and creeping up to kill us. I think I heard something scraping along over there, by that tuft – where the willow is.'

Elafi lifted a charm to his mouth and blew softly.

'Look there,' said the woman, after a moment. 'It's a deer.'

Something skittered through sedge and branches nearby, ending with a soft *plosh* in the water.

She swore. 'It was too quick for me.'

'And an arrow wasted, when we've none to waste. It's too dark for you to find it now. Let's get on then. Tide'll be coming back in. Venison would've been nice, I grant you, but all this talk of savages is making my skin crawl.'

They waited in silence under the willow as twilight dark-ened imperceptibly into night and the voices moved away.

'Keep silence,' said Elafi at last. 'That means you, Ki.'

He pressed the branches aside with his oar and they nosed
out of their hiding spot as the supple branches shushed over
them, tickling their skin and faces with the touch of new leaves
half unfurled all along the tree. With night came a hazy glamour hanging over the waters as though the clouds had drifted
down to meet the fens. It was hard to see. Yet Elafi knew
where he was going, and Stronghand felt the shift in current
where it was slowed by beds of reeds or the smell of salty
streams running beneath the smoother fresh water of the
surface. The ebb tide had reached its lowest point.

A pintail swished past. Ki bent to the cage sitting at her
feet in the bottom of the canoe. Beside it rested a hollow
branch. Deftly – heard more than seen – she eased a coal from
a hollow with copper tongs and set spark to wick, then released
the two pigeons. They fluttered up on the trail of the pintail,
and the scraps of candles tied to their feet swayed, slipped
loose, and spun down to the water below. Most sputtered and
died in the water, but a pair tipped and bobbed, still burning.

'Swamp lights,' whispered First Son of the Tenth Litter,
who had taken his turns on sentry duty at the borderland
where Weorod Holding sank away into the fenlands.

'A good trick,' agreed Last Son of the Fourth Litter, turning to watch the lights behind them.

Elafi lit a tiny lamp and held it beyond the prow of the
ship to light their way, while Ki lit other candles and set them
on the water, tag ends that guttered as the wake jostled them,
flared, and died. Out beyond the willow a true swamp light
flickered and vanished. Stronghand had to admire the cleverness of their use of misdirection.

They skirted the edge of a bed of reeds that gave them
cover as they came right up under the crumbling cliff face.
There rested an ancient willow tree, hoary with age, its trunk
as thick as a giant's leg and its lowest expanse exposed by the
ebb tide. This close, and with mist spreading its blanket over
the landscape, the noises of the island carried easily: a horse's
whinny, a barking dog, the rumble of a handcart over broken
rock, the laconic call of a sentry to his companion, a shrill
pipe accompanied by the patter of a drum and men singing

in harmony. The music spun through the fog like a thread winding around him, drawing him into the haze.

Rope chafes his wrists and ankles as he shuffles along, tugged awkwardly at intervals when the wagon to which he is tied speeds up. Once he slams into the back, not anticipating that it has stopped. Sharp rocks cut his feet, and he shifts in the hope of finding gentler ground.

A man curses him; a whip stings his backside more in annoyance than because he has hindered the line. The pain makes him flinch, but he does not cry out.

He has no voice. He cannot see.

Blind and mute.

The canoe bumped up against the willow's trunk as Stronghand threw his head back, searching the mist, but like the swamp lights the vision was already gone. Vanished.

What had happened to Alain? Where were the hounds?

He hadn't the luxury for questions. They were vulnerable to attack here at the foot of the island cliff; a sentry moved far overhead.

'What's that light?' the sentry called.

Elafi grasped the trunk of the tree. He eased his fingers under the peeling bark and pried a piece of the trunk open to reveal a gaping hole large enough to admit the boat. The willow was rotten inside but cunningly disguised so as to seem whole. Elafi and Ki pushed them through as, above, a second sentry replied to the first.

'Swamp lights. See, that one just winked out.'

They glided under the willow's gnarled roots and came into a chamber awash in mud and stinking of decay. Rocking the canoe, Ki leaned precariously out over the stern to close up the opening behind them.

'From here we must climb,' whispered Elafi.

They left the canoe, careful not to tip it, and waded through knee-deep sludge to a rock embankment. The air seeped like liquid into Stronghand's lungs; the mud oozed around his shins, slurping and sucking. He had never smelled anything so vile, and he was careful to keep the standard entirely out of the muck lest some poison in the sludge contaminate its magic.

Elafi's lamp illuminated the young man's face as he scrambled up the embankment. He lifted the lamp to reveal a maw ridged with huge teeth. The jawbone and teeth of some huge creature, yawning, made the archway through which they must pass into a low tunnel.

'What is it?' asked First Son as Last Son grunted with surprise.

'A wyvern,' said Ki, behind him. 'In ancient days the old sorcerers killed it and laid it here in the earth. A wyvern's bones hold magic. That's why it's never been found by our enemies.'

Stairs made of slate slabs had been laid into the earth, braced on one side against the huge spinal column. As the creature had died, it had rolled to the right, and it was the impossibly long rib cage of the dead wyvern that gave support to the tunnel's damp earth walls, so it seemed they were climbing up inside its belly. Only Ki and Elafi could stand upright; the RockChildren had to hunch over as they climbed the stairs by feel, since Elafi's body blocked most of the light.

Maybe it was the magic lingering in the wyvern's bones. Maybe it was the darkness, or the proximity of the stone crown. With each careful step up to the next slate stair, flashes of sound and sensation ripped through Stronghand.

'I don't like the sound of that!' says one of the men – they all smell rank, that much he does know. 'Move on! Move on! If we're caught here, we'll be slaughtered.'

His fingers slipped along a smooth rib, but he steadied himself and took another step up.

'Get up, bitch! Or I'll kill the baby.'

A woman sobs, crying for mercy.

He turns, seeking the direction of that despairing voice. Far away, as in a dream, he hears horses' hooves.

'Go! Go!'

'We'll split up and meet in the town.'

He gropes, finds the weeping woman's arm, and helps her up. A switch cuts into his ear, the one that throbs all the time, the swollen one, and he jerks back as pain roars through his head.

He staggered and barely caught himself, hand grasping at dirt, claws *shicking* out to scrape earth and send it spattering to the ground.

'Stronghand?' First Son sounded surprised, as well he might to see any sign of weakness.

Elafi hissed. 'Hush, now! Hush!'

They waited as Elafi went ahead into the darkness, the gleam of curved bone flashing above him with each step until the young man simply vanished.

Stronghand took a step forward to follow him.

'I'll take the woman.'

Screaming, she fights them. Her arm is torn from his grasp but as she is hauled away, she thrusts a bundle into his arms. The wagon lurches forward and he almost loses his footing as the rope snaps tight. He stumbles forward in its wake, clutching the bundle against him, wondering what it is. Moisture leaks onto his hands through cloth. For a while he has as much as he can do to trot along behind the rolling wagon, with staffs prodding him and the others who are bound.

There were more like him once, but over the course of many days – he can't keep track of how many – the rest fell behind or were taken away or died. He doesn't know. He can't see, and what he hears is often interrupted by gouts of pain that stab through his head.

He is missing something, though. He knows that much. Now and again he weeps with anger and despair.

As the wagon steadies onto a smooth forest path, the grassy track a pleasant tickle under his callused, battered feet, he pulls the cloth free and searches the bundle with a hand.

An infant. He is carrying an infant. Blood curdles in the hollow of its sunken chest.

It is already dead.

The torrent of sensation and emotion raged through him until he was overwhelmed, awash. He gasped for air as he staggered again, leaning on his staff to stop himself from falling. His feet slipped on something round and cylindrical, and he swayed as he struggled to regain his balance, to show no weakness before the others. The bone beads tied to the standard rattled softly. Stray bits of dirt spun past his nostrils and dusted his tongue.

'Careful.' Elafi's touch on his arm came out of the darkness. 'There are bones. You'll slip, just so. Just past here.'

The tunnel debouched into a corbeled chamber, dry and dusty and crammed with neat piles of bones laid into alcoves that gleamed fitfully as Elafi turned all the way around to shine his light into each one. Stronghand straightened, as did First Son and Last Son, and stared somberly at this burial ground. Ki's breathing sounded very loud, as if she were frightened – or awestruck.

Yet what was there to be frightened of? He glanced back at the tunnel, all but this last portion of which had been formed by the framework of the wyvern's skeleton. The living could find uses for the dead.

'The wise ones of our tribe are buried here,' said Ki.

'This will be my resting place,' added Elafi.

'You are a sorcerer?'

The young man smiled. Dirt smudged his cheeks and nose, and his eyes seemed very dark. 'Did you see a deer, out by the willow tree where we hid? The Albans did.'

Stronghand nodded. 'Are you more powerful than the tree sorcerers?'

'I am not unlike them. But alone, I cannot combat them. I am the last sorcerer in my clan.'

'And it's a good thing you have a clever warrior like me to protect you!' said Ki.

Elafi smiled as he set the lamp in the center of the chamber, under the highest point of the corbeled ceiling, and nodded at Stronghand. 'From here you must go on alone. What happens then is up to you and your gods.'

'Where is the stone crown?'

Elafi gestured upward. 'This chamber lies in the center, and the great stones beyond it, around it, with their feet in the earth. They chain it to the earth so the dead cannot escape.'

Did all stone crowns conceal chambers at their heart? Did the WiseMothers incubate human bones? Or something else?

Yet ever since Alain's return, he had suspected what the truth might be. He just hadn't decided what to do about it yet.

'Show me,' he said.

Elafi pointed to one of the alcoves. 'You'll crawl through there. The tunnel twists and turns back on itself, but I think you are slender enough to get through. You'll find a ladder. In ancient days it led up to the sorcerer's house, but you'll see that it's long since been covered over. That's why it's secret now. That's why the Albans know nothing of it. There's a trapdoor set in place by my mother's father's father's uncle. You can crawl through the old foundation. A new shelter has been built over the old one. From underneath you can look out over the stone crown without ever being seen. Or you can squeeze out and walk into the stone circle, if you dare. The Albans and their tree sorcerers fear the stone crowns. They do not venture there at night. These circle priests may be more bold.' He nodded at Stronghand. 'You wear their mark yourself. Maybe you know.'

'Maybe I do.' He stabbed the standard's sharpened end down into the dirt and fixed it there before turning to First Son and Last Son. 'Guard this.'

One alcove contained only animal bones, arranged just like the others so that with a glimpse they looked the same as human bones. Laid there, Stronghand supposed, because it was no sacrilege to disturb them as he did, crawling past. He eased along a narrow passage that twisted back on itself twice; the second time the crooked bend was so sharp that he had to back up, unfasten his ax, and push it ahead of him. The iron head rammed against earth, but he was able to adjust the angle and shift it around the bend. Dirt made his ears itch. He pushed himself around that curve and wriggled forward over the wood handle. The axhead had come up against a wall of banked earth, and here he touched the bottom rung of a wooden ladder. It was too dark to see, and he hesitated, wondering if the visions would come again, would even cripple him, but nothing happened.

It was impossible to know what had happened to Alain.

Without Alain's sight, he, too, was blind and lost in Alain's dreams. Yet it was still better than the lack he had suffered when Alain had vanished from Earth.

He got to his knees and slid the ax back through its loop before testing the rungs. One bent beneath his weight, but they held as he climbed. It was an unexpectedly long way up, with dirt pressing around him on all sides; the metal links of his long waist girdle scraped earth with a sound rather like a bird scratching for bugs. When he reached the topmost rung, he felt above him and after a bit found a metal latch. He fiddled with it until he identified the clasp that released it. Then he paused and listened.

He heard nothing at all.

After a while he braced his knees against the rungs, wiggled his ax up into his fighting hand, and released the clasp. He cracked it open to admit light and sound, but only darkness greeted him. Distantly he heard the muffled sounds of the camp.

It took a bit of doing to crawl out because the trap could not open fully; the ceiling above was too low and was in truth not a ceiling but a floor. The space had once been filled with dirt and debris – its film coated his hair and irritated his eyes – but one of Elafi's forebears, perhaps that same uncle, had dug a passage through it. He felt along it, pushing his ax before him, and touched not just dirt but potsherds, scraps of wood, two nails, and once a bit of wool cloth, all smashed down into the earth. A footfall sounded directly above him, muted by floorboards and yet another layer – rushes or yet more earth; he could not tell. He squeezed along until the slope of the ground dropped suddenly out from below his hands. Groping forward, he found himself with room to crouch and an unexpected view past warped planks to the stone crown. Torches burned, startlingly bright, but the circular ground that lay between the partially restored stones was empty.

Yet he heard voices.

'It gripes me that we are beholden to these heathens. I don't trust them. They're coarse and low. They're rude and arrogant.'

'Patience, Father Reginar.' The second man spoke Wendish with rigidly correct grammar but a marked accent and frequent pauses to negotiate unfamiliar words. 'As long as they control this crown by force of arms, we must ally with them.'

'You just arrived here, Brother Severus. You don't know what they are. They are in bed with the Enemy! Such things they do—! Did you see that the queen has more than one husband? Four, at least, old and young, fawning on her. She takes a different one to bed every night, and there are even two youths to warm the bed of the ancient one. It's sickening. I don't think God would wish us to—' He had the petulant voice of a man accustomed to his every whim brought to fruition, but Severus' sharp reply cut him off.

'We have no other choice. Where are their sorcerers?'

Chastened but not meek, the young man answered in a scornful tone. 'They refuse to come here at night. They say it is forbidden.'

'God Above! If they refuse to come up at night, then none of them can ever learn to weave the crowns!'

'Yes, Brother. So we have discovered.'

'Well. I have greeted their queen and made talk with her about an alliance between Queen Adelheid and Prince Henry and these Albans. Prince Ekkehard should prove docile enough to make a husband for her maiden daughter, if we can find him.'

'Wasn't my cousin offered to the church?'

'He may have been. If the skopos wishes him to serve her in this manner, none will protest.'

'No, indeed, Brother Severus. No, indeed. That she singled me out for this honor!' Only the young could fawn so enthusiastically. 'That she singled me out to assist her in this great undertaking—!'

'Indeed.' The snappish way Brother Severus spoke the word silenced the other man. 'Sister Abelia may prove more persuasive with the sorcerers, since they seem to defer to women. I detest waiting as much as you do, but we have no choice.'

Stronghand wiggled one of the planks until it shifted, and he turned it sideways and squeezed through, then paused, lying up against the building as the two men walked out of the house not three paces from him, down a pair of steps, and onto the grass, still talking.

'Was it a difficult journey, Brother Severus? The dangers are many in these times.'

'We had a delay, a detour. I had an errand to run for the skopos to the monastery at Herford, but we had swift riding after that and our crossing from Medemelacha went smoothly.'

Herford. Alain had sojourned at Herford. Memory niggled Stronghand like the annoying whine of a dog. Had he heard Severus' sour voice in his dreams?

'The war is going badly for the Albans, as you may have seen,' continued the younger man, pleased with his tidings. 'The queen's uncle and brother march to bring aid, but we've not heard yet from him, although there's a rumor now that his army was utterly destroyed by the Eika. Who can be worse? These Albans, with their pagan rites, or the godless Eika?'

'Our task is clear, Reginar. How God choose to punish the heathens matters nothing to us unless it interferes with our undertaking. It's true there are many dangers afflicting us, Albans and Eika, heretics and civil war. We avoided the Eika ships on the crossing, thank the Lord. I had to raise a small illusion—'

'But you taught us to detest the illusionist's skill as a tissue of lies, Brother! Unworthy of our talent and serious purpose!'

'So it is. But while one should rightly detest a lowly bard who sings for his supper and entertains the common folk with bawdy tunes unfit for cultured ears raised on the *Heleniad* and the *Philologia* of St. Martina, it is understood that God have created every creature with a purpose, however vulgar it may be.'

'I have met a few such base creatures in my time!'

'Indeed. It is our task to rule and theirs to serve. In any case, on our journey the Lady's justice traveled with us, or we would not have made it this far and in such good time.'

'That is a blessing, Brother.'

'So it is. Yet matters remain unsettled. There is much to

do and less time than we need. We have little hope of send-ing anyone north, if the seventh crown lies in Eika territory, as we believe it must. And although our brethren have found the Salian crown, the civil war there grows desperate. I fear Sister Abelia will not be safe when she travels there to super-vise the others. Their work on restoring the crown goes slowly. They are having a difficult time finding workers willing to toil when they are always in fear for their lives.'

Stronghand felt a very human urge to laugh. Truly, at times, it seemed forces far greater than he were at work, smoothing his path.

The two robed men crossed to the grassy sward lying within the great circle. The flickering torchlight weirdly shad-owed the upright stones. Of the seven monoliths, four had yet to be raised. A third figure appeared, hurrying toward them past one of the fallen stones.

'Brother Severus?'

'Sister Abelia.' They were mostly shadow, despite the torches; Stronghand could distinguish them by height and the distinctive way each one moved. Severus had arrogance, while the younger man, Reginar, moved with more boldness and less discipline. The woman had determination, at least; she was farthest from him and most difficult to see. 'How have you fared?'

'Poorly, Brother Severus,' she said with obvious disgust. 'It is as Father Reginar says. They will not enter the stones at night, no matter what argument I offer them. They say it is forbidden to them. I think they are craven.'

Stronghand rolled up to his feet and padded forward as the two men absorbed her words. He marked one sentry, a stocky figure mostly hidden behind a straggle of brush; an arrow's shot down the hill lay tents. Otherwise, they were alone.

The wind gusted, and a misting rain hissed across the grass, gone as quickly as it had come. The young man pulled up his hood, but the old one took no notice. He seemed to be fuming, rubbing fingers over his balding pate, impatient to get on with their task and put annoying obstacles behind him.

Stronghand walked right up behind them, testing the ax's

heft in his hand. The feel of the handle gripped in his palm always gave him a sense of well-being.

'What will we do, Brother?' asked Sister Abelia.

Seeing the shadow of Stronghand's movement, she gasped and clapped her hands to her face, too startled to flee.

Stronghand bared his teeth as the two men turned, utterly surprised, and stumbled back from him in terror. Humans were so physically weak, and these weaker than most, unarmed and unprepared.

Yet it never served to underestimate them.

'There is an easy solution to your problems,' he said in his perfect Wendish, before they could shout for help. He touched the wooden Circle that hung from his neck. 'Make a new alliance.'

2

Sanglant rode at dawn into the council circle with his sword sheathed, his back straight and shoulders squared and strong, an orderly retinue of some twenty attendants and noble companions behind him, and a satisfied smile on his face. The centaurs had shown him scant respect when he first arrived, but that was before he had seen Bulkezu killed, hooded a griffin, and bedded his wife.

The smile faded as he surveyed the waiting centaurs, a score of them led by the ancient shaman, and the wagon that concealed the Kerayit witchwoman, herself attended by a dozen men armed in the steppe way with short bows, spears, and curved swords.

To these foreigners he was about to give his beloved daughter – their price for alliance. Blessing was the sacrifice, and it tore his heart knowing that without their help she would certainly die. Might be dead already.

He glanced back to the wagon trundling along, Liath riding

guard beside it together with Anna, Matto, Thiemo, Heribert, the Kerayit healer, and a pair of soldiers.

Li'at'dano had freshened the paint on her torso. The green-and-gold stripes made a stark contrast to her silver-gray coat. She carried a bow, with a quiver slung across her back, and her attendants were armed in a similar fashion, although a few held wicked-looking spears, half tipped with obsidian and the rest with cruel steel points. They had striped their torsos as well and decorated their faces with chalky lines and ocher dots. He could imagine them, in their thousands, in a wild rampage through the streets of ancient Dariya, burning, pillaging, and killing.

Li'at'dano looked him over as she might a wild dog that has crept into camp hoping for scraps, and she waited with obvious indifference to his presence until Liath reined her horse up beside his. Only then did she stamp one foreleg to acknowledge their arrival. The other centaurs repeated the gesture and whistled softly.

Behind him, the two Quman who had agreed to come with him echoed that whistle. A partridge burst out of the grass, flying low over the ground, wings whirring as if in reply, and as it disappeared from view all the noise of their movements and voices faded until the only sound was that of the wind muttering through the long grass. Bugs chirred. Otherwise, it was silent.

Liath rode out into the gap between their two parties. She lifted a hand to gain their attention.

'We have little time, and few enough to undertake a dangerous task. This is what I know. Two thousand seven hundred and two years and some seven months ago the Ashioi were cast out of this world by human sorcerers working in concert through the stone crowns and under the guidance of a powerful shaman.'

She did not turn to look at Li'at'dano, but Sanglant did. The old centaur merely watched. Did she feel emotion in the same way humankind did? He doubted it.

'That spell caused untold destruction throughout the lands, and it did not work in the manner they had hoped it would.

It did not cast the land of the Ashioi into the void forever. Even now the land of the Ashioi follows a path twisted back on itself that brings it home again to Earth. According to Brother Breschius and Brother Heribert, who have kept track of the passing of days, today is the nineteenth day of Yanu, in the year seven hundred and thirty-four after the Ekstasis of the blessed Daisan. When the crown of stars crowns the heaven, on the tenth day of the month of Octumbre in the year seven hundred and thirty-five, the spell will be complete. The land inhabited by the Ashioi will return to the roots from which it was torn free. According to the workings of the universe, all things must return to their rightful place.'

As she spoke in Wendish, certain centaurs murmured a running translation to their comrades as did Gyasi to the Pechanek Quman – one man and one woman – who had braved the displeasure of their tribes' mothers to follow him. Now and again Liath would pause to let them catch up, but always, inexorably, she went on in that same calm voice, detailing the approaching storm.

'In nineteen months there will come death and there will come destruction. We have no way to escape the consequences of what was put into motion so long ago.'

She let them consider as she herself glanced over at Sanglant. He didn't smile at her. He didn't need to. He knew what he needed most to know of her: that she had changed and that she had not, the familiar weaving of her shot through with new threads.

That didn't make what he had to do today any easier.

'The mathematicus known as Sister Anne intends to weave this ancient spell again, to banish the Ashioi and their land from Earth a second time. Of a certainty I know it will condemn the Ashioi. Their land has been cut off from Earth for so long that it dies. They are few, and they are weak. There are almost no children.'

Here she hesitated and, with an effort obvious to her husband although others might think she merely paused for breath, she did not look toward the wagon where Blessing lay dying.

'Perhaps there are those among you who care nothing for the fate of the Ashioi. Let me argue, then, in this manner. What effect Anne's weaving will have on Earth itself I do not know, but I believe it will condemn many, many more people to die, countless people, and bring about wholesale destruction on a scale we cannot fathom. I have seen—'

She faltered as she was overwhelmed by memory, but she swallowed firmly and began again.

'I have glimpsed the past. I know what immense destruction the spell caused then. I believe that if it is woven a second time, it will cause a terrible disruption in the fabric of Earth far greater than if the ancient spell, the first spell, simply ran its course. Many will die regardless; no one can change that now. But what Anne intends is not only wrong but will bring upon us all ruin and desolation.

'I cannot command any of you. I only command myself. I have seen Taillefer's crown spread across the land. I have a good idea of where each stone circle lies that Anne must control to weave the spell. Yet since the spell needs seven crowns to function, it may be possible for us to disrupt it by halting the weaving at one or two or half of the crowns. I will travel as quickly as I can to the central crown, where Anne will lead the weaving. I will stop her. Or I will die.'

Resuelto flicked his ears back as Sanglant's hands tightened on the reins.

'Aid me if you wish. If you will not aid me, then I beg you, stand aside and do nothing to hinder me.'

She let out a great breath and lifted her chin. She was so bright as the sun's light cast its brilliance over her. She was so beautiful. As much as Sanglant simply lusted after her, he gazed at her now with much more complicated emotions: desire, love, anger still stirring in its dark pit, but respect as well and pride in her strength. A little awe, perhaps, for the dazzling promise of the power she had unlocked within herself.

It was true she could not command men, but she would go where she meant to go and by having the courage to take that path, others would follow the trail she blazed. He could not battle Anne on any sorcerous plane, but without the strength of an army to back her up, Liath might never reach Anne, and certainly she could never control the chaos and dissolution that would inevitably erupt across Wendar and the other countries in the wake of the cataclysm.

Maybe God had a hand in bringing them together – for surely without each other they could not succeed.

'I have spoken as clearly as I am able,' she finished. 'I have told you what I know, as simply as I can. I must set forth soon, and quickly. Today if I can; tomorrow if I must.'

She looked toward the wagon where Blessing lay surrounded by her faithful attendants, but she set her lips together in a thin line and lowered her hand. 'That is all I have to say.'

Silence followed her speech except for the ever-present drag of the wind through the grass. It was not warm, but today's strong blow did not make his bones ache with cold. Clouds gathered along the eastern crags, breaking up into smaller clots as the peaks tore them apart. Nothing else moved.

'You know I am with you.' Sanglant let Resuelto take two steps forward before reining him in. His voice carried easily. 'I will do what is necessary to stop Sister Anne.'

'What role do we play?' demanded Wichman, behind him. 'I don't like all this talk of sorcery.'

'Sorcery will not protect us from an arrow in the back. Anne will protect herself with soldiers as well as magic. That is why we need both griffin feathers and sorcerers. Without soldiers of our own, we are too vulnerable to those who possess Henry's army.'

Wichman grunted, and there was murmuring among those assembled to listen.

'Let's say it's true,' said Lady Bertha, 'for I've seen strange enough things that I'm less likely to doubt such tales than I was a year ago. Why should we help the Aoi? You say the land will return and that the one known as Sister Anne, who is also skopos over us all, will raise a great spell against the Lost Ones that will cause untold destruction. But what if this spell would make things better? What if it would banish the land of the

Lost Ones so that we need never worry about them again? Wouldn't that leave us free to fight our own battles and restore King Henry to Wendar? The Lost Ones have no allegiance to us. We can't know how many of them there are, and whether they'll be our allies or our enemies when they return.'

Liath nodded. 'A fair question, Lady Bertha.' Recalling Eldest Uncle's trick, she unbuckled her belt, holding it high in one hand. 'Imagine that this side of the buckle represents the land in which the Ashioi dwell.' She spoke the words much as Eldest Uncle had, giving the belt a half twist and showing how a two-sided belt became a one-sided belt because of that twist, and how the Ashioi land would return to the place it started. 'The spell Anne means to weave can only work if the land lies on Earth. This means that the destruction will happen twice – once when the land intersects with Earth, and a second time when the new spell casts it away from Earth again. This is what we must not allow. We must seek to mitigate the return, and fight to prevent a second sundering.'

Many among Sanglant's retinue spoke at once, calling out questions, but their voices quieted as Li'at'dano paced forward.

'What has been done, is done,' she said. 'I will aid you, Liathano, as well as I am able. Let me send my apprentice, Sorgatani, with you.'

'You will not come yourself?' Liath asked.

'My strength is bound to this land. If I leave it, I will die. I will send warriors in my stead, three hundreds of them, who will fight fiercely on your behalf.' She beckoned to a stocky mare with a cream coat and, on her woman's head, startlingly black hair. 'This daughter can be called Capi'ra. She will lead those who fight with you.'

'Does Sorgatani know that those who escort me stand the highest risk of dying? We will battle at the center of it all.'

'She knows.'

Liath nodded. 'Then we march as soon as we break camp.'

Sanglant broke in before the shaman could answer. Liath had courage and power, but she had little idea of what made it possible to move an army. 'We'll need help if we are to survive such a long and arduous journey. Can you supply us with guides? Food? Supplies?'

Li'at'dano shifted her weight and made a gesture with her hands that finished with a touch to her bow strap. Had she been a horse, he thought, she would have flicked back her ears to show dislike. She addressed Liath, not him.

'Two days' ride from here lies a stone crown. It is an ancient monument that was erected here long before my people came to these pasturelands. If you can weave the crowns, then you can travel from one crown to another directly.'

The glare of the sun sharpened. Wind snapped banners and pennants. He raced through the implications of the shaman's statement, and had to restrain a laugh even as he wanted to cry.

'Why did you not tell me this before?' exclaimed Liath, almost shivering with excitement. 'Anne will never expect an attack from that direction! I can do it!'

'With an entire army?' demanded Captain Fulk, then recovered and looked at Sanglant. 'My lord prince, if I may speak.' He pressed his horse forward. When the prince nodded, giving him permission, the captain went on. 'In this way Hugh of Austra saved Princess Theophanu and Queen Adelheid and their companies from an Aostan lord named John Ironhead, who meant to hold them as hostages.'

'Hugh!' One word from Liath, that was all. She looked away, hiding her face from Sanglant's view.

'Go on,' he said curtly to Fulk. He hated talk of Hugh.

'Yes, my lord prince. We numbered seventy-five men and fifty horses, many fewer than we have here, and even so the path was fraying as the last of us crossed through, according to the report of Sister Rosvita. She was almost lost as the pathway collapsed behind us. I think it unlikely we can move an army of this size through the crowns.'

'It is not possible,' agreed Li'at'dano. 'That any sorcerer accomplished what you speak of – to guide a group as large as the one you speak of – is astonishing. The crowns were meant to accommodate small parties only.'

'Hugh did it,' said Liath in a dangerously rash tone.

'With only seventy-five men and fifty horses,' said Sanglant. 'We have near a thousand. And a griffin, whose feathers are proof against magic.'

'Ai, God,' murmured Liath. 'I had forgotten the griffin. Can such a creature even pass through the crowns?'

'If I may speak, my lord prince,' said Hathui. 'My lady. Consider this as well. Sister Rosvita told me that months passed in the moment that they stepped through the crown.'

Fulk nodded. 'As many of us here can attest.'

She acknowledged him and went on. 'In that same way, I suppose, four years passed here on Earth while you experienced only a handful of days passing in the world above, according to your testimony.'

'Do you doubt her?' asked Li'at'dano.

Hathui's smile was sharp. 'Nay, Holy One, I do not doubt Liath, for I knew her before, if you will remember, when she was one of that company to which I hold allegiance.'

'Go on, Hathui,' said Sanglant. He had primed her for a speech, although she had cleverly adjusted her terms with the unexpected introduction of the stone crown.

'Sorcery is dangerous, my lord prince, and uncertain. It seems unlikely the entire army can pass through the crowns in any case. In addition, if all of us travel together, then how can we alert our supporters elsewhere? We ought not to move in a single group. It would be better to split up.'

'To split up?' he asked, knowing his lines as well as Hathui knew hers.

'When the storm comes, my lord, no one will be safe. Those who support the king and Wendar must know what to do. If they are not prepared, then whatever force convulses the Earth will be echoed by terrible strife among those who suffer and are afraid.'

Li'at'dano beckoned Hathui forward. 'You are wise, Daughter,' said the old shaman. 'I would look at you more closely, for it is not given to every creature to learn wisdom.'

'I thank you, Holy One,' murmured Hathui, but she glanced at Sanglant as if to say, 'save me!' No one doubted

Hathui's courage, but it was clear that the Horse people, and particularly the ancient one, made her nervous.

'Go on,' said Sanglant, not wanting any of his people to show hesitation, and Hathui – not without trepidation – nudged her horse closer to Liath's on the grass between the two groups, human and centaur, allied, yet in so many ways separate.

The shaman examined Hathui for a space before turning to Liath. 'She is a worthy daughter. Will you give her to me as part of our bargain?'

'She is sworn to the regnant,' said Sanglant irritably. 'One of his chosen Eagles. She must return to his hand at the end of her flight.'

'A pity,' mused Li'at'dano, but she made no further claim.

Liath saw the trap, but it was already sprung. 'Will you and I not travel together?' she asked Sanglant.

Sanglant had never done a harder thing than what he did now. 'To defeat Anne we need an army greater than the seven hundreds we have here. To defeat Anne we need an army greater even than that with which we defeated Bulkezu. A griffin brings me more than feathers to cut through the magic wielded by our enemies. It can bring me an army as well.'

Liath opened her mouth to protest, then fell silent. He went on.

'I must ride west to gather as many Quman as I can. Margrave Waltharia holds troops in readiness, waiting only for my return. From the marchlands I will turn south and draw more Wendish troops as I go. Brother Breschius assures me that the Brinne Pass remains passable for much of the year, if the weather holds fair. I'll cross that way into Aosta, and march on Darre to free my father.'

'But—!' Color had leached from her face, leaving her gray with shock, and her hands clenched the reins until her knuckles turned white. Her horse minced under her, sensing her tension. 'But that means we must—'

She could not speak the word. Neither could he. He could scarcely bear to think of it: *That means we must part. Must separate again, not knowing how many months or years would pass until they met. Not knowing if they would ever meet.*

It gave him no pleasure to twist the knife into her belly. 'It has to be done this way. Do you believe that a griffin can cross through the crowns?'

She shook her head despairingly. 'Nay. It seems likely its feathers will cut the threads of the spell. That way lies disaster for all who attempt the crossing.'

'Anne has woven her net well. She controls not just sorcery, and the crowns, but Henry's and Adelheid's armies as well. We must match her. This is the only way.'

She shut her eyes and said nothing, because she knew he was right. As much as he hated it, this *was* the only way.

'There remains one thing more, Holy One,' he said, unable to bear her silence and knowing that if Liath had a chance to speak he would weaken. He gestured toward the wagon. 'What of my daughter?'

Li'at'dano waited, and waited, but Liath neither spoke or opened her eyes. Tears wet her cheeks, but she made no sound, only sat there, rigid and suffering.

At last, the shaman inclined her head to Sanglant with a touch of disdain, yet just perhaps in the manner of a teacher acknowledging a pupil's apt question. 'I have pondered deeply about the child. It may be I have thought of a way that will give us time to save her.'

3

Although Anna was busy making ready to go, Matto still found time to pester her.

'Later, in the night, we could sneak out into the grass.'

'And be eaten by the griffins?'

'The prince did it. Out in the grass.'

She looked at him, and he flushed, shamefaced, and hoisted a chest into the back of one of the wagons.

Thiemo stalked over. 'Are you bothering her?'

'Is it any of your business?'

They both seemed to have puffed themselves up with air, trying to look bigger and bulkier than they were, although indisputably Matto had the broader shoulders while Thiemo stood half a hand taller.

'Stop it!' said Anna. 'Does it matter that you're jealous of each other? What will happen to us? Did you think of that? Will we abandon Blessing, or will we ask to stay with her?'

Stay with her. Out in this God-forsaken place, separated, perhaps forever, from their homeland.

She burst into tears. Matto and Thiemo shied away from her as she brushed past them, returning to the empty tent. Blessing had lain in the wagon all morning; no one wanted to disturb her, except for the healer who at intervals squeezed a bit of liquid down her throat through the reed.

What did it matter? Blessing was to be handed over to the centaurs, and the rest of them would journey back across the interminable steppe. It didn't bear thinking of. She began rolling up the traveling pallets, the last thing to go.

'I will not abandon her. But I don't want to stay here. I don't want to stay.'

So it went with those who served. Yet she hadn't fared any better before the Eika invaded Gent, when she had lived under her uncle's harsh care. The Eika invasion had freed her from her uncle's house, but hiding in Gent had not made her and Matthias more comfortable. Quite the contrary. Matthias had been eager to apprentice himself out as soon as he was given the opportunity; he saw the worth of an orderly existence, with the promise of a meal every day and shelter over his head at night. War and plague and famine might afflict him – there was no defense against acts of God – but being a member of Mistress Suzanne's household gave him a measure of security.

Hadn't God wanted her to go with Blessing? Why else would she have got her voice back just then? Whatever power earthly nobles held over her, it was but a feather on the wind, compared to God's power.

'Anna?'

'Go away, Matto.'

'Nay, Anna, we'll not go. We've talked it over.' Thiemo pushed in next to him, and they both knelt beside her where she was rolling up the last pallet. Everyone else had left the tent; after this tent came down, they would march.

'We've talked it over, Anna. We'll stay with you, both of us. No matter what. We won't leave Princess Blessing. Or you.'

She couldn't speak because of the lump choking her throat. She tied up the pallet and picked up another, while Thiemo and Matto did the same. In silence they carried everything out to the wagon while soldiers dismantled the tent.

They traveled all afternoon, first overland to the river and then upstream through tall grass. That night she slept restlessly under the wagon while Thiemo and Matto kept watch. She woke to hear footfalls rustling in grass as they paced; the wagon creaked as the healer sat the unconscious girl up and forced a precious bit of fluid into her, enough to keep her alive one day more.

That was all they could hope for.

She rolled over but could not go back to sleep. The constant irritation of breathing grass all day made her throat raw and painful. The wind had turned cold, and she shivered in her blankets, wishing she had a warm body to share them with. But whatever she did, whichever man she chose, the other would be angry and jealous. How could she balance one with the other? What if they lived for years out here, alone together among a foreign people? How was it possible that Matto and Thiemo would not, in the end, come to blows? Or worse? What if they decided that neither of them wanted her?

She waited until they converged on the opposite side of the wagon and wriggled out, got to her feet, and dashed into the grass, bent over so they would not see her. Although she met no sentries, she didn't go too far; she could not get the iron stink of the griffin out of her head. The hooded griffin paced along at the head of the procession, obedient to its master, and the big female flew overhead but circled down at night to curl up beside its mate.

She heard them before she saw them, their muted voices whispering, and she stopped at the verge of a stand of stunted poplars growing just beyond the river's edge. Through furled leaves budding on the trees she saw an amorphous beast perched on a rock overlooking the river. She froze, heart racing, knowing how foolish she had been to leave the safety of camp. If she did not move, perhaps the beast would lumber off without noticing her.

Its murmured laugh made her shudder until, too late, she realized that she watched no beast at all but the prince romancing his wife, huddled close against her with a cloak thrown over their shoulders. How would it feel to sit with his arm tight around her, to feel his lips pressed close, to hear the murmuring of his voice as soft as the caress of the wind?

She sidled closer.

'Why didn't you speak to me before? Why wait until the council, if you planned it all along?'

'If I'd discussed it with you when we were alone, you'd have persuaded me otherwise. I couldn't have done it. This way, there is no going back.'

'Ai, God. I can't bear to think of leaving you when we might never . . . If I die, Sanglant—'

'Hush. Hush.'

They hushed for a time, but eventually the lady composed herself. 'I'll need perhaps fifty troops to protect me. That should be enough to move swiftly, enough to provide a real shield, but not so many that they'll be at risk when they cross through the crowns.'

'Yes, twenty-five men and horses and twenty-five of the centaurs, and a few pack animals. You must take Breschius. For a captain . . . Wichman is daring and bold.'

'Scarcely better than a savage!'

'Then which other?'

'Bertha seems competent and even-tempered.'

'She's not even-tempered, but she knows when to stay cool.'

'And won't be raping every comely girl her retinue passes by, I should think.'

He chuckled. 'As to that, if rumor is true, I can't say.'

Liath made a sharp, disgusted sound and there was a flurry of movement beneath the cloak. 'It's nothing to laugh over. How can you think it funny?'

'Forgive me, my love. You're right. Wichman's behavior is nothing to make light of.' He bent his head and for a while, as Anna stared, knowing she ought not to, he kissed his wife. She couldn't really see them clearly; there wasn't enough moon, but she could see shapes and she could *feel* that kiss through the air, as though it were a live thing nudging against her body.

After a while they disentangled, if not by much, and Liath spoke cautious words as delicately as if she were walking on ice.

'I know you were alone for many years, yet it chafes me, a betrayal.'

'Who betrayed whom first?'

'I did not abandon you! I had no choice.'

He was silent. The night lightened as the gibbous moon drifted free of clouds. Its silver ran on the waters.

'How many lovers?' Liath asked.

'How many? Ah.' He hesitated, then sighed. 'Well, first—'

'Nay, I didn't mean you must detail each one.'

'Then why did you ask?' He got up, leaving her wrapped in the cloak, and paced to the river, where he scrabbled among the stones on the shore for a rock to toss into the rushing water. The plop of its splash was heard, not seen. 'Not enough. Too many. And none of them were you. I hated you for leaving me.'

And well you should have! Anna wanted to shout.

What woman could bear to abandon such a man? It was all very well to prate about necessity and duty, but if you really cared for a person that much, you would never leave them behind, no matter what.

Not unless they asked you to.

'Ai, God, Liath. This hurts more than any injury I've ever suffered. I can't bear to leave you again.'

'I know. I know. But what choice have we, my love? We

are prisoners of power. If we survive, we will be reunited. Now come. Don't stand so far from me.'

'Hsst! Anna!' The whisper made her leap right off the ground because it came so unexpectedly and from directly behind her. 'What are you doing out here?'

'I beg pardon, Captain Fulk! Just, um, just coming out to pee.'

'If you're finished, you might want to go back into camp. It isn't wise for anyone to walk beyond the sentry line.'

He pointedly did *not* look toward the river or the two figures now embracing. He waited until she sighed, and turned, and followed him back into camp.

The stone circle stood on what had been an island before the river had eaten a new channel. Now it lay on a point with one flank washed by the flowing waters. The old secondary channel had filled in at one end, creating a rock-strewn earthen bridge between the land and the low hill where the crown was erected. Soldiers led the horses to drink by turns in the slough while the prince, his wife, and the old shaman investigated the stone crown together with a dozen attendants.

There were few trees in this part of the world, and even the brushy scrub along the riverbanks was scoured low by the winter winds and heavy snow, so the crown was easy to see. The stones shone golden where the westering sunlight washed across them; a few glinted, light catching in crystals embedded deep, as if the stones were chiseled from granite or marble. There were nine in all, arranged not quite in a circle but in a figure that bore more resemblance to an oval. Two of the stones listed, and one stone stood perilously near a low bluff where the current wore away the earth. The grass between the stones had been trampled, revealing a hummock in the center.

'I've never seen a crown all standing in place, like that one,' murmured Thiemo, shifting from one foot to the other as he, too, watched from beside Blessing's wagon.

'It makes me feel prickly all over,' agreed Matto. The two youths shared a look that, all at once, made Anna feel left out. Then they both glanced at her and the momentary camaraderie vanished as they turned away, hands clenching, backs stiff.

No one moved to pitch camp. Like Anna they waited anxiously, not sure what would happen next. The bulk of the army formed up farther out on the grass, separate from the small party that would accompany Liath. Farthest back, a dozen soldiers stood guard over the hooded griffin.

'What will happen?' asked Matto, unable to stand the suspense any longer.

'Look,' said Anna. 'They're coming back.'

A strong, cold wind started blowing from the north, and the healer rose from her seat at Blessing's side to sniff at the air. With a frown, she shook her head.

'Snow,' she said when Thiemo looked at her questioningly.

As the prince and his entourage clambered up to the waiting army, Captain Fulk hurried away to talk to a cavalcade of sergeants awaiting his orders. The powerful centaur attending the old shaman trotted away to her own group, and, as Anna watched, the two lines began integrating, units of centaurs lining up between mounted horsemen, with Kerayit bowmen in the van and Fulk commanding the rear guard. Only Bertha and her two dozen soldiers stood their ground, together with a dozen centaurs, the wagon belonging to the witchwoman, and her Kerayit attendants.

The prince strode up to the open wagon where Blessing lay. He leaned over the side, reaching out to touch his daughter's pale face. Blessing breathed softly, but it was clear that it might well be only hours before her soul left her body. Liath came to stand beside him. A few tears glistened on her cheeks, and she wiped them away impatiently.

'We do what we must,' she said.

'I know.' He, too, was weeping, but he made no attempt to erase his tears. He stood there for a bit with his eyes shut and a hand resting on the girl's sunken, hollow cheek. Liath said nothing. Maybe, Anna thought uncharitably, she was heartless; she didn't seem as upset as she ought to be. Or maybe, just maybe, what she showed on her face wasn't the mirror of her heart.

Maybe.

At last the prince sighed deeply and withdrew his hand. His gaze ranged over Blessing's attendants. He seemed to be counting them off.

'Well, then,' he said. 'This task I will command none of you to accept, but I offer it in any case. One chance we have to save her – that she be placed in the barrow at the center of the crown in the hope that the spell woven by my wife will capture her in a kind of sleep.'

'Until when?' asked Heribert, stepping forward to stare broodingly at the girl.

Sanglant shrugged. 'Until the crown of stars crowns the heavens. That is what we hope for. This is all we have. Otherwise, she will be dead by morning.' He had to stop because of the tears, but he mastered himself. 'The Holy One tells us that for the spell to work there must be seven. That means we need six to attend her. I cannot promise you life, or death. It may be that nothing will happen, and that after Liath departs you emerge unscathed. In that case you will march west with us. You may die. Or you may wake in a year and a half out in this God-forsaken wilderness. If that comes to pass, then the Holy One has given us her word that some of her people will be here to rescue you. So.'

'I'll go,' said Heribert instantly. The terrible expression on his face made Anna want to weep, but it was hard enough to listen without running away in fear. It was hard, knowing what she must do and yet fearing to do it.

'I go,' said the healer in her broken Wendish. 'The Holy One command me.'

Gyasi stepped forward. 'We serve the blessing through life and into death. My nephews and I will go.'

'Nay, you I have need of, Gyasi. I need you as a guide and to interpret and persuade the Quman. You serve her better if you help me win the war.'

'Then take of my nephews as many as you need, lord prince.'

Sanglant nodded. 'So I shall.'

'I will go, my lord prince.' Anna's voice shook as she said

the words. She had never been so frightened in her life, not even when Bulkezu had taken her as a hostage.

'And I,' said Matto.

'I will, too,' said Thiemo, not to be shown up.

Sanglant nodded, his frown so deep that it looked likely to scar his face. 'One of your nephews I'll need, Gyasi. One who can fight.'

The shaman nodded.

Matto was white and Thiemo standing so rigid that he looked awkward. They said nothing, and looked not at each other nor at her, as if the merest meeting of eyes would shatter their resolve.

'She'll have to be carried in,' said Liath. 'They may as well take a few things.'

'Like a burial,' murmured Sanglant hoarsely. 'In the old days they buried queens and kings in this manner, stowed with their treasures.' He shook himself and pushed away from the wagon. 'Let it be done, then. I can bear this no longer.'

'I'll carry her,' said Matto.

'I will!' insisted Thiemo.

'Nay, neither of you,' said Sanglant sharply. 'I'll carry her.'

They made a ragged little procession, laden with bundles, as they crossed what had once been a sandbar thrown up by the way the current had dredged into the earth. No one called after them, bidding them safe passage. Anna kicked stones rubbed round by the tumble of the water and left high and dry when the current shifted and this channel turned into a backwater. Once they reached the old island, she slogged up a gentle slope through low scrub. Gnats and tiny flies swarmed, and she batted them away and was relieved, really, to step past the stones into the ring because, for a miracle, no gnats or flies passed that invisible line.

The hummock revealed itself to be a barrow constructed in a way familiar to Anna from ones left behind by the ancient ones along the river north of Gent. It was larger than it had seemed from the mainland. A passage grave made by stones had been covered by turf, now overgrown with grass, yellow violets, and, to her surprise, a rash of variegated irises. The spray of flowers reminded her of funeral wreaths placed on the coffins of the dead, but she only gripped her bundle of clothes and oddments tightly and kept marching. She glanced back once toward the army, forming up into a tight marching line, units close together and some of the wagons abandoned and rolled to one side, including the one in which Blessing had lain. Bertha's troop moved up behind them onto the sandbar, and halted.

'Let me kiss her now,' said Liath. She kissed her daughter on the brow, then drew an arrow from her quiver and retreated out of the stone circle, stopping at a sandy patch of ground that faced east, so close to the bluff that one more step backward would send her tumbling into the river.

As she might deserve to, thought Anna, then squelched the thought, afraid that such feelings would doom her. She had to pray, to focus her thoughts on her dying mistress, but her hands did shake so that the bundle seemed likely to drop right out of her grasp even though it was loosely swaddled and easy to grip.

'Anna?' Matto sidled close up against her.

'Nay, you just leave her alone,' muttered Thiemo.

'Stop it!'

Heads turned at her tone, but the solemn proceedings captured their attention again.

Li'at'dano sprinkled ocher over Blessing's limp body, then dabbed a spot on either of Sanglant's cheeks, drawing the spot out into a line, and finishing with a red mark on his brow. She marked the rest of them in the same fashion, and when it came Anna's turn, it was all she could do not to shrink away from the centaur. Those eyes seemed flat, and the pupils weren't shaped right, and certainly no trace of human emotion enlivened that creamy face. She could kill any of them with a kick, if she wished — well, any of them except Prince Sanglant.

And when they woke — if they woke — this creature would be her keeper. She didn't fear Li'at'dano, precisely, but the thought of living among the centaurs for untold years made her suddenly very queasy.

The prince knelt by the low entrance and, with his daughter clutched tightly against him, edged forward on his knees into the grave. Heribert followed him, carrying a lamp and a blanket, and after him went the Kerayit healer dragging behind him the heavy leather pouch in which he carried the tools of his trade.

Then it was Matto's turn. He took in a deep breath and glanced back at Anna and Thiemo, but he said nothing, only got down on his hands and knees and crawled in after the others. Once he was inside, Anna ducked down under the lintel, able to walk in a crouch rather than have to crawl as the bigger men did. The smell of earth overwhelmed her. The ramped floor sloped down and as she pushed the bundle ahead of her, unable to figure out any way to carry it, the ceiling above receded until she was able to raise up a little and walk bent over. The passageway seemed to go on for longer than ought to be possible, given the outward dimensions of the hummock, and when she reached the chamber, the flickering lamplight suggested a chamber far larger than it had any right to be. The corbeled vault was so high that Sanglant could stand upright. The walls were pockmarked with niches, but the lamp didn't give enough light for her to tell what was stored in them.

Thiemo caught her wrist as he crowded up beside her. 'Dead people,' he whispered. 'They bury dead people in here.'

A scream caught in her throat.

'I pray you,' murmured Heribert to the prince. The cleric had set down the lamp and now fussily arranged the blanket in the center of the chamber. With a grim expression, Sanglant laid his daughter on the blanket, tucking the ends around her feet, and kissed her twice.

The Quman youth crept in, staring about the vaulted chamber. He kept his hands away from his weapons, but it was comforting to see him armed together with the swords Matto and Thiemo carried and the knife she herself wore at her belt. Only the healer and Heribert carried nothing to defend themselves.

The prince lifted the lamp and shone it one final time into the face of each person there.

At last, he spoke. 'It makes no matter whether my beloved daughter survives, only that you six were willing to serve her even in the face of death. I will never forget that. When we meet again, you will receive a just reward. No one has done me a greater service than you.'

There was nothing more to say. Anna willed him to go quickly, so that she might not have to suffer his good-byes any longer. She might never see him again, the one she loved best in all the world. He held the lamp while they each of them sat down in a circle around the unconscious girl and once they had settled he placed the lamp beside Brother Heribert licked his fingers, and snuffed out the burning wick.

'Fare well,' he said.

He embraced Heribert last, then was gone. She heard his shuffling crawl up the tunnel.

'It's strange,' said Matto in a whisper. 'I can't see any light at all. We can't have come so very far, and there were no twists in the passage.'

She groped and found his hand, squeezed, and reached to the other side for Thiemo. There she sat holding on to each of them. The Kerayit healer crooned softly in a nasal voice. Although the words and the eerie tune made no sense, it was somehow soothing.

They waited.

The blackness was complete, drowning them. She could see nothing, not even Matto or Thiemo so close on either side of her, but the clasp of their hands comforted her. At length her trembling slowed and ceased. The cold grasp of reality overtook her; she might die, here and now, or she might not, but she had made her choice and now had only to wait.

It was strange to feel so calm.

'What's that?' whispered Matto.

'Hush!' said Heribert, who was now their leader.

A barely audible rumble vibrated the ground under her thighs and rump, more felt than heard.

'The army is moving,' muttered Thiemo.

'No,' said Matto. 'We couldn't feel them, they're too far from us.'

'Then what is it?'

'Hush,' said Heribert.

The Kerayit healer fell silent as a high, singing note thrummed at the limit of their hearing. A second voice joined the first, not a human voice nor even that of any living thing but of an entity so ancient and cold that its voice had great beauty but no warmth. Their harmony twisted through her bones and made fingers of cold fear race up and down her spine. She shuddered; the eerie counterpoint made her ears hurt, and the melisma of those voices stabbed her through the chest like knives whose blades had been soaked in icy water until they burned.

'Ai, God,' breathed Thiemo as in ecstasy.

Matto whimpered in pain.

Light flashed as swiftly as lightning, a blue fire, and in that instant she saw the six of them seated around the corpselike form of Blessing. The niches caught fire, blossoming into a labyrinth of passageways.

She saw into the tangle of the maze that flowered around them, reaching in all directions and in no direction, and anchored by a blazing stone pillar in whose heart lived past, present, and future woven each into the other in an unfathomable skein.

She saw.

A silver-gold ribbon winds through the heavens in twists and turns so convoluted that she cannot tell one side of the ribbon from another or if it even has two sides at all but only one infinite gleaming surface without end. The dazzle of stars blinds her, and then the glory of the heavens vanishes as a shadow looms, so huge that it covers half the sky. An immense weight bears down on her, crushing the air from her lungs. She struggles, but the weight passes right through her, and as she comes up gasping and choking and coughing for air, she sees

gnarled, hunched creatures clawing through tunnels of stone

a young woman, dressed in the most peculiar manner and with her face scarred, struck down by a spear made of light as she stands before a blazing stone crown a young lord asleep with six companions curled around him

a half naked warrior and his comrades striding along a path, stone-tipped spears in hand and revenge in their hearts; their bodies look like those of men and women but they wear animal faces: a wolf, a falcon, a griffin, a great cat, a curly-snouted lizard

a man attended by two hounds, his face obscured by shadow as he kneels beside a dead man whose flesh, horrifyingly, crumbles away until there is nothing left but bone

Blessing, grown into a young woman, seated on a golden throne

the Eika who caught them in the cathedral at Gent but let them go stands at the stem of a ship attended by grim warriors, his form outlined against the elaborately carved dragon prow; as the ship grinds up the slope of a beach he leaps out and at the head of his army assaults a creature half woman and half glittering wolf's-head. Bodies fall everywhere. Blood streams down the shore into the shallow waters where the churning makes them swirl and muddy until she sees, in their depths, the most awful sight of all:

Blessing's withered corpse, burning on a funeral pyre.

'No more!' she gasps as the visions wash over her in a flood and she drowns.

Blue fire swallowed her. Thiemo's hand convulsed in hers, and he fell against her.

Then, nothing.

4

The ships arrived in threes and fives, guided by the men who had paddled northeast with Manda's tribesmen through the fens to the sea. As the fleet gathered, the holy island on which the queen sheltered began slowly to become wreathed in an impenetrable fog that each day spread farther out across

the waters. Eight days after Elafi and Ki had guided him to
the secret path that led beneath the hill, Stronghand readied
his troops, detailed his plans, and moved his ships into position. He called for the attack at dawn.

Dawn never came, or so it seemed. The sun crossed the
threshold of night, but no light penetrated the viscous mist
risen from the fen. Even the ferocious dogs seemed subdued
by its weight.

'We should wait until tomorrow,' muttered Dogkiller. 'Our
ships will be scattered and our attack confused in this fog.'

'No. This mist smells of tree sorcerers. The tidal swell is
in our favor, high and strong. My ship will lead the attack.'

When Stronghand stepped to the stem of his ship, he thrust
his banner before him. As they rowed into the gloom large
drops of water condensed on the staff, and on the hull, as the
mist thinned. Soon water dribbled off every surface and
around and behind them shadow ships took form, more phan-
tom than real. As they pushed forward the fog shredded into
patchy wisps and the ships took on solid form. With a will
the men bent to their oars, stirring the murky water as they
skimmed across the wetlands. Dogs thrust their heads out over
the railing to sniff at the air, their glossy flanks trembling with
excitement. Now and again a ship snagged on a high lying
shelf or on a bank of reed submerged by the tide, but otherwise the shallow draught of their ships served them well.

Points of fire flared on the islands as the Albans prepared
for battle, but the water between them lay clear and open.
Stronghand leaned forward to taste the wind: was that the
scent of their enemy's fear, leavened with the stink of decay?
As he turned to survey his flanks, those ships sweeping around
to hit the island from the opposite side, the deck shook beneath
him.

Tenth Son, at the stern, called out an incoherent warning.
Behind them, other ships rocked, yet there was no wind
beyond a trifling early morning breeze. Barking and yelping
shattered the quiet; men shouted in alarm.

Darkly sinuous shapes writhed up out of the water.

The boat lurched sideways so suddenly that he fell against

the railing and barely caught himself with his free hand, almost
pitching right over the side. A dog skidded past him and
fetched up hard, rattling the railings. Tentacles snaked up
along the planks. He threw the standard onto the deck but
before he could pull himself upright a vise gripped his ankle
and he was tugged so hard he flew backward and plunged into
the fen.

The water swallowed him. Spinning, he got himself ori-
ented, but when he tried to stand his feet sank into silt. Roots
and vines wrapped around his legs. The keel parted the muck
above him. A flailing oar struck him on the head, and he staggered. The living roots embraced him, pulling him into the
slippery mud.

His breath was going. His lungs were almost empty. He
grabbed a root and drew his axe, hacking twice before cutting it through, yet for each one he sliced away another curled
up to take its place. He worked methodically and efficiently,
but his life was slipping away into the water.

Draining.

Darkness.

He was blind, hallucinating with something as close to
panic as he had ever felt in his short life.

*Chains scrape around his ankles and wrists, weighing him
down as his captor bargains with a merchant.*

*'It's true he's blind, but look at him. All his limbs work.
He's healthy. And he's as good as brainless. Doesn't even
remember his own name.'*

*The merchant grunts disgustedly. 'You'd offer me a lame
horse by telling me that it's easier for walking children to keep
up with it? Nay, twenty sceattas for him.'*

*'Twenty! Robbery! I'll take forty, but only because he's
blind. His hearing is sharp as a dog's. Look how strong he is!'*

*'Strong? Looks like he's in a stupor to me. He's probably
mute and touched in the head to boot.'*

*Moist hands test the muscles of his arms, squeezing and
measuring. They pause to tap at metal.*

*'What's this pretty piece? Bronze, and cunningly worked,
too. That would bring you a fair price down at smith's street.'*

'It won't come off,' replies his captor reluctantly.

'Won't come off?' Fingers grope at the armband given him by the skrolin, the last thing he possesses that links him to what he was before he forgot everything. 'What kind of fool – ai! Uh! Uh! Shit! It burned me!'

'You think we wouldn't have taken that off right away, if we could have? It's some kind of magic piece. A curse, maybe.'

'Magic! Curses! Fifteen sceattas is more than generous for the likes of him.'

'Fifteen! Thirty-five is my last offer.'

What are 'skrolin'? The word hangs in his memory, but he can make no image, can only remember the sound of clawed feet scuffling on stone. After all, he is blind.

The merchant's hands run down his flanks and prod his buttocks. Once he had clothing, but it has been stolen or sold. He wears only a loin-cloth and a frayed, stinking blanket thrown over his shoulders. The wind chills him, but it also brings to him a panoply of noise wrapping him around and drowning him.

'Oysters! Oysters!'

'Have ye heard the news? Two Salian ducs have each claimed the throne. It's said their armies are marching.'

'Are we safe here?'

A cart rumbles past. Chickens cluck. He smells the dusty aroma of unmilled wheat, tinged with decay – the last gleanings from a winter storehouse. He hears the steady, careful blows of a workman chiseling stone, the rasp of an adze dressing wood.

Two women laugh, but their voices fade as they walk on; like everyone else they take no notice of the interchange in progress. He is beneath notice, submerged into the background, just another commodity at the market town waiting to be sold.

A pig squeals as its throat is cut, an awful noise that goes on and on before, between one breath and the next, cutting off.

He shudders all over.

'Well, he can't likely escape if he's blind,' agrees the

merchant in answer to an unheard question. 'I think I know who could take a lad like this, dumb and witless and blind but otherwise hale. Thirty sceattas. Take it, or go elsewhere.'

'Done.'

The last root parted under his axe. He thrust up with his legs and burst out of the water, gasping for air, hollow with rage. From the other ships, men cried out in horror. Planks creaked as plants lashing up from the depths tried to pull apart planks and drag down keels. He sputtered and grasped the side of the listing ship. Tenth Son was first to reach him, hauling him up and over the side. He fell to his knees, grabbed the standard, which was lying untouched on the deck, and with his lungs on fire and his body shedding water and mud he struck the haft to the deck three times.

Roots withered and fell back into the muck. The churning waters stilled.

Next to him, a dog growled.

Still coughing, he surveyed the fleet. He had no time to dwell on the vision that had almost drowned him. One ship had capsized, its warriors and dogs lost to the swamp since RockChildren did not swim. Yet men would be lost to battle nevertheless. This battle had already begun as the magic of the tree sorcerers retreated before his talisman.

He lifted the standard. Drums sounded the advance as oars stroked to a beat. They closed with the shore. Flaming arrows shot by the Albans lit arcs through the sky and fell against shields held in place by warriors clustered on the foredeck of each ship. Before them the three islands rose out of the swamp. A hastily constructed earthen dike ringed the land, topped with a crude stockade neither stout nor tall. The enemy had scoured the island clean of vegetation for building, for fire, for fodder, and the stink of their overcrowded encampment drifted over the waters. Rising above all, at the height of the tallest island, the stone crown dominated the scene.

His ship scraped through reeds and grounded on the muddy shoreline. A second ship, and a third, slid up beside it. Dogs poured over the railing, eager for blood. His warriors leaped over the side and assailed the rampart. Unused masts were carried as rams, and soon they breached the stockade in a dozen places. Yet a hedge of Alban spears and shields filled every gap as soon as it was opened, and Alban archers darted to and fro behind the shield line, releasing shafts at deadly close range as they targeted the mass of dogs. With each push over the rampart, a countercharge drove the RockChildren back, but never all the way back into the water, never all the way back to their ships. More poured up on shore to support those in the vanguard.

The queen of Alba rose above the fray, her wolf's head helm shining and her banner held high behind her. A rank of tall shield-men as brawny as bears protected her, all armed with great axes.

'Tenth Son! Hold the standard and do not leave the ship. I'm leading a countercharge.'

Against the queen, Stronghand himself must be seen to prevail, just as he had at Kjalmarsfjord been the one to throw his challenger Nokvi overboard to the merfolk.

The sun rose high in the morning sky. Its light made the stones atop the hill seem to glow. From the other side of the island he heard the flanking ships engage. Shouts and cries rose up into the sky like startled birds.

'Now!'

He pushed into the front line, half a head shorter than most of his brothers. They struggled up over the rampart, clawed feet digging into the dirt to keep their purchase as spears thrust against their shields in an effort to drive them back. Arrows poured in on their flanks, and many of his warriors staggered back or fell, but the rest held their line as others filled in. The Alban line stretched and thinned under the onslaught. Here and there an inward bulge formed as the RockChildren pressed hard down off the ramparts. The toll was grim on both sides, but he had a larger army and one final surprise to unveil.

Once again the queen appeared. She drove headlong into the flank of one of those bulges, cutting the forward forces off from reinforcement. With a score of Hakonin warriors, Flint charged to meet the Albans, but these queen's men had such unusual size and girth that they could each one meet the charge of an Eika and hold their ground. With shield pressed against shield, the struggle became a stalemate.

Stronghand was caught behind his own shield line as a dozen men filled the breach and another dozen pushed against the Eika, straining, grunting, while all about them axes cleaved shields, spears thrust, and arrows whistled. One huge man stalked into view, looming above the battling line. The queen gave way to let him through.

He was massive, like a tree trunk animated and molded into the form of a man. His helm was closed over his face and only his beard could be seen, curly and green like moss. His ax crashed down onto the head of the warrior standing just to the right of Flint; the hapless soldier's skull split in two and blood poured out as the corpse collapsed, leaving a gap.

Three men sprang forward to meet the giant, but he swept them aside with a sideswipe of his shield as easily as a man dusts chaff from a table.

The earth beneath their feet trembled.

Again the ax rose and came down. Flint parried the blow with his shield, but the metal rim and wood body splintered and snapped and he dropped down like a stone under the weight of that awesome blow. Again the ground shook as if it would heave and buckle under the strain. The line shifted; the Eika, impossibly, lost heart in the face of such impenetrable strength.

The giant's ax rose again, poised to strike and break the line.

The knoll exploded in golden flame and green fumes. A roar to curdle any creature's blood vibrated through the air. Beyond the stones, the wyvern rose up from the cliff face where it had been interred for centuries, a skeleton no longer but fully fleshed. Deadly venom dripped from its fanged mouth. Its wings beat a thundering rhythm, and clouds of dirt and a spray of poisonous vapor blew outward from the tremendous wind made by wings. It curled its tail tight, using it like a rudder, and swooped down toward the Alban queen.

The dogs ran for the water.

Half of the Alban men fled blindly, although there was nowhere to run, struggling and pushing and trampling as they shouted and screamed in terror. The rest stood transfixed, and only a handful of her guardsmen had the presence of mind to turn to face the new threat.

'Now!' cried Stronghand triumphantly, and with a howl of victory the Eika surged forward to crush the Alban lines.

Flint leaped to his feet and buried his ax in the chest of the giant, then danced sideways as the huge creature toppled and fell flat, crushing two Alban soldiers under his bulk. Stronghand raced through the breach and with a dozen men at his side hit the stunned guardsmen and bowled them over. Above, the wyvern dissolved into a rattling, tumbling shower of bones, the illusion fading in a roar of sound no less impressive than the panicked screams of the vanquished Albans as the Eika killed as many as they could.

Stronghand lunged just as the queen made ready to flee. She parried him and swung a blow with her sword, but he dodged, ducked inside her reach, batted her shield out of the way, and cut off her head. The wolf's head rolled sideways and came to rest with its muzzle leering at the sky. Her heart's blood gushed onto the earth from her severed neck.

'Go!' he called to First Son, who was waiting for the command. A score of soldiers trotted off through the chaos toward the stone crown.

Tenth Son slogged over to him through the sea of dead to give him the standard. 'Not as good as Bloodheart's illusions,' he commented. 'The colors were too bright. But the poisonous spray was a nice touch. Do such creatures kill with venom?'

'I don't know. I've never seen such a beast before.' All around them the killing went on as the remains of the battle swept toward and then ringed the Alban encampment. At the water's edge, the boldest dogs turned and loped back into the fray. 'Come with me.'

The remaining Alban soldiers stood back to back in a tight shield wall that enclosed the central camp and the huge white tent that had sheltered the queen and her lineage. Two women wearing bands of gold around their foreheads stood under a white awning, one very elderly and the other so young she was still a girl. She wore armor but no helmet and did not look strong enough to heft the sword that she held in her left hand. Children cowered at the entrance to the tent, towheaded lads and lasses wearing the garb of noble kinfolk in stark contrast to the two score or more crudely garbed slaves huddled up against the walls of the tent. Caught, as Ursuline the deacon had once said eloquently, 'between the Enemy and the hindmost.' They alone were unarmed. Every adult in camp, not just the soldiers, had some kind of weapon in hand, shovels, picks, pitchforks, sharpened stakes, and many a makeshift club. Even the remnants of the tree sorcerers, young and old alike, held their leafy staves as if they were spears and not the staffs through which they wielded their magic. They knew their magic had failed them.

Stronghand beckoned to a trio of soldiers. 'Lift me on a shield.'

He set his feet at either side of the round shield, swayed as the soldiers hoisted him, and caught a fragile balance. His own warriors pulled back from the front line, and even the Albans fell silent, weapons at the ready, as they stared up at him. One archer shot at him, but he shifted sideways so the arrow grazed his left shoulder, the merest prick against his copper skin. The others held their fire.

'For some among you,' he shouted, 'there can be no mercy today. But those among you who are slaves, hear me. Cast aside your servitude and join us. Let the slave become the master, and the master become the slave. If you join us, you will live and be given land and the chance to start again. If you remain, then you will die with those who have ruled you.'

The girl queen lifted her sword to point at the heavens. Was it fear or fury that transfigured her youthful face? 'Kill them!' she shrieked.

Her armed countryfolk, all but the soldiers, turned as one mass and butchered the hapless slaves.

Stronghand leaped off the shield. 'No mercy!'

The Eika surged forward.

No mercy they showed, not this day when Alain had been shown no mercy. Black anger scalded his heart, and he himself killed the queens and the screaming, terrified children.

When all the Albans were dead, he sat in the queen's gilded chair and surveyed the islands while his soldiers assembled before him. Most of the corpses lay twisted on the ground, although he had ordered his men to string up the bodies of the tree sorcerers from the masts of their ships. The dogs fed eagerly. Tents lay trampled; piles of bodies marked episodes of fierce fighting; a few horses and sheep had been killed, and one of the ships had caught fire and now smoldered as his men heaved buckets of water over the smoking deck. The slaughter had an especially pungent smell because so many had died in such a small area.

A lone hound, lean and gray, nosed through the wreckage and paused to lap at a pool of blood, ears down and body cowering. A trio of Eika dogs caught its scent and raced toward it, and it bolted, yipping. The chase vanished from his view but ended in a spate of frantic barking and a squeal of pain, cut short.

It was a bloody field, truly, but all battlefields were in the end. Humankind might glorify war or twist themselves into knots to justify their conflicts as necessary and right, but he knew better. They were a means to an end, one choice made instead of another – effective, brutal, and if fought on the right battlefield with the right timing, decisive.

He had done what he needed to do to get what he wanted.

Yet he could not erase the stain of Alain's suffering from his mind. It seemed he could never exult in his greatest victories.

Out on the fens a score of small boats appeared: Manda and her people paddled toward the holy island they hoped to reclaim.

'It will have to be cleaned up,' he said to Tenth Son. 'I wonder if they prefer the corpses burned, buried, or drowned in the water.'

'Burning and drowning may pollute what is here,' said

Tenth Son. 'If I were them, I would ask that the corpses be conveyed to the mainland and disposed of there.'

Stronghand nodded. A score of his Rikin cousins approached, guarding his new allies, whom they had rescued from the shelter built up by the stone circle.

As he waited, he mused, and spoke at last to his companion.

'I am not the OldMother, to grant you a name. But neither am I Bloodheart or any of the chieftains of old, content with what they could grasp for themselves alone. Nay. Why should I stop here? Why should I hesitate?'

Soldiers moved aside to make way for First Son and their allies. They halted ten paces from him.

'As you commanded, Stronghand,' said First Son. 'None of the circle priests were killed.'

He moved aside to allow Brother Severus to walk forward alone, leaving his dozen attendants behind him under the protection, or custody, of First Son's cohort. It was clear that while some accepted their changing circumstances with a stoic calm, others felt less sanguine and the one known as Father Reginar, certainly, looked ready to vomit as he stared at the feeding dogs.

'Lord Stronghand.' Brother Severus spoke Wendish with a strong accent and an arrogant way of clipping off the ends of his words. If the carnage bothered him, he did not show it, but neither did he once look away from the matter at hand. 'We have abided by our part of our agreement. Now we expect that you will abide by yours.' He fished in one long sleeve and drew out a parchment scroll, freshly inked. 'We have written up a contract, detailing our agreement. It wants only your mark to seal our bargain.'

Stronghand rose, lifting his standard. With their usual patience, born of stone, the RockChildren waited. 'What is to stop me from killing you now that I have you in my power?'

Severus sighed with the weariness of a man who is plagued by the stupid questions of foolish children. 'We are sorcerers, my Lord Stronghand. You should fear our power.'

'But I do not.' He gestured toward the field of corpses that surrounded them and made sure to indicate the gruesome trophies dangling from the masts of his fleet. 'The magic of the tree sorcerers did not defeat me. Why should yours?'

The corners of Severus' lips twitched up, but he was not smiling. He lifted a hand casually, and a wind stuttered up from the earth. The awning heaved as though an invisible creature shrugged up beneath it. The cloth of the tents all around them flapped and fluttered. Pennants snapped. The corpse of the youngest queen rolled as a movement within the soil heaved it sideways, revealing maggots where her heart's blood had pooled on the ground beneath her. Every dog feeding yelped and leaped, as if stung, and like a flock of locusts they bolted into the water and there they stayed, whining but fearful as blood and offal oozed from their muzzles to further muddy the spoiled shoreline.

Stronghand bared his teeth, nothing more. This Severus was not one to be trifled with or underestimated. Unlike most men, he could not be intimidated, and he was no fool.

'We are not so easy to kill,' said Severus as wind rippled the waters and rocked the ships.

Stronghand let the sorcery subside without interfering with it. 'Had I wished to kill you, I would have done so already. Be assured that I make no bargain unless I mean to keep it.' He touched the scar on the back of his left hand to his own lips, remembering what had been sealed by blood when Alain had freed him from the cage.

Where was Alain now?

How could he find him, if he had no landmarks to show the way?

'I will mark your contract, but you must first read it aloud for my ears.'

'Of course. Reginar?'

The young man had lost the edge of his arrogance, but he had a measure of courage, too, because he took the parchment from Severus and read in a voice that wavered at first but at length became steady and strong.

'This agreement of mutual aid and alliance spoken and sealed between the Holy Mother, Anne, in the person of her counselor, Brother Severus, and the one known as

Stronghand, king among the Eika. In return for the help given to him by Brother Severus in defeating the queens of Alba and granting him material aid in claiming the queendom of Alba, Stronghand agrees to guard those who wish to restore the crown at Wyfell Island; they will abide beside the caretakers of the island in peace and will be allowed to study the ancient art of the mathematici within the confines of the stone circle. In addition, in return for our support and blessing, Stronghand will aid us in restoring and protecting the other crowns we seek, including one in the Eikaland and another in the kingdom of Salia. He will allow missionaries to move freely among his people and among the Alban heathens.'

The text was hedged round with prologues and appendices, legal wordings that had to do with humankind's propensity for complicating matters best left simple. At last Brother Severus laid the parchment open on a board and held it out for his mark. He wet his fingers in the blood of the young queen and drew two slashes beneath the neat letters, none of which he could read.

That would have to change. If he meant to treat with humankind, he must be sure they were not tricking him through his ignorance.

'It is done,' said Severus with satisfaction. 'We will continue with our reconstruction as soon as you provide us with laborers—' Even a man of such self-control flinched when he surveyed the bloody corpses, the ruin of the battle, the restless dogs. 'When the island is habitable again.'

'Just so,' agreed Stronghand.

He lifted his standard again, the gesture that brought quiet over his troops even to the limit of the islands. When he spoke, he spoke in the tongue of the RockChildren that few humans bothered to learn.

'Here we begin.'

He stared over the fens toward the horizon. The last wisps of fog dissipated under the sun's cold light and a bracing north wind off the distant sea. It had not taken so long, after all, to destroy the Alban queendom: a few seasons, one long campaign.

'Once, in the old days, the chieftains of our people would have plundered Alba and sailed home to celebrate their prowess, gaining nothing more than gold and trinkets. We have walked all of our lives in the old ways. But there is more to gain here than treasure. We need not be content with plunder alone. I say now, let us follow the old ways no longer.'

His army waited. They had learned that it was worth their while to find out what came next. Severus and his retinue backed up as Stronghand paced forward; not one among them did not look uncomfortable as they glanced around and, perhaps belatedly, realized the size and power of the people to whom they had just allied themselves. A hundred-score warriors here on this island and countless more spread across Alba or waiting their turn in the land of their birth, which the humans called Eikaland. For the humans would name each thing, because names were power.

'There is something every human possesses that all but the greatest among us do not. It is a thing few have thought to ask for, and many have feared to obtain.' In OldMother's hall, in a darkness dense with the scent of soil and rock, root and worm, the perfume that marks the bones of the earth, he had suffered her judgment and heard her words. He repeated them now, thrown as a challenge. 'Who are you?'

They watched and they waited, Rikin and Hakonin, Isa and Vitningsey, Jatharin, what remained of Moerin, and many more, hands shifting on axes and spears, feet nudging aside corpses so that they might shift to get a better view.

'By what name will you be called when the measure of the tribe is danced? When the life of the grass is sung, which dies each winter? When the life of the void is sung, which lives eternal?'

'It's wrong!' cried Jatharin's chief, speaking for the first time. 'You cast disrespect on the OldMothers, who alone can judge whether a son is worthy of a name!'

'Perhaps. But perhaps they are only waiting for us to take this thing for ourselves which up until now we have feared. We know each one of us his place in the litter from which we sprang. That place has defined us for long years. Why need it define us any longer? We are young in the world, and we will never grow old. Even the frailest Soft One can hope for a greater span of years than the strongest among us, my brothers.'

He paused to let them survey the bodies strewn across the ground, to let them examine the dozen clerics clustered around Severus. The loose robes worn by the circle priests could not disguise the weakness of their bodies – or the sharpness of their minds, honed by learning and the ability to plan and plot.

'Why do we wait? Why should each one among us *not* possess a name? Why should each one among us *not* hope to be named in the dance that is the measure of each tribe? Why should each one among us *not* seek to be named in the chronicles of the Soft Ones? Let them know the names of the ones they fear.'

He bared his teeth. He lifted his standard a little higher.

'Who is bold enough?'

Silence followed, dense and suffocating. It was one thing to follow the road of war and another to go against oldest custom, all the measure of safety they knew in their brief lives ruled by the OldMothers and the chieftains, strongest among them.

Tenth Son took a step forward. 'I will be known. I want a name.'

'By what name will we call you, Brother?'

'Trueheart.'

Others called out then so swiftly that Stronghand knew some among the RockChildren had brooded over this question.

'Fellstroke!'

'Sharpspear.'

'Longnose!'

'Ha! A good name for you, Brother!' cried Hakonin's First Son. 'I will be called Quickdeath.'

Some tapped their chests with a fist, claiming the name, while others merely spoke the word as if that were claim enough.

Many more remained silent, yet as the names were spoken, no one dared to object, not even Jatharin.

When the last namers fell quiet, he nodded and struck the haft of his standard three times on the ground.

'Alba belongs to the RockChildren whom humankind calls "Eika." We have work yet to do here in Alba to consolidate what is now ours, but we will not stop here. I turn my gaze east and I see Salia at war with itself, brother fighting brother. Where brothers fight, the land is weakened. So we know from our own struggles. That is why we were weak for so long.'

The fen waters gleamed under the sun's hard light, a cold spring day so clear that he could distinguish each separate reed stalk out where beds of reeds grew thickly around hummocks of land. A body floated in the water, the cloth of the tunic billowing as ripples captured it. North lay the wash and the sea, with no one to hinder their journey. Geese flew high overhead. One of the clerics whispered to Brother Severus, but the old man shook his head impatiently, cautioning the nervous one to hold still. Their allies were anxious, as they should be.

His army waited, restless as the geese, ready to be on the move again, to fight the next battle, but the discipline he had honed in them held fast. Even the dogs sat obediently, licking their bloody muzzles and paws.

They were ready.

'We are weak no longer,' he cried. 'From this island we will launch a new ship, and we will call it *Empire.*'

PART THREE

CAUDA DRACONIS

XXIII
INTO THE PIT

1

The ship lay at anchor beneath a cliff so high and sheer that it looked as if a giant had used a knife to slice through the island before carrying half of it away. To their right, the land dropped precipitously in ragged terraces and rock-strewn falls to the sea where it gave out in a curving line of islets and rocky outcrops thrust up to make of their harbor a sheltered bay. The water beneath them was, according to the ship-master, too deep to sound. Gentle swells rocked the deck. Zacharias found the motion soothing after so many weeks beating before a stiff wind out of the north.

The intensity of the light dazzled him. He shaded his eyes, peering up to a tangle of white houses perched along the top of the high cliff. What a view! It made him dizzy to think of living so high, staring each day out over the brilliant sea.

Marcus stood beside him, hands gripping the rail as he watched a boat work its way between a pair of scrub-crowned islets before heading, true as an arrow flies, toward them. Four men worked the oars of the craft; she carried six passengers, one scarcely larger than a child. When the boat drew along-side, a sailor threw down a rope ladder.

Wolfhere clambered aboard first, together with the Arethousan-speaking sailor who had gone with him to interpret. The old Eagle blew on his hands and examined them with a frown; the rowing had raised a pair of blisters. Next came a pair of servants, hardy looking souls, a man and a woman dressed simply but in the finest cloth. Below, the childlike figure was lifted into a sling tied around a third servant's torso, a man with the muscular build of a soldier. In this way, hoisted like a pack, she was brought aboard. Marcus hastened to the rope ladder. He had an odd expression on his face, one Zacharias did not recognize until the cleric clasped the hands of the ancient woman seated in the sling.

'You are looking well, Sister!'

He cared about her.

'Well enough for a woman who survived a shipwreck.' Though she was strikingly foreign in appearance, with black hair and dark skin, her accent sat lightly on her tongue. 'Two months on this island has been efficacious for my lungs.'

'I feared for you in Darre.'

'The air in that city would fell the healthiest of bulls. Its stink nearly did me in, but the sea air has revived me.'

Once she had been a beauty, black and lovely. Now her hair gleamed white, and her age-spotted hands trembled, but her gaze remained inquiring and keen. She caught Zacharias' eye and nodded. 'Who is this?'

'A discipla,' said Marcus.

'Ah.' Her bland expression made Zacharias twitch nervously. 'I will speak to him later.'

The servants unfolded a canvas chair, and as they transferred the old woman into this more comfortable seat, the last two passengers clambered onto the deck: a second female servant and a handsome girl no more than fourteen or sixteen years of age, strongly built and with a complexion darker than that of the Wendish servant's, but not as dark as the old woman's.

'Grandmother, I will see that the cabin is made ready for you.' The old woman and Marcus had been speaking in

Aostan, which Zacharias could understand better than he could speak, but the girl spoke Wendish.

'Elene, I wish you to acknowledge my comrade, Brother Marcus, of the presbyter's college. We will travel with him until we reach Qahirah.'

'My lady,' said Marcus with the politesse of a man raised at his ease among the nobility.

'Presbyter Marcus.' She inclined her head as between equals.

Whose child was this, so grand, powerful, and proud? So Wendish, yet with a heathen's looks?

He dared not ask.

'Will Brother Lupus stay with us, Grandmother?'

'For a time, but his task will lead him down a different road than the one you and I must travel. Now go below and see that all is made comfortable.'

As the sailors lifted several trunks on board, Elene allowed the ship-master to escort her to the tiny cabin in the stern that she would share with her grandmother.

'I did not think you could force a man like that to give up one of his daughters,' said Marcus. At the railing, sailors gathered to haggle with the local boatmen, trading from their personal stores.

'He is my son. He must do as I tell him.'

'And sacrifice one? Is this the one he loved least?'

'No. She is the one he loved most.' A flash of anger straightened Meriam's frail shoulders. 'You make light of a father's love, Marcus, since you knew nothing of it yourself. My father wept sorely when I was taken to the temple of Astareos to become an acolyte there. That was before I was sent north by the khsha;amyathiya as a part of the gift to the barbarian king. My son loves both his daughters as a man should. "A father's blood is made weak by sons but strengthened by daughters." They are both precious to him, since he will have no more by his beloved Eadgifu, may she rest at peace in God's light. But he knows his duty to his mother. He gave me what I asked for.'

'His duty to his mother, or to the church? What about his

duty to humankind in their war against the forces that threaten us?'

'When a man gives you the horse which will let you complete your journey, do not ask why he does so, in case the answer displeases you. Just be happy you got where you are going.'

'Is that what your Jinna kinfolk say? The intention of your heart matters more than the action of your hands.'

'Does the woman who gives grudgingly of a hundred loaves to the poor deserve less thanks than the man who gives only ten, but with a sincere heart? We may wish she gave out of a loving heart, but the bread feeds the hungry nonetheless.'

'Argued like a Hessi sage. Will you rest, Sister?'

'In truth, I would be glad to.'

The spectacle of Marcus showing affection and consideration astonished Zacharias. He watched amazed as the presbyter assisted the old woman to her cabin.

All the while, Wolfhere remained at the railing, silent, staring north over the sea.

Because the weather remained fine, Zacharias took his lessons on deck.

'How many hours are there in a week?'

'One hundred and sixty-eight.'

'How many points?'

'Six hundred and seventy-two.'

'How many minutes?'

'One thousand six hundred and eighty.'

'How many parts?'

These drills often took up half a lesson, Marcus testing him on what he had memorized previously before teaching him something new. If at intervals Zacharias chafed at the repetition, he reminded himself that, as a man ascends a mountain, they were making progress toward the summit.

'What is the period of ascent?'

'On leap years, from winter solstice to summer solstice the period of ascent is equal to the one hundred eighty-three days of descent from summer to winter. But otherwise the period of descent is shorter than the period of ascent because the Sun moves through the four equal parts of the universe in unequal times. From the winter solstice to the vernal equinox, ninety and one eighth days. From the vernal equinox to the summer solstice, ninety-four and one half days. From the summer solstice to the autumn equinox, ninety-two and one half days. From the autumn equinox to the winter solstice, eighty-eight and one eighth days.'

'An apt pupil.' Meriam reclined in a canvas sling rigged up near the stern so that she might take the air on deck. An awning shaded them, although its shelter offered barely enough room for four to sit together.

'He memorizes well,' said Marcus. 'Understanding has not yet taken hold. What are the zones of Earth?'

'There are five. Two arctic zones, one at each pole. Two temperate zones, where humankind lives. And a single torrid zone along the equator, within which no creature can live.'

'Yet some live there nevertheless,' remarked Meriam pleasantly. 'Tribes of humankind roam there, living in tents. Once it was said that sphinxes, the lion queens of old, made their home in the great desert.'

'They may have once,' retorted Marcus, 'but they are legend now.'

'Many things are called legend which may still exist unbeknownst to human sight.'

Marcus laughed. 'I am not as superstitious as you, Sister. I can only be sure a thing exists if I have seen it with my own eyes.'

'Have you seen God, Marcus?'

'God I must take on faith, but I would rather see Them with my own eyes, to be certain.'

Meriam smiled in her sharp way. 'So may we all hope to do when we die, but not while living. Do not let the others hear you speak so heretically. Men have been burned for less.'

'You can be sure that I do not intend to be one of them.'

Summer had come and gone; the autumn equinox had passed, and now the course of days uncoiled inexorably toward the winter solstice. They had escaped Sordaia somewhat after

midsummer and sailed south along the shore of the Heretic's
Sea to the harbor of fabled Arethousa. Zacharias had not been
allowed to disembark, but he had stood for two days at the
railing and stared in wonder at the great city on its hills while
the ship-master had supervised the unloading of timber, furs,
and wheat from Sordaia's market and taken up wine, cloth,
and iron knives.

In Arethousa, Wolfhere and Marcus had by unknown
means received a desperate message that sent them southeast
rather than west along the Dalmiakan coast toward Aosta. A
strong wind called the *halhim* had delayed them along the
Aetilian coast of the Middle Sea, forcing them to shelter for
days at a time among its many pleasant islands until they had
fetched up at an island the sailors called Tiriana, to rescue
Meriam and her granddaughter.

That Meriam was a mathematicus needed never to be said
aloud. Marcus informed the ship-master that they would
detour to the port of Qahirah before returning to Aosta.
Offered a bonus, the man did not demur. Perhaps, in truth,
he was wise enough to see he had no choice in the matter. In
the end, he served the skopos, who was rich and powerful
enough to command him despite the physical distance
between his ship and her throne. What mattered the intention in his heart as long as he did what he was told?

'Now,' said Marcus, 'we will continue with the spheres.
Earth lies at the center of the universe. . . .'

Bit by bit, the architecture of the cosmos took shape before
Zacharias, yet at times he wondered if it really matched that
awesome vision he had seen years ago in the palace of coils.
Remembering it, he still trembled, but he did not speak of
the vision to Marcus, who cared nothing for the experience
of others. Marcus knew what he knew, and that was enough
for him.

Elene never joined them. She took her lessons, if she had
any, privately with her grandmother. Otherwise, she stayed
in her cabin or stood on deck, staring north and east toward
the lands she had left behind. Often she had tears on her
cheeks, but she never cried out loud.

'Is she always this sullen?' Zacharias asked Wolfhere one afternoon as he watched the sailors changing tack as the wind shifted.

'Have you heard her speak a cross word to any soul on this ship?' Wolfhere spent as much time as Elene staring out to sea, but not in any fixed direction. Zacharias was as likely to find him staring south as north, east as west.

'I've not heard her speak more than ten words altogether.'

'Well,' said Wolfhere, as if that settled the matter.

But it did not, for Zacharias wondered how any soul could not rejoice in the company of such learned mathematici. Yet when he asked Marcus the same question as he settled down for his next lesson, he got a very different answer.

'Ten words? Why should the daughter of a duke and the granddaughter of a queen speak even one word to you, Zacharias? You are of no account to an illustrious noblewoman born into such a distinguished lineage.'

'Of course you are right, Brother Marcus. But as she is heir to a duke, *and* granddaughter to a queen on her mother's side, I am amazed that she could be torn from such a high seat and thrown like a common wanderer onto such a path as this one.'

'There is no path of greater consequence than the one we follow. Leave off these questions and attend.' Marcus stepped out from under the awning, shading his eyes as he gazed toward the cliffs, then shook his head impatiently and sat down again in the shade.

Elene appeared at the stern and placed her hands on the railing as she stared toward the distant land. After a moment Wolfhere joined her, and bent his head to listen. Jealous, Zacharias wondered what they spoke about.

'Pay attention, Zacharias!'

He started and shifted his gaze to the cleric.

Marcus had the most caustic smile imaginable, a curious way of turning up his lips and narrowing his eyes that made Zacharias squirm. 'Are you done?' He did not wait for an answer. 'To repeat. The ecliptic and the motion of the moon. Because the moon's path wobbles at an incline to the ecliptic, the moon crosses south to north and north to south at regular intervals. The points on the ecliptic where it crosses are called the ascending node and the descending node, or caput draconis and cauda draconis – that is, the head and the tail of the dragon.'

'Sail!' cried Wolfhere.

The lookout echoed the cry.

Sailors rushed to the railing. Elene leaned out until she seemed likely to pitch overboard, and her face was alight, as though she thought her father was coming for her at last. 'Pirates!' she cried eagerly.

A galley powered by oars cut through the water. There wasn't enough wind to save them, and although they could row, too, their sturdy cog could not hope to outrun a swift warship.

'It's a Jinna ship!' shouted Wolfhere. 'See the banner! They'll take as slaves those they don't kill.'

Zacharias rose but could barely keep his feet because his legs shook so much. He broke out in a sweat. The captain rushed up to Marcus and commenced gesticulating and shouting. Marcus merely looked annoyed as at an exasperating child who will not cease interrupting although he's been told to sit still and keep quiet.

'Enough!' he said, and the captain hushed. 'Bring Sister Meriam,' he added, and a servant went to her cabin to rouse her from her afternoon nap. 'Sit, Zacharias! You're in my way.'

Zacharias' rump hit the deck hard; he trembled all over. Sailors grabbed spears and poles and readied their knives. Wolfhere did not move, not even to touch the hilt of his sword. He stared so fixedly at the approaching ship that Zacharias wondered if he had been ensorcelled. Marcus tapped his feet on the decking, a pit-pit-pat, pit-pit-pat rhythm that made the frater want to scream.

The male servant emerged from the tiny cabin, carrying Meriam in her sling. When the man stopped beside Marcus, she assessed the situation as distant oars rose and fell and a drumbeat rang over the smooth waters.

'I see,' she said. 'Yes, that's a Jinna crew.'

'Let me raise a wind to our sails, then, and if you can cast aught to lessen their fervor, it will be the better for us.'

'Yes,' she agreed with such alacrity that Zacharias stared to see them work as with one mind, in no wise different than laborers who bend to the harvest in harmony to the songs they sang to make the work pass easily during long harvest days.

Oars flashed as the galley sped toward them. The wind flagged. The sail slackened, although the sailors desperately tacked again and caught the last dying gasp of the breeze.

'It's too late,' Zacharias whimpered. 'They'll catch us. We'll be slaves.'

Again.

'They've a conjurer on board,' commented Meriam. 'Elene! Fetch my pouch.'

Elene disappeared into the cabin.

'See if you can learn something,' snapped Marcus as Zacharias struggled to repress his tears. The frater hated himself for his servile cowardice, but the sight of those implacable oar beats filled him with such fear that he could not speak. The drum of the oar master shuddered through his body, each rap sounding his doom.

Marcus beckoned to the captain. 'Seek any tangled rope on board, especially that which was coiled neatly beforetime.'

The captain had not taken two steps away before an observant sailor shouted from the prow, and Marcus hurried forward to find the anchor rope so snarled and knotted that no man, surely, could have done the damage, and no sailor would treat rope so carelessly. Zacharias staggered after him, hard pressed to keep on his feet although the deck wasn't rolling any more than it had been before Wolfhere sighted the pirate ship.

The last breath of wind died, and the sail sagged and went slack. Becalmed, the ship creaked as waves lapped the hull. It was such a soothing sound but for the hammer of the drum that powered the Jinna galley, swooping in for the kill.

Marcus knelt beside the rope and placed his hands over the coils. Zacharias collapsed beside him as, in a low voice,

Marcus spoke words the frater neither understood nor recognized. Was his vision blurring, or did it seem that the rope began to slither in the manner of snakes?

A song rose from the stern, and he glanced back, surprised to hear a strong alto of such beauty where death came rushing to meet them. Sister Meriam stood at the railing cupping something in her hands that she blew softly against while her granddaughter, beside her, sang with such piercing clarity that it hurt to hear her.

'It won't be enough,' he whispered, not meaning to be heard.

'Do not underestimate our power,' said Marcus. 'You are not a man of faith, Zacharias. You doubt too much.'

The still waters, all that separated them from the oncoming galley, roiled and churned. The drum faltered once, but the steady beat resumed faster than before as the oars dipped and lifted in unison. The waters boiled up in clouds of steam. An angel rose from the sea as glorious as the dawn and towering as tall as their mast. Her hair streamed like sunlight around her uncovered head; her expression was grim and implacable. With each slow beat, her wings of flame shed sparks which spat and snapped as they plummeted into the salt water. She held a bow composed of shimmering blue fire, an arrow nocked and ready to fly.

The drum stuttered and stopped. From across the water, in counterpoint to Elene's song, shrieks and shouts of fear cut through the air as oars skipped across the waves. The galley slowed.

A snake slid roughly across Zacharias' hand. He shrieked in his turn, fell backward from knees to rump, but it was only rope uncoiling like a basket of snakes unleashed. A touch of wind brushed his cheek, a coy kiss, and the murmur of its passing whispered in his ear.

Wind filled the sail.

They left the Jinna pirates behind as the wings of the vast angel disintegrated into a shower of hot sparks that fell onto the deck of the coasting galley. Zacharias pulled himself up and crossed to the rail, watching as the Jinna oarsmen shifted their stroke and struggled to row backward out of that burning rain. A white scrap, like a butterfly, fluttered out of Meriam's hands and zigzagged across the water, growing so small that he should not have been able to see it as the gap between them opened – yet a hard shine kept it visible as it wove its erratic course.

The galley fell farther behind. The steamy mist risen with the angel spread to conceal it, but Zacharias saw a last wink as Meriam's butterfly vanished into a fog. Elene laughed out loud to end her song, and for an instant Zacharias thought she meant to leap into the sea to swim after that bright vision, now lost.

Marcus still knelt by the rope, a look of intense concentration on his face as wind boomed in the canvas. Wolfhere paced restlessly forward as the sailors adjusted ropes and sail, and laughed and joked, relieved at their escape but not relaxed. The sea lay calm behind them while an unnatural wind sped them forward.

'Well done, Brother Marcus,' said Meriam. 'The arts of the tempestari are difficult to master.'

'We must control the weather if we hope to succeed in the weaving.'

'Wolfhere, I pray you,' whispered Zacharias.

The old Eagle came to stand beside him. Spray off the water misted their faces and caught in his gray beard. 'It looked like Liath,' the old man muttered, his tone and expression distraught as his fingers opened and closed on the wood railing.

'Was it a real angel, or an illusion?' Zacharias asked, but Wolfhere would not answer.

The wind brought them across the wide waters of the Middle Sea and for five days they sailed along the southern coast with desert to larboard and the pale green waters to their right. Marcus slept most of that time, made weary by his labors, and Sister Meriam also kept to her bed, tended by her servants and her granddaughter. The only time Zacharias saw either of them awake they consulted with each other under the shade offered by the awning rigged up in the stern. What caused them such anxiety Zacharias could not know, but he watched from a distance as Marcus scrawled marks and signs on well-worn parchment, often scraping his notations off with a knife and marking again until the skin became translucent. If Zacharias tried to approach, Meriam's burly manservant chased him away.

'I have no time for lessons.' That was Marcus' only comment, delivered with a curtness that stung.

Nor would Wolfhere keep him company. His life was as barren as the land they sailed alongside. The desert shore rose and fell in curves, sand and pale hills with no sign of life, not even grass or scrub. Not even a man. During the day the sun's light made the sand and rock glint so brightly it was painful to look. Only the sea breeze made the heat tolerable. There was nothing to do but wait. Zacharias had grown accustomed to biding his time.

The wind at their back held until they came to the port of Qahirah. They sailed past a promontory where ruined columns rose along the backs of low hills and came into a bay ringed with flowering trees and gardens. The city of domed temples and whitewashed buildings shone under the autumn sun.

'It's a paradise,' he said.

Marcus, standing beside him, frowned. 'A lure, that's all. A temptation of the Enemy. It stinks with infidels.'

'You don't think it's beautiful? After the desert?'

'The desert is pure. It pretends to be nothing but what it is: a desolation. This fine garb conceals the rot beneath all.'

Yet the rot smelled so sweet, a potpourri of lavender, hyssop, jessamine, mint, and rosemary. Any Wendish city of such remarkable size would have stunk like an open sewer, but as the sailors slipped their oars and threw ropes to the waiting dockside laborers, who hauled them in against the pilings, Zacharias saw nothing but clean-swept streets beneath walls covered with the white flowers of the jessamine vine or gleaming as if they had been scrubbed and rinsed that morning.

Qahirah was a lovely city, well kept and hospitable.

A trio of customs officers boarded, and several hours went

by as each barrel, bag, and box must be opened for their inspection. Zacharias followed them as a scribe made a comprehensive list in the curling script used by the Jinna. At length they tallied up the impost, the tax levied by the ruler of Qahirah on all goods brought into the port. Coin and a few of those good iron knives traded hands, and the passengers were allowed to disembark under the escort of a youth who promised to guide them to the only hospice in town where foreigners were allowed.

It took the length of the walk from the ship to the hospice, placed at the outskirts of the city, for the ground to stop rolling under his feet. It also took that long for him to stop gawking. Because he had grown up in the countryside and spent years as a slave among the Quman, he had seen few cities and certainly no settlement that resembled Qahirah. Smaller than the city of Arethousa but grander in scale than Sordaia, Qahirah had an unearthly feel. No refuse stained the streets; old men patrolled with brooms and shovels. Women with scarves draped over their heads and falling down over their shoulders and men in modest robes that concealed the shape of their bodies went about their business in a tidy, efficient manner. The market they passed seemed crowded and lively, but there weren't any stray dogs scouting for garbage and, indeed, there was no garbage, not even peelings beneath the fruit stalls.

These unexpected sights hit like the slap of cold water, steadying his legs, and he could walk with a sure step by the time the guide indicated a closed double-doorway – trimmed with bronze – set into a wall that bordered the outer city wall. Both were constructed of whitewashed bricks. The Jinna youth waited for Marcus to gift him with a coin before making an elaborate bow and hurrying off.

Wolfhere rapped on the door. After a wait, it creaked open, they were examined by an old man of indeterminate years, and at length allowed to enter.

'But it's lovely,' said Zacharias as they came into a courtyard washed white with a profusion of flowering jessamine and tangles of pale purple-white dog roses. A fountain – all playful spouts and finger's-length waterfalls – rested in the center of the courtyard, ringed by benches. A few robed travelers sat on those benches, all staring as the party entered the hospice grounds.

The guest rooms surrounded this courtyard on three sides; along the fourth side stood an open-walled kitchen beside a built-up floor with carpets, pillows, and low tables. By the noise of squawking chickens and irritated geese, the complaints of goats and the whicker of a horse, Zacharias guessed that the stable lay next door, past an elegant archway. Even a prince would deign to bide in such a luxurious abode.

Marcus examined the courtyard with disdain as he waited for Meriam's servants to carry their baggage in from the street. 'I don't like the smell.'

It smelled of jessamine blossoms – and a fainter scent that Zacharias did not recognize.

'Is this a hospice for the wealthy?' asked Zacharias of Wolfhere.

The Eagle shook his head. 'This is a simple traveler's rest like many others I slept in when I traveled in these lands years ago.'

'You traveled through Jinna lands? Why was that?'

Wolfhere glanced at him, then away. 'I was looking for something.'

'Did you find it?'

'In the end I did.' His success, remembered now, held no apparent triumph. He strayed to the fountain and let water trickle over his fingers before wiping sweat from his forehead and the back of his neck. Zacharias followed him, made nervous by the stares of the other travelers, whose faces were concealed behind hoods and veils that left them free to scrutinize others without being examined in turn. He felt exposed. They might guess everything about him, staring so, and yet he could never recognize them even were they to meet him unveiled in a public market.

Better, really, not to allow men to conceal themselves so.

He splashed water on his face, glad of the cool touch on his hot face.

Wolfhere sniffed, casting back his head. 'It's said that you can smell thyme in any place where a murder has been committed. Can you smell it?'

'I don't know what it smells like. That strong scent – that's the jessamine, isn't it?'

'And the other – can you smell it? That is thyme.'

Zacharias glanced around. Meriam haggled with the hospice master while Marcus looked on contemptuously and her servants waited patiently with the baggage. Elene had pulled a scarf on over her dark hair, clutching the ends of the scarf in each hand just under her sharp chin. She stood in shadow with a fierce frown on her handsome face and anger in the stiffness of her shoulders.

The frater dropped his voice to a whisper. 'Do you think a murder was committed here?'

'I know one was. Long ago. I saw the body.'

'You've been in this place before?'

'I have.'

The hospice master was a middle-aged man with a lean face and skin twice as dark as Meriam's. He glanced their way, did a double take, and bowed hastily to Meriam before hurrying over to confront Wolfhere. He genuflected before grasping the Eagle's hand and patting it with evident joy.

'Friend! Friend!' he said in accented Wendish. 'Friend!'

Perhaps it was the only word in that language he knew. He returned to Meriam.

'What is he saying?' Zacharias asked as he watched the innkeeper gesticulate enthusiastically.

'I don't know. I know only a few words in the local speech.' But his narrowed eyes and intent expression, as he scrutinized the exchange between the innkeeper and Sister Meriam, suggested otherwise.

'Allowed to stay one night for nothing, no payment at all, and he will lend us a guide to escort us to Kartiako. All as recompense for a service you did him ten years ago. What might that have been?'

'Nothing that matters to you, Marcus, or to our purpose in coming here.'

The servingmen had settled their baggage in the spacious room to which the men of the party were escorted – the women resided in a separate wing – and now, as the sun set and lamps were lit, Marcus, Wolfhere, and Zacharias seated themselves on pillows while youths from the hospice brought around a basin of water in which they washed their hands before eating.

'Are there no chairs or benches?' Zacharias whispered. 'Do we not eat at a table like civilized people?'

'This is the custom of the country,' said Wolfhere.

'Where are Sister Meriam and Lady Elene?'

'They will dine separately.'

'Is it also the custom of the country to separate men and women as though men, like beasts, must be kept apart?' Marcus' lips curled in a sneer.

'No doubt the Jinna find Wendish customs as strange as we find theirs.'

Marcus snorted, but since trays laden with food arrived, he let the conversation lapse. He proved to be a fussy eater, scorning most of the dishes because of their spicy flavor, but Zacharias had suffered hunger too many times to let food go to waste. That one dish contained chicken he recognized, although the heat of the sauce burned his tongue, but he had a name for none of the other foods arranged before him. Still, he ate as much as he could stuff into his stomach and suffered for it later when he bedded down with the servants on hard pallets on the floor.

He tossed and turned, throat burning, and stifled his burps. His belly churned. In time he had to get up to relieve himself. He felt his way to the curtained door and slipped outside. The moon's light gilded the courtyard in silver, and he padded as silently as he could along the pathway that led under the archway into the stable yard, where the hospice's necessarium stood. Some kindly soul had left an oil lamp burning inside.

After he finished his business, he found he was not particularly tired. He crept back to the shadowed archway and paused there to look up at the stars. The air had a clarity here that caused the stars to look brighter than in the north, and the spherical curve of the rising quarter moon showed in stark contrast to the night sky.

Someone – nay, two people – stood by the fountain, speaking in low voices. He slipped from shadow to shadow until he crept close enough to hear.

'How can this be? You no longer trust him?'

'Sister Anne no longer trusts him. I found him in the company of Prince Sanglant. I tell you, he did not seem overeager to leave the prince and his retinue, yet he claims to have no knowledge of the prince's plans. He *says* he was kept an outsider to the prince's council.'

'It might be so. Prince Sanglant would have no reason to trust him. King Henry certainly did not.'

'Yet he did not aid me as he might have in securing the prince's daughter as a hostage. I wonder, too, about these old journeys he took many years ago, and his service to the Wendish king Arnulf. There is too much of Brother Lupus that remains hidden. He conceals himself just as these Jinna do. Concealment is the sign of a guilty conscience.'

'Perhaps. He was always the most loyal to Anne. Is he no longer?'

'Difficult to know. I believe he is still loyal to *Anne*. They were raised together, he to be her faithful servingman. How can he cast aside what he was raised for?'

'Then what troubles you?'

'I wonder now if he remains loyal to the Seven Sleepers. Does he still follow our cause? I do not know what is in his mind and heart any longer. We cannot trust him. That is why I cannot let him travel with you and Elene into the south. What if he betrays you?'

'I don't think he will. We need another experienced traveler, a strong hand, a keen eye. The desert is a hard place. We might come to grief in a hundred ways. I am an old woman, Marcus. My granddaughter is strong, but she is young and inexperienced. My servants are loyal and have great stamina, and we can hire a goodly retinue here in Qahirah. Still, I wish Brother Lupus to accompany us as well.'

'No. My plan is best. You will travel by means of the

crown, if we can use it, and thus you will not have to endure a long journey across this desolate land. If a gateway opens to the southeast, then you will pass through. If not, it means the southeastern crown is lost. Let us pray that is not so.'

'Let me take Brother Lupus. We need him. My grand-daughter likes him. It will make my task easier.'

'No.'

'You give me no good reason, only your own doubts.'

'Very well, then. Sister Anne commanded me explicitly to send him back to her. If it is her will, and after she has inter-rogated him, then she will send him after you. If not – so be it.'

'She no longer trusts him?'

'Her will is my will. I do not contest her in this, or in any-thing. Nor should you.'

'Well.' Sister Meriam's pause was as eloquent as her words. 'We must rely on such servants as we can hire here in Qahirah. I hope they are trustworthy. I hope the desert is not rife with bandits and monsters and storms.'

Marcus chuckled. 'You are not helpless, Meriam. Neither is Elene. You have taught her well.'

Meriam's tone was as dry as Zacharias had ever heard it. 'So we must hope.'

Beyond the fountain, along the opposite wall, Zacharias saw a slight movement, as much as a hunting beast might make when it eases behind bushes while stalking a bird. Marcus and Meriam, themselves scarcely more than shadows, took their leave and slipped away to their own rooms, but Zacharias remained, knowing it wise to linger until he was sure it was safe to move. Among the Quman, he had learned to remain still and silent for hours at a time, hoping to escape Bulkezu's wrath.

Yet in all that time he waited there, he saw no sign of that slip of a shadow. Who else had been listening? A breeze stirred the vines and he caught a hint of their perfume underlaid with that other, dustier scent. It was ungodly silent. He did not even hear dogs barking.

At length his legs grew tired because he was no longer accustomed to standing so still. Keeping to the shadows, he

slunk back to the room. The curtain brushed his face as
he slipped past, but his bare feet made no sound and no voice
rose to challenge him as he lay down to sleep.

In the morning Wolfhere was missing, his pallet empty
and his pack removed from the pile of baggage.

'Gone!' Marcus slammed a fist against the wall, then cursed
at the pain. But his temper calmed as quickly as it had flared.

'So be it,' he said to Meriam as they made ready to leave
for the ruins of Kartiako. 'He has revealed himself through
his actions.'

She said nothing.

Elene wept.

2

He smelled the choking scent of smoldering fires long
before his feet told him that they had left the loamy forest
path for a grimier track through ash and dust. Charred and
splintered debris crackled underfoot. Its acrid chaff coated his
lips. In the distance he heard the sound of men cutting wood,
echoes upon echoes of the throbbing in his head.

The throbbing swallowed everything. He couldn't remember how long he had been walking or where he had come from
or what he had been doing before being coffled together with
the other prisoners.

He wasn't cold – that was good – but his left foot still hurt.
A few days ago the pack mule had trodden on it, and it pained
him as he stumbled along grasping the rope that bound him
to the prisoner in front of him. Besides the merchant and his
two hired guards, there were six prisoners roped together and
bound for the quarries – or at least, he had learned to recognize nine voices over the days of their journey, and more than
once had felt the prod of the guards' staves. He would have

fallen a hundred times if not for the mercy of the two men roped before and behind him, a Salian criminal named Willehm and a captured brigand who called himself 'Walker.'

'Careful, Silent,' sang out Will, addressing him by the name the rest called him. A good enough name, since he had no memory of a name, only a hazy recollection of hot tears and shouted fury. 'There's a drop right ahead of you. Take a big step and brace yourself.'

From behind the rope pulled taut as Walker leaned back to brace him.

He swung his foot out and felt it fall, and fall, trusting to Will's directions. The foot struck loose earth, crushed leaves, and the slick remains of charcoal, and he slipped sideways, flailing. The rope snapped tight on either side of him, and he righted himself and dug his toes into the dirt for purchase. There was a reek about this place that tickled his nostrils and made his head spin and his blind eyes ache. His lungs burned each time he took in a breath.

'Get on!' The master's whip cracked so close that air snapped against his cheek, but he'd taken too many hurts and bruises to flinch.

Walker muttered a curse under his breath as Will tugged on the rope to guide him onward.

'We're walking through leavings scattered from two old charcoal pits,' said Will, who often described the scenery for him. 'They've burned down to the ground and been cleared off. There's a pit – no, two – burning off to the west. I see smoke through the trees.'

'It's a powerful bad stink,' said Walker. 'The air is nigh black with the smoke. Some kind of demons live here, I've heard tell. They burn iron out of the earth and smelt it with the blood of humankind.'

'Nay, that's not so. It's men I see, cutting wood. What are we for, then, if not to labor in the ironworks?'

'They'll kill us and pour our blood into molten spears and swords.'

'Work us to death, more like,' objected Will. 'Hauling ore. Digging pits.'

'Cutting wood, like them? That's work that makes a man strong enough to break his bonds and escape.'

'You think they'll give us axes, to cut our ropes?' Will laughed curtly. 'No, we're for the quarries and the shafts. I do so hate the dark.'

'I hear there's goblins who live in the ground around here. They eat the flesh of humankind when they can get it. When a prisoner's too weak to work, the masters lower him down into the deepest shafts and leave him for the goblins, and they pile silver and lead in buckets in exchange. They do love human flesh! They'll eat a man, bones and all! While he's still alive!'

'Where do you hear these tales?' demanded Will. 'I don't believe you.'

'You're a fool not to believe me. Haven't you seen those demons shadowing us? They look like great black dogs, a pair of them, but they have red eyes and fangs, and they feast on dead flesh! I saw the guards shoot arrows at them one evening. Haven't you heard them barking at night?'

'Many a starving dog roams the woods. Those who don't know the woodlands may see any kind of creature in its shadows, but that doesn't mean they're really there.'

'Believe what you will. I've lived five winters in the forests. I've seen dark shades prowling. I've seen elfshot shivering in the wind. I've fought off wolves. I've kissed forest nymphs, but their breath stank of rotting waterweed. If you'd seen what I'd seen, you'd not doubt.'

'The wolves I believe,' said Will. 'My aunt's cousin's son got et by wolves. Torn to pieces, and him walking home from mass, he was, at Dearc.'

'Wintertide,' agreed Walker. 'That's when wolves're hungriest. They'll eat anything. They like fat babies best, though.'

'Hush, you chattering crows!' snarled the man roped in back of Walker. He had a hard, nasty voice, one that stung when its sound hit you, and a particularly bad smell to him, all rotting sweet.

'Hush,' murmured Will, for the others were scared of that voice; their own voices betrayed them when they whispered

among themselves at night or responded to the man's retorts
or gibes.

To understand the world around him, he had to listen.
He had heard their whispered confessions; they often spoke
around him as if he weren't there. Will had stolen bread from
a biscop's table for his crippled parents; Walker had been
caught with a band of starving brigands stealing a lady's milk
cow; the rest were no better, and no worse — many were
hungry and the last two harvests had failed. But the one they
called Robert never confessed his crime to the other prisoners, and it seemed likely to them that he was a foul murderer.

Nearby, axes cut into wood, a man shouted a warning, and
a tree splintered, groaned, and fell with a resounding crash
that shuddered along the ground, vibrating up through the
soles of his feet. The breeze turned, taking the worst of the
scorched smell with it. No birds sang.

Fear crept along his shoulders. In some other place the
birds had fled, too. All gone. A horrible pain filled his belly
as he wept, remembering only that his hands had been slick
with blood. Where had he been? What was he doing?

Who am I?

Flashes of memory sparked.

*Ships slide noiselessly onto the strand, a shining sand beach
touched by the light of the morning sun rising over low hills.
Because they come from the west, the ships lie somewhat in
shadow — or perhaps that is only a miasma of death and
destruction that hovers over them. What pours forth from
them cannot be called human, yet neither are these creatures
beasts. They are fashioned much like humankind, with their
strange, sharp faces and the shape of their limbs and torsos,
but under the sun's light their skin gleams as if scaled with
metal — bronze, or copper, or iron — and the body of each one
bears a pattern of white scars or of garish yellow, white, or
red paint formed into bright sigils. Fearsome dogs yammer
beside them, leaping into the fray, biting and tearing. The
defenders of this quiet estate fight fiercely and with great
courage, led by a handsome young lord carrying shield and
sword, but the invaders outnumber them.*

It is only a matter of time.

The lord's hall catches on fire, flame racing along the thatched roof.

'Hey, there! Hey! You can stop now, Silent. We're here.'

'It's strange, isn't it, how sometimes he seems to be hearing us, and other times it's as if he's gone right out of his head. Maybe he's one of them whose soul got eaten by wights, just sucked clean out of him.'

'I pity him, poor man.'

'Well, friend, I pity us, for look and see what manner of a pit we've come to. A great gaping hole in the earth. Look at those pools of filthy water! Gah, it stinks! I don't mean to spend the rest of my life here, I tell you that.'

'Hush, Walker. We'll speak of that later when none can overhear. Here, now, Silent, sit you down. The master is talking with the foreman. God help us, this is a sour and ugly place.'

A hand pressured him downward, and he sat, numb, bewildered. Only when he dreamed could he see, and then he suffered visions of such a fearful host that it was almost a relief when darkness ate those dreams, as it always did.

Wind played across his face. Around him, the other prisoners murmured nervously. The dust of stones clotted the air, and everywhere around rang the sound of picks and shovels and the scrape of wheels along rock.

'There goes the master,' said Walker. 'Bound for home, a soft bed, good ale, and the next lot of sorry men like us. He must be glad to be free of this hellhole.'

'I hate you,' said Robert.

All the prisoners shifted as the words chafed them. He could feel the placement of their bodies, three to his left and five clustered to his right, with as much space as any of them could manage between them and Robert.

'I don't think he's talking to you,' whispered Will.

'The wights sucked out his soul, too,' murmured Walker.

'I hate you. No. No, you'll look! Look at the blood! Is that her bonny face?'

The anger and despair in that voice poisoned the air as

surely as did the dust and the drifting ash and the stink of distant forges.

He reached, groping, and found a hairy arm, well muscled, that belonged to Robert, but a hand slapped his away, and that voice cursed him while weeping, tears and fury together. He withdrew his hand, now wet with the other man's tears.

'Up! Up! You don't get food for sitting on your backsides! Listen here, you men. My name is Foucher, and I'm foreman of these workings. You'll be hauling stone from the quarry. Work hard, and you'll get fed and in two years' time your freedom.'

'Two years.'

Will's breath chased along his skin, carrying the murmured words.

'I'll not wait that long,' whispered Walker.

Willehm and Walker sat so close on either side that he felt protected, enclosed.

'Which is the blind mute? And the madman? Those two? Take them to the wheels.'

His comrades muttered oaths as footfalls approached.

'How can a blind man turn a wheel?' asked Will boldly.

'He'll be helpless if the mad one attacks him,' protested Walker.

'Move off, you two! What's it to you, anyway? Who better than a blind man to walk the treadmill, eh? It's all the same to him!' Foucher snickered. 'And we can't trust the madman with any tools, so he'll walk, too. Else he'll earn his keep by being thrown down into the deep shafts! As will the rest of you, any what cause me trouble!'

They muttered but moved aside. A hand pinched his elbow, dragging him up, while the ropes binding him twisted and pinched his skin as they were untied, then fell loose. The others remained silent as he was led roughly away. Each step jarred up his spine to rattle his head. Pain cut so hard up behind his eyes, beside his swollen ear, that he stumbled and tripped, hitting his knees against shards of sharp rock. Agony swallowed him. All the noises faded in a blur of sound like waves crashing over rocks.

Water surges through a narrow channel cut into the rock, then hisses along the hidden strand, a crescent shoreline composed of little more than rock and pebbles that will soon be covered by the rising storm. Here, among the isles that make up the Cackling Skerries, he and his retinue wait in a place between sea and land where neither he nor his allies hold the advantage. A pale back cuts the foaming waters, followed by a second. Rain spatters over the beach and drums against the rock columns that make up the chief portion of this islet, bones that cannot be worn down even by the endless tidal wash of the sea. Now and again through the misting rain he sees Cracknose Rock, the fist from which he launched his invasion of Alba.

Clouds and rain hide the coast, but he does not need to see what now belongs to him.

'There! Do you see that?'

'What is it, Lord Erling?'

'There!' cries young Erling, who takes a step back and at once realizes that he has thereby betrayed fear in front of the others, each one of whom is ready to notice any weakness displayed by his compatriots.

But the others, even his own kind, recoil as well. He alone does not fear what emerges from the sea.

Four of them drag themselves out of the water until only their tails remain in the surf. Waves sigh up to engulf them, then retreat with a murmur down through the rocks. Those flat red eyes betray no obvious gleam of intelligence, but this very strangeness is deceiving. They grin to display sharp teeth. Their hair twitches and churns, alive in its own way, because each thick strand boasts a snapping mouth that seeks air, or prey, or water, or some trace of his thoughts – who can tell?

The largest heaves itself up all the way onto the shore. Its huge tail makes it clumsy but nevertheless none of the landbound venture close. The claws and teeth of the merfolk can shred a man's flesh to rags in moments; not even the skin of the RockChildren is proof against their claws.

Its slit nose opens and closes as if sniffing. It speaks in a voice almost too low to hear, and the words sound oddly formed, too round and too flat, because its mouth and throat are not meant to voice human sounds. Yet they are able to speak the language of the RockChildren.

'We have come in answer to your summons.'

'So you have, and I thank you.'

'What do you want, Stronghand? We give to you aid. Food, you give to us. What do you want from us now?'

'I have heard a rumor that your people can swim upriver into fresh water. That you are not confined to the sea.'

It made no reply.

'If I had known that, I could have asked your people to be scouts. If I had a more efficient way to summon you, we could work together in this.'

'What more can you give us?' it asks.

'What do you want?'

Their reply comes in a hum so low that at first no words can be distinguished, but the pebbles all along the shoreline vibrate and actually begin to roll, grinding one against the other, slipping and shifting. Rocks tumble down from the high rock columns all around them and crash into the waters. Wind screams through the rocky inlet as the storm shoulders in. Rain falls in sheets, so cold and sharp that it opens a tiny cut on Erling's cheek as he hunkers down, drawing his cloak over his face for shelter.

'Revenge.'

'He's blind and mute, Captain.'

'Is he deaf, too?' Laughter followed. Men might laugh at drowning animals in such a way, not caring for their suffering but amused by their struggles.

He became aware of smells and noises and a cold draft rising up from below, the breath of the pit.

Where was he? How had he come here?

Distantly a hound barked, but the laughing man's voice drowned it out.

'All the better, Foucher. We'll put him on the deepest wheel where it will make no difference if he can see or no. No need for chains. Rope will do for him. How's he to escape if he's blind?'

'Are you sure he can work? He looks soft in the head.'

'He looks strong enough to me.'

'If he's too stupid to know what to do?'

The laughter sounded again, this time mixed with the smell of onions that flavored the man's breath. 'Prod him like a beast. He'll figure it out. Walk and he's let be. Stop and he's whipped.'

'I hate you.'

The comment caused a stir. He heard men whisper all around him. They were too many to keep voices straight, but their fear had a prickling scent that needled his skin.

'God Above, we'll need chains for that one,' said the one called Captain. 'They call him Robert. He's got an ugly look in his eye. We'll put him down with the blind mute. What the one can't see and hear, the other can't make trouble with.'

'You think the blind lad will last a week with that madman, Captain? He'll get shoved off the treadmill. He'll get et alive.'

'They're all dead men anyway, Foucher. What are you worrying for?'

'The duke is displeased we didn't meet our quota last year.'

'Due to the flooding. These wheels should fix that.'

'With all the troubles in the border country and the civil war in Salia, the duke wants more this year. More iron. More weapons.'

'Then get them down there and to work! What else did you bring me?'

'Criminals. The usual ruffians and wandering good-for-nothings. Thieves, mostly. I've sent them to the quarry master.'

'We may need more in the shafts to clear out those two rockfalls.'

'Better them than us. I fear that whispering, I don't mind telling you, Captain.'

'I won't send you down into the deep shafts, Foucher. You've served me well. Your bones won't be gnawed by the goblins!' He laughed again, so hearty a sound that were it not for the comment that had preceded it one might be tempted to join in.

Such cues gave him, the one called Silent, little enough to go on. The haft of a spear or staff prodded him in the buttocks, and he stumbled forward as the men around him roared to see his confusion. He was pushed to the brink of an open hole out of which air poured with a sharp, dry scent that he had smelled before.

What memory teased him?

Creatures scuffling in the dark.

He brushed his fingers over the bronze armband, his only possession, and images flared like lamplight illuminating a black cavern:

He drags Kel and Beor back from the brink of a gaping fissure while a searing wind rushing up from the abyss stings his eyes. His beloved Adica lives, and they have rescued her from the Ashioi, who stand cursing them on the other side of the fissure. In the shadows beyond the shifting light, skrolin chatter in whispering voices as they vanish into the rock. The bronze armband throbs against the skin of his upper arm; when darkness falls, it lights with the uncanny gleam of magic.

'Get on!'

A hand cuffed him on the ear – out of nowhere – right where it was swollen. The pain shattered inside his skull and broke his memory into a thousand shards.

'Go on! Set your foot on the rung. There. There! What a fool!'

'Go easy on the man, Foucher. He can't help he's blind.'

'Maybe so. Maybe not.'

'What's that armband he's wearing? It looks valuable.'

'Master Richard warned me of that. He said it burns any man who touches it.'

'Does it?'

'If you'd seen the look on his greedy face, you'd have believed him, too. I say we can wait and take it off him when he dies.'

'I wonder . . .' mused the Captain, but their voices faded as he descended into a clamor of rumbling and cracking and echoes.

A wooden rung slipped under his questing foot. He found purchase and climbed down, because he had no other place to go. Others led him, passing him from one hand to another down a shaft and down a second until it seemed the rock itself pressed around him, whispering of its age and of this violation of its secret parts. Now again he smelled burning oil and a gasp of smoke. Once he slipped into a ditch full of streaming water.

At length they chained him to stand on a curved wood walkway that was a huge wheel. They prodded him until he realized that they wanted him to walk and, by walking, turn the wheel beneath him. Water gurgled and sloshed, riding up from the depths and spilling away in a rush above him. The steady groan and rumble of other wheels turned above him under the tread of other feet.

He walked, chains rattling, and after a time got the hang of it, more sure of his footing, not fearing that he would stumble and fall and plunge endlessly into the darkness that lay everywhere around him. The wood slats of the wheel slid smoothly beneath his feet, worn down by the countless measured steps of the hapless slaves who had gone before him.

Had they died here, too?

Yet he found it so hard to think because his head hurt. It never stopped hurting.

It was easier just to walk.

After a very long time, they unchained him and led him to a hollow in whose confines he smelled the sweet gangrene scent of mad Robert. Curses echoed through the darkness as the madman was chained into the place he had just left. Here on this hard rock he was allowed to sleep, although Robert's ravings chased him through troubled dreams.

They woke him, fed him gruel, prodded him up, and chained him once more to the wheel where he walked again, forever, silent and in darkness.

3

'There,' said Marcus. 'That is what we seek.'

The ruins of Kartiako boggled Zacharias. Never had he seen such magnificence so spoiled. They walked half the morning away from the garden city of Qahirah into lands that ceased bearing life across a line so stark that on one side irrigated fields grew green and on the other, beyond the last ditch, lay bare ground. On three hills rising on the promontory that overlooked the sea rose the remains of a great city, now vandalized and tumbled into a shambles that nevertheless left those who approached it gaping in wonder at the columns and archways, the broken aqueducts and fallen walls, the intricate layout of a grand city that had once ruled the Middle Sea.

'You're looking the wrong way,' said Marcus to Zacharias as their party turned aside from the dusty path that led across the barren flats toward the hills and the city. Grit kicked up by the mules clouded the air. The locals hired by Sister Meriam pulled the ends of their turbans across their faces to protect themselves from the stinging dust. 'That way. Do you see?'

That way lay a low hill outside the crumbled wall that had once ringed Kartiako and, beyond it, the crumpled ridgelines of rugged country, rock and sand and not a trace of living things. On that hill bones stuck up from the hillside, but as they came closer, he recognized that these were rude columns set in an elongated circle. The flatland disguised the distance; they walked with salty grit in their teeth for the rest of the morning and did not come to the base of the hill until after midday. A narrow trail snaked up to the crest, and Zacharias blinked twice before he realized that the dark creature scuttling down the track was no insect but a man dressed in black desert robes and grasping a staff.

'Not one stone has fallen,' said Meriam.

The innkeeper had hired out his eldest son to guide them to the ruins, and this young man gestured for silence. He knelt, and the other locals knelt, heads bowed, as the old man of the hill halted before them. The robes he wore covered all but his eyes and hands.

He spoke in a surprisingly deep bass voice for one so small of stature. Meriam translated.

'Who are these honored ones? What do they wish, to come to this holy spot? I am guardian here. I can answer their questions.'

'I admit I am curious why the stone circle lies in good repair,' said Marcus. 'All of the others we have found needed at least one stone raised to complete the circle.'

By no means could Zacharias interpret any emotion in the old man's stance or face, because both were hidden. His eyes gave away nothing, narrowing now and again as Meriam put Marcus' questions to him and added, no doubt, a few explanations of her own.

When she finished, they waited in silence as the caretaker considered. Far away, beyond the dusty flats, green fields shimmered like a mirage.

'Come.'

'What did you tell him?' Marcus asked as they climbed the hill with their retinue walking behind them. Meriam rode one of the mules, led by a manservant.

'That we have come to see the crowns. He is an educated man. In this region, most of the people speak the local language and few have been educated in the priests' tongue. That he can speak it as well as he does means he knows more than we might otherwise imagine. He is no ordinary caretaker, sweeping and fussing. Be cautious. Be respectful.'

Marcus snorted.

'If you are not minded to respect him because he is an infidel, Brother, then I pray you be polite for my sake.'

'Very well, Sister. For your sake. I have no trust in the education of infidels.'

'You must bide among them many months more, Marcus.

Beware that your arrogance does not provoke them to turn on you.'

He chuckled. 'I will be discreet, and silent where I see fault.'

As they reached the crest of the hill, the wind off the barrens began blowing in earnest, and Zacharias was pleased to imitate the Jinna hirelings by covering his mouth and nose with cloth to keep out the dust. He had never tasted anything so salty, mixed with grit that ground between his teeth. Up on the hilltop they could see through the haze as far west as Qahirah and northwest to the bones of Kartiako.

The old man strode into the center of the circle, opening his arms and turning slowly to encompass the entire scene. As he spoke, Meriam translated.

'"You wonder why this holy place lies not in ruins. That is because the Jinna magi have kept it in repair. It is a holy spot. An ancient battle was fought here, a great battle against the invaders, the Cursed Ones."'

'Can it be that the story has lived so long among the infidels?' Marcus asked.

'Hush,' said Meriam. 'I wish to hear what he has to say.'

The old man walked to the eastern slope of the hill where it tumbled away sharply into a hollow that then folded up into the barren rock ridges that ran all the way to the eastern horizon. The nearest ridge side was pockmarked with holes.

'Down beneath the hills lie caves. The old ones lived there in the ancient days for a time, but now it is all ruins. Cursed. They worshiped idols and sacrificed children.'

The old man looked each one of them in the eye, as if delving for evil. Zacharias started back when that gaze met his; all his sins seemed to swarm up out of him, naked in the light. But without flinching the old man looked away to examine Marcus, and then Elene, and finally Meriam.

He nodded. 'All of these abominations Astareos enjoins us from committing according to the laws of heaven. Do you respect the laws of heaven?'

'Ai, God, Meriam, does he expect us to swear some heathen oath? We worship God in the proper manner. I will not suffer his maundering further, if you please. If the stone crown needs no repair, then there is no reason we cannot make our final calculations tonight and send you and Elene on your way tomorrow evening. The heavens will not slow their workings to accommodate our human frailties. There is much to do – and less time than we need, less than eighteen months until the day we have so long prepared for.'

'Do not be hasty, Marcus. What he knows may be of value to us when we least expect it.'

But although she spoke to the old man for another hour at least, in the end she admitted to Marcus that she had learned nothing beyond local legends of monsters, sandstorms, and lost caverns filled with eyeless snakes. The servants set up tents to shelter them from the winds, and as dusk came, the air quieted, the haze settled, and the stars shone with such brilliance that they looked close enough to reach up and steal.

Marcus took his stylus and wax tablet and sat cross-legged upon the ground, on a blanket, with a lamp burning at his right hand. He scrawled hasty calculations across the surface of the tablet before wiping it clean, muttering all the while.

Zacharias crouched beside him. 'Can I learn to do this?'

Marcus replied without glancing up. 'Can you write? Have you knowledge of numbers and sums and geometry? No? Then you must wait. I can only teach one step at a time. You must play Brother Lupus' part now.'

'What is Brother Lupus' part?'

'Cauda draconis. The tail of the dragon. Least among us. Be still.'

It was hard to be still. He wanted what Marcus possessed so badly that his desire was like the grit: everywhere, rubbing in the folds of his skin and at the creases of the corners of his mouth, caught in his eyebrows and worked deep into his hair. Each time he shifted his clothing shed grit, and it filtered through his leggings and his boots to grind between his toes. He had a blister, too, although he had thought his feet too tough to develop anything but calluses.

No man was permitted to build a fire atop the sacred hill, and a cold night wind off the desert wicked away the day's

heat. Zacharias shivered under his cloak as he paced under
the moon's light. To the east distant pricks of light marked
the walls of Qahirah, and he saw, surprisingly, the unsteady
waver of a campfire in the ruins of Kartiako, briefly glimpsed,
then lost. Had he only hallucinated those flames, or had they
been extinguished? The barren flat lay so dark and feature-
less that it seemed more ocean than land. Their position out
here, so far from human haunts, seemed precarious although
Meriam had hired fully twenty retainers to accompany her.
If bandits skulked in the lands hereabouts, surely they did not
roam so far into the wasteland.

What was there to kill?

His boot scuffed the ground, and a small object rattled and
rolled away from him, coming to rest where the ground sloped
slightly up again.

Were those finger bones?

He shuddered and turned back toward the lamp in whose
wavering light Marcus sat, with Meriam beside him, making
his marks and wiping them clean while the old woman whispered comments. Elene paced among the stones, lifting a staff
not longer than her arm and measuring it against the stones
and the stars. All of them glanced frequently at the sky.

An unholy cry rose from the east, a moaning that trembled through the clear night air. Meriam's servants leaped to
their feet, but the locals shouted hysterically one to the next
and grabbed staves and axes. One man wept.

That moan chilled Zacharias until he shivered, and yet he
broke out in a sweat, staring into the darkness. There was
nothing to see. A scent drifted over them, borne by the wind:
stinking carrion steeped with the sweetness of honey, so reeking and foul that he gagged.

The caretaker appeared from the shadows that half
drowned the stones and hurried over to the blanket where
Marcus and Meriam worked their equations. He called out to
the others, and the locals rushed in a group to huddle within
the stones, deathly quiet and obviously frightened.

'No light! No light!' The words came in recognizable
Dariyan, and the rigid mask of terror that tightened the

caretaker's eyes could be understood in any language. 'Go! Go!'

Too late Marcus pinched out the wick. Meriam's servants ran to fetch her and carried her within the stone circle as Marcus and Zacharias hurried after. An awful grinding, slithering noise rose from the east.

'Where is Elene?' cried Meriam.

The old man shouted words Zacharias did not know as he lifted his staff above his head. Light sparked from the stone columns. Threads danced between stars and earth to form a shimmering fence woven around the columns, and by that light Zacharias saw, sliding in and out of the light's verge just beyond the stones, a massive shadow writhing and twisting, first a woman and then a monstrous snake.

The men clustered behind him moaned in terror, crying out 'Akreva! Akreva!' and cast themselves on the ground as though prostrating themselves before the Enemy.

'By God's Name, Meriam, what is that creature?' demanded Marcus.

'Where is Elene?'

A figure darted forward from the hillside where it had strayed, but the hideous woman–snake slithered faster than any earth-bound creature could move and cut off Elene's retreat. The girl was stuck beyond the safety of the encircling spell, easy prey for the monster as it closed. She raised her staff, but it was a frail stick with which to fend off death.

The choking sound of grief and horror that came from Meriam's throat catapulted Zacharias into action. He would not stand by as he had when the Quman had attacked the party guarding Blessing outside the walls of Walburg. He would not run away.

Better to die than find himself a coward again.

He grabbed a staff out of the hands of a cowering servant and dashed past the glimmering net of the spell. The threads burned where they touched him; cloth blackened; his skin stung and turned white.

The monster reared up before the stunned girl, its tail lashing. Its scales were coated with a noxious substance that gave off a phosphorescent glow. Its tail bore a barbed stinger, and it whipped its tail forward, and struck. Elene darted sideways. The tail thunked into the ground. Dust spattered. The monster opened its mouth to trumpet its rage, a high, horrible scream echoed off the distant hills and vibrated the stones. The threads of light sparked and wavered. Behind their net of safety, men shrieked in terror.

Zacharias jumped forward and whacked the monster across the coils as hard as he could. It reared back, twisting to confront him. Its body was massive, as thick as a tree trunk and rippling with muscles, and it was shiny pale and so grotesque that he wanted to cry, or vomit. The stench brought tears to his eyes. The long snake body bloomed into a monstrosity, the grotesque semblance of a woman with round breasts and narrow face but so crudely formed that it seemed an ill-trained craftsman had botched the job.

Elene's voice rang out. 'Hear me, Misael, Charuel, Zamroch. Come to my call. I invoke you, Sabaoth, Misiael, Mioael. Prepare for me a sharp sword drawn in your right hands. Prepare for me seven radiant lights. Drive this evil creature from our midst!'

It struck.

He was slow, unlike the girl. The tip pierced his shoulder. He did not remember screaming. Suddenly he lay on the ground and a cold swift burning blew outward from the sting, turning his flesh to stone. He couldn't move.

It stared down at him, its youthful face like that of a girl but lacking all intelligence and emotion. It clacked sharp teeth together and drew its tail back for a second strike.

How strange, staring upward, that time should move so slowly. The creature had hair, of a kind, but in that last instant he realized that it was not hair at all but a coiling mass of hissing snakes writhing around its face.

A falling star flashed in the heavens. A burst of fire exploded before his eyes, and its brightness shrouded his vision. The monster screamed in such agony that the sound of it might as well have turned every soul there to stone. He could not move but shivered convulsively as that tail was dragged across him, drawn by what force he did not know, nor could he see, nothing except those heavy gray coils pressing their weight into his chest, the tail dwindling until the white stinger floated before his eyes, a bead of venom dangling from the barbed tip, ready to fall into his mouth.

It would burn off his tongue. He would never speak again.

The ground shifted under him. Hands gripped him and hauled him away over the rocky ground, then let him drop onto the hard ground as voices exclaimed in fear and excitement.

'It was a demon!'

'Nay, it was an angel, you fool!'

'It was a phoenix! Are you blind?'

'Not so blind that I don't know lightning when I see it! That was no creature at all.'

'Gah, gah, gah,' he said, but no words came.

'Is he safe?'

'He is stung, Sister.'

They conferred, but he could only stare up at the heavens where light burned just as it burned across his skin. He shivered, so cold. So cold.

'The old one says there is no cure for the sting of the monster?'

'So he says, but I am not so willing to give up on a brave man.'

When had it become so foggy? A haze drifted before his eyes. Yet those words blazed: *a brave man*.

Those words gave him heart.

'What do you suggest?'

'I am the only one skilled in healing among us. We will remain here while I do what I can.'

'We have no time for such luxuries, Meriam. In any case, the creature is wounded, but not dead. It may return.'

'Even if we go, you will still be in danger.'

'Perhaps. It is easier to protect one man than an entire retinue. You know I must change my plans because Brother Lupus deserted us. I can bide in Qahirah until Sister Anne sends a brace of soldiers to guard me, if that is necessary.'

'Soldiers cannot defeat such a monster.'

'Enough! You and Elene and your party must leave at dusk tomorrow.'

'Will you abandon him to death after he saved the life of my granddaughter?'

'Nay. He can be our messenger to Anne. He can still serve us, and in serving us may serve himself. . . .'

The wind's moan tore away the rest of Marcus' words.

Sister Meriam had called him a brave man.

It was better to die bravely than to live with shame.

It was better to die, but he lay there not precisely in pain but unable to move or see, with his skin on fire and yet not really hurting. He lay there and felt the sun rise, although the touch of light hurt him. They shaded him with a lean-to of cloth, and he lay in that shade while Meriam coaxed a bit of honeyed water down his throat, but the smell of honey nauseated him. That stench of honey-carrion that pervaded the monster welled up in his memory, in his throat, and he threw it all back up.

Elene sat beside him, staring at him with solemn eyes. 'I didn't look at him,' she said to her grandmother. 'I thought him beneath my notice. How strange that God should act through such a common, ugly, dirty man.'

'Even a cringing dog can bite, Elene. Look more closely at humankind. The outer seeming may not mirror the inner heart.'

'I know! I know!' said the girl impatiently, as though she had heard this lecture a hundred times before. 'That isn't what I meant! He just didn't seem to matter.'

'Neither did the mouse spared by the prisoner, who later gnawed through her ropes and thereby freed her.'

The shade drew a line across the girl's tunic as she smoothed it down over her knees; she had her head in the sun and her legs in the shadow. 'I'm afraid, Grandmother. I don't want to go into the wilderness. You don't know what we'll find on the other side of the gateway. What if there are monsters there, too?'

'We must be strong, Elene. We have been given a task. I

alone can speak the language of those who bide in the desert country, so I must go. So be it.'

'So be it,' she breathed, bowing her head.

'Gah,' he whispered, but the sound vanished in the trickling tumble of grains of sand down the sloped cloth lean-to as a wind blew up from the flats.

His body was ice, his thoughts sluggish. Somehow, the lean-to came down and he was rolled onto a length of cloth and dragged over the bumpy ground to be dropped again, left lying with a rock digging into the small of his back.

There he lay. A haze descended, and for a while he heard faint sounds, none of them distinct enough to identify. A drop of moisture wet his palm. Through the haze the sun shone as it sank low into the west, but its glare had the force of ice, creeping into his limbs.

He drifted. It was getting harder and harder to see people; they seemed so tenuous and insubstantial set against the pale hills and the darkening sky, which were older creatures by far, populated by ancient spirits that stalked the shadows. Light winked in the heavens; a star bloomed. Figures moved outside the circle, raising and lowering staffs and murmuring words too softly for him to hear or understand.

A spider's thread spun down from the heavens to latch to one of the stones, followed by a second. His heart sped as he realized they were engaged in the art of the mathematici, who could read the movements of the heavens and discern their secrets. Years ago Kansi-a-lari had woven a spell into the stones while he cowered and prayed, but she had woven it with the intent to keep them in one place while time moved forward around them. Marcus wove a gateway into the stones through which Meriam and Elene and their retinue might travel to a distant land.

The stone circles were gateways, each one a gate that could lead to any one of the others, but he did not know how to weave the spell. He wanted to know how to weave the spell. He tried to lift his head, to look, to learn, but none of his limbs moved and that waxing torpor dragged him down, and down, and down into the pit. A shadow bent over him; hands pinned parchment to his robes; the cloth on which he lay strained and tugged around his body and he moved into the web of light. Blind, he floated while all around blue fire burned with a cold breath that soaked him to the bone.

It is so cold that it burns. He sees branching corridors and down each one a vision, whether false or true he cannot say.

A man, grimy, thin, half naked, walks and walks as a rumbling wheel rolls around and around him, never ending.

Wizened creatures whisper and skulk in the depths of the earth, listening.

A merman glides through smoky waters, pulled by the wake of a slender ship.

A small party of robed figures strides hastily through the blue-white fog. Is there a familiar face among them? Isn't that the Eagle called Hanna, who was freed from slavery to Bulkezu? She turns as if hearing his thoughts and calls aloud.

'Who are you?'

Light flared, and died, and he hit hard ground, his back and head and hips jarred by the force of the impact. That flare of the light washed away until no light remained. Was it night? Or was he blind?

He could no longer move his lips. But he could still hear.

'Who is this?'

'See, there is a message pinned to his robes with a fine brooch. Ai, God! He stinks!'

'Feh! So he does!'

'This is signed with the name of Brother Marcus. Here is the man who dragged the filthy one. He has the look of a servant.'

'What's wrong with *him?*'

'I don't know. He looks as if he's been knocked cold, but otherwise healthy. We must take these two to the Holy Mother.'

'That's a long road.'

A warm hand touched his lips, then his throat, and last his eyes. 'God Above! He's like ice! I think he's dying. Hurry! Send for Presbyter Hugh!'

Their voices faded into a hiss, but that, too, fell away as he sank into the silence of the pit.

XXIV
HIS VOICE

1

It was raining again, a downpour that threatened to drown the newly planted seeds and sow the dreaded murrain among their precious sheep, for they'd heard rumors that the disease had blighted lands south of here. Ivar stood on the porch of the infirmary and listened to the gallop of rain on the sloping roof, accompanied by the coughs of the afflicted resting under the care of Sister Nanthild. Ermanrich, Hathumod, and Sigfrid were all sick with a pleurisy that had felled three quarters of their little congregation. One elderly nun had died, but the rest seemed doomed only to be miserable and weak for many weeks.

'There you are, Brother Ivar.' Sister Nanthild could barely walk with the assistance of two canes, and she never went farther than the porch of her infirmary, but she was nevertheless a fierce and wise ruler of her tiny domain. 'Still healthy, I see. Are you chewing licorice root?'

'More than I ever wished to, Sister.' The taste had ruined his appetite, since every food now stank of aniseed.

She chuckled. 'An obedient boy, even if you are a heretic. Is there aught Her Grace wishes from me? I can't let you in to speak with your comrades. We rely on your health, Brother Ivar. We must take no chance that you catch the contagion.'

'I know.'

'You don't like it.'

'Am I so easy to understand, Sister?'

Her smile was a well-worn crease in a wrinkled face. He had never seen her lose her temper, even with her most crotchety patients – and many tested her with their whining and complaints. 'I have seen every condition of humankind in the course of my years, Brother. You are no mystery to me!'

The comment frightened him, although he knew it ought not to. He had worked hard to quiet the demons that pricked him, but she saw into his innermost heart.

'There, now, child. I do not know all your secrets, nor do I wish to know them. I have secrets of my own.'

'Surely you have led a blameless life!'

'When I was a young girl I was allowed to kiss the hand of the sainted Queen Radegundis. It may be that a trifling measure of her holiness blessed me with a long life and few troubles. But I have sown my share of ills in the world, as do we all. Now, then. How goes it with Her Grace?'

'She says to tell you, "It is time."'

'Ah.' She went to the door and called to her assistant. 'Sister Frotharia, fetch me the satchel hanging from the hook behind my chair.'

Coughs and groans greeted her words as patients sought her attention, and she gestured to Ivar to stay put and hobbled back into the long hall where the sick lay on pallets. After a while, Sister Frotharia came out onto the porch and, without a word, handed Ivar a satchel, then went back inside.

Ivar glanced up and down the porch, but of course he was alone. No one ventured out in such rain. The ground was slicked to mud, and even on the gravel pathways rivulets and puddles made walking perilous. Their guards rarely ventured within the limits of the palisade that ringed their holy community.

The satchel weighed heavily on his arm as he hurried out into the rain. The infirmary abutted the main compound. The guards posted at the door to the biscop's suite stepped aside without speaking; they had served almost three months and glowered at him with the suspicion of men who have heard nothing but poisonous gossip. The guard was rotated through every three months; to this schedule Lady Sabella adhered with iron discipline. The usurper feared, Ivar supposed, that lengthy contact with Biscop Constance might corrupt the guards.

As it would.

Biscop Constance had certainly corrupted *him*. She possessed every quality that set apart those noble in spirit as well as blood: tall and handsome, prudent and humble, diligent and pious, farsighted and discreet, eloquent, patient, amiable, and stern.

'Ah,' the good biscop said, looking up as he entered. She sat as usual at her writing desk with two assistants beside her in case she needed anything.

Never in his wildest imaginings had he expected to become the familiar attendant and counselor to a noblewoman of such high station, one who wore the gold torque signifying her royal kinship at her neck.

'Are you sure this is wise, Your Grace?' he asked.

'I am sure it is not. If I cannot go myself, then I do not wish to put one of my faithful retainers into such danger.'

'It must be done,' said the young woman seated at the biscop's feet. She had riotous black curls that the nun's scarf over her head could not constrain. Sister Bona had been a foundling, discovered at the gates of the biscop's palace in Autun some sixteen years before. Now she was one of the prettiest girls Ivar had ever seen, and her houndlike loyalty to the biscop gave her a warrior's bold resolve. 'It must be done now! The rain will cover my tracks. The guards hide in their shelters. I can find refuge with certain farming families and loyal monasteries that are known to me through my travels with you, Your Grace. If I can reach Kassel, Duchess Liutgard's steward will give me aid and send me with an escort to Princess Theophanu. Even if I can get as far as Herford Monastery, I will be safe with Father Ortulfus. You know it must be done!'

'I could go,' said Ivar, but Bona fixed him with such a glower that he laughed nervously and took a step back.

'You are one of only seven men who abide in this prison,' said Constance. 'You would be easily missed.' Pain never left her. She shut her eyes, frowning, but with a deep sigh opened them again. 'Go, then, Bona. Make haste. Avoid the roads at all costs. Go with God.'

They embraced, then parted. Constance did not rise as Ivar gave the satchel to Bona, who slung it over her shoulder and hurried out into the courtyard, Ivar at her heels.

'I know the countryside better than you do!' she said, not looking back at him.

'It will be dangerous!'

'So it will.' She glanced over her shoulder, and her grin challenged and vexed him. No girl brought up in the convent ought to be so provocative, but no placid creature would have dared what Bona meant now to attempt. Sigfrid and Ermanrich had no difficulty adjusting to a celibate life as the only young men confined to this convent – there were also four elderly lay brothers who labored about the grounds – but Ivar felt the sting of itchings and cravings every day. He could never scratch.

At least it wasn't Liath he dreamed of every single night, but the procession of women who progressed through his dreams only made it worse, all of them succubi wearing familiar faces: Liath, sometimes, but Hanna, too, and Bona (too often), and that girl from Gent, and a dozen others glimpsed and forgotten until they returned to haunt him. He never dreamed of Baldwin, but that betrayal only plagued him in his waking hours when he wondered how much his friend suffered and whether he smiled or wept in Sabella's tender care.

On two sides of the courtyard the windows and doors opening onto the courtyard had been boarded up to keep Constance confined within the biscop's suite, but Bona had loosened a board and after a final, considering glance at Ivar, she wriggled through the opening, dragging the satchel behind her. He pushed the board back into place to conceal the opening and went out to stand in the cold rain beside the dry fountain, letting himself get drenched.

Six months ago he and his three companions had been

marched as prisoners into this place. How long would they bide here? Would they ever be freed? Or would they die here?

After a while he walked, dripping, back into the audience chamber.

Constance did not look up, but her quill paused. 'She is gone?'

'She is gone, Your Grace.'

She nodded. Her pen resumed its scratching across the parchment, driven with the same stern determination that had kept this tiny community going, although they might all so easily have lost heart.

He left and went outside, finding shelter in the mouth of the byre where the sheep sheltered during the winter. From here he had a good view of the palisade. This high fence had originally been erected across the mouth of the valley to keep out the enemies of Queen Gertruda, the founder of this tiny community dedicated to St. Asella but commonly referred to as Queen's Grave. Yet a refuge that kept enemies out might as easily be turned inward. Since Constance's arrival, the palisade had grown to enclose the community on all sides, zigzagging through woodland and running below the high ridge that closed in the valley at the far end. Guards patrolling the walls day and night kept them locked in. The high ridge walls and the palisade bounded their world, yet it was not precisely an evil existence, only a curtailed one.

What made it evil dwelled in the world, not in their hearts. Yet he could not believe that they were better off waiting in here than fighting out there.

2

For a long time Zacharias could hear but not see, could feel a jostling all along his torso and limbs that at long last and for no obvious reason ceased.

'Is this the one? He reeks.'

'Yes, Holy Mother.'

'He and the servant were found in the crown at Novomo?'

'Yes, Holy Mother. It took six days for them to convey him here in a cart. As you see, he is crippled, mute, and blind.'

'But not dead?'

'Not dead. The message speaks of a poison that both paralyzes and preserves.'

'This is the parchment that was pinned to his robes?'

'Yes, Holy Mother.'

'Brother Marcus has appended his name at the end. I recognize the imperfect curve of his "r's."'

'Yes, Holy Mother.'

The woman's voice lowered as she read the words in a murmur, phrases rising and falling out of earshot. '. . . akreva . . . Sister Meriam left this receipt for a nostrum that will counteract the poison . . . she has departed without further incident, but where she has landed I know not. She will send a servant back to me, but I do not know when to expect . . . I remain here to safeguard this crown and prepare for the conjunction . . . Brother Lupus' treachery . . . our calculations with the locations and angles necessary to locate each crown and link them together according to the ancient spell . . . but it will be necessary to double-check against these calculations from the tables of Biscop Tallia . . .'

The voice lulled him back into that stupor, prey to the touch of hands and the play of water and then cloth over his body as servants washed and dressed him and exclaimed over his mutilation. He knew when the haze lightened and became something more than a gray fog, when vague forms took on shape and he recognized forms as people bending over him to examine his skin and eyes. He knew when his sense of smell returned because of the unexpected scent of hot bread fresh from the ovens that caused him to salivate, and then to swallow.

The sensation of movement shocked him. Was he so utterly paralyzed? How had they been feeding him all this time?

Yet he was not dead.

When he tried his tongue, only that stubborn 'gah' sound clawed in his throat. Day after day he struggled against this muteness until he dared not attempt speech at all because it was worse to imagine that he had lost the ability to talk altogether. Day after day folk came to marvel, for what reason he did not know and could not ask. Mute. Speechless. Nothing could be worse. Even death was preferable.

But one day as the sober-looking servant called Eigio who always tended him rolled him to one side in order to change the bedding beneath him, he tried again because he could not stop trying to talk.

'Where have I come to?'

The man shrieked, dropped the half-cleared bedding, and ran from the room, leaving him propped up on his side like a board.

Was that truly his own voice, so rough and low? He tried again.

'Where have I come to? What day is it?'

Elation spilled tears from his eyes, streaming down his cheeks to spot the rumpled bedding. Emboldened, he tensed and rocked, overbalanced, and tipped forward to land facedown on the lumpy mattress at a tilt, caught between the mattress and the ridges made by the half-stripped blankets. A hollow cradled his face so he could breathe, inhaling the musty smell of straw ticking and coarse canvas cover moist with his sweat and effusions.

'Yes! He spoke as clear as can be, Your Excellency. God in Heaven! Look there! He's rolled himself forward.'

Hands gripped him by shoulder and hip and heaved him back against the wall. He looked up at the worried servant and, beyond him, a golden-haired man clothed in a fine pale linen tunic who gazed at him so pensively that Zacharias thought the man was about to weep.

'Can you hear me, Brother Zacharias?' asked this magnificent figure in a fine, mellifluous voice. 'Can you speak?'

'Who are you?' he croaked.

'Ah.' The man called to an unseen fourth party. 'Vindicadus, bring me my robes.'

'Yes, Your Excellency.'

The patter of footsteps faded as the lord examined Zacharias. 'What shall we do with you?' he mused. 'What shall we do? Two days yet until the king's ascension. Can you move?'

Zacharias tried to wiggle his feet, to move his hands, but nothing happened. He might as well have been stone, and it sickened him to think of lying here in helpless terror as each day spun into the next. 'Am I a cripple, Your Excellency?'

'His finger moved, Your Excellency,' said Eigio.

'So it did. Sister Meriam's nostrums have had their effect, as she promised us in her letter, but faster than expected. Strange.' As he bit his lower lip in a gesture more common to children puzzling over an unanswered question, he looked startlingly young and oddly frightening, but the shiver of fear passed quickly.

'Very well, Eigio.' He walked to the door and paused there. 'Let no person enter. Say his condition has taken a turn for the worse and that he is near death, and on no account let any soul hear him speak. Your meals will be brought as usual and a guard will be posted outside the door. You are not to leave this room again. Do you understand?'

'Yes, Your Excellency. It will be done as you say, Your Excellency.'

'I am sure it will be.'

Eigio shut the door behind him, closing them in.

'Where am I?' Zacharias asked, and the man looked at him in surprise, as if he had forgotten Zacharias was there.

'Nay, Brother,' he said, wrinkling his brow in distress. 'Only Presbyter Hugh is to speak to you, he made that clear. You may ask all you want, but I can say nothing.'

Zacharias had nothing left to do but wiggle his fingers and toes as he surveyed his domain: the bed, a bench and cot for the servant, a side table with a basin and pitcher of water, and a garland hanging over the door. On the bench rested a tray of oddments including a ball of bright red yarn and two large hooked wooden needles, a wine cup, a chess set carved of ivory, a bowl and spoon, a bundle of rosemary with a sprinkling of pale blue flowers among the spiky leaves, and a writing knife, stoppered inkhorn, and several uncut goose quills.

Two shutters leaned against the whitewashed walls beside a single embrasure. Outside it was day.

'Where am I?' Zacharias repeated, but Eigio turned mute and would answer none of his queries, only gave him a ghastly sweet mead to drink.

He slept, and when he woke it was dark, the chamber illuminated by a single candle whose light gilded the pale head of the lord Eigio had called Presbyter Hugh. He had pulled the bench up to the side table, on which a sloping writing desk had been set. He worked industriously, pen scratching as he wrote on vellum, his attention fixed on his labors as he copied onto the parchment from an exemplar out of Zacharias' sight beyond Hugh's left arm. He was a remarkably handsome man, with a face that light cherished and women no doubt swooned over, that wealth of golden hair, and his limbs and figure so well proportioned that he seemed more angel than man.

All at once Zacharias *knew* who the man was and, therefore, where he must be.

'Am I in Darre? How did I get here?'

Hugh set down the pen and used the penknife to scrape off a blot before turning to regard him with that same pensive expression Zacharias had seen before.

'I have been sitting beside you for half the night, Brother Zacharias. Did you know you talk quite volubly in your sleep? Yet in such a disjointed fashion that I am left puzzled. What can you tell me of Prince Sanglant?'

Almost he blurted out Hathui's accusations, but he stopped himself. He was helpless and alone. This was not the time to make enemies.

'I left the service of Prince Sanglant to become a servant to Brother Marcus. He promised to instruct me in the secrets of the mathematici.'

'Did he do so?'

'He did! He had begun to teach me about the motion of

the heavens and the glorious architecture of the world. When I had mastered those, then he promised to teach me how to weave the crowns.'

'Did he!' Hugh glanced toward the unshuttered window but looked back as quickly. 'Instead you were stung by a dread creature called an *akreva* and paralyzed by its venom. Brother Marcus saw fit to send you back to us, as the bearer of a message to the Holy Mother.'

'How came I here? Am I in Darre?'

'Brother Lupus, it seems, had deserted Marcus. He was to bear the message, but in his absence Marcus chose to send you – as you are now – instead. How did it happen that Brother Lupus abandoned his duty?'

'I do not know, Your Excellency.'

'You do not know Brother Lupus?'

'I do not know why he deserted the company, Your Excellency. He fled one night, while we slept in a hostel in Qahirah. That is all I know.'

'Is that all you know? Truly?'

His gentle smile made Zacharias shudder, and that movement spawned another as his hands spasmed and his feet twitched. It was a warning. If he could survive this paralysis, if it were wearing off, then he might hope to escape. He had no loyalty to Wolfhere, after all.

'We stayed at a hostel where Wolfh—where Brother Lupus had stayed many years before.'

'He traveled in Qahirah before?'

'So he said. I don't know why. The innkeeper recognized him. He had done the innkeeper a favor many years ago, so we were well treated and given a splendid feast that night and a palatable wine, as much as we could drink. That night I had to rise to use the necessary. When returning to my bed, I happened to overhear a conversation between Brother Marcus and Sister Meriam. Marcus no longer trusted Brother Lupus. He thought Brother Lupus had spent too long in Prince Sanglant's company and seemed unwilling to return to the fold. Sister Anne had commanded that Brother Lupus be sent back to her once we located the crown which lies beyond the old ruins of Kartiako. It was the next morning that we discovered he was gone. Perhaps he overheard their conversation as well. Perhaps he knew they were suspicious of him, and so he fled.'

'If so, it seems their suspicions were correct. *Wolfhere*.' He savored the name as he might a sweet wine. 'It seems that the king's distrust of him was deserved.'

So spoke the man who had, according to Hathui, corrupted the king by insinuating a daimone into his body! Zacharias held his tongue. It was all he could do not to blurt out the accusation just to see Hugh's reaction, but instinct saved him. Hugh was not Bulkezu but something different, better or worse he could not tell.

'Are you a mathematicus?' he asked instead. 'Can you teach me now that I no longer travel with Brother Marcus? He promised that I would receive teaching if I joined his cause.'

'Is that your wish, Brother Zacharias? To receive teaching?'

'It is! More than anything!'

'Yet you have not told me what you know of Prince Sanglant. And of an Eagle whose name is Hathui. You spoke her name while you slept. What do you know of her? Is it possible you have seen her? She was once King Henry's trusted counselor, but rumor has it she murdered Helmut Villam after a lover's quarrel and fled in disgrace.'

How difficult it was to remain silent! But Zacharias held his tongue. He struggled and writhed in his heart, but he held his tongue.

'A man who brought me information about this Eagle, Hathui, would be accepted as a trustworthy member of my household. Such a man could expect to receive training in any craft his heart desired. Even as a mathematicus. For I am one such. I could take him on as a discipla. I could teach him how to weave the crowns, and much more besides.'

At the price of betraying his sister.

Hadn't he once said: *'I will do anything for the person who will teach me'*?

He shut his eyes, and held his tongue, although he knew his silence betrayed him. Where desire and loyalty warred, loyalty won, and he possessed no glib words to worm his way out of this confrontation. He had probably lost the one thing he desired above all else – that he might learn the secrets of the heavens – and yet it mattered not. He had left Hathui behind, but he would never betray her.

Never.

'Ah,' said Hugh. 'I will leave you to think it over.'

He stoppered the inkhorn, cleaned the quill, and tidied up his writing things before he left. In his place, Eigio returned, blowing out the candle before he lay down to sleep.

In that darkness Zacharias smiled to discover what blossomed unexpectedly in his heart. Peace.

Hathui had accused him of never being content, but he was content now. He had saved Elene's life despite his fear. He had stood his ground in honor of the bond between him and Hathui. Weren't these the actions of a good man? A decent man? A courageous man?

In the morning, Eigio propped him up against the wall and he was delighted to discover that he could use his arms well enough to spoon gruel into his own mouth. He was ravenous. He had lost so much weight that his body seemed skin stretched over bone, and when he tried to stand, his legs hadn't the strength to hold him. Only a handful of days ago he could not swallow or speak. If he ate and rested, he would recover his strength.

The afternoon's meal of gruel and wine made him unaccountably sleepy. He drifted in and out of a doze as his skin burned and chilled at intervals and his tongue seemed swollen, choking him. Night came and departed while he napped and woke, head cloudy, hands tingling. Light returned, and he lay on his bed and struggled to move, but his limbs felt as heavy as stone, and his tongue stuck to the roof of his mouth.

Presbyter Hugh appeared suddenly, splendid in court robes and a scarlet cape that rippled like water every time he turned.

'Give him the antidote, and then bring him,' he said, and left.

Eigio poured sour wine down his throat. Half of it spilled down his cheeks and trickled along his jaw, but the serving man wiped him up and clad him in a plain shift, the kind of shroud a poor man would be buried in.

He couldn't move.

Servants arrived and rolled him onto a stretcher. In this manner he jounced down the hall, down stairs, up and down and in such a twisting, turning, crazy route that he became dizzy. Bile burned at the back of his throat, but he could not swallow it down or force it up. He could not even blink, but must stare up at plain and fancy woodwork both, and once a stretch of bright blue sky, until the jostling brought him along an arcade open to the air and surrounded by an ocean of murmuring water. Yet these were the mutterings of human-kind, because the servants bore him past multitudes whose faces flashed past as quickly as those of the painted cherubs laughing and weeping above him among the vaults.

A huge crowd had gathered, but where, and why, he did not know.

They crossed under a lintel and came into a space absolutely packed with women and men and rank with their perfumes and sweat and the headache-inducing bite of incense rolling in clouds past his streaming eyes. The ceiling flew away from him, arching up to an impossible height from which stared solemn angels and gloomy saints with huge eyes and glowing hands and heads.

Had he died at last and arrived at the Chamber of Light?

Whispers teased his ears as the servants bore him through the crowd.

'Look! That's the cripple who was found a month ago.'

'He can't talk or move, poor creature, yet he lives.'

'They say he's possessed by the Enemy.'

Male voices rose in unison.

The angel spoke to the chosen one:
Rejoice!
Receive the light for the glory of God illuminates you.
Rejoice!

A dome opened above him, the gulf of air so vast that he could scarcely see the painted figures gazing benignly down upon him, who was smallest and least. Folks gaped at him but his bearers did not falter and he was borne forward under the dome and crossed under a lower arch to the apse, where the crowd thinned and he was set down in the midst of a company of brightly dressed nobles. One man stood with his back to Zacharias, his figure limned by the light streaming through a tall window. He turned. The sun dazzled Zacharias' eyes as the man knelt beside him. He was clad in gold, and the gold cloth was sewn with gems; a heavy gold crown sat on his head and a gold torque encircled his throat. He had brown hair chased with silver and the calm, handsome, bearded face of a man in his middle years. Truly, he was as glorious as the sun.

Floating above, faces swam in and out of Zacharias' sight: a pretty young woman crowned and robed in splendor equal to that of the kneeling man; Presbyter Hugh; a woman robed in white with a delicate gold torque at her throat and an embroidered golden cap concealing her hair.

The choir finished. Silence trembled beneath the gulf of air.

The crowned man drew a red gillyflower across Zacharias' lips and after that a tickling branch of yew.

'If God favor this day,' he said in a powerful voice that surely carried all the way to the back, 'if the Lord and Lady look kindly upon the birth today of this new Holy Empire, I pray They will heal this poor unfortunate. Let my kiss be for him the breath of life.'

He bent down and kissed Zacharias on the lips. He reeked of a heady perfume so strong that it tickled in Zacharias' nostrils and made him, all at once, unbidden, unexpected, and just as the crowned man sat back, sneeze.

An audible gasp burst from the assembly.

'Catch it! Catch it!' cried a woman excitedly. 'The demon has been expelled!'

Zacharias burned all over as he stared up at the crowned man. Ai, God, surely it could only be one man, so glorious and so proud. The man whom Hathui respected above all others. Her king.

He struggled and found that his limbs worked after all. The crowned man rose to his feet, and Zacharias got his elbows under him and with immense effort, straining, levered himself up.

'Your Majesty!' he said hoarsely.

'He speaks! He speaks!'

'A miracle! The Emperor has healed him!'

All through the cathedral voices drowned him in a thunder of exclamations and joyful weeping. King Henry stared down at Zacharias without expression, his gaze that same calm facade, but suddenly he noticed that the king's eyes seemed first green and then blue and then green again as though he were both himself and some other creature entirely.

Hathui's anguished testimony crowded back into his mind, for with his excellent memory he had certainly forgotten nothing she had said to Prince Sanglant, although it was difficult to think with such a roar around him and so many bodies pressing forward to look at him, at the miracle. He was the cripple the new emperor had healed.

'Take him,' said Hugh's voice, almost lost in the uproar.

The stretcher rocked and he rose into the air, reaching, grasping, gasping.

'Your Majesty! Your Majesty!'

They shoved past the yammering hordes and hurried out through a side door and then by halls and courtyards heedless of his pleading to be let down, to return to the king who was not king any longer but now emperor. All that way he heard, fading, the noise of the multitude and, in counterpoint, a hymn.

Sing a new song of praise!
Lay the old man aside and take on the new.
Glory! Glory! Glory!

They came at last to a silent chamber where sunlight streamed through open windows to illuminate murals painted on the wall. They set him down on a pallet in a corner behind two handsome chairs placed on a low dais, drew a curtain, and left him alone except for two guards at the door.

There he wept, but for what reason he was not sure.

A miracle!

Maybe he wept for the lie.

3

Stronghand's ship sailed into Rikin Fjord on a calm day in late spring. Deacon Ursuline was among those who came to the strand to greet him, and she looked hale and healthy, as did all those who labored in the fields and pastures.

'My lord,' she said, inclining her head respectfully. He had learned to interpret human facial expressions and it appeared that she was actually glad to see him. 'We have received word of your triumphs in Alba. I pray that some few of the young people I am training in the way of God may be sent to that land to bring the Light to those who worship the Enemy.'

'The queen of Alba is dead,' he agreed, 'and her heirs with her. If there are any tree sorcerers left, they have fled into the wilderness and the high country. I do not wish to lose you, Deacon, because you keep the peace here in my birthplace, but if there are any disciplas you wish to send to Alba, I will see that they sail with the next ships that journey there.'

'You are generous, my lord.'

'Perhaps. If belief in your God makes the Alban people obedient and prosperous, then it is worthwhile to have them believe.'

'It is true that good deeds are most fruitful when they rise from a righteous heart, but you do the work of God despite your disbelief, my lord.' She looked past him at the group of clerics disembarking down a ramp. 'It seems you have brought clerics of your own, my lord. What are these?'

'They have come to seek the wisdom of the WiseMothers,

although I do not believe they understand what they will find. Make them welcome, Deacon, and feed them. I must give my report to OldMother.'

'Ah.' She nodded. 'She will be glad to hear it, my lord.'

He had taken a step away but turned back, caught by her tone and the odd choice of words.

She anticipated him. 'We have been good stewards of this land, my lord, as you will see, and have served you faithfully. You have been gone for a long time, so I have gotten into the habit of consulting with OldMother when I have questions.'

'Have you?'

'We have much to learn from each other.'

'As do I, it seems.'

She glanced at him sharply and pushed her scarf back from her head self-consciously. Although her face and hands were clean, her nails had dirt under them and the hem of her robe was stained, as though she had recently come from the gardens. 'Does this displease you, my lord?' Her tone was not at all submissive. Quite the contrary.

He bared his teeth, the merest flash, and had the pleasure of seeing her eyes widen in alarm and, an instant later, an ironic smile lift her lips.

'Had OldMother not wished to speak with you, she would never have allowed you to set foot in her hall,' he answered. 'So be it.'

Yet as he strode up to OldMother's hall, he puzzled over her words. It should not have surprised him that OldMother would speak with the one who stood as OldMother for the Soft Ones, weak as they were, but nevertheless the comment disquieted him. No son of the tribe entered OldMother's hall without her invitation, and her invitation came only to those sons who would lead, breed, or die. He had never heard of any time in all the long years since the RockChildren walked the Earth that one among the OldMothers had spoken to humans. Why now?

The SwiftDaughters had seen him coming by means of watch fires that burned along the fjord to alert the inhabitants of approaching ships, and they gathered outside the hall to welcome him. He had forgotten the unexpected beauty of their forms, or perhaps he had simply never appreciated it. Their hair shone with the gleam of ore, and this glamour wove veins of light into their skin as well, so that the midday sun made them shimmer. They moved with a grace no clumsy human limbs could imitate, and their cold lips and bright eyes held a wealth of expression as they danced in greeting. Yet like his cousins they were, as far as he knew, nameless; unlike most human females, they would never breed and produce hatchlings of their own.

Wasn't that the weakness of the RockChildren, who were stronger in so many other ways? Humankind would always outnumber them.

He crossed the threshold into the vast dimness of OldMother's hall, with its impossible sweep of stars glittering above despite the hall having a roof. As he walked forward, the ground transformed from beaten dirt to hard rock beneath his feet. An abyss opened before him, and he dared walk no closer to OldMother's high seat. A winter wind chilled his face and torso, blowing up from unimaginable depths. Ice formed on his braid and coated his lips.

Her voice scraped. 'You are bold, Stronghand. You set your ships onto the seas and fight to possess other lands than the one you were born to. You force the many chieftains to bow down before one leader, who is yourself. You seek both the living and the dead. You invite sorcerers into our homeland who care nothing for us although it is their kind who gave us life. What will come of these plans?'

'That remains to be seen. I use the tools I find.'

'In aiding the strangers, do you not put your own plans in jeopardy?'

'Perhaps. I will take the risk. They speak of a great cataclysm set into motion by their ancient enemies, whom they call the Aoi – the Lost Ones.'

Her silence encouraged him to go on, yet it seemed to him that she was not alone, that many more presences listened as he spoke. 'They seek a stone crown in these northern lands through which they desire to weave a spell that will reach across the lands from north to south, from east to west.'

'They will find what they seek,' she replied, 'yet it is not what they think it is.'

'They claim to seek only knowledge and wisdom, but I can see that they seek power as well.'

'In this you follow the path of humankind, Stronghand. Use caution.'

'I do.'

'You have a question.'

The statement caught him off guard, but he knew how to recover quickly, and he knew better than to attempt to deceive OldMother. 'Why did you not give your sons names?'

'Because they never asked for them.'

'Now they do.'

The blistering wind abruptly calmed, and ceased. He saw nothing, only darkness, but OldMother's presence enveloped him.

'An inescapable storm is coming, Stronghand. This my sisters and I know. Prepare yourself and those who shelter under your hand. In this storm long ago the RockChildren were born. The Mothers of our tribes do not wish our children to perish, but to survive, when it returns.'

'What must I do?'

'Step forward.'

He knew better than to disobey. One step plunged him into the chasm, falling and falling through blackness.

turning and turning and turning and a pause for unquiet sleep with the muttering of the madman infesting his dreams, and then up again, and again, and again, a hopeless round of labor that has neither beginning nor end, and still the wheel turns under his feet as he walks endlessly and never gets anywhere, the wheel rumbling around and around until he no longer recalls anything except this pit of darkness and the turning of the wheel.

Every time as he drifts off to sleep, the madman plodding in the traces whispers such a tale of blood and fear and anger that images pollute his dreams until all he sees is fire and weeping, although at times he has a momentary flash of surprise that he can see at all, even if only in his dreams.

'No, no, I pray you my lord leave her be she is just young yet an innocent my daughter if it please you she's never done any ai God the blood no you must look you will look I'll kill you look at the baby at her face I'm glad he is dead is that what you've done to her?'

The water drawn up from the depths to keep dry the shaft below spills endlessly into the ditch where it will flow onward to a pool where the next wheel draws it up to the next level and up and up, and the flood never ends, it just keeps turning and spilling.

'Nay do not you go there I will kill him dead and cut off his balls and why shouldn't I just look at the blood I hate you my poor child for it won't bring anyone back kill you kill you kill you.'

He falls because there is no bottom to this pit, it just goes on and on, and one day the pain of the madman reaches his tongue at long last, and a thing stirs there he no longer has a name for.

He speaks, although his voice is rough from disuse.

'Why do you despair?'

A horrible silence follows his words except for the rumble of the wheel and the splash and gurgle of running water and the echoes of the wheels above, whose turning never ceases.

Silence.

'Who are you?' asks the madman, although he does not stop walking the wheel which mutters under the tread of his feet, hard as fate. 'What happened to the mute?'

'I don't know.'

'Have they put a new one down here? Did the mute die? Are you a spy for them, come to wiggle out with my secrets? I know where the treasure is buried, it's buried with my treasure, my sweet, my innocent. And if I could have killed him who despoiled her I would have but he took what he wished and went his way for he was a lord among men and we are only the dirt he walked on. Did you see the blood?'

'I can't see. Was harm done to someone you cared for?'

'Don't mock me!' the madman roars, pounding his fists against wood. The wheel ratchets to a stop. 'Don't mock me! I protected her! All of them! But what could I do, for they had swords and spears and I only my hoe and shovel and them made of wood, nothing to do when they came round God I was helpless I was afraid I let them take the girl for fear of what they would do to the rest of us though she wept and clung to me and now I am punished for it, for wasn't I a coward, didn't I kill her with my own hands by not fighting them?'

The madman weeps, while above voices shout and there comes the noise of men descending to discover what has happened to the wheel. The one who was once silent rises from the cold pallet of stone where he rests and gropes along the passage. In an odd way he can see the walls, because his body senses the presence of stone so close that he feels its respiration, each breath seeping like the damp through its pores, as slow as ages upon ages. It's as if the stone wishes to speak to him but its voice can't quite reach him.

'Hurry,' he says as he feels against his cheek the upwelling of cold from the lowest shaft. He grasps the rim of the still wheel. 'You must walk. Or they'll whip you.'

'What care you for a man with blood on his hands? I am a murderer! I am! I am! I killed him, the one who done it! Not him, but his servant, for I couldn't touch him! I killed the one who took the leavings when the lord was done. It was all I could do. She was a good girl. She was a good girl. It was all I could do. My firstborn. My treasure.'

But the madman begins walking, weeping and blubbering until words and sobs meld together, for it is a different whip that goads him on.

'Ai, God,' he says as he listens to the roll of the wheel and the disjointed rambling of the madman. 'No wonder you grieve. I wish you may find peace.'

No chasm after all.

Stronghand stumbled into a ditch, and his feet slipped on gravel as water purled against his shins. The shock of spring water wrenched him into awareness, and he noticed how still it had become, as if the world held its breath.

Into this troubling silence OldMother spoke.

'We see into the heart of the Earth and we sense the threads that bind the heavens. Our memories stretch long, and long, into the past, but a shadow lies over our sight. We do not see everything. We are blinded where our memory most needs sight. The threads that weave heaven and Earth are not haphazard. Find this one who lives in your dreams. He has sight where we have none.'

'He is blind! He has lost his memory, even his name. How can he help you?'

'It is difficult to know who is lost and who is blind. Do you know?'

The question gave him pause. 'I do not. What of the foreigners I brought, the circle priests? They, too, have a quest.'

'My daughters will guide them to the fjall. There we shall see if they are wise or foolish, whether their plans threaten us or aid us. As for you, son of Rikin: Find him. He has seen what we have not. He can tell us what we need to know.'

4

Too weak to move, Zacharias lay on the pallet and stared through a gap in the curtain at the murals decorating the walls, scenes from ancient days of the first empire and before, the *Lay of Helen* and the triumphs of the Son of Thunder, and scenes he did not recognize of doe-eyed women riding on the backs of winged sphinxes. Because the servant hadn't completely closed the curtain separating him from the chairs, he could also gaze across the floor toward the doors that opened onto the corridor. The alternating pattern of white-and-black tiling on the floor made him dizzy, and he faded into a doze but started awake when a babble of voices surged. The doors were thrown open by guards. Folk streamed into the chamber. Their bright clothing and ringing voices made his head hurt so badly that he covered his eyes with a hand. Since he hadn't the strength to flee, he could only hope to remain overlooked here in the shadows.

The emperor and his consort ascended to the dais and seated themselves to the acclaim of the crowd, although many fewer people had the privilege of so close an audience with Henry in this more intimate setting. Clerics and stewards crowded around behind the chairs, and through their legs Zacharias watched as one by one nobles came forward, knelt before the emperor and empress, and pledged their loyalty.

A buzz of conversation undercut these proclamations. A pair of clerics whispered, standing so close that they almost stood on him, yet they seemed unaware that he lay just a foot-step behind the curtain.

'So, after all, the skopos chose the first day of Sormas, as I told you she would.'

'So you did.' Spoken grudgingly.

'That Bright Somorhas, the Fortunate One, should come into conjunction with the Child's Torque, signifies the right-ful ascension of the true heir.'

'That's true enough, but I thought the signs were most auspicious for the twenty-second of Novarian, last year.'

'The Arethousan usurpers still had a foothold in the penin-sula then. It would have seemed premature to claim an empire he did not control. It would have been tempting fate.'

'So the skopos said. Yet how could you or I or anyone have foreseen it would take three years to drive the bandits and usurpers and rebels out of southern Aosta?'

'That's all in the past. The last Arethousan heretic has fled, the Jinna bandits are dead, and Tiorno has capitulated at last – Look! But speak the name, and the Enemy winks into view! There is Lady Tassila and her nephew. Now that her brother is dead she is regent for the boy, but she intends to claim the duchy for herself and install her own children after her.'

'Can she do that?'

'Why not? Her brother fought against King Henry until

last winter. The boy might bear a grudge because of the death
of the father. He can't be trusted. There's this new campaign
they speak of, to take back the Dalmiakan shore from the
Arethousans. They'll need Lady Tassila's troops and her
loyalty in the army. I heard that Empress Adelheid—'

'Hsst.'

In a different tone, they spoke in unison. 'Your Excellency.'

Feet shifted. The cloth of their robes creased as the two
clerics dipped knees and heads, blocking his view of the
chamber.

'I pray you,' said Hugh kindly. 'If you would attend me?'

'Of course, Your Excellency! What do you wish?'

'Pray go to my chambers. Ask for my steward. He has in
his keeping a small chest that I need brought to me.'

'Of course, Your Excellency!'

They hurried off. Zacharias saw a fine, clean, strong hand
take hold of the curtain and, with a firm tug, twitch it entirely
shut, closing him into a tunnel of darkness. Beyond the muffling curtain the oaths continued.

For a long time he lay there, fretting and anxious. He knew
how to run, but he didn't know how to fight. He could babble,
but he could not talk himself out of the maze he had stumbled into. Hathui had fled because she had no real power in
the king's court except the king's favor, now turned against
her. Yet he had pledged his loyalty to Marcus in exchange
for teaching. His loyalties ought to lie here, but the bond with
Hathui clutched too tight. If he betrayed her, then he was
nothing but a soulless slave in bondage to those who meant
to ruin or even kill her.

After some time, he groped around the pallet and, as softly
as he could, rolled himself off into the gap between the mattress and a wall. He rested. When he could breathe normally
again, he pushed up to hands and knees and crawled forward
along the wall, trembling and sweating. He had not gone farther than the length of the pallet when he collapsed and lay
there for what seemed a year before he could try again. The
curtain that concealed the wall rippled as folk moved along
its length. Once or twice it sagged in so far that it brushed

him; the gap between curtain and wall wasn't more than the span of his arms.

No one noticed.

He kept crawling.

Maybe there were miracles, or perhaps the curtain only served to allow servants to come and go in concealment. A door revealed itself to his questing fingers, and with great effort he rose to his knees and pushed up the latch. It opened inward. He fell into the adjoining chamber and lay there stunned and aching and gasping with his head and half his torso on a carpet and his hips and legs on the other side of the threshold.

At last he dragged himself through and pushed the door shut with a foot. The latch clicked into place.

He sprawled with eyes shut, unable to move. Just lay there as his muscles twitched and he thought he might melt into the rug whose fibers pressed into his cheek. A friendly whippet nosed him, licked his face, and, when he did not respond, curled up congenially against the curve of his bent knees.

Perhaps he slept.

The next thing he knew, hands took hold of his arms and dragged him over the rug as the whippet whined resignedly. He cracked his eyes open to see that day had fled. Lamps lit a chamber hazy with shadows that congealed into things he could recognize: a table carved of ebony wood, a magnificent broad bed hung around with curtains, two massive chests, a woman dressed in cloth of gold trimmed with purple who turned to regard him with a faint expression of surprise on her pretty face.

'Is this the same one?' she asked as the hands released him, turning him over and dropping him supine on the floor a body's length from her.

'Yes, Your Majesty. This is the one.' Hugh stepped out of the shadows or perhaps through an unseen door. A servant scuttled past him to place a brazier full of red-hot coals next to a wall, then vanished back the way he had come. 'I cannot stay long. It must be done quickly.'

The empress nodded, still staring curiously at Zacharias,

but as she approached the bed, her attention shifted to the man lying asleep there, whom Zacharias had not seen before.

It was the emperor.

'Ai, God,' she whispered as she sank down beside her husband, her hands clasped in prayer. 'Can we save him, Father Hugh?'

'We can, but we must not falter, although the road seems dark. You have given him the sleeping draught?'

'Yes. He fell asleep just after the midnight bell. My servingwomen will not disturb us. They believe that he and I intend to make a new child tonight, one born of empire, not just to a mere king and queen. The four guards outside are those I would trust with my life. They will not betray us.'

'So we must hope. If they do, all is lost, for then the skopos will know what we intend.'

The shimmer of lamplight twisted across her face, making her look young and vulnerable, but there remained an iron tightness to the set of her mouth that suggested she was bent on a cruel course. 'Aosta belongs to Henry and me at last, Father. Henry would go north if he could. You know this.'

'I know this.'

'Yet now we are told that it is the emperor's destiny to ride east, into Dalmiaka to make war on Arethousa. And for what? For what? For a heap of stones, so my spies tell me! I had hoped we could be quit of this awful daimone by now, that we could restore him.'

'We dare not.'

A tear rolled down her cheek as she regarded the sleeping emperor. 'Look at him as he sleeps! Look at his beloved face!' She touched his cheek tenderly, brushed her fingers through his hair. 'Now and again I swear to you, Father Hugh, just as he wakes I see him, a glimpse of him, behind his eyes. He is angry. I swear this to you. He is angry that this cruel thing has been done to him! And done by the ones who love him most!'

'It was the only way to protect him. The Holy Mother will kill him if he does not do exactly as she wishes.'

'I know the skopos claims that this crown of tumbled stones

is all that will save the world from a terrible cataclysm. That our empire must hold the lands where the crown lies. So must we war against the Arethousans who control that territory now!'

'She is a woman obsessed with but one thing,' he agreed.

'Henry is not to be ordered about like a common captain, not even by the skopos! He would have insisted on marching north to Wendar now that our task here is through, now that the Empire is restored. He's heard the reports of all these Eagles, bearing dire tidings. But if we'd abandoned Aosta before, we would have lost it forever. Now that our work in Aosta is done, we can march north to Wendar safely. The skopos can lead an army herself into Dalmiaka to fight the Arethousans. The chronicles tell us of Holy Mothers who have sent armies to do their bidding. Who have accompanied their soldiers. Why must she force Henry to her will?'

'That's right.' As Hugh spoke, he moved closer yet to the bed where Henry slept and beautiful Adelheid bent in sorrow. 'We must protect him in the only way we can. Now, Your Majesty. I pray you. Just for this hour we must withdraw the one thing that protects him from any harm the skopos might do to him. He'll never know that his protection lifts. He'll never know when it is returned into his body, as it will be as soon as I have what I need.'

'So be it,' she murmured.

She drew the sign of the Circle at her breast and with a sigh moved to the foot of the bed. Hugh sat beside Henry's sleeping form while she watched over them. The way the shadow and lamplight played over the scene made it difficult for Zacharias to see exactly what was going on, only that Hugh had a ribbon wrapped through his fingers. He passed that hand over Henry's face as he murmured, and the ribbon came alive, writhing in his grip as if it were trying to escape him.

How could a ribbon move of its own will?

Henry's body relaxed so abruptly, although he still slept, that the emperor appeared oddly different than he had a moment before although his eyes did not flutter, nor did he give any sign of awakening. The young empress gave a gasp,

then bit her lip, but she did not move. She was as finely
wrought a statue as any Zacharias had ever seen, a lovely
woman in the prime of her youth and glorious in her empress'
raiment, golden and splendid. A true queen.

Hugh rose, crossed the room, and knelt beside Zacharias.
The red ribbon tangled through his fingers lashed and
slithered, but it could not escape. His golden hair shone where
the light gilded it. His smile was gentle.

'What do you know of Prince Sanglant, Brother Zacharias?'
he asked. 'What of the Eagle, Hathui?'

He was too weak to run, but he was strong enough to keep
silent. Never would he betray her.

Never.

Hugh touched the ribbon to Zacharias' lips and in his melodious voice chanted the names of angels, holy creatures, bidding them to come to his aid.

A cool sensation slipped down Zacharias' throat, insinuated itself in through his nostrils, and clawed its way into his
eyes.

There was something inside him.

He struggled, but he could do nothing. An aery presence
flooded him, twisting into his skin, into his vitals, into the
very hall where he stabled each of his memories, precisely
placed and uncannily accurate.

'Can you hear me?' asked Hugh.

'I can,' his voice answered. His tongue formed the words,
but he was not the one who spoke.

He fought, but in vain. He was both prisoner and slave.

'Tell me everything you know of Prince Sanglant. Where
was he when last you saw him? What are his plans? Where is
his daughter? What of the Eagle who escaped me? What does
the prince know? What did Hathui see?'

The daimone that infested him brushed through his memories and, one by one, with his voice and his tongue, told his
secrets.

Every one.

XXV

A MUTE BEAST

1

'... Brother Zacharias.'

He came to himself with a shock: he was free, untainted, unharmed, and alone in his body. The horror of that infestation thrilled along his skin, a million ants crawling, a thousand wasps stinging, too awful to contemplate.

'He cannot lie under the influence of the daimone,' Hugh was saying. 'So. The Eagle escaped me, and told Prince Sanglant everything.'

'True,' said Adelheid thoughtfully. 'But now we are forewarned and thus armed.'

Tears of shame streamed down Zacharias' cheeks. The others did not notice. They had turned their backs on him.

'If he seeks griffins and sorcerers,' Adelheid continued, 'and means to return with them and invade Aosta, then he must cross the Alfar Mountains over one of the three passes – St. Barnaria, Julier, or the Brinne.'

'Where is the Brinne Pass?' Hugh asked. 'I've not heard of it.'

'It's far to the east. Few folk use it, for it leads into eastern Avaria and the marchlands, and there's little trade in that direction. The road lies up the northeast coast and inland into Zuola, where Marquesa Richildis rules. She is loyal to us.' Zacharias heard the turn of her foot on the carpet. Her voice remained cool and collected, but her pacing betrayed agitation. 'That is what we must do. We must post men in each of the passes to keep watch for the prince and his army.'

'It could be months or years before an army appears, if it ever does.'

'So be it. That is the only way we can hope to gain warning of his approach.'

'If he returns from the east,' said Hugh.

'If he does not, then he is no threat to us.'

'Perhaps. If he chooses to foment civil war in Wendar, then the north might rise against Henry.'

'Henry will ride east with the skopos. When he returns from Dalmiaka, our position will be strong. That's when we can march north to restore his authority in Wendar and Varre. For now, all we can do is watch the passes and prepare ourselves.'

Hugh chuckled. 'You are a strategist, Your Majesty. It is well that you are, because you must fight this battle alone. I will ride north soon in preparation for the great weaving.'

'Why must you go?'

'Because the Holy Mother demands it.'

'What of Henry?'

'Anne will take the ribbon. She will watch over the emperor.'

'I don't like it. Dare we trust the Holy Mother with him? She might do anything without you or me there. That we hold Henry is the only sword we have to protect ourselves from her.'

'There is much in this world that we do not like that we must suffer because it is the only way to achieve the ends we seek. If we do not make a show of trusting her by giving her the ribbon, then she will know we do not trust her. She may come to believe that we act against her. She is more powerful than we are right now. We must be patient. We will bide our time. The day will come when all that we seek will come to pass.'

Too late, Zacharias searched for the door. He still lay on

his back, and the door lay a very long way away, an impossible distance but his only hope. If he could escape this chamber, he could warn someone – anyone – even fall at the feet of the skopos herself and use his tongue to condemn these two, who had forced him to betray his beloved sister.

'Very well.' Adelheid's footsteps sounded on the carpet as Zacharias hunched his shoulders to see if he could squirm backward.

'Will you kill him?' the empress asked in a cool voice.

'He is innocent,' said Hugh. 'Brother Marcus promised him that he would be taught the secrets of the mathematici. Yet, as he is, he is a danger to himself and to the emperor because he knows too much.'

Too late Zacharias realized that they no longer spoke of Prince Sanglant. It was Hugh who had come to stand next to him, not Adelheid; she remained by the emperor's bed.

'Is he so educated that he can learn the secret paths known only to the mathematici?' she asked.

Hugh's beautiful face wore an expression of compassion, but his eyes were cold. 'There is much he can learn. But, no, he is not educated. Yet it is precisely because he cannot write or read that we can show him mercy.'

Zacharias got his elbows under him and heaved himself up. On the bed Henry slept, yet a stiffness in his limbs suggested that the emperor did not rest entirely at peace. The red ribbon lay across his throat, unmoving.

'Will you teach me?' he demanded through his tears, then hated himself for succumbing even for a moment to that consuming desire. 'Nay! I will not be taught by you, who made me betray my sister!'

'I will teach you to weave the crowns,' said Hugh patiently. 'If you learn well, you can take my place as cauda draconis when the time comes.'

A grim exhilaration goaded him on. 'I'll not consort with those who mean harm to my sister!'

'I will need all four guards,' said Hugh to the empress. 'You are certain of their loyalty?'

'They wear the amulets you wove for them.'

'Ah. Then we need not fear that they will betray us.'

She went to the door, spoke, and four guardsmen entered the room, men with broad shoulders and powerful hands.

'Hold him down.' Hugh turned to the brazier sitting forgotten beside one wall, slipped a glove on his right hand, bent, and withdrew a knife from the coals. Its blade gleamed white-hot.

The guardsmen pushed Zacharias to the floor.

He thrashed against their grip. 'Ai, God! Ai, God! I pray you, mercy! I'll do anything you want! Anything you want!'

'So you will,' said Hugh. 'Hold him tight. One of you, take the head.'

Weak though he was, he struggled like a lion caught in a net, biting, kicking, scratching as the guardsmen cursed him, or laughed, each according to his nature.

They were stronger than he was. They were a vise. When they had him pinned and his head clamped between arms like iron claws, he still thrashed even if he could not move. He fought, and he twisted; he wept, and he begged, but they pried his mouth open and used tongs to fix hold of his tongue and hold it extended as Hugh brought the knife down. No glee animated that beautiful face, only the frowning intentness of a man sorry to be doing what was necessary.

When the blade touched, pain and fire exploded in his head, but the worst of it was that he did not pass out, not as he had that day long ago among the Quman when Bulkezu had mutilated him. He felt the knife slice, and he screamed.

It was the only speech he had left.

2

She stepped last of all through the archway of light that she had woven between star and standing stone. As the blue light enveloped her, it blinded her to the world below at the same time that it opened her sight into its interstices, paths leading off at every angle of past, present, and future. Yet her gaze remained fixed on a lodestone falling behind: Her daughter, a stranger to her, lay asleep on cold earth while each step took her farther away from the child because she had to follow the sparks made by the passing of Sorgatani's wagon. She dared not lose them.

As she was losing Sanglant for a second time.

She saw in him flashes. With each step he and his army receded; with each step her vision blurred, or his army got larger, a mass of soldiers attended first by two Quman banners, then four, then eight, a succession of images, glimpses into the future as days or weeks passed outside the weaving.

How long would it be until she saw him again?

Emotions shone in as many colors as the blazing stars, woven together to create the thread of her being: a sense of triumph at the ease with which she had woven the crown, a gnawing doubt that she had done it wrong and they would end up cast onto unknown shores, grief at leaving her daughter and husband behind yet again, anger at Anne, the weight of responsibility she had taken on, desire in thinking of him but that would distract her so it must not be thought of except that he had a very particular way of laughing when –

'Liath!'

She stumbled on uneven ground and went down on one knee. A strong arm steadied her as her head reeled and her legs gave out. She would have fallen flat if someone hadn't been holding her up.

'Just so tired,' she murmured, amazed.

A breeze chased her hair, whipping her braid along her shoulder. Dust eddied along bare earth.

'Where are we?' she whispered.

She looked up. Down the slope of a small mountain valley stood the familiar tower where she had studied for many months. She had left this place only days ago, or so it seemed.

Verna.

She went all hazy, breath punched out of her.

She woke to find herself lying on her cloak under the shade of an apple tree while Lady Bertha, seated beside her, cut worms out of apples. Bertha's padded tunic was blotched with sweat. A cord tied her hair back from her face, although the ragged ends didn't reach her shoulders.

'It's summer, no doubt of it,' Bertha was saying to someone out of her line of sight.

Liath stared into the canopy of an apple tree whose contours she recalled clearly from her time spent in Verna. She had eaten many apples off this tree. Once she and Sanglant had snuck out here at night and made love under these branches while the night breezes – or Anne's captured daimones – played around them. But he was far away now, lost to her. Months had passed for him while she had stepped through a single night. She could scarcely fathom it, yet the ache never left her and the apple tree reminded her bitterly of what she had left behind.

'If we're in the mountains, we must hope to find a pass that will lead us north to Wendar or south to Aosta,' Bertha continued.

Liath groaned and sat up.

'Liath!' Breschius loomed over her, a slice of apple crushed between his fingers.

'Don't look at me so! I'm well enough. Weaving the crown taxed my strength, that's all.'

'Do you know where are we?' asked Bertha.

'Ai, God. I fear I do. We've come to the ruins of Verna. In one night we've come from the uttermost eastern wilderness all the way to the centralmost massif of the Alfar Mountains.'

Bertha whistled appreciatively. 'It's true that with such power a man could strike all unexpected at his enemies. Eagles could cross vast distances with only a few strides.'

'Except for this matter of days and months passing in that night,' said Breschius, apparently continuing a conversation Liath's waking had interrupted.

'*When* is it?' Liath demanded. 'On this all our success depends.'

She set a hand on Breschius' shoulder and stood. The earth

stayed steady as she swept her gaze over the scene: Heribert's fine hall was charred and fallen, the old tower was blasted with stones crumbled at its base, and the sheds had burned down. Soldiers picked grapes in the riot of greenery that marked the vineyard, untended for several years. Fir and spruce covered the upper slopes of the valley except where fire had ripped through, leaving the skeletons of trees. Three mountains, Youngwife, Monk's Ridge, and Terror, towered above, their immense heights more rock than snow.

'Summer,' she said. From farther away, she heard the splash of water over rocks; many streams drained down into the valley to feed the overgrown garden and the pond, hidden behind a grove of leafy beech. The sun stood high overhead.

'It is summer, my lady,' agreed Brother Breschius, 'or so it seems.'

Their party had not set up camp, but the men had taken advantage of the slope and breadth of the valley to graze, water, and rest the horses. Sorgatani's wagon rested in the middle of a sward of new grass; her cohort of Kerayit warriors ranged around like a fence, although obviously the marchlanders had been warned to stay clear.

Liath's Jinna servants, Gnat and Mosquito, knelt a stone's toss from her, trembling like dogs straining against a leash; it was only after she nodded at them that they settled back on their heels to wait with more patience. Sorgatani's young serving-woman crouched in the shade of the next apple tree, watching Liath. Heat rippled through the mountain air, or was that an aery daimone? She had never been able to see them before, but now she detected flickers of movement.

'We arrived at dawn,' said Bertha, 'and you slept all morning.'

'We'll have to wait for nightfall,' Liath said. 'I'll try to speak to Hathui with Eagle's Sight, and after that I'll measure the stars. We must decide whether we march, or attempt the crowns again.'

'If I recall the lay of the land correctly,' mused Bertha, 'we can scarcely come much closer to Aosta than this and still tread quietly.'

'Nay.' She shook her head, disappointed with herself. 'Had I more experience weaving the crowns, we would not have landed here. I have seen the Crown of Stars laid out across the land. South and east of here, near the shore of the Middle Sea, lies the central jewel of that crown. That is where we must go, because Anne will go there as well. If we are not too late – if this is only a few months after we set out from the east – then there is time, a full year or more.'

Breschius licked the sticky remains of the apple off his fingers. 'We could march through Aosta and along the eastern shore of the sea to seek this crown.'

'So we could. And fight every step of the way, first through Aosta and then into Dalmiaka, which is ruled by the Arethousans. Should we survive, we'll have lost the element of surprise. That is all that gives us an advantage. I'll observe the stars tonight while the army rests and prepares. Tomorrow night we cross again.'

'I pray you, my lady,' said Breschius softly, 'teach me how to calculate the date by means of the stars. I know that when the Dragon rises at dusk it is spring-tide and that the Child rises to the zenith at midnight during autumn. Mok rides around the Houses of the Night every twelve years, and the Evening Star and the Morning Star are the same and rise and set according to a regular pattern. Can you teach me?'

She smiled at the frater. His answering smile gave his face a liveliness that revealed his strong heart, his courage, and an affectionate warmth that brought a touch of red to her own cheeks, seeing that he was a comely man, if rather old – certainly past forty.

'Yes, Brother. I will need my own schola of mathematici if I am to combat Anne.'

'A schola!' muttered Bertha in tones of disgust. Then she laughed. 'We have only one cleric. Is that enough for a schola?'

'It makes no matter to me whether a discipla is a cleric or a woodcutter's child, Lady Bertha. I will teach any woman or man who brings patience, a good memory, and a willingness to learn.'

By the lift of her head Liath could see she had startled the noblewoman. 'Any woman or man?'

'Any, no matter their station in life or what they are now, as long as they will work, for it is a difficult and dreary labor and few will have the taste for it. At dusk, assemble those who wish to watch and listen.'

'What will you do?' Breschius asked.

'I know what day we left the steppes because you and Heribert kept a close record of the days during your journey. It is possible we have skipped months or years by traveling through the crowns.'

'How can that happen?'

'I walked in the land of the Aoi for only a few days while years went by here on Earth. When we cross through the crowns, we touch the aether, where time passes differently than it does in the world below. I suppose there must be a way to calculate how much time any crossing would take. We know how long ago the Aoi land was cast into the aether. If we knew Eldest Uncle's exact age, we could discover how long a day in the aether expands into a day or month here on Earth. Then, if we knew how far we wished to travel between two crowns, we might predict how long we would spend within the crowns as we cross that distance. Unless there is some other factor that alters the measure of days. What if the time doesn't remain as a constant, if a day measured within the aether doesn't always equal a month on Earth but fluctuates—'

'Ai, God!' said Bertha, laughing. 'You've lost me! What if we've walked right past the cataclysm? What if it's already happened?'

'We would know if the cataclysm had rocked us while we crossed between circles. We would have felt its impact because of the thread that connects the exiled land and Earth. We still have time. I must see which of the wandering planets appear in the heavens, and where they walk. Then I can calculate backward to the places they stood when we first entered the crown in the east. That will give me a rough date.'

'The lore of the mathematici be no secret if any woman or

man is allowed to learn it,' said Bertha abruptly.

'What is hoarded among a few loses its power when more share it. Only think of what might happen if more than Eagles learn the trick of gazing through fire. If merchants can hire sorcerers to weave the crowns and allow them to cross over these mountains safe from avalanches and bandits. Only think of Anne's power, which she has guarded well. If there were more to combat her, she would not be skopos now, with the king dangling from a chain of her devising. Amulets protect us from her gaze, but they also cripple us because we cannot use my Eagle's Sight, lest it expose us. We can risk the sight once a day at most, as I arranged with Sanglant. If we did not fear, we would not be so weak. As I know myself, for I was fearful and weak once, too.'

'You would even teach the common-born folk?' Bertha demanded.

'Those who can learn. Why not? Da and I lived among highborn and lowborn alike. I saw no great difference between those born to a high station and those from the most humble. Some chose wickedness and some good. Some chose an honest path, and some chose a road paved with lies. Some were clever, and some had no more wits than a sheep. Any Eagle could tell you as much, for they are all of them born of low station yet they walk along paths frequented by princes.'

Bertha was looking at her strangely. 'You are born out of a noble line.'

'Am I? I am not Anne's daughter. I am not Taillefer's great grandchild. Da was born to a noble line, it is true, but I suppose they might have been free farmers digging a foothold into untamed land in the time of my great grand-mothers. Why should I be prouder than Hathui? Why should I hold myself above *her*? With the gold she claimed from the Quman she'll dower her nieces and nephews and who is to say that, if they prosper, their children's children might not marry a noble lady's sons and daughters? Or that a lord fallen on hard times might not send his youngest son into service as a soldier in another lord's army, and if that boy ever mar-ries and if his fortunes fall further, his children's children might be no better off than that of a servingman who obeys the will of a count.'

When she stopped, having run out of breath, she saw they were staring at her as though she had been raving, a lunatic run wild right before their eyes.

'I pray you,' said Bertha, 'fetch her some wine.'

Gnat and Mosquito leaped eagerly to the task, bringing a flask of wine and a tray of bread and cheese as well as a freshly plucked bunch of exceptionally sweet grapes.

Bertha left her under Breschius' care and went to walk among the troops.

'I have troubled her,' she said at last to Breschius. 'I didn't intend to. I wasn't thinking.'

'You have traveled a strange road, my lady. The touch of the aether must alter a person's vision.'

'It did.' She looked after Lady Bertha, who was laughing with a pair of soldiers. Yet she was master and they were servants, evident by the way they stood each next to the others, the amount of space between them, their postures as the noblewoman made a final comment and moved on. 'There is no going back to what I was before. Nor would I want to.'

Breschius nodded agreeably. He did not seem to think she was insane. 'It's true the blessed Daisan teaches us that all souls are equal before God.'

'Then why are they unequal on Earth?'

'Their position, not their souls, are unequal on Earth. God ordered the world so, my lady. That is why.'

'That's not really an answer, is it? Did God so order the world? Or did humankind order it so and give the claim to God to justify their actions?'

'You tread close to heresy, my lady.'

'Do I?'

He smiled, and she could see that he was not one whit offended. This was a man who liked to wrestle with difficult questions. 'You do. So I ask you this: What other order might obtain? How else can humankind prosper, if there are not some who command and others who serve? If we have no order in the world, then we will live in chaos, no better than the wild beasts. Even among the beasts, the strongest take what they wish and the weak die.'

'Beasts don't think, not in any way like to us,' she said stubbornly, but she could not answer his question. God had so ordered the world, with regnants above and slaves below and the rest each in their own place. How could she change it?

'Yet I will teach any person who comes to me, no matter their station,' she said, peeling the sour skin from a grape and tasting the sweet center. 'They must only show themselves willing and able to learn.'

He chuckled. 'Anyone, lady? Even these two Jinna idolaters?'

Gnat and Mosquito were watching her in the manner of dogs hoping to catch their master's intent and mood. She was still learning to tell them apart. Mosquito was the one with the round scar on his left cheek and a missing tooth. Gnat had broader shoulders, a broader face, and was missing the thumb on his right hand.

'Would you learn the sorcerer's skill, if you could?' she asked them in Jinna. 'Master the knowledge of the stars?'

They considered, looking into each other's faces as if what one thought, the other could read by means of a lip quirked upward or the wrinkle in a brow.

Finally, Mosquito spoke. 'Who would teach us, Bright One?'

'I would.'

Again they spoke to each other by means of expression alone, and this time when they were finished, Gnat replied. 'We will do as you command, lady.'

'But do you wish it?'

'Yes, lady,' they said.

Breschius smiled, watching them. 'What do they say?'

'I don't know whether they wish to please me, or to learn!'

'It is for this reason that princes must defend themselves against flatterers. Slaves are in some measure like courtiers, because they fear – rightly enough – that they have no existence without the good favor of the master. Therefore, it can never be known whether they speak truth, or lie to protect themselves.'

She smiled, liking him very well. 'Have some more grapes, Brother. I pray you, do not flatter me only because you think I desire it, for I do not. I think we should see if there are any likely *disciplas* among our party in addition to these two. If you agree to this task, I will expect you to teach what you learn to others, and to be my captain. If you will.'

He considered her with an unnerving intentness, as though he saw a different face hiding behind her own. 'Will you raise an army of sorcerers and become an empress?'

'I have no taste for empire. I do not wish to rule over others and make them do my bidding. I don't need a court of flatterers surrounding me! If I can defeat Anne, then I want to delve into the mysteries of the heavens and of Earth. There is so much to know and understand. That will be enough for me.'

A smile touched his lips, then vanished. 'You remind me of someone I once knew,' he murmured, 'who was dear to me.' He inclined his head, touched fingers to forehead in a gesture of respect, and met her gaze. 'I will be your captain, my lady.' His expression held a spark of laughter; he rubbed the stump of his missing hand and pressed it against his chest, over his heart. 'I will gladly serve as you command.'

Sanglant always had a hard time sitting still, but sit he did for the entire afternoon under the shade of a canopy that was all that sheltered him from a hot summer sun. The supplicants waiting for a turn to speak to him had no such shelter, but he had directed Captain Fulk to make sure that each soul there was given a cup of something to drink, although it depleted the army's stores. The stories had begun to sound the same, and yet every woman and man who knelt before him grieved his heart.

'I pray you, Your Highness. No rain fell all summer and the wheat died on the stalk. We've nothing to eat but berries and grass, and nothing to lay in for stores for the winter.'

'God help us, Your Highness. Bandits have raided our

village twice. My daughter and son were stolen.'

'It was the plague killed my family, all but me and my cousin, Your Highness. We didn't dare bury them, it was so bad. We had to abandon our village.'

'I pray you, Your Highness. Help us.'

Although he had nothing to give them, each one went away lightened, as if the touch of his hand alone could ease their troubles. As if the griffins he had tamed made him a saint. His mood was sour and his shoulders itched from the sweaty tunic, but he dared not show discomfort. His trivial cares were nothing compared to the suffering these people had endured.

The field in which his army camped lay in the marchlands, in border country where no person quite knew what land lay under the suzerainty of which lady or lord. Most of the folk here believed they lived in Eastfall, but few were certain; their concerns were more immediate and so pressing that they braved a camp inhabited by two gleaming griffins, one staked and hooded but the other roaming free.

'There's two noble families at feud, Your Highness. They've begun stealing our sheep although we're just farming folk. Their quarrels mean nothing to us. Can you stop them?'

'My lord prince, our monastery was burned by the Quman and half the monks killed, those who hadn't time to hide. All our precious vessels and vestments were stolen by the barbarians. We lost our entire crop, for there wasn't anyone to harvest it.'

The petitioner, Brother Anselm, clearly chewed his nails, and looked as if he wished he could do so now as he glanced toward that section of camp where war bands of eight Quman tribes had set up their tents. Their wings fluttered in a rising wind blowing up from the southeast; their banners snapped. Gyasi stood directly behind Sanglant with arms crossed, his blank expression more terrifying than any glower.

'Be at ease, Brother,' said Sanglant. 'These Quman serve me, not their former master. Go on.'

The monk bobbed his head too quickly and stammered as he continued. 'W—we live as well as we can in the ruins, but this summer two score foundling boys were left at the gatehouse. One was just an infant. No doubt their families can't feed them. The older ones are good and eager workers, but we need seed to plant winter wheat, and for next spring's planting as well, and stores to tide us over this coming winter.'

It was getting near dusk, with dark clouds piling up on that wind, and he had spoken to no more than half the folk who waited here, some of whom had walked for days upon hearing that his army was marching through this region. Twenty score or more of them camped nearby, perhaps most of the population of the surrounding region. A few seemed eager to join his troop or to follow along behind the rear guard. Many seemed simply to desire assurance that someone, *anyone*, meant to protect them from whatever disaster would strike next. He could promise them so little, yet that he listened at all, that he had set foot in this land, seemed enough for most of them.

It burned at his heart. Henry should never have abandoned Wendar to chase after dreams of empire. Henry was needed *here*. The time to chase an empire was when your own house was strong, not when it was tottering.

'My lord prince!' Hathui strode up, her cloak flapping as the wind gusted. She was damp but in good spirits, with a grin that seemed likely to split her face. 'I bring news from Walburg. And from the fire.'

Walburg meant Villam, but the fire meant that Hathui had at long last spoken to Liath through flame. He beckoned impatiently to one of his stewards. 'Bring the Eagle something to drink!'

A soldier brought wine. Although it was turning, so sharp he could smell the flavor of vinegar, she gulped it down as wind shook the awning and made the tents and banners dance all down the long slope where the army had pitched camp. There was a commotion at the far edge of the tents, where Hathui's escort was moving in and, no doubt, startling the new recruits who had joined up in the days since he had sent Hathui and her escort on their detour to Walburg while continuing his own southwestward march.

It was hard to wait, but he did; he reined himself in, tapping one foot on the ground in a staccato until she was at long last finished although it hadn't taken her more than ten breaths.

'What news?' he asked in a low voice. 'What news of Liath?'

'Each night at dusk I've lit a fire and taken off my amulet and looked into the flame, just as we planned, but I've seen nothing. Until last night. She's at Verna.'

'Verna!' The name rocked him; he pushed so hard with his legs that his chair teetered, and Gyasi leaned forward to stop it tipping over.

Hathui shifted to put more of her weight on her other knee, the one not plagued by an old injury. 'Verna. That's what she said. She thinks it likely they'll cross back into the crowns tonight.'

It chafed him, for he had no skill to speak or see through fire, but perhaps it was for the best not to have to see her and hear her voice. That would be torment. Even the centaurs were beginning to look attractive to him, and he did his best to keep women well away from him. It was the only way to keep his promise to her.

'We've been five months marching at a hard pace,' he said at last, 'yet she leaps farther in one step.'

'So be it, my lord prince. We have each chosen our own path. Had you willed it, you might have crossed through the crowns, but you needed to shepherd the griffins and raise your army.'

'So I did. What of Villam? Has Lord Druthmar returned with you?'

'He has. The milites who marched east have gone back to their farms, all but the soldiers. He comes at the head of an army of five hundred, which is all the margrave can spare. These are her words: "My lord prince, march south if you must, but be swift in this task. Wendar suffers and will break apart if you linger too long in the southern lands as does your father. Beware. There are those in the southern lands who know the gift of Eagle's Sight. They will spy you out if they can, and prepare where they must. Go in haste. Bring home the crown and the mantle that will rule Wendar in peace once more."

He grunted, and brushed his fingers over the gold torque

at his neck that Waltharia had given him, symbol of his descent from the royal line. 'Is it my father she wishes to rule Wendar, or me?' he asked softly.

Hathui's smile cut. 'The margrave wishes for prosperity and peace, as do we all. That her people have not suffered as badly as some is due to her wise and prudent stewardship.'

'What do you think, Eagle? Ought I to remain in Wendar and restore what I can?'

She would not be drawn. 'I am the king's Eagle, my lord prince. I serve Henry. It is to Henry that I desire to return. Free him, and he will return to Wendar of his own volition and set all things right.'

'Very well. What of supplies?'

'Ten wagons.'

He gestured to a steward. 'Let two bags of seed grain be given to Brother Anselm. Brother.' The monk crept forward, tears in his eyes. 'Husband this grain well. Your monastery must become a refuge to all folk who suffer in difficult times. Hold fast.'

The monk kissed his hand, weeping openly. 'Bless you, Your Highness.' The steward led him away.

'Let the next one approach.'

A brawny man with arms the size of tree trunks shuffled forward; he was lame in one leg. His face looked odd until Sanglant realized that he lacked eyebrows. His face was red, but his gaze was steady.

'I am a smith out of Machteburg, my lord prince. By name of Johann.'

'How goes it in Machteburg? That's a long walk from that town to this place, if I judge it rightly.'

'A long walk, it's true, but I came east hearing a report that my sister's village was besieged by barbarians, these Quman. By the time we came, we saw no sign of them for they'd ridden on west into Avaria.'

'Your sister?'

'Still living, thank God. I stayed to help her people rebuild their village and forge weapons. I married again, for my wife died two years back of the lung fever. But I found these things out in the woodland where we went to get trees for the palisade.'

He gestured to the trio of men who followed at his heels and they opened leather bags and poured out a treasure trove of armor, pieces large and small as well as two complete suits of mail. The prince picked up a shoulder piece stamped with a dragon rampant and turned it in his hands. A gold tabard had been washed and mended, but many small tears and cuts obscured the black embroidery that adorned the front. Last of all they set down a shield; its rim had splintered and half of the middle had been stove in, but it was still possible to make out the remains of a dragon rampant matching that on the tabard and the shoulder piece.

'There'd been a battle, my lord prince,' said the blacksmith. 'This is what we found.'

'Dragons!' His skin burned where he touched the armor, and he dropped the shoulder piece as though it had scorched him. Bile rose in his throat. He had lived as a beast among the bones of his faithful Dragons for a year; he had discovered their remains and the leavings of their armor in the crypt at Gent. His sight dimmed as he struggled to prevent memory from overwhelming him.

'Ai, God! Look at that sky!'

Thunder cracked.

'Hold on to the tents!' cried Captain Fulk in the distance as soldiers raced among the tents. 'This should blow through—'

A wall of dark cloud, almost green, bore down on them. Wind whipped the tops of trees, and the folk waiting on the open ground ran for lower ground. Many threw themselves down on the earth as the wind roared over them, and even Hathui crouched and bent her head, tugging her cloak up to protect her face, but Sanglant stood.

The world might cast a thousand arrows at him; his enemies might raise winds and storms to slow him down, but as the gale streamed around him, as the awning strained at ropes held by soldiers, he braced himself against the onslaught and let the blast of rain scour him. Wind screamed. Hail drummed across open ground as people cried in terror, horses neighed, dogs barked, the griffins screamed in challenge, and the wind howled on and on. The storm boiled over them like a huge wave.

He had faced worse, and would face worse still. Hail peppered his head and chest. It had been too hot to wear his cloak, and he had nothing but his tunic to protect him, but he minded it not. The storm broke free the regrets and cautions that infested his heart.

He missed Liath bitterly, but he had done the right thing, the only thing. He must strike south and strike quickly. Free Henry, and then turn his sights north to restore peace to the land. If Henry remained a prisoner in Aosta, Wendar could never be at peace, no matter who pretended to rule there. If Wendar was not at peace, then he and Liath could never live at peace.

The storm blew past as quickly as it had come in, leaving the land strewn with branches, leaves, torn canvas, lost clothing, and every manner of weeping and wailing and shouts as folk picked themselves up and ventured to measure the damage, then cast themselves back on the ground as the female griffin launched herself into the air with a thunder of wings and flapped off on the trail of the storm.

Hathui had thrown herself flat to the ground when the griffin sprang, and now she unbent and rose with a sheepish grin, helping up the blacksmith whose stalwart nerves had been undone by the sight of that beast leaping into the sky. The man had fallen into the pile of armor, whose polished iron surfaces were now scumbled by damp leaves and streaks of grass and twigs and even feathers. Pellets of hail had fallen in between the pieces, collecting in hollows on the ground.

'Whew!' said Johann. 'That was a strong one! We had a blow last month that near tore down the houses. And look there! Beasts ride the wind. Some folk say the end of the world is coming. Can't say I blame them.'

'Make ready.' Sanglant bent to pick up the shoulder piece. The rain had cooled the iron; it didn't burn him now. 'Take this armor. Build your houses as sturdily as you can. A storm *is* coming, Blacksmith. You and your people must be strong to survive it.'

It alone of all the daimones bound into service in the vale had not fled on the day when its elder cousins had come calling with a conflagration that had set even the heights of the mountains on fire. Though the thread binding it to Earth had been severed by the edge of a griffin's feather, although it was free to escape back to the sphere that had given it birth, it had remained to haunt the buildings and the orchard.

As a lower form of daimone, it had little memory and less will, easily bound and easily trained, more like a hound than a man and yet unlike because it was a creature whose aetherical body could not be touched by earthly ills and earthly mortality.

Yet its captivity had altered it, given it a semblance of human memory and will beyond that granted to its cousins. It persisted here, it waited, although it had forgotten what it waited for: A familiar touch. A familiar voice. A familiar presence. It lingered among the burned-out ruins.

One dawn as the sun rose the dead stones sparked and spit out a stumbling collection of mortal beasts, some on two legs and others on four, a confusing starburst of colors and heat and voices. It raced down on the wind to investigate, curling around the newcomers. None saw it; they were blind. Only there was one they kept enclosed in a little house on wheels, and this one had power to see both what lay above and what lay below and when it insinuated itself through a crack the creature spoke to it, so it fled.

It fled, but there remained a greater threat. The Bright One, child of flame, had returned, the one who had brought the conflagration down upon them. It concealed itself in the boughs of an apple tree, too frightened to approach the creature with a heart of flame yet so curious it wished to see what was going on. In the end apprehension mastered it, and it fled to the hut where it had in times before slept alongside the familiar presence of the one it longed for.

There it hid until nightfall, venturing out when darkness

might hide it from mortal eyes, but the Bright One and her retinue still inhabited the valley, and it feared they meant to stay and perhaps even to call the elder cousins down upon them all again in a terrible, incandescent bloom.

'That is the River of Heaven,' the Bright One was saying to an audience of eight shivering souls seated by the stones beside the remains of a dying fire. 'See how the Serpent is swimming across it.'

'It's so bright!'

'Those are the souls of the dead, streaming upward to the Chamber of Light. Or so the church says.'

'What else could it be?'

'The ancient writers had many explanations. Look there! Mok still resides in the Unicorn. There is Jedu – that red star – rising with the Penitent. I do not see the Red Mage or Somorhas. The moon hasn't risen yet, if it means to rise at all. The mountains block part of our view, as well. As the hours pass, we'll look for the other wandering planets, but already I can guess that about four to six months have passed since we left the east.'

'How can you guess that?'

'It isn't really a guess. The planets wander along the ecliptic in a regular pattern. Mok spends about one year in each house, Jedu from one to two months or as many as six months if it is in retrograde—'

Two voices spoke, overlapping.

'You've lost me!'

'What is "retrograde"?'

A ripple of laughter raced around the cluster of seated figures. The Bright One stood and went to lean against the wagon. Its door stood open, a stick propped against it to hold it wide, and a figure stirred, hidden behind a curtain of beads, peering outward.

'Nay,' said the Bright One as she brushed fingers over the beaded curtain. 'I'm going too fast. Let me start at the beginning. We stand on the Earth, which is a sphere. Earth lies at the center of the universe, so the scholars claim, which is also a sphere. But I wonder – nay, never mind that now. The

Earth is encircled by the seven planetary spheres and by the outermost sphere, that of the fixed stars. Beyond that lies the Chamber of Light.'

As her voice flowed on, the stars crept along their fixed paths across the heavens. Later, after the moon rose, the watchers slept, all except the Bright One and the hidden woman, who ventured outside, heavily veiled. These two spoke in quiet voices far into the night, and now and again held their faces close to the flames of a campfire, as if staring within.

Toward dawn, the veiled woman climbed back inside her cage as the camp roused. By torchlight and moonlight men and horses made ready to depart. The Bright One wove threads of starlight into the stones, and one by one the visitors crossed through the brilliant gateway and vanished.

Last of all, the Bright One turned, there at the verge.

'Who are you waiting for?' she asked. Then she was gone.

The blazing threads frayed and collapsed in a shower of sparks. Dust eddied around the base of the stones before settling. Shadows faded. The peaks dazzled as the sun crested the eastern heights and its light caught the blinding white snow fields. On one of those heights a cliff of snow calved loose and roared downslope in a tumble that shook the valley as a white haze rose off the mountain. The avalanche of snow and ice roared and boomed and at length slowed, gentled, and came to rest, still so high above the tree line that it was impossible to see any change in the shape of the mountain itself. The cloud of snow and ice sparkled and sank.

A leaf drifted in on the breath of the avalanche, spinning and dancing, at play among the stones, but although the daimone chased it, the leaf was a dead thing, its spirit fled, and it could give no companionship to one who was lonely.

Who are you waiting for? the Bright One had asked it, but only the wind moaning through the stones answered.

'Who? Who?'

3

'Your Excellency, we've had word that the honored presbyter and his party arrive today.'

Antonia set aside her book. The library in Novomo had so few volumes, even supplemented with those she had removed from the convent of St. Ekatarina, that she had been forced to reread St. Peter of Aron's *The Eternal Geometry* three times in the last nine months, although she still didn't comprehend more than a third of it. Lady Lavinia's steward waited beside the door, hands folded, as Lavinia paced to the unshuttered window. Light pooled on the table, illuminating the precious chronicle and the huge map inked onto a sheep's hide cured and treated but left intact instead of cut in sheets for vellum.

'He will bring news of my daughter. There was talk of marriage to one of the king's Wendish lords, although I would hate to see her forced to live in the cold north. Yet if Father Hugh thinks it for the best . . .'

Lavinia was a loyal and righteous woman and certainly devout enough that she insisted Antonia deliver the sermon in her household chapel every Ladysday, but she had long since developed an unfortunate infatuation for the handsome presbyter and treated him more as if he were God's bright messenger than one of God's humble servants.

'He would not countenance any alliance that might bring her to harm, not after saving her from Ironhead and introducing her into the queen's household. She is quite the queen's favorite, I hear. A marriage to a Wendish lord would improve the family fortunes. We could seek further alliances in the north for my kinfolk. But there is a boy of good family in southern Aosta, too, whose family has shown interest in a match with our house.'

As she rattled on, still staring out the window, Antonia cut quills. The lady's concerns were the heart of the round of life on Earth; a lady must steward her estates and prepare for the next season, breed her herds and tend her gardens. How her children married affected the prosperity of her household and the longevity of her line, and every noble lady and lord had a duty to perpetuate the lineage out of which they themselves flowered.

These toiled worthily in the service of God, who had created all, but they had not been fitted with the task of supervision. That task fell to the elite.

'With all this talk of the emperor and empress riding east to Dalmiaka to make war against the Arethousan Emperor – I don't know what to expect. None of us know what to expect.'

'Only God can see into the future, Lady Lavinia.'

'So true, Your Excellency! So very true!'

'Do not forget the tale of Queen Salome, who feared that a usurper would supplant her and so went to the witches and begged them to spy into the future on her behalf by raising the ghost of the prophet.'

'Yes, indeed. So it came to pass that for her impiety, a worthy successor took her place.'

'Yet was Queen Salome not a worthy regnant? She was humble. God Themselves raised her up to her high state. It was disobedience, not impiety, that caused her downfall. The witches did as they were told, and were not punished for their act. But the queen had disobeyed God's voice when God commanded her to kill the tribe of Melia.'

'She was a mother herself! She did not like to put children to death.'

'God may often call upon us to do things that may seem distasteful to our imperfect understanding, but we must never hesitate. Obedience is righteousness.'

With such lessons Antonia strove to educate Lady Lavinia and her household. Hugh had hidden her in plain sight, installed her as a member of Lavinia's schola, although in truth few visitors came and went from the lady's palace and fewer still from the court in Darre and least of all any clerics from the palace of the skopos, who might have cause to recognize and betray Antonia.

'Very true, very true,' said the lady distractedly as she leaned on the casement and squinted out into the molten Setentre sun. 'There! I see them.' She crossed to the door, paused, and turned. 'Will you come to meet them, Your Excellency?'

'I am not walking well today, Lady Lavinia. Best if I bide here and have a tray brought up for my supper.'

'As you wish, Your Excellency.' She hurried out.

Better if Hugh comes to me, as a steward attends his mistress. Perhaps the ploy was beneath her, but her position seemed weak and Hugh's all the stronger, and she felt it necessary to do what she could to remind him of her lineage and stature and the respect he owed her. She heard only such news as had trickled northward in the months since Decial, when she had arrived here still reeling from her imprisonment. Little enough to feed on, but she had learned to survive on scraps, and she now possessed the entire library hauled out of St. Ekatarina's Convent, most especially their chronicle, the work of many hands and many generations, a treasure-house of knowledge and observation.

She had read through the chronicle so many times that she had memorized entire passages, and as she shifted in her chair, she studied the map with immense satisfaction, knowing her work in deciphering the tangle of hints scattered throughout the manuscript like gems in a field of wheat had proved fruitful.

Sooner than she expected, Hugh came to wait on her. He, no less than she, knew they possessed information of incalculable value.

'This is it?' he asked, after a perfunctory greeting and after banishing his servants from the chamber. There remained only one beardless, thin man who cowered at the door looking ready to flee and never spoke one word as Hugh set hands on the table and studied the map.

From this angle, examining him, she understood why Lady Lavinia had cause to be grateful to this man beyond his service to the lady by saving her young daughter from rape. God favored few souls with such exceptional beauty. Yet he did not overplay his hand; he dressed plainly, without unseemly flourishes. He wore clothing of such fine weave it seemed invisible, his over-tunic dyed to a muted wheat gold and beneath it a reddish-golden under-tunic shining with the intensity of hot coals, barely seen but startling, the kind of detail that made you look twice. He wore three simple rings – emerald, citrine, and lapis lazuli – and his gold presbyter's chain and Circle of Unity. Only the gold chain, and his clean-shaven face, marked him as a churchman, although one might guess at his vocation because his hands were so remarkably clean, nails trimmed, and the skin smooth and unlined. No calluses or blisters marred his hands, but in truth they looked strong enough to throttle any soul who did not do his bidding. The mute manservant shifted nervously, took a step forward to get a look at the map, but when Hugh glanced at him, he slunk back to the door and quivered.

'This is the tale you gleaned from the convent's chronicle,' said Hugh at last.

'It is.'

The sheepskin had arrived six months ago with the known lands inked in by a master cartographer, the hinterlands marked in cruder dimensions – a sheep's head to represent the western island kingdom of Alba, the horns of a goat to suggest the northern reaches where the Eika barbarians nested, the blank emptiness of untracked deserts beyond the shore of the Middle Sea, and the geometric oblong marking the unknown reaches of the Heretic's Sea that lay north and east of the Arethousan capital. Dragons lay to the east and beyond them grass and sand and the distant glories of Katai. By careful measurement and guesswork, she had marked on this map each stone circle mentioned in the nuns' chronology.

'Every one you have marked here?' he asked.

'Every one, to the best of my knowledge of the land and as well as it is described within the text. The nuns of St. Ekatarina's recorded all things precisely. No fables and superstitions marred their pages. They set down what they heard as accurately as possible. I did the same.'

'Here.' He placed a finger on the map east of the Wendish marchlands and a little north of the kingdom of Ungria, although the borderlands of such places could not be marked with any precision, since they fluctuated with the season and the year.

She waited.

'Here,' he repeated. His finger covered a circle representing a known crown, with the number of stones inked inside. *Seven*. 'The Holy Mother has commanded me to journey east. I will oversee the crown discovered by Brother Marcus during his travels through the wilderness lands that lie north of Ungria and south and east of Polenie. Seven stones. One of the original crowns, so Mother Anne has decided.'

'How will you get there? That is a journey of many months' undertaking, through perilous country.'

He removed his finger. The servingman moved a foot, and a plank creaked, and the poor man winced, as startled as if a lion had burst out of the woodwork. 'I will travel by means of the crowns. Now that we have a better idea of the placement of each of the crowns, it is apparent—' He brushed a hand over *The Eternal Geometry*. '—that by using geometry the threads can be woven to open a passage from one specific crown to another. Depending on the rising and setting of the stars and their altitude at the time of passage, and allowing for angle and distance, I must reach east and north from Novomo using the threads from stars in those quadrants.'

'Other crowns stand between Novomo and this distant place. Might these not confuse your passage?'

'It is possible. If I can move swiftly enough, then I can correct for my mistakes and try again. I am confident that my calculations are correct. They have been double-checked by the Holy Mother herself. Her skills as a mathematicus are unequaled.'

'Except perhaps by her daughter.'

The felicity of his expression stilled and became rigid. He drew his finger south from the Ungrian border to the Heretic's Sea and farther south yet into desert wilderness surrounding the holy city of Saïs, west to the ruins of Kartiako, then west and northwest to the disputed lands lying between southern Salia and the Jinna kingdom of Aquila, yet north and west again to the sheep's head that marked Alba, and farther north yet to Eika country, inscribing a vast circle – a crown of sorts – across the continent of Novaria. By the time this was done he had recovered the mobility of his smile.

He beckoned. The servingman shuffled forward and handed him a brass disk engraved with marks and adorned with a bar on one side and a curling nest of circles, a smaller one superimposed on a larger, on the other.

'Except perhaps by her daughter,' he echoed. 'Do you know what this is?'

'I do not,' she admitted.

He did not offer to let her hold it. 'It is an astrolabe, which the Jinna use both as an observational instrument and a calculating device. It offers precision, and foreknowledge. I need only determine the altitude of a single star and with that information can tell which stars are about to rise and which have just set. You see there are several disks nestled here, each one a climate for a different latitude. If I am pulled off course, it will be quick work to forge a new path. I will get there.'

'Geometry holds many mysteries for me still, Father Hugh. Now that you must journey east, what thought have you given to my role here in Darre?'

After a measure of silence, during which the servingman shifted twice onto the creaking board before moving to avoid it, Hugh sat on the bench opposite Antonia and set his fine hands flat on the map, covering Wendar and Varre. 'The Holy Mother Anne has departed Darre for the east with the emperor and the army.'

'To the old imperial lands of Dalmiaka, so I have heard.'

'What you have heard is true. For many years Anne supposed the central crown of the great crown lay at Verna, but now she realizes she is mistaken. This crown—' He pointed to a mark lying on the shore of the Middle Sea about halfway between Aosta and Arethousa. '—must come into our control. Therefore, a conquest. Empress Adelheid is pregnant again—'

'Again!'

'—so she remains in Darre. I have encouraged her to bring you into her schola. Go there now. Prepare the ground.'

'Prepare the ground?'

'We have spoken of this before. The cauda draconis has a particular role to play when a great spell is cast.'

The cauda draconis died, but since he did not say so out loud, neither did she. She waited. Let him show his strengths and weaknesses first; then she would know how much to conceal and reveal.

'Yet we need not stand passively.'

'God's will must be accomplished,' she agreed.

'So it will be, Sister Antonia. But in order to accomplish God's will the righteous ones must wield power.'

She nodded. 'You are ambitious.'

He bowed his head. 'I serve God, and the regnant. That is all.'

He was lying, of course. Yet what difference did it make? In all the years of the church, no man had been skopos. Hugh had risen as high as he could. He needed her. For the time being, she needed him.

'I will journey to Darre and join Empress Adelheid's schola.'

'She will welcome you, Sister. You will be satisfied with the arrangements. You will be shown the respect due to you.' He picked up the astrolabe and rose. 'We must be patient, and cautious. Now we walk on the knife's edge. Now is the most dangerous time. It would have been best if I had remained with the emperor, but the Holy Mother has given me a different part to play. Be wary. Be strong.'

'You will not find me lacking, Father Hugh. I am aware that the hour of need draws close.'

'"All that is lost will be reborn on this Earth because of a Great Unveiling like to that Great Sundering in which vanished the Lost Ones." As it was said: "There will come a furious storm."'

'To overset the wicked.'

He shrugged. 'The innocent may drown in the same tide that sweeps away the wicked.'

'Then they were not innocent, if God did not choose to protect them!'

Because she was seated, he had the height to loom over her, and because he was beautiful, she felt, briefly, diminished, as though visited by the messenger of God, who stood in judgment upon her in all its glory and found her wanting.

Antonia did not like to feel diminished.

But his lips twisted up in an ironic smile, which betrayed his mortality and imperfection. 'I have never been sure of God's intentions,' he said softly. 'Much has been hidden from our eyes, and more than that is twisted and confused. Where we have seen a horse, perhaps we have mistakenly called it a cow.'

'Without conviction, there cannot be righteous behavior, Father Hugh. Be warned. Doubt is the tool of the Enemy.' She indicated the map. 'I know the shape of the world, and its place in God's plan. Do you?'

'I know what I want,' he said, and with that he made his farewells and departed.

4

The madman died soon after, leaving his corpse on the stone where he had slept. It was peace of a kind.

There came a string of screaming prisoners dragged down into the depths to walk the wheel, but none of them lasted more than a score of turnings. He discovered by searching with his hands several who died in their sleep, worn to nothing, so emaciated it was a miracle they had been able to walk. Another lay in agony with the flux for hours or days until at last he voided his soul as well as his guts. The sleeping hollow stank so badly afterward that the next four prisoners refused to sleep there, preferring the noisy ledge beside the wheel. Even the miners complained that the smell made them sick, so eventually a pair of workers dumped chalk in the hollow and after a few turnings swept it up again, but for many turnings afterward he shed chalk dust like skin and traced it into the creases of his body and rubbed it out of his hair, although in truth any substance in his hair was a relief against the crawling lice and the endless scratching.

One man slipped and broke his arm, and he died, too, for there was nothing to set it with and none of the guards cared to take the poor man back up, so the sweet sick smell of poison set in and the prisoner died suffering and babbling of nightmare visions. The next one leaped gibbering into the depths because he could not endure the darkness, and as the wheel rumbled on, strange noises echoed up from the pit where no miner walked – scraping and cracking, like dogs gnawing on bones.

Maybe it was better to be dead than living in this purgatory, which wasn't life or death but a state of abandonment in which neither the angels nor the demons could get their claws sunk into the flesh. He dreamed of sun and wind and the wide seas; he dreamed of the prows of dragon ships slicing through the swells as salt spray streamed against his face and wind snapped in his hair. But down here neither sun nor wind reached; he was buried, already entombed and awaiting only the final sentence.

The miners dug a transverse gallery and found, unexpectedly, a vein of silver-lead ore so rich that the levels sounded at all hours with the uneven staccato of picks and hammers at work and the rattle of four-wheeled barrows and the squinch of the windlasses hauling up filled buckets and the murmur of miners coming and going. They spoke of new shafts to be sunk and fortunes to be made, and yet always they whispered of the creatures that lurked in the pit where the richest deposits lay ripe for the pickings except for the danger of unstable tunnels and the fear of what waited below. Every day a bucket of purest silver was hauled up from the pit, and every day some dead creature or another pitched down into the darkness. Most of the dead men from the workings met their final resting place in this way although the overseer pretended that any prisoner who died while condemned to labor in the workings received a respectable burial and the blessing of a deacon.

All criminals were doomed to the Pit, surely, so what difference does it make if we trade their corpses for silver?

So they said, but their uneasiness wafted like the stink of the dead man's voided bowels through the levels until the mines reeked with guilt.

The wheels turned. He walked, because it was the only thing he remembered how to do. The dreams wicked away, swiftly come and swiftly gone, and if there had ever been any existence beyond the wheel, he had long since forgotten what it was. Whispers tickled him as smoke and steam did when a miner set fire to heat the rock and then poured water on it so it would crack. In these closed spaces he could smell and hear and taste every least tremor of life.

'They say he's protected by a twisted spell that looks like a bronze armband.'

'I think he's a demon.'

'An angel.'

'How else could he have survived so long? No man turns the wheels for as long as he has. Have you ever seen one last beyond two months?'

'Has he been down there two months?'

'Nay, three seasons or more.'

'I don't believe you!'

'I was here when they brought him in the spring. Mute and blind, if you please.'

'Hsst! It's almost winter! The levels make no difference to him! If he's touched in the head, he's like to an ox pulling in its traces. That would explain it. A mute beast.'

He walked, and he slept, and he ate, and walked and slept and ate, and again. And again.

Until the guards clattered down one turning and surrounded him, thrust a hapless, moaning prisoner into his place on the wheel, and hauled him up the ladders, up and farther up although it was no trouble to climb because he trudged so far every day, until a strange touch hissed against his skin and

he swayed, dizzily, as air opened around him and they emerged
from the workings.

So many smells! The perfume of earth made him reel. The
scent of fallen leaves and the stink of forges dug into his lungs
until he coughed. Sounds expanded, fading away into the
heavens, which were unbound by stone walls.

There were too many noises to sort through: the hammer
of picks breaking up rock; a man's shout; a goat's bleat; the
susurrus of wind; feet grinding on loose rock and squeaking
on damped down earth as a man halted before him.

Sour breath chased across his nostrils. The breeze carried
the rich tang of horse manure.

'Here's the one, Foucher.'

'Ai, Lord! What a stink! Best clean him up.'

'Do you think so? If we clean him up, no one will believe
he's survived below for so long. The duke won't be impressed.'

'Umm. True enough. But the highborn won't like the
stench.'

'Nor will any man, low or high. I can scarce endure it.'

'True words. This creature is something rarely seen. We've
got us a real prize here. He looks strong enough still.' The
point of a stick prodded him in the chest, but no hands touched
his body. 'He might last months more on the wheel.'

'Years more!'

'Do you think so, Captain? Think you so? That would be
a miracle!' Foucher snickered, enjoying this thought as
another man might enjoy the sport of laughing, innocent children.

'You feed on our misery,' he said to Foucher.

Silence from his captors, fed by drawn-in breaths.

'I thought he couldn't talk!' exclaimed the Captain.

A switch whistled, snapped against his ear.

Pain exploded in his head, that had for so long now been
a half-forgotten dull ache.

'So he shan't!' said Foucher. 'We'll take him over quickly.
Parade him before the duke and whip him if he speaks, then
haul him back down below.' Foucher hissed hard between
his teeth and the stick prodded him again, this time in the

stomach, but its thrust barely penetrated the pain raging in his skull. 'You'll keep quiet, Silent, if you know what's good for you!'

'Maybe this isn't wise—' protested the Captain.

'Nay, I already told the duke we'd a fine strange sight for him, so he's waiting. I hate to disappoint him.'

'Ai, indeed. He might do anything if we displease him. He's that angry already that there isn't more ore, nor did he like the sleeping conditions for the prisoners.'

'As if they deserve better!' The switch slapped against his buttocks. 'Get on! Get on!'

He stumbled forward. As the pain throbbed with each jarring step, vision flashed on and out as a man might catch glimpses in a dark room when a candle was covered and uncovered.

He saw feet so grimy and mottled with a scaly growth that they didn't seem human feet at all; then nothing, blinding darkness; then a swaying distant ocean of yellow and orange; then darkness; then the ocean again, but these were trees seen a long way away only it had been so long since he had seen trees painted with the colors of autumn that it had taken him this long to recognize them; then night as the clamor of the workings muted as they walked out beyond it; then mushrooms growing in sparse grass, only these weren't mushrooms but pale tents and graceful awnings sagging and rising in the wind with brightly colored creatures laughing and chattering and walking out under the sun. A magnificent, broad-shouldered lord stood among them whose skin was dirty yet after all not dirty but burned a deep brown complexion like that of Liath. Beside him clung a frail, pallid woman with hair the color of wheat. Her belly was swollen with pregnancy. She and her noble husband turned to see the curiosity that the foreman of the mines had brought for their amusement.

He saw her face. She was repulsed by the grime but otherwise disinterested. Yet he recognized *her*.

'Tallia,' he said, the word like the throttling gasp of a man as a noose tightens around his neck. A nail burned in his empty hand.

His voice woke memory in her. Her expression shifted and altered.

'She's pregnant,' he said. 'Tallia is pregnant.'

But it was a lie.

Her shriek cut through the pain. Darkness swallowed the brief stab of vision. He drowned.

'Conrad! Take him away! Make them take him away!'

'I pray you, Your Highness, we meant no offense,' gabbled Foucher. 'An amusement only, meant for your—'

'Lord have mercy!' swore the duke as the woman shrieked on and on and on, a grating wail that dissolved into hiccoughs and a whining sob. 'Take the creature away, Foucher. I know you meant no harm. It's a miracle, indeed, and he looks more like a goblin than a man with so much filth caked on him, although I wonder if you wouldn't get higher yields if your criminals lived under better conditions.'

'But my lord duke—'

'If I starved my soldiers and let them sleep out in the rain, they'd be too weak to fight. Why do you mistreat these poor souls?'

'The miners are hardworking free men, my lord duke. As for these others, they are only criminals. Half of them had a death sentence imposed on them for their sins but were shown mercy by being sent here instead.'

'A strange sort of mercy. It wasn't so bad last year, as I recall it. I never saw so many sickly creatures in my life. Look at the sores on that man!'

'He's no more than a mute beast, my lord duke. It's a miracle that he turns the wheel as well as he does. Think of it as his penance for the crime he committed.'

'Maybe so. No matter. Desperate times call for desperate measures. I have need of different miracles today such as more iron for my army and silver for minting coin. To add grief to all else we have word that the Eika have come back and are harrying the Salian coast! Take him away. Away! As for you, Foucher, my clerics will look over your records of the summer's yields.'

'Throw him into the pit! He should be dead! He's dead!'

'For God's sake, Tallia! Control yourself!'

A choked silence followed the crack of his words, and after it a sniveling whine that blended with the whisper of the breeze through distant leaves and the faraway noise of the workings and the sting of smoke from the charcoal fires set through the forest for leagues around.

'Should we throw him in the pit, my lord duke?' asked Foucher, voice trembling. 'He's a valuable worker. We've none so strong for the wheels as this one.'

'God Above! I hate wasting good labor. Nay, put him back to his task, as he was before. He's serving his sentence, just as we all are. Nay! Enough, Tallia! We'll speak no more on it!'

The switch stung his thigh. 'Get on! Get on!' said the Captain. 'This is all your fault!'

He stumbled, blind again, and tripped, and fell, but a hand grasped his arm, pinching his skin, and dragged him upright and hauled him away as he wept because she had betrayed him and he had betrayed Lavastine only he could not remember how. The past was closed to him. The blindness swallowed him up.

They came back to the workings, yet at the lip of the shaft a man's silky voice drew the Captain aside, saying, 'Here's two gold nomias for you, friend, if you'll cast that creature into the pit I hear tell you have beneath the levels, out of which no man ever emerges. You'll gain as well the favor of Her Highness Lady Tallia who, I should tell you just between you and me, will be Queen of Varre soon enough. Duke Conrad's war along the border against the Salians is going well. There's no word from Henry in Aosta. Varre will break free of the Wendish yoke soon. There's no one to stop Duke Conrad for he's born out of the same royal lineage as Henry, just as his lady wife is, and she with the right of primogeniture on her mother's side as well. Do what Lady Tallia wishes and you'll be glad of her favor in the days to come. Trust me.'

'Two gold nomias,' murmured the Captain, greed melting his voice until it wasn't a man's voice at all but that of the Enemy. 'I'll throw him in myself. Here, let me have them.'

'One now, one later when the deed is done. I'll go down with you and see you're given a second when you and I have come safely to the surface.'

'Fair enough! Fair enough!'

When they had pushed him and prodded him down the ladders past the turning wheels and their rumbling tumbling roar, they drove him to the edge of the Abyss where a cold wind blasted up from the depths and a smell of decay and sulfur swirled around his body. He did not fight them. He was too stunned because it had been a lie that she was pregnant; she had renounced the married state for all time and chosen to wed herself to God's service, hadn't she? God did not make bellies swell with pregnancy. Only men did that. What she withheld from him she had given to another man, and she had betrayed him to his death twice over, though he had loved her honestly and well.

With a thrust from the butt of a pick hard into his back, they shoved him over the edge, and he fell.

XXVI
AMONG THE DEAD

1

Silence did not come easily to Zacharias. Words screamed in his head every waking moment, but he had only vowels left him, a babble of ooo ah ee eh, all those strong glorious sounds shaped twixt tongue and lip cut clean off. He was a mute beast who could only moan and groan. It would have been better to be dead.

It would have been better to be dead than to have betrayed his sister.

Yet he did not die. Like a whipped dog he staggered at his master's heels cringing and slavering, communicating with gestures and a grotesque vocal mush that Lord Hugh sometimes deigned to interpret, for after all whatever Lord Hugh wished him to be saying surely was what he meant to say, wasn't it? He was a shadow, kept close by the iron chain that was Hugh's will and by fear. What if Hugh choked him again with the daimone?

At the end of a miserable summer they left Darre and journeyed north to the town of Novomo, where Novomo's mistress, Lady Lavinia, entertained Presbyter Hugh and his entourage lavishly and showered Hugh with attention and praise for his role in saving her daughter from an unnamed but obviously gruesome fate. Here they lingered only one day, however, because the heavens remained clear, and in the afternoon of the second day his retinue loaded pack mules and a pair of wagons with a king's ransom in provisions and traveling gear. With their escort of forty of Adelheid's crack Aostan cavalry they rode to a hillside outside Novomo where an old stone crown stood above slopes turned to white-gold after summer's searing heat.

The dozen servants, forty soldiers, and half a dozen clerics who made up Hugh's retinue waited in marching order as the sun sank toward the rugged western hills. Hugh led Zacharias forward to a patch of sandy ground – the only part of the hill not covered with brittle grass – and placed Zacharias directly in front of him, back to chest, placing into Zacharias' hand the arm's-length wooden staff used to weave threads of starlight into stone.

This mathematical weaving Hugh had been teaching him for months now, and tonight his learning, and his memory, would be put to the test. His knees trembled, his palms were damp, and his lips were cracked. Was it worth the price of his tongue to have the secrets he had so long wished to uncover revealed at last?

His tongue, perhaps. But not Hathui.

'There,' said Hugh. 'Do you see it? The first star. We must seek east and north to weave our path. We will hook the Guivre's Eye, rising to the northeast, and weave a net around the Eagle rising to the east.'

They would snare the Eagle, who had already been betrayed by her own brother. The staff quivered in his hand as rage shivered through him, but Hugh guided his arm. The staff rose as Hugh chanted words Zacharias would never be able to speak, although he now knew them by heart.

'Matthias guide me, Mark protect me, Johanna free me, Lucia aid me, Marian purify me, Peter heal me, Thecla be my witness always, that the Lady shall be my shield and the Lord shall be my sword.'

With Hugh's hand directing him as the first stars

shuddered into visibility in the purpling sky, he caught the threads of the stars with the staff and wove a pathway into the stones. The stars strained against this tether as the heavens churned inexorably onward, turning and turning with the wheel of night, and the entourage hurried nervously through the gleaming archway to vanish as if into thin air.

The threads pulled taut against the stones, stretching, thinning, and unraveling, before Hugh clapped him hard between the shoulders and shoved him forward after the final pair of riders in the rear guard. Zacharias stumbled through the gateway with the music of the heavens ringing in his ears and his legs as weak as an invalid's and his forehead and neck running with sweat. A steady throbbing buzzed up through his soles and all at once

he sees a girl asleep within a circle of attendants, a motley crew, certainly, for one of them is Anna to his utter surprise, and just as the vision flashes into darkness he realizes that it is Blessing, grown so large, trembling at the edge of womanhood

Sanglant rides at the head of an impressive army, Wendishmen and marchlanders and the ungodly banners, a dozen or more, of Quman tribes, a host of them to strike fear so deep that he wets himself. The prince does not ride in chains as their prisoner. He leads them, and yet he wears no griffin feather wings because he leads a pair of living griffins as easily as he might bring along a prized stallion and mare, their iron feathers gleaming so brightly that Zacharias is blinded

his head hurts

night drowns him as stunted shapes scuttle along rock and through tunnels, voices chattering and clacking as they converge on a pale corpse lying at the base of the shaft beside bronze-bound buckets half filled with nuggets of silver. They are so hungry that it gnaws his belly and he weeps with the pain of this constant starvation so many of them and all trapped here where they must labor in return for the merest dregs of foul nourishment without which they will all die and not merely the many who have already succumbed. They swarm, ready to descend on the corpse, but a sorcerous light bleeds from the arm of the dead man for he isn't dead at all

*and that precious totem they recognize as a sign passed down
through their generations. They back away, their whispers
echoing through the stone halls within which they are trapped*
    others walk in the labyrinth

    *he glimpses, briefly, the Eagle whom Prince Sanglant res-
cued from Bulkezu's horde, her hair gleaming like pewter as
she turns to glance around in surprise, as though she has seen
him. She vanishes down a side path, pushing a white-haired
woman along before her, but he does not see the older woman's
face before*

    *a wagon rolls far away, a tiny cottage on wheels with beaded
curtains rattling and smoke spinning upward from a hole in
the top, and beside it on a sturdy gelding rides a woman who
shines gloriously as the blue light pulses around her and all
at once refulgent wings blossom from her shoulders*

Zacharias fell hard up to his wrists in muck and pungent
manure, gasping and panting, chest tight.

'Liath!' said Hugh in a voice rough with passion, or anger.

'My lord presbyter! Your Excellency! We have been waiting for hours, Your Excellency! We despaired—!'

'God help us! He looks ready to faint. Grasp hold of my
arm, Your Excellency. Vindicadus, run down to the camp and
make sure my lord's chair is ready. Warm broth! This way,
Your Excellency.'

No one helped Zacharias up. Their voices faded as they
moved away from him, and it took some time before he had
the strength to lift his head and rise. Clouds chased across the
heavens. Below his feet the ground tumbled away into massive,
broken earthworks and farther down these leveled out to
become grassland and woodland and, to the north, a dense
forest of oak and pine. A river curved away until it was lost
among the trees. A piece of metal glinted far below on bare
earth, but when he shifted his weight onto his other foot, he
lost sight of it. His shadow fell before him, drawn long by sun
at his back. He turned, gasped in fright, and lifted a hand to
shade his eyes, but the looming figures that advanced on him
were nothing more than giant stones set into the earth – the
crown out of which he had staggered. Pinks, blue gentian, and

yellow stars bloomed on the grassy sward within the stones although whole stretches of ground consisted of dirt tamped down by a great weight now removed. Here and there cinquefoil speckled with yellow flowers crept through and around bleached bones lying scattered through the grass.

'Brother Zacharias!'

Two soldiers waited, arms crossed as they frowned at him. He stumbled after Hugh who, surrounded by his retainers, descended through the maze of earthworks.

A crude hamlet consisting of a dozen huts and several pit houses lay at the base of the hill, just within an eroded earthen gateway that closed off the labyrinthine earthworks from the open land beyond. There was such a dearth of refuse, with fresh pits dug close by for a necessarium and heaps of earth still crawling with worms and bugs, that Zacharias realized the tiny village was itself newly erected, not more than a year old and inhabited by two dozen or so dark-haired, pale-skinned folk. These natives cowered at the doors to their houses and, when Hugh appeared in his splendid garb, flung themselves prostrate to the ground.

Hugh studied them before speaking in an encouraging tone. His voice was no longer ragged with emotion, although he still looked pale.

'Brother Marcus said there was one among you who could interpret for the others – who would that be? Let that one come forward without fear. I am pleased with all I see and all that you have accomplished here. Fear no anger on my part.'

After a pause, a man raised up and by means of gestures indicated that someone was coming from outside the earthworks. One of Hugh's soldiers, by name of Gerbert, scrambled to the top of the nearest embankment.

'There's a small church half built out there, my lord,' he called down, 'and some men coming. They've a deacon with them.'

The gateway had once boasted a deep ditch crossing its opening as a form of defense, but the pit was now mostly filled in with debris although on one side recent scars showed where someone had started to dig it out again. Boards thrown over this sinkhole made a bridge. The procession that approached was led by a young deacon in stained and mended robes, who supported herself with a staff since she walked with a pronounced limp. She had a merry face and a cheerful smile that made her look extremely youthful, since her two front teeth were missing, and her bright, open expression sustained the shock of Hugh's presence without much more than a widening of her eyes and a trembling of her hands.

'My lord!' She knelt before Hugh. He offered her a clean, white hand, and she took it in a hand chapped and dirty from hard labor and kissed his fingers, but after this he squeezed his fingers over hers and indicated that she should rise.

'I am Presbyter Hugh, come from the skopos' palace in Darre with these retainers.'

'My lord.' She gazed at him with tears in her eyes, perhaps blinded by his beauty or overcome by the scent of rose water that clung to him. 'I am Deacon Adalwif, who watches over this flock on behalf of God, our Lord and Lady.'

'You are Wendish,' he said with surprise.

'So I am, my lord. My own people have their lands near Kassel, but after I came into orders, I walked east to preach among the Salavii heathens. Here you find me.' She nodded toward their audience, who watched in respectful silence. 'They are good folk, if rather simple, but their piety and hard work have proved them godly. You see that we have accomplished all of that task which Presbyter Marcus of Darre set before us two years ago. The stones are raised. Now we are engaged in erecting a church in order to hallow this ground and to keep the old heathen spirits away.'

'You have done well.'

'We do our best to serve God, my lord.' She hesitated as if to ask a question, but did not. 'Now you have come.'

'Here I will stay for the time being. I pray you, Deacon Adalwif, what day is it?'

She nodded. 'Brother Marcus told me that within the holy crowns the days might pass in different wise to that on the profane Earth. I have kept a careful track of days so that my flock may celebrate the feast days, as is fitting, and so that children may be named in honor of the glorious and holy saints. It is the feast day of St. Branwen the Warrior.'

He smiled, although a certain tension squeezed the curve of his lips. 'A glad day for arrivals! We departed Aosta most propitiously on the feast day of St. Marcus the Apostle.'

'St. Marcus!'

'It has taken far longer than I had hoped to come here.'

'Fully five months.'

'Almost six.'

'All these passed through in a single night?'

'In a single night,' he agreed, glancing up the hill, but the massive earthworks and the curve of the hill hid the crown from view. 'Yet,' he mused, 'what matter if six months pass in one night? We must wait here until Octumbre in any case, preparing for what is to come. I have a strong company to attend me, Deacon, as you have seen. We shall finish building your church. Then we will erect a palisade since this place was the scene of a fearsome battle not many years past.'

'True enough.' She nodded gravely. 'We remember those days well, my lord. Prince Bayan and Princess Sapientia brought a strong force here, but the Quman overset them and drove them northwest. In the end, so they say, Prince Sanglant saved us. All the Quman are driven out and will never return.'

A shift in the wind made Hugh grimace, chaff blowing into his eye, but he smiled quickly and gestured toward the neat camp his servants had already begun to set up. 'So we must pray, Deacon. If we are patient, and strong, all our enemies will be laid to rest.'

2

He drowned under the bones of the world. A whisper teased his ears, and he opened his eyes into a darkness relieved only by a gleam of pale gold light that emanated from his left arm.

Amazed, he waited for his vision to come and go in flashes, to fail again, but the gleam remained steady as he looked around.

He lay in a low chamber carved out of the rock by intelligent hands or shaped by more persistent forces. The floor had been swept clean of rubble. To his left the slope of the chamber created a series of benchlike ledges along the wall. Creatures crouched there, curled up with bony knees pressed to chests and spindly arms wrapped tight up against their shoulders. Many wore bits and pieces of ornaments slung around thick necks, odd scraps they might have scavenged out of a jackdaw's nest, most of which glittered with sharp edges and polished corners. The creatures had faces humanlike in arrangement, yet where eyes should stare at him, milky bulges clouded and cleared. He could not tell if they watched him or were blind.

With a grunt, he sat up. The movement made his head throb, and he had to shut his eyes to concentrate on not vomiting. At last his throat eased and his stomach settled, although the pounding ache in his temples pulsed on and on. The air was comfortable, not truly warm or cold; the air hung so still that he could taste each mote of dust on his tongue.

One of the creatures moved, arms elaborating precise patterns as it rubbed fingers one against the others, against its arms, and against the rock itself, clicking and tapping. The voice was not precisely voice but something more like the grinding together of pebbles.

'What are you?' it said.

'I am,' he said. 'I am . . .' It was like flailing in deep water as the riptide drags you inexorably out to sea. 'I have lost my name. It is all gone.'

'You wear a talisman from the ancient days,' said the creature patiently.

He saw now a dozen of the creatures seated like boulders around the chamber, sessile except for slight gestures whose subtle configurations and variations in sound began to make sense to him, flowing together and apart in the same way that seams of metal work their way through rock.

'The ancient days are only a false story! We must set aside comfort and dig for truth!'

'Despair is not truth. The ancient days are no false story, but a record carved in air to tell us the truth of the ancient days and the city whose walls speak.'

'You are a fool! A dreamer!'

'You are trapped by falls of rock that exist only in the mind you carry!'

They spoke by means of touch and sound, reaching out each to the others, passing speech down from one to the next and back again, punctuated by the scritch of fingers on dust and the rap of knuckles against rock or skin, by the push and pull of air stirred by their movements and the intake and exhalation of breath. The words they spoke were as much constructs he made through his own understanding of language as uttered syllables.

'The talisman bears witness to the truth! This creature bears the talisman! This catacomb traps us because in the watch-that-came-before we walk here seeking *luiadh*. To find luiadh we follow the veins of *silapu*. One element leads us to the next. This creature leads us to this talisman, or this talisman to the creature. Do not pretend one comes without the other. Listen!'

They quieted.

The one whose skin gleamed like pewter, the one who had spoken first, shifted and addressed him. 'What are you? The others of your kind, who descend from the Blinding, are empty when they reach us. You are not.'

'I am alive,' he agreed, before recalling the fate of the poor criminals cast into the pit. He shuddered. That shudder passed through the assembly like a venomous wind.

'It fears us!'

'It wishes to poison us!'

'It seeks silapu! Thief! Concealer!'

'Listen!' Pewter-skin stamped a three-clawed foot, and the others shifted restlessly before subsiding. When they crouched, motionless, they really did begin to blend into the rock so that he wondered if he still dreamed. They were only rocks, and he was hallucinating. But they kept speaking, and he kept hearing their words. 'Let it speak. What are you? Why are you not empty? Why are you cast down like the empty ones? Why do you wear the talisman?'

'I don't know.' Shards of memory flashed in his mind like lightning, burned into his eyes. 'You are skrolin. My people called you that once. It was one of your kind who gave me this.' He brushed his fingers over the gleaming armband, cool to his touch although its surface burned as though it were hot. 'I remember the great city. A shining city.'

'Ah! Ah!' They stirred, sighing and groaning, and fell silent again. Their milky eyes swirled and stilled. A few brushed fingers over rock before curling back up into their crouch.

Pewter-skin spoke. 'Tell us of the city.'

'Are you going to eat me?'

'Eat *you?*'

'The bodies of my people. They are thrown down here for your food, and then you give silver to the miners in exchange.'

They huffed, all their breath *whuffing* out. Dust stirred on the floor. First one, then a second and third, and finally all of them uncurled and with a rolling gait scurried out of the chamber, leaving him alone. He rubbed his filthy hair, shivering with fear and exhaustion as he struggled to get his bearings, to remember, but he could make sense of nothing. He possessed only scraps, like the chipped and broken ornaments the skrolin draped around their gnarled bodies. Nothing fit together.

Hadn't he seen a woman with wheat-colored hair, her belly swollen with pregnancy? She had betrayed him! But he wasn't sure how. It seemed as if anger and sadness had been his companions, but even they escaped him now.

He staggered to his feet, hit his head on the rough ceiling, and collapsed back to his knees while pain wept through him. It was all he could do to draw breath, let it out, and suck it in again. Once the world, every fiber of his being, had not hurt so much, but his head hurt all the time now. That was why he had been blind and mute. That blow to the head had damaged him.

When had it happened?

He couldn't recall.

A butterfly touch fluttered over his back. He jerked up, saw Pewter-skin folded into that boulder curl just beyond arm's length. There was something wrong with the creature's smooth skin; the lack niggled at him, but he couldn't place it. He couldn't remember.

'Come.' Pewter-skin used sounds, touch, and gesture to convey his meaning. 'You speak words that poison. The others turn away from you. We look away from the thing that offends us. But I think I first will show you. I think you are ignorant.' The skrolin unrolled and waddled away.

Walking made pain lance through his temple with every footfall, but he followed as the chamber narrowed on all sides. He walked in a crouch until the ceiling opened up and the walls fell away to a larger chamber. Pewter-skin led him to a low opening, where he crawled on hands and knees over coarse rock then cautiously down a steep incline to a larger chamber ribbed with veins of a mineral he could not identify. A well-worn path took them along a branching tube, past two shafts that plunged into darkness, three stone pillars with rubble heaped to one side, and four branches forking off the main corridor whose ceilings curved so low he could never have hoped to squeeze through them. The ceiling in the main tunnel remained high enough that he did not hit his head, and finally, where the floor ramped up, Pewter-skin scuttled through an opening and he scrambled up behind him, scraping his knees and palms although the soles of his feet were so callused that not even the rough rock edges could cut them. The ceiling and walls opened up with startling speed to a much larger cavern, and he sucked in a breath in surprise, inhaling a smell as thick as bubbling yeast in a closed, warm room filled with rising bread.

White growths, like huge mushrooms, grew in tidy rows and discrete clumps across the floor of the cavern. That powerful smell pervaded the air. He coughed, blinking back the stinging aftertaste of putrefaction that made his eyes water and his tongue turn dry. Life cannot grow from dead rock.

Corpses lay in stages of decay. The freshest bloomed

heavily with a funguslike mass; elsewhere, a few last sprigs decorated bones as the spongy fungus devoured the last shreds of the living.

Pewter-skin plucked a handful of the white stuff and ate it.

'We live in a trap. *Clavas* keeps us alive. The empty ones give nourishment to the clavas. So we trade silapu for the empty ones. We cannot eat the silapu, though some say we could in the time of the city. In that time, we were a strong and clever people, handsome and crusted with growths. Now we are sick and dying, even the free ones.'

'Where are the free ones? Why are you in a trap?'

'Come.' Pewter-skin beckoned.

He followed through the garden of corpses and bones and into a tunnel streaked with discolorations that glittered as he passed. By the glow of his armband he picked out veins and crystals grown into the rock. Sparkling grains slipped under his feet. Tunnels branched out to either side and crossed over and under where shafts pierced down or up until their path bewildered him and he knew himself lost. Pewter-skin led the way unerringly, and after an interminable time that might have lasted the length of a hymn or a hundred years they squeezed between twin pillars and he stared up in wonder. The ceiling and walls of this wide cavern shone where the light reflected off it, although the walls faded to darkness not so many steps away. The floor was unusually level. Here the skrolin had used scoured bones to build a strange architecture: a pyramid of skulls; an archway woven of thighbones cunningly trimmed and threaded together; a wharf constructed of linked rib cages; shoulder blades and pelvic bones arranged in a crude miniature temple or governor's palace.

'This is the tale of the city,' said Pewter-skin. 'We try to remember.'

'Why can't you remember?' he asked.

'The tale is told from one to another through many lives, but we forget if it is true, or if it is false.'

'The trap you speak of? Is that a true tale, or a false one?'

'Ah!' The sound cut, edged with rage, resignation, and sorrow. 'Come. Come.'

A trail bifurcated the bone city, leading them past the eerie structures to the far side where ceiling met floor. There, at the joining, a narrow passage ramped down.

'This is the trap.'

He smelled water. He got down on hands and knees and crawled forward into a tunnel far too low for him to stand upright. He hadn't gone more than a body's length when his hands met moisture. He touched liquid to tongue, spat it out, and wormed back out.

'It tastes like sea water.'

'Such water is poison to us. Through that tunnel many watches ago we come, thirty of us, seeking luiadh. The earth shivers. The feet of the wise ones far to the north shift and tremble. The waters rush in to trap us here where the tunnels run in a circle. We cannot get out.'

He had to sort through this speech. 'These tunnels you live in now are a dead end. The tunnel you came in through filled with water because of an earthquake. Now you are all trapped here.'

'Yes. Fourteen of us have emptied, but we the rest endure with the clavas.'

'So you trade silver to the miners in exchange for the corpses, which are the soil on which your food grows.'

'Yes.'

'It is this tunnel that leads back to your home?'

'Yes. Through this one we came. This tunnel is the path to the home, where the tribe roams the long caverns.'

'Is there no other path?'

'None. Many watches we have looked. Many watches we have dug. We wait in a trap.'

'Can you not climb to the surface? Find another entrance into the depths?'

'The Blinding burns us. The water poisons us. We cannot reach them. We are in a trap.'

'Can you not dig your way back? You are miners, are you not?'

'We dig in the earth. We dig, but slowly. We who came to be trapped here scout only when first we come here. We left the strong tools behind. Also, we are too few to dig so far within the span of our life. We will die here, waiting. One by one.'

He nodded. 'I'll go. I'll swim as far as I can and see if I can get to the other side.'

'The water does not poison you?'

'No. I can't drink it, but it does not poison me as long as I do not drink it.'

'Why?'

'I don't know why. The salt is too strong. That's why we can't drink it.'

'No. Why do you help us? Do you not wish to escape back to the Blinding?'

He sank down cross-legged, rubbing his eyes. 'Why would I not help you? You are trapped. Maybe I can free you by telling your kinfolk that you still live. If I climb back up the shaft, they will kill me, so I am doomed anyway. Maybe God sent me here to help you, seeing your need.'

'Who is *God?*'

He laughed, and the sound of laughter spooked Pewter-skin, who leaped backward and rolled up into the curled position, like a turtle retreating inside its shell. Yet his laughter acted like a knife, cutting one of the strands of the rope that chafed him. So many things bound him: his empty memory, his aching head, the mystery of his anger and grief. Still, laughter was its own enigma, a tonic to ease the burdens of life.

'Let me gather my strength first. I am so tired. I hurt. I need water to drink. Share your clavas with me, if you will. Tell me your stories while I rest. Then I will see how far I can swim.'

3

Zacharias' days fell into a routine. On fair mornings, Hugh presided over the schola, such as it was, with certain likely children seated on the ground before him as he taught them to write and read. Zacharias was never allowed to come close enough to listen, for if he had, he would have learned to write and thereby have a means to speak, and it was obviously Hugh's intention to prevent Zacharias from ever speaking in any form again. He had, therefore, to content himself with scratching letters in the dirt with a stick when he thought no one would observe him, and from these bent and crooked symbols he tried to puzzle out a meaning, for since he knew the liturgy by heart surely he must discover the secret that allowed words to be poured into letters, the Word that brought forth Creation according to the Holy Book in which he no longer believed. Yet there was something, surely, to the Logos, the thought and will that nestled at the heart of the universe, its kernel, its soul – if the universe had a soul. If any man had a soul.

Hugh had long since given up his soul, yet how might a man appear so beautiful and so kind and at the same time hide within himself such a poisoned heart? How could any great lord stand so patiently before a dozen dirty Salavii peasant children and teach them their letters? A pious churchman might, who hoped to see them become deacons and fraters in their turn who could minister to their countryfolk and thus bring their heathen relatives into the Light. Did that mean Hugh was a pious churchman? Or a cunning fraud? Yet he labored in support of King Henry and Queen Adelheid as their loyal servant.

These contradictions Zacharias could make no sense of. He did not understand a man of such elegance who could nevertheless live in this wilderness without complaint, keep his hands clean and yet bloody them with such cruelty as cutting out an innocent man's tongue, teach snot-nosed common children like any humble frater and yet walk among the great nobles in Darre with the arrogance of a man born to the highest rank. Be ruthless and yet seem so compassionate when mothers brought hurt children to his care, or his soldiers confessed their cares and worries and little crimes to him, for which he always prescribed a just penance leavened by the kiss of mercy.

If I did not hate him, I would love him.

The weeks passed as spring flowered around them. The church rose plank by plank, and many nights Hugh took Zacharias, Deacon Adalwif, and the other clerics to the crown where they studied the stars and the mysteries hoarded by the mathematici and prepared for the spell that would soon be their part to weave.

'What of the miracle of the phoenix?' Deacon Adalwif often asked Hugh as they walked back through the earthworks by lamplight.

'Did you see it with your own eyes?'

'Nay, I did not, yet these Salavii folk and I were spared by the intercession of a saint dressed in the garb of a King's Lion. The Quman army passed right by us while we were helpless and yet none were touched.'

'A miracle, truly. But why do you think this miracle is linked to the heresy you speak of?'

'I know it in my heart, Your Excellency. Do you not also? You do not condemn it, as you would if you did not doubt the old teachings.'

Hugh did not reply, but his arm tightened on the book he carried with him day and night. He watched over that book in the same way he watched over Zacharias, who was never left alone during the day and was by night chained to the center post of the tent.

The Feast of St. Barbara marked the first day of Avril of the year seven hundred and thirty-five. Thirteen days later the Feast of St. Sormas dawned with a shower of rain followed hard on by a balmy south wind that chased the clouds away. As the novices gathered for their schooling, two excited Salavii boys informed Hugh that the waters had receded enough with the coming of spring that he could, if he dared, creep into the burial mound.

'What does he mean?' Hugh asked Deacon Adalwif.

She shook her head. 'Nothing holy, my lord presbyter. This is an old grave mound such as the ancient ones erected over the bodies of their queens. That is why I insisted we build the church. I would have built it atop the hill to hallow the site and make it holy, but I could not obstruct the crown. Nevertheless, some of the children discovered a pool last summer and a hole that leads deep into the hill. They meant to crawl in, but I put a stop to it. There's no telling what might lie inside an old grave mound like this one.'

'Surely you are not superstitious enough to believe in evil spirits, Deacon?'

'Nay, nay, not at all, Your Excellency.'

'Best that I investigate for myself, if the way is clear,' said Hugh, although Zacharias thought his color unusually high. 'In that way I can drive out any lingering evil from this spot.'

'Of course, Your Excellency,' she said, looking relieved. 'It has not been easy to keep the older boys from exploring where they will. One poor lad drowned in the river last autumn.'

'Let the children show me the entrance. I'll take Brother Zacharias to carry a lamp and Gerbert to guard the entrance behind me so none follow.'

'You'll take no others in with you?'

'Have I anything to fear? The bones of the heathen dead have no power over me, Deacon. Nor over you either.'

'Yes, my lord. In truth, my lord, you have the right of it.' But she still looked frightened.

And why not? Zacharias had leisure to reflect as Gerbert waded into a knee-deep pool of water lying up against a precipice cut into the high face of the earthworks about halfway around the hill from the little village and their camp. A trickle of water had, over the years, eroded the face of the earth away to reveal an entryway, two stones capped by a lintel, once buried, Zacharias supposed, by the tumulus and now half concealed by a curtain of moss. If the children hadn't explored here, none of the others might ever have noticed. Gerbert hacked away the moss with his sword.

'Come.' Hugh held a lamp aloft as he waded into the water and squeezed through the opening.

The spring sun lay a warm hand across Zacharias' shoulders, quite in contrast to the freezing water that iced his toes and calves as soon as he followed Hugh into the narrow tunnel, which was just higher than his head and quite dark. His hand shook, causing the light from his lamp to tremble as it illuminated stone walls incised with spirals and lozenges. He was afraid of the dark, but Hugh frightened him more. The corridor widened enough that a man might slosh through the knee-high water without scraping his shoulders on either wall.

'What's this?' murmured Hugh.

Zacharias almost ran into a queer scaffolding that, twisting out of the water, was filthy with pale worms which after a moment he recognized as the remains of rotting feathers.

He retched, struck so hard by memory that he emptied his stomach into the water before he could stop himself.

'I pray you,' said Hugh, stepping sideways to avoid the stink, 'what is wrong, Zacharias?'

He couldn't answer.

'Ah.' Hugh groped in the water and fished up a skull patched with tufts of black hair. 'I take it these are the infamous wings of a Quman warrior, and this, I suppose, his head. He must have crawled in here to die after the battle. This certainly is no ancient queen laid to rest by her devout servants. Come.' If the matter now floating like scum atop the water disgusted him, he gave no sign of it, although it was difficult to interpret his expression in the shifting light and shadow that played across his face as he moved on.

Sweating and anxious, Zacharias waded obediently after. The tunnel floor sloped imperceptibly upward. The water receded and gave way to a shoreline and grainy earth as they walked cautiously into the darkness. Hugh halted to study the symbols carved into the stone: more spirals and lozenges, and long strips of hatching and even, here and there, dots and lines that looked like a calendar. What if Hugh found another daimone imprisoned here and let it capture Zacharias' body? He whimpered.

'What was that?' Hugh asked, pausing, then went on.

The tunnel opened into a broad chamber, a black pit made eerie because of the flickering play of their lights over the floor. The walls remained in shadow, and the ceiling lofted so high above them that it, too, was hidden.

'There she lies, poor soul.' Hugh walked a circuit of the chamber, shining his lamp into three alcoves built into the corbeled chamber. Shaking his head, he returned to the stone slab that marked the center of the chamber.

'I had thought I might find Blessing here with her attendants,' he mused, more to himself than to Zacharias. 'But perhaps that was a false vision, not a true one. It makes no sense. Why would Sanglant leave his daughter sleeping beneath one of the crowns? Held in safekeeping? Yet I can still find her. Surely that was Liath traveling in the same manner we walk – through the crowns. Who was traveling with her? A sorcerer of great power; I felt her power in my bones.'

He knelt beside the skeleton laid out on the slab. The dead queen gleamed under the light because the gold that had once decorated her clothing had long ago fallen in among her bones.

'What are these?' Hugh touched a pair of golden antlers that lay on either side of her grinning skull. 'Riches! Best we make no mention of this, Zacharias. I see no need to rob the dead. Let her lie in peace.' He leaned forward, still on his knees. 'Here, what's this?'

He reached past her to lift a crude obsidian mirror off the dirt; despite the passage of years, its glossy surface still caught the lamplight and flashed sparks into the concealed depths of the chamber. Where shadows moved.

They walk out of the alcoves, ancient queens whose eyes have the glint of knives.

Zacharias yelped in terror, stumbled, and dropped to his knees into a clot of rotting garments that crumbled beneath his hands. His lamp spilled to the floor, guttering as oil leaked onto the dirt.

'Don't be frightened, Zacharias,' said Hugh kindly as he lifted the mirror and with an expression of amazement and a clever grin directed light along the walls and up at the ceiling by using the mirror to reflect it. 'Of course. Of course. What if she was one of the ancient ones, a mathematicus? What if she used a mirror to capture the light of the stars? Why did Anne never think of this?'

The oil spilled over the ground caught fire and blazed up, and by this light Zacharias discovered himself wrist-deep in a heap of decayed clothing and rusted mail, the remains of a leather belt curled under his fingers and turning to dust as he stared. The fading outlines of a black lion exactly like those worn by the King's Lions rested a hand's breadth below his weeping eyes.

'Who's there?' said Hugh sharply, raising his lamp.

A chill breath of air coiled around them and the fires went out.

There are three of them. They are angry at this intrusion, but they are also intrigued by the exceptional beauty of the one who desecrates their tomb. They have not quite yet forgotten the memory of life that sustains their spirit. They have not quite yet forgotten the sweet perfume of the meadow flowers that bloom in the spring.

Zacharias lost all sense of up and down, and he fell, but only smashed his face into the bundle of clothing that dissolved all at once into nothing until, when he took a coughing, wheezing breath, it was as if he inhaled all the dust of what had once lain there, sucked up into his mouth and lungs.

The blackness chokes him. Salt water bubbles against his eyes and lips, popping in his nostrils. His lungs hurt, but he keeps swimming although the tunnel is entirely drowned. If he goes too far, he will not have enough air in his lungs to swim back, yet what difference does it make? Where else can he go? Without memory, he is dead anyway.

He is like the skrolin, trapped in a cul-de-sac whose tunnels only take him around in circles. He must go forward to free himself as well as them.

His lungs burn. His head slams into the ceiling, his fingers scrabble against rough walls, and his feet push along rock as he thrusts forward and all at once comes flailing to the surface. He drags himself out into air and lies spewing with his lungs on fire and his eyes stinging and the world hazing to darkness.

Agony slices through his body as a cold hand brushes the

top of his head and an icy finger tugs on his ear as if to drag
him back into the water.

He was no longer lying half in and half out of water but
rather on the dusty remains of the burial chamber.

A dry voice whispers through his mind. 'He has already
been claimed.'

Zacharias recognizes them; they are his grandmother's
gods, the young Huntress, bright and sharp, the Bounteous
One, and the Old Woman, toothless with age.

'I fear you,' he whimpers, although he cannot truly speak.
He says the words in his mind, and they hear him. 'You are
the gods my grandmother worshiped. She was loyal to you.'

'The days when we ruled on Earth are long forgotten. Our
power has faded.'

'I remember you!'

'You remember us. You are our grandson.'

He weeps, feeling their affectionate touch. Where his tears
meld with the dust, the earth speaks to him in a voice as heavy
as stone, reaching him through the ancient ones who linger
within the tomb.

Can. You. Hear. Us? Are. You. The. One. We. Seek? Help.
Us.

'I hear you. I will help you. Tell me what to do.' His lips
and his mind form the words although the breath that escapes
him is little more than a rising and falling of vowel sounds,
not real words at all.

The earth replies not with sound but with its voice throb-
bing up through his head.

Listen. Wait. You. Are. Not. The. One. We. Seek. But. We.
May. Have. Need. Of. You. The. Crown. Can. You. Reach.
And. Touch. The. Crown?

'I can.'

Light flared. Hugh cursed.

'Damn it. There must be a hidden opening somewhere,
to let in a breeze like that. Zacharias! For God's sake, man,
get up off the floor. Is the lamp ruined? And broken, too.'
His shoulders heaved as he sighed. 'Well, no matter. I'll take

this mirror. We'll leave the rest undisturbed.'

With some difficulty because of the pain still cutting through his body, Zacharias pushed himself up to hands and knees and, as Hugh's light bobbed away down the tunnel, to his feet. He bent to pick up the fallen lamp and such a wave of dizziness and disorientation swept him that he moaned.

Hugh's lamp stopped. There was silence.

From this distance and angle Zacharias could only see Hugh's face framed by the wavering light, golden and beautiful and utterly frightening. The presbyter studied him a moment more, then turned his back.

'Come quickly. I've no wish to linger. There's nothing here of interest.'

The ancient queens waited in the shadows, but they did not advance, only watched. He tingled all over, staggered, dizzy. Hurting.

Changed.

Hugh had seen and heard nothing. He had allies that Hugh knew nothing of, that Hugh could not combat.

'Zacharias?'

All his life Zacharias had struggled to keep silence, to speak prudently or not at all. All his life he had failed at this task. He had cast away his faith in God, turned his back on the Lord and Lady, on his kinfolk, and on the calling that had taken him into the east and slavery years ago. He had walked as a beggar through the world, starved for sustenance, fearful and cowardly. He had no words, he had lost his tongue, yet he had been changed utterly.

All the fear was gone. Vanished.

'Go, grandson,' the queens whispered as they faded into the tomb. 'Return to us when you can.'

He would return. He would sneak back into the tomb somehow, risking Hugh's wrath. The queens waited for him, and a nameless ally needed his help.

'Zacharias!'

That tone had once had the power to make him choke with fear. Now he only smiled to himself and, after a last glance around, followed Hugh into the light.

4

'The Word is the surest sign of God's grace,' Sigfrid said to
his audience, who were seated on the sloping grass with hoods
and shawls pulled up over their heads to protect them from
the glare of the afternoon sun. 'Only with words can we speak
to others and bring them into the light. Is it not true that those
who do not believe are, as the blessed Daisan says, "the prey
of every fear because they know nothing for certain"?'

Several heads nodded. Ermanrich sidled to the left to get
into the shade creeping out over the hollow where the community gathered.

'When the elements mingled and were corrupted by darkness, it was the voice of God, the Word of Thought, that separated darkness out from the others and propelled it into the
depths where it naturally belongs. Because it was the Word
that gave birth to this world, it is our words that give birth
to the community of believers on Earth.'

'Tell us the story of the phoenix and the miracle, Brother
Sigfrid!' cried one of the novices. 'Tell how God restored
your tongue!'

The others begged Sigfrid to tell the story yet again,
although in the last year and a half he had told it a hundred
times. Because Ivar stood at the back of the crowd, he easily
slipped away and climbed out of the gentle amphitheater composed by the natural contours of the ground. Here the inhabitants of the cloister assembled on fine days to discuss the Holy
Book and the ineffable mystery of God as well as the more tangible acts of humankind which had confined them in this prison.

At times like this, he just felt so unspeakably weary.

The amphitheater stood at the limit of the grounds, which
were measured on one side by the rocky ridge that closed off

the northern end of the vale, ringed to the east and west by a straggling line of forest and the steep slopes of hills, and opening to the south on a vista that looked up the vale over the buildings and fields of the cloister to the palisade. He shaded his eyes to peer into the distance. The estate had turned gold, with only a few greens to relieve the pallor. It had been a hot, dry summer, and the crops had suffered because of it. Dust smeared the sky beyond the palisade. Someone was coming, horsemen and perhaps wagons, if he judged the height and density of the cloud correctly.

He left Sigfrid and his listeners and jogged along the track that led past fields of seared wheat and rye and the withering vegetable gardens to the central compound. He trotted past the weaving hall and took advantage of the shady porch fronting the infirmary to cool his head before cutting across the last strip of open ground to reach the main compound.

The audience chamber lay empty, so he crossed it and walked out onto the portico that faced the inner courtyard. The fountain – a playful trio of dancing bears – had long since run dry, and buckets had to be hauled in every day to keep the herb bed and the roses watered. The grave post dedicated to poor Sister Bona had been freshly whitewashed; her ivory Circle dangled from a nail hammered into the wooden post. It had been over one year since her death, and yet the memory of that awful day remained as vivid as if it had happened last week – the first shock of it, like a punch in the belly, transformed into a numb ache.

One nun knelt among the herbs, weeding. The other attended the biscop, who sat in the shade at her writing desk, which had been moved out onto the portico because of the extreme heat.

Constance looked up, hearing Ivar's footsteps, and extended a hand to greet him warmly. 'What brings you here to me, Brother Ivar? You have deserted the company at the very hour when your discussions may yield the ripest fruit.'

He kissed her hand, then dropped to his knees before her. 'Someone is coming, Your Grace. I saw a cloud of dust as I stood outside the amphitheater.'

'Ah.' She smiled softly.

'I am anxious, Your Grace. I fear this cloud brings ill news.'

'It may be, but we can do nothing to prevent its arrival. Go to the gate, if you will, and see what comes our way. I will wait in the audience chamber.'

'Yes, Your Grace.'

'Sister Eligia, I pray you, assist me.' The young woman hastened to Constance's side, offering her the walking stick, supporting her arm, and helping her negotiate out from behind the desk.

'Do not hesitate to go before me, Brother,' said Constance. 'The community has more need of legs than my royal honor, which has not served us well these past two years.'

He sketched a bow and hurried out through the chamber, hearing the scrape of her ruined leg against pavement and the tap of her stick as she moved one laborious step at a time off the portico. He rapped on the door. The guards opened it, looked him up and down, then let him through. The door thudded shut behind him.

He was free – they all were except the biscop – to walk where he willed within the confines of the palisade. He strode down the track that led past the sheep pasture and the bramble fields where the goats made their home, arriving at the closed gates at the same time as the new arrivals. Harness jingled and a man cursed a recalcitrant mule. A pair of dogs barked. A woman laughed as the captain called down jovial curses from the parapet as a greeting for the soldiers come to relieve the last crop of guards.

'. . . bastard whoresons. It's quiet enough, I grant you, but all we have to amuse ourselves is dicing. There aren't even any fine ladies in want of swiving in the village, for they've sworn to have nothing to do with us on account of they've been corrupted by the prisoner and her lying words. You'll be wishing yourself off at the wars after a few days stuck here!'

'You must not have seen any fighting if you think battle is preferable to a quiet backwater like this.'

'I've seen fighting enough!'

'You must be Captain Tammus. We've heard of your loyal service to Lady Sabella.'

'It's true enough she can't trust every man who offers her service just because she has gold and swords, but I've long pledged my loyalty to her. She knows the worth of my oath. I've these scars and this stump to prove it. Who are you?'

'Captain Ulric, of Autun.'

'Ah. Yes, Captain, I recall you now.'

'I've brought relief for the men on guard here. I also have a message for the biscop.'

'Very well. Your men can leave the wagons here and choose accommodations in our camp — which you see is decent enough, warm in the winter and lots of wood and water, although the river is running low this year. I'll have my guards cart the goods into the cloister. Your men will need to know the lay of the land before they begin their guard duties. As for now, I'll escort you to the biscop myself.'

'Very good.'

When the gates swung in, Ivar concealed himself behind a stack of empty barrels and crates as a dozen soldiers escorting two wagons trundled past bearing the usual offerings of salt, oil, and candles. He recognized the name 'Ulric' from that unlucky day he and the others had entered Autun expecting to be tried for heresy and instead were sent off to smother in this cloister, their lives spared because of Baldwin's sacrifice.

Perhaps Captain Ulric had news of Baldwin.

He followed the wagon to the compound, then tagged along as Captain Ulric, Tammus, and two attendants walked to the biscop's audience chamber. Captain Tammus cherished the same surly frown he always wore, which went well with his belligerent stride and coarse language. He had indeed suffered horrific injuries in his lady's service, although Ivar didn't know what battles he had fought in: he was missing one hand and one eye, and nasty scars twisted across the right side of his face. In contrast, Ulric was a middle-aged man with a pleasant face, easy to look at, tall and well built with the bow-legged walk common to cavalrymen. His cheeks and nose were burned red and peeling, but the faces of his attendants were shrouded by the hoods they'd pulled up to shade themselves from the hot sun.

Ivar slipped into the audience chamber and stood along the back wall, unnoticed except by the biscop, of course, and by Captain Ulric, who glanced back as the door was shut on them and marked Ivar with a widening of the eyes and a stiffness in his expression.

He doesn't trust me.

Why should he?

Ivar had been named as Sabella's enemy, and Captain Ulric served her, or Duke Conrad, who was her ally. Even Gerulf and Dedi had vanished into Conrad's army; he had heard no word of them in eighteen months, just as he had no knowledge of Baldwin's whereabouts and whether he suffered or flourished under Sabella's care.

'You may come forward, Captain,' said Constance kindly, 'and kiss my ring.'

Tammus bent the merest angle, just enough not to insult her outright, and kissed her ring, although he sneered as he glanced back to invite Ulric to come forward. The cavalryman knelt before her chair and bent his head respectfully. Were those tears in his eyes? From this distance it was impossible for Ivar to tell, and Captain Ulric blinked, rose, and retreated, coughing behind his hand either because of dust in the room or to cover a strong emotion.

Ivar felt a swirl of dangerous currents at work in the chamber, but he couldn't identify their locus or the shifting eddy of these tides. He leaned against the wall, pretending to an ease he did not possess.

'What news, Captain?' Constance asked.

'I bring word from Lady Sabella. She means to visit you within the next fortnight.'

'Ah.' By no means could any person read Constance's reaction. She nodded, hands curled lightly over the arms of her chair, seeming relaxed. Or resigned.

'There'll be a great deal to be made ready,' said Captain Tammus. 'We'll have to deplete our stores to feed her retinue.

The village near here hasn't any grain stores left to them, and it's not harvest yet.'

'Harvest this year will not yield much,' replied the biscop. 'You've seen the fields.'

'I'll have to send men out hunting again. We'll take half a dozen sheep from your flock.'

Constance nodded, although she knew as well as Ivar did that their flock was sorely depleted. None of the ewes had birthed twins this spring, a sign, Sister Nanthild said, of drought to come, and indeed drought and unusually hot weather had afflicted them. What rains had come had arrived untimely, and in one drenching flood that had washed sprouts out of dusty fields, churned them into muddy lakes, and then hardened the land into cracked earth when the sun returned to beat on them as a hammer flattened red-hot iron on the anvil.

'It will be good for Lady Sabella to see the conditions of the lands hereabout, which have suffered greatly over the last winter and into this summer,' she said. 'Is there any other message, Captain?'

'That is all, Your Grace. Otherwise, as you know, I am under orders to make no communication with you or any of those residing under your care.'

'I understand the terms of my confinement well enough. It seems a long journey to come here all this way merely to bring me a single message.'

He looked at Tammus before risking further comment. 'I have escorted a new complement of guardsmen to replace the levy that has been here for three months.'

'Will you replace Captain Tammus?'

Tammus snorted.

Ulric shrugged. 'Nay, Your Grace. Lady Sabella has named him as your keeper. So he will remain as he has served well and faithfully these past two years.'

'So he has,' agreed Constance without a glimmer of sarcasm. 'I hope you will accept some wine, Captain, after such a long journey in these hot days.'

'That I will, gladly and with thanks.'

'Captain Tammus will show you the way.'

Ivar remained where he was as the two captains retreated to the doors and filed out with Ulric's escort behind them.

All but one.

As they passed through the doors, Ulric asked Tammus a flood of questions, while behind him the second of his hooded attendants sidestepped without missing a beat and by Ulric's misdirection managed to remain inside the chamber when the doors were shut behind the other men.

The stranger cast back his hood and strode forward to kneel before her chair, the movement accomplished so decisively that Ivar had no time to respond before it was done.

He could have knifed her, but instead he grasped her hand as a supplicant.

'Your Grace, I have only a few moments to speak with you. I pray you, heed me.'

She studied him, gaze shifting over his face and figure, and nodded to indicate that she recognized him. 'Lord Geoffrey of Lavas. How does your daughter, the young countess, fare?'

'Ill, Your Grace. Lavas county and all the western lands fare ill, and have done so ever since you were deposed. God are angry. This is our punishment: we suffer drought and untimely rains. Refugees fleeing north from the Salian wars confound us. Bandits have made the roads unsafe. There will be famine this winter. We hear tales of plague and murrain, although thank the Lord and Lady we've seen none of that in our lands, pray God that we be spared. There's even talk that my sweet Lavrentia is not in truth the rightful heir!'

'How can that be?'

'Nay, nay, I make no mind of it. It's only the idle talk of desperate folk.' With a shaking hand he drew the Circle of Unity at his breast. 'Another scourge strikes at us from the sea. The Eika have returned! They harry in Salia along the coast. We hear rumors that they are moving inland and north. I pray you, Your Grace. Lady Sabella usurped your rightful place, granted to you by King Henry, the true king. We will support you.'

'Do I understand that Captain Ulric is your ally in this?'

'As well as he is able. He was always your true and loyal servant, but he must protect his men.'

'Yes, he cannot fight Sabella and Conrad with only a single troop of skirmishers. Yet my position is weak, Lord Geoffrey, as you must observe. I am crippled. I rest here as Sabella's prisoner. It will prove difficult to throw off this yoke. Conrad is a powerful ally, and his ambitions do not accord with mine.'

Geoffrey had not yet let go of Constance's hand. 'So you see us, Your Grace. My wife's kinfolk have remained loyal to Henry through many difficulties, but now Lady Sabella has taken my wife's two children as hostage in Autun.'

'Even Count Lavrentia?'

'She remains in Lavas because of the rumors—'

'Which rumors?'

He clenched his hands, jaw tight, voice cold. 'That the rightful heir lives and waits, wandering in the wilderness until all Lavas cries out for his return. It is said there were miracles – but it's all lies! Even Lady Sabella sees how precarious the situation is, so Lavrentia remains with me in Lavas while Aldegund and our sons serve Sabella in Autun. Yet Varre suffers under Sabella's rule. Lavas suffers. And I dare not act against Sabella or Conrad unless we are certain we have sufficient backing to win.'

She considered him somberly. 'I have no means to communicate with those who might support me, and I have no army – only bands of faithful soldiers who need a commander in order to act in concert. What news of Princess Theophanu?'

'I hear rumor she bides in Gent. I have also heard a rumor that Prince Sanglant rode into the wilderness to raise a great army of savages in order to wrest Wendar from her, or to restore it to his father. But rumor is a fickle lover, as I know well. I do not know what to believe. They say Henry was crowned emperor in Aosta.'

'Emperor!' For the space of three breaths Constance was too shocked, or angered, to speak. 'Surely he commands a great enough army that he might come to our rescue rather than chase dreams in the south!'

'If only he knew our plight.'

'If only. I sent an Eagle, but none returned. I have no messengers to send, Lord Geoffrey. You must send one of your people to Gent.'

'Captain Ulric has offered me one of his men-at-arms as a messenger, Your Grace, but I have come to beg you to write a missive yourself and send one of your people with the soldier, with a message penned in your own hand and sealed with your own ring. Otherwise how can the princess believe us? She must know what Sabella and Conrad hatch between them. She will believe any messages of peace or war to be a trap laid to ambush her.'

'Emperor,' whispered Constance. 'Whether this bodes well or ill I cannot say.' Her gaze had strayed. Now she squeezed Geoffrey's hand and let it drop, indicating that he should rise. 'They will look for you, and if you are discovered here, all is lost. I can write a message, and perhaps, if we are fortunate and God favor our suit, I can smuggle it out to you before you depart in the morning. Captain Tammus has strict directions from Sabella to count our number each evening, as you will see, because Sabella fears precisely what you suggest – that one of these who swear loyalty to me will escape to take news of my plight to my kinfolk. I dare not risk it. The punishment is severe, as we have seen to our sorrow.'

'Punishment?'

'I sent a novice to carry word of my whereabouts to Princess Theophanu. She was brought back ten days later and dumped in my courtyard, mutilated and quite dead. Captain Tammus promised the same fate to any other member of my entourage who attempts escape.'

'I'll go,' said Ivar.

Lord Geoffrey started around, as startled as if he had forgotten Ivar was there.

Constance smiled grimly. 'So you have said many times, Brother Ivar. Yet by what means might you succeed when poor Sister Bona died so horribly?'

'They will not hunt down a dead man, Your Grace.'

'A dead man!' Geoffrey's skin washed so pale that Ivar feared the man might faint, as though Ivar's words had, for him, a deeper and more pernicious meaning.

'A dead man cannot carry my message, Brother Ivar. What do you propose?'

'We are prisoners, too, Your Grace. I have considered our situation at length, but it is only recently while in conference with Sister Nanthild that it has occurred to me that we may hold the means in our hands to smuggle out one brave soul. With Lord Geoffrey's plea, it seems the time may be right.'

'Sister Nanthild is a wise woman, it's true, but only God can restore the dead to life once the soul has left the body.'

'We need only the appearance of death, Your Grace.'

'I see.' Her gaze held him, and he looked away first, because she saw too deeply and too well. 'You are willing to take the risk, Brother Ivar? Knowing that you leave your compatriots behind, under my care, and that it is possible you will never see them again?'

'I am. These are desperate times, Your Grace.'

'And you chafe in these bonds, whereas your friends are content enough to rest here after the troubles they have endured. Very well, Brother Ivar.' She held out a hand, stained with ink and heavy with calluses where she gripped her quill, and he knelt before her and kissed her biscop's ring. 'I, too, am desperate. Lord Geoffrey, you must go. Appoint a rendezvous and have your man wait there for five days. If Brother Ivar has not arrived there in that time, he will not come at all. That is all I can promise.'

That evening Sister Nanthild brewed a concoction of valerian, pennyroyal, and two drops of a milky liquid she called 'akreva's sap.' In the morning, Ivar screwed up his courage and drank the potion in one gulp as Sigfrid, Ermanrich, and Hathumod huddled next to him, weeping and grimacing.

'You must take care.' Hathumod's nose always got bright red when she cried. 'I can't bear to think of losing you, Ivar, but I know you are doing what must be done. There isn't anyone else the biscop can trust.'

'Many she can trust,' said Sigfrid, 'but none as strong. Ivar must go.'

Ermanrich wiped his tears and said nothing, only held Ivar's hand and, after a moment, walked with him to the fields so that the convulsions would be witnessed by as many guards as possible.

Ivar hoed for a while, but his heart wasn't in it. He kept waiting, knowing each tremor that rippled through his muscles would be followed by a harder one. Once a shudder passed through him with such force that he dropped the hoe. When he bent to pick it up, he lost his balance, pitched forward onto the ground, and sucked up a quantity of dusty soil and a shriveled weed just an instant before hooked out of the earth.

'Ivar!' shrieked Hathumod.

He spasmed. A hot flood of urine spilled along his legs, soaking into the ground. He tried to rise, but his arms were useless; they would not respond.

'Plague!' shouted Ermanrich, weeping again.

Shouts rang in the distance. Shudders passed through his frame in waves, strong at first and then each one receding as his vision blurred and hearing faded.

In a waking dream he watched the sky pass overhead, a pale blue almost drained white by the heat of the sun. One cloud spilled past and was lost. He was awake and aware, but not really awake, still dreaming, because he could not move at all, could not truly even feel his own limbs or the rise and fall of his chest. Maybe this was what death felt like. Maybe he was dead, and the gamble had failed.

The ground juddered beneath him as the heavens rolled past above, and after a long contemplative interlude it occurred to him that he was lying in the cart that made runs between the village and the palisade. The shroud covering his body had slipped off his face, and the sun beat down hard. He'd be burned; he knew that much. Sun always burned him if he didn't keep covered, but he couldn't move to cover himself and there was some reason he ought not to. Some secret. He had a secret he was keeping.

'Whist! There! What's that, Maynard?'

'A whole cavalcade. Some mighty noble, I wager.'

'Must be the lady duchess.'

'Ai, yes, so it must.' Maynard hawked and spat. 'So. For her.'

'Careful. She'd as like ride her horse over you as spare you for the mines, so they say.'

The cart jounced over the ruts that made the road as the carters pulled their vehicle aside so the noble procession could pass unimpeded. He heard the clamor of the approach, hooves, talk, a smattering of song, and the rumble of wagon wheels, all wafting over him as the summer breeze did, felt and forgotten and beyond him, now, who was dead. Or so he remembered.

Sparks of memory clotted into recollection. He was carrying a message for Biscop Constance, written on a tiny strip of parchment that they'd rolled up in a bit of oiled sheepskin and which he now concealed within his cheek like a squirrel storing nuts against the coming winter dearth. He was only pretending to be dead.

That was a relief!

'Is that a corpse you're hauling?' a voice asked.

'Don't come no closer. One of the folk in St. Asella's died a nasty death, and they feared it's some manner of plague brought up from the south with the soldiers.'

'God save us! Have they all fallen sick?'

'Nay, none other. It might only be demons that chewed away the poor lad's vitals. But they're taking no chances so we're to haul him out to the woods where there's an old church abandoned in days gone. Our deacon'll say the rites over him there.'

'Let me see him!'

This new voice belonged to a woman. Ivar recognized that imperious tone, rankling and sour. A face loomed to one side. It was a woman past her prime, mounted on horseback, seen out of the corner of his vision and after a lengthy gasp of shade – for she blocked the sun – the light blasted him again and he would have blinked but he could not.

'He's not breathing, my lady duchess,' said another person. 'Ought we to turn aside?'

'Nay, I do not fear the plague. We've had no word of it in this region. No doubt some other ill felled him. Elfshot, maybe.'

'True enough, my lady. We've heard many a tale of shades haunting the woods in greater numbers than ever, bold as you please and afflicting the common folk who do fear even to seek wood and game though they've need of it. Do you suppose that's what felled this young fellow?'

'It might have.'

With the easy stream of their conversation flowing past, his thoughts began to coalesce into proper order, although their sluggish pace frustrated him. The carters would dump him in the wood at an old oak tree where the old gods had once demanded sacrifice. A chapel dedicated to Saint Leoba stood there now, proof against lightning, a boon to the righteous. As he must be, if he meant to carry word of Biscop Constance's plight to Princess Theophanu.

'Still, he looks familiar,' Lady Sabella mused, but although she kept talking her voice receded as she moved away, now disinterested. 'I don't see many folk with hair that coppery-red shade. He must hail from the north. . . .'

The shriek would have made any man jump, except one dosed with a potion that made him more dead than alive.

'Ivar? Ai, God. Ivar! It's Ivar! Nay, Lord, it can't be! Lady protect him! I thought he would be safe!'

'Lord Baldwin! Come back here!'

A figure hurtled over the cart's edge and landed so hard on Ivar that, had he not been paralyzed, he would certainly have betrayed himself.

'Ivar! It can't be! Ai, God! Ai, God!'

Tears poured in a flood. Baldwin clutched Ivar's hands and chafed them, repeating the same words over and over, crying and groaning, his pretty face twisted with grief. 'Ai! Ai! Ai!'

'Come, Lord Baldwin! This man may have died of the plague. Get off him!'

'Then I wish I would die, too. And so I would, if it would bring him back! I would share death with him if I could! Don't touch me!'

'Baldwin! Come!' Sabella spoke as if to a dog. Weeping, Baldwin tugged a ring off his hand and twisted it onto Ivar's right forefinger. 'Take something of me into the afterlife,' he sniveled. 'Ai, God! Ai! Ai!'

'Get him off there,' ordered the lady. 'I've had enough!'

Baldwin was hauled off, kicking and shouting, and dragged away while Ivar lay helpless, screaming inside, guts all knotted up with bitter fury and an ugly relief that the charade had passed the direst test of all.

Baldwin thought he was dead. Baldwin – who had sacrificed so much – would mourn him, although he still lived. Ivar would not suffer, but Baldwin would. The others dared not risk telling Baldwin the truth, not as long as he rode in Lady Sabella's train.

Not as long as he slept in Lady Sabella's bed, whether willing or no.

'Friend of his, you think?' said Maynard to his comrade.

'Didn't look like no brother or cousin, if you ask me. Mayhap they were fostered together.'

'No doubt. Whist! You stubborn ass! Get along!'

The donkey brayed a mighty protest, but the cart jerked and they set off again as the sun glared down, burning his skin, scalding his eyes, making tears run from the face of a dead man who wasn't dead at all.

But Baldwin would never know.

5

The merchants who lived and traded in the emporium of Medemelacha had wisely surrendered without a fight, warned by their Hessi compatriots that it were better to yield than die, but upstream on the Helde River the duc d'Amalisses had retreated inside a fortified town, seat of his power. By the time Stronghand reached the scene of the siege, Quickdeath had forced a battle by driving prisoners up against the walls at the point of Eika spears and, on their bleeding and mangled backs, swarming the walls.

The river was choked with corpses as the Eika burned and looted the town.

'This is not what I intended,' said Stronghand when Quickdeath came before him to gloat over his victory. 'This town cannot serve us burned to the ground. The fields cannot yield grain if no farmer is left to till and harvest.'

'But we are rich!' Quickdeath had brought a score of warriors and two score dogs as escort; they shouted and cheered, displaying the baubles, fine cloth, and silver coins they had plucked from the ruins. 'And the chief of this town is dead!'

Bodies dangled from the burning palisade. As the wind shifted, smoke chased away carrion crows come to seek their own fortunes.

'You are rash.' Stronghand did not rise from the chair where he sat. A choice few of his littermates stood at his back while the handful of chieftains who had joined up with him in Medemelacha kept their distance. Ironclaw stood foremost among them, watching and waiting. The bulk of Stronghand's army remained in Alba under the command of Trueheart, but in the months since the death of the Alban queen he had sent out smaller groups to strike hard along the coast, casting a net of terror as widely as they could. 'We are not yet ready to push inland. If we stretch ourselves too thin, we will break. War bands are more susceptible to ambush than large armies. Your orders were to harry the coast, nothing more.'

Quickdeath laughed, baring his teeth. 'And if I do not wish to heed those orders? Maybe I am rash. But you are too cautious!' He gripped his ax more tightly as his men pressed forward threateningly. If the lesser chieftains chose to stand by and not intervene, then Quickdeath's party easily outnumbered his own.

Stronghand did not smile. He no longer needed to make explicit threats, to puff himself up, to make himself appear bigger and fiercer for, in truth, Quickdeath was far more impressive in appearance than he ever could be. 'You mistake caution for cowardice because you do not understand it. A cautious man watches and guards, and uses forethought, a skill I do not think you have yet mastered.'

Quickdeath snorted disdainfully and hefted his ax, knowing he had the advantage in numbers. The blood of his men was hot with victory. Before them, Stronghand seemed so small.

'Yet it is true that any leader needs a reward,' continued Stronghand. 'Let this precious jewel serve to reward you as you deserve, for the victory you have achieved this day.'

'Do you think to bribe me?' asked Quickdeath, but like any Eika warrior, he hesitated.

Last Son brought the chest, carved out of ivory, banded with gold, and ornamented with cabochons of pale aquamarine and dark red garnets, and placed it on Stronghand's thighs, then retreated to stand by the others.

'I will not have it said I give grudgingly to those who fight in my army.'

Quickdeath flashed a smile, leaped forward with a laugh, and grabbed the chest off Stronghand's lap. 'Now both your army and your treasure will be mine!' he cried as he flipped open the lid.

Stronghand's men knew this as the signal. They froze in place, as did Stronghand, knowing stillness was his weapon now.

The rash ones did not understand caution, or stillness.

The ice wyrms were deadly, but fragile. Even starlight burned them. They were sightless, but Quickdeath's startled movement offered target enough. He dropped the chest. The tiny ice wyrm scuttled across the dirt to the closest thing that moved. And stung.

Quickdeath's scream pierced the heavens themselves. His warriors scattered in fear, except for two bold and loyal dogs who jumped growling into the fray, but the sun had already blasted the tiny creature to dust. Stronghand signaled, and Last Son struck down the dogs while Quickdeath twitched and croaked in agony as the venom coursed through his body. Their blood spattered his writhing body.

'Leave him,' said Stronghand, rising. He picked up the

ivory chest and frowned at it while two of his brothers collapsed his chair and made ready to leave. 'A pretty thing,' he said, 'but the knowledge possessed by the craftsman who made it is worth far more than the object itself, however brilliant these gems shine.'

The chieftains approached.

'Did you know he would challenge you?' asked Ironclaw.

'I knew he was rash, and scorned caution. That was all I needed to know.'

'How did you come by that ice wyrm?'

Stronghand bared his teeth to show the jewels drilled there, as sharp as starlight. 'Any one of us may brave the sands where the ice wyrms dwell.'

'Yet how many would think to do so? And survive the attempt?'

Stronghand let the chieftains think this over. Quickdeath's warriors would return in time, although by losing their war leader they had lost claim to their victory. They had learned their lesson. They would not rebel again.

'Come,' he said. 'I will see what remains of the town.'

The detritus of battle looked much the same whatever country he was in. The Salian dead cast into the river bloated just like any other; their blood stained the waters with the same hue. Their famished children bawled and whimpered in the same fashion as any freshly orphaned waif cleft so suddenly from its parent. Flames ate wood regardless, and the drought that had plagued Salia all summer encouraged the conflagration and made it burn even hotter so that by the time he reached the town gates, most of the buildings inside were on fire, smoke and ash rising into the sky to paint it a boiling gray. The gates had been razed, an impressive feat of destruction, and the defenders had created a second barrier with a jumble of carts and wagons, but these, too, had been smashed and pathways cleared through their remains where Quickdeath's troops had made their charge.

'Blow the horn,' he said to Last Son when he had tired of walking among the dead. 'I want all of our warriors to withdraw from within the walls.'

He gave orders that the last refugees were to be allowed to depart with whatever goods they could carry, stipulating only that any man carrying a sword was to be killed. Ash dusted his bone-white hair and coated his face and torso. The air stank of burning and death, yet it was not death that bothered him but the loss of this town's useful purpose, its craftsmen and storehouses, its gardens and tanneries, its merchants and smithies and marketplace.

The towns were the wheels that would drive his cart; the sails and oars that could propel his ships. A certain belligerent industry smoldered in the towns, at odds with the languorous round of existence that defined the countryside, where most of the common folk labored in the fields in some form of servitude to their noble masters.

'What will you do with this place?' asked Ironclaw. He had stuck close by Stronghand's side and seemed, perhaps, to regard him with a new respect.

'We must not overextend ourselves. But I would rebuild such towns when it is convenient to do so. Let them be filled with artisans and laborers who will pay a tithe to our coffers in exchange for freedom to work.'

'Why not make them slaves?'

'A man who is whipped is like a coal beneath ashes – still hot with resentment.'

'Then whip him until the spark dies.'

'If the spark dies, then he is no more than a beast, without spirit or thought. Nay, I will make slaves where it benefits me, but let artisans and freeholders grow in such soil that will provide me with a rich crop.'

'You are not like the chieftains who have come before you,' remarked Ironclaw, but the comment rang like iron in Stronghand's ears, a decisive stroke. Ironclaw's caution had yielded; his distrust had given way to approval.

'No,' he agreed. 'I am not.'

In the distance, out where stragglers fled into the surrounding woodland, a pair of beasts loped out of the forest. Something in their dark shapes triggered an avalanche of recognition. Around him, Eika dogs began barking, churning forward in a frenzy while their masters beat them back.

'Hold!' he cried, and his soldiers took up the cry as it carried outward so that no one there attacked the creatures who approached. He handed his standard to Last Son and ran toward them, and it was true, after all, that he knew them.

Their ribs showed, and dirt and leaves matted their black flanks. One had a torn ear and the other limped, but he knew them, and they knew him. They swarmed up with ears flattened and hindquarters waggling. Even starved and weakened, they were big enough to knock a man down and rip out his throat. His own dogs ringed them but stayed clear, warned off by the hounds' growls and snaps.

'Yes,' he said, grinning as they licked his hands. 'Yes, you have found me. Now you must lead me to Alain.'

XXVII

UNEXPECTED MEETINGS

1

Rosvita dreamed.

Prince Sanglant rides at the head of a great army up to a noble hall. Atop the roof flies the banner of Avaria: the powerful lion. A thirtyish woman regally gowned strides out to meet him. She is one of Burchard's and Ida's heirs; the hooked nose and the characteristic droop of her lips confirm it. She is cautious but not unwelcoming.

'We have much to speak of,' the noble lady says to the prince as she takes hold of his bridle in the same manner that a groom holds the horse so his lord can dismount. 'You know what grief my family has suffered. My elder brothers both dead in their prime, fighting Henry's wars. Now my mother and younger sister have died of the plague, my duchy is ravaged, and I fear that my father is being held against his will in the south, if he is not already murdered as they say Villam was. Henry has not remained loyal to us as we have been to him.'

A thunderclap shudders the heavens overhead, and Rosvita

is borne away on the dark wind, far away, until she sees her young half brother Ivar lying dead in the back of a cart, his body jolted this way and that as the cart hits ruts in the track. Grief is an arrow, killing her; then his eyes snap open, and he stares right at her. His blue eyes are the sea; she falls into the waters as night roars in to engulf her.

She swims in darkness as the last of her air bubbles out from her lips. Rock entombs her. She is trapped. The memory of starlight dazzles only to unravel into sparks that wink out one by one as the last of her breath fades and she knows she will drown.

A spatter of cold and damp brushed her brow and melted away, and a second cold splash kissed her lips, startling her into consciousness, but she still could not see, only heard the sound of the sea roaring and sucking around her as the waters rose and fell and rose again, battered against rocks. She was blind and mute and too weak to struggle.

Where am I? What has become of us?

Fortunatus' dear voice emerged unexpectedly out of the black sea.

'Sister, I pray you. Can you hear me? Nay, Hanna, it's no use. I can't wake her.'

'We'll have to carry her. We must go quickly, or we'll be captured. Those are King Henry's banners. How came his army here so quickly?'

'Better to ask how many weeks or months passed in the world while we walked between the crowns. They could not have known where we were going, since we did not know it ourselves.'

'The Holy Mother is a powerful sorcerer. Perhaps she can see into the future.'

'That may be, Eagle, but I think it unlikely since she would have to have known Sister Rosvita had the knowledge to weave the crowns. Best to ask ourselves where we are, and why the king and the skopos have led an army to this same shore.'

Hanna's laugh was bitter. 'You are right, Brother. No matter what the answer, we are in the place we least wanted to be! Hurry!'

Gerwita whimpered. Ruoda coughed, echoed by Jehan. These sounds roused Rosvita as no others could. They must make haste, or it would all have been for nothing. She could not expect mercy from the skopos for herself and particularly not for her attendants, for whom she was responsible.

'Ungh,' she said, clearing her throat, trying to force a word out. Her eyes were sticky, but she peeled one open to see a head swaying an arm's length above her, face turned away as it surveyed a sight hidden to her. The crown of his head was bald, and his hair was thinning, streaked with gray. Even Brother Fortunatus was growing old. A snowflake twirled down to become lost on his shoulder. He looked down, saw her waking face, and smiled as brightly as a child, a beacon of hope.

'Sister Rosvita!'

The others crowded forward, an ocean of faces, too many and yet too few. Where was Sister Amabilia? How had she got lost? Others seemed only vaguely familiar to her, as if she had known them once, a long time ago, and then forgotten them. Weren't those Hilaria and Diocletia from St. Ekatarina's Convent? Their expressions appeared so anxious that their fear gave her strength, and strength reminded her that Sister Amabilia was surely dead. The old grief, muted now if no less painful, gave impetus to her resolve.

'I can stand.'

It took Hanna and Fortunatus to aid her, and her legs trembled under her as she licked her fingers and used the saliva to wet her still-sticky eye until the moisture loosened the gunk that had sealed it shut.

'How long have I been unconscious?' she asked as she blinked to clear the blurriness from her vision.

The sky stretched hazy dark above them, and although she found it difficult to get her bearings, she fixed on the spray of light that blanketed the vista before them: a hundred fires, two hundred, even more, laid out in an unreadable pattern that sloped away from them to an unknowable horizon lost to night. Snow dusted the ground, and the wind had a bite. A few flakes spun past.

'Long enough to pray. It was dusk when we walked out into this place, with only a few stars in the heavens to draw us here. The clouds came in swiftly. We can't escape by the crown even if you were strong enough to weave it again.'

'Where are we?'

They answered with silence.

She attempted again to get her bearings.

In waking, she had struggled with confusion, but as she took in the ragged group she remembered everything. Heriburg still clutched the satchel that held the precious books, her *History* and the copy begun by Sister Amabilia and continued by other hands, as well as their copy of the *Vita* of St. Radegundis. Besides the clothes on their backs, a few knives, and Hanna's weapons, the books were all that remained of the possessions they had carried away from Darre. Jerome sat on the one chest they had filled with certain provisions and treasures saved by the sisters from the convent and hauled with them through the crown. For they had not escaped the convent alone.

'Mother Obligatia! Where is she?'

'Here I am, Sister.'

Sister Hilaria stepped aside to let Rosvita pass. With Fortunatus' aid she knelt beside the pallet on which the old abbess lay. Obligatia was so physically weak that it was always a surprise to hear how strong her voice was and to see the powerful spirit in her gaze – she bore the intensity of a much younger person.

'So,' said Mother Obligatia. 'A gamble, which you won, Sister. You have woven the crowns and brought us here.'

'If only we knew where *here* is!'

'There are not many stone circles with precisely seven stones, as this one has.'

'Seven in all or seven still standing?'

The stones rose at the brink of a cliff, and although she could pick out seven massive pillars she could not be sure if others lay toppled along the ground. They seemed to be standing on the edge of the world with the wind beating and moaning through the stones and the waters spilling over rocks far below, gurgling and whispering. Landward, the ground sloped away down a long, gentle distance that couldn't quite be called a hill. There might have been heights beyond where the army was camped, but without stars or moon it was difficult to tell what was shadow and what the land itself. Just beyond their group Teuda sat beside poor Sister Petra, who rocked back and forth babbling as Teuda soothed her.

'Seven in all,' said Mother Obligatia.

'How are we situated?' Rosvita asked. 'You saw the last of the setting sun.'

'The sea lies south, more or less,' said Hanna. 'We're looking north.'

'It's still winter, by the look of this snow. You're sure it is King Henry's army?'

'I am sure,' said Hanna. 'The skopos is with him.'

'How could they have journeyed here so swiftly?' Rosvita rubbed her eyes wearily. Fortunatus kept a hand on her back to support her.

Hanna went on. 'When I was in Darre, I was taken before the skopos. The Holy Mother spoke of a crown by the sea in Dalmiaka. Or we might have arrived in southern Salia or even as far west as Aquila.'

'As I remember from reading the chronicles,' said Obligatia, fingers still woven through Rosvita's, 'there are crowns with seven stones in all three of those places.'

'I wove east, or I meant to. This must be the Middle Sea at our backs.'

'We might be in the north,' said Hanna, 'but if that were so, we would be in Eika lands now. I don't see how King Henry could have marched here with such an army.'

'You agree this must be the Middle Sea at our backs?'

'It seems most likely, unless there are other seas we know nothing of. Yet then how could King Henry know of them? If we are come to Dalmiaka, this might be the selfsame crown that the skopos spoke of.'

'The simplest explanation is often the best one,' said Fortunatus. 'If a maiden's belly swells, it was more like a man who got her with child than a shade or an angel, no matter what story she tells the deacon. If the Holy Mother did not know where we were going, then isn't it likely she came here of her own accord not expecting to meet us?'

'Ill fortune for us,' whispered Gerwita, sniffling.

Ruoda coughed, and her spasms set off Jehan.

'Hush!' said Aurea from the gloom, where she kept watch. 'Look there! Torches!'

With a grimace, and aided by a spike of adrenaline, Rosvita got to her feet. Fortunatus kept hold of her elbow. Standing, she had a clear view of the land northward. A procession approached from the distant camp, no more than two abreast but more lights than Rosvita could easily count winding toward them.

'They are seeking us,' sniveled Gerwita. 'They know we're here!'

'They must have seen the threads of the spell sparking,' said Fortunatus.

'I pray you, let us go!' said Hanna.

'Where shall we go in such darkness?' asked Aurea, always practical. 'We dare not light a torch.'

'We do not fear the darkness,' said Sister Hilaria. 'If you can carry Mother Obligatia and the chest, then Diocletia and I can take turns leading the group. Night seems bright enough to my eyes. Teuda will bring up the rear. Let me take the staff so that I can test shadows and beat aside brush.'

'A wise solution.' Rosvita grasped hold of Gerwita's shoulders. 'Sister Gerwita, I am still weak from my labors. Fortunatus must help carry Mother Obligatia. If you cannot support me, then you must leave me behind.'

Gerwita's choked sobbing ceased. 'I shall never leave you behind, Sister! Here, let me put my arm around your back. Can you lean on me? That's right!'

Heriburg had the books, which she refused to relinquish. Ruoda and Jehan had themselves to care for, and it was clear that both of the young novices suffered from a severe grippe but would not complain. It fell, therefore, to Jerome to carry the chest and Fortunatus and Hanna to lift the pallet while Hilaria and Diocletia took the van, each carrying a staff. Teuda and Aurea brought up the rear, shepherding Sister Petra, who showed a tendency to stray if she were not led.

'Have you a rope that you might tie on her?' Rosvita asked gently, and after brief consideration Teuda used Petra's belt as a leash, so that the woman would not run off and delay them – or give them away.

In this fashion they stumbled east parallel to the cliff with the sea to their right and the wind stiff against their faces as it blew in off the water. It was cool but not cold. A salty damp pervaded everything, and as they walked, the fine blanket of snow faded into patches and at last gave way as a warm breeze rose out of the southeast. The ground was rocky and tremendously uneven, but there were few enough trees and large shrubs so Rosvita, walking directly behind Diocletia, did not find herself scratched and mauled too often as the nun flattened or broke off any offending branches. Even as Rosvita's eyes got accustomed to the dimness, she still felt half blind, but the nuns walked as confidently as if they held aloft torches to light their way. Gerwita steadied her, and indeed the girl trudged along like an old soldier, as surefooted as sin. Behind, Jerome tripped once, landing with a grunt of pain and the heavy thump of the chest, but he insisted he was unhurt and it wouldn't have mattered anyway. They had to go on. They all of them glanced back frequently, and Rosvita felt a great sense of relief when the lay of the land cut off any view they had of the torchlit parade that snaked its way ever nearer to the stones.

'Will they follow our trail?' Gerwita whispered.

'It may be, but we must pray they detect nothing until morning.'

'I hope so.'

'Careful,' said Diocletia, ahead of her. 'There's a cut in the ground five steps ahead. When I touch you, stop, and I'll help you over.'

Rosvita relayed the message back to the others. In four more steps she found herself passed from one strong hand to the next as Diocletia and Hilaria helped her over a ditch cut into the ground by a dry streambed. She and Gerwita waited on the other side while the pallet was laboriously handed across, and the rest followed, using the staffs for balance. After a brief rest, they moved on.

In this way, although she was so weary that she was shaking all over, they walked and walked and walked, pausing to rest only when they reached an obstacle of rock or earth or, once, a dense tangle of thorny burnet they had to detour around. Gaps appeared in the cloud cover, revealing stars and, intermittently, the waxing gibbous moon. No one spoke except to pass warnings down the line; once, Petra bleated like a goat, and they heard a distant answering blat from the night. Gerwita giggled nervously. Ruoda coughed.

Eventually, the ground began to slope noticeably upward and the noise of the sea receded as they climbed, pressing inland until they came to a forest of pine with a light layer of shrub whose spines and thorns caught in their clothing. When Jerome dropped the chest a second time after stumbling over a root, Rosvita insisted they stop and rest.

Every soul there dropped to the ground like a stone except Hilaria and Diocletia, who consulted with each other and then split up, Hilaria to scout forward and Diocletia to range back along their trail to make sure they weren't yet being followed. Gerwita fussed over Rosvita.

'I pray you, child, I am too weary to move, but perhaps you could see if Brother Jerome is injured in any way.'

'Of course, Sister!'

Hanna groaned and moved over to sit beside Rosvita, blowing on her hands. 'I'll have blisters!'

'How do you fare, Eagle?'

'Well enough. Mother Obligatia weighs so little. It's a miracle she still lives.'

'A miracle, perhaps, or stubbornness. Never underestimate the power of obstinance.'

Hanna chuckled, then sobered. 'Is it true she is Liath's grandmother?'

'Twice over.'

'Ai, God! I pray we find Liath again, and that Mother Obligatia survives long enough for them to meet.'

'I believe that it is that hope which keeps the good mother alive.'

They breathed in silence for a while, listening to the murmur of wind through the pines and underbrush, to the hacking coughs of the companions, to Petra's mumbling conversation held with herself. The scent of myrtle and wild sage gave the night a bracing flavor. Their party sat so close together that it was easy to mark all of them as much by feel as by sight, although by now the wind had blown the clouds into scraps that left the sky in tatters with the moon's face revealed.

'I can no longer hear the sea,' said Rosvita, 'yet that was all I heard in my dreams.'

'There was light enough to see when we first walked out of the crown. The stone circle stands at the edge of a great cliff. I got dizzy looking down to the water. It was so far below. And all up and down the coast I saw neither dunes nor beaches, but only a line of sheer cliff. It seemed strange to me, so sharp. I've seen the shore of the northern sea, and it's so very different, very flat. The waves creep in a long ways before they draw out again.'

'I've never seen the sea.'

'Not in all your travels with the king?'

Rosvita smiled. 'Are you surprised, Eagle? I expect you are better traveled than I am.'

'Although you ride with the king's progress? I wouldn't have thought so. You're from the North Mark, just as I am. The sea is not more than a day's walk from my village and your father's manor.'

'I was sent south as a child to enter the schola before I ever rode to the sea. Nay, I have never seen it, although I would like to.'

Hanna lifted her hands and blew on them to ease the raw skin. Rosvita shifted her weight from one buttock to the other; the litter of pine needles was a prickly cushion. Gerwita whispered to Jerome; Aurea brought round a skin of cider, almost turned to vinegar, which she offered first to Rosvita and then to Hanna, and it was only after she had gone on to Fortunatus where he sat beside Mother Obligatia that the Eagle replied.

'I have dreams, but they seem like true dreams, like visions of things that are happening, not dreams at all. I was told in a dream that I am the luck of a Kerayit shaman. Do you know what that means?'

'The Kerayit? Are they not a barbarian tribe far to the east? I believe that Prince Bayan's mother came of that savage race. Beyond that . . .' She shook her head. '. . . I know little enough, but I am always eager to learn more. What does it mean to be the luck of a Kerayit shaman?'

A nightjar churred, and Hanna started, half rising to her feet. 'It is the wrong time of year for a nightjar to call out to its mate!'

'Unless winter is past and this is the last snow of spring.'

'Hush!' hissed Aurea. 'Someone is coming!'

Brush rattled as Diocletia strode out of the underbrush into the clearing where they had thrown themselves down.

'Up!' she said, pitching her voice low. 'They are already on our trail. I saw a dozen or more torches back on our path. They were rising and dipping as the men holding them bent to examine the ground. We must move on.'

Fear lent them strength. Hanna pressed her palms to her cheeks before going back to the pallet. Gerwita hurried back to aid Rosvita in standing.

'I won't leave you!' she said predictably, but Rosvita only smiled and tried not to groan as she started forward. She ached everywhere. She was already exhausted.

'This way,' said Diocletia, heading into the brush.

'What about Sister Hilaria?' protested Heriburg.

'Come along,' said Diocletia, not waiting for them.

They had not gone more than a hundred paces when they stumbled out from under the cover of the wood into an olive grove where, under the light of the moon, Hilaria stood facing a brace of men armed with hoes and a trio of silent dogs standing at alert.

'I can take them,' muttered Hanna.

Hearing them, Hilaria raised a hand although she did not turn. 'I pray you, Sister Rosvita, come forward. These speak no language I know. Perhaps they are Arethousan.'

They were not, nor did they appear to recognize that tongue when Rosvita begged for aid. They had the look of farmers, stocky and powerful, and when they beckoned, Rosvita felt it prudent for their party to follow. Perhaps Hanna could dispatch them, but Mother Obligatia could not flee if anything went wrong.

Yet as they walked behind the farmers through the grove and then between the rows of a small vineyard, twisting and turning on a well-worn path, Rosvita did not feel that their captors were precisely suspicious but only wary. They neither threatened nor barked, not even the dogs. The path brought them to a village, no more than ten houses built with brick or sod in a style unknown to her together with a building whose proportions she recognized instantly: this squat, rectangular structure looked more like a barracks than a church, but by the round tower at one end and adjoining graveyard, she knew it was an Arethousan church.

A bearded man wearing the robe of a priest with a stole draped over his left shoulder waited on the portico of the church attended by a score of soldiers. Torches revealed their grim faces. The priest wore a Circle of Unity at his chest with a bar bisecting it, the sigil of the Arethousan church.

'I pray you, Holy Father,' said Rosvita in Arethousan, stepping forward once their party came into the circle of light and the others had set down their burdens. 'Grant us respite and shelter, for as you can see we are holy sisters and brothers of the church, like you, who seek a moment's rest before we go on our way.'

'You are not like me.' The priest's upper lip turned up with disgust as he looked them over. He had curly hair falling in dark ringlets almost to his shoulders but this angelic attribute did nothing to soften his sneering expression. 'You are Daryans. How is it you butcher my language, woman?'

She knew her grammar was good, but he seemed determined to remain unimpressed 'I am Sister Rosvita, educated in the Convent of Korvei. I pray pardon if I torture the pronunciation of your words.'

'Just as your people torture the words of our blessed Redeemer and blight the Earth with every manner of heresy. Only among we Arethousans have your false words been strangled and killed. Sergeant Bysantius, what shall we do with them?'

The sergeant had the look of a typical Arethousan, short and stocky, with black hair and a swarthy face, but he had a shrewd expression as he assessed them. He was obviously a man accustomed to measuring the worth of the soldiers he meant to send into battle. 'There's a Daryan army out there, Father, commanded by the usurper and the false mother. How are these few Daryans come here? Did they lose the army that shelters them? If so, how much ransom might we receive from the usurper to get them back?'

'Best to take them to the patriarch in Arethousa,' said the priest.

Sergeant Bysantius' gaze rested on the pallet and Mother Obligatia's frail form. 'Just so,' he said finally. 'We're pulling out tonight. I haven't the men to fight a force as large as that one.'

'Surely a dozen good Arethousans can slaughter their entire expedition! They are the feeblest of nations. The lord of Arethousa is the only lord who has stout soldiers and command of the sea.'

'True enough,' agreed Sergeant Bysantius, but there was something mocking in his tone that made Rosvita like but distrust him. 'I'll take these prisoners to the lady of Bavi and she can send them on to the patriarch. What of you, Father? Do you stay and fight?'

'My people expect me to stay. Not even the slaves and murderers who make up the Daryan army dare strike down a man of God! Take what you came for, and go!'

'Very well.' Bysantius turned away and gave orders to his men, who dispersed about their business.

'What did he say?' asked Hanna, and the others crept closer – as much as any of them dared move a single step – as Rosvita told them what she had heard.

A cart rolled up, and after loading sacks of grain, two barrels of oil and two of wine, and a cage of chickens into the back, the soldiers made room for Mother Obligatia's pallet, braced among the sacks in a way that would, Rosvita noted, offer the old abbess something resembling a more comfortable ride. It appeared that in addition to the provisions, the sergeant had come for recruits. As his party formed up, they prodded into line two frightened young men whose mothers and sweethearts, or sisters, wept in the doorways of their huts.

A pair of soldiers jogged into the village from the direction of the olive grove.

'Sergeant! There's a patrol of the Daryans, coming this way!'

'Let's be off, then,' said Bysantius. He had a horse. The rest walked, and so did Rosvita and her companions, trudging along the dusty road at a numbing pace, their way lit by the torches the soldiers carried, until at dawn the sergeant had pity on Rosvita and the coughing Ruoda and allowed them to sit in the back of the cart. Their party moved not swiftly but steadily, pacing the ox, yet as Rosvita stared back down the road up which they'd come she saw no armed band pursuing them. The countryside was sparsely wooded, and quite dry, although the ground was brightened by a spray of flowers.

'It must be spring,' said Ruoda quietly, voice hoarse from coughing. 'How long did we walk between the crowns?'

'Three or four months. I don't know the date.'

The girl sighed, coughed, and shut her eyes.

'Sister Rosvita.' Obligatia was awake; she too examined the road twisting away behind them, the sere hillsides, and the pale blue sky. 'Do you think we have escaped the skopos?'

'I pray so. Perhaps the priest put them off. Perhaps Henry's patrol believed that it had been Arethousan soldiers all along and gave up the chase.'

'In whose hands will we find safety?'

Rosvita could only shake her head. 'I don't know.'

They marched inland at this leisurely pace for three days, stopping each night in another village where they gathered new provisions to replace what they ate as well as a pair or three of reluctant recruits. Once an old man spat at the sergeant, cursing in a language Rosvita did not recognize. Gerwita screamed as Bysantius stabbed the offender, then left his body hanging from an olive tree, a feast for crows.

'I wonder if we would have found more mercy at the hands of the skopos,' said Hanna that night where they settled down to sleep in a cramped stable, enjoying the luxury of hay for their bed and cold porridge and goat cheese for their supper.

'"Learn the artifices of the Arethousans and from one crime know them all,"' muttered Fortunatus.

The sergeant kept a watch posted on them all night, and in the morning they set out again.

Today Sergeant Bysantius gave up his horse and during the course of the morning walked beside the wagon.

'So, Sister,' he said, 'how comes the usurper to these lands? Why does he wish to rob us of what rightfully belongs to another?'

'You must know I cannot speak in traitorous terms of my countryman and liege lord. I pray you, do not press me for information which I cannot in good conscience give. Even if I knew it, which I do not.'

He grinned. He had good teeth, and merry eyes when he was smiling. 'The Daryan soldiers that come marching in that army weren't just of the old city where the heretics will burn. They say the new Emperor of Dar is a northern man, an ill-mannered barbarian.'

She smiled blandly, knowing better than to rise to this trivial bait.

'He's a Wendishman, they say, king of the north. The masters like to say that Daryans and northerners are louts and liars, goat-footed and braying like asses. I've seen them fight, though.'

'Have you fought against them?'

He grinned again but did not answer, instead calling for his horse in a language she did not recognize, and for the first time it occurred to Rosvita that Sergeant Bysantius, like her, spoke Arethousan without the pure accent that the priest had scorned her for lacking.

2

In early afternoon the carters dumped Ivar out of the wagon beside the appointed meeting place, but it was only after they had rumbled away and their voices had faded into the distance that a young man stepped out from behind the massive oak tree that dominated the clearing. He was slender, with pale hair, and carried a bow in one hand and an arrow in the other.

'You're Brother Ivar,' the soldier said. 'I recognize you.'

Ivar spat out the tiny scroll concealed in his mouth, then groaned as he staggered, trying to catch his balance, and sat down hard instead. His limbs still weren't working right. 'How can you recognize me? I don't know you.'

'It's the red hair. I was there when you were brought by the prior of Herford Monastery to stand before Duchess Sabella for judgment.'

'Ah.' The memory of that humiliating day still made him hot with anger. The other man – no older than himself – squatted beside him. Ivar squinted at him, finding that his eyes hurt and his back ached and that he had a headache starting in like a mallet trying to pound its way out of his skull. 'I don't recognize you.'

'I'm called Erkanwulf. I belong to Captain Ulric's troop. We served Biscop Constance, and now—' Here his tone crept lower, ragged with disgust. '—now we serve Lady Sabella, whether we will it or no.'

'Had you a choice in the matter?'

'Captain Ulric told us we'd a choice whether to stick with him or go back to our homes. He said we had a chance to bide our time and wait for the right moment to restore Biscop Constance. He said if we rebelled against Lady Sabella now, we'd be killed.'

'So he chose to be prudent.'

Erkanwulf shrugged. 'That's one way to put it. We could have ridden to Osterburg. That's where they say Princess Theophanu has gone to ground. She's made herself duchess of Saony what with her father gone south and her sister and brother lost in the east.'

'Why didn't you do that?'

'Captain Ulric said he wanted us to stick close by the biscop, so that we might keep an eye on her, in her prison. Make sure she remains safe. Now that the king has abandoned us for the foreigners in the south, there's no one else to aid her. Here, now, let's get you out of the sun.'

He helped Ivar to his feet and led him to the shelter of the little chapel, which was no more than a curved stone wall roofed with thatch, open on one side to the air. The remains of a larger structure lay half buried in the earth around it. Inside the chapel a log had been split and each half planed smooth of splinters to make a bench; Ivar collapsed gratefully onto one of these seats. The altar consisted of little more than a mighty stump greater even than that of the remaining oak giant that dominated the clearing. A big iron ring affixed to an iron stake had been driven into the center of the stump, and spring flowers woven into a wreath garlanded the ring. A wooden tray had been set on the stump, laden with an offering of dried figs, nuts, and a pungent cheese that made Ivar's headache worse.

He was trying to remember what had happened to Sapientia and Ekkehard, but they had vanished with the rest of Prince Bayan's army that awful night, and he and his companions had found themselves adrift and lost, three years of traveling swept away in a single night punctuated by blue fire.

'Eat something,' said Erkanwulf, bringing him the tray. 'They said you might feel poorly. We can stay a night here, mayhap, but we'll have to move swiftly if we want to get out of Arconia before Lady Sabella's loyal soldiers wonder if there's anything amiss. If we can cross into Fesse, we should be safer, but, even so, Sabella's people have been growing bold.'

'Bold?'

'Duke Conrad pushes into Salia. There's a civil war, so they say, one lord fighting the next and the only heir a girl. Isn't it outrageous? A Salian princess can't inherit the throne, only be married to the man who will sit there.'

Ivar grunted to show he agreed, but he had to pee, and he was feeling distinctly queasy with that powerful stink of goat cheese right beneath his nose, yet he wasn't sure he had the strength to get up off the log bench.

'Do we have horses?' he asked finally. 'Or can you ride?'

'I can ride!' Erkanwulf slapped the tray down beside Ivar and moved away, his shoulders tense, by which Ivar deduced muddily that he had offended him. 'My lord.' He walked out into the clearing, quiver shifting on his back, and fastidiously wiped off the tiny scroll before tucking it into his belt pouch. Now he didn't need Ivar at all.

Who did, after all? Not even and not especially his own father, who had given him to the church as a punishment, knowing that Ivar had far different hopes and dreams, which by now had disintegrated into ashes and dust.

It was all too much. He retched, but there was nothing more than bile in his stomach, and after a few heaves he just sat there shaking and wishing he had actually died on that cart. He rubbed his hands together to warm them and caught a finger on the ring Baldwin had slipped on his finger – a fine piece of lapis lazuli simply set in a plain silver band. Ai, God! The token reminded him of Baldwin's stricken face; he had to survive if only to let Baldwin know he wasn't dead. It wasn't fair to allow Baldwin to go on grieving over a man who was still living.

Yet why did living have to entail so much misery?

For some reason he wondered where Hanna was, or if she were still alive, and the thought of her made him begin to cry, a sniveling, choking whine that he hated although he couldn't stop because his stomach was all cramped and the mallet in his head kept whacking away in time to the pulse of his heart. Just before he wet himself, he managed to push up and reel, stumbling, to the edge of the forest and there relieve the pressure. He shuffled back to the bench and curled up beside the stump, praying for oblivion.

Lady Fortune, or the saint to whom the chapel was dedicated, had mercy on him. He slept hard, without dreams, and woke a moment later although by now it was dusk. An owl hooted. He recognized that sound as the one that had startled him awake.

His headache was gone and although his mouth was dry and had a foul taste, he could stand without trouble even if every joint felt as stiff as if he needed a good greasing.

'Erkanwulf?' he croaked. 'Ho, there! Erkanwulf?'

There was no answer.

I've been abandoned.

Wind creaked the branches. Twigs rattled and murmured like a crowd of gossips. A pale light bobbed away among the boles, and he rubbed his eyes, thinking some mischievous demon had corrupted his sight to make him see visions, but the light still wove and dipped like that of a will-o'-the-wisp. He got a sudden creeping pricking sensation in his shoulders and back although he stood with his back to the curving chapel wall, which was a stout shield, a comfort to the righteous.

'Erkanwulf,' he whispered, but no answer came, nor did he see any movement except that of the ghostly light.

He heard voices. He took a step back and rammed up against the stump, tipped backward, and was brought up short by the huge iron Circle. The sharp cold of iron burned through cloak and tunic to sear his flesh.

A torch wavered into view, followed by a second, and a dozen soldiers thundered cursing into the clearing. They stopped and turned, standing back to back and holding out their torches to survey the lay of the ground.

'This must be the old church what the man said,' said one of them. 'But there's no graveyard, just this old tree and that bit of a ruin there.' He gestured toward the chapel, but evidently none of them saw Ivar hiding in the shadows. 'Captain was right. It were some kind of trick to sneak a man out—'

They stilled so abruptly that the hush that fell had a presence as though it were itself a vast and ominous creature stalking the stalkers. Light flickered deep within the woods. A breathy whistle broke the silence, then stuttered to a stop. Branches rustled. A cold wind brought goose bumps to Ivar's neck.

'Hai!' shouted one of the soldiers before pitching over onto his face. A thread of light glimmered in his back, then dissolved into dying sparks that winked out one by one.

Shades emerged from the forest on all sides, creatures that had the bodies of men and the faces of animals: wolf, lizard, lynx, crow, bear, vulture, fox, and more that he could not identify as their darts flew into the clot of soldiers, most of whom shrieked and ran while a few lifted shields and leaped forward to fight. Yet the shades had no solid substance, nothing to receive the strike of an ax; they could kill but were themselves immune.

Half of the soldiers escaped, blundering back the way they had come, thrashing through the woodland cover until the noise of their flight ceased. Half lay on the ground, bodies contorted and twisted as though their last moments had been agony, yet no blood marked their bodies where the elfshot had pierced their skin. Shades flowed away into the forest in pursuit, but a fox-faced man and a vulture-headed woman turned to stare right at Ivar. Both were stripped to the waist, wearing nothing more than loincloths across their hips, leather greaves and arm-guards decorated with shells and feathers, and stripes of chalky paint that delineated the contours of their chests. She was young; that seemed obvious enough by the pertness of her breasts, but whatever lust Ivar would otherwise have felt to see so much nakedness was killed by the cruel curve of the vulture's beak that was her face and the blank hollow behind its eyes.

They are masks, he thought, waiting as they raised their short bows and sighted on him. Instinctively, he raised a hand, although it would afford no protection against their poisoned darts. The lapis lazuli ring Baldwin had slipped on his finger winked blue.

They lowered their bows, glanced each at the other, and faded away into the forest.

He stood there shaking so hard he couldn't move as the

jolt of adrenaline coursed through him. It paralyzed him as efficiently as Sister Nanthild's concoction had mimicked death.

But after a long while it, too, faded, and the night noises of the forest returned piecemeal, first an owl's plaintive hoot, then a whisper of wind and the wrangle of branches, and finally the clear and loud *snap* of a breaking tree limb.

He leaped sideways and crashed into the stone wall, bruising his shoulder, but it was Erkanwulf returning with four horses on a string, two saddled and two laden with traveling packs filled with grain. Ivar could smell the oats even from this distance. The young soldier carried a lantern, and he stopped in confusion and fear as the light crept over the dead men.

'I-Ivar?'

'I'm here.' He stepped out of the chapel, shaking again, shoulder on fire and tears in his eyes. 'Where were you?'

'I hid the horses. What happened? How did they find us? Did you kill them?'

'No. I don't know. Shades came out of the trees. Ai, God! They're probably still wandering nearby! Let's get out of here!'

Erkanwulf's eyes got very round, and his mouth dropped open, then snapped shut. 'Here.' He thrust one lead into Ivar's trembling hands. 'I've heard they come back to eat their kills. We'll take the carter's track until light. They can't abide human-made roads.'

'A-are you sure?'

'I'm sure that elfshot kills.' He, too, started to shake with fear, making the lantern light jig across the corpses. The lack of blood made the scene more gruesome. The corpses had already begun to stiffen.

Erkanwulf snuffed the lantern, hoping that the moon would give enough light to guide them. They fled east along the track, walking until dawn with the nervous horses on leads behind them, but they were too afraid to stop. When dawn came after an eternity of walking, they found a deer trail that wandered east, and they kept going at a steady walking pace because, after all, fear prodded them on, so it was only when they reached a stream and had to stop the horses from drinking too much cold water while overheated that they remembered that while they might march on they had to rest and graze the horses.

'Why didn't they kill you?' Erkanwulf asked after they had watered and rubbed down the horses and turned them out to graze.

Ivar washed his face and drank from the rushing stream before he answered. 'I don't know.' He touched the ring, but its polished surface told him nothing. 'I just don't know.'

3

He lay winded and gasping, recovering from the panic that had seized him just before the last of his air gave out. For a long time he sprawled in blackness, his only reference points the touch of water on his toes and the grind of pebbles and sand against his skin where he had dragged himself out of the flooded tunnel. The ground sloped gently upward until, at the limit of his reach, it humped up into a curved shelf of rock. The air swelled thickly in his chest; it seemed as heavy as the darkness surrounding him. He could see nothing, not his hand, not the floor, not even the armband that had before this faithfully lit his way in the depths.

After a longer while he shouted, but the caverns swallowed his voice. He heard no answering reply nor the scuffle of curious scouts.

Again he called out.

Again, silence answered.

Buried deep under the ground one heard silence in an entirely new way. No sound but that of his own breathing disturbed the air. If he shifted, then his knee might scrape rocks; his toe might lift out of the cold bath of water and cause a droplet to splash. That was all.

He stood and reached above his head, searching, but could

not touch ceiling. He took in air, called out again, and a fourth time, and a fifth, and each time the sound of his voice faded and failed as he stood in a stillness so lucid that he finally understood that this was a dead place where nothing lived. He had swum into a blind pocket.

Without light, he could not explore to see how wide this cavern spanned or where tunnels might spear into stone to make roads that would lead him to light or help. He dared not move away from the water lest he could not find it again and, thus trapped, starve and die.

If he could not explore, then he would have no choice except to swim back to where his companion waited, where there was food and a chance to live buried in a gravelike prison. This taste, like defeat, soured in his mouth.

There had to be a way out.

'What are you?'

He shrieked and leaped backward, stumbling into the water, slipping, and falling to his knees. Then he began to laugh, because he recognized that rumbling whisper. The creature had been crouched in front of him all along, yet he had not sensed it. It made no sound of breathing. Now, it scraped away from him, retreating from the unexpected laughter, and he controlled himself quickly and spoke.

'I pray you, Friend, I am a messenger. I am come from your own tribesmen who are lost beyond this tunnel.'

'They are lost,' agreed the voice. 'One among us watches since the time they are lost. If the deeps shift, then the path may open. How are you come through the poison water?'

'It is not poison to me. I am not one of your kind.'

'You are not,' it agreed. 'We speak tales of the long-ago time when a very few of the creatures out of the Blinding dug deep. So do they still, but only to rob. Once they brought gifts, as it is spoken in the old tales. Once there was obligation between your kind and ours. No more.'

The words made his head hurt. Each phrase was a bar prying him open, cracking the seals that bound him; thoughts and memories spilled into a light too bright to bear. A great city. A journey through the dark.

Adica.

'No more,' he echoed, pressing his face into his hands as his temple throbbed and his skull seemed likely to split open. But despite his pain, he had a message to deliver. 'Can you help them? Some still live, beyond the tunnel, but they are trapped. Can you help them?'

'Come,' said the voice. 'The council must decide.'

It shuffled away, but he had to call after it.

'I can't see to follow you.'

'See?'

'I am blind in this darkness.'

It said nothing, and he tried again.

'The light above that blinds you, that you call the Blinding, is what I need to see. This place, where you can see without light, it is a blind place to me.'

Out of the blindness cold fingers grasped his arm, tapped the armband, and jerked back. 'Poison water!' It hissed and gurgled and went still, as though that touch had poisoned it.

He waited, and after a bit it spoke again.

'Such talismans we make no longer. The <magic> flees after the great calamity. Hold to me and follow like a <young one>.'

He reached out, grasped its cool hand, and trusting that it did not mean to lead him to his doom, he stumbled after it as it moved away with a strange rolling gait into a blackness so profound that he might as well have been walking into the pit.

The earth trembled beneath his feet, rocking him, then stilled.

'What was that?'

'The earth wakes,' said his guide. 'The wise ones shift their feet, and the deeps tremble.'

'Ah.' His head was hurting badly again, and so they walked for a long while without speaking. He had to concentrate on walking; because each step jolted the pain in his head to a new location and back again, he came to dread the movement although he had no choice but to go forward.

After a long, long time he had to rest.

'I must drink,' he said to his guide, 'or I will fail.'

'Drink?'

'I thirst. I must have water or some wine or ale, something to moisten my tongue and body.'

'Wait here.' The creature let go of his hand and before he understood what it was about, he heard it scrabble away over or along the stone and knew himself utterly lost.

He had no choice but to trust it – otherwise he certainly would die – so he lay down on the stone and slept. It woke him an unknown time later and put into his hands a bowl carved out of rock and filled to the brim with a brackish but otherwise drinkable water. When he had drunk it down, his head didn't hurt quite so badly and, although his stomach ached with hunger, he could go on. They walked on for what seemed ages upon ages or a day at least up above where the passage of the sun and the moon allowed a man to measure the passing of time. Time seemed insignificant here, meaningless. Twice more the stone shuddered and stilled beneath and around them, causing him to pause as he swayed, heart hammering with instinctive fear, although his guide seemed untroubled by the shaking.

The second time, as the shaking subsided, he heard the noise of a distant rockfall, a scattering and shattering echo upon echo that propelled in its wake an avalanche of memory in his own mind: He remembered two young men with wiry black hair and short beards, surefooted as they climbed across and up a vast swath of rockfall that had long before obliterated one slope of a valley.

'Shevros!' he breathed. 'Maklos.'

There had been another man with them, and two more companions, but to think, to struggle to name them, made his head throb.

'Come,' said the guide, tugging him along.

They walked for another day, perhaps, or so he guessed because in addition to the pain that crippled his head he was now growing weak with hunger and again faint and irritable with thirst. The darkness ate away at him until it filled him and he was empty, even those sparks of memory lost in that vast ocean where night reigns and indeed a thing beyond night because night is elusive and transitory and this blackness had no beginning or end. The armband abraded his skin where the last of the salt water still stung, and at last when they stopped for him to rest again – the skrolin needed no rest – he slipped off the armband and rubbed the inside with the filthy loincloth he still wore which had dried while he walked. He blew on it until it felt dry and clean – as clean as anything could be under such conditions – and eased it back up on his arm.

'Come,' said his guide, stamping twice on the ground as though impatient, and it seemed the stamp and the low rumbling growl that came from deep in the creature's body performed as an incantation, or else it had been the irritant of the salt that had poisoned the armband, because a soft glow rose from the metal and the darkness retreated.

He stared in amazement. They stood in a high tunnel whose ceiling was perfectly round while the path they walked on was level. No natural cave would appear so regular. If an arrow forged out of the iron had been shot by a giant's bow and pierced stone, it might bore a shaft such as this.

'Come,' repeated his guide. 'We are close.'

The creature had a pale cast of skin and a handful of crusty growths patching its squat body. It grabbed for his hand, but he took a step away, not meaning to.

'I can see.'

Pale-skin's huge eyes whirled as it regarded him. He had no way to interpret its expression. It had no expression, in truth, only features that mimicked those of humankind perhaps simply because he insisted on seeing the resemblance.

We recognize only that which we already know.

'I can see to follow you,' he said. 'I am steadier on my feet if I walk alone. But I will have to eat very soon, and drink again.'

'So much?' it asked. 'Your body is inefficient to need so much fuel.'

'I am no different than any other man.'

'You are a creature of the Blinding. So. Come.'

They walked on, but he was getting light-headed from lack of food, and his tongue felt swollen and heavy. Yet within ten hundred paces, not seen at first because the glow of his armband lit his way no more than a stone's toss in any direction, the tunnel's walls became pillars marking the advent of a hall of monumental proportions, so vast that the feel of the air changed as they walked through a forest of pillars, a woodland carved out of the stone, each pillar rising up to an unseen ceiling spanning far beyond the reach of the light, each pillar studded with gems that dazzled before fading into the darkness as he passed, a glimpse of riches soon gone.

'What is this place?' he asked.

'The old ones built it, so legend says.'

It was more like a forest than any building he had ever seen; there was no layer of undergrowth, and no sky, but the pillars marched out on either side in uneven ranks, and each column had as different a look to it as any individual tree might – some resembling each other as oak tree resembles oak tree, yet different in the pattern of gems or decoration on its surface or the width or smoothness or curve of the pillar itself. Pale-skin divined a path by means of touching each pillar and moving on to the next, sometimes backtracking before heading out in a new direction, but always moving into the vast forest itself, endlessly on, into the wilderness.

In the midst of the forest a clearing opened. They came to the rim of a shallow bowl cut into the stone so unexpectedly that he almost tripped and fell, stopping himself on the brim, teetering there for one breath, then stepping back. In that bowl, along the level base, a hundred boulders rested all helter-skelter, and that was only what he could see within the halo made by the light, for the bowl itself was too wide for the glow of his armband to illuminate the whole of it. When he blinked, he realized that of course these were not boulders at all but a congregation of skrolin.

His legs crumpled under him, and he sat hard on the lip, where the floor gave way. He was too dizzy and weak to negotiate the sloping side. There he sat while a low rolling scraping sound shifted around him, disorienting him, and he fought to stay sitting and not simply keel over.

After a long time he became aware that Pale-skin squatted beside him holding two objects in his hands: a loaf of clavas and a stone bowl filled to the brim with water. The smell of the water made his mouth hurt, and in fact his lips were so dry and cracked that the moisture stung them and they bled, the iron bite of his blood blending with the metallic taste of the water. He forced himself to drink less than he wanted, to eat only a corner, not to gorge, and afterward he was so tired that he curled up on stone and slept.

When he woke, he drank and ate again, and now he had the strength to stand, for it was apparent that the boulders – the skrolin – had moved while he slept, changing position to create a clear path for him down into the bowl.

The slope wasn't so steep that he staggered, but it was still difficult to keep his balance. Pale-skin followed him, bearing more water and clavas, acquired from an unknown source. The skrolin moved only their heads as he passed, watching him, and that shifting rumbling sound followed him as he descended because they all of them fell in behind. He came to a round amphitheater cut into stone with a series of circular ledges and, in the middle, a shallow pit like the fighting ground for cocks or dogs.

Most of the skrolin gathered on the ledges, but Pale-skin led him down by stages to the pit where eleven skrolin waited. Each one wore an armband, but his was the only armband that gleamed, and when he got close to them, he saw that the armbands they wore were pitted and faded and scratched and even tarnished green with age, ancient objects whose potency had withered.

He sat down cross-legged in the center of the pit. All around, up into the ranks of the amphitheater and beyond that into the darkness which the glow of the armband could not penetrate, he felt them watching him, the force of many gazes, of interest and curiosity and of something more besides that had the scent of hope or longing.

'I am a messenger,' he said. 'I swam through the poisoned tunnel to bring you a message from those who were lost when the earth trembled and drowned the tunnel through which they traveled. Some among them are still alive. Can you find them and help them to escape the trap they are in?'

His words brought silence. He listened. He heard his own breathing, nothing more. If they pulled air into lungs and let it out again, as did humankind, he could not hear it. They were as silent as the stone around them. They seemed more than half stone themselves.

Finally, when he thought there would be no reply, a rush of clicking and stamping and rubbing and tapping swept through the assembly. After a long while, the noise subsided. Pale-skin had retreated, and in its place one with a gold sheen and a dozen crystalline growths mottling its skin shuffled forward to confront him. It wore draped about its body a number of chimes and charms that rang softly. With a deft movement, at odds with its clumsy body, it stripped the armband off its own long limb and held it out for him to see.

'You wear a talisman,' it said. 'But the talisman you wear lives. The talismans we wear are long dead.'

A sigh of grief shuddered through the assembly.

'Is it true that the shining city existed in the long-ago time? Is it true? Or is it only a story we tell.'

He nodded. 'It is true. I saw it. I was there.'

'Tell us! Tell us!'

He told them what he remembered, which wasn't much, only flashes of sights and sounds, a memory of a vast city glimpsed deep in the earth, of pillars clothed in jewels, of a marketplace that lapped a river, of caverns streaked with veins of gold and copper and wagons that moved without horse or oxen to pull them. But as he spoke, the words took on substance, as though he were weaving the city right there before them, as if their listening and his words were the hands and the clay out of which a pot could be formed.

He created the world they had lost, and they believed him, because they wanted to.

'But it is gone,' he said. 'It was all gone. They destroyed it.'

Adica destroyed it.

The pain struck, doubling him over, because he could not

see or hear with the lance of guilt and grief assaulting him. Adica had destroyed it, but she had died in a wall of blue fire and after that he recalled nothing. Only her death, and the destruction of the world.

He fell forward onto the floor, body pressed against the stone, hands clenched and teeth gritted but the pain did not cease. Adica hadn't meant to do so much damage, surely. She hadn't meant to kill innocents in order to save her own, had she? Hadn't it all been an accident, a misunderstanding?

The magnificent cities of the goblinkin vanish in cave-ins so massive that the land above is irrevocably altered. Rivers of molten fire pour in to burn away what survives.

Adica had seen the skrolin cities. She had known they existed. Perhaps she and the others had not comprehended the scope of the destruction they would unleash. Yet if they had known, would they have gone ahead anyway? He could not bear to think that she might have, so it was a mercy that pain blinded him, hammered him, until he could not think.

But he could still see.

Rivers run deep beneath the Earth, flooded with fire. This is the blood of the Earth. These are the ancient pathways that mold land and sea and weave the fabric of the world. Far away down the threads woven through the depths of the Earth by the fire rivers lie intelligences of an order both keener and slower than his own, sensing the measure of time in whose passing a human life spans nothing more than the blink of an eye.

Their minds touch his down the pathways of fire. Their thoughts burn into him.

You. Are. The. One. We. Seek.

The toll of their words rings in his head like the clamor of bells oh so slow, slower than the respiration of the skrolin.

Tell. Us. What. You. Know.

They peel away his memories, which are opaque to him but somehow clearly seen by these ancient minds for whom the unfolding of a tree from sapling to a great decayed trunk fallen in the forest flies as swiftly as a swallow through a lady's hall at wintertide. He catches glimpses of their sight as they pillage his memories: the glittering archway that Adica wove; brave Laoina with her staff; wise Falling-down; crippled Tanioinin; the veiled one and the fearsome lion women; doomed Hehoyanah and Hani's mocking smile; dying Horn; the camaraderie of Shevros and Maklos who took him across the white path which marks the border of Ashioi lands.

He weeps, because he knows all that he loved is lost to him not just because it is fled across the span of years but because the old ones are tearing those memories away as they search. They are not done with him yet.

Will. The. Weaving. Save. Us. Or. Doom. Us.

They meant well, he says, but they killed more than they saved. They caused immeasurable devastation.

Ah!

They speak. They confer for hours, for days, for weeks, for months, for years, or for an instant only. He can't measure them.

This. Is. What. We. Needed. To. Know. Now. We. Can. Act.

They withdraw. On the wind of their leaving he sees beyond the borders of the Earth where the cosmos yawns, immense and terrifying. He cries out in fear and wonder because this abyss is both beginning and end, a circle that turns back in on itself. He hears its voice, not male or female and as vast as eternity: *I am what I was and what I am now and what I will be.*

And woke with jumbled, painful memories that faded into a merciful haze. All was gone, veiled and shrouded.

He was still lying on the floor of the pit, and he was so tremendously thirsty. The skrolin waited beside him as if no time had passed and yet by the measure of his thirst he thought that hours had passed or a day, but it was impossible to know. He found the bowl of water and gulped it down, and that gave him the strength to eat half the remaining clavas with the manners of a man, not a beast.

At length, he croaked out a word, and the skrolin tapped and rubbed the ground and each other in response.

'Where do you go?' asked Gold-skin, who now spoke for the others. 'What do you see?'

Only broken images remained in his head, which was beginning to hurt again. 'A terrible fire destroyed your city. What happened after that I do not know.'

'We know. We know. The tale passes from one to the next down the long watches. First the survivors fight for many watches, each with the others, one <guild> against the next. After long and long the fighting exhausts the few who are left and it is agreed that some will tunnel turnward and some will tunnel antiturnward. Long and long we seek in the depths, but the shining city is gone and so some speak of it as only a story. Across many watches an archive is collected, things found among ruins, in hidden corners, but the archive remains closed to us, as if it never existed. So the quarrels begin again. The shining city is a story only. It is the truth. No one can agree. Now we are scattered. The talismans are dead. The archives are lost to us without the key. This is how you find us, with your story of the shining city. We wish to believe. We fear to believe. Is it true?'

'It is true.'

All around they stamped their feet and tapped and clicked until Gold-skin lifted the dull armband it had once worn and everyone hushed.

'Proof,' it said. 'Bring one from the archives. Bring one. Bring two. Bring three. That will be proof.'

'What are the archives?' He touched the bowl of water, but he had drained it dry. Pale-skin, who had grasped his needs, picked up the bowl and hurried off into the darkness.

'They are proof. Closed to us, or open to us, they are proof. Or they are baubles, nothing more. Now we wait. Now we find out.'

Waiting among the skrolin took hours or days; he had entirely lost track of time. Pale-skin brought a whole bucket carved out of stone and filled with water as well as a dozen loaves of clavas. Many times he had to relieve himself by leaving the amphitheater and walking out into the pillars for privacy. He drank that entire bucket and a second one and ate all the clavas before a dozen skrolin returned bearing three massive scrolls forged out of metal – pewter, maybe, since it seemed too hard to be silver. They set these on the ground in front of him, unrolled them, and without further ceremony stepped back. The sheets were as long as his arm span, as wide as the length of his shin, and yet as thin as a leaf. How they could lay flat when they had just been so tightly rolled up he could not imagine.

One by one, the eleven skrolin who bore an armband came forward to press their talismans into a square etched into the center of each scroll. After a pause in which every creature there seemed ready for nothing to happen, yet something to happen, the skrolin would remove the armband and step back.

When they had finished, they all looked expectantly at him.

He saw the pattern, but he didn't know what it meant. He crouched beside the unrolled sheet, slipped his armband off, and pressed it onto the sheet.

Light flashed. The armband glowed red hot, and he yelped and released it, but it did not roll away; it was stuck to the metal. Light undulated down the length of the sheet in waves, a stark white light followed by successive ripples of gold, pale yellow, silver, and a last dark surge which drove furrows into the surface, gashes and gouges too thin to measure yet he knew what they were.

He recognized writing when he saw it, although these marks were alien to him.

No sound issued from the skrolin.

They stood, like stone, without speaking or moving, stunned or shocked or ignorant.

But he knew. He understood. The miracle had happened. All that had separated them from their ancestors was their access to the knowledge that their kind had accumulated in the ancient days. These scrolls held their memories, closed to them for untold years and centuries. In this same way the pain had choked off his own life from him, glimpsed in snatches as transitory as the tales the skrolin had told themselves over and over since that day when the great weaving had destroyed them.

How long they stood in silence he could not measure. In

the depths of the earth, he possessed no gauge by which to quantify time.

They stood in silence for as long as they needed to absorb what he had wrought. They stood in silence while he unrolled the other two sheets, pressed his armband to the centers, and watched as these, too, revealed their secrets.

At length, Gold-skin turned to him.

'A life for a life. A payment. An obligation. You do not belong here, you consume too much fuel. We will trade. One among us will lead you to the Blinding so you can return to your own kind. That is your life, in exchange for the talisman.'

My own kind.

He no longer knew who his own kind were. He could only remember the wheel, and the garden of clavas growing among the rotting flesh of the dead.

'What of your kinfolk?' he asked. 'The ones who are trapped? What of them? Can you rescue them now? I can help you. I made a promise to them.'

They gave him no more speech. Pale-skin clasped him tightly, pinning his arms to his side, and hoisted him with awkward strength.

'What of them?' he called, desperate for an answer, but none came.

For hours or days Pale-skin carried him through the labyrinth that is utter night, stopping three times to give him water and clavas, and depositing him at long last, and unceremoniously, on a shelf of rock where grains of soil slipped beneath his fingers although he still could not see.

'Climb up,' said Pale-skin. 'Climb up. You have done us great wrong. You have done us great good. We will not forget.'

It rattled away, and he was left alone in the pit. But he probed and touched and sought for handholds, however useless it seemed, because he did not want to die in the pit. So he climbed up and up and up and just when he thought he had been abandoned at the base of the Abyss and must climb for an eternity without ever reaching the top, he discovered a certain alteration in the darkness revealing contours across the rock. He saw a crack of light far above.

He climbed, although he had to rest frequently and more than once slipped and almost fell. When he squeezed out through a narrow cleft, scouring his back against the rough rock, he spilled down a short escarpment, scraped through a bramble bush, yelping and cursing, and came to rest in the shade of a tree on a layer of decayed leaf litter. A bird shrieked a warning and fluttered off through the branches. The light hurt his eyes, but it gentled and mellowed as he caught his breath, dizzy, gasping for air. It was hot and muggy, but there was ease in it and the savor of freedom.

He eased up onto his forearms. He lay on a hillside overlooking a valley a quarter cleared and the rest wooded. A half dozen unseen hearths spun fingers of smoke into the darkening sky. In one clearing a pond faded to a pewter gleam. It was hard to see more detail than this because the sun was setting, the far horizon bathed in an orange-red glow so beautiful that he wept.

4

For three days they trudged overland along an old Dariyan road still used by the locals for market traffic, of which they saw little. This was the driest country Hanna had ever seen. Nothing that was truly green grew, only prickly juniper, the ubiquitous olive trees, and so many varieties of thorny shrub or broom that she wondered what they had to protect themselves against besides goats. She and the others soon became coated with a film of dust. Her mouth was always parched. Her lips cracked, and the sun was merciless.

They changed direction, turning east at dawn on the fourth day so that they marched into the rising sun, and for the next three days followed a trickle of water running over rocks which Sergeant Bysantius persisted in calling a river. Every chance she got, she sluiced its waters over her head, neck, hands, and red, swollen, blistered feet until she was streaked with sweat and dirt never completely washed away by the water. Yet for moments at a stretch that cool touch relieved her skin and the headache that continually plagued her.

Where a hole in the ground swallowed the stream, they turned up a defile with jagged, steep-sided hills rising to either side. After two arduous days on a rocky trail, making poor time and less distance, the wagons were left on the path with a guard while Sergeant Bysantius pointed the rest at an impossibly steep trail that led straight up the side of the hill. His soldiers rolled a dozen barrels out of the wagons and with great difficulty lashed them to stout poles and lugged them up. Two other men carried Mother Obligatia on her stretcher up that twisting trail which switched back and forward and back while the rest of them strung out behind, falling farther and farther back. It took hours, or years, before their footsore and exhausted party reached a row of buildings perched on a ledge cut into the cliff face.

'I almost feel that I am home again,' gasped Sister Hilaria with as much of a smile as she could muster. Her lips were bleeding, as were Hanna's.

Certainly, the monastery resembled St. Ekatarina's in its inaccessibility, high up along the cliff face with a forbidding rock ridge above and only the trail leading up to it. An army might besiege this small settlement to no avail since it possessed, as they discovered, a spring within the walls.

'Quite at home,' added Hilaria, who smelled water when they passed a stairwell cutting down into the rock. 'I only need a pair of buckets and a shoulder harness, and I'll be ready to set to work hauling up water.'

Instead, they settled Mother Obligatia in the pair of adjoining rooms – cells, really – where they were herded and shut in. The two chambers were built of stone so cunningly fitted together that it appeared the builders had not needed to use mortar. The floor was dirt, as gritty and dry as the air. Six pallets lined the walls. The second room had four actual beds with rope strung between the posts for a mattress. It was smaller than the first but opened onto a tiny, triangular court-yard where they could take air and sun; this courtyard boasted a high brick wall too high to see over and a single olive tree under whose inadequate shade stood a stone bench. There was not a single other living creature in the courtyard except ants and flies. They couldn't even hear birds singing.

'Here you will rest until I return to fetch you,' said Sergeant Bysantius to Rosvita. 'The monks will care for your needs. I leave as well ten of my men-at-arms as guards. Do not, I pray you, be fearful. I mean you and your companions no harm.'

'A fine sentiment,' said Rosvita when she translated his speech for those who could not understand Arethousan, 'but we cannot trust him. We must scout out our surroundings and make ready to escape.'

Yet when Hanna surveyed their company, she knew they had traveled as far as they could. Ruoda and Jehan were so weak it was a miracle they had come so far, and Jerome and Gerwita had only made it up the trail by stopping to rest every ten paces. All four of them lay on the pallets, utterly exhausted. Even Fortunatus and Heriburg were flagging, even *she* was, and the old ache in her hip had returned. They hadn't the strength to run, not now.

For the first ten days they mostly slept, talking little, recovering their strength, with rock and a hard blue sky their only companions. Sister Petra insisted on sitting outside in the direct sunlight until her face was burned and blistered from the sun, and then she suffered under a terrible fever for days.

They saw only two monks, both of them withered old men as wrinkled as the raisins they sprinkled onto the porridge given to the prisoners twice a day. Neither spoke, not a single word, but one knew herb-craft, and he brought ointments for Sister Petra, a foul brew for those suffering from the cough that relieved their congestion, and a spelt porridge for Mother Obligatia along with sage steeped in wine.

'We must keep up our strength,' said Rosvita one evening in the courtyard after they had finished a noble and astound-ingly filling supper of beans stewed with parsnips and fennel.

With the help of Hilaria and Fortunatus, Hanna climbed

up onto the top of the wall – and shrieked. The courtyard was carved into the last triangle of the ledge, an acclivity whose bounds were cliff above and below. She hung over the wall, feet drumming on the bricks while Fortunatus held her ankles, and stared straight down into the defile as though the wall became the cliff face. The gulf of air made her dizzy. Dusk swept in from the east; the valley below was already drowned. A fly buzzed by her ear, but she dared not slap at it. So far away that it was only a speck, a hawk glided on the wind. If only they could fly, they could sail right out of here. Then she looked down again, and fear choked her: the whole wall might collapse under her weight and send her plunging.

'We can't escape by this route. Too steep to climb above, and too steep and too far below.' She kicked out and jumped, landing with knees bent as Fortunatus steadied her. She wiped her hands on her leggings, but they were so dry that she wondered if the dust would adhere permanently to her skin. Her heart was still racing.

'The sun will kill us if we escape without a good store of water,' said Aurea, always practical.

The rest were silent, waiting for Rosvita to speak. Both Gerwita and Heriburg had come down with the cough, but they didn't suffer from it as badly as Ruoda and Jehan, who were only now beginning to recover the color in their cheeks although they still slept most of the day and night.

'Until we are all strong, I think we must bide here quietly,' said Rosvita at last. 'I will ask the guards to allow us to take turns hauling water up from the spring. Surely they tire of performing this task, and it will allow us to gain strength by climbing the stairs with full buckets. When all of us can manage the feat—' She smiled at Mother Obligatia, lying on a pallet beside the open doorway, since it was understood that Obligatia and Petra would be exempt from work. '—then we choose between what opportunities seem open to us. Meanwhile, I will ask the guards if we might obtain quills and ink and a table and bench for writing. As well make good use of the time, if we can.'

5

With fewer than fifty picked troops at his back, the boldest and most reckless, Stronghand struck inland, following
the hounds. The trail took them east and northeast through
northern Salia. The war between the Salian heirs had already
ravaged the countryside, but they still fought a dozen skirmishes before they came to a ferry crossing on the banks of
a great river which marked the limit of Salian territory.

The Hessi interpreter nodded at the river and the garrison stationed on the far bank.

'That is Varrish country, part of the duchy of Arconia,'
Yeshu said. He had spent much of his childhood in Salia under
the tutelage of an uncle and knew the country well. 'Under
the rule of King Henry and his sister Biscop Constance. But
those in the garrison are flying the sigil of Duke Conrad. You
see? The hawk of Wayland. We heard rumors in Medemelacha
that King Henry is dead, or has abandoned the north to linger
in the old city of Darre, seduced by dreams of empire. Biscop
Constance is said to be a prisoner of her half sister, Lady
Sabella. Sabella married her daughter to Duke Conrad. Maybe
this is true. I haven't seen it for myself.'

Hessi merchants liked to see things for themselves before
pronouncing them true or false. It was one of the reasons
Stronghand found them useful to work with. If he dealt fairly
with them and allowed them to expand their trading networks,
then they returned a fair profit in information and taxes in
exchange.

'We'll need ships to attack that position,' said Stronghand,
'unless you know another ford that can be crossed.'

'Duke Conrad is vigilant, so they say. He has ambitions in
eastern Salia, I have heard.'

'Yet such a river makes a powerful border. It would be hard to rule both sides of the bank if you haven't enough of a foothold. Duke Conrad sounds like a prudent commander.'

'It is said he is. He has allowed my people to trade in his cities. He does not demand more of a tax than other nobles.'

'So he is a man who will watch his back.' Stronghand turned to Last Son, now his second because he had left Trueheart behind in Alba as governor. 'We'll need fifty sheep or cow bladders. Call as little attention to yourself as possible. Eat your fill.'

They moved upstream under cover and once they were out of sight of the garrison he unstoppered the precious flask the merfolk had given him and let fall two drops of spoor into the streaming water. They ate well that night, careful not to gorge, and remained concealed in the woodland all through the next day, scouting upstream for the likeliest place to cross. A bend in the river offered the best conditions; the twenty human soldiers could swim it and the Eika cross with the aid of inflated bladders. By dusk they were ready to go. He left four men behind to wait for the merfolk.

Now they would have an escape route if the hounds led him farther inland than he hoped. They were a small group, fashioned for speed and a quick strike, not for a prolonged campaign.

He let the hounds support him across. Swimming made him nervous, as it did all Eika because they did not float like humankind. And because he knew what lurked in the depths. Although he had an alliance with the merfolk, he did not trust them. Their desires and goals seemed too alien from his.

But as he clambered up on the far shore, these reflections made him grin. Certainly humankind feared and hated the RockChildren for the same reason. What we do not understand makes us afraid. What does not look like us on the outside must remain suspicious. Yet how much harder it was to see past the outer seeming into the inner heart. The merfolk wanted restored to them what they had lost.

Was that so difficult to understand? Any soul might feel

compassion for what they had suffered – if it were a soul that could feel compassion.

The hounds shook themselves off. His soldiers deflated the bladders and carried them along in case they had another river to cross. The hounds cut back toward the ferry crossing to find their trail, and once again they speared east and south through woodland. After a pair of days the land became broken and hilly, and the fields and settlements they had been careful to avoid fell away. Up in the hills no one farmed.

On the third day he smelled the smoke of smelting fires and in the late afternoon they crept up to the verge of a great scar dug into the land. The forest had been cleared back; the reek of charcoal tainted the air. Shafts pitted the land, and steam rolled out of their depths. Men dug and hauled and hammered, most in chains and a few with whips and spears and knives set as guards upon the others.

'These are mines,' said Yeshu. 'Silver and lead if we're in the Arbeden Hills, as we should be. These are the richest veins of silver and lead in the northwest, so it is said. King Henry controls these mines and feeds his treasury out of their bowels. But you see, there.' He pointed to a log house set at the eastern edge of the clearing, where two banners could be seen through drifts of smoke. 'Duke Conrad's hawk flies beside a guivre. The guivre is the sigil of the duchy of Arconia.'

The hounds whined, ears flat, bodies tense. They wanted to charge forward, but they looked up at Stronghand, awaiting his command.

'We'll move swiftly,' said Stronghand, gathering his men close. 'Some man out to relieve himself will stumble upon us soon enough. We'll strike first to free those in chains and kill as many of the guards as possible. Some of the slaves will join us. Others will flee. The confusion will divide the attention of the guards. I will follow the hounds. Once we have my brother, we grab anything we can carry and retreat. What you grab is yours to keep or trade, and all of you will have boasting rights. Is that understood?'

They nodded. He had been careful to pick those who liked

daring and risk but who had no obvious pretensions to rule. For this troop, including young Yeshu, the hazard itself was the reward. Such a gamble made the blood sing.

He grinned and gestured. 'Move out. When I release the hounds, that is your signal to attack.'

They split up into smaller groups and spread out to surround the clearing. He waited, counting off the interval, and with the sun a hand's span above the western horizon and the guards and workers beginning to slacken their pace as they readied themselves for the evening rest, he released Sorrow and Rage.

The hounds bolted forward. Silent, as was their custom, his troops broke from the woodland cover and sprinted across the open ground, overwhelming the first guards they came to before those men could raise the alarm. The scuff of feet on earth; a shout; the ring of hammer on chain as a slave struggled to free himself; a grunt as a guard doubled over, skewered on the end of an Eika spear. Rage leaped, bowling over a guard who had turned, in surprise, a shout of alarm twisting into a scream as the weight of the hound bore him to the ground.

Guards, free workers, and men without chains grabbed their picks and raced toward the log house.

'To arms! To arms!'

'We're attacked!'

'Beasts! Fire! Run!'

Many scattered into the forest. Others barricaded themselves into the log house. His men swarmed the open ground, which was a carpet of ash and dust and chipped, wrinkled, rutted earth from the tread of feet, the dragging of chains, and the press of wheels. Twenty surrounded the log house, using the dips and levels of the uneven ground as cover; his human archers shot at any sign of movement within the house. Others spread out to stand sentry along the woodland's edge or to stand guard over the shafts, not knowing if men might clamber up from the depths.

Yet the scene of this swift victory gave him no pleasure. The stench of the workings stung like poison on his skin. The land had been stripped to bare earth, and even that soil had been mauled into an ugly facade. To steal treasure out of the earth they had created a wasteland.

The slaves, chopped free, ran for the trees, but his soldiers captured about a dozen, driving them forward in a herd. The hounds loped up to the lip of a big shaft and yipped and whined at its edge.

'I'm looking for a man known as Alain,' he said to the slaves cowering before him. 'I'll give a handsome reward to any man who leads me to him.'

They responded with frightened silence.

'He is so tall, more or less. Black hair, fair skin. He may have been blind or mute when you saw him. The hounds belong to him. Perhaps you recognize them.'

From the crowd a low voice murmured. 'What kind of reward?'

Stronghand grinned, showing the jewels studding his teeth. 'Your life. Is that not enough? Your freedom, which I grant you regardless. If you will have more, I must have more. I deal fairly with those who serve me faithfully, but I also punish those who believe they can cheat me.'

A stocky young man stepped forward out of the crowd, trailed by a second, taller companion. They wore rags that shed dirt with each step; they were themselves so filthy it was difficult to make out their features. But he liked the look in their eyes: although they feared him, they each had a keen gaze and an intelligent expression. Their captivity had not beaten them down. They hadn't given up yet.

'We came here with a fellow we called Silent, for he couldn't speak or see,' said the stocky one. 'They took him into the shafts to walk the wheel. He might live yet, or he might not. The slaves who tread the wheels don't live long.'

The taller one nodded. 'He was a decent fellow, poor lad. But the Captain would know if he still lives. I heard a rumor that the Captain had him cast into the pit in exchange for a pair of gold nomias.'

'The pit?'

'Only dead men are cast into the pit.'

The slaves shuddered, hearing these words; the pit scared them more even than he did.

'I don't know who would have wanted him dead, though,' added the taller one, 'a blind mute as he was.'

His stocky companion nodded. 'He wasn't just an ordinary prisoner. Someone was trying to get him out of the way. He knew something, I'd wager.'

'Where is this wheel? Where is the pit?'

But he already knew. The hounds whined and scratched at the lip of one of the shafts. They knew where their master had gone.

The ones who had made Alain suffer would suffer in their turn. With cold fury in his heart he turned to Last Son. 'Kill every man here except the slaves we have freed. They may go free, as they wish. Burn the rest alive.'

Last Son nodded and called out to the archers. By the time Stronghand reached the shaft and turned to clamber down the ladder into the workings, the log house was already ablaze and he heard the shouts and screams of the men inside as they made their final charge, out the door, in a vain attempt to escape.

As he descended, darkness swallowed him. He had his men bring torches such as the miners used, and with rather more difficulty the hounds were lowered after him, down each level and farther down until they reached the lowest wheel. Here, by the wavering, stinking light of pitchblende torches, Sorrow and Rage snuffled all around the wheel and up a low tunnel to a cold, damp hollow worn into the stone where rags and leavings and waste had collected.

Their tails beat the walls, wagging. They stuck their noses into the garbage and whined. Alain wasn't here, although by the testimony of the hounds he once had been.

'Hsst!' Yeshu stood beside him, head cocked. 'Listen!'

They heard the clamor of metal striking stone. A shout, followed by a harsh scream. A few moments later two of his soldiers padded out of the blackness dragging an injured man with a third soldier holding a torch to light their way.

'He and his companion attacked us,' they said. 'The other one is dead.'

The captured man moaned, lifting his head. 'Mercy,' he croaked. Blood pooled at his shoulder and dripped to the floor. 'Mercy, lord. We are only poor miners, defending ourselves.'

'Where is the pit where you cast dead men?'

The man sniveled. 'I'll show you! I'll show you!'

'You'll come down with me. Bind up his wound.'

He cried and pleaded as his wound was bound up, and it puzzled Stronghand to see that his fear of the pit outweighed his fear of his captors. What lay down there? Ought he to be afraid also? Yet the unknown had never frightened him. He feared only where he knew danger threatened him, and the unreasoning, babbling terror of this man made him curious.

'Please don't make me go down!'

The workings lay eerily silent, all sound muffled, the weight of earth heavy over their heads. Water trickled down side passages. Torchlight illuminated ancient scars mottling the walls where stone had been chipped away as miners sought new veins. These rich workings could supply a great treasure-house. It would be worth a great deal to him to possess mines like this.

The captive staggered to a halt at the edge of a shaft plunging down into the earth. Light did not penetrate far; it was pitch-black below, empty, although a faintly sulfurous wind skirled up from the depths like the breath of a buried giant long asleep.

'We'll need rope,' said Stronghand, understanding the risk he took. If his men were not loyal, they could strand him there. But OldMother wanted Alain; he wanted Alain. He had to take the chance. And, in truth, the gamble made his blood sing.

With rope lashed around his torso, he allowed himself to be lowered down and down and down, using his feet to balance himself away from the sheer wall and probing ahead with his spear until he found rock beneath him. He untied himself and tugged twice on the rope, then waited as both hounds, the miner, young Yeshu all strung about with coils of rope, and a Rikin soldier laden with four torches, an ax, and more rope arrived.

They were ready to explore. They tied more rope to the main rope and strung it behind them as the hounds sniffed forward into a labyrinth of passageways, blind alleys, one breakdown where blocks of stone littered the passageway, and a dead end – a sloping cavernous chamber ridged with ledges where the hounds snuffled with great interest for a long while before turning and leading them back in a different direction.

They scooted down a steep incline while the miner moaned under his breath until the sound so grated on Stronghand's nerves that he whirled around and brought the edge of his knife to the man's throat.

'There's nothing here.' He knew the words as truth as he spoke them. No living scent touched his nostrils. He heard no echo of footfalls, no whisper of scuttling movement, no monster's slither or the fluttering breath of an ancient evil lying in wait.

The pit lay empty. Deserted.

He snarled, low, and the hounds echoed his anger with growls of their own. They, too, knew the truth, but they led the party on regardless as the miner gulped down his sobs and Yeshu exclaimed at every pillar and shaft and new texture of rock. A new smell assailed them as they scrambled up a ramp into a large cavern.

'Bread!' Yeshu exclaimed as he ventured forward into the space, the light of his torch dancing over a field of mushrooms. Spoors settled where their feet kicked dust up.

'Corpses!' said Far-runner, the Rikin brother who accompanied them. 'They're growing mushrooms on corpses!'

The miner fell to his knees and vomited.

'There was someone here, then,' said Yeshu. 'Someone who could think, and drag these bodies to this place, and plant them. There is an old legend among my people of a race of men who delved under the earth because of a curse placed on them by their enemies. I know lots of old stories, most of them nonsense. Maybe this one is true!' He laughed, delighted, and probed among the field with his staff, shifting bones, uprooting a clump of the fleshy white growth that was bound to a rib cage with pale tendrils.

'God protect us!' wept the miner, and retched again.

'Come,' said Stronghand, because the hounds were pulling him on, padding to the limit of the light and yipping, eager to move forward.

He quickly outpaced the others, hearing Yeshu's voice behind him exclaiming over some marvel or another as they passed through glittering caverns and skirted sinks and trenches that gave out into other levels beneath. Another day he might wonder, but he felt himself close – so very close. Torchlight illuminated a wide cavern peculiarly ornamented with low structures constructed out of bones, but the hounds trotted down a path and he hastened after them even as Yeshu and Far-runner came out of the passage and broke into startled exclamations at the sight of this city of bones.

In the darkness the ceiling met the floor; where they met, a tunnel ramped down. The hounds scrabbled forward, Rage pressing into the tunnel with Sorrow nudging at her hindquarters, tails lashing. Then they barked and in some confusion backed out of the tunnel. He got down on hands and knees and, thrusting the torch before him, pushed into the tunnel.

A foul-tasting water had swallowed the passageway. The route was blocked.

The others came up to him as he stood and furiously kicked at the nearest house of bones, sending it rattling and clattering down. He would have smashed them all, if he could have.

'Is that wise?' asked Yeshu. 'There might be a spell on those bones.'

'Gone,' he said. 'Out of my reach. There's no one down here, and Alain is gone.'

The walls ate the sound of his voice, but the rock could not absorb his anger and the blinding grief that, for the space of ten breaths, took hold of him. He choked out a breath and sucked one in, then turned to the miner.

'Pray you can swim,' he said. 'We'll tie a rope to your ankle and you'll go in. If you reach the other side, you may flee, if you dare, or you may tug on the rope and we'll haul you back. If you succeed, if there is a way out, then I'll reward you with silver and riches, as much as you can carry.'

The man wept and gibbered, but Stronghand himself tied the rope to his ankle and drove him forward into the water. The rope paid out, and paid out, and paid out, and Yeshu said:

'No man can hold his breath that long.'

It ceased moving, then slackened slightly. They waited far past the point where a man might live so long underwater.

'Draw him in,' said Stronghand at last, and Far-runner took the line in hand over hand, hauling with all his strength, but a weight fetched up somewhere within the tunnel, and although all three of them yanked, they could not dislodge it.

'He's fled, or drowned,' said Stronghand.

'That's an awful way to go,' said Yeshu. A spark of fear brightened his expression as he looked at the creature he served.

Stronghand nodded. 'I am not like you, Yeshu, but I deal fairly and I use the tools I have. Come. There's nothing for us here.'

His loyal soldiers hauled them up; outside, in the blessedly fresh air, the log house was still smoldering, ringed by a garden of corpses. His men had methodically looted what they could, and as dawn shaded the trees from black to gray, scouts raced out of the forest.

'A war band approaches, flying the banner of the hawk.'

They had nothing to wait for, nothing to fight for. They had taken the chance and lost the gamble. Alain was still alive – he knew that – but the hounds had lost his trail and he did not have a strong enough force to fight off determined and organized resistance.

They ran west, and when three days later they reached the ferry, four ships waited by the far shore, just out of sight of the garrison. The merfolk had come when called and brought him a swift means of escape.

'What do we do now?' asked Last Son as they set sail, letting the current sweep them downstream toward the distant ocean. Oars beat the water to keep them in the main current. Stronghand stood at the rudder, watching the shoreline pass. The hounds lay at his feet, heads on their forelegs; they seemed as despondent as any creature he had ever seen, but they trusted him enough to return with him to the ships. At the stern, Yeshu and Far-runner had gathered an audience while they told their tale of wandering among the dead bones of the Earth. Men and Eika huddled together, shoulder to shoulder, comrades rather than enemies as they listened appreciatively. Because he looked closely, he saw two new faces among the assembly.

'Aren't those two of the slaves we freed at the mines?'

'So they are. They followed us and were strong enough to keep up. They desire to join the army.'

'Is that so?'

'Will you take them?'

As he watched, he saw the stockier one, the more talkative of the two, raise his voice to add to the story being woven by Yeshu and Far-runner. The others did not shout him down. 'It seems I already have. A man bold enough to run in our pack is bold enough to fight with us.'

Last Son nodded. 'They call themselves "Walker" and "Will". I've kept my eye on them.'

As he had not. He had thought of nothing except Alain, except how water and rock had defeated him, who was mortal and short-lived, unlike the Earth. Stronghand considered while oak forest slid past on the banks. In battle it was usually necessary to act precipitously, but in council a measured decision gave the best results. It was necessary to always keep your eyes open, to examine your position from every side before you chose your course of action.

He had not kept his eyes open.

But Last Son had.

'Why did you not take a name?' Stronghand asked.

Last Son grinned, displaying his teeth. 'Last Son is a good name, too,' he said. 'It's the name I want. What do we do now?'

'My brother Alain wanders out there. To find him, I must plan carefully and not overreach. The Salians will fight us. The Wendish are strong. We will use Medemelacha as our foothold and we will push step by step inland, consolidating as we go, just as we are doing in Alba. That way we will find Alain but also gain more land for our empire. Piece by piece.'

'Yes,' said Last Son, nodding. 'That is a good plan. That is why we follow you, Stronghand. Because you are not like the chieftains that came before you.'

6

'They say the end of the world is coming, Sister Antonia,' said the empress.

Adelheid gripped the railing of the balcony, knuckles white as she stared out over the city of Darre from the second story of the royal palace. Roof tiles baked under the sun. Heat shimmered. At this time of day, in the middle of the afternoon, the streets were deserted but the stink never abated; on a day like today, with no wind, it only subsided a bit with no breeze to spread its miasma over the palace hill. Perhaps the stench wasn't quite so bad this year because so many people had fled the great earthquake and returned to the villages and fields of the countryside, where they felt safer.

In truth, Adelheid wasn't looking at the city at all. She looked west toward the hills that bordered the sea. They all looked west when they had the courage to look. It was now possible to see the smoking mountain at all hours of the day and night, belching ash and sparks.

Antonia said nothing. She had a comfortable seat on an Arethousan–style couch, she was fed, and a servant stood beside her waving a fan so she didn't get too hot. She knew when to be patient. She hadn't caught her fish yet.

'If you get my daughters, and me, and the emperor through it safely, then I will give you anything.'

Ah. The line twitched.

'Anything?'

'Yes.'

Hooked. Now she needed only to reel her in. 'Very well. You are at risk in the city. You and your daughters and household must move to a villa outside the city, but keep troops under the command of Duke Burchard garrisoned in strength in the city to protect your position here.'

'No. I would be a fool, and a coward, to abandon Darre and leave a Wendish foreigner, however loyal, in charge.'

Stubborn creature! Antonia suppressed a grimace of irritation. She knew better than to let anger show. People didn't like to be reminded that they knew less than she did.

The empress went on speaking, oblivious to Antonia's silence. 'Henry has been absent for over a year now, fighting in Dalmiaka. If I leave Darre as well, then the people will say we abandoned them. I will not go.'

'It won't be safe.'

'It will be less safe if I flee. The people of Darre want an Aostan regnant, not a Wendish regent. They will not tolerate Duke Burchard.'

'Leave an Aostan lady in control of the palace.'

'If I do so, the people will rise up and crown her queen. How does it benefit me to save the cow but lose the farm?'

Adelheid had a tendency to be pigheaded. In Antonia's experience too much soft youthful prettiness gave girls an inflated notion of their importance. In addition, she listened too much to the common folk and spouted their rustic wisdom as if she were born to it; as if the rabble had the wisdom to rule themselves!

'If you will not go, Your Majesty, then at least send your daughters to a place of safety.'

A rumble whispered under their feet, shivering the ground. The balcony swayed, and the servingwoman who was fanning Antonia shrieked and then laughed as the rumbling subsided as quickly as it had come. A vase brimming with lavender teetered but did not fall.

'Just a small one, Your Majesty. Your Grace.' The servant curtsied nervously.

'The fan,' said Antonia. With a last anxious chuckle, the woman resumed stirring the air. 'Your Majesty, I pray you—'

Adelheid had a pretty face, but when she clenched her jaw, she betrayed her obstinacy. 'I cannot leave Darre. Look how they swarm out onto the street. They are frightened, Sister. They fear. If I abandon them, they will seek a different strong hand to rule them. To give them hope and strength. Henry charged me to stay. This is the empire we have won together, the heart of our regnancy. I cannot leave.'

'Your daughters would be safer in the countryside,' continued Antonia, sensing that the tremor had offered her an opening. 'Take a dozen girls from the city to act as servants and companions and you will please the common folk, who will see you acting on behalf of their daughters as well as your own. Send them out of the city. They will be safe even as you suffer the same dangers as your subjects.'

There was no wind to cool them, but Adelheid endured the heat without wilting. These sweltering late summer days did not make her face mottle with unsightly red blotches, as it did Antonia's; her complexion remained smooth and lovely. Her hair stayed neatly coifed under a linen scarf, held in place by a slender gold circlet that she wore at all times except for formal audiences, when she placed the heavy imperial crown on her own head. Sweat stippled her brow but otherwise she gave no sign in her silk robes of being hot, not as Antonia was.

'I don't know . . .' she mused, still staring down at the city.

Voices called out in the hallway. The door into the chamber slammed open and a girl ran in, sobbing.

'Mama! Mama! Make the shaking stop, Mama! I'm scared!'

Adelheid turned as little Mathilda flung herself against her mother's skirts and clung there, arms wrapped around her hips, shoulders heaving and shaking with far more violence than the tremor that had precipitated the girl's outburst.

The nursemaid hurried in, accompanied by two guardsmen. She was an older woman, breathless from the run. Her bones popped and creaked as she knelt before the empress. 'I pray pardon, Your Majesty. I let the princess run away from me.'

'What of Berengaria?' Adelheid asked sharply, one hand stroking her crying daughter's head. 'Where is she?'

'She slept through the tremor, Your Majesty. Such things do not trouble her. She is still an infant.'

'Very well.' She wiped Mathilda's tears away with her thumb and tipped her head up so that the girl looked up at her. 'Should you like to go to the countryside, Tildie? Would you like to be a shepherd?'

Mathilda sniffed hard. At four, she had a face both more handsome and less pretty than Adelheid's, and was already tall and strong for her age, brown-haired, snub-nosed, with an endearing dimple in her left cheek.

'I should like that, Mama!' she cried, her tears forgotten. 'I would much rather run outside. I hate Darre! I hate it!'

She was a passionate child. Antonia smiled as Adelheid melted before her daughter's fierce will, so like her own. Yet Mathilda possessed her father's famous ability to rage outwardly, whereas Adelheid held her feelings on a tighter rein, pulled tight, concealed behind a prettiness that disarmed her antagonists. Henry was stronger, but Adelheid more dangerous.

'You hate the hot summer air and the walls,' said Adelheid sternly, 'not the city.'

'Yes, Mama,' said the girl meekly. 'I love Darre. Just it's so hot and stinky. I wish I could climb trees like we do in Tivura.'

'So be it.' Adelheid nodded at Antonia to show that she had accepted Antonia's advice. 'You and Berengaria will go to Tivura for the rest of the summer, until Octumbre at least.'

She clapped her hands, then stilled. 'But what about you, Mama? Won't you come with us?' Her lip trembled. Tears brimmed.

'I must stay in Darre until Octumbre. You know our duty is to rule. It will be your duty one day.'

'Yes, Mama.' She struggled and got the tears under control. At four, she already comprehended her destiny. 'When will Papa come home?'

Adelheid glanced again over the city. 'We must pray that the Lord and Lady grant him success very soon, and that he

return swiftly. Go on, then. Go make ready. You will leave
tomorrow.'

'Yes, Your Majesty,' said the nursemaid. She grunted and
rose with some effort, wincing at the pain in her limbs. 'Come,
Your Highness. You must pick out which of your animals you
wish to take with you.'

Adelheid kissed her daughter's forehead and watched as
she skipped out of the room, now holding onto her nursemaid's hand and babbling happily about lambs and foals and
how she absolutely must take all five of her whippet puppies.

'I am not sure you understand Aosta, Sister Antonia,' said
Adelheid quietly once the doors had shut. She came back into
the room and sat on a couch, took a cup of wine from a servant, and sipped. 'This is not Wendar, where nobles rule and
the common folk till the ground and pay their tithes to
whichever lady commands them. The "rabble," as you call
them, speak loudly in Darre, and if we ignore them, then they
will rise against us. That is why I cannot leave, or leave Duke
Burchard as regent, no matter how affectionately I admire
him. The people have suffered much – the earthquake, two
bad harvests, the shivering sickness. Many have fled to the
countryside, but others from the country walk in rags to the
city walls hoping to be given flour from my granary. I must
feed them, or they will riot. They love me because I never
deserted them, because I came back to save them from
Ironhead. I will not desert them now.'

She tucked her feet up onto the couch, curled up like the
leopard it was rumored she had once kept as a pet – lost when
she had fled John Ironhead's siege of Vennaci. She was small
but lithe and alert; no fool, indeed.

Antonia did not trust her.

'I respect Lord Hugh, Sister Antonia. He supports Henry
and myself because he is Henry's loyal subject, and because
we allow him influence beyond that granted to most men who
are dedicated to the church. I am not naive, although you may
think me so because I have a pretty face. Lord Hugh recom-
mended you to me. That is why I have admitted you to my
councils.'

No other reason. Adelheid did not say the words; she didn't need to.

'Lord Hugh is an ambitious man.'

'He is a bastard and a churchman. He cannot rise higher than presbyter. He can never hope to become skopos. He can never cast off his robes and become a lord and sire children to inherit after him. His sisters inherited Olsatia and Austra. He is trapped as he is now.'

'Do you not trust him, Your Majesty?'

'I know what he is, Sister Antonia. I think you do as well. I trust him as I did my beloved cat. Cats are not dogs. They serve you if they wish. Their claws are sharp.'

'They are among God's most beautiful creatures.'

'Are they?' Adelheid's smile was as sharp as the rake of a leopard's claws. 'I have never thought any man as desirable as my dear Henry.'

Maybe it was even true. Hugh had never had the power to give Adelheid an imperial crown.

Antonia swallowed a sigh of irritation and speared a slice of melon with her eating knife. 'Let us be honest, then, Your Majesty. What do you want of me?'

'You are educated in the arts of the mathematici. Your knowledge can be of value to me and to the kingdom. I hope you will agree to go with my daughters to Tivura and educate them. Mathilda is destined for the throne. Berengaria, however, must go to the church. It would be better for Mathilda if the two sisters never quarrel over what is already ordained. The elder must go before the younger. That is the way of the world. Teach Berengaria what she needs to know so that she can support her sister when they have come of age and into the inheritance that Henry and I mean to leave them.'

The servants had retreated to the door, standing silently, heads bowed, as they awaited Adelheid's commands. Only the woman fanning did not cease, as Antonia could not endure the heat if the air remained still. The tick of the fan's rising and falling was the sole sound in the chamber. From outside there came a shout. Much farther away, the noise of people who had rushed out onto the streets in the aftermath of the tremor faded as folk retreated indoors. The sun's hammer struck more mightily than their fear. They had grown used to the tremors, to the daily sight of the smoking mountain and its sparks and clouds of spitting, hot ash blown in by the west wind. The market would open as afternoon melted into dusk. In summer, the city was more lively in the evening than during the heat of the day.

In this way, the Darrens were a practical people.

Horses whinnied in the courtyard below. Adelheid drained her cup, beckoned, and a servant hurried over to refill it. Antonia popped the melon into her mouth and savored its sweet moisture.

The infant Berengaria could walk and speak a few words. She seemed biddable and clever, although she was not yet two years of age. Adelheid's plan had merit, although the empress might not comprehend the full magnitude of Antonia's ambitions. Berengaria could serve her in many ways, as could Mathilda.

Yet they were so young, and she was old. She would be dead before Mathilda ruled.

Unless, of course, both Adelheid and Henry died untimely deaths.

'I will go to Tivura if you command, Your Majesty,' she said, bowing her head obediently.

'I trust my daughters with you, Sister, because you need them. Care for them as if they were your own, bring them safely through the days to come, and I will see that you receive that which you desire most.'

'What do you suppose I desire most?'

Adelheid made a sweeping gesture toward the unseen portion of the hill where the other palace lay. 'I will make you skopos. Is that enough?'

'I have underestimated you, Your Majesty,' said Antonia with a curt laugh, because Adelheid had surprised her, and she did not like to be surprised.

There was silence, and for a moment Antonia thought she had offended the empress, but Adelheid made a little noise in reply, half laugh, half thoughtful sigh, as she rose and went back out onto the balcony. It was the vantage point she liked best. 'I am a small flower, Sister Antonia, but a hardy one. Drought and sun and wind and snow will not kill me.'

'All things die, Your Majesty.'

'As God will it, so shall it come to pass. But are we not creatures of free will? I acquiesced to my first marriage. I thought I had no choice in the matter, I thought those who chose for me must know best, until I discovered that my noble husband was no better than a rutting stag, bellowing and roaring. I swore never to acquiesce again.' Her white scarf fluttered as a wind rose off the river, bringing with it the stench of the city's sewage, but Adelheid did not flinch, although Antonia felt compelled to cover her own nose with a corner of her sleeve. 'Nor will I. Now that I have tasted the sweetness of freedom, I cannot return to the bitter plate.'

'God demand obedience.'

'God demand that we do what is right.'

'The Enemy tempts with sweet things.'

'Yet so do God, for what is right must seem sweet to us. So the blessed Daisan preached.'

Voices rang in the hall beyond the closed doors. The servants leaped aside as the doors were flung open and a captain wearing the tabard of the palace guards strode in, dropping to his knees before the empress. Like all her captains, he was a solid, competent man, neatly dressed and devotedly loyal to his young queen.

'Your Majesty! A messenger from the north. From Zuola.'

'Zuola!' The county of Zuola lay north and east of Darre, near the border with Dalmiaka, on the plain below the easternmost extent of the Alfar Mountains. 'Is it news of the emperor?'

'Alas, no, Your Majesty. Ill news, I fear.' He looked back toward the door, hearing the jingle of mail, and a weary man clattered into the room with a guard on either side. The messenger's dark hair was plastered to his head with sweat, and sweat had made runnels through the dust staining his face. Dust spit from his boots with each step; he shed it from his clothing onto the rugs.

'Your Majesty,' he croaked.

'Give him wine,' said Adelheid.

'Nay,' he insisted, kneeling beside the captain. Dust shook from him. Antonia coughed. 'I'll take wine after, if it pleases you, Your Majesty. Dire news.'

She was pale but not cowed. 'Go on. Is it the emperor?'

'Nay, I have heard nothing of the emperor, Your Majesty. I am one of those you posted in the Brinne Pass.'

'An army! Has it come?'

'A large army, Your Majesty.' He began coughing too hard to continue.

One of the guards was so excited he could not contain himself, but blurted out rash words. 'Rumor says it is led by a sorcerer who commands two griffins.'

'Griffins!' The servants exclaimed in wonder.

Adelheid's face changed color, but she said nothing.

'Hush!' Captain Falco gave the guard a sharp look, and he flushed, shamefaced, and stepped back.

'Rumor delights in false words.' The empress turned her attention back to the messenger. 'What is your name?'

He bent his head, acknowledging her intent notice, the honor she did him by asking who he was. Most men and women lived and died without ever coming to the attention of their noble ruler, and often this was to their advantage, but Adelheid was a different kind of ruler, one who liked to know to whom she spoke, even if they were the lowest laboring serf.

'I am called Milo, Your Majesty.'

'Drink first, then tell me only what is known for certain.'

He dared not disobey, and in truth it was clear that he was grateful to drain two cups of wine and wipe his neck and face with a damp linen cloth. Adelheid waited patiently, as still as a cat watching a mouse which has not yet realized that it is intended to become dinner.

'It is better to consider your words than to speak in haste. Captain Falco, send for Duke Burchard, Count Tedbald, and Captain Lutfridus.'

He sent a guard on the errand, then knelt again beside Milo. Already word had run through the palace that a messenger had come bearing ill tidings, and a murmur of voices betrayed the gathering of servants, guardsmen, and courtiers come to lurk outside the doors, although none dared enter the empress' private apartments without explicit permission.

'Go on, then, Milo. Do not fear to speak before me.'

'Your Majesty.' He wiped his forehead one more time, more for courage than to cool himself. 'We camped many months in the pass. The winter wasn't so hard, for it snowed less than usual. We placed ourselves with a good view of the trail, so we might see scouts or the van of an army coming long before they might chance to see us. So it proved. A large army is crossing the pass. In truth, they may have come down into Zuola in the days it has taken me to ride here, although over the months we rigged traps to create as many obstacles as we could manage. My comrades have ridden according to our orders. I came here.'

'Describe exactly what you saw.'

'A great army.' He trembled and for a time was so overwhelmed by exhaustion, or recollection, that he could not go on. She waited. A commotion stirred the company waiting beyond the doors. Duke Burchard entered, leaning on his cane and attended by one of his nephews. Adelheid moved aside on the couch to let him sit next to her, and she patted his aged hand fondly, had a servant bring him wine, and bade him listen to the messenger's report.

Milo drank another cup of wine and went on.

'A great host of armed men. It is true there are a pair of griffins, for I saw them myself. They are huge beasts! They shine in the sun! There was a horde of barbarians with wings sprouting from their backs, although others say they aren't true wings but only crude emblems constructed out of wood. They looked like wings to me. And there were other foul creatures as well – men with the bodies of horses.'

'Bwr! Bwr!' The cry erupted, torn from the listening multitude, for certainly a mass of people now pressed into the chamber and crowded the broad hall beyond. More folk came, a staccato of footsteps and a clamor of voices calling back the news to those who pushed at the rear.

'Silence!' cried Adelheid. One by one and in groups they fell silent. Maybe the entire palace hushed, waiting on her words. 'Barbarians? An invasion from the east? Are they Arethousans?'

'Nay, Your Majesty. Most of them seemed to be Wendish.'

'Wendish!' exclaimed the old duke. His hands trembled because of age, not anger or shock. His sojourn in Aosta and two bouts of the shivering fever had weakened him.

'They fly the banner of a black dragon.'

'The Dragons!' said Burchard. 'It was Duchess Yolande's rebellious brother Rodulf who was sent east to lead the King's Dragons into the field against the Quman. Can it be the Dragons have come to aid Henry?'

Adelheid's small hand closed on Burchard's wrist just as the duke opened his mouth to speak, and he looked at her, surprised. What message passed between them, read in lips and eyes, Antonia could not interpret, but the old duke bent his head, obedient to the young empress' will, and kept silence.

'Go on,' said Adelheid. 'What else did you see and witness?'

'There were other banners as well, a dozen or more. A silver tree on a blue field—'

'Villam!'

'A gold lion on a black field.'

'Avaria!' The old duke moaned, and Adelheid called for a linen cloth and wiped his damp brow herself. 'My Avaria. What means this? Have my heirs turned their backs on me? On the king?'

'If they are friend,' said Adelheid, 'then they do not threaten us. If they are our enemy, then we must crush them before they reach Darre. Burchard, will you march out with me?'

'Do you mean to march against this army yourself?'

'I did not surrender to John Ironhead. Henry still fights in Dalmiaka. I will protect Aosta. I will not run.'

'If there are Bwr, Your Majesty . . .' said Captain Falco. 'Bwr!' He was a brawny soldier, a man of action who served his lady bravely, but the name had the power to make a man as stalwart as he was shudder. The crowd murmured. This was how fear sounded, like water washing all resolve out of their hearts.

The empress rose, lifted a hand, and commanded silence. Antonia did not trust Adelheid, but she admired her. It was a pity the empress was not as malleable as her young daughters, but God did not place obstacles in one's path in order to make life easy. The road to heaven was paved with thorns and barriers. One had to climb them and not be afraid of getting scratched up.

'Heed me!' she cried. 'The Bwr once burned this city, but they will not do so today, nor will they do so as long as I rule over you and protect you! I will ride to meet them. Let every man or woman who can carry arms go to the north gate. Together with the city guard under Captain Lutfridus, they will guard the walls in my absence. I will ride out with my army, and with Duke Burchard's and Count Tedbald's faithful men.'

That Burchard had been too old and Count Tedbald too untrustworthy to ride to Dalmiaka with Henry and Anne she did not say, although Antonia and most of the others knew it.

They cheered her because she was their beloved queen, young and brave and pretty. Being pretty always helped.

When they had dispersed to make ready, Adelheid turned to Burchard and repeated her question. 'Will you ride out with me, Duke Burchard? It seems that the obedient son has turned rebel.'

'I cannot believe it,' said the old man. 'Do you truly believe that Prince Sanglant has taken the field against his own father?'

'A black dragon?'

'Saony flies the red dragon. It must be the prince. Just as you warned me.'

'He has turned against Henry. Will you ride with me, Burchard?'

He wept quietly, but his gaze on her was steady. Like most men, he adored her. 'I will ride even against my own children, Your Majesty. I will not waver. You know that.'

She nodded. 'We will ride together, old friend.'

All were gone except the servants. Antonia relished the solitude. The bees had buzzed so frantically, maddened by fear and uncertainty, but now the chamber lay quiet, the only noise the beat of the fan against the air. That rhythmic pulse was so soothing. It was cooling off as the sun set. In the city, the markets had opened and folk walked the streets, hunting their suppers.

Adelheid went back out onto the balcony. 'See!' she called. 'Have you seen it, Sister Antonia? It is brighter tonight. There it is, burning in the heart of the Queen.'

Antonia knew what the empress pointed at. She sighed and rose. The only good thing about the heat was that her joints didn't ache as much as they did in the cold.

As the sun set, darkness rose in the east and the accustomed stars slowly burned, one by one, into view. In the constellation known as the Queen, now at zenith, a comet shone.

'The Queen's bow is pointed at the Dragon,' said Adelheid. 'Others have claimed this comet portends the end of the world, but now I know it signals my victory over Prince Sanglant.'

Lamplight stippled the battlements of the distant city walls as well as the nearer palace walls that ringed the hill on which the two palaces stood. Dusk waned to twilight and twilight faded to night as they stared at the comet, which was noticeably brighter than it had been three nights before – the night the queen's clerics had first marked it. Three nights ago it had burned in the Queen's Bow.

'It moves quickly across the sky,' said Antonia. 'How can you know what it portends? It might only portend God's displeasure because of the manifold sins committed on Earth by the wicked.'

'It might.' Her tone changed, and her head tilted provocatively. 'Do you know what is whispered in the streets? Some say the comet is a warning that God mean to punish us because the church mothers suppressed the truth.'

'Which truth?'

'That the blessed Daisan was brought before the Empress Thaissania and condemned to death, that he had his heart cut out of him while he yet lived.'

'Heresy! Foul heresy! You must pray that your ears should be burned off rather than another whisper of such foul lies touch them! This is the Enemy's work!'

'Do you think so?' Adelheid's voice was as light as that of a laughing child's although her words were as heavy as lead. 'The ancient Babaharshan astronomers said that a comet portends change. I will have need of you, Sister Antonia. One task.'

'If I can aid you, Your Majesty, I will.'

The queen nodded, as though she had expected this answer. As though she knew Antonia had few other options at this moment. 'I fear it will come to battle, but we are ready, because we have been forewarned. Because we have already prepared the trap. Yet force of arms alone cannot win the day.'

At once, Antonia understood what Adelheid wanted. 'What you ask is not a pleasantry, Your Majesty. Only blood can summon the galla. You are the one who must give me the lives I need to work the spell. Have you considered your part? Are you willing to do what is necessary? Are you willing to be the executioner?'

The queen placed a hand atop Antonia's. Her fingers were surprisingly strong as they tightened on Antonia's. 'I will do what I must so that I and my daughters survive.'

XXVIII

HOLY FIRE

1

At dawn he shook the leaves off his body that he'd used to make a nest for sleeping. The air was cool but promised heat later. He licked his dry lips. After he slaked his thirst, he could search for food. A haze blurred the valley, but he smelled water close by, and pushing through thickets he got in under the canopy of beech and headed downhill. The beech began to give way to a mixed wood of oak and hornbeam in the full leaf of summer; the shade made him shiver. The sun hadn't yet risen high enough to penetrate the cover.

He heard a stream and kicked through wood-straw and fescue to the bank, where he knelt and drank his fill. For a while he lay on the grassy verge while insects crawled on his body and the sun's light warmed his face, but at length hunger drove him on.

He followed the stream as it plunged down the hillside and found himself in a broad clearing where the water emptied into a pond. He paused at the forest's edge, seeing movement not too far from him, out in the high grass: a man was cutting hay with a brush hook. There was a child, too, and a dog playing with a stick on the far shore of the pond within sight of the laborer. The man bent and cut, rose, bent and cut again. At once, suddenly, without warning, the iron hook tore free of the handle and flew spinning through the air to land with a splash in the pond.

At first there was silence, only the chirp of a bird and the lazy humming of insects; then the man cursed so loud and long and so despairingly that the child and the dog left off their play and came running.

'What happened, Uncle? What's wrong?'

'Some damn fool didn't fix the handle to the hook. Now it's flown off and into the water. We'll never find it! That was the iron blade I borrowed from the steward so we could make our tithe this month by bringing in straw for the lady's stables.'

'It's lost?' The child's voice quavered as the enormity of the accident struck home. 'But we can't replace an iron blade, Uncle. Can we?'

The man shook his head, unable to speak through his tears. He and the child went to the shore. Neither wore shoes or leggings. They waded through the reed–choked waters, the man pushing the stick along under the surface, the child groping through the vegetation.

'Where did it fall?'

'Ai, God! It happened so fast! What will we do? Ai, God. What will we do when the steward demands recompense?'

He stepped out from the trees.

The dog barked at once and trotted forward to greet him, snuffling into his hands as the man stood and pulled the child against his body, shielding it.

'What is it, Uncle?' cried the child. 'Is that a wild beast?'

'It's a man!'

'That's not a man. It looks like a goblin!'

'It must be a beggar, child. God enjoin us to give bread to beggars.'

'Even if we've none to feed ourselves? What if he's a thief or a bandit?'

'Hush, now. See how Treu greets him.' The man pushed the child behind him. He stood to his knees in the water, and from the safety of the pond hoisted the dripping brush hook handle so it could be seen he had something to use as a weapon. 'Greetings, stranger. You're welcome to our steading if you've a wish for a hank of bread and a cup of sweetened vinegar.'

'Give me the handle,' he said as he approached. He held out his hand, and the man got the strangest look on his face, puzzled and wary at the same time, but as he waded into the water with Treu wagging his tail happily at his side, the laborer let him take the handle.

'I saw where it fell.' He thrust the handle into a stand of reeds, and after pushing it here and there for a little bit the stub jostled something hard. He reached into water made murky by all the wading. Groping through pond scum, his fingers skimmed over a curved blade.

'Here.'

The laborer wept when he lifted the hook out of the water.

'Bless you, Friend! Bless you! You have saved my family. Come, I pray you. Come with me to my home, and we'll feed you, for you look sorely in need of feeding.'

'So I am,' he said wonderingly. The water had sluiced a layer of dirt off his fingers and arms, and he could see his nails grown long, packed with dirt under the cuticles where before he had merely seen an encrustation of filth formed in the crude shape of a hand. His bare thighs and chest were equally filthy. A scrap of grimy cloth concealed his hips. Otherwise he was naked.

What was he?

He lifted his head to stare at the man, thinking that the laborer's gaze might tell him something he needed to know, but the other two had already clambered out onto the shore and the child kept its distance, although the dog seemed eager enough to accept his strokes and patting.

'Come,' said the laborer.

He led the way through feather grass whose golden heads were stippled with black. The ground had a moist, squishy feel under his feet, as if it never entirely dried out, but the dew on the grass had burned off and it was beginning to be hot and humid. They crossed into the woodland and walked

on a well-worn path in glorious shade. Here the mark of
human hands shaped the land; where larger trees had been
chopped down for planks and logs, light speared into open
spaces lush with saplings and shrubs. No fallen trees rotted
and there weren't many branches on the ground either; the
villagers had picked the ground clean for firewood. Some pigs
rattled away over the ground, squealing.

'Pigs haven't done well this year,' said the laborer, squinting after them. 'Some of the sows went dry and there wasn't
a litter that half didn't die though we did what we could to
save them. It'll be hard going this winter. Four of the steward's cattle died over the winter beyond what was picked out
for the Novarian slaughter. Two of the steward's mares lost
their foals, too.'

'My mam died just last week,' said the child. 'She saw
demons and they made her fingers and toes burn until she
went crazy. So did the deacon and six other folk in the valley.
It was witches what cursed them. They gave me and all the
other kids a tummy ache for days, too, those witches. And
my fingers got all cold.'

'Hush now, Brat.' He said the word fondly. 'I beg pardon,
Friend. We don't mean to burden you with our troubles.'

'Was there a murrain among the cattle?' he asked, because
he had a sudden unexpected memory of sheep with weeping
hooves and a crying farmer who was set to lose everything,
but he couldn't recall how it had all fallen out.

'God forbid!' The laborer drew the Circle at his chest.
'We've been spared that curse at least. We've had too much
rain, and it's been cold. This sickness that's haunting the
valley, that's troubled us. But we're no worse off than many
other folks, I'd wager.'

'My dad died,' said the Brat kindly. 'But that were two
winters ago, when we hadn't enough grain or stores to last all
winter and the new lord didn't bring more, not like the old
one always done. So all our troubles didn't just start this year!'

'That's right,' agreed the laborer. 'They started when the
rightful heir was dispossessed by that greedy Lord Geoffrey,
for he wanted the county to go to his infant daughter instead

of the lord's true son. That was when all our troubles started. Every one of them.'

Maybe the root shrugged up out of the ground and wrapped its tendrils around his foot and tripped him. Maybe his scattered thoughts skipped, jostled by these words, so that he stopped paying attention to the uneven trail.

He stumbled and went down hard on his knees, bruising his knees, his hands, and an elbow.

The child cried out. Treu barked, then came to lick him, and while he lay there half stunned and aching, he heard the laborer speak softly to the child.

'I've never seen Treu take to a man like that. Never.'

'And him such a wild beast!' whispered the child agreeably. 'He stinks!'

'Hush, Brat.'

They did not want to touch him or get close enough for him to touch them. With a grunt, he sat back on his haunches, then rose, shaking himself as a dog shakes off water. He was indeed so filthy that dust and matter spattered onto the ground around him as water droplets might spray. They stepped away, and the laborer gestured awkwardly toward the trail and kept walking. It wasn't difficult to keep up with them looking back every five steps, although he hurt all over. The fall had jarred him badly and his head throbbed; each step jarred more pain loose until he thought he was going to go blind.

The hamlet appeared where woodland ended in open ground striped with fields of rye and a trio of soggy gardens ringed by high fences to keep out deer, goats, and rabbits. Farther down, at the valley bottom, trees grew thickly along a small river's winding banks. Three more dogs came running out to greet them; tails wagging and ears high, they swarmed around him and he patted them all.

'Where is this?' he asked, staring over the straggle of buildings.

'Shaden is what we call it. Just my father and his brother and sister and two cousins came out here thirty year back when they were young, with the permission of the count, and cut back the forest and tilled the high ground. I heard tell

from the deacon, before the sickness took her, that the count
– him who died just a few year back – had a new plow so
strong it could cut through that good earth down at the bottom
of the valley, but we've never heard tell of such since he died,
God rest him. It's said he meant to share out plows among
the countyfolk, but the new lord hasn't done so. That land
would make good tillage. We had such a hard rain these past
two year that the best soil got washed down to the river, and
we got black rot in the rye stores, and it come up in the grain
again this year.'

'It's my job to pick it out,' said the Brat cheerfully, 'but I
don't get it all.'

The hamlet boasted five houses and one common stable in
addition to six lean-tos, a chicken coop, and a broken-down
corral missing half its fence, with the inside grown to weeds.

Every soul in the village turned out to see the marvel: a
visitor. Even the old one – the Brat's grandmother – got up
from the bench on which she sat in the sun and hobbled over
to examine him with the expression of a woman who has seen
too much not to be skeptical of a gold coin pressed into her
hand.

'This beggar did me a good turn,' said the laborer, 'and
I've promised him a bit of bread and something to drink in
recompense.'

He went over to the corral and sat on a listing log. He was
so weary. A passel of tiny children stood at a safe distance
and stared at him, with an older girl keeping watch to make
sure they didn't venture too close. The dogs scratched at the
dirt before settling down at his feet. The adults seemed to be
conferring among themselves, out of earshot, but the Brat
lugged over a big ceramic pot sealed with a lid and a wide
basket tipped over her head like a hat. She settled down on
the ground near him and gestured to the other girl.

'Won't you come sit by me, Lindy?' She smirked when
Lindy shook her head and took a step back.

After setting the basket down beside her, she took the
wooden lid off the pot to reveal grain. 'It's not gone down to
the miller yet, but that's a two-day walk,' she said as she ran

her hands through the grain. 'Uncle goes tomorrow.' She began to pick through the grain, tossing black kernels onto the ground. The dogs snuffled at them but did not eat. 'Whew! This is a bad one!'

'Here,' he said, 'let me.' He slid off the log before she could say more than a startled protest, and the watching children shrieked and scuttled backward, but the Brat only scooted away, not running, as he crouched beside the widemouthed pot. The top layer of grain was indeed contaminated by monstrous black kernels grown to twice the size of the regular kernels. He sifted them through his hands into the basket, but the farther down he got, the cleaner the grain became until there wasn't a trace of black rot.

'Look at that!' The Brat had slid closer by degrees and now she peered over his shoulder and whistled with awe. 'Nary a bit wasted! That'll be enough flour to get us through to harvest, after miller and lord take their tithe.'

'Brat!' Uncle called, and she hopped up, poured all the grain back into the pot, covered it, and hoisted it up to haul back to him.

Chickens came over, pecking for the discarded grain, but he shooed them away and swept dirt over the black grains. They looked evil to him, although he wasn't sure why. He'd seen black rot before, just never so heavy. Indeed, staring through the hazy day toward the fields it seemed to him that the entire field was poisoned by black rot, as thick as flies on honey, and he heaved himself up and walked, weaving because he really was getting light-headed from hunger, out to the fields and down those long strips brushing his hands over the heads of rye. They tickled his skin. Black grains tumbled to the earth like rain.

Harvest tomorrow, or next week – wasn't that what the girl had said? He couldn't recall. The dogs followed him patiently down one strip and up the next and after a while he remembered that the villagers had promised to feed him and he wandered back through golden fields unstained by rot into the hamlet. Here he found a wooden platter waiting for him with a cup of sweetened vinegar that made his eyes open wide, a cup of onion soup, and an entire half a loaf of rye bread, very dry so probably some days old, but by soaking it piece by piece in the soup he softened it and gulped it down. It sat like a lead weight in his stomach, the vinegar fizzing and bubbling, the onion burning, and he was suddenly so tired that he had to lie down. He crawled over to the stables where he would feel more comfortable with the animals, but of course what animals the villagers kept were out grazing in the pastures, so he found a filthy pile of straw for his bed and slept.

2

The griffins could take the cold, but they didn't like the elevation, and despite the uncanny number of trees blocking the road and rockfalls whose shatter-trail had to be cleared before the wagons could pass, it was the griffins who slowed them down most.

'It were a warm, wet winter,' said their guide, an old Avarian man called Ucco who had crossed the pass at least fifteen times in the last twenty years, leading merchants out of Westfall and southern Avaria who had slaves, salt, and Ungrian steel to trade in northern Aosta. 'That makes the avalanches worse, mind you. If it's cold, it don't melt. But it weren't so bad earlier this year, for I crossed back in Quadrii with a Westfall merchant who's been trading Ungrian slaves for Aostan spices and cloth. I don't know where all this rockfall come from, or how these trees come to fall. It weren't here two month ago.'

'Might there have been storms?' the prince asked. 'We got hit by a dozen strong storms out of the south. I lost a dozen men, and saw a village flattened by wind.'

'Nay, not so I recall except that one thunder boomer in Cintre that blew a bit of snow on it off the peaks. But for that, it hasn't rained much the last two months. See how the streams are low. Look at all that bare rock on the heights. Where's the snow? That'll bring drought, mark you. Drought this summer already, and drought this autumn, and worse to come if there's not snow this winter.'

He was a voluble man accompanied by an exceedingly pretty granddaughter who seemed delighted to flirt with a noble prince who was, once again, without his wife. It was at times like this Sanglant missed Heribert most, but in truth Hathui proved a stronger fence; she had a hard gaze and a way of snorting with laughter that suggested amusement at the foibles of mankind.

'The men have cleared the trees away, my lord prince,' Hathui said now, riding up to him where he waited on the road. She eyed the granddaughter, rolled her eyes, and went on. 'Two were felled by axes. You can see the bite of a blade in their trunks.'

'Bandits?' he asked.

'No bandits up here, my lord,' said the old guide, 'unless they've come north from Zuola because of hard times there. No man winters up here. That's a death sentence.'

'The monks winter over at St. Barnaria's Pass.'

'Well, they ain't rightly men, are they? Clean-shaven like women – begging your pardon, my lord – and women can take the cold better, that's for certain.' He patted his grand-daughter fondly. She was a sturdily built girl of no more than fifteen or sixteen years with the thick buttocks and legs of a person who hikes and climbs every day. She smiled at Sanglant, displaying remarkably even, white teeth, sign of strong stock. Hathui snorted. He flushed and hastily turned his attention to other things, tilting back his head to survey their route.

They had reached the pass' summit yesterday after strug- gling through a complex warren of stones cast across the road in stages that had seemed to be the remains of three differ- ent rockfalls. Now the road wound almost level at the base of a barren valley, which they had mostly climbed out of before this latest barrier had brought the vanguard to a halt. They had crossed through a land of rugged mountains capped with bare rock which dropped down on this side in north-facing slopes where green alder bushes grew along the furrows and alpine rose on the higher slopes where water did not collect. There were no patches of snow on the slopes at all, not even in the shade. According to Ucco, they had come three quarters of the way across and tomorrow would start their final descent through the foothills of Zuola and, beyond that, down through steep valleys onto the northern coastal plain of Aosta.

'Is it possible they know we are coming?' he asked, eager to discuss war rather than lust.

'They might know,' Hathui admitted reluctantly, 'if it's true Wolfhere betrayed us.'

'We must suppose that he did. To believe otherwise is folly.'

Her frown was answer enough to a question she didn't like the sound of, no matter how many times it bowed before her. 'Wolfhere is a good man,' she insisted.

He shrugged. Behind, the male griffin huffed, and Sanglant dismounted.

'We'd best stop for the night,' he said, wiping his forehead. There hadn't been rain for weeks. Even Ucco had difficulty finding enough drinking water for their entire army and all their stock.

'I'll let Captain Fulk know, my lord.' Hathui reined her horse away.

The male griffin was limping, and even the female – bigger and stronger – suffered from the altitude.

'I didn't think they'd hurt like this just from climbing,' said Sibold, standing clear of the huffing griffin as he watched the prince approach. 'They never seem to catch their breath.'

'Domina hasn't flown once since we reached the mountains,' said Sanglant. Lewenhardt had shot a bear yesterday and Sanglant fished a hank of meat out of a barrel and walked right up to the griffin so that it fed out of his hands. He respected the sharp curve of its beak, but more and more he had come to think of Argent as a cross between his horse and a jessed eagle. Though it loomed larger than a warhorse, and could send him flying with a swipe of its foreclaws, it never did, and he felt easy around it now, although Domina still held herself aloof. After Argent fed, he stroked its downy head-feathers until it rumbled with pleasure deep in its chest, rather like a cat. Still, its breathing was labored, and it huffed twice more, too much like the dry cough of a man who has caught a fever in his lungs and can't squeeze it out.

'We'll stop here for the night and let them rest. It's not more than two days' march to Aosta.'

'Thank God,' said Sibold. A few other soldiers had gathered, those brave enough to stand watch on the griffins, and they echoed Sibold's words. They wanted out of the mountains. They wanted action, not this endless long journey.

Yet Aosta wouldn't bring peace.

They set up a rough traveling camp. The Quman had a way of pitching canvas lean-tos to hold off the prevailing wind that the rest of the army had adopted, and after feeding the griffins Sanglant made a tour of the camp: the Villam auxiliaries under the command of Lord Druthmar; the Saony contingent who chafed under the difficult rule of Lord Wichman; a ragtag collection of fighting men out of Eastfall and Westfall whom he had placed under the able command of Captain Istvan; Lady Wendilgard and her Avarians; the centaurs and their Kerayit allies; the Quman clans, stolid and silent, and their strings of horses; his own personal guard, now numbering more than two hundred.

His soldiers had grown used to the routine of the long march. The horses were cared for first while sentries took up places along the road. A line formed at the infirmary, mostly men complaining of loose bowels and sore feet. There was plenty of light for men to collect mountain pine for firewood, although little enough meat or porridge to cook over those fires. They would live off the land in Aosta and make enemies by doing so, yet he could not regret that they would march down onto the Aostan plain at harvest time, when they might be assured plenty to eat and bread every night.

'You're quiet, my lord prince,' said Hathui when they returned to the van where the griffins had settled down to rest like big cats curled up for the night.

'So I am.' He shaded his eyes to sight west along the

mountain ridges, then turned to examine the wandering line of camp stretching north along the roadway. The rear guard lay out of sight because of the curve and dip of the valley. 'We're vulnerable, strung out along the road like this. Ah! Look there!'

A rich harvest of herbs grew beyond the alder, and until it grew too dark to see he plucked saxifrage, chervil, and wolfs-bane.

'What virtue do these herbs have, my lord?' Hathui asked, working alongside him to his direction.

'Different virtues for different plants, but all of them can aid men who take wounds in battle. Wolfsbane can do more.' He glanced up at the sky, which was darkening as night swept up the valley. Only the peaks were still lit. 'It can poison a man, should it come to that.'

'Poison is a traitor's weapon.'

'Some name us traitors. Would you poison a man, Hathui, if it meant that a thousand men would be spared death in battle?'

She sat back on her heels. 'You've taken me off my guard, my lord prince. How can we measure one man's life against a thousand?'

'We do so all the time. Every day.'

She chuckled as she tied up the herbs into tight bundles. 'Perhaps we do. Shall I hike back down the trail and light a fire for Eagle's Sight, my lord? Liath may have reappeared. It's been three nights since I've looked.'

He shook his head. 'I don't feel easy. We're too close to Aosta now. Liath knows what her task is. We must stay hidden.' He grinned as an unexpected mood of reckless jollity swept him. 'It is an irony, is it not? Isn't that what the poets would call it? The regnants of Wendar kept secret the knowledge of the Eagle's Sight so that they could make use of the advantage it gave them. Now, protection against that sight has become so commonplace among those of us who know of its existence that the sight no longer serves any function. Yet I find I prefer knowing that I will make my way unencumbered by sorcerous aids or obstacles.'

'Not even those wielded by your wife?'

He laughed, because it was both painful and sweet to think of Liath. 'I don't know. I only know that without magic Anne and Adelheid and Hugh could not have ensorcelled my father.' He gathered up the herbs. 'Come,' he said, rising. 'Only protect me from our guide's lovely granddaughter, by whatever means necessary, and you'll have my thanks.'

Thoughts of Liath stirred his dreams, and he woke more than once, restless, discontented, until those disturbing visions melted into broken dreams of war. A hammer beat out a sword, cruel and jagged in shape. Sparks flew from the glowing iron with every stroke, and each spark drifted heavenward on that holy fire, spiraling and dancing, to become a star.

All at once he started awake, hearing that ringing beat, but he realized he was listening to the chuffing of the griffins. From the half-open tent he saw the stars twinkling above, yet a haze began to obscure them as he watched, growing murkier, covering the sky. The canvas rustled as if a rain were rolling in, but the air was dry and no thunder sounded in the distance.

Something is coming.

As he slipped on his boots and buckled his belt, an odor that reminded him of the forge crept into the air, blown in on that wind. Memories like bright sparks snapped in his mind. The dark spirits, the galla, that he and his mother had battled at Verna three or more years ago had brought with them the stench of the forge.

He faced into the rising wind. Up and down the camp came awake. Horses stamped and neighed. Dogs barked. Men called out each to the others or pounded extra stakes and rope to fix down flapping canvas. The wind whipped his hair around his neck as he turned to face south toward the height of the road ahead where a dozen soldiers stood sentry duty. The chuffing of the griffins grew in pitch until it became a cross between a yelp and howl. Others woke, grasping their weapons. From the hill they heard the somber tolling as of a bell.

'What manner of storm is this?' asked Captain Fulk, coming up beside him.

'Nothing good. Let an alert be passed all the way down the line. We must be ready.'

He pushed past the men to the hooded griffin; Domina had scattered men by stalking through the tents to stand with its eagle's head upraised as it called out a piercing challenge.

A horrible screech answered that call, carried on the wind from the sentries at the forward edge of camp where the road disappeared over a rock rise.

The sound of a man dying told much about how he was being killed. A quick blow on the field of battle might produce a subtle sigh. A gut wound often elicited screams, a mixture of pain and the realization that one's life was ending. This scream was that of a man dying in increments as his flesh was flayed off still living bone. Through the darkness, for now the stars were all but gone, Sanglant saw the shadows of men fleeing their posts. One figure, caught in mid-stride, was lifted from the ground where he flailed as if drowning, while he screamed and screamed until his silhouette against the deep blue of night was extinguished. A scatter of bones fell to earth.

'Torches!' cried Sanglant, coming fully awake at last.

While few men had senses keen enough to see or smell the galla or taste on their tongue the scent of the blood of dying men which carried on the wind, all could hear. All realized that they were set upon not by a mortal foe but by wicked demons.

'Your Highness!' Fulk ran up beside him, and even he, who rarely sounded shaken, could barely speak from fear. 'I don't think steel or fire can banish such creatures!'

Panic bled backward from the vanguard as men cut loose their horses and fled north along the road, or up the slopes, anywhere; a rout unfolded around him in the space of two breaths. Like a rolling mist, the galla came over the hills that sheltered the camp; few of the sentries stationed at the perimeter of camp were swift enough to escape, and as he finally got an arm to move, a leg to move, those slowest in their flight were flayed to the bone and their remains scattered on the gale.

The griffins howled in unison, and Domina turned her head back to chuff at her mate. Her iron feathers glimmered where the wind ran through them.

'Fulk! Take the men and horses and retreat north at full speed. At dawn if you've had no signal from me, gather our forces. If I am dead, let Lady Wendilgard take command. Save my father.'

'My lord prince.' Fulk did not hesitate; he was too good a soldier. He called out. Anshelm raised the horn to his lips and blew. The call rang above the screams and chaos and soon the tide of men flowed north along the road in a steadier stream, pushing the rear of the panicking army before it. Even the centaurs and the Quman fled.

Sanglant ran to Argent. 'This is your fight!'

He cut the trusses that held the hood and as the cloth fell away and Argent shook its head to cast off the remaining tangle of ropes, he sawed through the restraining ropes. The toll of bells rang through the air. The hot iron scent of aetherical bodies descended upon them. He heard his name in their heavy voices. Turning, he raised his sword as the ranks of galla swept down.

'Sanglant! Sanglant!'

'This earthly realm of pain is no gift, let us free your soul!'

Their forms were clear, towers of darkness and vaguely humanlike, although their features were blurred and faceless. They had grasping claws and could rend flesh. The smell of iron overwhelmed him as he staggered backward, unable to stand against such an onslaught. A wave of heat washing down before them completed the feeling of being cast into a blacksmith's white-hot hearth. He struck with his sword, but it passed through a wispy form and a quick hop backward was all that saved him from its touch. The rocky ground twisted under his feet, and he stumbled and fell flat.

The griffin sprang. It leaped not like a warrior plunging into battle or a wolf in a last burst of speed as it brings down an elk, but rather like a kitten chasing a moth around a candle, surprised at the ease with which the moth is swatted down but greatly pleased when another comes along to play. Its mate yelped and danced along the slope, wings outstretched as she sliced through the crowded galla.

The galla felt no fear, and so they came on, much to the griffins' delight. They shrilled no death screams, only whushing sighs of relief as their earthly forms splintered where griffin feathers cut through them; one by one, they were banished from Earth and fled back to the abyss from which they sprang.

Some few of the galla pursued the army, but with great bounds and gliding leaps the griffins cleared the camp and took off in pursuit of the pursuers. As they overtook each of the galla, they made a great spectacle of pouncing on the shimmering spear of darkness, and with each snap of release, each galla vanquished and banished, the griffins released a rumbling noise that could be mistaken as nothing but the sound of elation.

Sanglant climbed to his feet. He stood alone amid the ruin of camp and laughed to watch the griffins at play while his heart wept for those of his men who had been murdered in such a foul, cowardly manner.

And yet, and amazingly, when the galla were all gone and every trace of that iron sting had been blown into oblivion, the griffins circled around and padded back to him. They loomed over him, and Argent bent its head and shoved him playfully as if to say: will there be more?

'There will be more,' he promised. 'So I fear.'

As soon as it was light, he rode south with two dozen men along the trail while leaving Captain Fulk to set the army in order. The path made by the galla was easy to follow: all living things were dead where they had passed, even the plants. About an hour's ride south he discovered a hollow lying east of the road where the massacre had happened. Vultures and crows led him to it, for they had gathered in great numbers. Within this bowl of ground fifty or more men had had their throats cut and then been abandoned. Blood spattered everywhere, and it stank. The birds had pecked out all the soft eyes already, and the feast was so rich that he had to kill one before the rest fluttered away reluctantly only to roost close by, waiting.

Hathui and several of the men were sick; he himself could scarcely stand to look. It was one thing to kill in battle against an armed opponent. This was murder, plain and simple.

They returned to the army in a grimmer state of mind than they had left it, rejoining them at midday. Captain Fulk had the ranks set in marching order, and as soon as the prince arrived, he made his report.

The guide and his pretty granddaughter had vanished, but more than one man reported having seen them running north with their packs bouncing on their backs. All but forty-eight men were accounted for, yet the bones they had collected on the hillside and along the road where the galla had attacked seemed to add up to no more than nineteen men. Most likely some had lost heart and run for home. Still, not one among the Quman, or the centaurs, deserted him. Of his own men, Den and Johannes were missing and presumed among the dead.

'My people took the brunt of it!' Lord Wichman complained. 'Twelve men posted on sentry duty in the van, and only poor Thruster is left of them. Look at him!'

Lord Eddo had a bad reputation and was not liked even by Wichman and his cronies, but Sanglant had to pity the man now. He was a wreck, babbling and weeping without end about demons and fearful whispers and the claws of the Enemy raking into his guts until a potion got down his throat made him sleep.

'This may be the least of the losses we'll suffer,' said Sanglant, looking at each of his commanders in turn. 'If there are any without the heart to go on, now is the time to leave, without shame.'

His captains looked beyond him to the two griffins, who lounged up on the rocks, taking the sun, sated and satisfied. Unbound and unrestrained, they had not flown off.

Captain Fulk laughed. 'If such creatures follow you of their own volition, why would we poor frail humans turn away? Your army is ready to march, my lord prince.'

3

Uncle pushed the handcart and its precious container of grain plus a beautifully carved bench for trade along the windy path that led out of the valley. The Brat padded alongside, chattering nonstop about each least sight; she had never left the valley before, not in her entire life. The trail rose, crested a ridge, and descended out of the hills into open country beyond. That journey took them all morning and into the afternoon. Treu followed at his heels the entire time and now and again licked his hands.

'Look at how wide open everything is! Look, there's a hamlet! Look, I've never seen those people before! Hey, there! Hello, there! We've come walking all the way from Shaden! What's this place called? Obstgarten?' In a lower voice. 'Isn't that a peculiar name, Uncle? Just calling themselves "orchard"? Look! I've never seen an oak tree so big! We could live inside that trunk if it was hollow! Is it much farther to the miller?'

His stomach hurt. Although the others had taken cheese and baked eggs for the journey, he was so hungry he couldn't wait for midday so he had eaten another half a loaf of old bread that morning, the last of the hoard stored in the deacon's cupboard, too precious to waste although it had become so dessicated that it tasted like rocks and gritted between his teeth.

This countryside seemed vaguely familiar to him, although he wasn't sure why, but every time they came around a curve in the path the sight of that particularly unmistakable oak tree whose broad, leafy crown seemed to hide half the sky, or an apple orchard, or a hollow lush with alder made his eyes hurt and his head throb until he thought he would go blind again. His fingers were cold, although it was a late summer day so hot that the heavens had a tendency to shimmer.

'Storm,' said Uncle, pausing to rest while he wiped sweat off his brow. He pointed southeast where the land was most open. 'Coming up that way.'

Thunderheads piled up to form a huge wall of cloud, white at the top and an ominous green-gray color along the base.

'We'd best take cover,' added Uncle.

'Can't we make it to the miller?' asked Brat anxiously, biting on a grimy finger.

'We'll go a bit farther. I don't see any likely place here and we passed that village too long ago. I don't feel rain yet.'

'I'm hungry.'

'We'll eat when we've reached shelter.'

The leaves danced on the trees, spinning and whirling until he thought he saw daimones at play in the rising wind, laughing and teasing as they sported in the branches of the broken woodland through which they traveled. Meadows and fallow fields cut the woods into clumps and strips where humankind had hacked out a place for themselves; they could never leave well enough alone. They delved deeply where they weren't wanted and chopped down the forest because it made them fearful, and in time they would flatten and consume everything like rats set loose in a storehouse of grain.

He walked behind Uncle and Brat and the cart, wondering why his fingers, which had been so cold, were now beginning to burn as if he had thrust them into flames and yet here he just walked and there wasn't a fire anywhere except maybe the one in his head because his head was burning, too, a conflagration so fierce that although he could see, it wasn't like true seeing where a man touches an object with his vision and notes and measures that it is there and thinks about it and makes a judgment or a decision of what to do regarding what he has seen, only there were objects before him moving or not moving and he wasn't sure what they were any more only that he had to avoid smashing into things which was getting more and more difficult.

'What's he babbling about, Uncle?'

'Hush, child. He's a holy man. Don't offend him.'

'He's scaring me, Uncle! He's a crazy man! Fire and judgment and the world burning. Is he seeing the end of the world?'

'Hush, Brat. Hush. Look there! Thank the Lady. It's the miller.'

A little river glimmered in front of them, but it was the turning wheel that made his head spin so badly that he staggered sideways until he stumbled up against a fence, which he hadn't noticed. Two white clouds moved in the field: a pair of sheep running away from something.

'Why are they building that wall, Uncle?'

'I don't know, Brat. Best you keep quiet and let me do the talking.'

Rain spattered, flecking the dirt road. The wind tossed the boughs in a stand of apple and walnut trees lining the path. A pair of ripening apples fell and bounced on the ground. A branch heavy with walnut fruit whirled past on a gust, sank as the wind dropped off abruptly, and landed on the earth with a thump and crackle.

'Hey! Hey, there, traveler!'

A pair of men dressed in the coarse tunics of workmen strode out from the settlement, which consisted of a pair of houses and the laboring contraption that was the wheel and the grinding house. A half-built stone wall rose between the mill and the path like a fortification. Treu loped forward to place himself between Uncle and the men, barking.

'Quiet!' scolded Uncle. Treu whined and flattened his ears.

'Big storm coming in!' cried one of the men, having to shout to be heard as the wind roared behind them. 'Hurry!'

They ran, but not quickly enough. Rain lashed their backs. They were pummeled by loose branches and debris as the wind gusted so strong that it pushed Brat right over, and she stumbled and fell while Uncle struggled to keep the handcart from tipping over.

He grabbed Brat's wrist to drag her up. A stick came down on his arm.

'Leave off her, beast!' cried one of the workmen, brandishing the stick as if it were a sword. The other man hauled

Brat up and they ran for the door of the miller's house, where a stout woman stood crying out and beckoning although her words could not be heard above the howl of the storm. Thunder rolled, but it was the shriek of the gale and the drumming of rain that deafened them. He staggered to the shelter of the half-built wall just as Brat tore away from the man holding her and dashed back to him.

'Come on!' she screamed. 'You can't stay out here!'

Maybe the mortar hadn't set yet. Maybe it was the wind, because a cruel gust actually tore thatch off the roof of the miller's house and sent one line of fence clattering into sticks.

The wall tumbled down on them. Heavy stones hit his legs and head but, because the Brat had been crouching under the highest part, the stones buried her entirely. Only one strand of her pale brown hair could be seen, and a pair of fingers, twitching once, then still.

Bruised and dizzy, afire as his hands burned and his head was struck again and again by flying debris, he shoved stones off his legs and heaved the stones that had covered her to one side as the gale tried to flatten him. Beyond, he heard faint cries like the whimpering of birds. He glanced that way only once. Treu had been blown over against the mill itself; the gale pressed the poor dog against the wall of the outer housing, and if he barked, the scream of the wind drowned him.

Uncle dropped down beside him, hair whipping wildly against his face, half blinding him, but he, too, tossed stones aside until Brat was revealed, crushed, lying as still as a dead thing. The second workman fought over to them, holding tight a blanket that seemed ready to take wing. A branch hit him square on and he went down to one knee and crawled forward. They managed to roll her body onto the blanket, but even so she seemed likely to be blown away on that gale as they carried her at a run back to the houses, going to the shed, which hadn't lost half its roof.

The door banged shut. Inside the storehouse they huddled as the wind tore at the roof and whistled through cracks in the logs. More than once the whole structure shuddered as if it was being shaken in the claws of a monster.

'Ai, God!' moaned Uncle, bending over his niece's body. The gloom hid much, for the shed hadn't any windows, but it was obvious that the collapsing wall hadn't just broken all the bones in her body but crushed them. Horribly, she was still breathing. Blood bubbled on her lips, and one eye was open while the other was purpled and swelling shut so fast they could see the skin rise and blood rush up under it.

He wept over her, although he burned. His tears burned, as bright as petals of flame where they struck Brat's mangled body. The dark shed flickered with sparks of light flashing in and out of existence. Angels had come to visit them, bringing holy fire.

'I pray you,' he murmured, beseeching them, 'heal her.'

But the angels tormented him, pricking and stinging his skin, and the wind piped a tune around the frail shed that forced him to dance although there wasn't much room among the barrels and sacks and the shelves piled with rope and tools shaped by the millwright's lathe.

'He's a madman!' cried the workman who still wielded the stick. 'He threw that wall down on her!' He poked him back, and back, slapping at his thighs and body until he was driven up against the door.

'Leave him be!' cried Uncle, still weeping. 'He's a hermit, come out of the forest. Just a beggar. The wall fell because of the storm, or because of your poor workmanship! Leave be!'

'We didn't! I won't!' cried the workman. 'I'm not feared of madmen. I fought in the army of the old count, God save him. We saw plenty of worse things than filthy beggars, didn't we, Heric?'

The stick pressed him against the door while, beyond the planks of wood, the wind battered and beat, the strength of it thrumming against his shoulders. He twitched and jerked, needing to dance, anything to shake the sparks free that snapped open and closed all around him.

A shadow rose beyond the dying girl, a face that exploded into bits only it was still there, staring at him with a twist of its lips and a jaded gaze. 'I recognize him.' The workman shook his head. 'Nay. Can't be.'

'Let me go!' he begged. 'Can't you see the angels? It's all fire! Ai! Ai! It burns!'

'What, that filthy creature?' asked the other man.

'Leave him be,' said Uncle, but weeping had crushed his voice to a monotone and he did not look up from his niece to see what they were doing.

'Uncle?' whispered the girl, the sound of her voice almost lost beneath the noise of the wind.

'It looks like that stable boy, the one the old count took for his son and who was fooling him all along, the cheat.'

'Nay! Do you think so, Heric? I've heard all kind of stories – that Lord Geoffrey's daughter ain't the rightful count and that there wouldn't be such bad times if that son had stayed on. Wouldn't Lord Geoffrey be happy to show the doubters that the cheater was nothing more than a madman? There might be a great deal of silver in it for us, if we took him along to Lavas Holding.'

'Silver! Don't you remember how he tossed us out after all that time we'd served the old count, bless his soul? Why shouldn't Lord Geoffrey cheat us as well even if we did do him a good turn?'

The wind was dying. Far beyond, he heard the bleating of sheep and Treu barking and barking and barking, but the snow of angels had turned to flowers winking and dazzling in front of his eyes until the whole world turned the white-hot blue fire of a blacksmith's flame, searing his body.

'As if we can live with what work we can find now, eh, Heric? Building walls for a bowl of porridge. That's no way to live!'

''Least we eat almost every day.'

'You lost your spirit in the war.'

'I lost my spirit when Lord Geoffrey threw us out to make room for his wife's uncle's war band! Didn't even give us a loaf of bread for our pains and our wounds.'

'Why not try? It's a gamble. It might not be the same man. Lord Geoffrey might want nothing to do with him. But we might win something.'

'Why not?' said Heric as light showered down around him,

obscuring his face. The wind moaned in through the cracks in the shed and up among the rafters. 'Why not, indeed? The stable boy never did me any favors, did he? Even tried to take my girl, before she left me for a man who could give her a meal every day. Here's some rope.'

4

'After hearing this news of Princess Theophanu's troubles, and after reflecting upon his triumphs in the south, the king decided to settle his affairs in Aosta and return north to Wendar.'

When Heriburg's quill ceased its scratching, the young woman looked up. 'What next, Sister Rosvita?'

Rosvita sighed and looked over her company. They had become accustomed to long stretches of silence, and in truth this prison was a remarkably silent place, with the sound of the wind and the occasional *skree* of a hawk almost the only noises they heard. Now and again a guard might laugh; at intervals they heard wheels crunching on dust; the monks never spoke nor ever sang even to worship. She had come to believe that the brothers who lived here had all had their tongues cut out.

Prison was a species of muteness, too, but she had rallied her troops and kept them busy marking the hours of each day with worship, discussing the finer points of theology and the seven arts and sciences and memorizing the histories that they knew and the three books they possessed, her *History*, the *Vita* of St. Radegundis, and the convent's chronicles. Fortunatus proved especially clever at devising puzzles and mental games to keep their minds agile.

Now Fortunatus, Ruoda, Heriburg, Gerwita, Jehan, and Jerome all looked at her expectantly. The Eagle was out fetching water – of all of them, Hanna had the least ability to remain peaceably within such monotonous confines, although when Rosvita taught the others to understand and speak Arethousan, which she did every day for several hours, Hanna had shown an unexpected facility for that language.

Sister Hilaria was sitting with Petra out in the courtyard while Teuda continued her fruitless attempts to garden. Sister Diocletia and Aurea were in the next chamber massaging Mother Obligatia's withered limbs, a duty done in privacy. She heard one murmur to the other, and a stifled grunt from Obligatia, followed by a chuckle and an exchange of words too faint to make out.

'In truth,' said Rosvita finally, 'that is as far as I have got. I confess that when I composed the *History* in my mind, while in the skopos' dungeon, I stopped there. I could not bring myself to speak of that night when I saw Presbyter Hugh murder Helmut Villam. I had not the courage to record the queen's treachery. As for the rest, I must rely on your testimony to construct a history of the months I was imprisoned in the skopos' dungeon. What remains to be written beyond that has passed unknown to us, or has not yet to come to pass. Now we write the events as we live them.'

Seventy-three days they had remained confined at the monastery, each day a hatch mark scratched onto a loose brick pried out of the courtyard wall, but since the monks remained silent, it was impossible to find out exactly what date it was, although they might all guess that it was summer. It was so blazing hot that each trip down into the rock to fetch water from the hidden spring was a relief and, even, a luxury. At first only Hilaria, Diocletia, Aurea, and Hanna had the strength to complete the climb, but eventually every one of them except Petra and Mother Obligatia could negotiate those stairs.

Fortunatus bent over the table to examine Heriburg's calligraphy. 'A sure hand, Sister, and much improved.' He glanced at Rosvita as if to say 'yet never as elegant as Sister Amabilia's.'

She smiled sadly at him. How many of these truehearted clerics would survive their adventure? Amabilia certainly was not the first casualty of these days, nor would she be the last if all that they had heard predicted actually came true. It had proved far easier to write of the great deeds that formed history than to live through them.

'We must pray we survive to see the outcome of these events,' she said at last.

Sister Diocletia came into the chamber, rubbing her hands. She had connived olive oil out of the guards and it was this she used to manipulate and strengthen the old abbess' limbs.

'She'll sleep for a bit,' she said, 'but she's well today, as strong as she has been in months. However much it has chafed at the rest of us, this long rest has saved her.'

'Bless you, Sister,' said Rosvita, knowing that the young ones needed to hear such words, to believe that the confinement wasn't wasted; that they hadn't doomed themselves. They hadn't fallen into Anne's grip yet. There was still hope.

From far away, as if the sound drifted in on a cloud, they heard muffled shouts. Soon after, footsteps clattered outside. The door creaked open on dry hinges, and Hanna burst in, her face red and her hands empty, without the buckets of water they depended on.

'Sergeant Bysantius has returned!' she exclaimed. 'He's taking us to his commander. We leave tomorrow!'

The broad valley had so much green that it made Hanna's eyes hurt, and she could actually see flowing water, a dozen or more streams splashing down from surrounding hills. After ten days spent crossing dry countryside, Hanna inhaled the scent of life and thought that maybe they had come to paradise.

The others crowded up behind her to exclaim over the vista and its bounty of trees: figs, olives, oranges, mulberries, and palms. But Sergeant Bysantius wasn't a man who enjoyed views. He barked an order to his detachment of soldiers, and the wagons commenced down the cart track toward the land below. He was still the only one riding a horse; the wagons were pulled by oxen, slow but steady, and they had a trio of recalcitrant goats whose milk kept Mother Obligatia strong.

As she trudged along beside the foremost wagon, exchanging a friendly comment or two with the carter, Hanna shaded her eyes to examine the valley. Its far reaches faded into a heat haze, although certainly the weather was not as hot as it had been through much of their time confined to the tiny cliff monastery. In the center of a valley a small hill rose, crowned with ancient walls and a small domed church in the Arethousan style, almost a square. Beyond and around the hill a formidable ring wall appeared in sections, half gnawed away by time or by folk needing dressed stone for building. Tents sprouted like mushrooms on the plain around the old acropolis and mixed in among what appeared to be the ancient ruins of a town now overgrown with a village whose houses were built of stone and capped by clay-red tile roofs.

'Tell me what you see, I pray you,' said Mother Obligatia, who lay in the back of the wagon on her stretcher, wedged between dusty sacks of grain.

'It's a rich land, with more water than we've seen in the last three months altogether, I think.' She described the vegetation, and the layout of the buildings, and last of all described the tents. 'It's an army, but I can't make out the banners yet.'

Mother Obligatia thanked her. 'If they had meant to kill us, they have had plenty of opportunity. I suppose we are meant to reside as hostages. Yet among whom?'

'I wish I knew,' replied Hanna, 'but I fear we shall discover our fate soon enough.' She clasped the old woman's hand briefly, then let go in order to negotiate a badly corrugated stretch of road over which the wagons jounced and lurched; she lost her footing more than once, turning her ankle hard and gritting her teeth against the pain.

By the time the path bottomed out onto level ground, she was limping and could no longer see anything except the high citadel walls in the distance, which did indeed resemble a crown set down among the trees. Yet down here in the valley the wind had a cool kiss, and there was shade, and ripe figs and impossibly succulent oranges to be plucked from trees growing right beside the rutted road. They crossed two streams, and the sergeant was gracious enough to allow them to pour water onto their hot faces and dusty hands, even over their hair and necks, before he ordered them onward.

They crossed a noble old bridge with seven spans, water sparkling and shimmering below, and passed under the archway of the ring wall. A lion, like that sacred to St. Mark, capped the lintel, although it had no face.

Once inside this wall they walked on a paved road with wheel ruts worn into the stone at just the wrong width for their wagons. Fields surrounded them, most overgrown and all marked out by low stone walls. There were more orchards and one stand of wheat nearing harvest. She heard ahead of them the shouts and halloos of a host of men, and the braying, barking, caterwauling, and neighing of a mob of animals. Where the road turned a corner around an unexpected outcrop of rock, they came into sight of an old palace of stone, still mostly standing, where three grand tents sprawled with banners waving and folk here and there on errands or just loitering. Men forged forward to gawk at them as their party lumbered in.

'Isn't that the two-headed eagle of Ungria?' Hanna asked, but before she got her bearings or an answer two handsomely robed men with beardless cheeks and shrewd expressions rushed out from the central tent to meet them.

They spoke to Sergeant Bysantius in Arethousan, while Rosvita crept forward to stand beside Mother Obligatia and whisper a translation, although Hanna found that she could pick up much of what they said herself.

'They know we are coming and ask if we are the prisoners whom the king and his wife have asked for. The lady is pleased. We are to be escorted in at once, even without pausing to be washed.'

Soldiers trotted forward to hoist the stretcher out of the wagon. Sergeant Bysantius herded the gaggle of clerics forward. Heriburg clutched the leather sack containing the books, but Jerome left their chest behind. It contained nothing so valuable that it couldn't be abandoned. Except for the books, they possessed nothing of value except the clothes on their backs – and their own persons.

Who would ransom them? Who would care? Aurea crept up beside Hanna as they were pressed into the anteroom of

the central tent, and clutched her hand. Her palms were
sweaty, her face was pale, but she kept her chin up.

'Take heart,' said Rosvita softly to the girls. She exchanged
a look with Fortunatus. He nodded, solemn. Even Petra had,
for a mercy, gone silent, eyes half shut as though she were
sleepwalking.

The anteroom was crowded with courtiers dressed in the
Arethousan style but also in the stoles and cloaks of
Ungrians. There were a lot of Ungrians. It seemed a face or
three looked vaguely familiar to Hanna, but she wasn't sure
how that could be. She caught sight of a man short but power-
fully broad with the wide features and deep eyes common to
the Quman, enough like Bulkezu that she actually had a jolt of
recognition, a thrill of terror, that shook her down to her feet,
until she realized a moment later that the ground was shaking,
not her.

A rumble swelled, then faded, a shiver through the earth
like a great beast turning over in its sleep.

The crowd in the anteroom fell silent. Outside, a woman
laughed, her high voice ringing over the sudden hush.

'Just a little one,' whispered Gerwita, her voice more like
the squeak of a mouse. She let go of Ruoda's hand.

Blood-red curtains shielded an inner chamber from the
anteroom. A eunuch, resplendent in jade-green robes,
appeared and held a curtain aside for them to pass. It was dim
and stuffy within the inner chamber, which was lit by four
slits cut into the tent's roof and by two lamps formed in the
shape of lamias – sinuous creatures with the heads and torsos
of beautiful women and the hindquarters of snakes. A couch
sat in the place of honor, raised on a low circular dais constructed out of wooden planks painted the same blood-red
shade as the heavy curtains. Two young men, stripped down
to loincloths, worked fans on either side of the woman reclining there at her leisure. She eyed the new arrivals as though
they were toads got in where they did not belong. She had a
dark cast of skin and black hair liberally streaked with gray,
and she was fat, with a face that would have been beautiful
except for the smallness of her eyes and the single hair growing

from her chin. A blanket covered her body from her midsection down, and Hanna began to labor under an obsessive fancy that the noblewoman might actually herself be a lamia, more snake than woman.

A dark-haired, homely boy of about ten years of age sat at the base of her couch, holding a gold circlet in his hands and trying not to fidget. A general outfitted in gleaming armor stood behind her, striking because he had one eye scarred shut from an old wound while the other was a vivid cornflower blue, startling in contrast to his coarse black hair and dark complexion. He stood between the two slaves, so straight at attention, hands so still, that he might have been a statue. But he blinked, once, as he caught sight of Hanna's white-blonde hair, and then a man laughed, such a loud, pleasant, hearty sound that Hanna's attention leaped sideways to the king and queen seated on splendidly carved chairs to the right of the Arethousan lady on her dais.

Nothing could have shocked her more – except the appearance of a lamia slithering in across the soft rugs.

The king and queen sat on a dais of their own, rectangular and exactly as high as that on which the Arethousan noblewoman presided. Two banners were unfurled behind their chairs – the double-headed eagle of Ungria, and the red banner adorned with eagle, dragon, and lion stitched in gold belonging to the regnant, or heir, of Wendar. Behind the queen stood three grim-faced Quman women, one young, one mature, and one very old. They wore towerlike headdresses covered in gold, and when Hanna looked at them they made signs as one might against the evil eye.

The king laughed again. He was a big, powerful man not quite old but not at all young. 'It's as if a breath of snow has come in. I've never seen hair so white!' He turned to his queen, taking her hand, but her expression was as sour as milk left too long in the sun.

'That's just what your brother used to say,' Princess Sapientia said. 'She is my father's Eagle, but I don't trust her. Nor should you.'

Hanna gaped, but she knew better than to defend herself.

'These folk are known to you, King Geza?' asked the Arethousan lady. Behind her, the one-eyed general was smiling at a jest known only to himself.

'They are known to *me!*' said Sapientia. 'That woman is Sister Rosvita, one of Henry's intimate counselors. I have never heard an ill word spoken of her, although it's true some are jealous that the king honors her so highly when her lineage is not in truth so high at all.'

'Will she know the usurper's mind?' asked the lady.

'She might.'

They spoke Arethousan slowly enough that Hanna could follow its cadences; Geza and Sapientia were not fluent, and the noblewoman evidently disdained to use a translator.

'Sister Rosvita, step forward,' said the lady.

Sister Rosvita took one step, halted, and inclined her head respectfully. 'I am Sister Rosvita. Although I could once claim to be one of Henry's intimate counselors, that is true no longer.'

'So she says!' snorted Sapientia.

'Yet we have seen rebellion in plenty,' said Geza, 'not least in the person of your charming brother, my dearest Sapientia. Henry loses support and his authority falls to pieces. Is that not the sad fate of those who do not rule well, Lady Eudokia?'

The lady's smile thinned her lips. Hanna almost expected her to flick a snake's forked tongue out of her mouth. 'We need but one great victory to gain the support of the people here in Arethousa, it's true. We must drive the usurper's army out of Dalmiaka. After that, we will turn to the golden city in triumph. My aged cousin will retire to a monastery and allow my nephew to take what ought to be his.'

'Is that when I will become emperor, Aunt?' The homely child sitting at the foot of the couch spoke in a piping voice, peculiarly loud. He looked as if surprise were his normal state as he spun the circlet between his fingers. Obviously he would rather be playing than sitting in on this grave council.

'Yes, Nikolas,' she said dismissively. The general did not move, not by one finger's breadth, although he had developed a disconcerting habit of flicking his gaze now and again back to Hanna. 'Tell us again, Sergeant Bysantius, in what condition you found this sad party?'

'In my opinion, Exalted Lady, they were fleeing from the usurper's soldiers. If not, then they should become actors and go on the stage, for they have fooled me.'

'I pray you,' said Rosvita in a strong voice, 'we are a small group of clerics, harmful to no one. We have both crippled and ill among us.

'I did not give you permission to speak!' snapped Lady Eudokia. Rosvita pinched her lips together over a retort, yet otherwise her placid face did not change expression. Rosvita was a mild woman, but she was probably smarter than the rest of them put together.

Hanna was surprised to find herself shaking a little, indignant on Rosvita's behalf. Where had this loyalty sprung from? When had she lost her heart to the cleric, who did not *command* the loyalty of those around her but claimed it nevertheless?

Rosvita would never desert them. She would never stain her own honor.

That was what her companions all knew. That was why they followed her. In her own way, she was a prince among men, too, but the army she led bore different weapons: the quill, the steady mind, the slow accumulation of knowledge put to good use.

'Do you know why the usurper came to Dalmiaka?' demanded Lady Eudokia.

'I do,' said Rosvita evenly. 'I must have some assurances regarding the safety of my people before I will speak honestly with you.'

'Will you betray my father just as my brother has?' cried Sapientia, face flushed. She began to stand, but Geza's hand tightened on her wrist and she subsided at once, trembling so hard that it was noticeable, as though that mild earthquake still gripped her.

'I have never betrayed Henry, Your Highness. Others betrayed him, but never me. The task which lies before us all is much graver, and will afflict high and low, Arethousan and Wendish and Ungrian and Dariyan regardless. What date is it, I pray you?'

'This night begins the feast day of St. Nikephoras,' said the attendant in the jade-green robes. 'In the two hundred and thirty-sixth year as acknowledged by the Patriarch's authority, and recalling the foundation of the Dariyan Empire, of which we are the only true heirs, one thousand six hundred and eight years ago.'

'I pray you, what date according to the calendar recognized by the Dariyan church?'

The beardless man sneered. Lady Eudokia looked offended and had actually to drink wine before she could bring herself to express her disgust. 'You have forgotten the proper rites and observances! Can it be that an educated churchwoman of the apostate church no longer recalls St. Nikephoras, who was patriarch and defender of the True Church?'

Geza called forward a steward from his entourage who, with great reluctance, admitted to knowing and keeping track of the calendar of the apostate Dariyans. 'Begging your pardon, Exalted Lady,' the man said to Eudokia. 'This is the day celebrated by the false shepherd in Darre as a feast day of one of her ancestors, called Mary Jehanna, who also donned the skopal robes in defiance of the rightful patriarch. Rebels and heretics, all!'

'That means it is already the equinox,' exclaimed Rosvita. 'We were six months or more within the crown!' Her color changed. She swayed, and Ruoda and Gerwita steadied her. 'Nay, not six months at all!'

She was so stunned that she was talking to herself out loud, the workings of her mind laid bare for all to see. The secret method of their arrival in Dalmiaka, too, was betrayed, but she was profoundly shocked. 'The Council of Addai took place in the year 499, and if the Arethousan church has counted two hundred and thirty-six years . . . then it is not the year 734 but rather 735. We wandered within the crown for fully eighteen months! How it can be so much time slipped away from us?'

'What does she mean?' murmured Geza, face tightening with suspicion.

Lady Eudokia leaned forward, her hand greedily gripping the blanket that covered her legs. 'The crowns! How comes it that you have gained this ancient knowledge long forbidden to those in the True Church?'

Rosvita glanced at the girls. The flush that had reddened her face began to fade. 'I pray you, Sisters. I can stand. It was a trifling blow.'

Hanna hardly knew whether to breathe. They all stared at each other, trying to comprehend what Rosvita had just said. Was it true they had lost eighteen months in one night? Was this the cost inflicted by the crowns for those who thought to spare themselves the effort of travel? Fortunatus' lean face had gone gray with fear, and the others muttered prayers under their breath or gazed in astonishment at Rosvita. Mother Obligatia had closed her eyes, although her lips moved. Only Petra appeared unmoved; she swayed back and forth, eyes still half shut, singing to herself under her breath.

Rosvita drew in a shaky breath and clasped her hands before her in an attitude something like prayer. 'Exalted Lady, I have learned many things in my time. What is it you want of me? If you wish to learn what I know, then I must get something in return.'

'Your life?'

Rosvita shrugged.

'The lives of your companions?'

'That I will bargain for, it's true, yet they are free to choose their own course of action. If the intelligence I know is true, then it matters little what coercion you choose to inflict on me, or on them. "The sun shall be turned to darkness, and the moon to blood." A storm is coming—'

'So Sanglant claimed!' retorted Sapientia.

'So he did,' said Geza. 'He may have been obsessed, but he is no fool. *We* would be fools to discount what he said.'

'It was a ruse! A lie to catch us off guard! He meant to abandon me in the wilderness all along. I would have died if it weren't for the Pechanek mothers! I never believed his story of a cataclysm!'

'I do,' said Lady Eudokia in a voice that commanded silence. 'Our scholars have studied the ancient histories. We in Arethousa escaped the full fury of the Bwr invasion that destroyed much of Dariya five hundred years ago, but we remember it. We recall bitterly the anger of the Horse people, who swore to avenge themselves on the descendants of the Lost Ones because in ancient days the Lost Ones ripped the Earth itself asunder in their war against humankind.'

Eudokia spoke with as much passion as if the event had occurred last month, but Hanna could not fix her mind around such gulfs of time, years beyond counting. In Heart's Rest a woman was considered rich in kinship who remembered the name of her grandmother's grandmother.

'Now this Prince Sanglant seeks an alliance with the Horse people. How can we know whether he seeks to aid humankind, or his mother's kinfolk, the Lost Ones? How can we trust any creature who is not fully human, as we are? Who does not worship God as we do?'

The crowd remained silent, not even a whisper, but Rosvita was not cowed by the lady's zeal. 'What do you want of me, Exalted Lady? Your Highness? Your Majesty? We are nothing, we fourteen wanderers. We matter not.'

'You fled my father,' said Sapientia. 'That means you are guilty of some crime. You are guilty of sorcery! You admit it yourself!'

'No need, Cousin,' said Lady Eudokia to Sapientia. 'It matters not what crime she was accused of back in Dariya. We march to Dalmiaka with or without her and her companions.'

'I think it wisest to keep them close by,' said Geza thoughtfully, with a respectful nod toward Rosvita.

'If it is possible her knowledge can aid us, then I think we must march with her and hold her in reserve,' agreed Eudokia.

'When our victory is achieved?' Sapientia asked. 'What, then?'

'Do not disturb yourself on that account, my dearest,' said Geza, whose gaze never flicked by the least amount toward

Eudokia, although any idiot could see that he and the Arethousan lady had cozened Sapientia between them. 'You will be restored to your rightful place. His Exalted Lordship will be placed on the throne that belongs to him.'

'That's me!' cried the boy with a big grin.

'All will be well,' finished the Ungrian.

'And you, King Geza?' asked Rosvita boldly. 'What do you gain from these ventures?'

He did not smile, but he wasn't angry either. He had Bayan's ability to be amused, but his was a character much deeper and murkier than Bayan's had ever been. 'Certain territories along the Anubar River, which has for many years marked the disputed border between Arethousa and Ungria. And justice for my wife, who sought my aid after being abandoned by her brother in the wilderness.'

Sapientia smiled brilliantly at him; her eyes sparkled with unshed tears. He patted her hand, but no wise differently, Hanna thought, than he would have patted the head of one of his favorite dogs. Bayan had treated Sapientia with more respect.

Yet how could she know where the fault lay? Had Sapientia thrown herself into Geza's arms, or had he taken her by force? The princess had marched east with her brother, and without asking questions that an Eagle hadn't the right to ask as a prisoner, Hanna couldn't know what had transpired to set Sapientia so fiercely against Prince Sanglant except perhaps the prince's refusal to execute Bulkezu.

This thought of Bulkezu surprised her. The old familiar revulsion and hatred still clung, like a stench, but after her time in Darre she could see now that necessity might force a man's hand, might bring him to spare the life of a man he detested for the sake of the greater good.

Have I forgiven Sanglant? The revelation startled her. His name evoked no fury in her heart, only resignation. Only a wry smile.

She had changed. She had come through the fire, and she had an inkling of the fearful vista opening before them that could make their former trials seem light in comparison.

'Let them be taken away, Basil. Let them be fed, and given decent accommodation and a wagon to ride on as we travel, but do not allow them to escape or I will have your head.'

The general chuckled, and perhaps he blinked just as Hanna looked at him, or perhaps he winked at her. She averted her gaze quickly.

'Yes, Exalted One.' The man in the jade-green robes turned with a flourish and beckoned to a trio of men as beardless as he was, if not quite as elegantly dressed.

They were led to a tent whose dimensions and accoutrements seemed royal after the spare monastic cells in which they had remained confined all summer. The exhaustion brought about by unremitting anxiety and the stunned recognition of their changed circumstances, as well as their discovery of that unexpected passage of time within the crowns, made them a quiet group as they each found a place to sit on the chairs, benches, and pillows carried in for their comfort. Tea and honey cakes were brought, and bread, and a porridge of mashed peas spiced with rosemary, which was, in truth, overdry and had a bitter aftertaste. They ate in silence. Even Rosvita said nothing as she drank wine and, at intervals, rubbed her head as if it hurt her.

When all were sated and sitting slumped and slack-faced, Hanna dared speak. 'What now, Sister Rosvita?'

Rosvita's smile was more ghost than real. 'It is an irony, I think, that we find what proves to be a kind of refuge with one who is enemy to our regnant.'

'Sapientia is his rightful heir!' protested Fortunatus.

'So she is, yet he has claimed Mathilda in her place, under the influence of Adelheid. Princess Sapientia has not necessarily made a foolish bargain with King Geza and the Arethousans, although she may come to regret it. It may be that she believes this to be the only way she can hope to restore herself to the position she has long assumed she would one day possess. Yet we know as well that the Henry who speaks and rules in Darre now is not our regnant but a puppet controlled by outside hands. Who, then, is the enemy, and who the ally?'

'Will you tell them so?' asked Hanna. 'How much do we dare say to the regnant's enemies?' Inside the walls of this pleasant tent, a finer bower than any place they had rested for the last many months, Hanna felt at ease, although she knew Rosvita was right. 'It seems to me that we face enemies on every side. How are we to know what to do and whom to trust?'

'Sanglant claimed that the crown of stars would crown the heavens on the tenth day of Octumbre, in the year seven thirty-five. I do not know the means by which the mathematici arrived at that date, or if they are correct, but that date falls next month. We now camp in southwestern Arethousa, I believe, just north of Dalmiaka. This army plans to march into Dalmiaka, apparently to face the Holy Mother and Henry themselves. Yet I know not whether we must turn the Holy Mother Anne aside from her task at the crown in Dalmiaka, or aid her in succeeding to weave her mathematicus' spell.'

Throughout this discussion Mother Obligatia had remained silent. Hanna had even thought her asleep. One of those shivering tremors shifted the ground beneath them, so that Gerwita cried out, then giggled nervously as the quake subsided as quickly as it had arisen. As if the earth had roused her, Obligatia lifted her head and braced herself up on her elbows. Sister Diocletia came to her aid, supporting her. They all turned respectfully to hear her.

'The old can be blinded by sentiment.' It was always a surprise to Hanna how strong a voice could issue from so frail a form. 'I know this, for I have seen it. I have regretted it. Yet I do believe that I saw my son Bernard's daughter, and that she saved us against the galla, although she was too late to spare Sister Sindula.'

'Liath!' whispered Hanna.

The abbess nodded toward her before continuing. The tent grew dim as shadows lengthened, as the sun set and the blazing temperatures abated with the coming of twilight and the promise of night. They had no lamps.

'If this woman, this skopos, who calls herself Anne is truly Liathano's mother, then that is where Liath will go. Seek out the Holy Mother Anne, and we will find the one we seek. That is where I wish to go.' Tears glistened on the old woman's cheeks, and Diocletia tenderly wiped them away. 'I am content with this turn of events, my friends. I am old, at the end of my life. The world will end for me whether a storm comes or not, and now I see that all along I have been self-ish.'

Although outside the tent's walls the camp grew lively as night fell, inside a hush contained them. The twilight wind fluttered along the canvas.

'I want to meet my granddaughter before I die.'

XXIX

THE TRAP SHE HAD LAID

1

In Verna, Liath used an arrow to weave a net of magic through the crown. The threads pulled down from the heavens thrummed through her arms. This was joy. She felt transported and alive; her body hummed with the touch of the stars and the music of the spheres, the ever-turning wheel of the cosmos singing through her from top to toe.

Lady Bertha rode in the van, leading her thirty mounted men-at-arms in ranks of two through the blazing portal. Sorgatani followed, her wagon driven by the two slave women who attended her while her Kerayit guard rode behind. Last of all, Gnat, Mosquito, and Breschius paused, glancing back at her, and she willed them to forge forward. She dared not speak or move for fear of shifting the portal as the stars spun slowly westward, tugging at the threads.

The subtleties of direction and distance were harder to control than she had imagined, but with practice – indeed! With practice she could master this skill. The stars could speak through her; she could sing with them. She could dwell on Earth among those she loved and still touch the heavens.

As long as they defeated Anne.

The three men dashed forward through the archway at last. The ethereal threads quivered as if in a gusty breeze as the men passed under them and vanished, and as she pulled the threads in behind herself she paused on the threshold and looked back. The daimone waited in the valley, hiding itself, but she could see its pale form quavering against the fading night. It had hovered nearby all night.

'Who are you waiting for?' she asked, but it did not answer, so she turned her back on Verna and stepped through as light cascaded around her. It seemed in that passage as if all those threads drew the spheres in behind them, the entire cosmos – stars, the sun, time itself – swirled as the light from one body blurred into the next.

She sees Sanglant marching out of the mountains at the van of a great army. He rides at the front on Resuelto with Hathui behind him and noble ladies and lords surrounding him. On either side pace the two griffins. The male no longer wears a hood. It lifts its eagle's head and shrills a call that echoes down the valley. No clouds soften the hard blue glare of the sky. The view is glorious, and the road lies clear before them, all the way down to the coastal plain.

An Eika prince sails on choppy seas, brooding at the stem of his ship. He stares across the gray waters, hand clenched around the haft of a standard laced with bones and beads and feathers. Two black hounds lie at his feet. Behind him, a deacon prays.

Ivar rides along a woodland path beside a young man who looks startlingly familiar. Erkanwulf? Wind ripples through the leaves, turning her down a new path.

She sees Hanna sleeping.

Hanna!

The threads whip and crack her sight down new passageways, a maze that pulls her in a hundred directions as it splinters into manifold paths.

She has lofted far above the world, and she sees how the threads of each life are intertwined with all the others, a chain linking every soul and every thing and every place.

A filthy beggar with hands and feet chained is shoved into a cage. Shadow obscures his face.

A creature half-man half-fish swims in calm waters, hair writhing like eels.

Sister Venia wipes her brow, standing among two score corpses. She has blood on her hands, and a disfiguring anger suffuses her expression.

In the depths of the earth, a wizened beast crouches before a sheet of metal and runs its fingers across a glowing sequence of lumps and etchings. Others cluster behind it, clicking and humming, tapping the ground.

Snakes hiss. A phoenix stirs in its deep cavern. The ground trembles.

An owl hoots. She turns to see Li'at'dano looking right at her through a stone burning with blue fire 'Beware!' the centaur cries. 'Beware the trap she has laid!'

Seven crowns of seven stones form the loom on which the great spell was woven in the long-ago days, laid out across the land to make the points of a vast crown. She glimpses each circle in turn, and she sees:

Meriam.

Hugh.

Marcus.

Severus.

A middle-aged woman in presbyter's robes, completely unknown to her. A stranger.

An arrogant young man wearing the robes of an abbot. His face looks vaguely familiar with a family resemblance to Duchess Rotrudis.

Where is Anne?

Why can't I see Blessing?

She hears the surge and suck of a sea as waters rise and fall against rock close by.

She stepped through.

'At them again!' Bertha's voice rang out above the clash and clamor of arms.

Liath stumbled out of the circle and into madness. In the

light of the waning sun it seemed that beyond the stones on all but one side stood a forest, tightly packed and denuded of branches, ringing them in like a rank of men with a tightly linked shield wall. Scattered in no particular pattern on three sides were tents and a profusion of campfires. Torches glared. Men, most on foot, charged back and forth, shouting, and because she was staring at them in shock and amazement, she did not watch her feet. She tripped and fell forward over a dead man who had been killed by an arrow in his throat. Blood eddied into the dirt. Two more dead faces grimaced at her, one by each of her outflung hands. The first she recognized as one of Lady Bertha's soldiers; the other wore a tabard sewn with a gold Circle of Unity on a black field: the sigil of the guardsmen who protected the skopos.

Now she understood what she saw. They had come through the crown into the middle of an armed, fortified encampment set up to protect the stone circle.

'To me, to me!' Bertha's voice sang above the din. Again she drove her small force against a knot of footmen who had formed up but were not yet ready to receive a charge. They scattered, some falling, but some taking horse or rider down with strokes at a horse's legs or clever thrusts to the rider's exposed rib cage. There wasn't enough room for Lady Bertha to swing her cavalry around and get the full weight of their horses behind them. More infantry surged up from behind to attack them. Arrows whistled out of the twilight. They were surrounded.

Ai, God. She struggled to her feet and readied her bow, but they were hopelessly outnumbered. She drew, shot, and took down a valiant sergeant who had just then gripped the stirrup of Bertha's charger. A second man fell, mortally wounded, with her second shot.

'Push that way!' cried Bertha. 'There! Where the stockade is unfinished!'

Had the Austran lady already lost half her men? Liath fell in behind Kerayit guardsmen as they pushed to make a path for Sorgatani's wagon to the breach in the wall. Breschius ran at the back, a dagger glinting in his hand. She couldn't see

Gnat and Mosquito. She grabbed a pair of arrows off the ground and shot, and Lady Bertha got her surviving soldiers pulled in around her and threw them forward to support the retreat.

Gnat and Mosquito appeared out of the stones and sprinted for the wagon, bent low, dodging arrows and spear thrusts with astonishing agility.

'Here!' she cried as she leaped over bodies and fell in with the others. She looked around for a spare horse, but too many soldiers pressed forward against them. She hadn't time to do more than grab arrows off the ground, to duck away from a sword blow that swept past her head. She shot a man in the gut not a body's length from her, and he jerked backward, screaming, carrying two of his fellows with him as he flailed.

Yet as they closed on the south end of the camp, toppling tents and cutting down stray soldiers, they seemed as one to realize that in fact the stockade was finished. It ringed the camp. The sound of water grew, but the open ground did not expose the side of a steep hill but rather became the edge of a cliff that plunged far down to the sea below. The stockade finished at either end with a pile of stone and earth; beyond that, only air. They were trapped. No one could climb down that cliff.

The Kerayit guards reached the stockade first, and one hacked in vain at green logs as his fellows formed up around Sorgatani's wagon and Lady Bertha called on her soldiers to dismount and make a shield wall. Arrows fell among them, some chipping up the dirt; a few thudded into the logs. She felt one whoosh past her cheek; another found its mark, and a man shrieked. A horse bucked and spilled its riders.

They were trapped.

She reached out and called fire. First the canvas of tents burst into flame, then, brushed by billowing, roaring canvas, a hapless soldier who had boldly stepped forward to urge his men to advance caught fire. He spun screaming as flames wrapped his body.

She had no time to regret his death. She reached into the green logs of the encircling palisade. Fire slumbered deep within. She pricked it, and again, harder, until flame exploded up from a dozen logs in the stockade right where the Kerayit soldier stood chopping at the wood. The fire blackened and consumed him in an instant; he didn't even have a chance to scream. The other guards dragged the wagon back one turn of the wheels, but they understood what she meant to do. They braved the heat, waiting for their chance as the logs burned from inside out.

Fire was the only thing that would keep them alive. The enemy had fallen back away from the burning tents, and now with her party clumped next to the blazing wood, easily seen, the archers set arrow to string and began to shoot at will.

She set her will to the bows the archers held, one by one, and yet for each man who cast his bow aside when flame licked along the curve, the next might find his arm ablaze, his tabard streaming with fire. Their screams burned her, yet she could not flinch.

Wasn't this war?

Didn't men die just as horribly stuck deep in the guts by spears or their heads sliced open by swords?

She was too slow. She could not stop every archer, not quickly enough. Arrows peppered the ground. Lady Bertha's soldiers hid behind their shields, but the horses were easy targets and their enemy happy to cause havoc among them by shooting for their bellies. The poor beasts kicked and screamed and half a dozen bolted for the enemy line. It was not the battle but the fire that panicked them. She still held her own bow, but where she aimed, she called fire. A flight of arrows burst into flame above and rained ash down over their party.

The stockade roared.

The enemy pushed forward step by step, calling out, readying a charge.

'Go, Arnulf! Go!' cried Bertha.

Liath glanced back. They were twenty still standing, no more. One of Bertha's soldiers, a giant of a man with massive shoulders and thick arms, threw a cloak over his head and braved the flames with ax in hand, hacking at the wood. The cloak began to burn, but the logs crumbled into flaming splinters. The heart of the wood had burned away.

'Move!' screamed Bertha. 'Go! Go!'

'Charge them, men!' bellowed a captain among the enemy. More massed behind that front line. Archers with burning hands wept. A horse thrashed on the ground beside her, pierced by a dozen arrows.

The Kerayit slave women drove the wagon headlong into the burning wall, their horses frantic with fear as they plunged through the fiery gap. Under the press of the wheels, logs crumbled like burning straw, and the flames that licked along the painted wagon guttered and failed as Sorgatani's magic killed them. The wagon was through! A cheer rose from the survivors as they pressed forward in its wake, seeing escape.

A roar unlike that of fire rose from the enemy.

'Forward!' The captain took a step, then a second. 'Forward, you cowards!'

The line doubled, swelled, gathering strength for the charge.

'You must go, my lady!' cried Bertha, coming up beside her, still mounted. Her horse's eyes were rolling with fear, and it was streaked with ash and flecks of charcoal, but it held its ground. An arrow dangled from its saddle, fixed between pommel and seat. Bertha's shield had been lopped in half, and she cast it away.

'Mount up behind me!' she cried.

'Go on!' shouted Liath. 'I'll hold the rear. Hurry!'

Bertha did not hesitate as Liath delved into the iron rimming of shields; she sought deep within swords for sparks of fire bound tightly within. Boot and belt, hair and bone, all bloomed as fire scorched through the front line, and yet they came on and on, screaming, shrieking, while those behind them yelled and cursed and some ran toward her all over fire like torches.

I am a monster.

One passed by her and threw himself on a Kerayit who hung back with a few others to protect her back. She saw their faces change shape as fire ate flesh down to bone. Their eyes were black pinpricks, bursting open at the moment of death.

The tents within arrow shot burned so bright it seemed like day. Yet nothing touched her. She was the center, the sun.

'Fall back, my lady!' cried Bertha far behind her. 'Or we shall all surely die waiting for you!'

Had they all gone so quickly? She retreated, step by step, holding the enemy at bay simply because she existed. More than two score men lay in ruin around her, some dead, their fingers and arms curling like charred twigs. A few, the unfortunate, writhed on the ground, whimpering, moaning, skin melted off or hanging like rags. Smoke, sweet with scorched flesh, drifted in a haze around her so it seemed she moved backward into a miasma.

So I do.

She fought an urge to run. To turn her back would be certain death as arrows still rained around, many burned away within an arrow's length of her body. Hundreds of furious, fearful men kept their distance but moved with her, pace by pace. She saw her death in their gaze. They hated her for what she was.

'Liath!' cried Breschius from far away, but not so far, where moments might seem like an hour, where three strides might seem like three leagues The stockade still burned; she heard the rattle of the wheels of Sorgatani's wagon crunching away over dirt. Had she taken more than ten breaths between the collapse of the stockade and now?

She was almost there. The heat of the burning logs whipped along her back.

'Bright One! Run quickly!'

Gnat's voice came from the wrong direction. She lost track of her footing. With her next step she tripped over the leg of a fallen horse.

She was able to catch herself as she rolled onto the body of the beast, but before she could rise, an arrow struck through her thigh, piercing her flesh and burying its head deep in the horse's belly.

She screamed. Pain bloomed. Flames spit up from the earth. As she twisted, seeing fletchings protruding from the leg, a second arrow hit through the same thigh, at a different angle.

Mosquito appeared, dodging through burning tents, ducking behind a fallen horse. 'Mistress! I come!'

Fire shot up in a wall, driving her foes back. Horsehair singed, its scent stinging her.

'Go!' she screamed. 'I command it, all of you. Gnat! Mosquito! Retreat! Save Sorgatani!'

She grabbed one of the arrows, but her touch on the shaft sent pain shooting up her spine and down her calf. She choked down a scream; she knew what she had to do.

Let them run, she prayed. *Let them retreat and save themselves.*

She grabbed each shaft, closed her hands around them, and called fire. The pain inside her thigh flared; it bit; it flowered. It stunned her with its ferocity, eating at the flesh from inside. She wept. Tears spattered her face with cold fierceness. There was a terrible strong wind blowing in off the sea. Thunder rumbled.

Or was it the earth trembling beneath her?

Fire guttered as rain splashed, yet it wasn't the rain that cooled the flames but the sparkling wings of butterflies, a thousand winking shards. Where they fluttered, flame died.

The first arrow crumbled away into ash. Blood from the wound gushed down the belly of the horse. Ash and blood in a muddy mixture dripped onto her feet. She tugged on the second arrow and almost passed out, but it did not break. It had not burned through.

'I've got it, Mistress! I'll put it out.'

Mosquito was the one with the round scar on his left cheek and a missing tooth. Gnat had broader shoulders, a broader face, and was missing the thumb on his right hand.

And, damn him, there he was, scuttling in beside his brother. He shoved a knife between her thigh and the horse, levering it in until it hit the shaft.

She thought the pain of that movement alone would kill her. The heavens dazzled; stars spun webs, and Mosquito yelped with fear as Gnat sawed and she moaned. A glittering net drifted out of the sky an arm's length above them. Butterflies skimmed across her cheeks.

Anne stepped out of the line of soldiers and halted a stone's toss in front of her. The skopos was crowned and robed in the splendor of her office, wearing white robes embroidered with red circles. No ash marred the purity of that linen. A gold circlet rested on her brow, mirroring the gold torque that circled her neck, the sigil of her royal ancestry.

Anne regarded her in silence for some moments. Because the light of the burning tents blazed behind her, her face was in shadow, half obscured. Yet Anne had always been obscured; if there was passion beneath that cool exterior, it, like coals, had always been buried beneath a layer of ash.

'Shoot the servants,' she said.

Five arrows flashed out of the burning night. Three thudded wetly into flesh: two into Mosquito and one into Gnat, just above his collarbone. He fell back, choking. Mosquito had collapsed without a sound.

'I am disappointed in you, Daughter,' Anne said in that mild, flat tone. Anne never raged. 'You cost me so much. Yet now I have nothing to show for it.'

'Did I cost you so much?' The agony awash in her thigh, the sting of the blade's edge pinching her mangled flesh where the knife was still wedged between leg and horse, was nothing compared to the pain in her heart. 'I cost you nothing. My mother and father are both dead. What cost was there for you in my conception? In my mother's death? In my father's murder? Except that you had to lie to the others all these years, pretending that I was born from your womb.'

'Ah.' Even with the truth cast on the ground for them both to consider, with the charred bodies of men smoldering around them, Anne did not flinch or falter; she showed not the least tremor of emotion. 'Well, then. Certainly there is no hope of a rapprochement if you have discovered the truth. Yet I wonder. How do you know these things?'

'Well, then,' echoed Liath, mocking her. Mockery was all she had, surrounded by the ruin of her hopes. 'It seems you have told me more than I have told you, since you have now confirmed what I only guessed at. I have nothing further to say.'

The first strands of that net brushed her hair and settled over her shoulders. The fire that burned inside her, her mother's spirit, shrank from its cold touch.

'You need not speak, Liath. Your plans are an open book to me. You may have a fire daimone's heart, but you are weak, as Bernard made you. You were easily captured and will be easily held in my power. With this same net of sorcery I caged your mother.'

The net was a cage for fire. But she was only half born of fire. The rest of her was common human flesh, Da's heritage.

She grabbed the arrow and wrenched. The pain blinded her, but only for an instant. Gnat's knife had done just enough work, weakening the shaft, which snapped, half charred, half splintered. She rolled sideways over the smoking body of the horse to fall between her wounded servants.

She grabbed their arms and, of a miracle, they scrambled up although it was impossible to know how they could still walk. They ran, staggering, bent over, while men shouted and gave chase.

One glimpse only she caught of the smoking gap in the stockade, of Anne's soldiers pouring through the opening in pursuit of her own people. Rain swept over them. Hail burst, thundering over the ground. Lightning flashed to display in one sharp vision the broad expanse of sea, waves churning up as a storm drove down on them from across the waters. Whitecaps foamed.

A wall of men blocked the gap in the stockade. Anne's net brushed the skin of her trailing hand, leaving bloody welts.

'This way!' cried Mosquito, but his voice was liquid; the second arrow had punctured his lung and blood frothed on his lips.

They wavered on the edge of the cliff, poised there, staring down and down to the water below. There was no beach, only the sheer face of the cliff and a scattering of rocks showing above the waves. Out in the sea, mer creatures swarmed, their ridged backs parting the choppy waters as if they sensed the battle, or the magic, above and wished to discover what was going on.

'There is no other way,' murmured Gnat. 'It is better if they do not have the chance to mutilate our bodies.'

He leaped, and his brother jumped after, and she did not think or hesitate as she followed them over the edge, springing out as strongly as she could so that she might not fall straight down to the deadly rocks below.

Her wings of flame shuddered, flared and unfolded, and for two breaths she had lift. Gnat hit the water and vanished under the waves. Mosquito was gone an instant later, swallowed by the sea. The wind blasted her sideways. Thunder crashed.

Her aetherical wings had not the strength to hold her. Their substance collapsed as the wind battered her. The inexorable weight of the Earth was like grief, dragging her down.

I'll never see my beloved, or my child, again.

She plunged, wingless, lost, and tumbled into the sea.

2

Hammers rang. Axes thunked into wood. Shovels scraped into dirt followed by the spitting fall of earth thrown up onto the growing ramparts, the sound like hail spattering against the ground. The music of these labors accompanied Stronghand as he toured the new fortifications at Medemelacha. Eika and men worked together if not always side by side.

With his escort of the five dour merchants whose families controlled most of the commerce in the town, a dozen men-at-arms, and his most faithful attendants – the two hounds – he walked down to the strand where the shipyard bustled. Axes and adzes rose and fell. Men hammered wedges into a huge trunk to cleave it in two. Four boats lay propped up on stumps and posts, the newest no more than a keel while the most complete was being fitted with a side rudder. Soon it would be ready to launch.

Medemelacha had doubled in population in the last six months as folk swarmed to the trading town to get work in the shipyards and on the fortifications. Barracks had been built for the workers and to house the garrison. The farmland for a day's walk on all sides lay under his control, enough to feed the population as long as the harvest was good. He had given up inland strikes in favor of consolidating his position on the Salian coast and in Alba.

Yet the failure of his rescue gnawed at him. He had no peace; he could not savor his triumphs.

'There are three men in the customhouse who await your pleasure, my lord,' said Yeshu as they lingered in the shipyards and the merchants began to fidget.

He tore his gaze away from a young Alban man, his pale hair tied back with a strip of leather, who under the hot harvest sun had stripped down to a loincloth as he carved out a stem with an ax. It was sweaty work. He worked in tandem with an Eika brother, a handsome, brawny fellow whose skin gleamed with silver and who had taken to wearing a tunic in the human fashion, covering him from shoulders to knees. They worked easily together, making a comment now and again, picking out splinters, blowing away sawdust; laughing once, as comrades do. A young woman came by with a skin of ale; he could smell it from here. She had her hair concealed under a scarf and her skirt robed up for ease of movement so that her pale calves and bare feet were exposed. They joked with her, Alban and Eika alike, although it seemed she was Salian and could barely understand them. Yet she did not fear them. She, too, laughed.

This was prosperity – that folk laughed while they worked because they did not fear hunger or war.

'My lord,' repeated Yeshu.

He returned his attention to his companions. The merchants murmured among themselves. One was a veiled Hessi woman; she stood away from the others, who were Salians once beholden to other noble protectors. Out in the bay, a longship was being rowed toward shore, and its oars pulled in as the sailors made ready to draw up on the beach. It flew

Rikin's banner. He sighed, and as he turned to address the others, he stifled a nagging sense of regret that he could no longer stand where the Lightfell plunged down the mossy rock face, far down into the still, blue fjord. Hadn't he known peace there once?

Maybe not. Maybe he had never known peace from the day he was hatched and began his struggle to live.

'What matter needs my attention in the customhouse? Is there not a council of elders to consider such things?'

'Yes, my lord. But it seems two of these men are suspected of being smugglers, and the other is a merchant from north up the coast, out of Varre. It's thought you might wish to speak to him. He may know something of the disposition of Duke Conrad's forces.'

'Very well.' He whistled the hounds to him. They came obediently. They suffered him, but they pined for their master, and so each time he patted their heads he was reminded of his failure.

They walked past the new jetties to the customhouse, an old long hall that had once belonged to a Salian lord, now dead, who had taxed the merchants and sent a tithing to the Salian king while keeping the balance for himself. He hadn't been well liked. Indeed, his skull was stuck on a post out in front beside the door, stripped of most of its flesh and trailing only a few tatters of straggling brown hair.

Inside, the hall had been cleared of its old furnishings and transformed into something resembling a cleric's study with shelves, tables, benches, and a single chair set on a dais. He sat in the chair. The hounds settled beside him, Sorrow draping his weight right over his feet, but he didn't have the heart to move him.

'Bring them forward.'

All work ceased, clerics scritching and scratching with pens, women and men arguing over the worth of their trade goods, merchants counting by means of beads. They feared him, as they should, but he found their fear wearying. He tapped his free foot, waiting.

Two men were dragged forward. Their hands had been

tied behind them; they were cut, bruised, and terrified. Four witnesses came forward to testify against them: they'd been caught north of town in an inlet setting out in a rowboat laden with cloth that had been reported stolen two days before from the house of Foxworthy, a respected merchant.

The thieves begged for mercy. They were young, they were dirty, and they looked hungry and ill-used, shorn of hope, but the penalty for stealing trade goods from the merchant houses was death and all men knew it. He called forward the scion of the house, a middle-aged man with red hair and beard dressed in a fine linen tunic whose border was embroidered with fox faces half hidden amidst green leaves.

'What is your wish in this matter?' Stronghand asked. 'They do not deny the charge. Do you wish to make a claim against them?'

The merchant considered thoughtfully. 'There's always need of labor in the mines, my lord. If they are sold to the mines, then I will take whatever price they fetch as recompense for the crime. The cloth was recovered in good condition. No permanent damage was sustained by my house.'

'Very well.'

Rage heaved herself up and nudged his hand. He remembered the mines. He wanted those mines. But not yet.

Not yet.

Patience had served him well. It would have to continue to serve him. If he moved too quickly, he would overreach and lose everything.

The criminals wept, but they had sealed their own fate by becoming thieves.

'Bring the other man forward,' he said, feeling the curse of impatience draining into him, although he fought it.

Where was Alain?

Sorrow barked, just once, like a greeting, a demand for attention. Rage whined.

There!

He rose, he was so startled, but an instant later realized he was seeing things. It wasn't Alain at all; it was the shadows within the hall that had tricked him. This was an older man of middle years, dark hair well streaked with gray, who walked forward between an escort of two soldiers. He looked nervous, but he had a proud carriage and an alert gaze. If he was shocked to come before an Eika lord, he showed no measure of his surprise on his face.

He knelt before Stronghand as though he were a petitioner, not a prisoner. He spoke Wendish, not Salian. 'I am called Henri, my lord. My sister is a householder in Osna Sound. I carry her goods to market once a year. We came late this year due to the troubles, and I find myself held as if I am a criminal although all my dealings among the merchants here have been fair and perfectly ordinary. I pray you, my lord, I am a simple man. No merchant complained of the goods I traded. I had quernstones, very high quality, and good quality wool cloth woven in my sister's weaving hall. That's all. I am taking home wheat and salt in exchange. Nothing more.'

He looked at the hounds, expression clouded with doubt, and after a moment tore his gaze away from them to meet the dark eyes of Yeshu. He nodded, to show he was done speaking, and waited for the translation to begin.

'Have we met before?' Stronghand asked in his perfect Wendish.

The man started visibly, as if he had not thought an Eika could form human words. 'I–I think not, my lord. Many years ago Eika burned the monastery near our village.' He stammered again, realizing that he might have offended. 'The-the count as was then drove off another group of invaders that year. He captured one of them, rumor said, but the creature later escaped. My foster son was at Lavas Holding at that time, but we heard the story from others. I've met no Eika face-to-face. Not in all my years.' He twisted his fingers through his beard in an anxious gesture, realized that he did so, and lowered his hand. 'My lord.'

'Have you heard other news of Eika this summer? Have you heard news of Duke Conrad? Of the Salian war?'

His hands were clenched, and he nodded in a manner so suggestive of resignation, of a man who has given up hope of a successful enterprise, that Stronghand felt a stab of compassion. 'In truth, my lord, we at Osna have been beset by our own troubles for the last year or two. We've heard nothing of the world.'

'What troubles have plagued you?'

'Harvests have failed. It's rained too much. There's no trade at our little emporium, none at all these last two years, although we showed signs of prosperity before. Refugees from the Salian wars have overwhelmed us. There were four murders in the village last year. Unthinkable!' He shook his head. 'Lads have gone off to join the war and never returned. Laborers beg for a crust of bread. There's been a sickness among the outlying farms and among the poorest – they call it "holy fire" because their limbs burn and the poor afflicted souls see rivers burning with blood. Our new count has deserted us. He hides in his fortress, fearing enemies on all sides. Some say he's not our true count, that the rightful heir was disinherited, cheated of his place.'

'Do you think that's true?' asked Stronghand, intrigued by the man's complex expression which grew yet more grim, leavened by sadness.

'Nay, my lord. If any man cheated, it was him who claimed to be the rightful heir. Yet I'll not say the new count has courted God's favor either, for his folk fare ill in these days.' He shifted on the plank floor, setting his left knee on the floor to give his right a rest. 'I pray you, let me go. I am no spy. I have no grand knowledge to reveal to you. If we eat once a day, we count ourselves fortunate. It's true we've heard tales of troubles along the coast and seen sails passing, but they did not stop. I sailed south this year to Medemelacha because we have become desperate. I pray you, my lord, let me return home.'

'Let him go on his way!' said Stronghand brusquely. The man's speech had shaken him, although he wasn't sure why. 'I see nothing suspicious in his arrival here. Are there any here who have a complaint of him?'

There were none. The man was known as one of those who traded once a year at the market, bringing in a few goods from the countryside which lay north up the coast. He had always dealt honestly over the many years he had come to Medemelacha. He had only been detained today while loading his small boat to leave, because it had occurred to someone that he was a foreigner and might therefore be a spy.

'He has nothing of importance to tell us. Go!'

The man hurried out, although when he reached the doors, he glanced back toward Stronghand. As if in answer to an unspoken question, Sorrow heaved himself to his feet and barked again, and he and Rage trotted over to the door as if in pursuit. The sunlight streaming in through the doors hid the man in that haze of light as soon as he stepped outside.

'Osna Sound,' Stronghand murmured. He whistled, but the hounds did not return.

Because he was seated, others came forward to press him for a decision on trifling matters, disputes and arguments that a strong council ought to have disposed of. Yet they tested him; they wanted to know if he was as clever as rumor made him out to be. He had to listen, to ask questions, and to judge.

Yet the name teased him as petitioners came forward and retired in pairs, as trios, in groups, now and again a single person. A disputed fence that marked the border between two fields; a bull that had gored a child; stolen apples; a knife fight between feuding suitors.

Osna Sound.

He had heard the name before. Wasn't that where Alain had come from? He wasn't sure; he didn't know the Varren coast well, not as he had learned the Eika shore and the settlements and roads and landscape of Alba or the fields around Gent. In Varre, when he had been captured, he hadn't been quite awake; he had only vague memories of those days when he was little more than a ravening beast like his brothers. The cage had changed him. It had woken him, and Alain's blood had quickened him, and since then he had been plagued by this restlessness, this lack of peace, and yet he could not wish for it to have transpired in any other way.

'Where is that man's boat laid up?' he asked Yeshu when the tide of petitioners ebbed.

'Which man, my lord?'

'The one from Osna Sound who was brought forward to be questioned.'

'Most of the local merchants beach their boats up by the north wall, my lord. By the mill. They do most of their trading at Weel's Market.'

'Go find him. Bring him to me. I've a mind to visit this market and see what goods he brought with him.'

He rose, and his escort gathered behind him as he strode to the door. He hadn't asked the right questions. He had missed an important clue. Had this man known Alain? Hadn't he said his name was *Henri*? For a long time Stronghand had assumed that Alain was the king's son, for the king of the Wendish was called Henry, but Alain could not be both a king's son and a count's heir, could he?

He had let himself be distracted. He had failed to follow the scent when it was right before his nose.

Where had those damned hounds gone?

At the door, a large party of Rikin brothers hailed him cheerfully. A short, plump woman stood authoritatively in their midst, one hand slack at her side and the other cupped at her waist. It was clear these fierce Eika warriors followed her lead, although they towered over her and might have crushed her with a single blow of an ax.

'My lord prince! I bring a message of utmost importance. I pray you, let me speak.'

The sun dazzled him. He turned aside to stand under the eaves. 'Deacon Ursuline!' The world tilted; a cloud covered the sun

as the waters stream around him, but he has to walk against the current because his hands are bound and they are dragging him through the flowing river of blood that burns so brightly that the heat forces tears from his eyes.

The blood is everywhere, drowning the land. Its rushing roar obliterates every noise. No matter how loudly he cries out, how he shouts or sings, he cannot hear himself. He cannot hear anyone, only the river's furious flood and the rumbling tremor that afflicts the earth beneath him where pebbles slip under the soles of his feet and he slides and slips, dancing to keep upright.

Buildings rise around him and through an open doorway he sees into the interior of a dim chapel. A lord lies there with a steadfast hound curled asleep at his head and terror at his feet. He fights free of his captors and darts into the church, flinging himself weeping against the lord, but no human flesh embraces him. He is all stone.

Everything is stone or fire.

'Get him out of there! He profanes the holy chapel.'

'Madman,' they cry.

They drag him outside and pour water over him.

Ai, God. It burns.

Coarse brushes scour him until his skin bleeds. Everything is bleeding. The world is bleeding.

There is a man sitting in a chair with a child beside him, a girl, sweet-faced and quite young, but the blood had got into her bones and she turns red. She is burning.

He struggles to reach her, to save her, but they pin him down and beat him.

'It is him,' says the man. 'So am I vindicated. Let all the folk who have whispered under their breath see what he has become. He lied about his birth. He tried to cheat my cousin. He has now tried to assault my daughter, who is the rightful count. Put him in a cage. Restrain him, so that he can't hurt anyone. Let an escort be assembled. I will make the folk who scorn to bend their knee to my daughter see what he truly is.'

'My lord?'

He fell, caught himself, dizzy, and his claws extruded as he slammed a fist into the log wall, thrusting deep. He stuck there a moment, and only after he shook his head did he wrench his claws out of the wood.

'My lord prince?' she asked again.

'The light blinded me,' he said. 'I walked too quickly from inside the hall into the open air.'

His head rang with the sound of that roaring, the unceasing stream. *I know where he is!* It was difficult not to shout aloud with joy and triumph.

'Are you sure you are well, my lord?'

He attacked with questions, to give himself time to recover.

The scent of blood had been so strong. The hallucination had almost subsumed him.

'What brings you to Medemelacha, Deacon Ursuline?' he asked. 'I am surprised to see you.'

'No less surprised than I am to be here, my lord. I was sent at the command of OldMother.'

This was staggering news, but he knew better than to let his amazement show by any gesture or expression. 'What message do you bring, Deacon?'

Yet his heart raced, and he could scarcely quiet his trembling limbs. Alain was at Lavas Holding. Now he could sail to rescue him, and do it quickly, before worse harm was done to him. What had sent him mad? Why was he being punished in this way? Or was it punishment at all? There were other plagues abroad; they spread among humankind as maggots in rotting flesh. No man, or woman, was immune. Alain had wandered into places where he might well have taken sick.

All the more reason to save him and take him to the WiseMothers, as they had commanded him to do.

'Yes, my lord,' she said, as if he had spoken out loud. 'OldMother wishes you to sail to Alba at once, to the stone crown where Brother Severus has left several adepts to perform the ceremony on the tenth day of Octumbre. There is little time left if you are to reach there by the proper day.'

'What about Alain?' he demanded. His passion startled her; she took a step back, and the Rikin brothers crowded around to listen circled nearer, pressing forward, as if they expected to see blood spilled.

Rivers of blood.

The wind was rising. A cloud covered the sun, blown in off the sea, and out beyond the harbor he saw rain coming in across the water, changing the color of sea and sky.

'OldMother said nothing of a person called Alain,' Ursuline said after a moment's consideration. 'Is that one of Brother Severus' adepts? I can tell you, I do not care for these noble clerics. They sneer at a woman like myself although my lineage is perfectly respectable. They think themselves above the work of shepherding the common folk from birth to death, although certainly the blessed Daisan spoke of the importance of the ordinary work of living, of choosing what is useful and good instead of what is evil. Every person faces this struggle, not only the high and mighty!'

She was indignant. Her expression gave him pause.

'OldMother made no mention of Alain?' he asked again.

Yet OldMother *knew*. OldMother herself had told him to find Alain.

'She said this.' Her voice changed pitch, deepened and roughened. '"Stronghand must go at once to the Alban crown, there to set in motion what is necessary. Now we understand what we need to do."' I am to go with you.'

'Said she no more than this?'

'Is that not an express command?' she demanded of him. 'Yet if that is not enough, then she bade me give you this to remind you of her power.'

She unfolded her right hand to display four ephemeral items: a tiny white flower, a lock of downy infant's hair, the shards of an eggshell, the delicate wing bone of a bird. These things he had once placed in the hand of the youngest WiseMother as she climbed the path to the fjall to join her grandmothers.

'My lord Stronghand!' Yeshu jogged up, face red, tunic plastered with sweat. 'The man's gone. His boat's already put to sea, that's what they said, him and two big black dogs, but he can't be far yet. The tide's not with him. He must be moving right up along the coast. Do you want men sent out in pursuit? We'll catch him soon enough.'

He reached for the precious items cupped in Ursuline's hand, but she closed her fingers over them and pulled her hand away gently, so as not to seem defiant in front of the others.

He saw now the trap Ursuline had laid.

'No. Let him go. No matter.'

Ursuline was born out of humankind, weak and soft, but like the WiseMothers she bore within her the capacity to gestate life. Therefore, the mothers ruled. They alone could create life, and destroy life before it came into autonomy.

She understood their power, and now she challenged him. The stab in the back he had long expected had come from the most unlikely place. Ursuline had shifted her alliance. She obeyed him not for himself alone but because he obeyed the wishes of OldMother. She knew who ruled the Eika; he was simply their servant. For some strange reason, caught up in the exhilaration of war and conquest, he had forgotten.

Of course he had no choice. To go against OldMother was beyond him. He bowed his head, knowing he had lost Alain and the hounds. He had failed his brother.

'I am OldMother's obedient son,' he said. 'Tomorrow we sail for Alba.'

3

As she hit the water hard and went under, the remnants of her wings held her aloft just long enough that the impact did not knock her out. She fought to the surface, gagging and spitting, and gulped air.

Storm waves crashed against cliff. One of the brothers bobbed up next to the rocks. It was difficult to tell whether he was alive or dead, and she kicked to swim over to him, but the movement sent such a shock up her leg that she almost passed out, floundering. All at once, too suddenly, his body vanished into the waters.

A swell off the storm washed right over her. She swallowed sea water, panicked, and slid under. Nightmare memories of the battle choked her as she struggled.

I am a monster.

A blow slapped into her rump. A large body shoved against her. She spun in the water, thinking it was one of the brothers, but there were other creatures in the water with them. Her eyes were open, and as lightning split the darkness she saw the limp bodies of Gnat and Mosquito, who were not even flailing as two huge men-fish glided gracefully around them.

Was it a dance? Was it curiosity?

Her air was giving out. She clawed for the surface, but not soon enough. Not before lightning flashed again, and she saw what was happening.

Gnat and Mosquito were being eaten, flesh ripped from their bodies. Already their faces had lost shape and the bone of their skulls gleamed in patches where the flesh had been gnawed away. Their eyes were gone.

They hadn't been dead when they'd leaped into the water.

She came clear into the air gasping and heaving, and a face emerged from the seas just as lightning again illuminated the heavens. It had lidless eyes and horrible writhing hair that was a mass of eels with tiny sharp teeth nipping at her face. The monster loomed so close that the shock of seeing it made her forget to paddle. She sank beneath the waves again. Yet drowning gave her no surfeit from a broken heart.

I led them into a trap.

She thrashed, trying to find the surface, but everything had gone topsy-turvy.

A second body undulated underneath her kicking legs. She burst out of the water and, flailing, found a muscular arm under her hand. A rough hand gripped hers. She tugged, trying to break free, but it yanked her along after it. Spray and waves broke over her. The storm howled and thunder made her ears ring. A squall of rain passed over them, pounding on her head.

Must fight.

That claw closed around her arm and the monster dove, dragging her under.

I have been trapped.

She struggled, but the wound had drained her. She had no reserves left, and they were too far under the water for her to fight back to the surface if she could even figure out which way to swim. Her lungs emptied; her vision faded and sparked into hazy blotches as bubbles rolled past her eyes.

A face loomed. A lipless mouth fastened over hers, and a

thick, probing tongue forced her mouth open. Now it would
feed on her, consume her from the inside out as she had woken
the fire that had consumed from the inside out the logs and
the poor, doomed soldiers who had died screaming. Razor
sharp teeth pressed against her own in an ungainly kiss.
Pinpricks jabbed in her hair as the eel-mouths sought flesh.

Air.

Ai, God. Air filled her lungs, breathed into her by the
monster.

The creature unfastened its mouth and dragged her
onward, down and down, breathed air into her lungs a second
time, and when she thought they could go no farther, it swam
into a tunnel opening deep in the rock, far underwater, felt
not seen because by now she was blind. They were trapped
in a drowned hole in the ground and when her head scraped
against rock, the pain washed down her body like knives. She
passed out.

Eyes swollen shut, she woke when the ground shivered
beneath her. Her tongue was so thick it seemed to fill her
entire mouth. Clammy fingers pried her lips open and a foul
liquid trickled into her mouth. She spat, and struggled, but
she hadn't the strength to fight. As the potion soured in her
stomach, she slid back into darkness.

*Speak. To. Us. Bright. One. Speak. To. Us. We. Know.
Where. You. Are.*

'Dead, is it?'

She swam up from the depths. Her face hurt, and her ears
rang from a hallucinatory dream of ancient voices afflicting
her. Her body throbbed with pain. The earth beneath her
trembled and subsided. She opened her eyes and saw a double
image wavering in front of her, but at long last she realized
that she saw two distinct creatures who were speaking Jinna
for some odd reason.

She hadn't spoken Jinna since the years she and Da had
lived in Aquila among the fire worshipers. Those had been

good years. Da had been happy there. That's where he had
got the astrolabe, a gift from his noble patron. There had been
chopped dates and melon at that banquet. She recalled it well
enough, the feasting and the singing, the poem that had taken
five nights to tell about a bold queen and the wicked sorcerer
who had opposed her; she had known that poem by heart
once, it had amused the court poets to teach her because of
her excellent memory, but a veil clouded her sight . . . the
palace of memory lay under a fog. She couldn't recall the
opening line.

In the beginning. No.

This is a tale of battle and of a woman.

No.

Wisdom is better than love.

No!

In the Name of the God who is Fire I offer my tale . . .

'Bright One!'

Gnat and Mosquito, her mind told her hazily. Certainly
they pestered her mercilessly enough. One pinched her so
hard on the arm that she croaked a protest.

'Not dead,' observed the first.

'Bright One, wake up! You must drink.'

She drank. The water cooled her tongue, and she could
talk almost like a person. 'It was a trap.'

'A trap, indeed, Bright One. They were waiting when we
came through,' said Gnat.

'Maybe so, Brother,' retorted Mosquito, 'but we don't
know if they were waiting for us or if they were waiting for
anyone!'

'How many sorcerers can weave such a spell, you idiot?
Who do you think they expected?'

'Where is Sorgatani?' she asked, managing to get up on
her elbows.

The ground she lay on scraped her skin, and it hurt to
move at all, but no pain could equal the shock of looking up
with her salamander eyes and remembering that Gnat and
Mosquito were dead; they had been fed to the fishes. Where
their bodies had gone she did not know, but the creatures

who stared back at her were not the Jinna brothers at all but mermen, the same beasts she had seen devouring her hapless servants in the stormy waters.

They had the torsos of men but the hindquarters of fish, ending in a massively strong tail. They had arms both lean and powerful, and their scaly hands had webbing between the digits and claws at the tips. Monstrous faces stared at her, with flat eyes, slits for noses, lipless mouths, and hair that moved of its own accord, as if a nest of eels was fastened to their skulls. Yet they spoke Jinna with the inflections of Gnat and Mosquito.

'The Hidden One?' Mosquito shook his head, and looked at his brother, although it was too dark in this pit for any normal man to see, and they were not men to have lips or wrinkles from which to read thoughts and emotions.

Gnat shook his head like an echo. The eels that were his hair woke and hissed, then settled. 'We don't know. Her wagon went through the gap. Then we came back for you.'

'What of Breschius?' she asked, choking on the words.

'Those who were still living ran out through the stockade. We came back to help you.'

'You are dead!'

Again they spoke to each other by looking alone. Water made a sucking sound in a hole nearby, rising and falling. Lichens growing along the walls of this cavern gave off a slight luminescence, and this dim light allowed her to see that the two mermen rested half in and half out of water where it funneled away into a tunnel sunk into the rock, an old flooded passageway. She lay farther up, almost in the center of a cavern no larger than a royal bedchamber. It looked high enough to stand in, and she thought there were three passageways opening into the rock on the far side of the chamber, if she could only get so far. Yet to move seemed an impossible task. Her head felt muzzy and her ears clogged. Her leg hurt so badly that she could barely think.

'Many are dead,' agreed Gnat somberly. 'Many more will die. We died for you, Bright One.'

'How can it be you speak to me now?' Her words echoed

through the cavern. The ground shivered in response.

'The Earth is waking,' said Mosquito. 'The Old Ones speak. We are your servants. What do you wish us to do?'

Ai, God. She wept. She had not feared to risk her own life, but she hadn't really considered what it meant to allow others to die on her behalf. Gnat and Mosquito were dead, pierced by arrows and then eaten alive, yet some portion of them remained living within the bodies of these creatures.

Was she their prisoner, or their master?

'Where are we?' she said when she could talk through her tears. Her voice shook, or perhaps it was the ground trembling again, the shudder of a chained beast. Fear washed through her, its taste as harsh as sea water. As the quake subsided, a second followed hard on it. Did the shaking never stop?

'Beneath,' said Gnat.

'We are at the heart,' said Mosquito. 'Lay your head against the earth, Bright One. Close your eyes. Let the Old Ones speak to you.'

Liath sat up. Pain shot through her injured thigh, but she gritted her teeth and endured it. 'Who are the Old Ones?'

They shook their heads and, after another wordless consultation, Mosquito spoke. 'We don't know. They live in the Slow, just as you do, but they live even beyond the Slow for the passage of their life is not like that of flesh, which feeds us.'

Flesh fed them, mind and body. If they consumed her, would they ingest her knowledge and her memory and her way of speaking? Even if they did, how were they, who fed as all creatures must feed, any worse than she was? She had killed men this day in the most horrific fashion imaginable.

Who was the monster?

'Very well,' she said, although she couldn't bear thinking of closing her eyes again. If she closed her eyes, she might see the blackened bodies of comrade and enemy alike. But what else could she do? She was at the mercy of these creatures who spoke like Gnat and Mosquito and who had not yet devoured her. Who knew how long they would claim to be – or seem to be – the brothers. She would drown if she tried to escape back the way she had come. She might not have the strength to walk, and there might be no way to escape to the surface from this cavern in any case.

'We know of a plant that will soothe the wound. Rest. Listen to the Old Ones. We will bring nourishment, and brackweed for healing.'

'So be it,' she said.

Mosquito rolled sideways, got most of the way into the water, then vanished with a heave of his tail. Water boiled up to her toes before subsiding across the uneven floor. He was gone. Gnat remained, silent and watchful.

She stretched full length against the earth and laid a cheek against the ground. The surface abraded her skin. For a long time she remained there with eyes open, just breathing, emptying her mind, trying not to remember the battle. Or Sanglant. Or Blessing. Or Hanna. Or Da. Or the fire daimones.

Let. It. Go.

She shut her eyes.

Hers was not a nature that took easily or eagerly to earth. Earth buried fire. Earth cast on flames choked them. But with each breath she let her awareness sink into the earth, and she remembered those slow voices that had spoken to her in her dream. How long ago was it? How far must she travel? How deep must she go?

Stone was only a blanket covering the deeps of the Earth where fire flowed in vast rivers hotter than any forge. The Earth churns around a dragon's heart of fire and a cold, heavy mass at its innermost core.

Listen. Swift. Daughter. Listen. The. Storm. Is. Coming. The. Earth. Will. Crack. To. Pieces. If. We. Do. Not. Aid. Her. Make. Room. Make. Room. Will. You. Help. Or. Hinder. Speak. Daughter. Can. You. Hear. Us.

The fires within the Earth were a conduit linking her to the Old Ones who spoke through the earth, who were part of the earth and yet apart from the earth, slow as ages yet with the sharp intellect of humankind and the powerful dreams of creatures long since vanished from Earth who were called dragons, children of fire and earth.

'We must stop the weaving.' Her whisper carried on the thread of liquid fire deep into the earth and away, into the web that wove all things together.

No. No. So. We. Thought. First. But. Now. We. Know. Better. This. We. Have. Learned. From. The. Fallen. One. The. Weaving. Must. Open. To. Allow. The. Song. Of. Power. The. Resonance. Between. Land. And. Land. Make. Room. Or.

They had no words for what came next. It was an explosion of images beyond anything she had ever seen, beyond even the destruction wrought by Adica and her companions twenty-seven hundred years before. A scorching rain would blast the countryside; the earth itself would buckle and heave, spilling forth rivers of fire to drown land and sea alike. All creatures, dead. All life, obliterated.

'What of the Ashioi? Are they doomed?'

Make. Room.

Open the weaving to make room, to soften the blow, but close it before Anne could cast the Ashioi land away again.

'How?' she whispered as hope bloomed in her heart because now she recognized where she was. She knew how the threads connected them. She lay directly below the central crown. She lay buried in the earth, and they called to her through the ancient resonance that linked all the crowns each to the others. What they spoke of made a sudden, awful sense. She had to trust that they were her allies. She had no other choice, not anymore.

'How can we do this?' she asked.

They told her.

4

They bound him to the wagon's bed with chains that rubbed his ankles and wrists raw. Each jolt as the cart hit ridges and ruts in the road slammed him into the railing until his hip and torso bruised all along that side. Splinters stung in his bare arms, but he hadn't enough give in the chain to be able to raise his hands to pick them out. When it rained, he got soaked; the sun burned him where no clouds protected him from its glare.

It was still a merciful existence because, slowly, over days or weeks, the rivers of blood receded from his sight. He was weak, and so dizzy more often than not that he could barely stand. He had long since forgotten what was real and what was hallucination: a hamlet might rumble into sight and children might throw rotting fruit at him, laughing and screaming, the two sounds too close to untangle because of the desperation ringing in their voices, and yet as he stared trying to make sense of the scene or wincing at the impact as a wormy apple struck him full in the abdomen, a flood would crash down drowning the huts and casting beams and thatching into foaming waves like kindling, but if he blinked, he might be staring at forest again or at the sea, for it often seemed he stood at the stem of a dragon ship with oars beating away at the waters and the wind blustering in his bone-white hair.

'Who are you?' cried the guardsmen who attended him as they jerked the wagon to a halt on the commons and folk ventured in from the fields or out from their workshops and cottages to see what their lord had brought 'round on procession. 'What's your name, noble lord?'

The words smirched him no less than the rotten fruit, but he could not answer their questions or defend himself. If he spoke at all, the words that poured from him made his audience laugh, or weep.

'We'll never know peace. What is bound to Earth will return to Earth. The suffering isn't over!'

'See what a count's progress this cheat and liar makes now!' called Heric, who had bread every day and a new tunic for his reward as well as the pleasure of accompanying the cage as it made its rounds through villages and farms that at times seemed familiar to him although he could put no name to anything if it were not spoken within his hearing. The only name he remembered was Adica's. She was dead.

His only companions were rage and sorrow, invisible but always crouched at his side, and the shackles bound him close against them. He could never escape.

At least the rivers of blood had stopped flowing.

'Yet blood will cover us again,' he said to the villagers as he tried to blink away the glare of the sun. He had to make them understand even though there was nothing they could do to save themselves. 'The cataclysm is coming. She set it in motion. She didn't know what she was doing. She did know, but she couldn't have understood. I loved her. She couldn't have wished harm on so many.'

She couldn't have.

No matter how many times he said it, he knew he would never know.

Because of the chains, he could not wipe dust from his eyes. Tears ran constantly as the dirt of the road was kicked up into his face. His tongue tasted of grit. Now and again they gave him porridge poured onto the floorboards of the wagon so he had to kneel and lap it up while curious folk watched and whispered. Once a child threw the end piece of a moldy cheese at him, and he barely caught it and wolfed it down even though it was so hard it was like eating rocks. Even apples rotted to a brown mush inside the soft skin were welcome. He picked the skins off the bed of the wagon where they had splattered. He drank rain, licking it from his hands.

'He's no better than a wild beast!' said Heric. 'Yet this creature claimed kinship to our noble count! For shame! For shame that any of you once bowed before him!'

Fear shamed them. He saw right into their hearts. They were afraid of their new lord, the one they called Geoffrey, yet they feared *his* raving words and filthy appearance even more and so they hated him. He spoke aloud of the terror that slept within each one, songs of despair whose melody was the end of the world.

They believed him but did not want to. He heard their murmurs as they spoke among themselves of the harbingers that had plagued them for the last few years, ever since the

lamentable death of the old count. Troubles beset them with
refugees on the road and children starving and holy fire burning their limbs and plague rife in the south, so rumor had it,
and the harvest blighted and the storms as fierce as any in
living memory with hailstones so large they destroyed houses
and lightning that had burned down a church and untimely
snows in late spring which caught travelers and householders
and shepherds unprepared.

They believed him, and therefore they cursed him. Lord
Geoffrey rode into each village in his wake with his young
daughter beside him, and they bowed and genuflected before
the young countess and pledged their oaths, because Geoffrey
was better than the end of the world.

'No one will escape,' he said to the air.

'Especially not you!' crowed Heric, and the guardsman
called to the carter who controlled the reins. 'Here, now, Ulf!
Time to move on! We've a long way to go today before you
and I will get our feast and a longer way to go before the
usurper gets his fill of his just reward.'

The wagon lurched forward as Ulf the carter got the oxen
moving. They jounced down a forest path. The leaves of the
trees had begun to turn to gold and orange, and as the wind
rattled through the branches, leaves spun loose and danced
in eddies and spirals. Ahead, Heric called out. The wagon
jolted to a stop in a clearing carved out of the woodland where
stood half a dozen wattle-and-daub huts roofed with sod.
Fences ringed vegetable gardens, each one neatly tended
although most looked recently harvested. A stand of rosemary
flowered; a few parsnips remained in the ground. A score of
ragged folk stared as Heric launched into his tirade and the
other guardsmen poked at him with sticks to emphasize
Heric's words.

'. . . claimed to be the son of the count, but it was all a
lie. . . . God have punished him . . . found as a madman roaming the countryside stealing a deacon's bread and trying to
murder a girl . . . no better than a beast.'

A woman stepped out of the crowd, holding tightly to the
hand of a small child. She was thin and wasted, and the child

was not much more than skin stretched over bone, but both had a fierce will shining in their expressions, not easily cowed by Heric and his arrogant companions. Strangely, although she dressed in rags like the rest of the villagers, she wore over all a sumptuous fur-lined cloak more fitting to a lord than a pauper. It was this cloak that gave her authority among the others. It was this cloak that made his eyes burn, and his head reel.

'We know what you are about,' she said to Heric with the calm contempt of a woman who, having stood at the edge of the Abyss and survived, no longer fears worldly threats. 'Leave us, I pray you. Do not mock us by this display. We know who walks among us. We know who he is.'

Some of them wept, and their compassion silenced him. He did not condemn himself by babbling but only watched as Heric angrily swore at the carter and got the procession moving again down the forest path. The trees closed in around them. The hamlet was lost as if it had never existed, and maybe it hadn't. Maybe it was just a vision, not real at all. His head hurt. In the distance he heard the rumble of thunder that heralded a gathering storm.

XXX

THE NATURE OF
THEIR POWER

1

'I pray you, Sister Rosvita.'

Rosvita started awake. 'I dozed off,' she said, brushing a
fly off her cheek. The warmth of the sun soaked into her back,
which ached from lying on the ground. Despite the late date
– by her calculations, it was the ninth of Octumbre – the sun
glared ungodly hot. Beneath her body the earth trembled.
Horses neighed. Dogs barked. As the noise subsided, a stillness sank over them, as taut as a drawn bowstring. There was
no wind.

'That was a little stronger than the others,' said Ruoda,
but there was an odd tone in her words, a warning.

Rosvita sat up. Her little company sat like rabbits caught
under the glare of an eagle, all but Mother Obligatia, who lay
beneath the shelter of the awning on a pallet. The old abbess
was also aware, raised up on one elbow to watch. Hanna stood
beside her with her gaze fixed on the five men waiting at the
edge of their little encampment, one of whom was the one-
eyed general, Lord Alexandros, wearing a handsome scarlet

tabard and, under it, a coat of mail. He did not speak. Such an exalted man had servants to speak for him.

'Sister Rosvita.' Sergeant Bysantius inclined his head respectfully. 'General Lord Alexandros requests the attendance of the Eagle at his tent.'

'Very well,' said Rosvita, knowing they had no way to protest if the general chose to drag Hanna off by force. 'I will go with her.'

'Those are not our orders, Sister.'

'I pray you, Lord Alexandros.' Rosvita turned her attention to the general. 'She is under my protection.'

'I know what he wants,' murmured Hanna, who had gone ashy pale. 'It's my hair. These eastern men are obsessed with pale hair.'

'I can't let you go, Hanna! I'll let no man abuse you. I am not so weak or cowardly.'

'Nay, Sister.' Hanna moved up to take her hand and whispered into her ear. 'I am not without weapons of my own, although you cannot see them. Let me go. Better if I go now. We may need to rebel on a different day than this.'

'Soon,' Rosvita agreed, but such a tight fist clenched in her chest that she despaired. Soon the world would alter, and they were prisoners and helpless to combat it.

'We must survive,' murmured Hanna. 'That is all we can hope to do. If I do not come back, do not despair. If I can escape, I will.'

'Go with my blessing, Daughter.' Rosvita kissed her on either cheek, then on her forehead, and wiped away tears as the Eagle left the circle of rope and went with the general and his escort. Hanna did not look back, but Fortunatus went right up to the rope and gripped it in his hands, staring after her. Rosvita joined him there.

The day was so hot. 'This is not natural heat,' she said. The guards glanced at her, but since they could not understand Wendish, the conversation did not capture their attention. 'I feel all the Earth holds its breath.'

Another rumble danced through the ground and faded so swiftly that it might have been no more than a fly buzzing at her ear. No clouds softened the hard blue sky. The sun dazzled over the ranks of white tents arrayed in neat columns. They had settled into this campsite four days ago and not moved, and she did not know why, although she suspected that over the last weeks they had marched well into Dalmiakan territory and now waited close to the sea.

They camped on the slope of hills that crumpled up the ground to the north and west, and it seemed likely that the hills rolled flat to become a plain to the southeast, but since they rode in the midst of the army and camped in the midst of the army, it was hard to get a good look. No vista opened before them, only the rugged outline of hills burned to a pale yellow by the autumn heat. The quartermaster's tent blocked their view to the west. Under the glare of the sun, the camp lay quiet. A man walked between tents hauling two buckets of water from a pole balanced over his shoulders. A dog slunk out from the shade of a tent and trotted, ears flat, after a scent too delicate for her to catch.

Lady Eudokia, too, was waiting. That was why she had ordered her army to leave off marching and set up camp. That catch in their air was the false calm before a storm breaks, the worse for having held steady for three days. Often the noontime sky lightened from blue to a shade nearer white, and on occasion she thought it actually rippled the way tent canvas ripples when wind runs across it. She hadn't heard a bird for days. Even the bugs had fled.

'I am afraid, Sister,' said Brother Fortunatus.

She put her hand over his, then glanced back at their tiny encampment. The young clerics had fashioned a writing table and took turns copying to her dictation or from the pages of one of their precious books while the rest clustered around watching or offering commentary. Gerwita read aloud to Mother Obligatia in a voice so soft it was inaudible from a stone's toss away. Teuda and Aurea were washing shifts in a bucket of water, now gray with dust, and chatting companionably as Aurea labored to improve her Dariyan. Petra slept, as she did more often these days.

'A peaceful scene,' said Rosvita. 'Deceptively so.'

'What will become of us?'

'I have told Princess Sapientia what I know. If she chooses not to believe me, I can do no more. It is in God's Hands now.'

2

In the general's tent there was wine as well as sherbert cooled in a bowl of ice crystals, all arranged on an ebony table placed beside a couch covered with green silk. Lord Alexandros indicated that Hanna should sit. At first he sat beside her, taking her hand in his as he examined her emerald ring and fingered her hair, but quickly enough he rose, went to the entrance of the tent, and spoke in a low voice to a person stationed outside.

Hanna ate the sherbert, seeing no reason to let it go to waste. It tasted of melon; it melted on her tongue and sent a shiver through her as she braced herself for what would come next. Besides the table and the couch, the tent was empty. A sumptuous jade-green carpet, embroidered with pale-green Arethousan stars, covered the ground.

A servant – one of the beardless eunuchs – brought in a bowllike brazier glowing with coals and opened up its tripod legs. He arranged sticks in a latticework over the top and, receiving a nod from the general, retreated. The curtains swayed back into place. The general frowned thoughtfully at Hanna, standing with hands clasped behind himself as he surveyed her, his gaze lingering longest on her hair. She waited, holding the empty cup in one hand and the silver spoon in the other. Even a spoon could be used as a weapon, if need be.

He chuckled. The injury to his eye – not visible beneath the patch – had affected his facial muscles; when he smiled, he had crow's-feet only on the unmarked side of his face.

'I know what you think.' He spoke so softly that she had to listen closely to distinguish words out of his heavily accented Dariyan. 'I have a wife. You're not that pretty.'

She flushed and with an effort did not touch her hair. The curtain lifted; Basil the eunuch entered and held the cloth aside as Lady Eudokia was carried in on a chair by two brawny men adorned with bronze slave collars and wearing only short linen shifts and sandals. An embroidered blanket covered the lady's legs. The slaves set her down beside the still smoldering brazier. Smoke trailed upward, but the latticework of sticks had not yet caught flame. A spark popped out of the coals and spun lazily to the carpet. Hanna shifted her knee to grind it out. She couldn't bear to see a hole burned in such a magnificent rug.

'I understand you can see through fire,' continued Lord Alexandros without greeting the lady. He did not look toward Eudokia, as if he had not noticed her entrance. 'The Eagle's Sight, they call it. Show me.'

Hanna grunted under her breath, both amused and outraged, but she supposed it mattered little. They could not see what she saw unless they had themselves been trained in Eagle's Sight. As she knelt before the low brazier on its tripod legs, Lady Eudokia cast a handful of crumbled herbs onto the fire and flames blazed up and caught in the sticks. The heat seared Hanna's face, and she sat back on her heels, but the general had already moved, as quick as a panther, to draw his sword and rest the blade flat across her back.

'If you see nothing,' he said, 'then you are no use to me. I will kill you here and now. If you see, I spare you.'

All her breath whooshed out. She set her palms on her knees as she steadied her breathing, however difficult it was with the pressure of the blade along her shoulders and the chill of the threat hanging in the air. *Fear not.* She had survived worse trials than this.

She focused her thoughts and stared into the flame. Whom should she seek? What could she see through fire that would not betray them?

Yet what betrayal remained? Rosvita had told the truth, but Sapientia and her companions had not believed her. Her thoughts skittered. The general loomed over her with his sword held close to her vulnerable neck.

Ai, God, where was Liath?

In the depths there is only shadow, a darkness so opaque that she imagines she smells the wrack of seawater; she imagines she hears the sigh of wavelets lapping on a stony shore. A sound catches her, the scrape of cloth against pebbles as if a limb moves as a person shifts in sleep. Down, and down, she falls, following that sound, until the flame itself becomes one with a river of fire that rages in a tumult, pouring over her.

She starts back. Iron confines her movement and shoves her forward again, and she breathes his name, whom she has sought for so long.

Ivar.

He kneels before a lady crowned with a circle of gold. A gold torque grips her throat. She is tall and sturdily built, a powerful woman with brown hair and the broad hands of a person who rides and does not fear to wield a weapon.

'Go, then,' says the lady.

Hanna knows that cool voice well: It is Princess Theophanu. She is seated in a hall with banners hanging from the beams and a crowd of courtiers about her, most of them women. There is another young man with Ivar, but Hanna does not know him. 'Take this message and return to my aunt. I am shut up here in Osterburg. My influence ranges no farther afield than Gent and the fields of Saony because I was left as regent without enough troops to maintain my authority. I dare not leave the ancient seat of my family's power. It may be all we have left. Famine and plague have devastated the south. I have sent into Avaria and the marchlands, but now I hear that they have cast their lot with my bastard brother, and that they, too, have marched to Aosta in pursuit of Henry and the imperial crown! I cannot ride against Sabella and Conrad. They are stronger than I am.'

'What must Biscop Constance do, Your Highness?' Ivar asked despairingly. 'She is their prisoner.'

'She must pray that deliverance comes soon.'

'So it is true.' Lady Eudokia's voice jerked Hanna out of the fire, but Lord Alexandros' sword still pressed against her back. She wasn't free, and might never be so again. 'How much more is true if this is true?'

'Queen Sapientia believes the cleric's story is not true,' said the general.

'She is easily led. Geza has gained a pliant coursing hound to bend to his will.'

'As long as he keeps to his share of our bargain, we are well served by this alliance.'

Eudokia smiled, and Hanna pretended to stare into the waning flames so they could not guess she understood them. 'General, I do not criticize the alliance with the Ungrian barbarians. I only speak the truth. It is the truth we must discover before we decide whether to attack the usurper and the false skopos or to retreat. The portents speak of an ill tide rising. Does the fire speak the truth? Does it speak only of this day and this hour, or can it see into both past and future? Do we strike now? Or protect ourselves until the worst is over?'

The sword shifting against Hanna's back betrayed a gesture on his part, which she could not see. She dared not turn her head. Hairs rose on the back of her neck. How easy it would be for him to kill her here where she knelt, yet surely they wouldn't want to spoil the carpet with her heretic's blood. She had betrayed the Eagle's Sight to foreigners. What more did they want of her?

Eudokia fished beneath the blanket covering her legs and drew out a bundle of straight twigs, none longer than a finger. She leaned forward and scattered a dozen onto the dying fire. Flames curled and faltered, then caught with renewed vigor, and the smell that burned off those twigs was a punch so strong that Hanna reeled from it and would have fallen if the general had not closed a hand over her shoulder and wrenched her upright.

'See!' he commanded.

Smoke twined about the licking tongues of fire and dizzied Hanna until her eyes watered and she could no longer tell if she saw true or saw hallucinations brought on by the taste of the smoke.

'*Camphor* will lead her,' said Eudokia, but Hanna was already gone. Her head throbbed and she broke out in a sweat,

coughing, while her awareness seemed sharply stimulated. She
felt the pile of the carpet through the cloth of her leggings;
she heard the rustle of silk as the general changed position
behind her; the wasp sting burned in her heart while Lady
Eudokia murmured words under her breath, a spell like a
snake that drew the smoke into a mirror into whose smooth
depths Hanna fell

*Holy Mother Anne stands in a circle of seven stones on
the edge of a cliff. Through the stone crown she weaves
threads of light into a glimmering net reaching far across the
lands. Its apex explodes in*

*fire and lightning so bright it stings her eyes, it blinds her
the Earth burns*

*the Earth splits and cracks open and a yawning abyss swal-
lows the Middle Sea, and she is choking as a wall of water
sweeps inland, drowning all before it*

'Enough!' cried Eudokia, voice rising, cracking with fear.

Hanna was flung backward and hit her shoulders and then
her head, although the carpet cushioned the blow somewhat.
Yet sparks shot from the brazier and spun like fireflies, raining down as the general leaped forward to shove Lady
Eudokia's chair out of the way, chair legs catching in the
carpet and dragging it up into stiff folds. An ember ghosted
down to light on Hanna's cheek. No vision, this. It burned
into her skin and, with the heavy incense clouding her lungs,
she gulped for air, coughed helplessly, and passed out.

'Hanna, I pray you, wake up.'

She fought those hands, knowing that the fingers that
closed around her neck would choke the life out of her just
as the smoke had.

'Hanna!'

A jolt threw her sideways into a hard wall. After this new
pain resolved into an ordinary scrape and bruise, she found
herself staring into the grain of rough-hewn wood. She
recognized the scrape of wheels and the lurching gait of a
wagon. She lay in its bed with the heavens splayed above her
almost gauzy, they glared so whitely. Because the sight made

her eyes hurt, she looked down. Fortunatus strode alongside, peering down anxiously at her.

'Hanna? Are you awake?'

The taste of the incense still clogged her throat.

'Hanna, what happened?'

Other faces crowded around as they jostled to get a look at her: Ruoda, Heriburg, Gerwita, Jerome and Jehan, the sisters from St. Ekatarina's, the servant women, all sliding in and out of her vision. Then Rosvita came and the others melted aside so the cleric could walk with one hand upon the wagon. Her gaze on Hanna had such a benign aspect that Hanna gave a sigh of relief, though it hurt to let air whistle from lungs to mouth.

'Let her be, comrades.'

'But what happened?' cried the others, voices tumbling one on top of the next. 'Where are we going in such haste? Why are we traveling back the way we came as though we're fleeing the Enemy?'

'Can you tell us what happened, Hanna?' Rosvita's tone was mild but her expression disconcertingly tense. She touched Hanna's cheek with a finger, flicking at the skin; Hanna winced, feeling the scar where the ember had burned her. 'Ah!' murmured Rosvita sadly, as if she had only now realized that Hanna bore a new injury.

'I saw it.' She did not recognize her own voice. The smoke had ruined it. 'Fire. Burning. A flood of water as mighty as the sea unleashed.' Tears made her stammer. 'T-the end of the world.'

3

The company of thirty handpicked soldiers and their charge fled down onto the coastal plain in blistering heat to rejoin the queen's army, and on the evening of the fifth day they rode into a camp situated near the shore in the hope, perhaps, of catching a breeze off the waters. Yet the tide was far out, exposing rocks and slime, and despite the lowering twilight there was no wind at all, only the heat.

In the center of camp Antonia dismounted from her mule and fixed Adelheid with an exasperated gaze as a servant showed her to a seat under an awning. Adelheid indicated that all but Duke Burchard and her most faithful retainers should depart to give Antonia a few moments to relax in peace.

'How long will we suffer in this heat?' Duke Burchard asked the empress, as if continuing a conversation halted by Antonia's arrival.

'It is part of the skopos' plan. If clouds cover the sky, then she cannot weave her great spell. Or so I understand.' Servants fanned them, but it was still almost too hot to breathe.

Burchard grunted, sounding uneasy. 'When I was young, the church condemned tempestari. They said such magic interfered with the natural course of God's will.'

'One might say the same of swords and spears,' observed Adelheid, 'for otherwise enemies would do much less damage each to the other when they went to war, and battles would be a far less bloody business. Sorcery is a tool, Burchard, just like a sword.' She turned to regard Antonia, who had finished drinking her wine while a servant wiped her sweating brow and neck with a damp linen cloth. 'You were not successful, then, Sister Venia?'

She was dusty, sore, hot, tired, and thoroughly angry. 'He has griffins!'

'So the scouts reported,' said Burchard with an uplifted brow. 'Didn't you believe them?'

'I did not comprehend the nature of their power.'

'What is the nature of a griffin's power?' The empress sat with feet tucked up under her in a most unbefitting informality; one blue silk slipper peeped out from beneath the gold drapery of her robe. She leaned forward now, lips parted, eyes wide, as innocent as a child and most likely just as stupid.

'They have the power to banish the galla. It is said griffin feathers can cut through the bonds of magic.'

'Did the galla not throw confusion into his army?'

'A score of men may have died, more or less. I viewed the attack from a safe distance. We have not stopped him.'

'But we have slowed him down.'

The queen's prettiness had never irritated Antonia more than at this moment. How soft those pink lips looked! How pale and inviting were those lovely eyes! Adelheid had not sullied her hands with blood, since the criminals she had handed over to Antonia were marked for execution in any case. But Adelheid had the knack of getting others to do her dirty work for her so that her hands remained lily white. She had scribes to write her missives; loyal guardsmen to wield swords in her defense; stewards to bring her food and drink and a host of fawning courtiers like that old fool Burchard to sing her praises. Beauty was a perilous gift, so often misused. Even as a girl Antonia had scorned those who with their ephemeral beauty got their way even when it was wrong for them to have done so. She had never possessed winsomeness. She had studied righteousness and the game of power to achieve her ends, molding herself into God's instrument.

That was a better kind of sword, one whose reach was infinite and whose span was eternal.

'We cannot stop him,' said Antonia. 'Have you not considered what the failure of this attack means? The galla were our most powerful weapon.'

'Think you so, Sister Venia? I would have thought that surprise was our most powerful weapon.'

'The galla surprised him, yet he overcame them.'

Adelheid sighed, shifting her feet. Her hair was uncovered as relief from the heat, and her thick black hair braided in as simple a fashion as any farm girl. 'I hope you do not despair. I do not.'

Antonia knew better than to say what she thought. She had her own plans, and it would not do to anger the empress. 'What do you mean to do, Your Majesty?'

'I mean to send you back to my daughters. You will reside

at Tivura until I call for them. I believe you can protect them with your galla, if need be. You have proved your worth. I know you will do what you must to protect them. I hope you do not fear the journey back to Darre. There may be dangers now that Prince Sanglant's army descends into our land.'

Burchard was nodding in time to the queen's recital. Antonia had once had more patience for this kind of nonsense, and it was difficult to endure it now, but even so she knew how to smile to gain another's confidence and goodwill. Adelheid needed her, and for now she needed Adelheid. 'I am well armed, just as Prince Sanglant is, Your Majesty. And your plans?'

'We will march east through Ivria along the coast.'

'Away from Darre?'

'Prince Sanglant will not march on Darre if we challenge him elsewhere. Darre is not the heart of Aosta. I am. He must capture me to have a hope of capturing the empire.'

'Rumor speaks that it is his father he seeks, not you, Your Majesty.'

'No man refuses a crown if it is dangled before him.'

Antonia frowned. 'Do you want Prince Sanglant, Your Majesty? Is this a feint to capture him?'

Burchard snorted. 'The queen is loyal to her husband!'

Adelheid laughed and reached out to pat Burchard's trembling hands. That sweet laughter had captivated a court, a king, and an empire, but it did not fool Antonia. 'Hush, Burchard. My loyalty to Henry is not in question.' She settled back and turned her bright gaze on Antonia. 'Of course it is a feint to trap him, Sister. What else would it be? Eagles fly swiftly. I am not the only one who received news from a messenger ten days ago speaking of Sanglant's approach over the Brinne Pass.'

4

Adelheid's army retreated in good order a half day's ride out in front of them through the worst heat Sanglant had ever suffered and at last took shelter within the walls of the seaport town of Estriana while his army laid in a siege. Few Wendish towns boasted strong stone walls; most had wooden palisades and a stone keep. These were ancient walls erected in the days of the old Dariyan Empire. The town stood on an outcrop that thrust into a shallow bay with waters flat and glassy beyond and the belt of surrounding fields shorn of forage. Her forces had worked efficiently, leaving nothing more than dusty stubble, plucked vines, and a number of gnarled olive trees. To the east the ground rose into rugged hill country and west the wooded coastal plain stretched into a haze of heat and dust. To the north lay hills as well, and where a tongue of a ridgeline thrust out onto the narrow coastal flat a river spilled down onto low land and thence out to the bay, joined halfway by a smaller stream winding in from the eastern hills. Because this bluff lay less than half a league from the town walls, they used it to anchor their siege works to ensure access to water.

As the camp went up in a huge half circle around the town, he sat down under an awning and held court. No man could stand out in the sun's glare for long without succumbing to dizziness and fainting and, indeed, the report of his chief healer and head stable master made him feel light-headed with concern.

'Five men have died since we came out of the mountains,' said the healer. 'I swear to you, my lord prince, this heat is worse than the cold of the eastern plains. I've a hundred men or more with blistering burns and a fever, or who have collapsed on the march.'

'I wonder if the Aostans have as many words for heat as the Quman do for cold. What of the livestock?'

The stable master had dire news as well. 'We've lost twenty-two horses over the last ten days, my lord prince. While it's good that we're digging in so as to keep the river within our lines, there's so little water trickling down from the higher ground that I'm wondering if the queen's forces haven't diverted it upstream. We just don't have enough water for the livestock.'

'There's a drought on this land.'

'Truly, there is,' he said, wiping sweat from his forehead, 'but if this is the same river we rode beside yesterday and the day before, it had a great deal more water in it then. It would be good tactics on the queen's part to deprive us of water, especially if they've access to a spring within their walls.'

'Lord Wichman.' Sanglant called the duchess' son forward. 'Will you take fifty men and venture to find this dam, if there is one, and destroy it?'

'With pleasure!'

'Do you think that wise?' asked Hathui as Wichman strode out of the gathering, eager to get on the move. 'He'll be alone in enemy countryside. The heat is ruinous.'

'Then I'm rid of him and the trouble he causes, or he solves our water shortage. Captain Fulk?'

The captain stepped forward. 'We're setting up our perimeters on both sides, my lord prince, and digging two rings of ditches, one facing out and one in. That bluff to the north holds one flank. The spot where the stream meets the river fortifies the second. We can't do anything about an attack from the sea, if one comes, but we've set the wagons in line as a palisade. I've got a score of men strung out as sentries well into the countryside. We've heard a rumor that King Henry marched east many months ago into Arethousan country – a region called Dalmiaka. If it's true, his army lies east of us. If not, he could come up from the southwest.'

'Very good.'

'I pray you, Prince Sanglant.' Lady Wendilgard of Avaria came forward with a dozen of her best soldiers at her back.

Although her nose and cheeks had been burned red by the sun, her face had the pallor of a woman held under a tight rein. 'We have come from the forward line.'

When she knelt before him in an uncharacteristic show of humility, he smelled trouble. The way she had set her mouth, teeth clamped shut and lips pressed thin, bode ill. 'I pray you, go on.'

In the distance he heard the griffins shriek. Lady Wendilgard remained silent too long, and when she spoke, she spoke too quickly.

'I have been to the forward line, my lord prince. I have seen the walls of Estriana. My father's banner flies beside that of Aosta. He rides with Queen Adelheid. I cannot fight against him.' For once she could not look him in the eye, knowing what he was: bastard and rebel. 'I cannot.'

Silence was a weapon, and she employed it better than he did.

He spoke first. 'It may be a feint. How do you know your father himself rides with the queen?'

Like her parents, she was proud and with a few breaths regained her composure enough to look him in the eye. 'I called out to the guards on the wall, my lord prince.' Such formality from a woman who was near enough his equal in rank condemned him. He knew what she would say next. 'My father was summoned. I saw him on the walls, hale and alive.'

He tapped a foot on the dirt, stilled it; a surge of energy coursed through him but he had to remain seated and in control. 'So,' he said, temporizing, but he had already lost this battle and it was too late to change the course of the defeat.

'So be it,' she replied, again too quickly. 'I gave you my oath, my lord prince, which I will not forswear. I will not draw my sword against you. Yet I must remain loyal to my father. I and my Avarians will withdraw from the army and return home.'

XXXI
THE LOST

1

He could not let it be. The lady and her soldiers rode out in the late afternoon while Adelheid's men gathered on the walls of the town and jeered those who remained, although the griffins prowling between ditch and wall gave the enemy pause. One man shot an arrow which fell harmlessly short of Domina.

The Avarian defection dealt the siege a grievous blow. Men frowned as they dug the ditches that would protect them. Soldiers muttered and fell silent as he passed. They gazed north, toward home. They argued about who had the camp next to the Quman contingent although Fulk had already assigned places, and Gyasi was forced to order his nephews to stake out a rope to encircle the Quman encampment and bind it with charms and bells to keep Wendish and Quman apart.

Worst of all, the griffins flew off suddenly, and although they had done so before in order to go hunting and had always returned, this time their departure smelled of defeat. Men watched them go and turned muttering back to their tasks. On the rocky shoreline, five dead dolphins washed up, their

corpses half decayed and infested with tiny worms. In the
wake of this omen the seawaters began to retreat as though
draining away into a sinkhole. Fish flopped and gasped in
shrinking hollows on the exposed seabed, and his soldiers
waded out into the muck to retrieve them in baskets – yet one
man wandered too close to the walls and three arrows pierced
him before his comrades could drag him to safety. He died
shortly after, as the sun was setting, and no sooner had the
one piece of ill news made the rounds than two horses suffering from colic had to be slaughtered.

Sanglant took Hathui aside as the camp settled in for an
uneasy night punctuated by curses and jeers from Estriana's
walls and the too-distant sigh of the sea, whose waters receded
finger's width by finger's width although by now the tide –
if there even were one in the sheltered Middle Sea – ought
to be turning to come back in. Drought on the land and an
uncanny ebb tide at sea. What next?

'Saddle a mount. I'm riding after Wendilgard.'

She began to speak, but after making that first sound – no
recognizable word – she shut her mouth.

'You know I value your advice. I pray you, Eagle, say what
you think.'

'Only this, my lord prince. Best that you persuade her to
return. The Avarians make up a fifth part of the army. Lady
Wendilgard commands respect because she, too, rode south
not for glory but because of loyalty to her father. Now folk
are reminded that you are a rebel. They do not like to think
of fighting against the regnant they love.'

'How is it, then, that you dare think of it, Hathui?'

Her steady gaze matched his. She held her ground. 'I witnessed what they did to the king. Who is to say they have not
ensorcelled Duke Burchard in the same manner? Isn't it a
form of sorcery if he doesn't know the truth and instead
remains faithful because of a lie? How is it rebellion to raise
weapons against false dealing?'

By the time they rode out along the road that cut into the
wooded hills left of the bluff, it was night with only the waxing

crescent moon to light their way and a wind blowing in hard off the water. He took fifty men, half of them dismounted and walking on foot with torches. The road plunged into a pine-and-oak forest open enough that they could see the stars twinkling through the foliage. Wendilgard had ridden farther than he expected, and the moon had set by the time he called his soldiers to a halt and went on with only Hathui.

The Avarian sentries heard him coming and let him pass into the center of the encampment, which had been hastily thrown up in the lee of a solitary hill with the slope at their backs and a ravine, not much more than a ditch, protecting their left flank. Wendilgard had set up her tent beside a jumble of boulders and dressed stones as big as a man's torso. These had once rested higher up on the hill where the face of a long abandoned fortress was being eroded by degrees. She greeted him with reserve. Wind tossed the branches of the trees, and they heard a roar of wind sweeping in from the east.

'Come,' she said, beckoning him into the tent as her men raced for cover under the trees or where fallen walls made a windbreak.

A gust raced through camp so swiftly that men had just begun yelling by the time the wind abated and Wendilgard and Sanglant came out of her tent to see half a dozen tents flattened. Horses had bolted free of their lines. Men scattered to search. Distantly, they heard the rumble of thunder, but no herald of lightning lit the sky. There was no rain.

'So,' said Wendilgard as they stood by the ruined fire her stewards had lit earlier. Its coals were scattered, and servants stamped out sparks. 'What do you want, my lord prince?'

'I want you to come back.'

'Impossible. I cannot fight against my sire.'

It was too dark to see her face well. All of the torches that had earlier lit the camp had been doused by the wind, and the soldiers searching for the lost horses had claimed the first to be relit. The glimmer of their flames winked and vanished and reappeared like the dance of will-o'-the-wisps in a summer forest in the north, spirits that would lead a man astray if he followed them into the dark.

'You knew I meant to lead an army against King Henry. If your father fights with those who corrupted Henry, is he not more of a rebel than we are?'

She said nothing at first. She had the knack of keeping still, like stone. He tapped his own thigh repeatedly with one hand because he could not pace.

'I do not disagree with you,' she said at last. 'But when I saw my father, I knew I could not raise my sword against him. I could not ask his Avarians to press into battle against their brothers and cousins. I could not do it. How do you know, Sanglant, how you will react when you meet your father on the field?'

'If I do. If he is ensorcelled, and I believe he is, then I would be a traitor not to free him.'

'Yet wouldn't you wonder? What if there is no enchantment? I tell you frankly: I doubt, where I did not doubt before. Are you sure of your information? Or are there other ambitions driving you that whip doubt away?'

'I am not ambitious,' he said impatiently. 'I have always been an obedient son.'

'Have you? Rumor has it you married against your father's wishes. I hear whispers that the end of the world is upon us, that drought and famine and plague and even the Quman invasion afflict us because of God's displeasure. Because of a curse laid on humankind by the Lost Ones many ages ago. Now I am no longer sure. You are only half human blood. Are you my ally, or my enemy?'

'I was abandoned by my mother! My loyalty has always been to my father!'

He hadn't meant to speak so sharply. All around the camp men raised their heads and looked toward them. A few touched swords and spears; a dozen moved closer, but Wendilgard waved them away. She was a prudent woman, not easily cowed and rather older than he was, a late child of mature parents and after the untimely death of her younger brothers and older sister the only remaining direct heir.

'I am on the knife's edge,' she said quietly. 'If I choose wrong, then I doom my own people as well as my father.

Avaria has suffered badly these last few years. I weep when folk come before me and tell me their tales of hardship. I have not protected them.'

He reined in his temper, hand clenched now and rapping a staccato rhythm against his leg. 'Caution will not save us.'

'Maybe not, but I have come too far. Or rather I should say: I have come as far as I can go. My soldiers will not fight, Sanglant. They have seen my father's banner. Some among them have seen my father, as I have, and now all know he lives and rides beside Adelheid, who is, after all, Henry's wife. If I press them, they will mutiny. I cannot help you.'

'Without your forces, Henry may be lost.'

'If I rejoin you, my forces will be lost because they will rebel against me.'

'What will come is something far worse than fears of rebellion. If we do not save Henry and turn against Anne, we are lost.'

She shook her head. 'You ask too much of me and of my soldiers. Thus are we caught. There is nothing I can do.'

She would not be swayed and in the end he had to retreat to save face, but he did not go gladly. He fumed, although he spoke no word of his vexation aloud. He went graciously, because anger would lose him even, and especially, her respect.

But he was angry. He burned with it, and because he could not even stay seated in the saddle without risking too hard a hand on Resuelto's mouth he walked and soon outpaced his own guardsmen whom he waved back when they jogged up to catch him. Hathui he tolerated because he knew that she, like a burr, would cling unless he tore her loose and he hadn't the energy, had too much energy, to pry her off.

'My lord prince,' she said as they walked down the path where it hooked and crooked among oak and pine and underbrush, 'this is the wrong turn. We're going back the way we came. Can you see there, through the trees? That dark shadow is the hill where the Avarians camped. Those are their torches.'

'Damn her!' He kept walking. 'Will she now be a threat to our rear? Will she try to lift the siege? Should I attack her at dawn and take her men prisoner? Can I trust her to retreat north and leave us, so that she's neither threat to me nor aid to Burchard and thus to Adelheid? God Above, Hathui! I have trusted your word this long. Is it true my father is ensorcelled? Am I driven by other ambitions? Did I sell Sapientia to elevate myself? No doubt she's dead now, and I'm no better than a murderer who kills his own sister to gain the family lands.'

She said nothing, only followed as they blundered on. He couldn't listen, although he knew he ought to. Branches scraped his face. The brush layer crunched beneath his boots.

'My God,' Hathui said, and stopped dead.

He thrashed on for another ten paces through the undergrowth until he glanced up through the trees. The heavens bled fire across them, whips of pink, orange, and a drowsy red light that writhed like serpents. A drumming like rain swept out of the north, and as they stood there, a second tempest swept over them.

While in the distance his men shrieked in fear, they were pounded by hail the size of fists and he shrank under the shelter of an oak tree whose trunk was laced by a thick cloak of ivy. Hail pummeled him, even through the branches, tearing leaves loose, ripping ivy from the trunk. Hathui cursed and cried out. He called to her and, when she did not answer, dashed out to find her. He held his arms over his head as the hail bruised him all along his back and shoulders. The brunt bore him down to his knees because it came so fiercely. He crawled, seeking shelter under a bush that smelled faintly of honeysuckle, and there, strangely, no hail struck him although it slammed down on either side. A peculiar gleam painted vague shadows along the lacy architecture of the bush whose branches arched over him. His hands scrabbled in the moist leaf litter. He dug away several old layers to reveal dry earth beneath, white grains like sand, and beneath these chalky smears a paved stone road. He tasted the sting of magic on his tongue.

The front passed as swiftly as it had come, and when he staggered out with his palms and knees weeping sodden leaves, he found Hathui trembling so hard beneath a black pine that he actually grabbed her shoulder to stop her. The heavens were bright with stars but otherwise perfectly normal as though no strange strands of color had ever shone there.

There were no clouds.

She could not speak because she was shaking so hard.

A ghostly half moon floated in the sky, fading in and out of focus, although the crescent moon had already set. It was too dark for him to see, but he could hear. A few animals braved the quiet: two squirrels scrabbling up a rustling branch, three pigs, a deer. Their scents brushed him but faded as they fled away through the forest. The whisper of footfalls was itself like a breeze, carried on the air. No scent of humans touched him, yet someone approached from the northwest traveling through the woods without dust or actual sound.

Hathui stared past him, gone rigid.

He turned.

Light shone in a thread whose unwinding ran right across the spot where he had crouched beneath the bush during the hailstorm. That pale ground was part of a path no wider than his outstretched arms, glittering now with sorcerous light. Shadowy figures appeared on the old road, marching south. He slid his sword from its scabbard and pushed Hathui backward, staying between her and the gleaming path.

The shadows walked at a steady pace, not quickly, not slowly, but with the certain stride of folk who have walked a long way and mean to reach their destination. As they walked they sang in a lost language, the rhythm of their song timed to the fall of their feet on the ground. The words were unknown to him, yet the meaning seemed clear, as if he had absorbed this secret out of his mother's body during that interval when he had existed not as a self but as part of her.

They sang of a land lost, which was their home; they sang of families never forgotten, of love unfulfilled. They sang of war, and of vengeance unsated. Yet a note of hope twined through their song, as if they had sung it for a very long time but believed that a final cadence would soon signal its end. Although he hadn't Liath's salamander eyes, he saw them clearly as they passed him in a line that straggled along the path. Old men led children. Strong warriors both male and female masked with animal faces strode proudly, armed with bows or spears or strange swords forged not of metal but rather edged with black glass. Stout old women balanced on their hips baskets woven of reeds and jars decorated with spirals and hatch marks, white paint on red fired clay. They were all of them shadows walking amid shadows; they weren't real, they hadn't substance, not as he did. Yet they were as perilous a people as he had ever met.

They were the Lost Ones, the Ashioi. His kinfolk.

For a long time he watched them pass. Hathui spoke no word. He could not even hear her breathing because the unearthly hush that had fallen over the wood muffled all earthly sound. It seemed he and the world slipped into shadow as the shadows marched. They passed, one after another after another and on and on, so many he could not count but certainly more than a tribe, more than a town. They were a host, journeying southeast on the gleaming path.

The stars wheeled above on their appointed round as the night wore on. The world lay still, waiting, as did he. He had a wild notion that he could fall in at the end and join that line, although none seemed to notice him – he might as well be a shadow to them, as they were to him. Was he only dreaming? Would he see his mother among them?

He did not see her. As the first gray tiding of dawn filtered through the trees, the last of the line passed him, brought up, in the rear, by a proud young man of stature very like to his and a face that seemed eerily familiar, a man's face molded out of the lineaments of his own mother. He was clad in a cuirass molded of bronze whose surface shimmered. The young warrior halted and stared at the prince. His hip-length white cloak swirled in an unfelt breeze. Leather tasses clacked softly about his thighs.

'Kinsman!' he called. 'How is it you watch us pass and do not join us? It is near. It is close. Can't you feel it?' He faltered, shifting his entire body as a shudder passed through him. 'How can it be?' he demanded, voice changed. 'You are not one of us, yet I recognize you. Who are you?'

This was no language Sanglant knew, yet he understood it anyway. It melted into him like the heat of the sun, which shines on all folk whether they know to call it the sun, or whether they are blind.

'I am Sanglant,' he replied, taking a step toward the path. 'I am son of Henry, king of Wendar. I am son of Uapeani-kazonkansi-a-lari.'

The other man lifted his spear in a gesture of warding, or astonishment. Beaded sheaths covered his forearms and calves, and in the twilight they flashed, catching the attention of the warriors who had gone on and now paused, turning.

'Hasten! Hasten!' they called. 'The time is near! We must hurry.'

'I know you!' cried the young warrior, tense with frustration. 'Yet who are you? How do you claim descent from a name that cannot exist? Uapeani-kazonkansi-a-lari is the name my brother's daughter would have carried had he ever sired a girl child, but he is many lifetimes gone, lost to me. Who are you?'

'Are you dead or are you living?' demanded Sanglant. 'To my eyes you are a shade, a ghost. Yet you speak as if others have died while you survived.'

'We are dead and we are living. We are caught in the shadows, torn out of Earth yet not killed when the witch Li'at'dano guided the hands who wove the great spell that exiled our land and our people.'

'I am your kinsman! I am trying to help you—'

'It is too late. What is done cannot be undone. The exiled land will return.'

'Nay. Another cabal of sorcerers seeks to weave that ancient spell a second time, to cast the land back into the aether.'

'Do they still hate us? Does the witchwoman still brood over our ancient war?'

'She aids me. She is no longer your enemy.'

The other man laughed. 'If she says so, then she lies to you, or you are foolish enough to believe her. How can she even be alive? We have seen ages pass. No one who lived in the time of the Exile can still be alive!'

'You are alive!'

'I am a shade, but I hope to live once more so that I can take my vengeance. Enough!' His comrades, a dozen masked warriors waiting a bow's shot away, called again to him. The rest of the procession had vanished into the trees and dawn's twilit haze. The man followed.

'Heed me!' called Sanglant angrily. 'Do not turn your back on me! I do not lie. You know less than you believe you do. I have met the Horse shaman you call Li'at'dano. I have spoken with her. She still lives. She spoke freely of the ancient weaving, which she now regrets. She strives to prevent those who would banish the Lost Ones again. We must act as allies—!'

The warrior heeded him no more than had Lady Wendilgard. From down the path his comrades called to him, but their voices were too faint even for Sanglant to hear.

'I must go,' the warrior said. 'The day dawns.' A strange note changed the timbre of his voice. He looked once more, piercingly, at Sanglant, then jogged away on the ancient road to join the others. As light rose to scatter night, they faded into the trees.

Hathui collapsed to the ground in a dead faint, completely limp, and he gaped, taken by surprise, then heard a clamor of voices as his escort fought their way through the forest to reach him. He knelt beside her, and she opened her eyes just as Sergeant Cobbo ran up with a worried expression on his face and a big dent in his helm.

'My lord prince! We've been searching for you all night. We thought we'd lost you when that gale blew through! That wasn't anything natural! What's amiss with the Eagle? Was she struck down?'

She rubbed her head and groaned, sitting up. 'I got hit in the head by hail. I don't remember anything after that.'

The prince looked toward the path, but he saw only butcher's-broom and buckthorn beneath a spreading canopy of ivy-covered oak. The trail that had glimmered so clearly last night was invisible, and when he walked over to the bush he believed he had sheltered under, he found no trace of those chalk-white grains nor, when he kicked aside layers of matted leaf litter, did he uncover an old stone roadway. The drought had baked the dirt until it was as hard as rock.

'My lord prince?'

They watched him in the manner of folk who are not sure if the dog is crazy or only needs a few moments to relieve itself. Far away they heard a shout. He still held his sword, and with a murmured curse he sheathed it and returned to them.

'Come,' he said. 'Best we get back to camp without disturbing Lady Wendilgard's peace.'

Wichman returned at midday having lost a third of his men. His horse was in a lather, and he dismounted and flung its reins into the face of a waiting groom. The prince stood on a rise looking over the city walls and the coastal shoreline where the retreating sea had uncovered all manner of ancient refuse – slime-covered rocks, bones, an encrusted anchor, the ribs of several boats, as well as what appeared to be the old straight track of a paved road. Evidently when the road had been built what was now the bay had rested above the waterline.

'Cursed bad news!' cried Wichman with a coarse laugh as he strode up. Men scattered from his path as he shoved aside one fellow rather than stepping around him. He halted beside Sanglant, glanced incuriously toward the sea, and turned to regard the men hard at work filling in the gaps in their defenses.

'Why hasn't Queen Adelheid attacked?' he demanded. 'That ring of wagons won't hold off a determined sally from within the town walls. You haven't half the ditches dug that'll be needed.'

'Well met, Cousin,' said Sanglant, changing the ground before Wichman could get started. 'What of the river?'

Wichman shook his head. 'Drought. Someone tried a diversion of the trickle that was left up above the bluff where there's a bit of a waterfall, but in truth there's just no water coming down from the mountains. Fields are drying to nothing. We saw some mighty odd lights in the sky last night, I'm telling you. I lost six men to elfshot.'

'Elfshot!'

'That's what the sentries said, but I'm thinking it was partisans skulking in the woods, scouts for the army that's marching right up on us as we speak. We heard shouts and screams in the distance, over to the west of our position.'

Sanglant's escort turned. Each man and woman there stared at Wichman as though he had sprouted feathers.

'What do you mean?' asked Sanglant softly. 'What army?'

'The one whose forward scouts caught a dozen of my men watering their horses at a pond this morning, that's who. A damned big army, for I saw them myself.'

'I pray you, Wichman, slow down and speak more clearly. Is there an army marching this way? From what direction? How many? Who are they?'

Wichman grinned, enjoying the attention. 'It seems you called, Cousin, and Papa heard you. There's a large army moving this way from the east out of the highlands.'

The sky hadn't a cloud in it, but a rumbling roar of thunder shook through the heavens at that instant as though Wichman were its herald. The ground shuddered, rocked, and stilled. Men cried out, rushing here and there as if they could find steadier ground a few steps to left or right, but just as the yelling in the camp subsided a new noise arose as sentries pointed to the north above the distant line of trees. The griffins flew toward camp, growing larger; behind them, well into the woodlands to the northwest, a thread of smoke curled up into the sky. Was Lady Wendilgard marking her position for her father?

'What banner does this army fly?' asked Sanglant, voice tight.

'They're flying the banner of the regnant of Wendar and Varre as well as the crowns of Aosta, and a new flag as well.'

'That of the skopos?' It was difficult not to grab Wichman by the throat and choke the information out of him.

'Nay. I saw no banner bearing the mark of the skopos. Only one I have seen a single time before, in the chapel at Autun: a banner embroidered with Taillefer's imperial crown.'

Henry had crowned himself emperor!

All around the men whispered: *Emperor.* The word itself had magic, one that griffin feathers could not dispel.

Their murmuring died as they waited for Sanglant's response. The day, too, had gone utterly quiet, a strange, hard pressure in the air that made his ears seem full and muted his hearing. No wind stirred the banners in his camp; even Adelheid's pennants up on the walls of the town hung limp, curls of color. The world seemed to be holding its breath. The blue of the midday sky had faded to an eerie silver cast until he felt he stood on the inside of a drum, waiting for the thump of a stick overhead to wake them up. To shatter the silence.

To bring Liath and Blessing back to him alive.

From far away, too faint for any man born solely of humankind to hear, a horn's ringing call caught his ear.

'To arms!' he cried, breaking the spell. 'Sound the horn.'

He wore mail at all times, but with battle imminent he allowed his guardsmen to add extra protection, the mark of the heavy cavalry that were his strongest pieces on the chessboard. He stood while Sibold strapped on an iron breastplate over his mail shirt and greaves on his calves. Chustaffus waited, fully armed, with the black dragon banner held in his left hand. The rest of his personal guard clustered behind, mounts saddled and ready. All of them had iron helms and most had greaves and breastplates – his strongest troops. While Sibold armed him, Captain Fulk gave his report.

'Our choices have dried in this heat, my lord prince. We cannot flee without water, nor can we withstand an assault from both town and field with our defense not yet set and the emperor's army so large.'

As they spoke, stakes were being hastily set in the remaining gaps of the inner defense, between the circling wagons, to prevent a sally out of the town from breaking through their line.

Sanglant looked at Hathui. 'Wendilgard's retreat has cost us. Shall we surrender and beg my father's mercy? He is renowned for being merciful.'

She lifted her chin. 'Truly, Your Highness, if it were King Henry, we might expect mercy. But the man we face will only wear Henry's face and speak with his voice. I saw what manner of daimone they forced into his body. I heard his voice condemn Villam, but I know King Henry would never have done so. If we surrender, we will be baring our throats to those who will show as little mercy to us as they did to him!' Without leaving him, her gaze shifted focus, seeing onto a scene he could not share: the events which had led her to take refuge with the regnant's rebellious son.

'So be it.'

Sibold stepped back, having finished, and Sanglant mounted Resuelto and took his lance from Everwin. Raising it, catching the attention of the men making ready to fight, he called out in the voice that would, soon enough, ring above the fray. 'Upon every field, there is a victory to be found. Let us find ours.'

Malbert handed up his helm, burnished, trimmed with the figure of a dragon so like the one he had once worn as captain of Henry's Dragons, back in the days when he had been his father's obedient son. So he was, still; it was Henry who had changed, not him. Yet did it matter what story he told himself, now that the hour was upon them? Last night, with Wendilgard's departure, he had felt angry, sullen, worried, irritable. All that sloughed off him now. The decision had been made. He had ridden a long way to reach this moment. Now. At once. The anticipation of battle lightened his heart and lifted his mood. The griffins beat past overhead, heading out over the town.

As he rode with his escort behind him to the southern apex of such siege works as they had had time to throw up, he held his lance so the pennant tied on the shaft could dance in the breeze made by Resuelto's pace. He was already sweating freely. There wasn't a breath of wind.

The infantry had dug in to the northeast of the river along a line leading from the bluff where the river left the forest all the way to the shoreline. Because they had wanted to keep a portion of the river within their lines – if this trickle of water over stones still warranted such a noble title – the river split his force. Even over the course of the single day they had camped here the water level had fallen. When he pressed Resuelto down the bank and into the channel, the water came scarcely higher than the gelding's fetlocks. Companies of Wendish, marchlanders, Quman, and centaurs followed him to the field, muddying what remained of the waters.

The infantry manned the defensive works, such as they were, with some of the ditches only half dug. There were too few soldiers to withstand an attack at multiple points. Still, infantry weren't the strength of his army. They crossed beyond the defensive works into the dusty open ground where he had room to maneuver, most of it level but crossed by a dry streambed that had once been a tributary of the river. He and a dozen men from his entourage rode up onto a rise from which they could survey the field while his army took their places.

He had thirty centuries of cavalry, more or less. The Quman clans formed up on the left flank and marchlanders on the right. His Wendish cavalry, a motley crew nominally under the command of Wichman but actually controlled by Captain Fulk, held the center – which should have belonged to Wendilgard's Avarians. What remained as a reserve force spread out as a second rank, broken up in groups of fifty to a hundred riders made up of his marchlanders and renegade Ungrians under Captain Istvan, Waltharia's picked heavy cavalry under the banner of Lord Druthmar, his own personal guard, and the Bwr. The griffins had flown out over the exposed flats to the water's edge, where they began to make their ponderous turn to come back in.

Few epics from heroic ages past ever sported such a strange array of beings and peoples. No poets had ever sung of such an army, many kinds joined together against a common foe.

Certainly he had had problems on the march. He had heard mutters against sorcery. He had heard men whispering that it wasn't right to consort with pagans and heretics, or whether it was right for a child to challenge a parent or a lord to challenge the wisdom of the skopos. But their fear and their doubt was also their strength. They had, most of them, thrown over their old prejudices out of loyalty to him. The Wendishmen might distrust the Quman, but they granted them a measure of respect. And frankly, for the men, there was something heartening about fighting alongside centaurs, that ancient race that had once burned the holy city of Darre. Their inhuman nature was always visible to any man with eyes, yet they had a kind of beauty as well. Now and again Sanglant had seen a man stare dreamily at one of their Bwr allies, and more than a few times he had caught himself admiring their robust figures clad in nothing beside the accoutrements of war and wondering at the mystery of their existence. Now and again he had to remind himself that they weren't women at all. Now, like the rest of his army, they waited with spears or bows or swords held ready.

It was so damned hot. He prayed that he had not moved too soon, that this wait in the stifling heat would not sap his army, and indeed it was midafternoon before Henry's army marched into view and began to form up in battle array. Two well ordered contingents of infantry, one wearing the tabard of the King's Lions and the other Wendish milites out of Saony, flanked a mass of cavalry riding under his father's banner, the conjoined sigils of Wendar and Varre. The banner displaying the imperial crown flew gloriously above all the rest as a bannerman hauled it back and forth to let the fabric stream.

Henry's farthest left and right flanks were held by alternating bands of cavalry and infantry belonging to various nobles from Aosta. Missing was the banner of Duchess Liutgard of Fesse. Wichman had noted this force but a few hours ago and now they were gone.

Indeed, Wichman left the center and rode back to inform him of this fact, galloping up onto the rise with a gleeful grin on his face.

'D'ya see that?' he called breathlessly as soon as he came within shouting distance of the prince. 'That bitch will have taken a force around our flank. They'll go north into the woods and swing around to hit our defensive line from the northwest, where we're thinnest. Best to send the reserve to meet them.'

'Do you think so?' Sanglant shook his head. 'Henry will

stall to give her time to arrive. He'll have her attack at the same time he'll signal Queen Adelheid to sally forth from the walls.' *Check,* his father would say in a confident way that encouraged one to resign the game right then. 'Nay, Wichman. The next move is mine. We'll not spread ourselves thin. We'll win this battle before Liutgard can get all the way around our position.'

Wichman snorted. 'Henry outnumbers us! That's just what's on the field. Who knows how many wait with the queen to attack us from the rear.'

'Numbers aren't everything. We have winged riders, and Bwr, and griffins. We are bold, not cautious.' He stood in his stirrups, lifting his lance as he gestured toward the imperial banner, then shifted his gaze to stare down his cousin. 'I challenge you! Will it be you, or me, that captures the banner bearing the sigil of the crown of stars?'

Wichman laughed outright, outraged and delighted, and reined his horse around before Sanglant could say another word.

'Look there,' called Hathui. A dozen riders rode forward from Henry's front line bearing the Lion, Eagle, and Dragon flag of Wendar. 'They want a parley.'

Sanglant nodded at Chustaffus, who lifted the black dragon banner once, twice, and thrice. They rode down the rise and advanced to the forefront of the host, dust spitting up where hooves struck. As they passed through the Wendish line, a cheer rose and continued until he gestured and Chustaffus raised the banner for silence. They stood at the edge of the tributary stream. Across the cracked and stony bed waited those who spoke for the emperor.

He recognized three of these noble courtiers, two armed and one a cleric.

It was the cleric, one of Henry's schola, who spoke. 'Sanglant, the emperor Henry, your father, begs you to lay down your arms and embrace him as a son should. Have you forsaken God and parent alike? How can you rebel against the one who gave you life? He weeps, wondering what madness possesses his beloved son.'

All suffered under the sun's hammer. Sweat flowed freely. Resuelto twitched his ears. The heat would drain them long before courage flagged.

Sanglant rode forward four paces and cried out in a voice meant to reach as great a distance as possible. 'Know it to be true: Henry is not himself. Those who call themselves his allies have abused his trust and insinuated a daimone into his body, so that he walks and talks to their command. If you do not believe me, then wonder why Henry did not return to Wendar when his Eagles brought him news of troubles in the north. He is a puppet dancing to the command of those who use him to their own ends. I have ridden across months and leagues to save my father, not to fight him. Will he come before me so that I may look into his eyes and know that he is truly himself?'

'The parent does not attend on the child! You are the one who must beg forgiveness of your father, my lord prince!'

'So I will, when he is free!' He turned to Sergeant Cobbo. 'Sound the advance.'

With his heels he urged Resuelto forward. The horn blew three sharp blasts, but before the second blast finished, Wichman was halfway across the stony bed at the front of the charge.

Taken completely by surprise by this breach of etiquette, the parley band broke into a full rout and raced helter-skelter back to their line. One mount stumbled, spilling the cleric to the earth. He rolled to his feet and ran.

Resuelto surged up the far bank, muscles bunched, ears forward; behind, Sanglant's guard pressed the charge. Before them the Wendish cavalry of Henry began to lumber forward, for they were heavily armored enough that it was difficult to get speed quickly, then rolled forward in a wedge, slow at first but gaining momentum. A cloud of dust rose behind them, blocking the view of the emperor's banner. From away to the left rose the eerie whistle of Quman wings as the winged riders began their own attack.

The lines met with a roar.

Sanglant veered left and thrust right to gain the unshielded side of a Wendish knight. *My countryman.* The thought was fleeting, vanishing as quickly as it sparked in his mind. He struck true; his lance pierced the man through his abdomen and passed clean through his body. With a backward yank Sanglant tried to rip the lance free, but the mail links of the other man's shirt held firm and their grip pulled the lance out of the prince's hand. Now the clamor of battle joined swallowed him like a wave.

He unsheathed his sword. Its point rapped against his shield as he drew it over his head, that tiny sound in counterpoint to the cries of men and the screams of horses, each a melody of exhilaration or surprise or death. Slashing ever forward he drove on. No man could stand before him. In truth, each poor soldier he faced, however briefly, seemed incapable of grasping his peril amidst the dust and chaos, as if they loitered there expressly to be cut down in their confusion. Lifting his shield he caught a man across the face, unhorsing him as he hacked across the hindquarters of a mount, causing the beast to buckle and collapse to the ground. His eyes burned from the dust, and the heat, as he cut his way through the mass of cavalry in search of Taillefer's crown.

The glint of jewel-bright colors caught his eye: the stars in Taillefer's crown rising above the haze. He made for the banner, but slowed, seeing a wall of infantry placed between him and his goal. Turning to his left, he faced another stalwart wall of unmounted Lions, advancing one measured step at a time. To his right another wall of infantry bristled with spears. Too late he realized he had pressed forward of his own troops.

'Yaaa aaah!' The cry came from behind him as Wichman, at full gallop, charged into the front wall, his mount leaping at the last moment. Fully half a dozen spear points pierced the horse's belly but its collapse created a huge breach. Sanglant and a dozen others pressed through the gap, which widened as men were cut down or broke formation. A last knot of horsemen stood between them and the emperor's banner, yet the regnant's banner of Wendar and Varre was nowhere to be seen nor was Henry and his distinctive armor and white-and-gold tabard anywhere in sight.

The defenders fought bravely and with skill but could not stand before Sanglant and his men. Yet as their numbers dwindled, so did Sanglant's, and even as he hacked his way closer to the imperial banner, so did the Lions re-form and close in behind them. Out beyond, within the dusty haze, new figures appeared, a fresh line of cavalry, and they charged.

Sanglant parried a blow, cut a man down as he thundered past, but as he was twisted to one side wrenching his sword free a spear slid past his thigh deep into Resuelto. The gelding convulsed, yet struggled forward bravely. Slowly, they fell away from the spear, as if it were possible to escape a blow already struck. Slowly, Resuelto crumpled. Blood gushed over Sanglant's leg, and he flung himself forward to escape being crushed, falling across Resuelto's neck as the horse collapsed completely, blood pumping from its flank. His sword skittered out of his hand. A broken lance rolled between Resuelto's forelegs, maybe even the same one that had killed him. A horseman leaped right over them, striking down.

Sanglant ducked under the broken remains of his shield, then grabbed the hilt of his sword and brought it up hard. He wasn't sure what he hit; blood had got in his eyes, but he tumbled sideways as the horse stumbled to the ground and when the rider pitched forward Sanglant took him under the arm, cutting into the unprotected armpit.

'The crown of stars, the crown of stars!' The cry rose up from the Saony milites who hemmed them in, yet his countrymen seemed hesitant to strike down one of their own. The imperial banner had fallen and was lost from view.

Of his own soldiers he saw none, only a crowd of unfamiliar tabards and sharp blades. He jumped forward, lashing out first to his left and then to his right to keep them off-balance. His shield was shattered and his body pierced by inconsequential cuts, but he fought on.

Checkmate, his father would say.

He sensed it coming, but in his fatigue he was slowed. He spun to parry, but he was late. The point had just tipped his mail below the heart, inevitable in its trajectory, when it went flying as if by magic and the rider who wielded it was carried backward off his horse. The butt spike on the shaft of the imperial banner had taken the man down, and grasping this most noble of spears was Wichman, dragging the huge banner and its brilliant crown of stars in the dust.

With a smile, blood leaking from his lips, he spun the shaft in his hands to lift the fabric off the ground. 'I win!' Wichman shouted.

They stood in an eddy, in that moment cut off from the ring and hue surrounding them, locked in a silence and stillness that captured them within its net.

Wichman laughed. In truth he blazed, shining in his glory, and the enemy scattered and shrieked, scrambling backward as the sun itself plummeted to the battlefield, so bright Wichman had to shield his eyes against its unexpected glare and Sanglant stepped back as the downrush from their wings struck him.

When the griffins landed, the earth shook. Their feathers gleamed even through the swirling dust that coated every man, every horse, and every weapon.

They pounced, falling upon the nearest men as hawks would upon a nest of baby mice. Their talons, and the touch of their feathers, shredded flesh and metal. Undone by this assault, many soldiers – ai, God, his own countrymen – fell to their knees to pray while others dropped their weapons and ran.

Sanglant sheathed his sword and shook the remnants of his shield off his arm.

'Wichman! Follow me!'

He ran for Domina and leaped up onto her back, swinging a leg over and pushing himself up onto her shoulders. His armor saved him from the worst lacerations, but he bled all over her feathers from a hundred tiny gashes, and where his blood touched her plumage, it sizzled and gusted as tendrils of steam. Wichman ran for Argent, but it leaped skyward before he could reach it, and Domina with a harsh cry launched herself awkwardly at the same time, legs dragging as she thrashed to gain height with so much weight bearing her down.

The wings beat dust into his face. He lost sight of Wichman and the banner as the griffin rose into the air although he heard the duchess' son cursing, and he almost lost his seat as she swayed and plunged and rose again. Arrows chased them into the sky.

Below, the field of battle was chaos, obscured by dust so thick that he couldn't tell where his line ended and Henry's army began. It was quieter along the camp's inner siege wall, but Adelheid's defenders were firing blazing arrows into the ground in front of the line of wagons. Small fires scorched the dry grass, sending up billows of smoke, but the fires didn't threaten the wagons. Not yet. Behind the worst of the dust, the reserve held its ground, waiting for a signal.

It was a bumpy ride, nothing like a horse and far less comfortable. He had never been so frightened in his life, wondering if he were going to pitch right off and fall to his death, and although his gaze took in the scene below he found he could not utter a single word or call out to those below, so choked was he with fear.

At last, as the griffin circled in toward Fulk's position in the center rear, Sanglant caught sight of Henry's banner. It had moved far to the left, heading toward the woods. About ten centuries of cavalry rode with his father, a substantial force. Through the heat haze he saw the front rank of Liutgard's troops moving slowly up and over the wooded bluff. They hadn't yet negotiated the steeper downward slope on the western side. He couldn't count her forces because the trees concealed their numbers.

Ai, God! Taillefer's banner had been a feint all along. Henry played chess with a subtle mind and a strong will. He would never let himself be taken easily, but he had taken his own son for a fool and dangled a line and caught him.

So be it.

He had only one course of action left. Already the sun sank quickly toward the west. Night would come, but Henry would not wait for dusk to make his final move.

The griffin shrieked a warning and landed with a rattling thump. Horses bolted; soldiers ducked; the impact shook him so hard that he slid, slipped, and tumbled to the ground. As soon as his weight was off her, she launched herself back into the air with a *whuff*.

Fulk came running, helmet off and hair matted to his head with sweat and grime. Blood streaked his right hand, and as Sanglant got to his feet, Fulk turned and joyously signed toward a soldier coated with dust. It took Sanglant a moment to recognize Sibold through the filth. The young soldier whooped out loud, seeing the prince, and hoisted up the black dragon banner, torn, bloody, and stained, but not lost. A ragged cheer went up from the defenders. His troops pressed forward with renewed vigor.

'My lord prince! We thought you were lost!' cried Hathui, weeping, coming up in Fulk's wake. She handed him a square cloth so that he could wipe the dust and blood out of his eyes.

His palms and hands were sticky with blood. He was cut everywhere mail had not protected his skin, cloth torn and tattered, but the gashes were shallow, a mere nuisance. He bent down and carefully picked up two gleaming griffin feathers. Shoving his knife between boot and leggings, he thrust the feathers into its sheath, although the leather showed signs of splitting where their edges sliced.

'How many of my men returned?' he asked.

Hathui stepped back to let Fulk approach. 'None, my lord,' said the captain, 'except Sibold, who took the banner out of Chustaffus' dead hand.'

There was no time for grief. Later, sorrow would stalk him, but he had to act now.

'What news?' Blood spattered the dirt around him. His tabard was in ribbons. Malbert ran up and offered him a full wineskin. Taking a swig, he rinsed his mouth and spat before swallowing an even larger mouthful.

'The men are falling back as we arranged, to hold the siege line. I've thrown Lord Druthmar in at the hinge where the streambed meets the river. Bands of Aostan light cavalry had broken past and were harrying the camp. One group of Bwr has lent support to the center.'

The captain in charge of the centaurs, a big, stocky mare

whose cream coat and blue-black hair made her stand out from a distance, galloped up to him. 'My lord prince.' She had been designated captain in part, Sanglant supposed, by reason of age and seniority, in the manner of mares, and in part because she could speak Ungrian. 'We thought you lost.'

'I am not, Capi'ra, as you see. How many of your folk have yet to be committed to the field?'

She stamped one hoof. 'Two centuries wait.' She indicated the Bwr reserve just visible behind the clouds of dust that marked the field of battle.

'Ride with me to the wood. Fulk, I'll need a new mount. Fest, if you have him close by.'

The bay gelding was being held in reserve, and when he was brought forward, Capi'ra eyed him sidelong. Like the other centaurs she had unusually mobile, elongated ears, which she flicked now, but he could not discern emotion in her bland expression. 'Have you no pura to ride?'

'No.' He said it more sharply than he intended.

'What is your plan, my lord prince?' Fulk asked.

He took a last swig of wine. 'We must hold our line on this field at whatever cost. Adelheid's forces will attack at a prearranged signal, so be on your guard against it. I think they will wait until Liutgard can flank us. That will be the crux of the battle. Right now her forces are strung out through the woods. We must rout them there before Henry can catch up to them. I need a shield.'

'Your Highness.' Hathui stepped forward. 'Would it not be better for you to command from the rear? Send someone else?'

Sanglant's mood changed and he laughed. 'Nay, Eagle. I trust Fulk for his steadiness, and steadiness is what is needed on the field. If we're not quick, we'll be engulfed. As well, there is a chance I may meet my father in the woods.'

He took the shield Malbert brought, and as soon as the captain called her troops in, they rode, the centaurs falling in behind him and Capi'ra.

'We must rout Liutgard's forces quickly and turn back to support the Quman left,' he told her.

The centaurs had exceptional stamina, and the heat did not seem to bother them as much as it did him and Fest. They raced up along the western side of the river to the bluff, moving in among the trees below the western slopes. Their pace slowed once they were in the wood, where shade gave relief from the sun. It was now the hottest part of the afternoon and Sanglant knew that as many men would fall to the heat as to the enemy.

It seemed that they traveled well into the forest before the lead scouts of Liutgard's troops were spotted with the rest of her riders strung back along the path, hidden from view, moving single-file or two abreast. The Bwr communicated with snorts and stamps whose meaning was unintelligible to him, but they moved away to form a line two deep winding through the woods parallel to the path. Those in the second rank had bows at the ready while the front rank held spears and shields.

Too late Liutgard's forward troops realized the threat. Capi'ra blew a sharp blat on a ram's horn and her centaurs closed at a trot. The Bwr had horn bows and they loosed arrows as they advanced, surprisingly agile at fending off tree branches and leaping around or over bushes as they plunged through the woods. Their skill with a bow was unsurpassed even by the Quman, who were renowned and dreaded as horse archers, and this skill began to take a toll. By the time he reached Liutgard's vanguard most of the forward soldiers were down although only one horse had been hit. There was no one to fight. Fest leaped corpses as he followed the centaurs back into the trees; the gelding had steady nerves but lacked imagination and thus was well suited for this kind of skirmish. Their group wheeled around to attack again.

He heard Liutgard's voice – he could scarcely fail to recognize it, since they had grown up together at court – as she shouted for her people to form up for a charge. Yet as the centaurs drove forward again, shooting at will, whistling and calling in their high-pitched voices, the mounts belonging to the human soldiers did not shift, as if under a spell. Liutgard and her soldiers were stuck on horseback, unable to move, absorbing one after another flight of arrows. Her men began to panic as the front line of Bwr closed with spears lowered.

They hit the central rank of Liutgard's line with a resounding crash. Spears that did not strike flesh stuck in shields, and as the centaurs passed through the line, cutting to each side with long knives or thrusting with their spears, the horses began to buck and kick. Riders were dumped onto the ground. Men trying to fight back could not hang on or even get in a good blow, but it was the betrayal of their mounts that panicked them most. In ancient legend it was said that the Bwr spoke to horses, and now it appeared to be true. One by one, unhorsed, Liutgard's soldiers broke into reckless flight.

'At them,' cried Sanglant, encouraging the pursuit. The centaurs answered with shrill, inhuman calls. He pressed Fest forward. The pursuit must be swift; Liutgard could be allowed no time to regroup. Yet the forest favored men on foot. Sanglant himself traded only a few blows, wounding one man before that one and his two companions leaped into a bristling thicket of thornbush and scrabbled away through its branches where he could not follow without dismounting.

Some centaurs pursued men through the woods while others shot arrows into those clumps of men hiding in the underbrush. Circling, the centaurs chose each shot carefully, seeking the best angle around a shield or a favorable gap in the branches.

They had not the numbers to keep the advantage for long. Behind the skirmishing line rose a cry.

'To me! To me! Fall back to the Eagle of Fesse!'

Duchess Liutgard, still mounted on a black mare and herself carrying her banner, rallied her men. A shield wall swelled around her as dismounted men overcame their fear. It was natural to him that the ebb and flow of battle would dictate each move, each objective. Liutgard and her banner must fall to complete the rout.

A bristling wood of spears formed up in front of the duchess. A dozen centaurs joined him as they probed around the right flank of Liutgard's position. He saw his cousin clearly, just as she saw him: she was a proud, experienced fighter who knew how to shift ground in a skirmish depending on changing circumstances. She shouted commands, directing men to fill gaps or pointing out targets for her few archers, but it was obvious she knew exactly where Sanglant was.

He charged, not at her line but at a group of men seeking to join her, scattering them and dropping two before he continued around to the thinnest point in the wall of spears and shields.

'We must take her! Now!'

Capi'ra sounded her horn. More centaurs joined him, and they pressed forward through the trees as others attacked from the flanks. He was almost unhorsed when he glanced aside for one moment only to be thwacked hard on the helm by a tree limb. He fell sideways, caught himself on Fest's neck, and dragged himself upright in the saddle.

In close formation, the dismounted men had the advantage over the centaurs, but Capi'ra urged her troops on and they went without hesitation. He chased after them, ears still ringing, and where the clash unfolded he pushed forward to try to break a gap through to Liutgard herself, who had retreated a few paces back on the path. The melee had a muffled sound, arrows fluttering through leaves, the grunt of a man absorbing a spear blow to his shield, a yelp where a centaur was hit, the crack and snap of branches and dry leaf litter under the press of feet and hooves as soldiers shifted their position or fell. Some among the centaurs sat back and took leisurely aim, but with shields held close it was more difficult to pierce the enemy's ranks. This slow dance of attrition would not aid his cause. He pushed forward and struck hard to either side. Men gave way before him. He punched spear thrusts away with his shield. The line bowed inward as they gave ground.

Liutgard's voice carried above the fray.

'Sanglant! Give up this rebellion! Throw down your arms and your father will show you mercy!'

He could not answer. He broke through and with a dozen or more centaurs behind him galloped along the path, bearing down on Liutgard. She was easy to mark: she wore a surcoat of white and gold, royal colors, although her banner was furled for the ride through the trees. She had loosened the straps of her helmet and pushed it back the better for her voice to be heard.

As Sanglant closed, she pulled her helmet down and braced. Five men stood between him and the duchess, and he fought furiously to reach her. He took the arm off an ax man and punched another aside with his shield, kicked a third man in the face who was attempting to rise after being bowled over by Fest.

He closed, and he met Liutgard's defiant gaze.

She is my favorite cousin.

The thought fled, and in its passing he hesitated. Then he struck, but the eagle banner swept down over him before his blow landed, blinding him, trapping him in the cloth. She had caught him. His blade rang against hers as she parried, all the while pressing the banner against him that he might not escape it or bat it aside.

'To the Duchess!'

'Get him!'

'For Fesse!'

A spear slammed against his breastplate but did not penetrate; a sword glanced off his greave. The ululations of the centaurs guided him as he cut into the banner pole's shaft. The cloth slithered down off him, falling to the ground and clearing his sight.

The press of men around him forced him back together with the centaurs who had come to his rescue. They formed a small phalanx and he shouted, calling others to join up with them. Liutgard fell back. Her ripped banner, its broken haft grasped by a sergeant, rose to shouts of triumph.

From up on the bluff a horn rang out three times. She had only to hang on until Henry reached her.

'Mark her! Mark her!' he cried to the centaurs at his back. If Bayan could die with an arrow in his throat, so could Liutgard. Fesse arrows struck his shield and one stuck, quivering there. Fest veered and stumbled as a spear grazed his withers.

Two centaurs fell; the others ululated and first Liutgard's horse and then the others around her went crazy, and she could not run or fight. He closed.

A horn sounded to his left. Out of the woodland to the north swarmed many more men, some on horseback, some running. They wore the colors of Avaria.

'For Henry!' they cried. 'Murderer! You murdered our lady! Traitor! Deceiver!'

In another ten breaths they would be upon him. A glance told him what took his breath away: These were Wendilgard's men.

Avaria's heir had betrayed him.

He had no choice but to retreat or else sacrifice what remained of his strike force. They lost three centaurs pulling out, but with the enemy fighting their own mounts and using the cover of the trees they were able to pull back out of range where he found Capi'ra bleeding from a dozen shallow wounds.

He caught his breath while she tallied her forces. His mouth was parched and his neck and back soaked through with sweat. The pursuit came close behind; they had to move on, and quickly. He had to decide what to do. If he stopped even for a moment to think, to consider that he had been so close to murdering his own kinswoman, he would lose all.

'No worse than I expected,' Capi'ra said in such a stolid and unemotional voice that her calmness struck him like a slap in the face. 'No more than twenty dead. Yet we cannot take on such a large force, even broken up as they are within the woods.'

'No,' he agreed. The truth hurt, but he had to face it. 'No. Henry closes in. Wendilgard has moved against us. Adelheid will attack our rear. We must pull the entire army back west and north through the woods before we are surrounded. We've lost the battle.'

XXXII

WORSE YET
TO COME

1

In Alba, at twilight, Stronghand strolled up to the stone crown and stared out over the fens. The horizon on all sides and most of the flat waters and half-drowned hillocks were hidden by a thick haze shrouding the land, but the sky above was so clear that it seemed stretched and thin, almost white. The sun was sliding into that haze, drowning. Soon the stars would come out.

He ruled Eika and human alike; his ships roamed the seas and struck the coast at will; all of Eikaland lay under his rule, and most of Alba had capitulated and was falling into line. But when OldMother commanded, he must obey. He had reached Alba three days ago. Thoughts of Alain chafed him, always, but he had been given a task to complete.

'Father Reginar,' he said, greeting the young churchman who waited eagerly and anxiously beside the stone crown together with five other clerics.

'Prince Stronghand.' Reginar was young, callow, and arrogant, and hadn't the ability to hide his scorn, but he was no

fool. Stronghand's soldiers guarded him against those who
might interfere with the spell he and his comrades meant to
weave this night. For that reason, Reginar tolerated the Eika.

Stronghand bared his teeth, noting how the clerics flinched
and stepped away from him. The sun set, and the first stars
blossomed in the vault of the heavens. Far to the east, lightning stroked through the sky, although they were too far away
to hear answering thunder.

'I pray you,' said Reginar's companion, a woman holding
a short staff. 'If you will allow us, my lord prince, we will
begin.'

He nodded and retreated ten steps down the slope of the
hill. There he clasped his hands behind his back as the woman
took her place in the weaving circle. Three of his brothers
joined him, as silent as mist. Ursuline waited in the camp
below, leading the evening song. He heard many voices joined
together, singing a hymn. Some of those who sang were
RockChildren.

So. Now it would begin. The alliance the WiseMothers
had made would prove wise, or foolish. No matter what transpired, the world would change, as he was already changed.

There was no going back.

When evening fell, the allied armies of Lady Eudokia and
King Geza made camp in a protected hollow partway up the
slope of the drought-stricken hills in Dalmiaka. There was no
water to be had for prisoners, only a single flask of vinegary
wine passed around between them, a few sips for each member
of their party but no more than that. They weren't given any
food at all, not even a dry scrap of wayfarer's bread.

Hanna was parched and her head ached from hunger and
the unremitting heat. Mother Obligatia lay with a hand across
her eyes, pale and breathing shallowly, while Sister Diocletia
wiped sweat off the abbess' face with her own robes. Rosvita
stood with a hand on Fortunatus' elbow as they stared south
into the darkening sky. The others clustered behind them,
dead silent.

There were no clouds, not a wisp. The air had such a flat

heavy cast to it that it seemed an unnatural color, almost green. The lay of the land allowed them a magnificent view out over a plateau to the south of their position. South lay the sea, although they couldn't see it from here. A huge lightning storm played across the southern expanse of the heavens, bolts lighting the entire sky, crackling sideways or down to strike the earth. Distant thunder rolled in waves. A net of light sparked and dazzled in the sky as lightning danced around it.

'We are too late,' said Rosvita. 'We have failed.'

Hanna wept.

Folk along Aosta's coastal plain northeast of Darre were frightened by the terrible omens that had plagued them in increasing numbers over the last months and weeks, but they welcomed a kindly old woman garbed in simple deacon's robes and attended by a pair of humble fraters. They did not realize that she was cloaked in a binding that made men's eyes skip past her and find her unremarkable unless she claimed their notice. They did not see that the fraters carried swords beneath their robes. They fed her and her escort, stabled their mounts, gave her their best bed to sleep in, and in the morning sent her on her way toward Darre with bread and cheese for her midday meal.

It was often difficult for her to sleep. The amulet blistered her skin, and this evening in particular it burned with a stinging touch that caused her at last to leave the soft feather bed of her hosts and go outside in the hope that the night wind might cool her. Although the skin, where the amulet touched, was red, only a single blister had raised tonight, like a bug's bite. Nothing to worry about, then. She had only to remain vigilant. Long ago her clerics had woven amulets under her guidance to protect Sabella's army from the guivre's stony gaze, and they had developed a terrible leprosy. Certainly in Verna she had learned more sophisticated and careful means of enchantment and sorcery, so most likely the clerics who had aided her then had not been righteous enough to withstand the corrupting effects of the binding's secret heart.

No doubt they had got what they deserved.

Outside she found no relief from the windless heat, however. She stood in the dirt yard between crude door and garden fence and stared at the heavens. Her guards crept out from the stable, rubbing sweat from their foreheads, and after a time every soul in that tiny hamlet – twenty or more, half of them children – staggered from their pallets to stand on the dusty track and stare up at the uncanny lights that played across the stars and the lightning flaring in sheets and chains across a cloudless sky.

The villagers wept with fear. Even her stalwart soldiers, chosen for their steadiness and loyalty to Adelheid and her daughters, cowered as they watched.

Antonia did not fear God's displeasure. She welcomed it. She would survive the coming storm. She would rule the remnant, and all would be well.

The road Ivar and Erkanwulf followed ran straight west through the Bretwald, a vast and ancient forest in western Saony close to the borderlands where Wendar met Varre. All day, clouds gathered and the sky turned black as a storm approached. At dusk, rain poured down so hard it tore leaves off trees and gashed runnels into the ground. They were stuck out on a path in the middle of the forest, riding in haste, trapped by nightfall, and now sopping wet.

'We'd best find shelter,' said Ivar. He dismounted and held his nervous mare right up at the mouth, trying his best to calm her, but the storm seemed to shake the entire world.

'Do you think we'll survive the night?' Erkanwulf's voice trembled and broke.

'Come on!' Fear made Ivar angry. 'I've survived worse than this! We'll get back to Biscop Constance. Princess Theophanu charged us to do so, and we mustn't fail her.'

'Charged us to take a message, but sent neither help nor advice! And how are you going to get back into Queen's Grave when you left as a corpse?'

'We won't fail her,' Ivar repeated stubbornly, even though he wasn't sure it was true.

The rain hurt as it pounded them, and it didn't seem to

be slacking up. He'd never seen it come down like this, as though rain from every land round about had been pushed over this very spot and now, letting loose, meant to drown them. They pulled their mounts under the spreading boughs of an old oak tree. Acorns thudded on dirt and hit them on the head. Rain drenched them. The horses tugged at the reins. Water streamed around their feet, and already the path had turned into a muddy, impassable canal, boiling and angry.

'Look!' cried Erkanwulf. 'Look there!'

Out in the forest lights bobbed and wove. Erkanwulf took a step toward them and called out, but Ivar grabbed his cloak and wrenched him backward.

'Hush, you idiot! No natural fire can stay lit in this downpour! Don't you remember who attacked us before?'

'Ai, God! The Lost Ones! We're doomed.'

'Hush. Hush.'

The lights turned their way.

When you have lost, discipline is everything.

Sanglant allowed himself a grim smile of satisfaction when he reached the edge of the forest with what remained of his army just as dusk spread its wings to cover them. They hadn't routed. When the call came to retreat off the field, they had moved back in formation and in an orderly manner, without panic. Now, perhaps, night would aid them and hinder Henry. So he hoped.

He had chosen to remain with the rear guard, letting Fulk lead the battered army northwest alongside Capi'ra and her centaurs. The remnants of the Quman clans, Waltharia's heavy cavalry, the Ungrians, the marchlanders, and his Wendish irregulars and cavalry followed Fulk and Capi'ra. He held shield and sword, with stalwart Fest beneath him and his banner and the last surviving members of his personal guard close at hand. Together with the griffins, a tight line of Villam infantry and marchlander archers under the command of Lewenhardt was all that separated him from the press of Henry's army. Although he had no real way to communicate with the griffins, they had sensed his need and during the entire retreat across open ground had roamed along the last rank roaring and shrieking whenever Henry's pursuing army came too close. Once or twice they pounced, but the press of spears and swords against them was heavy, and they did not like to get so close. Even iron feathers weren't proof against steel, although few arrows had enough force to pierce their skin.

Hathui stuck beside him despite the danger from arrows and the occasional spear chucked at them from the front line of Henry's advancing army. Henry's banner he could not see, but he recognized Henry's presence with each step that he retreated and with each lost, dead soldier he had to leave behind.

'He isn't pressing us as hard as he could,' he remarked.

There was some jostling of position as the infantry shifted formation in order to move from open ground into the woods. A man in the final rank fell forward to his knees as a halberd hooked his shield and dragged him out of place. An ax blow felled him, but his fellows screamed and leaped forward to yank him back to safety. A moment later the injured man was carried out of the line past Sanglant and his mounted guard to the wagons, which trundled at an agonizingly slow pace down the narrow road that led through the forest. Two days ago they had followed Adelheid's army through more open land just south of the forest, on the narrow coastal plain, but open ground gave Henry's superior forces too much of an advantage. The forest offered cover, yet it had its own dangers. Sanglant recognized this road as the one Wendilgard had used yesterday when she had pulled back her troops.

His conversation with her, and his encounter with the shadow prince, seemed ages ago. An eternity had passed since she had turned her back on him. If he had known that she would betray her word and attack his rear, would he have cut her down when he had the chance? Could he kill his own kinfolk? Had his hesitation when confronting his cousin Liutgard sealed his fate?

Doubts would prove fatal. All this he could reflect over later. Right now, with Sergeant Cobbo at his side holding a torch aloft and the tramp of feet and murmur of men calling to each other to check their positions, he could concentrate on only one thing.

'It was a trap all along,' said Hathui.

'My father has not lost his sense of strategy.'

The thought gave him pause. If Henry could still outplay him in the game of chess, did that mean he had recovered his own mind? Had Hathui been mistaken in what she thought she had seen in the palace in Darre?

No. He believed Hathui. She was an Eagle, trained to witness and report.

The forest stymied the griffins and with a shrill call they leaped into the air. The downdraft from their wings sent men flying, and with a rush the last rank got itself together and pulled into place as Sanglant waited under the outermost trees for them to move in under the canopy. At Hathui's urging he moved forward behind the last wagon where the freshly wounded man groaned and moaned beside a half dozen of his injured comrades. The soldiers who had lugged their companion away from the line paused before the prince.

'My lord prince!'

'Your Highness!'

He gave them a blessing and they hurried back to take their place in the rear guard. It struck him, in that gloaming, how strange it was that men were willing to die for the sake of another man's honor or ambition and yet would struggle to stay alive in the oddest circumstances imaginable, in the teeth of any sort of vile disaster. A drowning man who battled to stay afloat might turn around and sacrifice himself without a moment's thought so that a comrade could reach safety. A mother would hang on with an iron will through weeks and months of starvation only to give the scrap of food that would save her to her beloved child. God had made humankind's hearts a mystery, often even to themselves.

Stars glittered above, seen in patchwork through oak boughs. The moon rode high overhead, but it wasn't bright enough tonight to offer much illumination. Far away to the east beyond the dark mass of the highlands the sky lit and flickered, then went dark. Although he strained to hear, he heard no answering thunder.

Within the wood they had perforce to spread out between the trees to protect the wagons. The horses had easier going on the road, although it was slow in any case. All around he heard branches snap, leaf litter crunch beneath boots, and men curse as they lost their footing or were slapped in the face by a limb let loose by the man in front of them. Harness jingled. Horses whickered. Some man's dog whined. Once he heard the griffins call, but he had lost sight of them. Now and again an arrow whistled out of the darkness. Torches burned all along their route as men on foot lit the way for those with horses. These lights burned far ahead and out to either side, marking the limits of his army, while behind the enemy brought up torches as well, so that the forest seemed alive with fireflies.

In truth, they were an easy target, but although Henry's forces harried them, the king – the *emperor* – did not press an all-out assault. Henry, too, was impeded by night.

'He's holding off,' said Sanglant to Hathui. 'He's waiting. For what?'

'We're deep in enemy territory without support. Why should he risk losing more men than he needs to if he can pick us off piece by piece at less risk to his own? Too, I think his men are afraid of the griffins.'

'As they should be. But the griffins can't help us now.'

Lightning turned the sky to a ghastly gray-white. The silhouettes of trees leaped into prominence, and were gone, all except the afterimage. Distant thunder rumbled, then faded. His ears felt full, as though ready to pop. An arrow whooshed past to bury itself into the wood of the wagon just in front of them. Out in the forest, a man yelped as he was struck.

They held their position as they trudged along. The lightning storm flashed and boomed off to the east as they kept moving in formation, not breaking ranks. They had lost far too many men in the field, but he dared not number or name them now. They had retreated over the corpses of their own, but they had not left behind any wounded man who could be moved. Yet the heat had sapped them, and they had abandoned more horses than men. Half their supplies had been lost. Even at such a slow pace and with the mercy of night they could not go on much longer. He was still sweating; the night hadn't cooled down, and the air got thicker and more humid until it seemed difficult to take in a breath.

The sky lit so brightly that it blinded him. Thunder rolled in over them, wave upon wave of it, and a bolt of lightning ripped through the sky and hung against blackness for what seemed forever, burning itself into his vision so that when it flicked out he still saw it against the starry heavens like a twisting road delineating the path on which angels descended to Earth to collect the souls of the newly dead.

There were so many dead.

'My lord prince!' A man appeared out of the darkness with a comrade leaning on him, an arrow in his thigh. 'Terrence here can't walk, but there's no room in the wagon.'

Sanglant dismounted and broke the shaft off near the leg. The man gritted his teeth and did not scream. 'Put him on the horse,' he said.

'My lord!' cried Hathui.

Malbert and Sibold protested. 'Ride our horses, my lord. We'll walk.'

'Go on,' he said. 'I'll stay with the rear guard. We'll all get free, or none of us will.' He had seen the bones of his Dragons covering the flagstones in Gent Cathedral. He had no wish to be the last to remain alive, not again. No wonder his mother's blessing was in truth a curse. To survive might be a worse punishment than to die. How many people had he led to their deaths while he remained among the living?

A gust of wind rattled the trees and showered leaves and twigs down on them. As the line moved forward, he fell in with the last rank. The torches held by Henry's soldiers flared a spear's throw behind, but Henry's men did not speak, only followed. An arrow hissed out of the night and struck his shield, hanging there to join the stump of the arrow left by one of Liutgard's archers earlier that day. Lewenhardt moved up behind him, took aim, and shot. His arrow skittered away through brush. He heard laughter, followed by a captain's command to draw back.

'No more,' he said quietly to Lewenhardt. 'Save your arrows for daylight.'

'Yes, my lord prince.'

The archer stuck behind him, unwilling to leave, and Sibold came up as well, having given his mount to another man. Malbert might have come as well if he hadn't been carrying the banner. Except for a dozen men with Captain Fulk, they were all that was left of his personal guard. Lightning flashed, illuminating a straggling line of men following their trail, a hundred or more within view and the noise of thousands marching up from behind. They were gone again as night returned, their line shrunk to the pitch fire of torches.

Lewenhardt whistled softly. 'I never thought there would be so many.'

No one faltered. No one stepped out of line or wept with fear. They were good soldiers, the best. It was a curse to lead men to their deaths. He understood that well enough. He had done it so many times.

'Not this time,' he muttered. Anger built. Like the pressure in the air, it throbbed through him. Not this time. He might have lost this battle and far too many men and horses but he would not lose his army no matter what he had to do to save them.

To the north, from the van, he heard a cry. A horn blatted, sounding the alarm. Had Henry sent men through the forest to surround them?

Wendilgard and her banner had not yet been seen, although some of her force had reinforced the Fessians. Did she still hold the old ruined fortress to their north? Had his army retreated into another trap?

'Sibold. Lewenhardt. Hold this line together no matter what. Keep a slow retreat until you hear from me. Hathui! Sergeant Cobbo! You'll come with me!'

Wounded Terrence he put behind the soldier now riding Sibold's horse. Leading Fest, he jogged up along the line with the sergeant lighting his way. It was narrow going. Often there wasn't room between wagon and trees and sometimes he had to wait with frustration welling while a wagon trundled past a gap before he could follow through; other times he cut through the undergrowth although Fest didn't like the darkness and the footing. He passed wagons, marchlander infantry with spears resting on shoulders and grim expressions on their dust-stained faces, a quiet group of Ungrians with heads bowed, and at last he negotiated past the awkward wings of the Quman clansmen, not fit for the confines of woodland travel.

'Prince Sanglant!' Gyasi rode at their head. 'I smell a powerful weaving taking shape. We must take shelter.'

The heavens caught fire, white and bright, but as he blinked everything went dark again. Thunder cracked over them. A net of lights sparkled high overhead before fading in spits and sparks.

Shouting broke out ahead on the road, echoed by the sudden ringing clash of a skirmish opening up at their rear. Lightning flashed. Thunder rolled. There was still no sign of clouds. The stars seemed so close he thought he might pull them down from the sky simply by reaching; they pulsed as if to the beating of his heart.

Something is coming.

He ran, dropping Fest's lead line and leaving Eagle and sergeant behind, stumbled, tripped once and fell hard, jolting himself right up through his shoulders. One greave, rent from a sword blow, pinched at the back of his knees. Drawing his knife he cut the straps as he picked himself up and ran on. If Wendilgard were there, he would slay her for her treachery. No quarter, no ransom.

Lightning flashed, and again, and again, and in each flash he saw the faces of his men, haggard, drained, but determined as they marched on into what fate they did not know, only believed that he would lead them to victory or to shelter.

Out in the forest an uncanny path gleamed. He saw it now, crossing the road at an angle. Not too much farther up the trail Wendilgard had camped yesterday, and beyond that, having lost his way because of anger and doubt, he had encountered the Lost Ones. Surely they had moved on.

He ran. The transition from woodland to open space came abruptly. One moment branches whipped past him, the next he bolted out under the stars and right there, just beyond the last tree, he tripped and fell hard across a body, caught himself on an outflung arm. Lightning flashed again and he saw that he lay on top of the corpse of a man wearing the sigil of Avaria's lion, one of Wendilgard's soldiers. Dead with no apparent wound, no blood staining the ground around him, and quite stiff, which meant he had died many hours ago, long before Wendilgard's forces had attacked Sanglant's forces below the bluff.

Avarian dead lay scattered across the clearing throughout the ruins of Wendilgard's bivouac, under the shadow of those ancient walls. Again a flash illuminated the clearing. A stone's toss from him lay the torn remnants of her proud banner and, across it, her body. Her red-and-white tabard was dusty but otherwise intact and unstained; her lips were pulled back in a rictus grin, and her eyes stared at the heavens although it was quite obvious she no longer saw anything.

Wendilgard was dead.

She had died fighting – but not against him. The Ashioi had killed her, the same ones he had met in the forest, and her Avarians had blamed him and taken what revenge they could by aiding Liutgard.

He jumped up and ran out into the clearing. It was dominated by a low hill on whose height a fortress had once stood, although it was now only shattered walls and fallen stones. He crossed the outer works of the fortress, so fallen and moss-covered that it appeared to be little more than a garden wall. Sanglant plunged right into the midst of a skirmish, his own men screaming and shouting as they fell back before the determined onslaught of the Ashioi. By the light of their torches he glimpsed the scene: the Lost Ones poured out of the fortress.

They had taken refuge there at dawn – so he guessed – as though it had been their place long ago and they defended it now against interlopers.

Night slammed down again. He rushed forward to the front ranks where men stumbled back, some falling to shadowy darts that dissolved as quickly as they struck. He pushed past the ragged line where Fulk and a few others held their ground to let the others retreat. He had thought the battle lost, but now he realized he had forgotten the one chess piece he had thought he would never dare to play, that he would, in fact, never want to play.

Hadn't his mother abandoned him? Had she loved him at all? Yet her blood had mingled with that of his father to create him. She would always be part of him, and never more so than now.

He pulled off his helm, gulped in air, then shouted. 'Cousin! I pray you, Cousin! Heed me, who is son to Uapeani-kazonkansi-a-lari. I need your help!'

'Prince Sanglant!' Fulk called him back.

He jumped into the gap and raised his sword as the clearing lit again, casting a pallor over the melee. A rank of shades stared at him, many wearing the bodies of men but the faces of animals. They paused as he called out once more.

'Cousin! I am the son of Uapeani-kazonkansi-a-lari. Heed me! We are cousins. Kinsmen. Why do we fight?'

The shades drew back to let the shadow prince approach. He and Sanglant stood among the corpses of Wendilgard's troop and a few fresh Wendish ones, facing each other with their soldiers at their back, all of his living and solid and all of the Ashioi insubstantial shades.

'You stand in our sacred ground, a fortress once dedicated to She Who Will Not Have A Husband. These others camped here, so we slew as many as we could and drove off the rest. Now we must hasten.'

'I pray you, aid me, and I will aid you. I am pursued by an army of humankind who seek my destruction and who seek yours as well. Listen!'

A bolt of lighting scorched the sky, hanging in the air for three breaths before it flicked out, leaving behind an after-image that cut a blazing line across the rank of shadow elves who stood listening. Waiting. He saw trees through the outline of their bodies. Far back, he heard a horn call ring out and the sound of clashing weapons, and a horse's screams.

'Why do you fight your own kinsmen?' asked the shadow prince.

'We fight those who are weaving a spell to cast your exiled land back into the aether. I am not a sorcerer. I do not understand by what means such a spell can be woven into being.'

The other one laughed. 'No more so am I a mage's apprentice, although my brother was. I prefer to hold a weapon in my hand. A spear is something I can comprehend. What is your name, Cousin?'

'I am called Sanglant, prince of Wendar and Varre, son of Henry and Uapeani-kazonkansi-a-lari. Who are you?'

'I am called many things. That is the custom among my people. Some called me Younger Brother, while others called me Gets-Into-Trouble. But you may call me Zuanguanu-kazonkiu-a-laru. Or Zuangua, for I know that humankind has difficulty with our names.'

Sanglant laughed. 'I not least among them. So, Zuangua. Will you aid us against our enemy? I have no wish to harm them, only to drive them off so that I do not lose more of my men. The king I must capture alive. He has been made a prisoner by the sorcerers who also wish to harm your people. I carry two griffin feathers with me that will cut the threads of magic. Once he is free of the spell that binds him, he will no longer fight us.'

The prince grinned, and Sanglant recognized that grin for he had felt it on his own face many times, born of a reckless and bold impulsiveness, the willingness to throw oneself forward into an unknown battle where the outcome was in doubt. 'Will he not? What if I desire battle? I have waited a long time to kill humans in revenge for what they did to my people. But very well. The time is near. If aiding you will aid my people, then I will aid you. If it does not, then I can kill you as easily as any other mortal man.'

Zuangua lifted his sword. Lightning flashed, making his white cloak blaze before night returned. A woman standing beside him fitted out in warrior's armor and wearing a hawk's mask pushed up on her head brought a jewel-encrusted conch, bigger than her hands, up to her lips. She blew. The sound arched up just as thunder cracked, but where the thunder splintered and rolled away into silence the mournful note held on and on. The Ashioi warriors scattered into the woods, quickly lost in the darkness.

When the call faded, Zuangua gestured toward the ancient walls on the height. 'Find refuge there for your wounded. The rest, range below. Together, we will fight.'

'My lord prince!' cried Fulk as lightning shot white fire through the air. His anxious expression lit, and vanished, as blackness crashed down.

Sanglant shouted as thunder pealed right on top of them. 'Go! Form a shield wall with those who are strong, and put the injured up in the fortress. Do not touch any of the Lost Ones who bide there. Go! Go!'

He himself turned back to Zuangua. 'Will you hunt with me, Cousin? I seek my father, and I mean to free him.'

2

On the afternoon of that day – the tenth of Octumbre – when Hugh led them up through the maze of ruins that surrounded the tumulus to wait beside the stone crown, Zacharias was ready. The high grass had been scythed for fodder. They waded through its stubble single-file with Hugh in the lead and Zacharias walking behind him, head high. He would make Hathui proud, although she would never know it.

The waxing crescent moon rode high in the heavens as the company spread out around the stones. There were two score guardsmen, Deacon Adalwif, a pair of Hugh's servants, and himself. Zacharias knew well the sandy patch of ground from which the threads were woven; he and Hugh had practiced here many nights in preparation. As the sun sank westward,

Hugh nudged Zacharias to this patch and placed the weaving staff into his hands, then stood behind him. The light faded and the first stars winked into view in the darkening sky: the Diamond, Citrine, and Sapphire that graced the Queen's Sword, Staff, and Cup, with the Diamond so close to zenith it made him dizzy to stare up at it. It was cold, and bitterly clear; with a cloak Zacharias felt the fingers of winter clutching at his bones, but such trifles meant little to him this night.

No rain had fallen for two months and the river that ran below the tumulus was no more than a trickle over its stony bed, while livestock and villagers alike suffered from thirst. The young wheat, recently planted, had not yet sprouted, and the deacon and her villagers despaired, fearing it might never do so without autumn rains to germinate it. Obviously Holy Mother Anne and her tempestari had done their work well, keeping the heavens clear for the weaving across so vast a span of land. Just as obviously they cared nothing for the consequences that fell hardest of all on the common folk. His folk. His kind.

Before his birth a King's Eagle had ridden through the Wasrau River Valley, where farming families crowded the arable land cheek by jowl, all paying heavy taxes and yearly service to one lady or the next in return for protection, right of way, and a pittance of grain during lean years, not always delivered.

King Arnulf the Younger had decreed that any family willing to risk the long journey east to the marchlands, there to farm rich upland country never before touched by a plow, would be freed of the yoke of lady's and lord's service, owing allegiance only to the regnant of Wendar. Most people stayed put: everyone knew that the marchlands were hard, dangerous country, close to the barbarians, where you were as likely to die in a Quman raid or have your daughters raped by Salavii or be eaten by griffins and lions as you were to prosper. His grandmother had packed up her household without looking back once.

His grandmother had understood the way of the world. She had journeyed east because she had hated the yoke of servitude more than she had feared danger and hardship. Now, for the first time since his captivity among the Quman, he was truly her grandson. Her heir.

'Ah,' said Hugh, more breath than word.

At the hazy western horizon, still tinged with a fading gold, bright Somorhas winked briefly before heaven's wheel dragged her under. Mok, the Empress of Bounty, shone high in the southwest, on the cusp between the Penitent and the Healer.

'There,' said Hugh, and *there* Zacharias saw, rising as the wheel turned, the cluster of seven stars known as the 'Crown.'

Tonight the Crown of Stars would crown the heavens.

I pray you, Old Ones, give me strength.

You are strong, grandson. Do as we have taught you.

Zacharias felt Hugh's chest against his own back, as close as that of a lover, but when the presbyter's hand closed on his elbow his grip was iron, the chain by which he bound his servants to his will. He held Zacharias' hand, and thus the staff, steady.

'Now you will weave as I have taught you, Brother Zacharias. With this spell you will see into the heart of the God's creation itself if you do as you are bid. This, I promise.'

Zacharias grunted; he had many sounds left to him, but without a tongue few of them made words. The Old Ones understood him nonetheless. They had offered him strength – and with strength came the opportunity to avenge Hathui's betrayal. He quieted his mind as Hugh began the chant.

'Matthias guide me, Mark protect me, Johanna free me, Lucia aid me, Marian purify me, Peter heal me, Thecla be my witness always, that the Lady shall be my shield and the Lord shall be my sword.'

The staff caught the thread of the Crown of Stars and bound it into the circle of stones, and as stars rose and others set Hugh directed his arm so the staff wove these strands into a net that dazzled his eye and throbbed through his body.

Or was that the ground itself trembling? The moon set. Night passed more quickly than he had imagined once they were enveloped within the web of the spell, pulled one way as heaven's wheel strained at the stones, as each ply drew taut and, before it could snap, was directed elsewhere to spin the pattern on into a new configuration.

There were rents in the sky, huge gaps, like tears in a tent wall through which a man might glimpse the world beyond.

He sees the ladder of the heavens reaching from the Earth high up into the sky, glimmering in a rainbow of colors, rose, silver, azure, amber, amethyst, malachite, and blue-white fire burning so hot that he cannot look at it directly. Disquiet assails him. The ladder is empty. All the aetherical daimones who once ascended and descended from Earth to the heavens and back again are absent. Or fled.

They have fled the power of the weaving. For an instant he quails. He shrinks. Fear swells. Then he recalls Hathui and the voice of the Old Ones. He is Brother. He is Grandson. He will act. He will be strong.

'Sister Meriam!' said Hugh.

An answering voice thrummed within the web of the spell; he glimpsed her frail form, supported by her granddaughter, in the midst of a wasteland of sand and shattering sky. He felt her body beside his, although he knew it for illusion.

'I am here. I am here.'

'Brother Marcus!'

The ruins of Kartiako rose as ragged shadows along a distant hillside before Marcus' tense figure blocked the view.

'I am here.'

The heavens turned. Night crept westward across the Earth although they were by now drowned in darkness, marching on through the early night hours toward midnight. So it was true, he thought, heaven and Earth stretched those threads out, and out, until they were as thin as a length of hair. It was true that the Earth and the heavens were spheres, for otherwise night would come all at once and at the same time in each place but instead the heavens turned and the stars rose above the horizon first in the uttermost east and later as night crept westward over the Earth.

The rents opened wider as the threads pulled taut.

Stars burn, each with its own color, each with its own voice, each with its own variegated soul.

He wept with joy at their beauty. The music of the spheres rang through his body as the spell caught him within its weft and warp.

'Hugh! Meriam! Marcus!'

He faltered, hearing a voice colder than any nightmare. The Holy Mother had joined her presence to the web.

'I am here,' said Hugh, and Zacharias could say nothing, but of course now it seemed obvious that Hugh had lied to him. Why give Zacharias the glory of weaving the spell when Hugh could take it all to himself? Why did he want another man standing in for him?

Yet what did it matter? He had to concentrate on the weaving. Patience. Soon this joy would end. What matter what came after? He knew what fate awaited him.

Every spell demands a sacrifice.

A fifth voice joined them, a man's voice unknown to Zacharias although he spoke his name: *Severus.* Hugh still chanted, but his hand fell away from the staff as Zacharias wove the threads. Hugh eased backward out of the net as a sixth woman wove herself into the spell, who called herself 'Abelia.'

The seventh crown waited, still silent, but within the song of the other crowns he sensed the net, yawning wide. He felt on his shoulders a prickle like the breath of impending doom, a great weight bearing down on them not precisely from the sky but from a place beside the sky, inside the sky, unseen but ready to explode out of the air.

The scatter of stars known as the Crown of Stars had already climbed most of the way to the zenith, although it seemed he had only drawn six breaths in the interval since nightfall. Mok and the Healer sank down toward the south-western horizon as the Penitent made ready to lay down her burden. In the east, the Lion poked his nose above the horizon while the Guivre flew aloft in triumph. The River of Heaven streamed right across the zenith, rising in the southeast and pouring its harvest of souls into the northwest.

Each star glittered like a jewel, etched onto the black vault of the sky. Each one sang in his heart as the seventh voice joined them out of the crowns.

'Reginar.'

'I am here.'

Hugh stood a hand's breadth behind him, no longer touching him although his chanting did not falter as he sang a tune as melodic as a hymn and far sweeter.

With the touch of the seventh circle, the crown lit with fire, burning heavenward, blue white and so brilliant that it hurt Zacharias' eyes although he felt no heat. The heavens shuddered. He stared into their depths and saw the shadow of a vast weight hurtling down on them not as rain falls from clouds or as an arrow is loosed from on high but approaching from within the net of the spell.

The spell buckled under the strain, but it did not break. The seven mathematici drew their strength together, making ready to seal and close the crowns, to cast the exiled land back into the aether. To close off Earth forever.

The stars splintered into rays of color, stems banded along their length with variant light, some streaming blue and some red. The Earth groaned. Mountains shifted; the waters churned. Because he was woven into the spell, he felt cracks racing out from the crowns into the deep places far beneath the surface of Earth, down and down to where rivers of fire steamed and crackled.

'Now!' cried Anne. Her voice rang through the seven crowns.

Out of the depths a voice called as though in answer.

Now, Grandson.

He cast himself through the archway. Because he still held the staff he dragged the threads in after him, tangling them, pulling them all awry and thereby disrupting the spell. It had to be disrupted at as many of the crowns as possible, so the Old Ones had instructed him. Without Zacharias, their plan could not succeed.

In the distance down the pathways of the spell

he sees an island crowned by stones. A young abbot standing on the weaving ground gasps and turns just as he is cut down by an ax, but another cleric leaps forward to take his place, grasping the threads before they can unravel. Yet she, too, falls beneath a shower of ax blows. Beyond the crown, the ground heaves and collapses in on itself as half the island shears away. A huge winged creature rears up from underneath the dirt

he hears Severus' voice crying out in fear and shocked anger as the glittering sand beneath his feet comes alive with translucent claws: 'What means this! What?' The claws drag him under.

Blue-white fire enveloped him, burning him. No earthly flesh could withstand such heat, yet he felt no pain, only the cold grasp of death engulfing him. He would never see Hathui again unless they met on the Other Side.

With his last breath: *There.*

Through tears he sees into the infinite span that lies beyond the heavenly spheres. Folds of black dust form shapes like shifting clouds. Two suns spin each about the other, linked by pathways of red fire. A nautilus of light churns around a dark center. A spiral wheel composed of numberless stars whirls in a silence so vast it has weight. He is afraid, but he was once always afraid. Life is fear. Let it go.

So much light beckons, and yet gulfs of emptiness swell between the great wheels. This is the Abyss, into which all humankind falls in the end.

Let it go.

Death comes to all creatures, even to the stars.

He let go. He fell.

3

Now.

For a long time she lay in a state between sleep and waking, kept alive by bitter seaweed and an astringent juice brought to her by the brothers. At intervals she explored the passageways that led out of the cavern, using a trail of pebbles to

mark her path, but even with her salamander eyes to guide
her she at length came to labyrinthine tunnels without any
illumination whatsoever, and so she returned, always, to the
cavern.

It wouldn't have mattered anyway even if she had found
a path that led to the surface. She had a task she had to complete.

When she slept, or lay in a stupor, the old ones spoke to
her; what a person might say in an hour took them days or
even weeks. She couldn't be sure.

She held on. She would have one chance. She might never
again see those she loved, but what did love matter when
weighed against duty? She knew how to seal off her heart;
she did so now, so that sentiment would not distract her. That
skill she had learned from Anne.

Now.

The tremors came constantly, as if the Earth were adrift
on a vast sea like a ship rolling and yawing on the waves. Deep
in the Earth the old ones worked their ancient magic. They
could not touch Anne; they could not even move, it seemed,
but they had other means at their disposal. They channeled
the deep rivers and spoke to those who had the patience to
listen and the ability to travel.

*We. Are. The. Children. Of. The. Cataclysm. We. Are.
Guardians. Of. Our. Own. Children. We. Are. Born. Of. Stone.
And. Dragon's. Blood. And. Human. Flesh.*

She roused as the sting of magic melted down through the
Earth from the land above, winding her in a ghostly net of
blue-white fire. She staggered up to her feet. Gnat and
Mosquito lifted their heads to stare at her with flat eyes.

'Go far out to sea with your kinfolk,' she said to them.
'You will not survive if you remain close to shore.'

They looked at each other. The eels that were their hair
twitched and writhed, hissing, as though motion were speech.

'Go,' she repeated.

They dragged themselves to the flooded passageway, slithered in, and vanished, leaving her alone. She knelt, pressing
palms against the ground. She let her awareness fall as the

net of magic twisted along her body and snapped in her hair, making it stand on end. She pierced with her mind's eye far down into the molten fields lying beneath the grinding crusts of stone. Where rivers of fire flowed, she swam, making her way out of the eddies of viscous pools into faster-moving streams so red-hot they melted their own path through rock. These rivers raged at flood stage, pushed and prodded by the Old Ones in their circles. Beneath the seeming solidity of the ground, a tumult of liquified stone seethed and boiled.

As night crept westward across the land and the stars rose, the weaving caught within the stones of seven circles, the great crown that spanned the northern lands and the Middle Sea. The net of the spell blazed. Through that net she saw the shadow of the Ashioi land manifesting out of the aether not as a stone drops from on high but shifting out of one aetherical plane of existence back into the world of mortal kind. Through the widening gaps aether poured down into the world below, invisible to mortal eyes but blazing with power that Anne and her cabal gathered into their loom.

She heard Anne's voice reaching out to the rest of the Seven Sleepers who wove the spell: Meriam, Marcus, Hugh, Severus, Abelia, Reginar.

'Now!'

A surge of emotion coursed through that net, its own kind of magic that works against those who oppose the one who is about to win: Anne knew that she had triumphed and that her enemies had lost. The warp and weft of the spell wove together into a vast glittering net that interpenetrated aether and Earth.

'Now!' echoed the Old Ones.

Now.

The Old Ones had searched and commanded, and at the three northern crowns their agents leaped into action. To the north, ice wyrms consumed Brother Severus. To the northwest, an Eika prince called Stronghand cut down the clerics gathered at the Alban stone circle. To the east in the wilderness north of Ungria, Hugh – nay, it was not Hugh at all. Hugh had set another in his place to absorb the back-

lash he knew was coming, a tattered, mute cleric named
Zacharias. That other man flung himself bravely into the
crown, knowing it would kill him, but by tangling the threads
he knotted them all across the northern span of the weaving. One side of the spell began to unravel.

Anne did not falter. She was stronger than Liath had imagined any mortal could be.

'Marcus! Meriam! Abelia!'

They did not fail her. Across the southern span the net
held steady and with its thrumming architecture to bolster
her Anne bent her will to the north and from her place in the
center of the crowns she painstakingly wove the threads back
together. The spell shuddered back to strength, weakened
along that line but not shattered. The Earth groaned and
quaked. The heavens ripped, turning white as lightning
scorched the sky. The waters of the sea were sucked out and
farther out yet by an unnatural ebb tide until a broad swath
of shoreline was laid bare, exposing ancient foundations, old
roads, shipwrecks, and gasping fish.

There was no one in place to halt Meriam, Marcus, and
Abelia because they could not reach them even with the Eika
ships. They hadn't had time. Yet the Old Ones left no con-
tingency unplanned for. Age gave them an advantage Anne
did not possess: they knew how to think things through from
beginning to end. They had one force left in reserve.

One last weapon.

Liath was only sorry for Meriam's sake, because Meriam
had been kind to her, but it had to be done. Best not to think
about consequences.

Swift. Daughter. Act. Now.

Aether poured through the net of the spell down to the
Earth. Liath drew this bright, heavenly substance into her
and used its power to unfurl her wings of flame. When those
wings enfolded her in a sheltering cage of aetherical power,
she reached down and farther down yet to the burning rivers
– and called fire out of the deeps.

4

Along the outerworks of the ancient fortress Fulk ordered the men. Those who could still heft a shield formed a tight line behind the tumbled stones. As Bwr, Quman, and Ungrians filtered in, they were sent out into the clearing to cover the flanks to ensure safe passage from the line of retreat to the fallen arch of the gate. A dozen wagons trundled up, but the roadway leading up to the gate was impassable because of fallen stones and broken pavement, so after their cargo of supplies and wounded were hauled up into the ruined fort, they were rolled against the others to form a barrier, yet another makeshift wall to hold off Henry when he arrived.

'We'll be surrounded by Henry's army,' said Fulk, following Sanglant up the ramp with men bearing torches before and behind.

'Perhaps. The Ashioi are powerful allies. They can't be killed because they aren't truly alive.'

'That's so.' The captain glanced from side to side nervously. Shadowy forms – old women clutching baskets and jars, lean children with eyes as bright as stars – glared at them from the alcoves and hollows where they had taken shelter. When lightning flared, they almost dissolved away entirely into the light. It was easier to detect their presence when it was dark.

'Can you smell it?' At the gate that led into the inner court, Sanglant paused while wounded trudged or were carried past into the shelter of what appeared to be a fallen chapel. 'There's water here. We'll not be driven out by thirst, at least. You're in command, Fulk, unless Lord Druthmar is found.'

He hurried down the ramp and back into the clearing, running once he gained level ground, careful of his feet given the many corpses littering the open space. To the south, where Henry's forces pressed the assault, Sanglant saw signs of his own stragglers losing order and flying. Men passed by, some weaponless, most wounded. Seeing their prince, those without weapons took heart and moved to go back to the fray, prying swords and spears out of the hands of corpses, but Sanglant ordered them up to the walls. They were being overwhelmed, yet the shadow elves would soon turn the pursuit upon the pursuers.

'Hai!' called Zuangua. 'Make haste. We haven't much time!'

He left Fest with Hathui and Sergeant Cobbo and followed Zuangua as best as he could, but it was hard going once they got into the forest. The shadow prince moved so gracefully between branches that his armor or cloak never snagged and his face was never scraped. He was unhindered by the poor light lent only by shaded starlight, setting moon, and irregular flashes of lightning. He was also silent and odorless in a way most disconcerting to Sanglant who knew men and beasts as much by their sound and smell as their faces and color. He existed, but he had no earthly substance, and more than once Sanglant slammed up against an unnoticed tree that Zuangua effortlessly avoided.

They passed Malbert, still carrying the dragon banner, and a ragged group of grim soldiers marching double-time in tight formation. 'Make haste, my lord prince!' Malbert called in an uncanny echo of Zuangua's words. 'There's one group behind us. I fear they're lost.'

At last they came upon the rear guard huddled around an overturned wagon. Wounded men had spilled out on the ground, and while some crawled or limped away down the path after the retreating line, Lewenhardt, Sibold with an arrow pierced through the meat of his neck, and six others held out around those of their injured comrades who could not move themselves. No few soldiers wearing the eagle of Fesse or the tricolor of Wendar lay dead or dying from their attempt to overrun these last few guardsmen, but a fresh assault pressed out of the trees on the heels of those who had fallen.

Zuangua danced up to the soldiers, startling them as he jumped up on the wagon and sliced the air with his obsidian-edged spear. The cut left a trail of sparks in its wake.

Lewenhardt, with an empty quiver at his back and his last arrow nocked, stood stunned, unsure if he should loose it at the shadow or at Henry's men.

'Lewenhardt! Sibold!' Sanglant came up beside them out of the gloom. 'Take every man you can carry and go. We have new allies. We'll cover your retreat. There's a fortress ahead where Fulk's in command. Go!'

Sibold did not answer because the arrow in his neck, while not seeming to hinder his movement or threaten his life, shut him up. Seeing Sanglant, Henry's men shook off their doubt and with cries and shouts pelted forward. Lewenhardt released his arrow, taking one man in the thigh, then scuttled backward with the rest.

Out in the woods to either side, shrieks rent the air. The Ashioi had reached their prey. Sanglant braced. He was not used to fighting on foot, but he could hold his own. Spears jabbed at him, but the light wasn't good enough for his enemies to hit true. Above, on the wagon, Zuangua swept his blade above the swarm of men, then struck among them like black lightning. His spear passed through armor and shield and deep into the bodies of his foes. With every blow a man fell, struck not through flesh but through soul, killing the being that animated the mortal shell. Lightning flashed, and flashed again, and a third time in quick succession, and as if it had torn a gap in the stillness a gale blew across their position out of the east. The trees creaked and no few swayed dangerously in that tempest. Leaves and branches rained down, striking men in the head and knocking them flat. A leafy branch crashed right down through Zuangua, and though the wind drove some men to their knees, although Sanglant had to dodge blows and branches alike, the shadow prince stood balanced upon the wagon's side as if it were a calm day. Men struggled to fight him, but none of their blows had any force against a shade.

Sanglant laughed, knowing how cruel an irony this was.

He had found an army that death could not claim.

Lightning flashed and thunder rolled; this time the Earth itself trembled beneath their feet. Men screamed out among the trees. The world had gone black except for bolts of lightning that lit the sky. The moon was gone and all torches blown out by that wind. Only the firefly lights borne by the stalking Ashioi darted within the wood.

As quickly as it had come, the gale stilled. Zuangua trilled a war cry and that cry was echoed a hundredfold throughout the woodland. That cry had no words but every soul within earshot knew anyway what it meant:

Vengeance.

The Wendish army fled except for the few who fell to the ground speaking prayers or simply weeping at the judgment now laid upon them.

'The hour is at hand, Cousin! The sacrifices are ours to take.' Zuangua leaped from the wagon, thrusting at will deep into the bodies of the men who had fallen to their knees. He gave no mercy; he sought none. Sanglant ran at his heels as a second gale crashed through the forest. The shouts and screams of men rose in counterpoint to the crash of falling branches and the roar of wind in the leaves. They pressed on as branches fell all about them, as the ground shivered beneath their feet, as lightning dazzled in wave upon wave until day and night melded and splintered and here and there in the forest trees exploded into flame where lightning struck and dry limbs and dry leaves flashed and blazed. Smoke curled among the trunks. Men ran, and fell where hissing darts pierced their bodies. A fiery rain pattered down around them, but it was only burning leaves. There was no rain, no clouds. It was as hot as it had been in the daytime with the sun overhead.

There, unexpected, waiting unshaken in the road with a brace of noble companions at his back and his banner planted beside him, stood Henry.

The emperor needed no torch to light his way. He *was* a torch. His eyes gleamed with an unearthly light, cold and brilliant. A nimbus cloaked him, shedding that inner light onto the path and into the air. Where wisps of smoke trailed around his feet, the smoke glowed a ghastly silver.

Sanglant stumbled to a stop. Zuangua paused next to him as a dozen Ashioi ghosted out of the woodland to take up positions at either flank. The hawk-masked woman slipped into place at her prince's right hand with her bow drawn and her lips pulled back in a feral, unavian grin.

'This is your father?' Zuangua murmured. For the first time he sounded uncertain and even afraid. 'I did not know any woman of my people would embrace a daimone of the lower sphere.'

Sanglant wept to see him. Of course Hathui had told the truth. He could smell that this was not his father but an inter-loper residing within his father's shell. Perhaps Henry's noble companions suspected something was amiss, because they stared at the emperor in shock and then belatedly recalled that they must keep track of their enemies, now gathering before them. No human man could shine so brightly, not even one granted the luck of the king. Yet a lingering trace of his father still existed, hidden away beneath the daimone's presence. If he could reach the man, he might give him the strength to fight against the creature that possessed him.

'I pray you, Father,' he said. 'Let us call for a truce. Let us end this war.'

'Kill him,' said Henry.

Sanglant took one stride, another, and broke into a run. Behind, he felt the hesitation of his kinsmen; he marked it, but he was already at full speed and dared not stop. Would not stop.

He would rid Henry of the daimone. He would rescue him.

Henry's guard shouted. Several lords leaped forward to place their bodies between prince and emperor, but Sanglant took one in the thigh, shattering that man's mail, and another in the guts, thrusting so hard it split the man's mail shirt. He twisted the blade and pushed him aside with his foot. Three others fell to bolts of elfshot.

Henry had not even drawn his sword. He stared indiffer-ently at the death of his companions.

'Damn you! You're not Henry!' Yet Sanglant could not

strike his father. He seized him by the gold brooch that clasped his handsome cloak and yanked him, but he might as well have been pulling on a mountain.

Henry did not move until he himself struck. The back of his hand caught Sanglant under the chin and sent him flying backward, lifting him right off his feet. The prince landed hard, jaw cracking. Blood rimed his lips.

Zuangua lunged, but Henry dodged and raked Zuangua with a mailed hand. Bronze armor gave way as three wide furrows of blood opened across Zuangua's chest as if Henry's hand bore unseen claws. Astonished, Zuangua leaped back, still grasping his spear. Although the stark wound did not seem to hurt their leader, the Ashioi were now less eager to press forward.

Sanglant clambered, wincing, to his feet.

'Traitor,' said Henry in another creature's voice. His voice had the timbre of a bell and it carried far into the forest, out to the ranks of his terrified army. His companions took a step back from him. 'You have all along plotted with your mother's kind. Now we see the truth of it. Duke Burchard. Duchess Liutgard. My noble companions. My captains. Do you see it? Do you mark him for what he is?'

'Murderer!' cried Duke Burchard, rallying. 'You betrayed my daughter!'

'Traitor!' cried Liutgard more passionately. 'I believed that you were loyal!'

Sanglant stood, unsteady, as the ground shook and he struggled to focus his eyes. His ears were ringing and ringing although there was no thunder. Silence gripped the land, or he had gone deaf but for a whooshing that resolved itself into the griffins, circling above.

Ai, God! The feathers! He grabbed for his knife's sheath, but in the course of the battle the feathers had torn it right open. They were gone, and half the sheath with them. If only one feather would come drifting down from on high into his hand, he could succeed.

Henry — the daimone — laughed cruelly and lunged forward. Just in time Sanglant stepped aside and parried the blow, but that blow hit his shield so hard that wood disintegrated and he was sent reeling, and tripped, and stumbled, and barely fended off another cut from one of Henry's captains, then went down on a knee. The captain gasped sharply as a dart sparkled in his shoulder.

Sanglant got to his feet. Zuangua had leaped to cover him and now danced back and forth as Henry struck blow after blow, attempting to get through him to Sanglant. The shadow prince was bleeding from face and leg and gut, and still he fought while his warriors pressed back the nobles.

Sanglant pulled his knife out of his boot and leaped in to grab Henry from behind. He kicked him hard at the back of one knee as he wrapped his arm around his father's throat and pulled him backward. But the daimone caught the blade and just the touch of that hand shattered the iron blade into shards that sprayed out, caught fire, and spattered against the ground in a hissing hail of sparks.

Henry reached back and wrenched Sanglant's helmet right off his head. Before the prince could react, Henry twisted his fingers into Sanglant's hair. Sanglant squeezed harder, trying to choke him, but those fingers ground into his flesh and twisted as though to yank his head right off his neck. What claws had cut open the aetherical substance of Zuangua's shade had no purchase on mortal flesh, but the cutting edge of Henry's iron gauntlets cut into Sanglant's skin and seemed likely to sever tendons.

He struggled, but it was futile. Henry's unnatural strength could not be bested, not even by him. The pain made spots flash and fade before Sanglant's eyes. The world hazed as the daimone throttled him. His own grip slackened. He could not hold on.

Zuangua's black-edged spear stabbed right through his father's head. He felt the whisper of its passing as a hot tingle below his own chin.

Clutched so close, he actually felt the daimone die as the shadow blade pierced its soul and released it. That inhuman strength snapped and with an ungodly shriek it vanished into the aether, banished from Earth. He recoiled and collapsed onto his back with his father on top of him and his arm still wrapped around Henry's throat.

His gaze was forced heavenward as he fought for breath. Through the boughs he saw stars swollen to twice their normal size. The Crown of Stars stood at zenith, so bright it hurt his eyes. The wheel of the stars throbbed and pulsed until that music reverberated through his head and sank into his very bones, making him weak, shaking the Earth itself with a roar filled with bangs and loud knocks and tremendous booms rolling on and on and on and on. Successive waves of a sickly, nacreous light washed across the sky.

'For Henry!' shouted Liutgard behind him.

'For Wendar!' cried Burchard. 'And the empress!'

Then it hit.

A wind blasted out of the southeast. Trees snapped and splintered as they were scythed down. Men tumbled to the ground. Horses screamed as the gale sent them flying. The gale scorched the air and turned the heavens white, and the leaves of a butcher's-broom shriveled, curled, and disintegrated right before his eyes. His skin hurt.

He rolled to get his father's body beneath him, to protect him from debris, and in that movement saw Zuangua and his companions staggering backward and their bodies shifting and changing as the wind howled over them, as if that wind were filling them with substance, with earth, with mortality. Liutgard had flung her spear before she was herself hurled to the ground; the weapon carried on the wind but held true, piercing Zuangua in the shoulder where he clung to a toppled tree trunk.

The Ashioi prince screamed, who had gone untold generations without any pain except that hoarded in his heart. Blood as red as a mortal man's gushed from the wound.

The wind died abruptly, although Sanglant heard it tear away across the land, moving outward. He sat back on his heels. *We must take shelter,* Gyasi had said, and he knew it to be true: there was worse yet to come.

A horrible orange-red glare shot up into the heavens along the southeastern horizon. It looked as if the world had caught on fire. It reminded him of Liath, and a wave of sick dread coursed through him. Was she dead?

Henry groaned.

'Father!' He pulled off his father's gauntlets and helm, chafing his hands, staring into his eyes, which looked like any man's eyes in this strange half-light. 'Ai, God! Father!'

Henry lifted an arm weakly. 'Hush, son,' he said in a voice entirely like his own familiar beloved voice. His hand brushed Sanglant's hair and stroked it softly. 'Hush, child. Go back to sleep. You are Bloodheart's prisoner no longer.'

Sanglant wept.

Around him, folk began to shake out of their stupor, those who had not been knocked unconscious by debris or falling trees. He heard a thrashing out in the forest as men and horses came to their senses, got up, then fled or shouted for help or moaned in pain, depending on their injuries. An unseen soldier yelled out an alarm, but it was too late. A dust-covered, blood-soaked nightmare of a man stumbled out of the trees, laughing as coarsely as a madman. This creature steadied himself on the shaft of a banner pole from which hung a tattered banner so stained and ripped that it was almost impossible to mark what sigil had been embroidered thereon.

Almost, but not quite: it was a glittering crown of stars set on a sable field representing the night sky.

'Cousin! I have found you at last! God Above, you bastard, you abandoned me on the field! But this time I bested you. I won!'

Zuangua had roused; now he spoke a word. The hawk-masked woman leaped forward and, before Wichman realized what she meant to do, pulled the banner out of his hand. In an instant she stood back beside her captain, spear raised. Other Ashioi clattered in from the woods to form a grim wall made up of flesh and blood bodies and expressions filled with an ancient hatred.

The air was utterly still, the only sounds the cries of men and animals out among the trees, the snap of a weakened branch and the rustle and crash of its falling, and the steady filtering patter of falling ash.

'Let him go,' said Liutgard sternly. She had regained her feet although she had lost her horse. Burchard lay on the ground, not moving; Henry's companions shook themselves off or writhed on the earth, and at least one had been crushed by a falling tree.

'Ah!' said Henry, blinking his eyes. 'I'm dizzy. Sanglant, what has happened?'

The prince rose, but he knew already what faced him, standing as he did between the two sides and with what remained of his army, he prayed, safe within the fortress – but out of his reach. He was no different than his dragon tabard – one half smeared and grimy with earth and the other stained with blood. As inside, so outside.

'Now it is time to make peace,' he said.

Liutgard scoffed at him. 'Traitor and murderer! How is it you can speak their language if you have not long conspired with them? This disaster is your doing, Sanglant! Let your father go.'

Zuangua laughed harshly, for it was obvious he could not understand one word Liutgard had said. 'Peace? Nay, now it is time to make war. Who do you choose, Cousin? Humankind, or us?'

'Neither,' said Sanglant furiously. 'Both.'

'Stand back, Liutgard,' said Henry in a stronger voice. He attempted to rise but could not. Blood leaked from the wound in his head. He choked on blood, coughing and spitting, and raised an arm. 'Sanglant! Help me. Help me sit up at least.'

'Ai, God.' Sanglant knelt beside him, still weeping. 'Father, you must rest.'

'Nay, I have rested long enough. I have suffered. . . .' He coughed again; with each pulse of blood he grew weaker. Burchard groaned, and a captain helped him rise. The nobles drew closer to attend the king. 'I have suffered under a spell! I saw Villam killed by traitors. God! God! My own dear wife conspired against me.'

'Adelheid?' croaked Burchard as he knelt on the other side of the king. He had taken off his helm. 'Not Adelheid!'

'What do you mean, Your Majesty?' Liutgard asked, coming up behind Burchard. She glared at the Ashioi, who held their position, as ready to strike as she was. 'Yet it's true you were shining in a most unnatural way, there on the path. Is it true, what Sanglant claims? Were you ensorcelled and chained by a daimone?'

'Presbyter Hugh and Adelheid between them . . . with the approval of the Holy Mother . . . Anne . . . to force their own schemes forward. They thrust a creature into me . . . into the heart of me. . . .' He shuddered. Blood pumped from the wound. He sagged into Sanglant's arms. 'Hurry,' he whispered. 'Hurry. Listen!'

They crowded forward. Behind, Zuangua snorted at this display, but he held his place and his peace for the moment.

'These are my wishes . . . my last wishes . . . my dispensation, as is my right as regnant. All my life I have wished . . . but custom went against it.' His head grew heavier against Sanglant's arm, yet through sheer force of will he kept speaking although his face grew ghastly pale under the weird orange-red light as his life drained out of him through the hole made by Zuangua's spear. The shush of falling ash was the only sound beyond his labored breathing and the footfalls of men creeping closer to listen, to see, to seek comfort within the orbit of their dying king.

'What are you saying, Your Majesty?' asked Liutgard.

'My right . . . as king . . . to name my heir.'

'Princess Mathilda is your heir, Your Majesty,' said Burchard, troubled now, wiping ash from his face. 'You named her yourself.'

'Under duress . . . even Sapientia not worthy. This one.' He reached across his chest, found Sanglant's other arm, and clutched it tight. 'This one. Swear to me. Give me your oath. You will follow Sanglant. He becomes regnant after me. Swear it!' He choked and convulsed, but he held on. 'Swear it!'

They swore it, each one of them, because Henry was their king, the one they had followed all this way.

'Ah!' he said when last of all Burchard and Liutgard knelt and gave their oath. He looked up into Sanglant's eyes. His own were free of any taint. 'Ah! The pain is gone. My son. My beloved son.'

The light passed out of him. His soul was released, there one instant and in the next gone utterly.

Sanglant bowed his head, too stricken even to weep any longer. At first, the rustling seemed part of the strange night, more ash falling, perhaps, or leaves tickling down through dead and blasted branches. Then he looked up.

They had knelt, all of them; all but the Ashioi, who waited. Tears streaked Liutgard's cheeks. Burchard sobbed silently, shoulders shaking. Beyond, as far back into the forest as Sanglant could see, captains and sergeants and men-at-arms knelt to honor their dead king.

Out of the gloom stumbled two recognizable figures – Lewenhardt and Hathui. The Eagle cried out and flung herself down beside Henry's corpse.

'He died as himself,' said Sanglant as she wept, and she shook her head to show she'd understood because she could not speak through her grief. 'He died as regnant.'

'Tell me, Cousin,' said Zuangua a little mockingly behind him. 'What does this display of passion and weeping portend?'

Even Wichman had knelt, but he sprang up at the sound of Zuangua's voice and with a roar leaped forward and ripped the imperial banner out of the hawk-woman's grip. He stuck it into the ground behind Sanglant, and he laughed.

'What is your command, Your Majesty?' he said, the words almost a taunt.

Sanglant laid his father's body gently on the ground. He rose, shaking ash from his shoulders. Henry's blood streaked his hands. His sword, shield, and lance were gone, but his father's last gift to him had been the most powerful weapon of all.

'The storm is upon us,' he said, letting his voice carry. Ash and grief and exhaustion made him hoarse – but then, his voice always sounded like that. 'I do not know what else we will have to endure to gain victory.'

What I will have to endure, he thought, *if Liath and Blessing are dead.*

'We have allies.' He looked at Zuangua, but the Ashioi prince only shrugged, unable to comprehend his words, holding himself aloof. *I hope we have allies.*

'We have enemies. Some of them are those we trusted in the past.'

And some, like Adelheid and Hugh and Anne, don't yet know what they have lost.

'Who follows me?'

'Your Majesty,' said Duchess Liutgard and Duke Burchard. Said the noble companions who remained. Said the captains still living. Said Lewenhardt, speaking for his own faithful soldiers.

Henry's army echoed them, every one. They were his. He ruled them now.

5

Anne ruled the heavens. Her net of magic spanned the Earth as the exiled land belonging to the Lost Ones shifted out of the aether in its attempt to return to its earthly roots. That net quivered under so much weight, but it held. Even lacking three crowns it would hold, it would cast the Aoi land back into the aether, but beneath the weaving the first intimations of doom swept across the land as lightning torched the sky and earthquakes shuddered across the entire continent of Novaria. What the Seven Sleepers did not understand and refused to understand and cared nothing for was that by dooming the Lost Ones they were dooming Earth. They could not change their course now. They would not. They had won.

Anne's triumph was as palpable as sand – and like sand, it could be washed away with one tidal surge.

Liath called fire from the deeps.

The eruption of molten rock exploded straight up through the heart of the stone circle that was itself the heart of the weaving. Liath felt Anne die. She felt Anne's life ripped from her. The skopos hadn't time even for a single startled exclamation. Between one breath and the next she was dead.

The souls of all of Anne's retinue and Anne's army were torn from their bodies as the power of the blast vaporized every living thing that stood or moved within a league of the crown. It stripped away the topsoil to expose the rock beneath. Ash and pulverized stone sprayed upward. The rock hammered to earth in a hail that struck up and down the coast and made the Middle Sea foam for leagues outward. The ash rose into the heavens as a churning plume that soon covered half the sky. Lava poured over what remained of the cliff face into the waters, where clouds of steam boiled upward to meld with ash and smoke.

Inside the shelter of her wings Liath witnessed all this and more, the massive destruction she and the WiseMothers had wrought in order to rip apart the spell. The stone crown was obliterated. Anne and her retinue were dead, utterly gone.

And this was only the beginning. This was not even the worst of it. As you sow, so shall you reap. Humankind and their Bwr allies had sown two thousand seven hundred and four years ago and now their descendants faced a bitter harvest.

The storm was coming.

Now.

She bound her wings tightly around her as the impact reverberated through the earth. Shock waves coursed deep through the ground. Out of the ruptured sea rose a vast wave that radiated outward in all directions and which crashed against the cliffs of the erupting coastline in a blast of hissing vapor which at once cooled and heated and poured yet more impetus into the towering plume rising above the land. In a short time, or in hours, the wave would reach the other shorelines. There was nothing Liath could do to warn the thousands who would drown.

The displaced air from the impact swept outward in a vast ring that rolled over land and sea on all sides, uprooting trees, burning grass, and what close by resounded in an eerie silence

was heard as a roar of bangs and knocks and booms far away
and even in so distant a place as Darre itself. Folk stopped in
the streets in terror and fear only to see a worse horror as the
earth began to shake and the volcano long smoking and rumbling to their west erupted with a slurry of ash and mud.
Down the western coast of Aosta other sleeping volcanoes
shuddered into life. There was nothing Liath could do to warn
those living too close to this rim of fire, now woken.

I had no choice.

No doubt Anne had spoken such words, too, as she convinced herself to take on the task that had led to her destruction, although she had believed herself all along to be the
righteous one. To stop Anne, Liath had made herself into
Anne.

No matter.

The deed was done.

She cast herself onto a streaming river of fire and let it
carry her to the surface, just in time, because already the flow
abated as the WiseMothers withdrew the press of their minds.
Already the salt water cooled and stiffened the outer layer of
the flowing lava. Already the flood of aether out of the heavens diminished, and the strength of her wings weakened; they
began to shred and fall apart as the Earth reasserted its pull.

She found herself, naked, clutching only her bow, on a
stairway formed out of the crust of a lava flow, all swirls and
coils in the hardening skin. Everything else had burned off
her, even the Quman quiver, even Lucian's friend – her sword.
She ran up into the open air. A thin crust sizzled against her
feet, cracking under her weight. Smoke hissed up from
narrowing vents. Any other creature would have died in such
heat and such fumes, but she was born half of fire, and this
was her element.

A blessedly cool wind greeted her as she climbed to the
rim of the crater made by the eruption and, reaching the top,
wiped sweat from her brow. The wind that had blasted outward had left the air clean beneath a heavy layer of ashy cloud
extending to all horizons. The sky turned a hideous red in
the east, heralding sunrise.

She heard the shush and slap of a distant shoreline, which had once lain directly below the stone circle, and she wondered whether Gnat and Mosquito had survived. She wondered if anyone had survived, because standing on the crest of a ragged ridgeline with desolation on three sides, she felt she was alone in a vast new world.

Nothing is permanent except change.

There the shoreline had once gnawed at the base of cliffs, but no longer. She stared out over new land extending as far as she could discern to the south and east into the Middle Sea. Mist wreathed its heights and valleys in a silvery gleam. Far away, felt more than heard, a moaning call rose out of the mist, the cry of a horn summoning the lost.

The Ashioi had come home.

EPILOGUE

In the distant haze where sky met sea, islands rose out of the sound like teeth marking the horizon. The water gleamed, as still and smooth as burnished metal; seen from the height of the ridge, the swells were lost under the glare of the sun. The carter and the guardsmen paused on the path to wipe their brows against the terrible heat.

He had no shelter and no water to slake his thirst, and anyway over the numberless days of his captivity he had grown accustomed to the sun's hammer. Today was especially hot and humid although he had an idea that it ought to be cooler, but he couldn't remember why, and there was no wind at all, only the expectation of wind and a pressure in his ears as though someone were squeezing the air all around them. The heavens to the west and north were hazy along the ocean but clear above, while thunderous clouds had piled up and up in a black mass to the east and south.

'Don't like the look of that,' said Heric to his fellows, nodding to the east. 'Must be a mighty tempest. Hsst! I've never seen clouds like those, not in all my life.'

'Let's get on,' said Ulf the carter. 'I don't like being exposed up on this ridge.'

'Dragonback, the townsfolk call it!' snickered Heric. 'No doubt some girl or other does creep up here on a dark night with her lover to make dragonback! I'd do it!'

Ulf sighed. 'The folk in Osna village weren't too friendly, neither. I didn't see no girls making eyes at us. I wish we was going back to Lavas Holding and rid of this stinking creature.'

'Soon enough,' said Heric. 'We've a few holdings and villages yet to ride through before we're safe home.'

Ulf snorted, scratching his nose, then spat on the dirt. He

was not an unkind man, but he clung to his superstitions. 'If we get safe home! Those clouds look ugly to me. These locals aren't any too happy to see us, neither. They're too worried about bad weather and a poor harvest to mind that foul creature.'

'It's him what ruined their harvests with untimely rain and cold snaps! Brought about by his sin!'

'Maybe so.' Ulf shrugged. The other three guardsmen yawned; they followed Heric's orders and ate their food but otherwise hadn't any enthusiasm for the job. 'But enough's enough, that's what I say.'

'Get on!' said Heric irritably. He had a willow switch and with this he slapped his mount's croup to get it moving.

Ulf had a softer hand on the oxen. The cart lurched forward and they creaked down the path at a steady clop. A scatter of buildings lay beyond the tail of the ridge, arranged around a roofless church and a stone tower, which was still intact. For a bit they lost sight of the ruins as the path reached the base of the ridge, wound through a tumble of boulders and then, turning to loam, struck through a quiet forest, but soon they emerged into overgrown fields and trudged up past broken gates to take shelter for the night in the tower. Ulf watered the oxen at a stream and set them to graze, and the horses were given their oats and let wander within what remained of the fence that had once kept livestock within the compound.

Before building a fire for their supper, they rolled the wagon up along one side of the church, offering a bit of shelter if it stormed. From here he could stare at the curving ridgeline or out over a stony beach onto the sound. The water was so still that it seemed like solid ground, where a man might walk for leagues and leagues on its surface out into the wild lands beyond the guardian islands. Out there, strange creatures traveled and wept, or so he remembered. There were fish with the faces of men and men with claws in their hands who raced across the sea on ships as sleek and effortless as dragons.

Memory came in flashes as sharp and as brief as lightning.

That window, half obscured by a rosebush run wild, opened into the scriptorium. The monastery boasted a precious *Book of Unities* bound between covers plated with gold and encrusted with jewels.

'I know this place,' he whispered. He saw in his mind's eye an old man leaning on a stick, dressed in monk's robes. But he was dead, wasn't he? Hadn't they all died? The storm had come in off the sea and slaughtered them all and burned and destroyed their home as it would sweep in again.

'Shut him up, will you?' demanded Heric. 'All that babbling about dead dead dead makes me want to hit him across the face, and I will!'

'Poor mad soul,' muttered Ulf, but the carter brought him a crust of bread to gnaw on and, quite unexpectedly, a skin of ale so rich that he had to sip at it and not gulp it down lest he spew it all back up. At first it unsettled his stomach, but then it warmed him enough that he could curl onto the hard bed of the wagon amidst the remains of dirty straw, shut his eyes, and doze as the guardsmen gossiped by their fire in the shelter of the deserted tower.

He heard their voices.

'Don't like the look of the sky.'

'What, them clouds? Not enough wind to blow them over us.'

'Nay, look at the color of that sky. It's not natural. There's some terrible nasty storm coming, mark my word.'

'What bitch's tits did you suckle from? You've been harkening to the madman's voice.'

'Oh, shut up, Heric. What have you got against him anyway?'

'He stole my girl!'

'A filthy beast like that? Not likely.'

'He was all cleaned up in a lord's tunic and bright jewels. Of course he stole her! Thief and cheat—'

Thief and cheat, he slipped into darkness and he dreamed.

A noble youth sleeps in the midst of a heap of gold and gems with six companions surrounding him, but out of the shadows creep gnarled figures whose skin gleams like pewter, whispering and tapping, seeking.

Seeking, rivers of fire forge new paths deep within the Earth, and the world trembles.

The storm is upon them.

The Holy One bends her gray head as she watches the sun set. From her vantage point beside the stone crown, the farthest east of its kind, she watches the weaving plotted and planned in ancient days come to life once more in the hands of those who are now her enemies, not her allies.

She is so weary. A part of her hopes this night will be her last, that she is too old to endure the force of the storm. She does not weep, because she has lived too long and made too many difficult choices to weep any longer along the trail of years, a path down which she can never return or retrace her steps.

But there was one whom she loved unforeseeably, inexplicably. Sorcery exacts a cost, although humankind in their immense arrogance have not always understood this principle, and each gesture, each choice, will be counterbalanced by a consequence of equal weight. Yet affection drowns reason. Although she knew it for a foolish act, she reached onto the paths of the dead and expended more power than she ought because she wanted to make happy the one she loved like a daughter. Adica. She had no daughter of her own among the Horse people; that was forbidden. She loved too well where she should not have loved at all, and that act of love rebounded on her in a way she never anticipated or desired. By meddling in the paths of the dead she dislodged the stream of her own soul.

For so long death has been denied her. She witnessed the unfolding effects of her great undertaking, and all did not transpire as she hoped it would. She lived while her people slowly died off and diminished, as humankind migrated into their ancient homeland, stole or gelded their puras, and hunted down their daughters one by one. She wants to sleep, but she must stay wakeful in order to save her people, whom she doomed although she never meant to. She will stay awake one more night and then she will lie down and die and let others carry the burden she has carried for so long.

Be careful what you wish for

'Now!' cries Stronghand, heeding the command of the

WiseMothers. He leaps forward with ax raised high. The blade
glints and where light flashes
    Lightning turns the sky white and in the place of thunder
he hears a hoarse, gleeful battle cry as the ground begins to
shake

'Ai, God! Ai, God! Get the horses!'
He shuddered awake, startled up by the earth shaking
under him, and jerked to the end of his chains as he stared
at the shadows of men chasing their mounts off into the forest
to the north. Even the oxen tossed their heads and trotted
away, spooked by that earthquake; Ulf, cursing, ran after
them. Iron bit into his wrists and ankles, drawing blood, as
he strained after them, but they had forgotten him.
Overhead, the sky was a sheet of lightning that veiled the
stars, painting the heavens a color as loathsome as that of a
corpse, life and soul drained from it. Along the shoreline the
water had receded far out past the line of ebb tide, exposing
the seabed and a line of sharp rocks along the curve of the
ridge. Fish flopped in the shallows. He drew in breath,
although the air felt like soup in his lungs.
A rumbling roar shook the ground and pitched the cart sideways so hard that it tumbled over onto one side and the post
to which he was bound cracked and broke in half. The tower
groaned as it leaned sideways and then in a roar collapsed
entirely. Dust and grit rolled over him, choking him. He lay
stunned, hearing the screams of panicked horses far away.
The wind dissipated the cloud with a sudden fierce blow
that blasted the shroud of dust out over the sea.
The ground hadn't done shifting. It pitched and yawed
as though it were alive and when he was able to lift his pounding head, he saw the great Dragonback Ridge splinter as
sheets of rock cascaded onto the waters of the sound. It
buckled. The noise of its shattering deafened him. The booming and crashing hurt his ears so badly that it brought tears
to his eyes.
It moved.
The dragon's tail lashed sideways, snapping trees. As its

flank heaved up, dirt roared into the sound and buried the old shoreline. Where it lifted a claw and set it down, the earth shook. Atop a slender neck, its head lifted into the heavens. It slewed round its vast body, bent its neck, and lowered its head down to the ground not a stone's toss from his cage where he lay trapped by his chains.

He struggled to his knees to face it.

It had scales the color of gold, so bright that he squinted. Its eyes had the luster of pearls. A single tear of blood squeezed from a cut on its belly, splashed, then coursed down through the furrows made by its claws to gush over him. That viscous liquid burned right through his rags, down to his heart.

My heart is the Rose. Any heart is the Rose of Healing that knows compassion and lets it bloom.

He stared in shock at the creature's beauty as it blinked, examining him in return, then huffed a cloud of steam, reared its head up, and opened its vast wings. Their span shadowed the entire monastery. It bunched its haunches, waited a breath, ten breaths, a hundred breaths.

He heard the gale coming before he felt it; he heard it cutting through the forest, downing trees, a wailing wind out of the southeast.

The wind hit. The dragon leaped.

The gale whipped over him. The dragon's shadow passed, the weight of its draft battering him down. The sea raged out beyond the shore. God have mercy on any soul caught out in this storm, but every soul on Earth was caught in this storm whether they willed it or no, whether they huddled in shelter or braced themselves against it out in the open. The stars had gone out. All he could see above was a swirling haze mixed of dust and ash and wind and blowing foliage and trailing sparks from the vast net of the weaving that Adica had made and that was now at long last finished.

Someone would have to pick up the pieces.

The roar of the sea filled his ears and a huge wave swept over him although no wave could ever possibly wash so high up on the ground. He rolled in surf, caught under water, pinioned by the chains.

He drowned.

On the northeastern shore of the Middle Sea where the center jewel in the Crown of Stars blazes in glory, the Earth opens up to engulf the crown in a pillar of molten fire. Across the land the Crown of Stars and the spell woven through it tangles and collapses in on itself. A shadow emerges out of the air to materialize up against the knife edge cliffs that abut this shoreline of the Middle Sea.

All down the western shoreline of the great boot of Aosta the ridge of volcanoes shakes into life. Lava surges out of the earth. Cracks yawn in once quiet fields. Mud and ash bury slopes and towns and streams.

The ocean churns as all the water displaced by the returning land floods outward, heading for distant coasts. Where the tidal wave hits, the shoreline is utterly drowned.

The Earth groans. Along the northern sea the mouths of rivers run dry as the land jolts a finger's span upward to counterbalance the abrupt weight that has slammed into the Middle Sea. In places, rivers run backward. Ports are left high and dry.

Everywhere the ground shakes. The windstorm that raked across the broad lands dissipates in wilderness where there are only dumb, uncomprehending beasts to sniff at its last gasping residue.

Deep in the earth, goblins race through ancient labyrinths, seeking their lost halls.

Out in the ocean, the merfolk circle, diving deep to escape the maelstrom above.

Out on the steppe lands, the Horse people hunker down in hollows that offer them some protection against the howling wind. The magic of the Holy One shelters them even as it drains the life right out of her.

Those who were most harmed in ancient days ride out the storm, for they have the least to lose now. It is humankind who suffer most. Maybe Liat'at'dano knew all along that this would be the case; maybe she planned it this way, harming the two greatest threats to her people – the Cursed Ones and her human allies.

Maybe the WiseMothers suspected humankind would take the brunt of the backlash. Maybe they had no choice, knowing that the belt was already twisted, that the path was already cleared through the forest on which their feet must walk.

They speak to him through rock and through water, although the salty sea almost drowns their voice.

It. Is. Done. You. Have. Saved. Us.

The link retreats, and their presence withdraws.

The tidal wave sucked back into the sea, pulling every loose piece of debris with it into the sound. At first, the wagon was caught in that riptide, but the church wall trapped the wagon among its fallen stones and the chains held him. Battered but alive, he was left wheezing and choking on sodden ground as the water receded.

The sun came up. It was a cold, cloudy day; there was no blue sky visible, and an ashy haze muted the daylight, but nevertheless the world had survived. He had survived. He was weak and exhausted and sopping wet and hungry and thirsty and filthy and yet despite all this at peace.

It was done.

He had seen the beginning and now the ending. The crown of stars was obliterated. The Ashioi had returned from their exile.

'Lord save us!' said a man's voice, heard as through a muffling cloak. 'Can anyone have survived that? Go on, then, boys!'

Hounds barked. He heard them pattering through pools of muddy water, paws slip-slapping on the ground. He tried to open his eyes, but a salty grime encrusted them, and it wasn't until tongues licked him, wiping away all that blinded him, that he could see again.

'Sorrow!' he whispered. 'Rage!'

They whined as they bumped up against him, waggling their hindquarters in ecstasy. They were thin, and scruffy, and overjoyed. The salt had cracked the bindings that shackled him, and as the hounds swarmed over him, the chains fell away.

A man loomed into view. He uttered a gasp of shock, or a murmured curse, or perhaps a prayer.

'*Alain?*' He knelt beside him but didn't touch him, not yet. Instead he dragged the heavy chains off his body. He was weeping. 'I heard, lad, but I had to see for myself. They said you'd gone over the ridge. And that storm! Ai, Lady. There's at least three dead in the village and I haven't been back home yet to see how Bel and the others fared. My God. What man could be so cruel as to treat another man in this way?'

He cracked open his eyes. 'Father?'

Henri looked much older; he had many more lines on his face, and his hair was gray. But the face was so blessedly familiar, so beloved. There were tears on the merchant's cheeks.

'Ai, God, lad, can you forgive me? Even though you weren't the old count's son, you never deserved this. I raised you better than to lie and cheat in such a way. I suppose the old count chose for himself and how could you say him nay? There was a girl he'd bedded who bore a stillborn child near or about when you was born. He might have thought otherwise, might have insisted you were his. Old sorrows take men that way sometimes. I should have trusted you. I should have known you better. That's how I failed you, Son.'

The words spilled out in a rush as strong as the tide, leaving Alain stranded and out of breath. He was still dazzled and shaken and stricken, and the hounds were laying half on top of him, pressing as close as they could.

Henri frowned, wiped away tears, and spoke again. 'Off, you brutes!'

Amazingly the hounds crept back meekly, their soft growls more like groans of protest. Hesitant, as if he wasn't sure he had the right to touch him, Henri laid a hand on Alain's arm. 'Here, lad. Come now, get up. Lean on me.'

With help, Alain was able to stand, although his legs were shaky. The sea churned, the water a foamy, dirty gray, and the islands were half hidden within the murky haze. The ruins had been washed clean by the tide, and debris littered the old shoreline, but the strangest sight of all was the new

inlet carved out where Dragonback Ridge had once risen.
Trees lay tumbled like so many scattered sticks down a
ragged, rocky slope that was cut, where the earth met the
water, into channels separated by the heaps of dirt and rock
that had sprayed out into the sound when the dragon woke.
Along the curve of the bay, distant and mostly obscured by
haze, he saw the tiny cottages and longhouses marking Osna
village up on its rise overlooking the strand. The village was
more or less intact as far as he could tell from this distance.

Henri stared, too. The hounds sat patiently. 'I've never
seen such a night as that,' said the merchant in a quavering
voice. 'That dragon come alive. That tempest. That wave off
the sea. It took Mistress Garia's granddaughter with it. Maybe
it's the end of days, after all. Maybe so.'

'It is the end,' said Alain, surprised at how steady his voice
was. He glanced down at his naked body and was shocked to
see how wasted and thin he'd become. 'It is the beginning,
too. There'll be hard times to come. But I pray the folk of
Osna village have faced the worst. I pray they will be spared
any greater hardships.'

Henri looked at him searchingly, and with an odd expression of respect. 'Do you know of this? Do you know if it were
God's hands that brushed us?'

'I know of it. It was humankind caused this, not God.'

The merchant reached up and wiped at his cheek, then
frowned. 'What's this mark on your face? You hadn't such a
birthmark before. Is it a scar? It looks like a rose.'

The Lady's Rose. For so long he had misunderstood what
it was – or maybe the Lady of Battles had. Maybe she had
misled him. Maybe the Lady of Battles was not his patron
but his enemy.

'It's the Rose of Healing, Father. It's to remind me of how
much there is to do. Adica didn't mean to cause so much
harm, but now someone has to try to pick up the pieces. I'll
do it. I must. But if I could just sleep a little first. If I could
just eat something. . . .'

'Bel will have my head! You've been starved and treated
no better than a wild dog. Here, now, come along.' He began

walking. Alain had to lean on him to stay upright, but it was easy enough; Henri had a strong arm. 'I've a cloak to cover you and a horse for you to ride. You look too ill and worn to walk so far.'

'Where are we going?'

'Home, Son. We're going home.'

SHADOW

K. J. Parker

Book One of The Scavenger Trilogy

A man wakes in the wilderness, amid scattered corpses and inquisitive crows. He has no memory of who he is or how he came to be there. The only clues to his former existence lie in his apparent skill with a sword and the fragmented dreams that permeate his sleep.

The evidence of his past must lie somewhere, but masquerading as a God in the company of the mysterious Copis seems an unlikely place to start looking. Yet as their journey leads north answers begin to emerge. Each one points to a riddle far more complex than he could ever have imagined and a truth he may not wish to believe.

Shadow is the first book in a series that takes fantasy fiction into remarkable new territory.

WIT'CH FIRE

James Clemens

Book One of The Banned and the Banished

Long ago, the Mages of Alasea, beset by a dark and implacable evil, made a last desperate stand to preserve some remnant of their once-beautiful land. Knowing their own destruction to be inevitable, the Mages gathered the last of their magic and stored it away against the need and peril of a distant time. In doing so the Mages gave the people of Alasea a future and a hope – and damned forever . . .

Now, five centuries after their destruction, a young girl, Elena, inherits the powers that the Mages had so carefully hidden from their enemy. But though the Mages are long dead their ancient foe is not – and when the Dark Lord learns of Elena's power he turns all of his terrible strength against her. Desperate and alone, fleeing from disaster, escaping into darkness, Elena seeks out the allies and knowledge that can help her to master her bitter gifts and cast down the evil that shattered the land of Alasea.

Wit'ch Fire is the first volume in a spectacular fantasy series by James Clemens

Orbit titles available by post:

❏	King's Dragon	Kate Elliot	£7.99
❏	Prince of Dogs	Kate Elliot	£7.99
❏	The Burning Stone	Kate Elliot	£7.99
❏	Child of Flame	Kate Elliot	£7.99
❏	Shadow	K. J. Parker	£6.99
❏	Pattern	K. J. Parker	£6.99
❏	Memory	K. J. Parker	£10.99
❏	Wit'ch Fire	James Clemens	£6.99
❏	Wit'ch Storm	James Clemens	£6.99
❏	Wit'ch War	James Clemens	£7.99

The prices shown above are correct at time of going to press. However the publishers reserve the right to increase prices on covers from those previously advertised, without further notice.

ORBIT BOOKS

Cash Sales Department, P.O. Box 11, Falmouth, Cornwall, TR10 9EN
Tel: +44 (0) 1326 569777, Fax: +44 (0) 1326 569555
Email: books@barni.avel.co.uk.

POST AND PACKAGING:

Payments can be made as follows: cheque, postal order (payable to Orbit Books) or by credit cards. Do not send cash or currency.

U.K. Orders under £10	**£1.50**
U.K. Orders over £10	**FREE OF CHARGE**
E.E.C. & Overseas	25% of order value

Name (Block Letters) _____

Address _____

_____

Post/zip code: _____

❏ Please keep me in touch with future Orbit publications

❏ I enclose my remittance £_____

❏ I wish to pay Visa/Access/Mastercard/Eurocard

Card Expiry Date